Part one

Chapter 1

When death reaches for you, it's over. Your fa[illegible] they want to say at your funeral, of course they'll talk about all the good things you've done. They never talk about the bad.

How could they?

You're dead.

Who could ever speak ill of the dead?

We wonder if there truly is an afterlife, we hope and pray there is, but that's all we can do. If there isn't, we go to nothing. But what's so bad about that?

If there's nothing, we no longer have to deal with the weight of our burdens, the pain we felt throughout our lives. With death on our minds, we must never forget to live: wake up and spend time with your family and friends, meet new people, and do the things you love.

Never stop living.

Live.

No matter how many times you've died.

Live.

Samantha Knight tossed and turned, the morning sun shining in on her sleeping form through the loose curtains. Flashes of dark hair ran through her mind, the laugher of children, the terrified screams of a crowd. Throughout the 20 years she's been alive, she always had the same dream of a little boy running to her from the bottom of a hill as she stood at the top.

She had never seen the boy outside of her dreams but the way he looked was burned into her mind: his brown hair and hazel eyes shining as he looked at her, a wide smile on his face.

It wasn't merely a dream though, she stood in a tiny form, the body of a child, and she would speak words she didn't understand.

Perhaps it was a memory.

"Sam!" A familiar voice called to her and her eyes flew open to find her mother looking down at her. Her blue eyes were filled with confusion as her blonde hair fell over her shoulders as she leaned down. "You need to go pick up Mina."

Sam's eyes widened as she shot up, the coils in the bed creaking as she got to her feet. Her body had yet to adjust to being awake and it didn't help that her dreams of the little boy had made her toss and turn all night. Her mother watched as she quickly rummaged through the drawers to find something to wear for the day.

Sam turned and met her mother's curious gaze, she had obviously seen her uncomfortable state when she was still asleep. She had made the mistake of telling her parents about her dreams, but there was no hiding it. She would wake in the middle of the night screaming as the dream ended, her heart fluttering and grief filling her. Her parents sent her to therapists and doctors and they prescribed medicine for her take to ease her anxiety but none worked.

She had to persevere on her own, the dreams wouldn't ease no matter the treatment.

"I have to get dressed." She said with an hint of annoyance, her mother didn't need to stand there as if she was too crazy to be alone.

Her mother turned after giving her one more questioning look and shut the door behind her.

Sam sighed as she pulled off her blue tank top and patterned pajama pants and replaced them with jeans and a black T-shirt. She wiped her hazel eyes and she pulled her long wavy brown hair out of her pale face into a pony tail. She looked in the mirror at the corner of her room and noticed how tired she looked. She had to drive to the city to meet her best friend Mina whose semester at collage came to an end. Sam had been friends with Mina since they were in grade school and while Sam decided to stay at home and work at a local car shop, Mina went off to beauty school.

Mina's parents were strict and would have picked their daughter up themselves but both had to work and they trusted Sam enough to do it instead since they had known her since she was little.

Mina didn't have a car and neither did Sam if you didn't count her motorcycle.

Her parents were allowing her to take the car that she and her brother shared. They were polar opposites and he wasn't happy she was taking the car.

Sam sighed as she turned from the mirror, the little boy still on her mind as she walked out of her room and made her way down the stairs.

As she rounded the corner to the living room, she was met her father as he sat on the couch, his eyes on the morning paper. They shared the same hair color but his eyes were dark brown instead of hazel. Her brother who sat at the kitchen table that could be seen from the living room was the male version of their mother.

"Be careful and call me when you get there." Her mother instructed as she rounded on her, her blue eyes filled with nerves.

"I will." Sam assured her, even at her age her mom still had the right to worry.

She turned to her father who she wasn't close with, her dreams had put a strain on their relationship. She turned back to her mother, gave a small smile, then made her way to the kitchen where she grabbed the keys to the car at the table beside her brother who continued to eat his cereal quietly. She stepped out the front door with her mothers voice following her as she repeated what she had just told her inside.

She made her way to the black car that sat in their long driveway as she called back that she would do as her mother said.

After setting her phone on the map to her destination, she drove out of the driveway and made her four hour drive to pick up her best friend.

She pulled into their meeting place and turned the car off and closed her eyes since Mina wasn't there yet. The deal was that Mina was going to take a taxi to a rest area so Sam wouldn't have to go all the way to the city. Mina knew about her dreams, of course she would tell her best friend her problems, she never worried about being judged when it came to Mina.

She thought of the boy again and clenched her jaw. A knock on the window made her jump and as her eyes flew open, she realized the culprit was Mina. She had a wide smile on her face and Sam returned it as she got out of the car and the girls wrapped their arms around each other as they exclaimed. Sam pulled away and took in her friends blue eyes that looked larger due to the makeup she was wearing and her blonde hair was done up in loose curls.

"Look at you!" Mina laughed as she looked Sam up and down, her voice girlish. "I can tell you're still practicing that fighting stuff you like."

Sam had taken taekwondo classes when she was younger to try to deal with her anxiety and although she couldn't stick with it, she practiced what she had learned at home.

"And I can tell you've learned a lot at school." Sam pointed at her friends perfect cat eyeliner and Mina smiled until she saw the bags under Sam's eyes. "You're still having that dream?"

"It's nothing." Sam assured her.

Mina inhaled sharply as she nodded, she understood that Sam didn't want to talk about it.

"I'm surprised my parents even allowed this to happen," She lowered her gaze to her bags that laid at her feet. "Especially with everything going on..." her voice broke and Sam frowned.

There've been disappearances in their area, mostly people between the ages of eighteen and twenty five and there was no sign of the people that were taken, not even a body.

With these large scale kidnappings, the police suspected the culprits to be traffickers.

"Maybe it could be the demons-" Mina started but Sam interrupted her.

"There's no such thing." She shook her head as she placed a hand on her friends shoulder. "And you know it."

She wasn't speaking literal demons of course, she was talking about the creatures the government and their parents had told them about.

Over twenty years ago these creatures supposedly attacked cities and towns and they left a path of destruction and death in their wake.

After years of tormenting people, the creatures suddenly disappeared and haven't been heard from since.

"It's just something they made up to keep us in line," Sam assured her as Mina's blue eyes filled with worry. "I have a feeling the cause was the government and these *demons* are the cover ups." She gave a small smile. "I'd be more worried about the traffickers."

Mina returned her smile and she seemed reassured from Sam's words.

What were the chances of them being kidnapped anyway?

"I already called my mom and told her I'm going to take my time going back home." Sam told her as she lifted one of her bags for her. "Call your parents and tell them we're making some stops on the way."

Mina's smile widened, "I want to go to Stacy's burger joint."

"Your wish is my command." Sam joked as she opened the back door, placed Mina's heavy bag's inside, and the two started their journey back home.

By the time they were done with their day of catching up, it was dark and after trying to convince Mina's parents it was alright, they made their way to Stacys where Mina would get her hamburger. After the girls got their food, they sat under a street lamp as they ate.

"We need to talk about it." Mina said finally as she chewed her cheeseburger.

"About what?' Sam asked as she played with a fry.

"Your dreams."

"I don't want to-"

"I know you don't." It was Mina's turn to interrupt. "But while I was in the city, I talked to a girl who saw a psychic and she told her there's a good chance she had a past life."

They sat in silence for a moment and Sam's mouth hung slack. "A what?"

"You might have been reincarnated." Mina declared as if what she was saying might've been possible.

"Does this girl have dreams like I do?" Sam asked, her nerves filling her voice.

"No, but-"

"It must be a coincidence." Sam flicked the fry off her plate "My mind is a piece of shit anyway."

"Sam-" Mina started but stopped as her eyes drifted to the right of Sam to the road where a rusted gray van was idling.

While Mina looked on with fear as it's headlights shined on them, Sam looked with narrowed eyes. As more people came with their food, the van revved it's engine and took off, leaving the girls paranoid.

Sam turned back to Mina and she was about to crack a joke when she sensed her friends fear and her heart thumped.

"Im terrified." Mina's voice shook. "I know I can't stay home and hide forever but I'm terrified it's going to happen to me."

Ah, the kidnappings.

"It's not." Sam left her food behind and sat beside Mina. "It's not going to happen to you, we're going out tomorrow like we planned and we're going to make it home safe and sound." She pinged her head and Mina yelped. "Do you think I'd let anything happen to you?"

Sam had always defended Mina from anyone who had thought it wise to pick on her.

"No," Mina sniffled. "Of course not."

Sam leaned against the bench they shared. "It's not gonna happen anyway."

When Sam got home she was surprised to see the still lights on. She knew her mother would be waiting up for her but would have gone to be bed while doing so. She stepped out of the car, the keys swinging from her fingers as she made her way up the front porch. She opened the front door and stepped into the kitchen, her black ankle length boots clunking against the hardwood floor as she pulled them off. She flipped the kitchen light off as she watched her mother, father and brother in the living room as they watched the television.

They turned to her as she walked in.

"How's Mina?" Her brother asked as he sat on the back of the couch behind their parents.

"Good." She said with a confused look as she turned to the television to find what they were looking at, the newscasters voice ringing in her ears.

They were reporting another kidnapping and Sam's heart thumped as she noticed that it happened only an hour away.

First an image of a girl with long blonde hair, fair skin, and blue eyes flashed on the screen followed by a dark skinned girl, her dark curly hair falling over her shoulders.

Lastly a photo of a male came on the screen, his skin tan, his hair black, and his eyes dark brown.

All of them had smiles on their faces and it made Sam's chest ache.

Under their pictures were their names: The blonde haired girl was Carma Connelly, the other girl was Emily Watson, and the male's name was Cale Harper.

The reporter stated that they were taken earlier in the night and the police were working tirelessly to look for them. At the close of the report, the female newscaster appeared on the screen, her red hair in a fancy style as she announced that the police believed the culprits were traffickers.

"You're not going anywhere tomorrow." Their father declared as the news changed to the weather. "Neither of you are."

"We're going to be fine." His son scoffed as he got up from the couch, he was supposed to go to the movies with his girlfriend at the mall.

"Why don't we go together?" Sam suggested and the three of them looked at her like she was crazy for suggesting such a thing. She and her brother didn't get along especially when his girlfriend was around since he acted like a different person.

"We're safer in numbers and we'll stay inside and near other people when we go outside."

The three thought about it but Sam knew she had won.

"You stay close to each other when you're outside and no arguing." Their father demanded and Sam smiled at her brother who agreed as long as he could go out.

That was easy.

"Yes sir." She nodded as she turned to go and made her way upstairs where she took a shower and got ready for bed.

She laid with her laptop on her stomach, her wet hair in a bun and the smell of berries filling her nose from the shampoo and soap. She looked at the pictures of the three that were kidnapped earlier, a lump in her throat as she took in their smiling faces. She wondered where they were and if they were ok, she hoped they were.

She closed her computer and placed it on the night stand as sleep called to her. She closed her eyes as she leaned into the pillow, trying to calm her breathing as she prepared herself for another night filled with dreams.

Chapter 2

She sat at the top of a hill, her small form casting a long shadow behind her. She was between the ages of six and eight and her long wavy hair fell to the middle of her back. Her hazel eyes were filled with awe as she gazed at the city in the distance. Her parents never let her go see the sights and although she was ok with their living situation, she longed to be normal.

"Hey!" A young boy with brown hair that matched her own smiled at her

as he climbed the hill.

She smiled gently. "Mom and dad want you to keep an eye on me?"

"That's not it." It sounded like he was pouting but he wasn't, it was just his childish tone. "Our brothers are mean."

Her eyes dropped, "I know."

Her brother sat beside her and the long grass reached the top of his knees as he brought them to his chest. "You wanna go to the city, don't you?" He asked as they looked at the large buildings in the horizon.

"I do." Her voice squeaked. "I don't know why mom and dad won't let us."

"Because of what we are."

The dream changed and all she could see was blood and the sound of people screaming filled her ears.

She woke with a start and she inhaled sharply as her throat felt like it was closing in on itself.

As she swallowed, she found that it was raw and she knew she had screamed during the dream. She hoped she held off long enough for her family to leave for work but knowing her luck, she didn't. She grabbed her phone that laid charging beside her to check the time.

9:00am

She had slept in and she was thankful that today was her day off. As she continued to look at her phone, a text from Mina came in:

Mom and dad said it was fine, took some convincing because of last nights news.

Sam typed her reply, her fingers gliding over the touch screen.

I had to do the same, I wish I didn't have to ride with my brother but it's better than nothing.

She placed her phone back down and stretched, she had the house to herself for the day and she was going to spend it doing what she liked best: going for a run and practicing her taekwondo moves.

She pulled on her earphones after she was dressed and she made her way to the front of the driveway. She wondered if it was smart to be running alone but she convinced herself that the amount of cars going by would make it hard for someone to grab her.

She mentally smacked herself, she was the one who was starting to worry now.

When she got back from her run, she was covered in sweat but instead of washing up, she made her way to the backyard where she practiced her fighting moves.

Nothing worked better than making her body work to help her forget her dreams. The strain on her body made her forget the strain in her mind.

After hours of doing just that, she made her way inside to shower and get ready for the night.

She pulled on a band shirt and a pair of black jeans and she spent the rest of the day until their departure for the mall relaxing in the house. They were going to meet her brothers girlfriend and Mina there and Sam couldn't wait for the awkward car ride to be over.

After their parents warnings to be careful and to stay with each other while outside, they were good to go.

When they got to the mall the two walked to the entrance where his girlfriend was already standing: she was a pretty girl who stood a head shorter than him, her hair dark and her skin pale. Although they could have gotten away with leaving her, they stood with Sam until Mina arrived.

Sam watched as Mina tried convincing her mother it was alright and she ended up waiting for the girls to get inside before taking off.

"See ya!" Sam's brother took off with his girlfriend and they made their way through the foodcourt to the movie theater at the other end of the building.

"That was easy." Sam shrugged as she and Mina made their way through the mall until they got to Mina's favorite store: The makeup place.

That's what Sam called it at least.

Sam's nose filled with the smell of perfume as Mina picked through eyeliners, lipsticks and mascara's while she watched. She didn't get bored while waiting on Mina to look at the things she didn't care for, she knew it was something she liked.

Mina had always joked with her that she didn't need makeup anyway and Sam would brush it off and say that she didn't need it either. No one needed anything to look better, it was about what someone wanted for themselves.

"Can I?" Mina popped a fresh eyeliner pencil out of it's casing and Sam gave her a confused look. "I just wanna see what you'll look like."

Sam had a problem with telling Mina no.

After putting the eyeliner on and adding a bit of tan eye shadow, Mina had a smug look on her face as she took in her friend. "Yep, I knew it would make your eyes pop."

She had Sam look in the mirror and she certainly agreed, it did make her eyes pop.

After Mina bought her makeup and she handed Sam the eyeliner she had used on her, they made their way through the rest of the mall. They stopped at a bookstore and although Sam didn't mind reading books, she didn't do it much.

Mina looked through the magazines while Sam wandered around and took in the book covers.

She stopped at a cover that had a goat on it but it was built like a man. There were curved horns sprouting from it's head and it eyes glowed a deep red, a pentacle carved into it's forehead.

The title read: *Lucifer's conquest.*

As Sam examined the black backdrop behind the beast, she couldn't help but think that the cover got the devil's look wrong.

'That's creepy." Mina rested her head on her shoulder and her warm breath hit her neck.

"...Yeah it is." Sam agreed as she turned away from the book.

For the rest of their time at the mall, they had shopped at a meditation store where Mina tried pushing a book to see if it could unlock the mystery of Sam's dreams but she declined.

After spending some time in the other shops, Mina had bought some summer clothes while Sam found herself empty handed.

By the time they were done, it was almost time to go to their designated meeting place in front of the mall and Mina called her mom to pick her up as the girls made their way there.

The people in the mall were thinning out as closing time approached and when they made it to the front, Sam leaned against a wall as she waited for her brother and Mina did the same across from her as she waited for her mother.

After 15 minutes the mall was almost empty and all the food stands had closed down making the two the only ones in the area.

Her brother's movie was running late or he was too busy messing around with his girl.

Sam rolled her eyes to the end of the food court where she noticed a man clad in all black heading towards the exit, his hood covering his phone as he talked into the device.

"Yeah, right now." he said with a deep voice and Sam found herself leaning curiously forward to see what he looked like but failed. It was easy to get a creepy feeling from a person with their hood up on a warm day in a public area.

Mina and Sam who had been talking before the man came into view found themselves silent as they got an uneasy feeling not just because of the man but from setting.

An engine roared outside and it made Sam's attention go from the man to the clear doors. She saw nothing but parked cars illuminated by the street lamps but she could hear an engine idling close.

Where did she hear that sound before?

Dread filled her as she leaned against the door to see the edge of the rusted van from the night before.

"Min-!" she started but the hooded man came running and grabbed Mina as she tried to run away. The shock of the situation had made her vulnerable and he caught her.

The man gripped onto her and she kicked, thrashed and screamed as he started pulling her out of the automatic door. It had happened so fast but Sam sprung into action and ran outside after the kidnapper and her friend. She punched and kicked him and his grip loosened from the continued efforts of both girls. When they thought they had a chance, two more men came from the van and joined the hooded man who ignored Sam and continued to grab Mina.

Mina was their target.

"Run!" Sam yelled but Mina was a slow runner and the hooded man scooped her up from behind as the other two came for Sam. They obviously saw her as the bigger problem.

They both towered over her and she couldn't make out how they looked due to the dim light and their hoods. She didn't bother to return their hits, she only focused on dodging them as she made her way to her screaming friend and her captor.

"LET GO!" She roared as she grabbed the eyeliner pencil from her pocket and slammed it with enough force that it went through the captors shoulder and he yelped as he let Mina go.

"RUN!" Sam screamed and Mina ran back into the mall with tears and regret flooding her face from leaving her friend behind.

None of the men went after Mina, they rounded on Sam instead.

"You're gonna pay for that, you fucking bitch." the man she had stabbed said with malice and she gulped. She was clearly outnumbered but she wasn't going down without a fight. She ran at the opening between the two larger men but in what felt like lightning speed the hooded man kicked her to the concrete and she felt some of her ribs crack.

"You..fu..ck!" She gasped.

"Don't touch her." the hooded man told the others as he leaned over her and she tried to get up but the pain in her ribs shot through her body.

"She's mine." he continued as he grabbed her collar and pulled her up a fraction. Another gasp escaped through her gritted teeth as the pain sharpened.

"Don't kill her, she's useless to us dead." One of the lugs warned him

"And the boss won't be happy if you do." The other added.

"Don't worry," The hooded man's voice was filled with venom. "I'm just gonna shut the bitch up for awhile." Sam could feel the anger flowing off of him and she stiffened.

She didn't regret what she did as long as Mina got away.

"Hurry before someone comes." She could hear the others making their way to the van and a rusty door shut.

She could see the hooded man's features now as the headlights shined on him: he looked like he was only a few years older than her and his eyes... it had to be a trick of the light.

She didn't have time to reflect on it as he grinned and his fist smashed the side of her head, knocking her out.

Chapter 3

She was leaning over her mothers body whilst sobbing into her hair. "Mom!" she cried. "Please..."

Her voice cracked as she looked up to see her four older brothers, the oldest had brown hair and hazel eyes like his mother and the twins had blonde hair and blue eyes like their father. The three had shocked looks but instead of falling to their knees and crying, they just stood there.

The youngest of the four boys who had brown hair and hazel eyes like his mother, oldest brother, and sister fell to his knees like his sister had.

"They're gonna pay." She turned to her three oldest brothers, her cheeks stained with tears. "It looks like you're gonna get what you wanted."

Sam's eyes fluttered open and she winced at the pain in her ribs and head. She tried to look around but everything was black. She began to bring her hands up to pull off whatever was blocking her vision but a rough cord was wrapped around her wrists.

"Welcome back." A man's voice startled her and it took her a moment to remember what had happened. She didn't say anything as she accessed the situation: She was leaning against something and her bound hands were behind her back. The van was moving and she could feel the small bumps that it hit as it traveled and whenever it hit a pothole pain shot through her.

As the pain continued to get worse the adrenaline she once had disappeared and the seriousness of the situation set in. Her heart raced and she felt like she was going to be sick as cold sweat dropped down her brow.

"I'll give you props," The man began. "Out of all the people we took, you're the only one who put up a fight."

She could hear the rustle of the other captors as she ignored the loud mouthed one.

"...Where are you taking me?" the question was stupid, they weren't going to tell her. It was a generic question that people asked in scary movies and she was stupid enough to ask it herself.

"To your new home." The talkative man answered and her heart thumped as she thought of what her new *home* was going to be like.

Was this really human trafficking?

"You really pissed Kellen off," she could hear the amusement in the man's voice to the left of her. "That was the first time I've seen him loose his cool like that."

"Shut the fuck up." another voice that she recognized immediately rang from the other side of the van: the hooded man's name was Kellan.

Sam jumped at the venom in his voice.

"You hear me bitch?" he asked her when he saw her reaction."You're lucky I didn't kill you."

"Arthur wouldn't like that." The babble mouth spoke again.

Kellen's laugh was frightening "She's just another pawn, maybe he'll give her to me if it doesn't work out."

"She's a fiery one so I think he'll like her."

"Fiery ones have a hard time obeying orders." Kellen answered simply and Sam could feel their eyes on her. Arthur was obviously the ring leader, the mastermind behind all these kidnappings.

"What's the point in all this?" her voice was hoarse.

"You'll find out." Kellen answered and she could hear the smile on his face.

It obviously wasn't good.

She was definitely an idiot for what she was about to say.

"You fuckers kidnap people for God knows what and you don't even have the balls to tell me what's going on?"

"Damn!" The man to her left exclaimed. "You're the first one to fight *and* talk back."

She didn't say anything, she thought Kellen would have said something out of anger but she could tell he was watching her.

They hit the biggest bump so far and she couldn't muffle her pained cry and she could tell her captors were amused by her pain.

"You'll get your answers soon." Kellen said finally with amusement in his tone.

Sam spent the rest of the ride internally freaking out about her situation, her heart thumping in her ears and her throat dry. Her brother would know by now what had happened, did her parents know? She pictured her mother crying and her father trying to hold it together while talking to the police. Tears formed in her eyes but she couldn't let them fall, even with the blindfold, she wouldn't allow them to see any weakness in her.

It wasn't long before they stopped and she could feel movement around her.

"Here." she heard a new voice as a door creaked open. She perked up as if she could see what was going on, there was no way they were at their destination already. How long was she out for? She wanted to ask but she figured it wouldn't matter much since it couldn't have been that long.

"Get up." Kellen was the one to grab her and he purposely jabbed her in her injured ribs.

"You *fucker*." she gritted her teeth.

She didn't need to see to know that he had a triumphant look on his face as he yanked her roughly out of the van and practically dragged her along with him.

She could hear the other two walking in front of them and the sound of the van roaring to life and taking off behind them.

She struggled to pull away and she let her feet drag to make it harder for Kellen to pull her. "You're a second away from me breaking more of your ribs." Kellen threatened and she stopped being so difficult.

"I'm going to warn you girl," one of the men in front of them started. "Our boss isn't as nice as us so watch your tongue."

She gulped, they certainly weren't nice so their boss had to be some kind a demon.

Demon.

Sam shook off the thought before it began, this was not something mystical, it was impossible.

"I see you caught one as well." A voice she didn't recognize called and her attention was brought to her unseen surroundings. She was so lost in her thoughts she hadn't noticed someone approaching.

"Another easy one." The newcomer announced and Sam could hear the person he kidnapped struggling against him.

"This one fought." The blabber mouth told his ally and she knew he was talking about her. "She wasn't the one we were aiming for but she sacrificed herself to save the girl we were going to take."

"We better tell them to get the rest ready." The newcomer advised and Sam was sure they were talking about the people they had already kidnapped.

One of the men turned on a radio and the buzz made her jump.

"We have the last two… get ready." He demanded then turned the thing off.

They continued on and after a minute, Sam realized they were going upward, her breathing becoming labored as she tripped over rocks and loose plants, her ribs screaming with each step. The other prisoner begged and pleaded for his captor to let him go all the way up the incline.

What felt like hours had passed when the radio came to life again. "Camilla, we're here." One of them spoke into it and a females voice replied. *"We're all set."*

Kellen pushed her roughly forward, their footsteps beginning to echo as they stepped inside something and the first thing that came to mind was a cave.

Water dripped from somewhere and it echoed along with their steps. The cool air made a shiver go up her spine but fear might have had something to do with it as well.

Kellen forced her to take a sharp turn and she whimpered as her ribs twisted.

They came to a stop and she could feel more eyes on her and the sound of nervous breathing as Kellen straightened her. The prisoner that came in with her continued with his begging to her right.

"Shut up." His captor commanded and the boy went quiet in fear of getting hit.

Sam could hear people moving, sobbing, and praying in the hollow room and she knew they were the people who had been kidnapped before her.

She wiggled to test her restraints but Kellen who still stood behind her leaned into her ear.

"If you do anything stupid I'm going to snap your ribs one by one." his breath tickled her neck and she stood still from that moment on.

She could feel Kellen stiffen when two more sets of feet echoed through the room and satisfaction went through her only for it to be wiped away at what sounded like twenty lackeys greeting their leader.

"Keep them quiet." a deep new voice commanded and she knew it belonged to the leader. A couple steps echoed through the room and after a pause, he spoke again. "Cell C."

The boss made his way down the line of people and as his footsteps echoed to each person he announced a cell letter from A to C.

As he got closer, Sam had already counted twenty two people that he had sorted so far. The boss and the person who had been following him while he sorted continued on until they were at the person to the right of her.

"Cell A." He commanded for the third time and Sam was getting restless as the boss took one step and he was right in front of her.

She thought her heart was going to explode as the cloth was pulled from her eyes and she blinked at the sudden fluorescent light.

Her hunch was correct: They were in a cave.

Her eyes moved to the man standing in front of her: He was only an inch taller than her and the florissant light made his already pale skin paler. His brown hair shined in the light along with his hazel eyes as they widened with shock as he took her in.

Sam narrowed her eyes and she did the dumbest thing she had ever done in her life: She spit in his face.

The room filled with gasps but she didn't bother to look, she only had eyes for the now spit covered man in front of her.

The man behind all of this didn't look surprised anymore, his face had lost all it's emotion.

Kellen stepped away from her.

"Arthur." the man beside him warned and as Sam turned to see the source of the voice, the leader known as Arthur struck her so hard across the skull that it cracked on contact and she fell to the ground as she lost consciousness.

Chapter 4

Spots covered her vision as she came to and as she tried pulling herself up, she collapsed back to the hard rock underneath her.

Gasps and cries rang around her as her head screamed and blood poured from it to the ground beside her and she looked up slowly as her sight came back.

"Mother… fucker…"

She met Arthur's eyes and her heart practically stopped: They were completely white.

His hazel irises were gone along with his pupils, they were both consumed by the whites of his eyes.

Kellans eyes from back at the mall weren't a trick of the light, they really were what she had seen.

"This is your fate," Arthur started as he kneeled in front of her and she flinched. "The humans like to call us demons but they are misinformed," he sounded amused but it was quickly covered with a chilling tone. "We are *gargoyles*."

He shot up at his declaration

"Cell A." he said simply and Kellan appeared behind her again and pulled her to her feet.

"Tried to warn you." he snickered into her ear and her aching head brought tears to her eyes as more blood poured from her cracked skull.

Arthur took one look at the boy that had came in with her.

"Cell C." he said without even bothering to take off his blindfold.

Sam's lips twitched as she watched him leave into one of the tunnels that were scattered around the cave. The person who had followed

Arthur as he sorted was a dark skinned man and he was adorned in a white doctors coat. He didn't look much older than Sam and although he looked gentle, sweet even, he was here with these beast's.

He looked at the situation around him."Take them to their cells and we'll go from there." He said as he turned and trotted after Arthur.

The captors stood behind their prisoners and they began to push them down the separate openings, it was like a labyrinth and it was obviously carved by these gargoyles.

Sam's head spun when Kellan pushed her around to the opening behind them to follow the others that were also sorted into *Cell A*.

"How's the head, bitch?" Kellan snorted as they stepped through the dimly lit tunnel and it was so narrow that you had to walk one person in front of other.

"How's your shoulder feel?" she snapped back but quickly regretted it as a pang of pain went through her head.

"It feels great." He flipped her around and she almost threw up from the pain but the shock that hit her was even worse: He had pulled his shirt off his shoulder and the wound she had caused with the eyeliner pencil was completely healed.

"I'm a gargoyle too, sweetness." he flashed a quick grin and flipped her back around.

The demon theory was wrong but it was also true in a way, they were monsters no matter what they were called.

Sam thought of the grotesque creatures on top of buildings and she felt like she was going to be sick from the shock that filled her.

As they approached the end of the tunnel, the other guards were standing in a line in front of a cell with three people trapped inside, the bars planted into the ground.

Sam couldn't make out their faces due to the dim light and as she and Kellen approached, a female guard grabbed ahold of two bars and pulled them apart almost effortlessly.

All Sam could do was blink before Kellen threw her through them and she rolled to the ground for what felt like the hundredth time that day.

She hadn't noticed that the ropes that had been tied around her wrists were gone until she tried pulling herself up but she collapsed again.

After the pain in her ribs and head dulled to a constant ache, she looked at her captors. "Wouldn't it be easier to add a door?"

Two of the men left at her words while the female and Kellen remained.

"Easier to keep you in." Kellen leaned on the bars that had already been set back into place and Sam had to fight the urge to go over and deck him.

This was the first time she had gotten a good look at him with his hood down: He was handsome with a head full of blonde hair and his eyes were currently his normal color, a deep shade of blue.

The woman that stood beside him had a pixie cut and shared his hair color. She was small and petite and Sam would have been surprised by her strength if she didn't put two and two together that she was a gargoyle as well.

"I hope you guys get along…You'll be seeing a lot of each other." The woman had a high pitched voice that made Sam want to hit her as much as she wanted to with Kellan.

With that, the two of them walked back down the hall with smiles on their faces, leaving the cellmates alone to bond.

Sam didn't bother to get up as the adrenaline started to wear off again and the pain was getting so bad that she almost didn't notice one of her cellmates coming from behind her.

"You're insane." A girls voice echoed and Sam slowly looked up to see Carma Connelly, the girl she had seen on the news. Her now messy blonde hair fell over her shoulders as she bent down and examined Sam's wounds.

"I was going to school to be a CNA before *this* happened." Carma sounded extremely frightened but she put her fear aside to check Sam's wounds. "Can I?" She asked permission first and Sam locked her jaw and nodded slowly.

Two more approached from the darkened back of the cell to reveal that they were the two shown with Carma on the news: Cale Harper and Emily Watson.

Sam couldn't believe how this was turning out. She had only just seen them on the news the night before and she had worried about them all night just to be in the same situation as them and in the same cell.

Cale Harper looked the same as he did on the newscast, his skin tan and his eyes and hair were dark. Sam glanced at him with an eye closed, he was tall and it was easy to tell that he stood over six feet tall.

Emily Watson's curly hair reached past her shoulders unlike in the picture they had used on the newscast but other than that, she looked the same.

"Why'd you do that?" Emily kneeled on the other side of her.

"Because I'm stupid." Sam replied simply and the girls looked between each other while Carma examined Sam's wound.

Sam watched as Cale moved to the bars and he peered into the hall until he turned back to the inside and sighed. "I can't believe this."

"None of us can." Carma's voice shook along with her hand as it touched Sam's wound and she flinched. "…It's cracked open."

"I don't see her getting any medical attention in here." Cale said as he sat against the bars. "*Gargoyles…*" He brought his palm to his face. "And I thought that demon stuff was bullshit."

Sam leaned her head down as Carma pulled away and sat along with her friends.

"I felt the same…" Sam closed her eyes as her broken skull ached. "This doesn't feel real."

"It doesn't…" Emily sniffled and rubbed her eyes. "But since we're cellmates…" She started shakily. "We might as well introduce ourselves."

They could tell she was trying to change the subject.

"I know who you are." Sam looked at each of them and they gave her curious looks. "You were on the news last night." She picked her head up a fraction and she noticed their looks that meant they understood but their expressions quickly changed to fear.

"It happened so fast…" Carma started after she swallowed the lump in her throat. "We were outside the mall talking and messing around… we grew up together and wanted to catch up after being away for so long but a green colored van pulled up and five people got out."

She turned between Cale and Emily as she relived the moment in her mind.

"We thought they were walking into the mall but they blindsided us and they threw us in a cell with ten other people until we were taken out to be sorted." She brought her eyes to Sam as if she were saying *your turn*.

"I'm Samantha Knight… Sam for short, and my situation came about the same way as yours."

She drew a shaky breath. "My friend came home from college and we wanted to catch up... We saw a rusty van and got nervous but didn't think anything of it until that guy that brought me here tried taking my friend and I fought him until she was able to get away."

"That's a lot more heroic than our story." Carma seemed impressed but her voice was sad.

Sam shook her head. "I'm not heroic, I just wanted to save my friend even if it meant I was taken instead."

The cell was silent until Emily broke it, "And so here we are..." her voice trailed off and her anxiety spread across the cell. "What do you think they want with us?"

"I don't know." Cale replied as his jaw shook and he laid his head in his hands.

"Maybe they're going to eat us?" Carma gulped and Sam looked at her, she looked pale but she knew she looked worse.

She turned to Cale and Emily, she had only just met them but she felt like she had to protect them.

"There's more to it." her head pounded hard and her vision blurred, "If that was the case, they wouldn't have sorted us, and we would likely be dead by now." She gasped from the pain and she felt like she was going to throw up.

Carma placed her hand on her back and started rubbing. "*Breath.*"

Sam listened but her breathing came out labored, she desperately wanted to lay down and she thought of her soft bed at home and longed for it.

"Grab the pillows for her." Carma instructed but Cale was already on his feet and he placed the pillow he had grabbed under her head as Carma helped her lean back against the hard ground.

It was cold but the pain in her head was worse and she had forgotten about her injured ribs.

"So nice of them to leave us pillows." Cale growled sarcastically.

Sam closed her eyes and she thought of what the gargoyles could be planning to do with them until her mind drifted to the dream she had after she was knocked out the first time. She couldn't seem to remember it well as if there were pieces missing.

She wished she understood what the dreams meant but she didn't think much of it because she fell asleep while listening to the others talk softly around her.

She woke up to arguing, she had a dreamless sleep and she hoped everything that had happened was a dream and she would wake up in her bed. Her heart sank as her eyes adjusted and the pain in her head and ribs came rushing back.

She brought her head up slowly, trying not to cause any more pain, and she found Cale standing at the bars arguing with the woman who had locked them in there.

"What are you going to do, young man?" she grinned then chuckled as she cocked her head. "Even if you were on this side of these bars, I'm sure you wouldn't be able to do much."

"I don't know why we're here or what you want to do with us but she's hurt and she needs to see a doctor." Cale growled and he was met with another chuckle.

"Cale." Emily said nervously from beside Sam and he turned to see that she was awake.

"Ah! she's awake!" The woman's face filled with glee. "But she really does look like shit." she admitted.

Sam shakily pulled herself to her feet and Emily rushed to help her.

"What's your name?" She asked the woman as she leaned her head against a bar next to where Cale stood and the woman grinned. "Camilla"

She was the woman who had been called to get everyone ready.

"Well, Camilla." Even with her being taller, Sam had to incline her head to meet her eyes since she slouched from the pain. "I would like you to send your boss here."

Camilla's laugh echoed through the cave as she took in Sam's words.

"He'll be here soon." She turned to walk away but looked back. "I like you two." she grinned at Sam and Cale and with a gleeful snicker, she left.

Sam turned to Cale, "Thanks for that." she smiled gently and he frowned. "It didn't get us anywhere."

She shook her head. "No, it did."

She turned around and sat on the ground near her pillow while the three watched her with curious expressions.

"What do you mean?" Carma asked as she blinked.

"I mean that even though they're the ones that did this to me, they can't afford to lose me... not yet at least." Sam bit her lip as her head continued to throb. "I know there's more to this, they're not trying kill us, they need us." She brought her hand to her face and did the nervous tick that she always did whenever the going got tough. Starting from her forehead, she pulled her hand down to her chin until it fell into her lap. "I'm not going to lie though, I'm scared as hell of what that might be."

"I'm strong," she thought to herself. *"I'm not gonna let this conquer me."*

But how strong could she be in this situation?

"Why do you think he's coming here so soon?" Carma questioned while looking around at her companions. "You'd think he'd make us sit in here for awhile… It's only been two nights for us and one for you and lets not forget the others."

The four remained quiet for a minute.

"He needs to get what he's planning done," Cale suggested while looking at the ground as he thought. "He's doesn't have time to wait."

"But what does he expect from us?" Emily looked around nervously and the cell went quiet again aside from the sound of dripping water and the occasional noise from down the hall.

Sam thought it was nice that even though she didn't know them well, they talked about their situation like they had known her for years.

Perhaps being kidnapped by gargoyles would do that to a person.

They had to be prepared.

A few hours passed and they were beginning to think that Camilla had lied about Arthur being there soon. Sam was looking worse as the minutes ticked on and she thought that maybe she was wrong about her assumption.

Once in a awhile they would hear the cry of another prisoner. Sam said that she was surprised that they weren't making more of a racket and the others told her they already had but it didn't get them anywhere.

Cale punched the rock wall and Carma kneeled beside Sam to check her wound again.

"This is bullshit." he gritted his teeth and Emily who had been sitting in the corner praying to God let out a sob.

Sam regretted agitating Arthur as the ache continued and she leaned her head back and found refuge in the fact that Mina was safe.

"We're gonna die here…" Emily sniffled and Carma sat beside her.

"We won't." she comforted her friend but the lie was clear in her voice as she held back a sob.

Cale who had been standing at the bars walked over and sat next to Sam but left his eyes on the hall. "You said you saw us on the news?" He asked suddenly and she nodded. "I'm sure you're on there now." He bowed his head.

"But they won't find us." Her voice trailed off and her head snapped painfully to the hall as she heard footsteps. She tried getting up but couldn't find the strength so Cale helped her and they faced the bars together. Carma emerged beside Cale while Emily stood behind Sam who could feel her shaking against her back.

Camilla popped into view followed by Kellan and Arthur's assistant then the boss himself.

"Look! they're friends!" Camilla beamed as she grabbed ahold of a bar and yanked it as if she was going to pull it open but it didn't budge.

Sam didn't pay attention to her, she only had eyes for Arthur and it seemed he was the same as his eyes set on hers.

"Thanks for this." she smiled at him and his hazel eyes moved to the wound on her head.

Sam glanced at Kellen who had a triumphant look on his face. "Hey fuckface." she greeted him and his smile broadened.

"God damn, I love her." Camilla pushed her head between two bars and Sam thought it would be hilarious if she got her head caught.

"Why are we here?" Carma asked shakily but otherwise held her composure.

"I think we should make them suffer before we tell them." Camilla pulled her head out of the bars and glanced at Arthur and the others.

"They're going to suffer anyway." Kellan seemed to relish in this. "But I won't complain if you gave us permission to make this one suffer more." He placed his sight back on Sam and her eyes narrowed.

"You're just pissed that I hurt you, maybe you shouldn't underestimate us humans." She gave him a satisfied look and he looked like he was going to try agitating her more but Arthur stirred and everyone's attention went to him.

He stepped forward to get a closer look into the cell. "Humans are weak and selfish creatures who have no right to live the way they do." He looked Sam in the eyes and she hobbled over until she was face to face with him.

"Humans are shit," she gritted her teeth as she looked into his face. "This world is shit, and you are too." she stretched to her full height so she was on the same level as him, the extra inch that he had on her meant nothing.

"Humans are exactly what you say they are and even though I don't know everything you've done, I do know you killed innocent people and you're abducting people to do God knows what with them now." She didn't know why she talked of God when she didn't believe in the being but the saying seemed right. "You have no room to talk."

Arthurs features changed into something she couldn't read as he took a step back and with a simple nod, Kellen pulled the bars apart with a ear ripping screech. In the next second, he grabbed ahold of Sam.

Cale reached for her but his fingers fell through hers as Camilla kicked him into the back of the cell and he landed with a harsh thud. Carma who was about to help Sam as well froze as he blew past her. Sam resisted as Kellan pulled her from the cell but screamed as he wrapped his arms around her lower chest and squeezed her injured ribs. Her screams could be heard through the cave as he carried her down the narrow hall.

Camilla pulled the bars back into place then skipped behind the rest as Sam started to whimper as the pain and fatigue hit her like a train.

They entered the large opening as they followed Arthur and his lackey and Sam could hear her newfound friends yelling behind her and the desperation in their voices.

She wasn't sure if she meant that much to them since they had only known each other for a few hours, but she figured they felt fear in what was going to be their own fate.

Sam was the sneak peak.

They entered the hall that Arthur had exited into earlier before she had even adjusted to the light in the large opening. The new narrow hall looked like the one she had just been in but instead of a cell, the hall ended with a small room as bright as the main opening.

There were cabinets running along the walls and in the middle was an I.V drip standing next to an examination chair that you'd normally see at a doctors office. Only there were straps built in to hold the patient in place.

Sam swallowed, she had acted out and this is where it got her.

She could feel her heart beating against her injured ribs and her brain was pounding with anxiety. She didn't notice that she had stopped with her attempts to get out of Kellen's grip as she took everything in.

"What is this...?" she asked quietly and she was answered with Kellen pushing her into the chair and Camilla strapped her down while he held her in place.

Arthur watched as the man in the lab coat rummaged through some drawers and Sam continued her struggle to get free but it was to no avail. The gargoyles were much stronger than her and had restrained her with ease.

"Leave." Arthur ordered and like a whip, the two snapped and left the room.

"What is this?!" Her voice shook as she pulled her wrists and ankles against the straps as if they could break with her laughable strength.

"I'm sure you can access the situation." Arthur replied and Sam desperately wanted to do her nervous tick and unconsciously tried to raise her hand to do so.

She had an idea of what was going on but she didn't want to say it out loud.

She bit her lip, "Tell me what I'm thinking."

Arthur exhaled sharply as his hazel eyes met hers."I'm turning you into a gargoyle."

Her heart felt like it was going to explode as her fears came true.

"...Why?" She could barely get the word out.

In answer, Arthur began to circle her. "You don't need to know yet."

Sam's heartbeat was shallow and she could barely feel the pain anymore as she focused on Arthurs words and she gulped, "You can explain a little you asshole, you're trying to turn me into a monster and I want some answers."

Arthur laughed and her hair stood up as she felt him behind her until he stepped in front of her and stopped. "All of my followers were once in your position, only they did this voluntarily."

Sam's eyes drifted to the man going through the drawers and she watched as he closed one with a slam then went to a cooler to his left.

She brought her attention back to Arthur, "Why do you need us? Are you planning on turning every human into a monster?"

Arthur closed his eyes and smiled, "There's that word again... *Monster*... No, I'm not turning every human into a monster, you're my last bunch." he started circling again and Sam thought of a shark circling its prey.

"I had my followers go out and hand pick those who looked like they had promise." He continued to explain and she listened with wide eyes. "Two nights ago, Kellen brought me a picture of two girls sitting in a parking lot. One with long blonde hair and the other couldn't be seen due to a glare."

She could hear his breath hitch as he stepped behind her. "I told them to get the blonde girl but they brought you instead." He stopped in front of her again."But I'm far from angry, I heard what you did and you're exactly what I need."

She could see in his eyes that he was hiding something since she could oddly read him but she kept the current conversation going.

"Why aren't the monsters you already have good enough?"

"Because we need all the help we can get." He said simply and turned.

Sam had the feeling that was the most truthful thing he's said so far.

"You won't bend us." she said confidently.

"You? Perhaps not, them? Sure I can." He replied without looking at her as he made his way to the doctor.

"This is Archie, he's what you call a doctor." he turned to face her again as Archie pulled a bag of blood out of the cooler and Sam started fidgeting again.

"He used to be at least, until he joined me." Arthur continued and gestured for his comrade to approach her. "He's human by choice but still supports our cause."

Sam's lip twitched as Archie carried the blood filled bag over to her. "If you're human why are you doing this?!" she tried to pull away as he hung the bag on the drip.

"At this point, you wouldn't understand." he said simply and turned to rummage through another drawer.

How was blood going to make her into a gargoyle?

"This is my blood," Arthur approached again and Sam turned to meet his gaze as she fought her tears from falling. "Gargoyle blood is stronger than human blood, my blood will consume your's and you'll change into a *monster*." He explained with a small grin and Sam's body was shaking uncontrollably now. "H-how did you find this out?"

"It took a few trial and errors but Archie is smart and managed to figure it out."

"You sick motherfuckers..." she pulled against the straps but they continued to hold her in place.

She was wrong, she was weak after all.

Arthur leaned against one of the drawers and crossed his arms as he watched Archie feel for a vein in Sam's arm as she pulled and yanked. She hoped the movement would restrict him from finding one but he managed and stabbed a vein.

She didn't flinch but gasped because she knew what was going to come next. She pulled frantically, if she somehow got lucky the needle would fall out but the damage was already done. The deadly liquid was already streaming through her body and she could feel it eating at her insides.

During the beginning stages, she simply gasped at the sensation until they turned into pain filled screams that could be heard throughout the cave.

Tears splashed onto her cheeks as her eyes darted around the room until they landed on Arthur who was watching her with an even expression but his jaw was clenched.

Her teeth chattered between screams as the blood burned her insides and her heart lurched as her vision went blank and her head fell to the side.

Even with her being out cold, her body still spasmed and screams escaped her lips.

Chapter 5

She stepped through the blood soaked town as screams filled the air. She had grown numb to the sound of death and a part of her relished in it. The night was still young and she could hear her brothers having their fun around the town. She didn't care for the theatrics of the kill that her brothers so enjoyed, she just finished the job and went to the next.

She had just killed a man who ran from her, it didn't take much for her to catch him, humans were slow.

She came to a stop and sighed as she turned towards a liquor store and when she dropped her eyes from the flashing sign, she was met with her own reflection in a large window.

Staring back at her was a young woman, her brown hair braided to her scalp on the right side and blood was splattered over her skin. Her black trenchcoat, pants, and knee high boots were covered as well but the liquid blended with the dark color.

She looked away, uninterested in her own looks, and she continued her assault on the city.

When her eyes opened she was met with florissant light again. Her head ached and a strange feeling ran through her limbs, it was as if a electrical current was flowing through her veins. Her ribs no longer ached and her head injury was gone.

She picked her freshly healed head up from the chair and she was met with Arthur who was leaning against one of the cabinet's with his arms crossed.

"What did you do to me?" she exhaled, the question was stupid, it was already explained to her.

"I made you better." he said matter of factly and uncrossed his arms

His plan had worked, Sam was now a gargoyle. She didn't know what that meant but she did know that she was now a monster.

"Show her." Arthur demanded of Archie who was typing away on a laptop at the far end of the room. He rolled his chair back and grabbed a vanity mirror as he made his way to her.

Her jaw clenched. "Show me what?"

Her eyes were on Arthur until Archie placed the mirror in front of her and she flinched as she took in her eye color: Her pupils and irises were gone and only the whites remained.

Arthur who had been watching her reaction with a emotionless mug spoke. "We have another white eye."

Sam's sight went to him again, she couldn't look at herself anymore.

Archie moved away and went back to his laptop.

"What do you mean by white eye?" she struggled against her restraints. "I thought you all had white eyes?"

"No," like a switch, Arthur's hazel eyes changed to match Sam's. "Eye color signals strength for us, black eyes are the base color, strong but more common. White eyes are stronger and much more rare. Only Kellan, Camilla, and myself have them, though there were more in the past."

Sam listened intently to his explanation, she hated his existence and every word out of his mouth made her want to strangle him, but the need to know about her situation was more important.

"There was another," his jaw clenched. "A black and white eyed gargoyle that was stronger than the other two colors combined. One eye was white while the other was black, it was rumored that there were two in total, one that appeared over a hundred years ago but died, and another that was born not too long ago but died as well."

"They don't seem so powerful to me." Sam felt a smirk spread across her lips and she didn't bother to hide it. "For someone so strong, it's almost hilarious that-" she stopped after she saw the terrifying look on Arthur's face, she had obviously struck a nerve.

"Gargoyles only age until a certain point," he began with a hard tone. "For example, I stopped aging around the age of twenty five but I'm currently over forty years old. "

Sam took in Arthur's features again and she found it hard to believe his true age when he didn't look a day over twenty.

The two of them didn't look too far off in age but he had been around for so much longer than her. A part of her had wondered how someone so young could be the head of this group, even his strong stature did nothing to ease her wonder but now she knew.

His mind was that of a seasoned gargoyle while his body told another story.

Was she immortal now too? He said they stopped aging but did that apply to the new gargoyles? She thought of the black and white eyed gargoyles that he said had died.

They were immortal but they could still be killed by an outside source.

He pushed himself off the cabinet and Sam fell back into the chair as he walked past her, a glare directed at her as he left the room without another word.

She rose a brow at the strangeness of Arthur's departure and she found herself grinding her teeth as Archie's typing began to get on her nerves.

He must have noticed her anger as he stopped his typing and got to his feet then made his way to her. His eyes were dull but she could see a bit of sadness in them.

"Why?" she asked angrily but a tinge of her own sadness could be heard in her tone.

"I'm sorry." he said simply and Sam twitched as she pulled against her restraints, the anger that flowed through her threatened to explode.

"Don't give me that bullshit." She spat. "You're no better than that bastard."

He watched as she pulled the leather straps. "I'm sorry but you are misinformed," he bowed his head and his dark eyes fell. "One day you'll know the truth."

"I don't wanna be informed." she snarled and she felt something forming in her mouth and she flinched as that something pierced her tongue.

Archie stepped over to the cabinet where he had left the mirror and when he returned, he placed it in front of her again.

What she saw in her reflection shocked her more than her eyes: Her teeth had formed into points.

"If you don't control yourself, you really will be a monster." Archie looked into her eyes without an ounce of fear from her monstrous look.

Sam thought about his words and breathed slowly to settle herself down.

Archie turned on his heel, setting the mirror down as he walked away, and as Sam's heart calmed, her eyes went back to hazel and her teeth retracted.

Tears began to fall and she closed her eyes as she lowered her head, letting her hair fall over her face to hide them. She fought to keep her sobs muffled, she didn't want to give anyone the satisfaction of seeing her cry. She bit her lip so hard it bled but it sewed itself shut as soon as the blood slid down her chin.

"It'll get easier." Archie assured with his back to her.

"Take me back to my cage." she growled and as if on cue, Kellan strutted into the room and her head shot up. "Arthur tells me you have white eyes." his smug face was obviously a result of her suffering. "Congrats."

She lowered her ahead again, the fight she had in her was essentially gone.

"You disappoint me." he scoffed at her lack of argument as he undid her restraints and forced her up. Her legs felt like jelly and she almost fell but he grabbed under her arms and pulled her back up.

"All set, doc?" he asked as he craned his head towards Archie who nodded. He grinned as he turned turned away from the doctor. "I'll bring the next one."

The next one...

Her head wobbled as he pulled her out of the makeshift hospital room into the dimly lit hall.

"Don't tell me that's all it took to break you?" he huffed as he pulled her into the hall her cell was in.

She remained silent until he pulled one of the bar's out of the way and pushed her inside the cell. She hit the ground hard and she could hear the shuffle of her cellmates approaching her.

"Look at me." she demanded as Kellan began to walk away and he gave her an expecting look. "The silent one's are the one's you have to watch out for, so be wary of me being quiet." She warned as she felt a strange pressure in her eyes and Kellan relished in the threat.

"I'm glad." he exclaimed as he walked away.

Carma knelt in front of her and placed a hand on her shoulder as Cale and Emily knelt beside them.

"Sam.. what did they do to you?" Her voice shook. "We heard you screaming then everything went quiet… we thought…" she gulped. "…they killed you."

Sam shook her head, she didn't want them to see what was under her eyelids so she kept them closed.

"It's worse." She swallowed and Carma tried lifting her chin so she would look at her.

"This is what's gonna happen to us too." Cale told her gently but she could hear the fear in his voice. "We want to know what that is."

He was right, they deserved to know.

She opened her eyes slowly and with her heart racing, she revealed her two white orbs.

Her cellmates gasped as they saw them, the eyes that were once hazel and human were now the eyes of a gargoyle.

"This is our fate." Her lips trembled. "They're turning us into gargoyles."

"No…" Carma's voice echoed through their cell. "This can't be happening.."

"I'm sorry." Sam closed her eyes again and the pressure started to diminish with her despair.

"We have to get out of here…" Emily's eyes were wide with fear and she started to shake.

"This has to be a nightmare… I have to be dreaming." she got up and ran to the bars and Carma followed. "We can't be turned into monsters… we can't… We heard you screaming…" Her voice broke. "Oh God, we won't even survive it."

Carma grabbed ahold of the bars alongside Emily and they pulled like they had the chance at moving them.

"Let us out!" Emily screamed and it echoed through the cave. "We'll do anything! Please!" Before long the other prisoners started begging along with the two girls.

Sam brought her gaze to Cale who kept his head bowed as he shook.

Sam was a freshly made monster, a sneak peak to her cellmates of what their fate was.

She brought her attention back to the begging girls and for some unknown reason it brought her back to her most recent dream. Although she didn't remember much, she did remember her own reflection. It was the first time she had seen herself in a dream and she was surprised that even with everything being so unfamiliar, the figure in the reflection was her.

But it wasn't at the same time.

The girl looking back at her was the same height, had the same hair color, and had the same build, but she was different in so many ways.

Sam averted her gaze from the girls but continued to listen to them as they begged and she knew one of the guards would be there soon to shut them up.

This was not the time to be thinking of dreams, it made no difference for her reality.

She had to find a way to get out of there, but as she began to plan, she heard the screaming of a suffering prisoner mixed with the girls begging.

The others heard it as well and they listened quietly with terrified expressions. The screaming was blood curdling and Sam recognized it immediately as the way she had sounded not too long ago.

She got to her feet but felt dizzy so she struggled along the wall to the bars to keep herself upright. Through the bars, she could see Camilla making her way down the narrow path towards them. She had a smile on her face and her blue eyes were filled with satisfaction, it was like the pain filled screams were a melody to her.

"What's with the yelling?" she stopped in front of the bars, "And I'm not asking about the lad in the docs room."

"Y-you have to let us out of here." Carma stammered.

Camilla blinked. "Why would I do that?"

The yelling died down as the girls began to beg again and Cale, who Sam noticed got up in the corner of her eye, placed his hands on his friends shoulders. "She's not going to let us out, we went through this when we first got here."

Sam imagined them being thrown into a cell upon their arrival and the three of them doing what the girls were doing now. Carma fell to her knees while Emily backed away from the bars and fell against the hard wall as their despair turned into silence.

Sam and Camilla gazed at Cale, Sam's face filled with sadness while Camilla's was filled with amusement. If Cale was feeling like his friends, he didn't show it.

"You can leave now." He spat but Camilla shook her head, her short bangs sweeping back and forth across her forehead.

"No can do, one of you needs to come with me."

Sam Gulped.

"No!" Carma screamed and Cale positioned himself protectively in front of his friends.

"It hurts like hell but once it's over, you'll feel brand new." she brought her attention to Sam who was struggling to move to help Cale.

"Fuck off." She snarled as she wobbled.

"That'll wear off," Camilla acknowledged her clumsiness."You're only in the beginning stages, there's so much more waiting for you."

"Leave them alone." Sam finally made it to Cale and she stood straight.

"Stop messing with them and grab one." Sam turned at the sound of the new voice and she noticed a man walking towards them. He was tall and his blonde hair was darkened due to the dull light in the hall. His blue eyes matched his sad tone.

"You're boring." Camilla sulked like a child but pulled on a bar as the man watched. "I think I'll go for one of the girls." She snickered and there was a commotion as she stepped into the cell as the man guarded the large hole between the bars.

Sam and Cale tried getting Camilla away from Carma and Emily as they cowered but Cale was no match for a gargoyle and Sam was too new to her power to make a difference.

"Stop!" Cale yelled as Camilla grabbed ahold of Carma by the collar of her shirt.

The cell went quiet as their attention switched to Cale where he was leaning against the left wall alongside Sam where Camilla had pushed them.

"...Take me instead." his voice shook but he held onto his fake strength.

"You can't save them forever." Camilla shrugged as she pushed Carma to the ground and walked over to Cale, her face still bright with excitement. She grabbed the front of his shirt and slammed the back of his head into the rock wall so hard that it knocked him out.

"Cale!" Sam reached for him as he fell to the ground but Camilla pinged her and she fell beside him.

"Oops." She chuckled as she grabbed ahold of Cale's collar and pulled his unconscious body from the ground.

"He was willingly coming you *bitch*." Sam growled as Camilla flung him over her shoulder, if the situation wasn't so dire, the image would have been funny: A six foot tall man slung over the shoulder of a five foot tall woman.

"Just to make sure he doesn't try anything." Camilla winked.

Sam's knees buckled as she tried getting up, she desperately wanted to help Cale but her stupid body was too weak.

"You'll get used to it my friend." Camilla smiled as she stepped out of the cell and the newcomer pulled the bars back into place.

"We're not friends." Sam gritted her teeth as Emily and Carma tried running for Cale, their screams filling the hall again.

With a pit in her stomach, Sam watched as Cale's head bounced off of Camilla's back until they were out of sight.

Chapter 6

The cave was filled with the echo of Cale's screams and out of anger, Sam punched the cave floor and she was surprised to see a little crack where her fist had landed.

"I'm so weak!" Carma roared and Sam watched as she paced the bars.

Carma's attitude had turned around as soon as Cale's screams could be heard.

"Sam." Carma rounded on her as she sat on the cold ground with her arms around her knees, her head resting on them.

"It's already happened to you, what's the probability of Cale living through this?" Sam looked into her watery blue eyes and weighed the question in her mind.

"For the little time that I've known Cale, I've learned that he's strong." It was a strange thing to say, not that Cale was strong, but the implications it had, that you had to be strong to survive. Sam didn't feel strong but she had survived.

Carma nodded as if she was assuring herself.

The yelling died down like it had with Sam and the other new gargoyle and the cave went silent again.

Sam closed her eyes, her body felt strange but she didn't have time to dwell on it while she worried for Cale.

Emily who was leaning against the rounded corner of the cave looked dead inside as she looked at the wall with a blank expression.

Carma made her way over to her and placed a comforting hand on her shoulder then they threw themselves into a hug while Sam watched. She felt out of place, her only friend was safe at home because of her and even though she was stuck in here and she now had a monsters body, she wouldn't change the fact that she had taken Mina's place.

"Sam." Carma said after she pulled away from the hug and Sam resurfaced from her thoughts. "We're sorry, it won't happen again."

Sam tilted her head in confusion. "What are you talking about?"

"I was weak." She walked over again and knelt down in front of her, her blue eyes meeting Sam's hazel. "I'm going to protect Emily and Cale."

Sam nodded. "And I'll help."

The girls looked at each other with determination in their eyes but it was broken when they heard footsteps echoing down the narrow hall leading to their cell.

Sam started to pull herself up and when she had trouble, Carma helped her and she nodded in thanks. The girls walked to the bars and Emily followed. Sam listened as the steps came closer and she noticed a dragging sound along with them. Her eyes widened as she looked at the other girls to see if they could hear it too but they didn't seem to notice.

"Hey!" Camilla said as she came into view and behind her was Kellan who was dragging Cale's unconscious body by the back of his shirt.

"Cale!" Carma and Emily began to pull on the bars to get to their friend while Sam watched with wide eyes.

"Get the hell out of the way." Kellan demanded as Camilla pulled the bars apart and the girls caught Cale as Kellan threw him in.

Cale's head rolled to the side as Carma helped him to ground and Sam watched as the girls fussed over him to get him to wake up. She was so focused on the others that she didn't notice the two gargoyles watching her.

"He has black eyes in case you wanted to know." Kellan's bored face changed to humor as soon as he started talking to Sam. "Look at you," He continued. "If you saw yourself right now, you wouldn't know what to do."

"What's that supposed to mean?" She questioned but didn't get her answer as Cale woke and the girls cried in relief as he groaned from their weight as they hugged him.

Sam kneeled down in front of him as Carma and Emily pulled away.

"I'm fine." he assured them with a small smile but Sam knew he was bullshitting them, she could tell from the look in his eyes.

He moved his weak gaze from the girls to Sam.

"When does this feeling go away?" he asked softly and she figured he was talking about the burning feeling in his bones.

She shook her head, she was about to disappoint him. "It hasn't yet." she replied and to her surprise, he grinned sheepishly. "Figures."

The girl's helped him to a wall so he could lean against it and Carma demanded for Sam to do the same since she still wasn't looking good. Sam turned back to Camilla and Kellan before doing so but the hall was empty.

She stumbled a few steps as she made her way to the wall but Emily wrapped her arm around her shoulders to keep her upright. She leaned on the wall next to Cale after Emily helped her down, the cold rock felt good against her burning body.

"I'm so sorry I panicked, I-" Carma blurted as she leaned over them but Cale silenced her with a raised hand.

"Don't." The simple gesture seemed to take all of the strength out of him.

Carma lowered her head. "I'm going to let you guys rest…let me know of you need me."

Sam watched as Carma made her way to the other side of the cell and laid down on her side, her face away from them. Emily had laid down in the middle of the cell and Sam could hear her teeth chattering. She glanced sideways at Cale and she knew he could hear it too, even though it was a soft chatter, the two of them could hear it.

"How are you holding up?" she broke the silence after watching him watch his friends for a few moments.

"I feel like shit, emotionally and physically." he drew a shallow breath. "I can't believe this is happening…"

Sam wasn't good with comforting people especially with her feeling like shit herself, so she said the first thing that came to mind.

"Me too…"

Sam woke with a start and tried getting up but stopped as she expected to be sore from falling asleep unexpectedly against the uncomfortable rock but she didn't feel sore at all.

She rolled her shoulders and was surprised at how light they felt.

After thinking about it for a moment, she realized that the burning feeling had disappeared.

She felt brand new, like her body wasn't hers. She didn't even have a strange dream, if she wasn't in this situation, she would have enjoyed the feeling.

She turned to Cale and found that he was still asleep, his face had returned to it's normal color and he looked so peaceful that she didn't want to wake him. Besides, she didn't know if it was night or the middle of the day, it was hard to tell in the cave.

She moved her sight from him to see if Carma and Emily were still asleep but she was met with empty space. Her heart thumped as she started to feel sick.

"C-Cale." she mumbled breathlessly but it was too low for him to hear while he was asleep so she tapped him on his cheek with her index finger.

He opened his eyes and blinked a couple times, "Sam?" he leaned forward and she dropped her hand.

"They're gone..." Her voice shook and she watched as realization filled his face as he looked around the empty cell.

He jumped to his feet and ran to the front of the cell, "Carma!" He roared. "Emily!" He pulled on the bars and Sam helped but neither of them knew how to use their new power.

"They took them out from under us!" he roared as he continued to pull.

"They knew we were weak so they took the opportunity..." Sam's voice drifted as she watched Cale slump to the ground when he realized his efforts were useless.

Her heart thumped as she watched him place his face into his hands and she heard a sob escape his lips. "All I wanted to do was protect them but I knew this was inevitable." he looked up, his eyes meeting her's and she noticed that they had turned pitch black.

Sam thought of how she had saved Mina from this fate, it wasn't because she was strong nor was it was destiny, it was all due to chance.

She kneeled down and for once the consoling part came naturally as she rested her hand on his shaking shoulder. As if the action calmed him, his eyes returned to normal, the black dissolving like ink into the sides of his eyes.

"They're gonna get through this...We're gonna get through this." she removed her hand from his shoulder but she kept her eyes on his, "I'm going to make all of them pay." her gaze was sharp, her eyes like daggers, and Cale nodded with a determined look.

"When they get back, we're gonna make a plan." She smiled. "We're gonna get out of here."

"I'm happy we ended up in here with you." Cale smiled sadly.

She rose a brow. "Why's that?"

"You're different, If you were in the corner crying we definitely wouldn't make it."

"I feel like shit though," she closed her eyes and leaned her head back. "But I can't let this conquer me, not until everyone is out of here at least."

But that seemed impossible, she was likely to go insane in there.

"We have a long time to get out." Cales voice woke her from her thoughts and she glanced at him with her head still leaned back.

"You know gargoyles don't age?" she asked as she leveled her head.

"The doctor or whatever he is told me before he turned me into a gargoyle." he shivered at the thought.

Sam kept her gaze on him as she thought of all the things she had been told by Arthur and Archie, what were they gaining by explaining this to them now? They explained enough to keep their prisoners informed but it was obvious that they were still hiding so much. Anything that left their mouth's could be a lie.

"I need to know everything." She said.

"Knowing everything can make a person insane." Cale warned and his gaze moved from Sam to the end of the cell where shadows could be seen moving towards them.

Sure enough, the sound of footsteps filled their ears.

The two shot up as they started to hear dragging along with shallow breaths. Sam closed her eyes and drew a breath, there was only one person being dragged and that could mean two things... She opened her eyes and looked at Cale who she knew at first glance was thinking the same thing. The two waited as the steps grew closer and their nerves grew more restless until Kellan came into view along with Camilla and Emily in tow.

"You fuckers blindsided us." Cale growled as he reached through the bars for Emily who was barely awake and she groaned as Kellan grabbed a bar as per usual and Camilla threw her in. Kellan pulled the bar back into place within seconds, giving them no time to escape.

Cale had moved out of the way to retrieve Emily before she hit the ground and he patted her cheek as her eyes flickered between her normal brown and pitch black.

Sweat dripped off her and she shook with each breath, she had taken the transformation harder than Cale and Sam.

"It was easier that way." Kellan answered with a shrug and Sam who stood over Cale and Emily turned her head to see the two gargoyles standing in front of the bars and it looked like they enjoyed the view.

"I swear to God I'll fucking ruin you." She gritted her teeth but was met with laughter.

She bit her lip and she could tell that her teeth were expanding from the anger she felt.

Their laughter echoed through the cave and when Sam thought she was going to go crazy from the noise, they finally quieted down. Kellan sniffed like his outburst of laughter had almost brought him to tears.

"By the time we're done with you, you won't believe there's a God." his voice was steady but she could still hear the amusement.

"I already don't." she replied roughly, she didn't believe, she never had.

"Where's Carma?" Emily groaned and Sam turned back to see her trying to get up. "She got changed before me..."

Cales eyes widened. "What..?"

"I thought…they already brought her back." she gulped as she slowly looked around the cell then back and forth between Cale and Sam.

Cale rushed to his feet and gripped the bars so hard that Sam could hear the steel whining under his touch.

Emily leaned on her elbow "Cale…please."

"What'd you do to her?!" he roared and Sam watched with wide eyes as his tan skin turned to a grayish color and the top of his ears grew into points. His mouth was now filled with pointed teeth that were bared at Kellan and Camilla. He was looking more monstrous by the second and Sam thought of the stone gargoyles that rested on top of buildings.

Kellan and Camilla smiled "It's not what we did to her, it's more of what Arthur has planned for her." Kellan explained with a pleased look then turned to Sam, "It seems you're not the only white eye in this batch."

Sam's jaw clenched.

"Why does that matter?!" Cale began yelling again. "Sam's eyes are white too, what makes Carma different?!"

Camilla merely shrugged, "We don't know why our boss does what he does."

Cale gripped on the bars so tight that his veins began to pop out and Sam's heart skipped when the sound of one of the bars moving filled her ears. The organ gave a gleeful jolt as she saw the bar bend. The achievement was short-lived as Kellan punched Cale square in the face through the bars and Cale was flung all the way to the back on the cell with a loud crash as he landed against the cave wall. Small rocks fell around him as he landed on the ground and Sam unconsciously covered her ears from the sound.

"Cale!" Emily crawled weakly over to him.

"Chill out." Kellan's voice was harsh and it was enough to send chill's down their spines.

"You act like you don't know anything but I'm sure you have some details." Sam turned away from Cale and Emily who both looked devastated. Cale had returned to his normal look, Kellan's hit must have helped with that.

Kellan's eyes were white from the power he had exerted to hit Cale and Sam thought of the night she was captured and the fear she had felt at what she thought had been an illusion.

Now she carried the same illusion.

"He's interested, that's all." he replied with relish while extending his arm and rolling his wrist.

"I'm a white eye too and he sent me back here." She used Cale's argument.

"You're not that special princess." Kellan grinned then laughed as Camilla did the same, her short hair bobbing as her laughs echoed through the cave.

The diss itself didn't bother Sam but her heightened hearing proved to be a problem without having control over it, their laughs made her ears ring.

"I'm hurt." she replied sarcastically and gritted her teeth.

"You'll see her again, don't you worry." he looked down into her eyes as they returned to their normal blue. "She won't be the same, she might not even be whole, but I assure you, you *will* see her again."

"It'll be so much fun when you do." Camilla chimed in, she had been quiet aside from her laughter. It was as if she was trying to keep her mouth shut.

"You're a loudmouth but you've been awfully quiet." Sam set her sight on Camilla and she felt her pride swell at the sight of her being caught off guard.

"I said this once and I'll say it again…you're all going to pay for this." she could feel the pressure in her eyes and she knew they had changed again. "You better hope Carma is alright or I'll make sure your suffering is slow." she could hear the venom in her own voice and it scared her.

Kellan chuckled, the fear obviously didn't reach him. "You're awfully bold." he leaned down and got so close to Sam that they were almost touching noses. "The same goes for you, I remember what you did when I caught you and I won't be satisfied until you're begging for mercy."

"Not going to happen." she growled and she thought of her own stupidity, she was going to get herself killed.

All Kellan did was grin as he walked away while Camilla followed. The mouthy woman was definitely holding her tongue and as Sam watched them leave from view and was about to turn back to Cale and Emily, Camilla's voice echoed through the tunnel.

"We'll make sure her screams won't keep you up!" Her tone was filled with glee and it made Sam sick.

"NO!" Emily lost it and Sam gulped as she turned to see their reactions: Emily was shaking with her right hand covering her mouth and her tears splashed onto her fingers. The hand did nothing to cover her sobs.

Cale had his left hand over his eyes and his mouth was in a straight line, Sam noticed his shoulders bobbing as he tried to hold back his emotions.

Sam sunk to her knees, she didn't know Carma well but she had been there for her since the moment they were thrown into the cell together.

She wanted to help Carma but how could she help her when she couldn't help herself?

The pressure in her eyes disappeared as sadness washed over her. The situation was getting more and more dire and the little hope that she had of getting out of there was washing away.

She closed her eyes, she had succeeded in consoling Cale before but there was no way it was going work this time.

Chapter 7

No one knew how many day's had passed since Carma was taken, the cool and dark atmosphere of the cave made sure of that. They hadn't seen any sign of Arthur, Kellan, or Camila since that day as well. Only fodder guards would come by as Sam would call them to check on the prisoners and they brought food consisting of crackers, cold soup, and water.

They had heard screams throughout what they had guessed was a few days, but not once did Sam think it was Carma. She didn't want to ask Cale and Emily their opinion on the matter so she would look at them to see their reactions and they never once gave her the hint that it was Carma.

They were currently sitting on opposite sides of the cell as they listened to another innocent human being turned into a gargoyle. They'd been distant from each other since Carma was taken so sitting alone was normal for them.

The cell was cold and Sam constantly had goosebumps as she sat against the wall and she would constantly think of ways to get out there but with every idea she had, the bad outweighed the good.

The three of them had seen better days: They were weak and hungry, their clothes were stained from sleeping on the dirty ground and Sam had dried blood from her healed wounds.

The males screaming filled the cave as the three sat with what looked like uninterested expressions. Although the screams reminded them of the pain they had felt when they were changed and of the situation they were in, they seemed numb to it all.

Sam had her arms around her legs and her head against the wall. She was planning again but as usual, she wasn't going anywhere with it.

She opened her eyes when the thinking got to be too much and sighed, her breath coming out as vapor in the cool cave.

She frowned, she hadn't had any dreams since her last and she vividly remembered it.

Her frown deepened as she turned her head to look at Cale and Emily through the dim light of their cell. They hadn't spoken much to each other since Carma was taken.

Sam closed her eyes again and pursed her lips, she had to change that.

"What did you guys do before you ended up here?" her voice sounded hoarse from the lack of use. Emily looked up absentmindedly as if the question didn't register and Cale looked surprised that Sam was trying to start a conversation.

"Let's not fight who gets to go first." Sam awkwardly smiled.

Cale and Emily turned to look at each other as if they could communicate silently.

Maybe Sam should have kept her mouth shut and as she was about to go back to her thinking, Emily's voice filled the cave and she sounded like a mouse from the lack of talking.

"I was going to college for physiology."

Sam was happy they were willing to talk.

"What does that mean?" She considered herself knowledgeable to an extent but she was nowhere near intelligent.

"I study the functions in living organisms and how the human mind works." Emily seemed to perk up and Sam was glad that she had helped with that.

"She's wicked smart." Cale told Sam while smiling gently, he knew what she was getting at.

Emily got flustered and shot Cale an embarrassed look. "I'm not that smart."

"It would seem you are," Sam grinned. "I'm not going to college at all." she turned to Cale "What about you?"

"I joined the military instead," He announced. "I was home on break when I was taken." his smile dimmed. "All I could think of was home when I was at training but I knew I'd be able to go back, but now… I'm not so sure." He looked at the ground. "I miss home."

"Me too." Emily sighed as her lip quivered.

"What's it like where you live?" Sam wanted to try to keep the mood she had planted.

"I live with my adoptive father," Cale replied. "I don't remember my adoptive mother because she passed when I was young." he drew a breath and continued. "My father got a job as a teacher in Japan so I pretty much lived by myself. I couldn't believe it when he told me he was going, he even wanted me to go with him but I wanted to join the military."

He lifted his head and looked at an empty space as he pictured the memory.

"Now I wish I'd gone." He paused for a moment as he thought of his choices. "We have another house that we were fixing up after my aunt left it to me…I never got the chance to stay in it since I was gone."

Sam was genuinely intrigued with Cale's story but sad at the same time, she had no right to complain about her living situation, at least she had a family and someone to come home to.

"Your father seems like a great man." She had to talk over the yelps of the man being changed.

"He was a teacher long before I was born, it was something he had always wanted to do and I was happy that he finally got the chance." Cale averted his gaze. "He must be worried about me."

"We've been friends since middle school." Emily hurriedly tried to change the subject. "Mr. Harper was my teacher in seventh grade, he's actually the reason why Cale, Carma, and I became friends."

Cale laughed, "Because Carma and I sucked at math and he had you tutor us."

Emily snickered. "Your father was a math teacher but he couldn't even teach you."

The two laughed and Sam found herself joining in. She thought of Mina and how she could be herself around her like Cale, Emily, and Carma could be with each other.

"What about you, Sam?"

She almost jumped at Emily's question, she didn't think about telling her own story.

"I live with my mom, dad, and brother and I work as a receptionist." She flicked a pebble that had fallen from the side of the cell.

"Well, I guess I *used* to work there." she pursed her lips and glanced upwards, this was the first time she wanted to talk about her dreams. The urge was sudden and maybe the fact that Emily had studied physiology had triggered her.

She didn't want them to think she was crazy.

But maybe she was.

"...I know this is random." She inhaled sharply. "But have you dealt with anyone during your studies that had dreams that were random and recurring?"

Her heart leapt as Emily considered her.

"Yeah there's plenty of cases like that." Emily started and Sam felt a twinge of relief but it was short-lived as Emily continued. "But what kind are you having? Are they nightmares? have you been to the places in your dreams when you were awake?"

"No..." Sam started gingerly. "I've never been to these places and the setting feels-" she couldn't think of a way to word it. "...Old."

Emily rose a brow, not in a judgemental way but in a *I want to know more* way.

"People have odd dreams but most of the time they're in a place they've been to in real life."

Sam could tell that Emily was weighing the options in her mind and she turned to Cale who seemed intrigued but not as much as his friend.

"Did you watch any movies that could have triggered it? Any books you read?" Emily questioned finally and Sam shook her head, there was more that she could explain but chose not to: That she had seen someone who looked just like her. The image of her blood splattered self filled her mind and it was all she could think about.

Her eyes widened.

Blood.

Why was there blood?

An idea popped into her head.

"Cale." She called and Emily jumped as the mood changed while Cale perked up.

"What kind of training did you have while you were in the military?"

"Hand to hand combat, defense, how to use a gun…why?" He leaned forward and his elbows rested on his knees.

A light was going off in Sam's head, she had thought about this before but not to this extent.

"I've taken Taekwondo to help with my anxiety…I wonder with our new abilities and with our knowledge with fighting, that it could give us a chance?" she looked down into her opened hand.

"They don't expect us to go out of our way to teach ourselves how to be gargoyles." She looked up again and met their eyes. "I don't want to force you to do this, I plan on keeping my humanity, but this needs to be done to get out of here." She swallowed. "We need to get out of here before they decide to move on with their plan."

Cale didn't think about it and by the way he acted, it seemed like he had been thinking the same thing. He got to his feet and turned to look at the bar that he had bent days before. Kellan nor Camilla had bothered to fix it.

They needed to bend it the rest of the way to get out of there, they had tried but with the strength they currently had, they had failed.

They had tried breaking the bars with rage or any emotion that caused the power to swell, but with no control, there was no chance for them.

Sam finally saw an opening at the end of the tunnel, *no*, the cave.

With Cale having combat training and with her low tier fighting experience, the thought she had refused for so long finally shined bright.

They had to learn how to be gargoyles, they had to learn how to be monsters.

Chapter 8

Sam had started Taekwondo when she was twelve. She was forced by her mother to go to a nail salon with her and the small spa was located in a plaza along with a pizza joint and a taekwondo school. By the time her mothers nails were done, Sam had persuaded her to let her join but not without begging. Her first class was nerve wracking, she made mistakes and it took her awhile to get the moves down but once she got used to it, it came naturally.

While the others kids went to shows, Sam only used her training as a means of escape from her anxiety. She thought of the night that she had taken Mina's place and had gotten herself into this mess. She had been distracted because of the danger and had forgotten everything that could have helped her. The result would have most likely been the same but the thought still bothered her.

"I'm not going to be as good as you guys." Emily warned as she watched the other two as they stood only a foot apart. They had decided to try emotion control before training how to fight. Their emotions proved to be a problem and it caused them to transform when they didn't mean to and they would lose control. Cale's partial transformation from the other day was an example of that.

"I'm sure it has more to do with focus than fighting ability." Cale assured Emily as he kept his eyes on Sam. They had decided to keep a close eye on each others eyes to see if there was even a hint of a change.

They tried anger and while it worked and their eyes changed to their respective colors, there seemed to be an edge to their power. As they tried pulling the bars, their strength seemed to be cut in in half. Whatever Cale had felt when he had bent the bar was still unknown, it was hard to believe there was anything other than anger.

"What else did you feel?" Sam had asked after they forced themselves to calm down.

"All I can remember is wanting to rip Kellan's head off." Cale replied breathlessly and Sam huffed "Believe me, I know the feeling."

Even though she knew the feeling, her anger seemed to center around Camilla after her fiasco with Carma.

They tried sadness next but it didn't get them anywhere other than into a worse mood.

Sam groaned and let herself fall to the ground, what the hell were they going to do?

She reached for her face and did her nervous tick and through her fingers, she saw Cale making his way over to Emily who watched with a disappointed face as her friend sat beside her.

Sam dropped her hand, her fingers hitting the cold rock with a *thump* and her cold fingers ached.

"This shit's not working." Emily made an exasperated noise and practically banged her head on the rock behind her.

Her exasperation quickly turned to sadness.

"...We're going to die in here." her voice shook and Cale nor Sam had the strength or will to comfort her and they felt worse because of it.

"I don't know what to do." Sam rolled her head to the side and looked into the hall.

They had no experience being gargoyles, they were forced into this. It was almost funny that just days ago, Sam was talking about demons with Mina and it turned out that the creatures were actually gargoyles. Maybe the government called them demons because they resembled them so much.

"We can practice our combat skills for self protection in the meantime." Cale suggested."It won't help much but if we're not getting anywhere with learning our transformations, we can learn how to fight for when we do." His words woke Sam from her funk and she nodded.

"Yeah…" she agreed as she rose to her feet and Cale followed suite.

"You too, Emily." He gestured for her to get up.

She looked exasperated, "You know I can't do this." she protested but got up anyway.

"Won't know until you try." Cale said simply.

"I know." she agreed as she stood at the back wall and the three looked like they were in a triangle: Emily at the top while Sam and Cale stood at the bottom.

Emily swept her arm in front of her as if she was saying *Get on with it* and Sam and Cale looked at each other. They were the only ones with fighting experience but neither seemed to want to be the one to start. As Sam was about to suggest that Cale go first, he beat her to it.

"Show us what you know." He told her.

He seemed like he was genuinely interested in what she could do and she didn't blame him, she wanted to know what he could do as well.

She exhaled nervously and looked out into the hall to see if the coast was clear even though she could've just listened, she guessed old habits really did die hard.

She brought her attention back to Emily and Cale, "I took Taekwondo for awhile and I practiced at home even after I stopped." She met their eyes. "I did it to get my mind off of stuff."

She motioned for them to come closer and they complied.

"I'm going start off with simple self defense moves that I learned when I first started."

Cale looked determined while Emily was noticeably nervous. But that's why she was starting off small.

"Unfortunately when push came to shove, I failed at using what I'm about to show you." Her eyes fell. "I let the adrenaline get to me and I need to work on that." It was hard to hide the disappointment that she felt in herself. "Sometimes it's easier to run but if they grab ahold of you…well I'm not sure how well this will work against gargoyles, but you hit them where it hurts: The eyes." she took her index and middle finger and pointed them at Cales eyes as if she were about to poke them. She listed off the throat, nose, knees, and groin and as she did so, she pointed to each part but dropped her hand when she listed the groan.

That was too awkward.

Emily seemed to calm at the simplicity of Sam's directions but she still had a frown on her face.

They practiced the art of escape and they made it as real as possible by taking turns grabbing each other. They found even though they didn't know how to use their abilities, they could still feel the difference in the person being the aggressor as they grabbed ahold of them. Their strength clearly wasn't human and it practically knocked the wind out of them.

When getting out of their aggressors hold, their jabs were faster than a normal human and it hurt a hell of a lot more than it would if a human had done it.

Cale did well at the exercise since he had learned it at basic training and Sam wasn't too far off although she was a tad rusty since she had no one to practice with for so long. Emily caught on after a few tries.

When they got free, they would would run and the aggressor would chase them and that's when they had their mini sparring session.

By the time they were done, the three of them were sore in the spots that Sam had listed.

No one had gone for the groan thankfully.

They had tried being gentle but it proved to be difficult with their lack of control.

Emily sat on the ground while Sam and Cale leaned against their respective walls.

"Ow." She exclaimed then surprisingly grinned, her smile turning into laugher.

Cale and Sam looked at her as if she was crazy but found themselves chuckling at her, her change in attitude spread to them as well.

Why are you laughing?" Cale asked her after she was finished.

"Have you ever hurt yourself and instead of yelling or crying, you laugh instead?" she asked as she wiped her eyes since tears had formed from her laughter.

"I think everyone has done that." Cale reached to help her to her feet when she stretched her arm to him.

"What else do you have to teach us?" Sam was surprised that Emily was the first to ask and she looked into the hall again and listened for anyone coming. After assuring herself that the coast was clear, she brought her attention back to her cellmates.

"Quite a bit."

Sam leaned her head against the cold wall and listened to the water dripping in their cell. It had taken her a few minutes to differentiate between that and the sweat dripping off of her and the others. It was freezing in the cave but their movements had warmed them up and then some.

Sam had taught them every taekwondo move she could remember and she had no idea how rusty she was so she didn't stop practicing until she had every move as good as she had it before. After her instruction, Cale showcased all of his military training.

Which was a lot.

By the time they were done, it felt like several hours had gone by and they all sat down as exhaustion weighed them down. Sam had made the assumption that their transformations had helped them in being able to train longer. She was sure they would have been done long ago if they were still human.

Steam rose from where their skin met the rock and Sam welcomed the cool stone.

"I don't know how you guys do that." Emily groaned as she got to her feet and leaned against the wall. Cale who was in more shape than both Sam and Emily since he had only been back from basic training for only a couple weeks still looked tired. Even with them being supernatural creatures, Sam figured that the lack of proper nutrition and the environment took it's toll on them.

"I don't know to be honest with you." Cale chuckled softly and Sam smiled at the friends. It seemed wrong that they smiling with Carma being gone but they were planning on saving her. Laying around and crying wouldn't do anything.

Sam knew Cale and Emily were feeling the pain of Carma's absence but they were also holding onto hope that she was going to be ok.

At the end of the day, Carma was more useful alive than dead.

Sam jumped as she was caught off guard with the sound of footsteps echoing at the end of the tunnel. The three jerked their heads towards each other, they had done this every time they heard someone coming down the tunnel but more often than not it was a guard bringing them their food.

They were hoping for Kellan and Camilla to return and Sam wasn't sure about Cale and Emily but she was also waiting for Arthur to show his face as well.

If any of them were to show up, they could try getting answers about Carma and what they were going to do next. Though Sam was sure they weren't going to get a straight answer, she wanted to know more about Arthur's plan, his real plan to be exact.

Finally the man that was with Camilla when she had taken Cale came into view and he looked at them with an uninterested expression. It was as if he was counting to see if all three of them were in there. He kneeled down and pushed three bowls of cold chicken noodle soup through the bars then he stood back up and left. Sam waited for him to leave the hall before she grabbed the bowls and handed two of them to Cale and Emily and kept one for herself.

As she sat down, she sloshed the pieces of chicken around in the broth and she sniffed the soup. It was far from appetizing and they hadn't eaten it the first few times but as hunger won over their stubbornness, they finally took a taste.

As Sam took a sip of her current bowl, she gagged as the cold liquid touched her throat.

She forced herself to swallow and her eyes watered as she coughed through her gags. She turned to the right where they had left the jug of water that the guards had supplied for them and took a swig. After composing herself, she got to her feet to hand the bottle to the others.

Her legs felt like jello from getting up again so she wobbled as she made her way to them as they too were having a hard time ingesting the soup.

"We have to find Carma and get the hell out of here." Cale's voice had an edge to it as he gulped down his share of the water.

Emily swallowed her share and wiped her mouth where the soup had slopped on her.

"I hope she's alright." Her voice drifted as she thought of her friend.

Sam could see the sadness in their eyes and in a chain reaction, she grew sad as well.

Carma had shown her kindness and she was sure they would have became good friends if she wasn't taken.

She sat down in front of the two, "I don't know what they're doing..." she started then took another gulp of water as Cale handed the jug back to her. The salty tasting soup was burning her mouth and the feeling reached all the way down to her chest. "They haven't been back to taunt us about her and you know that's strange for them, especially Camilla."

They considered this for a moment. "If they were hurting her, they would be here trying to break our morale." Emily agreed.

"They would do that even if they weren't hurting her." Cale added and looked out into the hall.

Sam and Emily turned to where Cale was looking and they found themselves watching a candle flickering back and forth as if it was entertaining.

Sam blinked once she realized what she was doing and turned away.

Maybe they were starting to lose their minds.

Some time had passed and sleep was creeping in on them but a loud boom from outside of the cave was keeping them awake. After the initial shock of the noise, they realized that it was thunder. The cave had hollowed the noise and made it sound more terrifying.

While Cale and Emily waited out the storm, Sam sat in the front corner of the cell as she tried to calm her nerves by keeping her breathing even and begging her heart to slow down.

She had been scared of thunder since she was younger, there was no cause that she knew of, she was just scared.

"Are you ok?" Emily called over to her when she noticed that she was looking pale.

"I-I'm fine." Sam drew a shaky breath as she lied."...I don't like thunder."

The loudest crack so far made her jump and she started shaking as a result, she felt like she was going to be sick. She could have handled it easier at home with a pair of earphones and the music on full blast but she was locked in this cave with nothing to distract her.

Cale and Emily watched her with pitiful expressions and she hated it, she was a weak girl that couldn't help herself and the people around her.

She was a weak girl that was afraid of a simple thunderstorm.

Cale got up and sat next to her then he slowly placed his hand on top of her's and she flinched at the touch.

She turned slightly to him."I-I'm fine, you don't-" she was cut off by Emily as she made her way over and she sat beside her on her free side. She leaned her head on Sam's shoulder and it strangely calmed her down.

None of them said anything as the storm thundered on and when Sam jumped, Cale tightened his grip on her hand. She couldn't believe their kindness, the feeling was foreign to her as Mina was the only who had comforted her like this. Even with being sick with panic, it made her happy that there were others like her childhood friend and it was unfortunate that the feeling wouldn't last long.

Even when the storm had passed, the three remained together, they hadn't said a word to each other since they sat but they needed this.

Silence was a virtue right now.

Sam was feeling the side affects of her mini panic attack and she couldn't get her mind off the thunder. She knew it would have been worse if Cale and Emily hadn't been there to help her.

She could feel Emily's even breathing against her and she figured she had fallen asleep.

She leaned her head slightly against her's and closed her eyes. She didn't want to think about getting out of this cell right now, she didn't want to plot her revenge, she wanted to rest.

She opened her eyes and looked at Cale who was still awake. He was staring at the wall opposite of them, he was obviously lost in thought. Sam looked down to find that his hand was still on her's and she wasn't sure if he knew that it was.

"Cale." She whispered.

He blinked a couple times as he brought himself back to reality then he turned to look at her.

She raised her arm slowly while trying not to wake Emily then patted her empty shoulder.

It took a second for him to realize what she was doing and he awkwardly shook his head. "I don't wanna bother you."

"Easier to stay warm." The corners of her mouth twitched and even though he looked taken back, he moved to lean against her. Though he didn't lean his head on her like Emily had.

"...You're right." he said after a moment. "About this being easier to stay warm."

"...Yeah." She replied as she leaned her head back on Emily's and closed her eyes.

She had never liked touching anyone nor anyone touching her. She didn't like hug's let alone someone leaning on her but she welcomed it now.

This was far better than being cold, alone, and lost in her thoughts.

She could feel Cale take a deep breath against her and after a few moments, his breathing evened as he fell asleep. Sleep was drawing in on her as well and she let it take her, unaware of what was waiting for her in her dreams.

Chapter 9

The universe was formed with a bang or what you would call an explosion. Not a literal explosion of course, when you think of an explosion, you think of disaster. This explosion was an expansion, everything formed from it and from nothing it rained down.

The universe had began with an explosion and her life had ended with one.

An ear deafening bang rang out and she screamed, her heart racing as every part of her shook.

Her eyes had been closed but when she opened them, she was met with more darkness and she couldn't even see an inch in front of her. She was kneeling and she desperately tried to get up but where could she go if she couldn't see anything? Besides, she was shaking so much that she wasn't even sure if she'd be able to walk. Her ears were ringing from the loud noise but she could hear someone walking amongst the pitch black.

She stiffened and gulped, the buzz in her ears was making it difficult to pinpoint where the being was and it was too late by the time she realized that it was in front of her.

What felt like a human's hand touched her forehead, only it was much warmer than a human's normal temperature. She gasped at the touch and flinched away only to be met with a light so bright that her eyes burned. She squinted as a sky formed from the light followed by the rest of the landscape.

She looked for the person who had touched her but like in the darkness, the figure was nowhere to be seen.

She felt something pull her and she found herself watching a town below a mountain top, her long wavy locks blowing in the gentle breeze. She closed her eyes and used her extraordinary hearing to listen to the children yelling below and their parents laughing.

People enjoying themselves, living their lives.

"NO!" A familiar voice rang out and she kept her eyes closed.

Her mouth twisted into a sad smile. "I'm sorry…"

An explosion went off and her body was torn to shreds…

"Sam!" Emily and Cale called for her to wake up as her dream caused her to thrash and scream in real life. The two had moved away from her when she started thrashing but came back to comfort her. She swatted at them as they approached her and they flinched away but remained close in case she needed them.

She wasn't Sam at the moment, she was the embodiment of fear.

"Ex-" she started as she tried to get up but fell as her knees wobbled with anxiety. "*Help me*!" she screeched.

"It was just a dream." Cale assured her but she didn't even hear him as she finally got to her feet by pulling on the bars.

"I don't want to do it!" she screamed so loud that Cale and Emily slapped their hands over their ears and looked at each other as if the other had the answers to her erratic behavior.

"You have to breath." Cale's face was filled with worry as he made his way to her but as she felt his touch on her shoulder, she flipped around and hit him so hard on his shoulder that it cracked on impact and he was flung into the back of the cell.

His pain filled grunts filled the cell as he pushed himself from the ground and gripped at his injured shoulder as Emily ran to him with tears in her eyes.

Sam's eyes had turned white as she thought about being torn apart by the explosion. She screamed the loudest she had so far and her brain ached as she pulled on the bars and they moved a fraction each time she yanked.

"I'm sorry!" she sobbed as she let go of the bars and clenched her fists, her nails that had changed into sharp daggers dug into her palms and blood poured from where they punctured her. She started screaming uncontrollably and saliva poured from her mouth as her canines sharpened. She couldn't hear Emily calling to her and Cale whimpering from the injury she had caused.

There were multiple footsteps running down the hall leading to their cell. There was no doubt that the guards were on their way to see what all the commotion was about.

Sam grabbed ahold of the right side of her head, her fingers twisting into her hair and a nail dug into her scalp as she roared. "GET OUT OF MY HEAD!"

Arthur, Kellan, and Camilla came into view and stopped in front of the cell as she got done damaging the side of her head and blood poured from the wound down the side of her face.

When she spotted Arthur, her eyes widened and her panic escalated.

"I'm sorry!" she cried. "I failed!" Tears poured from her white eyes and crashed to the ground.

Arthur's face whitened and if Sam was in her right mind, she would have been surprised by his reaction.

"I'm sorry!" she whined as she brought her claws to her now blackened veins.

Instead of their usual entertained faces, Kellan and Camilla watched with wide eyes as Sam came undone.

Arthur grabbed the bars and pulled them apart as Archie came into view with a syringe filled with some kind of liquid. He yanked the syringe from Archie's hand as he stepped into the cell and he tackled Sam as she started to dig her nails into her arm.

She fought against him as he knocked her to the ground, tears running down her cheeks as he pinned her and stabbed one of her veins with the needle. He pushed down on the lever with his thumb and the liquid entered her. It didn't look like a safe dose to give a human but she wasn't human anymore and within seconds she began to calm aside from a few spasms and fresh tears poured from her now hazel eyes.

Arthur turned to his subordinate. "Go." he demanded and Archie ran down the hall with no hesitation.

Kellan and Camilla stood with shocked expressions until they slowly turned into interested ones. Kellan's eyes gleamed as Arthur turned back to the cell and his eyes found Cale and Emily: Cale's teeth were gritted not just from the pain, but from being face to face with the man who was responsible for all this.

Arthur returned his gaze to Sam who was whimpering underneath him. She looked him in the eyes and more tears fell.

"I'm…sorry." she whispered weakly.

His eyes widened for a second but he quickly got off of her and picked her up, her limbs swinging like a rag dolls.

"Ex…" she mumbled as he stepped through the bars and Kellan closed them behind him as he ran down the hall with Sam shaking in his arms. "Ex…" her eyes were starting to feel heavy, the sedative was working it's way into her system.

Arthur carried her into the main clearing then to the hall that led to the miniature hospital room. The bright lights in the room made her already stinging eyes throb and she felt dizzy. Her brain felt like it was shaking against her skull.

"Plos.." Her teeth chattered as Arthur laid her on the examination chair.

Archie was in the corner rummaging through a cabinet as Arthur stayed beside Sam and he watched as she mumbled. "Explos…" more tears fell.

Archie approached and examined her head: The deep single claw mark bent down toward the end of her eyebrow like a hook. The wound was trying to heal but since it was done by a gargoyles nails, nonetheless her own, it was having a hard time.

Saliva dripped from the side of her mouth as she shook.

"Why isn't she asleep?" Arthur questioned worriedly as Archie looked at the nasty head wound as it gushed blood onto the floor.

"It's taking longer since she's in a panic." Archie looked at his boss as he replied then went back to his cabinet to rummage more.

Arthur didn't take his eyes off of Sam as she turned slowly to look at him. She was at her last wit as the sedation finally hit her.

"Ex..." she drifted. "Ex...plos...ion." she finally got the word out even though it was broken.

She got a final look at Arthur's face before she lost consciousness and he looked like a ghost.

She woke without opening her eyes, they felt so heavy and her limbs felt numb. She felt strangely calm but that changed when an image of the mountainside where she had died flashed into her mind.

Died?

Her eyes flew open as panic rushed through her and she tried to get up without realizing that there were restraints around her wrists and ankles. The spot above her right eye ached as she continued to pull.

"Calm down, calm down, calm down..." she thought desperately to herself.

"Calm down or you'll rip out your stitches."

She froze as she recognized the voice and she turned to find Arthur sitting beside her in the rolling chair that had been at the desk. His hands were pressed together as his elbows rested on his knees.

"W-why am I here?" she questioned, she had no recollection of what had happened.

"You don't remember?" His usual cold expression had returned.

Her eyes widened a little. "Remember what?"

The ringing in her ears returned and she remembered the dream she had. Her heart began to race and she began hyperventilating. She vividly remembered going temporarily insane and hurting herself and Cale.

She felt like complete shit, Cale had tried helping her and she hurt him. They were going to hate her when they only just started getting closer.

"Get a grip on yourself." Arthur rose from his chair but didn't move from where he stood.

Sam wondered if he had been there watching her the whole time she was out. More of her memories were returning and she thought of how Arthur brought her here and the pale look he had. Why did he look like that? She was a pawn, why would he go through such lengths to help her? She figured that he only did it because she was an important pawn since she had white eyes. Not only that, but she was also harming the others.

Her heart sank even more at the memory of Cale's pained face as she hit him…She felt like she had been in someones else's body as she looked back on the events that had transpired.

"Your file said that you had anxiety but I didn't know it was that bad." Arthur examined the stitched up wound over her eye.

"...I was never that bad." she had no fight in her, all she could feel was remorse for hurting her new found friends and embarrassment that Arthur, Kellan, and Camilla had seen her so vulnerable. She didn't even bother to ask how he knew that she had anxiety. He was a gargoyle and he worked with a doctor, he had found a way to somehow learn about his prisoners.

"You're something else." his tone had a twinge of humor. "You injured yourself with your claws and now you'll have a scar." his gaze moved from her injury to her eyes. "You didn't use your normal nails to do it, it's like you knew that you could only do damage with your gargoyle nails." his face filled with anger and Sam flinched. "I-I didn't know anything…"

Why was she explaining herself?

Arthur's expression evened but Sam could still feel the anger coming from him.

"You gonna spit on me again?" He asked with annoyance and she quickly shook her head, she valued her skull being together.

He turned away from her and walked past the examination chair without another look. He made his way to the opening of the room but stopped just before stepping out into the hall.

"....You're always going to punish yourself, aren't you?" he stepped out of the room without another word. Sam blinked and her mouth hung open from his words.

"What the hell?" she whispered out loud.

"What the hell indeed!" She jumped and her wrists and ankles cracked against the restraints as Kellan stepped into the room.

"You really put on a show for us!" he gleamed. "I appreciate it! it was getting kind of boring here."

"What the hell do you want?" she hissed and her head ached from the strain.

"I'm here to bring you back to your cell, if you're done with your mental breakdown that is." he relished in this and she hated it but the guilt and embarrassment made it hard for her to fight back.

He cockily made his way to her and released her from her restraints, humming to himself as he did so. Sam's head still buzzed from the side affects of the sedative and her limbs felt like jello as he pulled her up and dragged her out of the room.

"That's going to leave a scar on your pretty face." he snorted.

She bowed her head as she wobbled beside him and as she was beginning to fall, his grip tightened around her arm and she could feel his nails digging into her skin. She clenched her teeth to stop the yelp from escaping her lips.

"You're a masochist." He declared but Sam kept her head down to avoid an argument.

"I stayed back when Arthur took you and checked on your friends so you should be grateful." her heart began to race at the mention of Cale and Emily. "I'm sure they lost all their trust in you, the boy's shoulder is hurt pretty bad."

Her jaw began to shake as her teeth pressed together, the force she was using was so strong that she thought they were going to break.

"You'll fit in with the rest of us." He kept up with his taunts and he waited for a reaction. "Nothing?" He seemed disappointed. "That's too bad."

They got to the cell and Kellan used his empty hand to pull a bar out of the way and pushed her in with the other that was already on her. She landed on her knees and kept her head down to avoid Cale and Emily.

"You're boring me." Kellan told her with a rough tone as he pushed the bar back into place and left.

Sam wrinkled her forehead as she waited for her presence to be acknowledged. She wished that Kellan had put her in a different cell, preferably one by herself. She could hear shuffling towards the back of the cell and she stiffened.

"No!" Emily protested nervously as Sam heard someone approaching her, it was sure to be Cale. She wasn't sure how much time had passed since she had injured him, was it ok for him to be up? She swallowed, she had injured one of her comrades instead of the people she needed to fight.

She slowly lifted her head and flinched as she realized that Cale was already in front of her and reaching out a hand.

At first she thought he was going to return the favor but instead of hitting her, he used his uninjured arm and placed it on her shoulder as he kneeled down to get a better look at her. Even while kneeling, their eyes didn't meet because of their height difference.

"Are you ok?" he asked with an uneasy tone.

Sam had her head turned to the side so her eyes couldn't meet his but it jerked towards him at his question.

"Am *I* ok?" her bottom lip trembled. "What about *you*?"

Her eyes moved to his shoulder: It was hunched slightly compared to the other but no pain showed on his face as he rolled it. He glanced at the wound and shook his head as he met her face again "You weren't yourself."

"That's the problem." her chest rose and fell rapidly. "I don't know who I am anymore..."

She didn't allow the tears to fall, she couldn't let them feel bad for her after what she had done. Cale's face fell, he felt the same as Sam, they had only just started to trust each other and this ruined it.

Sam looked past him and saw Emily watching cautiously at the back of the cell, her jaw was clenched shut and her chocolate brown eyes were wide with fear.

Sam could tell that she hated the fact that Cale was near her and Sam didn't blame her.

They were safer away from her.

She started to pull away from Cale's touch but he tightened his grip. "I'm not going to let this ruin everything we've worked for, we can still get out of here together."

She started to shake her head but his hand tightened again and she met his eyes for the first time.

"I'm not afraid of you, I'm only afraid that this is going to set us back." his voice was calm and it eased her nerves a bit. Not enough to make her forget about what she had done, but enough to bring her back to the way she was before her breakdown.

She had to continue with her efforts to get free but she had to be careful.

Cale's words were genuine but you didn't have to be experienced in tones and expressions to know that he was apprehensive. She could lose her mind again at any moment, especially in her sleep. She agreed with him, they had to continue with their training and if they got out, they could go their separate ways and they wouldn't have to worry about Sam's inability to stay sane anymore.

Their days spent in the cell started to show on their bodies. They all looked malnourished and worn down. Cale's dark hair had grown and it almost fell into his eyes and Emily's curls had turned into waves from the lack of maintenance. Sam's hair, that was considerably long before, had grown and it got in the way as she sparred with Cale. Emily had refused to go near her so she only sparred with Cale. She had resorted to tying her hair in a knot but the effort failed every time as her silky hair slid from the tie.

"You need to sleep." Cale said as they sat at their respective sides of the cell.

He was right, her eyes were heavy from the lack of sleep and they looked bruised and puffy. She raised a hand and swept it like she was swatting at a fly.

"I'm fine." she claimed but she was getting sloppy with her training and she didn't last as long as the others. She had chosen not to sleep since Kellan brought her back to the cell. She wasn't going to take the chance, she would fall asleep for a few minutes but she would always wake with a start.

"Try not to dream if you fall asleep." Emily suggested as if she could control it.

Sam bit her lip as her eyes dropped to the ground and Cale turned to give Emily an annoyed look. They hadn't asked her about the dream that caused her to go insane, though she knew they wanted to. She knew she had to talk about it with someone but she wasn't ready.

Who would think she was sane after she had a dream of her own death?

Her mouth felt dry and she felt a pressure in her chest as she thought about it.

She glanced at Cale's shoulder, even though it had healed and he said that he didn't have any pain, it still leaned down more than the other. It served as a constant reminder to Sam of what she had done and it gave her strength to stay awake.

She turned her head away from Cale and Emily as they silently argued and she closed her eyes to only rest them for a moment… to help her think.

She had a hard time thinking lately, whenever she tried to make a plan, her mind would wander back to her dream.

For some reason every dream aside from the one with the little boy was vivid. She would only remember a few details: The boy seemed to have been her brother and there were three others. She had also remembered her reflection. Other than that, she could barely remember what happened in the dreams or what the boys looked like. She only knew that they were there.

The dream of her death felt as clear as day though and she found herself thinking about Mina's intrigue with past lives. She shook her head slightly then leaned her head against one of the bars, the cool steel sending a shiver down her spine.

She could hear the boy that had been in her dreams for so long, his childish tone echoing in her ears. She couldn't make out what he was saying but as he continued, his tone changed as if he was aging. It went from soft spoken to rough and before she could pinpoint the voice, she opened her eyes and was met with Cale and Emily who were watching her with curious expressions.

She swallowed the lump in her throat. "What did you say?"

"I said your name." Emily rose a brow at her strange behavior. "You really do need to sleep."

"I'm fine." Sam insisted then went back to leaning on the bar and closed her eyes, her mind wandering again. She chewed on the inside of her cheek as the boys voice rang in her ears again.

She wanted to know who he was and why he was in her dreams but he could very well be a part of her imagination.

Her heart slowed and sleep washed over her, there was no control over it now and she didn't know that she had fallen asleep until she woke hours later to the sound of Cale's angered voice.

Her vision returned as the sleep left her eyes and she took in the scene in front her: Cale was standing at the bars with his hands clenched into fists, his brows furrowed and his teeth pressed tightly together in anger. On the other side of the bars stood Kellan with a grin on his naturally smug face. Emily was standing behind Cale and was trying to pull him away from the bars by the hem of his shirt. She looked shaken by whatever Kellan had said to make Cale so furious.

"You tried this shit when Sam had her panic attack and you're trying it now, I'm not believing a word that comes out of your mouth." Sam could hear the venom in Cale's voice and even she felt intimidated. A question rose in her mind, what did Kellan say about her?

"I don't care if you believe it, I just thought I'd let you know." Kellan shrugged. "Carma won't mind either way."

Cale reached though the bars with lightning speed but Kellan was faster and he stepped out of the way before Cale had the chance to grab ahold of him.

Sam's heart quickened at the mention of Carma, this was the first new piece of information they'd been offered since she was taken.

"What are you talking about?" She demanded as she got to her feet and Kellan's face lit up at the sight of her.

"Perfect, I'm sure the crazy girl will love to hear the news." he looked down at her with a mischievous smile as she made her way to him.

She rose a brow as she gave him a look that looked like she was telling him to get on with it.

"Your friend Carma has decided to join us." he explained and Sam blinked. "That's bullshit." she turned to look at Cale and Emily and she froze at how distressed they looked.

Cale had just said that he didn't believe Kellan, but they looked like they did.

Were they keeping something from her?

She brought her sight back to Kellan and said the most logical thing that she could come up with. "If that's the case, I'm sure you threatened her to make her join you."

Multiple footsteps could be heard coming down the hall and Kellan turned towards the newcomers. Sam and the others leaned their heads forward to get a good look but they weren't prepared for what they were about to see: Carma walking alongside Arthur and Camilla.

She didn't look like she was there against her will, she didn't even look like she had been beaten or tortured. She looked clean and refreshed, her blue eyes glimmering.

She kept her gaze on Cale and Emily as if they were something foreign to her then she turned to Sam who looked back to see that her once kind eyes had turned sharp.

"Are you alright?" Cale stepped over to stand in front of her but she didn't take her eyes off of Sam. Sam broke her gaze and turned to Cale and Emily to see if they were seeing the same thing but she found her eyes stopping on Arthur instead who was watching the exchange with his usual expression.

"Please say he's lying." Emily's voice shook, Carma's answer was sure not to be good.

Carma finally turned from Sam and brought her attention to her friends and Sam was thankful that she had, she was starting to feel uncomfortable.

"It's true, every word." she confirmed lazily, even her voice had changed to fit her new eyes.

"You're doing this again?" Cale's anger was replaced with disappointment and sadness.

Sam flinched, what did he mean by *again?*

"Why?" he questioned and Carma smiled. "For power of course." her eyes turned white and she brought them back to Sam. "And to kill her."

Sam just stood there, she knew Carma was trying to scare her with her partial transformation but all she could think of was why she would want to kill her.

She felt a twinge of jealousy at Carma's control over her ability.

Carma licked her right fang, "But I'm not allowed to yet." her eyes returned to normal and she looked at her friends with a grin. "Arthur wants to pit us against each other to see who's stronger."

Cale opened his mouth to speak but Sam interrupted him.

"You need a willing fighter to do this and I'm not going to play your game." she kept her eyes on Arthur and likewise as he kept his on her. She broke their gaze as she rolled her head to Carma."You'd do this to your friends?" Her tone was harsh. "For power?" she looked her straight in the eyes with as much intensity as there was in her tone. "You can have all the power in the world but you'll still be weak…I know you're full of shit."

Carma suddenly grabbed the bars to get to Sam but Kellan, who was enjoying the squabble, grabbed her wrists.

"Arthur said to wait." He warned.

It looked like it took nothing for him to hold her back and he let her go when she pulled roughly away. Her eyes were white again and black veins crawled down her cheeks.

"I'm going to kill you, bitch." she spat and stomped down the hall.

What the hell was happening?

Sam watched her leave as a chill ran down her spine and her head jerked towards Cale and Emily.

"I-" she was going to apologize for angering Carma but Cale was hugging Emily who had tears streaming down her cheeks.

Sam's nerves were on fire as she turned back to Arthur who motioned for Kellan and Camilla to follow Carma.

"What the fuck did you?" She was starting to feel like her reckless self again, it was amazing what a few hours of sleep could do for a person.

"She woke up acting like that." he explained.

"Don't fucking lie." Cale warned him.

"I'm not." Arthur took a lazy step as if Cale wasn't worth his time. "I'm sure you know about your friends problem."

Cales eyes widened as Emily bit her lip and Sam watched closely.

By the way they were acting, it was obvious that they indeed knew of Carma's *Problem*.

"Don't blame other people for the lack of effort to get rid of it, That's on you and her parents." Arthur continued his mental assault.

"That's enough." Sam warned. "You turned her into a monster and made her *problem* worse. Don't act like you're innocent when your sadistic plan did this."

The side of Arthur's mouth twitched as if he was trying to fight a smile.

"You want to talk about being sadistic?" His hazel eyes flashed. "Humans cause war, fight, kill, rape, and maim." He narrowed his eyes. "They harm innocent creatures and torture emotionally and physically for their personal gain. Every living creature on this planet is sadistic in their own way." He took a step back as he watched her reaction to his words and it took her moment to think of a reply.

"I refuse to believe that we're all sadistic, but you are." she kept her eyes on his uninterested face, trying to see if any of the emotion that he had shown the other night would reappear.

"You kidnapped and turned us into gargoyles all because you want to kill humans, you talk about all the wrongs people commit but you're no better…You're a damned hypocrite."

His expression didn't change and it was aggravating her to no end. She needed to think of something to change that.

She squinted her eyes as she took another step forward and that's when she had her *aha* moment.

Cale watched with curious eyes and Emily stepped away from him.

"You're plan is pretty shitty." she grinned mischievously. "You forced this upon us, what makes you think we'd join you? Plus there has to be another reason why you're doing this, taking down the humans doesn't make sense to me, that was in the past…You have an ulterior motive."

It wasn't much, but Sam was able to see it: A twitch of an eye and a discreet bite of the inside of his lip. She was reading him like an open book and he hated it.

"Sam…" She could hear the nerves in Cale's voice and she didn't need to ask what was wrong since the answer stood in front of her.

The air around her seemed to freeze and she couldn't seem to breathe. Arthur's eyes had turned white for the third time since she had met him but it was different this time.

So this was the true power of a gargoyle?

Sam gritted her teeth to stop a gasp from leaving her lips.

"This-" Arthur started and a gasp finally broke from Sam's mouth. "- Is power."

He picked up his hand and looked at his clawed fingers. "My motives are a secret, yes. But you know nothing of how well my plans are going." He stepped forward and stood face to face with her.

Even with him only being an inch taller than her, she found herself looking up at him as she tried to lean away from his power.

"Things *will* go my way." he smiled and all of his teeth ended with a sharp point.

Sam took a step back as she imagined his teeth sinking into her neck, ripping out her jugular, and leaving her to bleed out.

"I have the *power* and the *will* to make things go my way." he finished and as if someone had snapped their fingers, he went back to his human form.

His ease to transform and to turn back to his human form shocked Sam at first but of course he would be great at it, he was born a gargoyle.

"That is just a fraction of my power, remember that the next time you think you can read me." he turned on his heel and left like none of what had just happened had an effect on him.

Sam fell to the ground and placed her right hand over her mouth, her eyes were wide and she shook with fear.

The possibility of beating Arthur was gone, there was no way any of them could beat him. He said that he had the power and the will, what did they have?

She inhaled sharply and shot to her feet. It was strange but it seemed like a light was going off in her head, like something was telling her the answers to her question's.

She needed the will to have control.

She glanced at Cale and Emily who were watching her with curious eyes as a small smile appeared on her lips.

She wanted to get everyone out of there, to save them from the fate that Arthur had planned for them. She thought of Mina's smiling face and her tears as she ran to get help before Sam was taken in her place. Sam wanted to protect Mina at all costs, she had the will, she just needed the power.

Like something had snapped inside of her, the pressure she was looking for built around her eyes and they switched to white. The Power coursed through her veins and she brought her arms up and flexed her fingers. There was no change in her nails or teeth but that wasn't the point. She just wanted to use the strength that being a gargoyle gave her.

"No way." Cale exclaimed breathlessly and he smiled while Emily watched with a light in her eyes, a shimmer filled with hope.

"Use your will… your reason to get out of here." Sam pointed at her eyes to show the result. "Don't think about anger or sadness, think of your reason for changing into a monster. Emotions taint the transformation, you need to think of an outcome."

It was almost funny how easy it was now that they found a way to change, but even more funny was the fact that Arthur was the one who had given her the idea on how to do it.

Cale closed his eyes and kept them shut for a moment. The girls watched as his eyelids twitched and when he opened them, they were pitch black.

He had already shown promise, it was easy to understand how he had gotten it so easy.

Sam supposed she was lucky even though they both had a long way to go.

Cale was flexing his fingers like she had from the energy and as he lifted his head to look at her, he grinned.

"What now?" Emily breathed.

This was the first time they had gotten a clear look at each others eyes without a haze blocking their way. It was amazing how a controlled channeling of their powers helped with their thinking and their outlook on their transformations.

Their eyes didn't look monstrous, they were oddly beautiful.

Sam pivoted to face the bars that were holding them in.

"We're getting out of here."

Chapter 10

They listened for a sign that the guards were near. They wanted to avoid a fight at any cost since they were still inexperienced and it wouldn't go well for them if they were caught.

Their hearing had gotten even better after they learned how to channel their strength. Not only did they hear the occasional guard making their way past the tunnel, they could also hear the other prisoners. There were cries and soft whispers, angry voices, and the occasional prayer.

This only fueled Cale and Sam's desire to get out.

Once there was no sign of guard, the two nodded to each other and Cale glanced back to Emily to make sure she was ready and she nodded hesitantly. She was to stay close to them but was advised to run if things went south.

They couldn't get their hopes up but they also couldn't let their doubts keep them from trying.

"Do you think we can do this?" Cale whispered since they had decided to talk softly so they wouldn't be heard though it might not be of much help.

"No." Sam admitted.

"Same." He laughed anxiously.

"I can't believe we're doing this." Emily paced behind them.

Sam inhaled sharply as she grabbed ahold of the bars and she jerked her head towards Cale and nodded. There was a chance that pulling the bars apart wasn't going to work.

Maybe all they mastered was the ability to change their eye color.

The two started pulling and at first the bars didn't move and their arms ached from the friction. They were using their human strength when they should've been using their gargoyle strength.

Sam's canines sharpened as she finally released her inner monster, Cale did the same and the bars pulled apart.

The three didn't even have time to feel proud as they chanced a look at each other before they jumped through the bars into the hall.

They ran down the dimly lit path, they knew the guards had heard the bars being pulled apart and there was no time for sneaking. They could very well be on their way to Kellan, Camilla, or even worse, Arthur.

They slid to a halt at the end of the tunnel and Sam glimpsed into the large opening to see two guards making their way to them.

Only two?

The guards were a brown haired man and a blonde haired woman that had checked on them many times and they were approaching fast. Sam turned and nodded to Cale and his face hardened. Emily had been hanging onto Cale's hand but let go as she saw the guards approaching.

As the male guard stepped into the tunnel, Sam grabbed ahold of the collar of his coat and flipped him over backwards with ease. He would have yelled but Sam knelt down behind him as he tried getting up and placed a hand over his mouth. She wrapped her free arm tightly around his neck to cut off his breathing.

Cale grabbed the woman and slammed her head into the wall, not hard enough to kill her, but enough to knock her out. She fell to the ground as the man that Sam had taken on fell limp and she let him fall the rest of the way to the ground.

Emily who had stepped back into the darkness of the tunnel came into view with a hand over her mouth. "D-did you kill him?" she squeaked and Sam was hurt that she only asked her.

"No." she replied flatly though she didn't mean to.

"I wish I didn't get the woman." Cale looked down at the frail looking woman who was passed out in front of him. A trail of blood running from her forehead.

They'd heal anyway, they had gargoyle blood to think for that.

They stepped into the opening, their eyes squinting at the change in light but it didn't take long for them to adjust. There was no sign of the other guards and it didn't sit right with Sam.

What the hell was Arthur up to?

She was sure they were aware that they had broken out of their cell but she didn't have time to think into it.

"You guys get out of here, I'll stay back and get the others out."

Cale gave her a stern look. "I'm helping you and you're not going to change my mind."

Sam considered him for a second, they didn't have time to argue.

"Fine." she agreed quickly and rounded on Emily. "You stay close to us." she demanded and Emily nodded nervously.

Sam could hear her heart along with Cale's thumping in their chests and she found that her own was doing the same.

There were four tunnels other than their own and the one that led to the makeshift hospital room. Sam listened for the other prisoners to know what tunnel to choose and she narrowed it down to a cell to her right and to her left.

"I'll go to the right and you go to the left." Cale said before she was done listening and she spun around.

"We have to stay together." she was worried that if they separated, something would happen.

"It'll be quicker this way."

He was right, it certainly would be quicker.

She nodded hesitantly as Cale turned to Emily.

"You go with Sam." he directed and Emily refused right away. "I'm not leaving you."

"I need you to go with her so I don't get distracted, I'm not as focused as she is."

Sam awkwardly watched their conversation.

Emily's jaw locked as she turned on her heel to face Sam.

"You better hurry." she demanded sharply to Cale without taking another look at him.

"I will." he promised but Sam could tell that he wasn't sure if he could.

For assurance, Sam was going to listen to make sure everything was going well for him and she was sure he was going to do the same.

They glanced at each other one last time then went their separate ways. Emily was so close to Sam that she almost stepped on her heels as they ran.

At the end the tunnel was an exact replica of their own cell only there were ten people cramped inside. Some were squished together while others leaned against the walls.

A girl with long black hair looked up at the sight of the newcomers, her eyes were as blue as the ocean and almost glowed in the dark. "Haven't seen you before." she said flatly as she got up and made her way to the bars "What do you want now…?" her eyes widened from what Sam was sure was her white eyes. "You're-"

"I'm not a guard." Sam assured her as several people gasped and quickly got to their feet.

"She's telling the truth." Emily stepped into view, she was far less intimidating than Sam who stood a head taller and currently had the eyes of a gargoyle.

Sam imagined Cale having the same problem only he didn't have Emily to make the situation better.

The girl looked between Emily and Sam as a few more people made their way to the front.

A boy with a football players build and light brown hair stopped beside the girl, his eyes looked tired but it didn't hide his fear. A chubby man stopped to the girls left, he was short with soft features and his hair spiked naturally at the front.

"How can we believe you?" he asked shakily.

"You can believe me or not but I'm sure you'd rather get the hell out of this cell."

Sam rolled her eyes and grasped the bars, she was better this time as she pulled them apart with a quick motion but the sound of steel being pulled made her grit her teeth. Her heightened hearing proved to be a problem as much as it was a blessing.

The prisoners stood there with puzzled looks on their faces, maybe they thought this day would never come. Sam didn't blame them, she had felt the same at one point.

"Stop gawking and get the fuck out." She yanked the chubby boy into the hall.

He looked at her like she was going to eat him.

"Follow me or stay here, I don't care at this point." Sam grabbed ahold of Emily's arm and started back down the tunnel while listening for Cale and any guards that could be coming their way.

She obviously cared whether or not they followed but she had to make them desperate. She had to make it look like she didn't care and she especially had to make it quick.

To her surprise, her lie worked.

She could hear them running behind her but her relief didn't last long because when they got to the end of the tunnel, a guard blocked their way.

"My oh my where are you going?" his voice echoed though the hall and Sam recognized him as the third man that had taken her with Kellan and the others. He was the one that always ran his mouth.

"Get out of the way." Sam grumbled over the gasps and whimpers behind her.

"Y-you lied… this was a test, wasn't it?" a female prisoner whined and a vein popped in Sam's head as she let go of Emily's arm who had nervously took a step back.

Sam took one long step towards the guard.

How strong was he? She hadn't seen him fight but she couldn't remember him being much of a threat when they took her.

She walked a few more steps then picked up a jog that turned into a run as she made her way to the enemy.

He smiled cockily and extended his hand towards her then smashed her into the wall as she got into range. He did it so quickly that she didn't have time to react.

She gnawed on her lip as the pain in her back set in and a pained gasp escaped her lips.

She fought through the pain and wrapped her legs around his waist and grabbed his arm. Her fingernails extended into points and they dug into his arm. He hadn't done any real damage to her, he wasn't strong but he was fast.

All she had to do was to not let him get away from her and even though the position was uncomfortable, she held true.

The two struggled against each other, the loud mouth trying to get her off while she struggled to hang on. His pitch black eyes pierced into her but her white remained unfazed.

The dim light made it hard to see the possibilities but Sam figured an old trick would work. She acted like she was struggling harder than she really was and she squeezed her legs even tighter around his waist. A hiss escaped his lips and when he tried to fight harder, she let go of his waist and he fell backwards into the wall behind him.

Sam gathered her new found energy and kicked him into the wall where he left a human shaped indent. He fell with a rough thud and a trail of blood rolled down his lip where he had bitten it. Rocks crumbled onto him and the noise irritated Sam as she blinked at the dent.

It was hard to believe that she had done that.

She shook her head and listened to see if there were more guards coming but she was met with Cale's voice along with the small talk of other prisoners as they ran down their tunnel.

Sam turned and motioned for the others who were watching with shocked expressions before she bursted out of the narrow tunnel into the large opening.

The ten prisoners groaned and blinked at the sudden change in light but in the moment it took for Cale to get there with his group, they had gotten used to it.

The longer they stood there the more sick Sam felt. They had to hurry or someone they couldn't handle was going to show up.

Cale and Sam's eyes met as he ran into the opening and as if they were moving in slow motion, she turned on her heel to face the tunnel that was separate from the others.

Within seconds, she was running towards it with Cale and Emily in tow. The other prisoners following closely behind them.

The tunnel was far shorter than the others and had a large boulder blocking their way to freedom. The outside world was shining where there were cracks.

Sam gulped, could they move something that big?

Cale leaned down and placed both hands on the rock without saying a word and she did the same. The two pushed and pushed but the boulder proved to be a harder challenge than the bars. They had to transform now, but how were they going to do that without losing control?

Sam breathed in through her nose and out through her mouth.

She thought of everyone here and Mina and like the thought gave her strength, a small growl left her throat and the pressure in her eyes deepened. The power tempted her to give in and to go on a rampage, but she couldn't let that happen. They had to get the boulder out of the way.

She glanced at Cale and his features had changed as well, he was having the same struggle she was having. He shakily turned his head to see if she was ready and she had to admit that she was startled by the way he looked and by the look on his face, he felt the same.

She nodded and they set to work at pushing on the boulder again and this time, it pushed away from the opening a few inches at a time. The two half gargoyles walked after it as they continued to force it out of the way.

The sun shined on them as the boulder no longer blocked their way. The cool spring air stung their faces and above all, the coast looked to be clear.

Sam and Cale laid against the opposite walls and motioned for their fellow prisoners to leave but they stood frozen from what they had just seen.

Emily who had waited for the others to get out of her way sprang through them and left through the opening with an excited hop and the others finally followed.

Cale reached into his pocket as the others left and pulled out a couple of touch screen cellphones and handed one to Sam.

"How did you-" She blinked at the object like it was foreign to her, she had forgotten about her own cell phone.

"There was a small room in the tunnel with our belongings. They were all shut off so no one could track them, I found mine and grabbed an extra for you."

She looked up at him, impressed with his discovery.

"My number is in it in case you want to meet up." He nodded with a smile.

Her heart thumped as her gaze moved to the shoulder that she had injured. Even after what she had done, he was still willing to meet with her again.

She smiled and nodded. "Thanks." She pocketed the phone.

They turned to go, they had wasted too much time already.

Cale stepped through the opening as Sam chanced a look down the tunnel and her mouth went dry as she noticed that Arthur was watching from the middle of the large opening. His eyes were on her but he showed no sign of going after her.

She certainly wasn't going to give him the chance.

She leaped into the blinding light without another look back and ran like hell.

Chapter 11

Her throat stung as she breathed in the moist air and the sun burned her eyes. She blinked rapidly to adjust and when they finally did, she noticed that Cale and Emily were waiting for her at the entrance of a tree line.

When she was within a foot of them, they turned to run into the shaded woods. The ground was hard to tread since they were on a incline and there were many loose rocks. As they ran, they slid and almost fell multiple times. Emily had practically face planted but Cale grabbed her arm and pulled her back up and they started off again as if it had never happened. They chanced looks back to make sure they weren't being followed and even though they were sure their captors would be trying to catch them, they seemed to be home free.

It didn't take long for the three of them to catch up with the other prisoners, most of them had fallen from the looks of the scuffs on their clothes but none of them broke skin.

It took Sam until she saw a marker in the distance saying how much longer until the top that she realized that they were on a mountain side. A mountain that she had climbed many times when she was still in school: Prospect mountain.

She yelled for the group to stop and after a few failed attempts, she finally got them to do so. She told them to go to the marker and that it would bring them to the bottom of the mountain.

After a bit, Sam got worried that she had pointed them in the wrong direction but when they got close to the bottom, she noticed a bridge that she had crossed before.

The old looking thing was placed over the thruway and it led to a parking lot, she couldn't believe how close to home she was.

They ran across the bridge and the drivers in the cars passing below watched the sudden surge of people coming from the mountain.

They ran down the steps into the parking lot and while the others kept running to nearby houses for help, Sam, Cale, and Emily stopped to catch their breaths and to think about their next move.

The three heaved from all the running and Sam felt like she was going to pass out from anemia. She turned to look at the path leading to the bridge and there was still no sign of anyone coming for them.

"What now?" Emily asked through her heavy breaths as she looked between Sam and Cale.

"We can't go to the authorities," Cale looked around as if to see if anyone was listening but the parking lot was empty aside from the three of them. "We'd just be asking to get experimented on."

"My parents wouldn't understand." Emily's mouth trembled, it was obvious that she longed to go home, they all did.

"I'll call my dad to let him know that this was just a misunderstanding and if it turns out that he didn't make it home yet, we can go to my new place." Cale's face fell.

Sam watched the two while they weighed their options, she already knew what she had to do. As she continued to watch, she noticed how tired they looked and they both had a layer of dirt on their skin and clothes.

She found herself looking down at her arms and finding herself equally as dirty, only she also had dried blood plastered on her.

Suddenly, she thought of the reflection she had seen of herself in her dream.

"We'll go to my place." Cale pushed his dark hair out of his face. "You're going home, aren't you?" he turned to Sam and she nodded.

"I need to let them know that I'm alright but I'm not going to stay."

"You're welcome to come to my place until we figure stuff out. It won't be safe very long and I have to get rid of this phone before we're tracked but I'll keep it on me until you call." He smiled gently. "We've got a long road ahead of us but we'll figure something out, I just can't believe we made it out of there." he didn't seem to believe his own words.

Sam nodded again, she didn't know what to say so she settled for *Thank you.*

She watched as they walked away, it wasn't goodbye so they didn't bother to say it but they did say. *See you later.*

Sam decided she would call a cab and she waited for the others to be out of view before getting one last look at the trail leading to the mountain top. She had been locked in there for God knows how long and had been changed into something grotesque. Up there stood her greatest enemy and his legion of monsters. She pulled out the phone that Cale had given her and dialed for a cab while walking away from the trail.

She watched with a lump in her throat as the men's lifeless bodies swung back and forth. Their broken necks wobbling side to side, exposing the noose wrapped tightly around them.

Their eyes were glazed over and blood dripped from their nostrils and mouths. The gasps and cheers of the crowd around her made her eyes wander and she stopped on the man behind her: Instead of the expression she was expecting, he had a sadistic smile and the pupil in his dark bottomless eyes glowed red.

"Miss?" a foreign voice called. "Miss?"

Her eyes flew open, she didn't mean to fall asleep in the cab but drowsiness had washed over her.

"Is this the place?" The cab driver, an old balding man with a beer gut turned in his seat with a brow in the air. He had been giving her judgemental looks since he pulled up to the curb a few blocks away from the mountain. She didn't blame him, she was dirty with hints of blood and her hair was matted.

She had to look in the rearview mirror multiple times to make sure her eyes weren't white anymore, though she was sure his reaction would have given it away.

She looked out the window to see her house up the long driveway.

"Yes." she grabbed a few dollars out of her pocket that she had managed to not lose during this whole ordeal and handed them to him. "Thanks." she said as she got out of the car without taking another look back.

She walked up her driveway and listened as the taxi driver pulled away. She stopped for a moment and looked into the second story window to her room.

Her mother was walking around up there, perhaps cleaning up her daughters stuff and as she walked by the window, she saw her missing daughter standing outside.

Sam could tell she was yelling something and with her hearing, she could tell that she was yelling for her husband and son. She looked like she about to cry as she turned from the window and ran out of Sam's room. Sam waited for her family to meet her and as they ran from the front door, she was surprised to see how desperate they were to get to her.

They wrapped their arms around her and practically knocked her over.

"How are you here?!" her mother sobbed into her hair as her father and brother pulled away.

"Mina told us what happened." Her brother placed a hand on his sisters shoulder as if to console her. Sam had kept her hands to her sides since she was worried that she wouldn't be able to control her strength.

"Yeah…" She replied simply, she had to make this brief. "They were traffickers." She lied. "I got away out of sheer luck."

That wasn't a lie.

They seemed to believe her but she sensed something was off as the three looked between each other.

With her mother still doting over her, the family of four made their way into the house.

"We have to call the cops." her father stated as he made his way to the phone.

"No." Sam grabbed his hand. "Not yet." she knew this was coming and they could call the cops when she was gone but now she had to grab a few things.

"Look at you!" her mother started with the tears again. "You have dried blood on you and you look so tired and dirty!" she reached for the dried blood where Arthur had struck her then moved to the stitches on her temple that were falling out. "They need to pay for doing this to you."

"How long was I gone for?" Sam asked simply and her mother looked shocked at her daughters lack of emotion.

"Two weeks." her brother answered since his parents were busy looking at Sam like she was a hollow shell.

Sam looked between the three of them, "I'm going to the bathroom."

She skipped over the bathroom and went straight for her room: It looked the way she had left it all the way down to the unmade bed. She grabbed her lilac backpack and placed five shirts and five pairs of pants in it along with other necessities.

She walked to her nightstand where her laptop was closed with the charger still attached to it. She grabbed both and squeezed them into the little space that she had left in her bag then made her way out of her room but not before grabbing a few hair ties.

She went into the bathroom and looked in the mirror: She looked tired, dirty, and bloody but most of all she didn't look like herself.

Her hair was still brown, her eyes still hazel, but her skin was paler and she stood straighter. Her eyes were like daggers as she judged her own reflection and she remembered the way she looked in her dream.

Her heart thumped and she was brought back by a nasty smell that she realized was coming from herself. Staying in a cell for two weeks laying in your own filth would do that to a person.

"Ah." she looked into her eyes: There was a sliver of gray in the corner of her irises.

"Two weeks, huh?" she sighed to herself, she didn't have a grasp for time while she was locked up but it felt a lot longer than that.

She longingly looked at the shower behind her reflection but she had no time. She picked up her bag, unlocked the door, and made her way down the stairs into the living room where she saw her mother and brother sitting on the coach silently and her father on the phone.

He was whispering so low that a humans ears wouldn't be able to make out his words but she technically wasn't human anymore.

"She won't tell us the truth." he whispered quickly. "I don't know what they did to her but she's different, I'll see you when you get here." he hung up the phone and Sam could hear the cut of the line.

"Called the cops?" she asked while placing her backpack where it's name implied and stepped the rest of the way down the stairs.

She expected this, she knew the government knew about the gargoyles or the *demons*.

Were both creatures real?

Surely demons would be if gargoyles were, Sam didn't know what to believe anymore.

Her family gave her exasperated looks as they turned to see her walking into the room, they obviously didn't expect her to be done so soon. Maybe they had expected her to take a hot bath? Check her emails?

Her father made his way over to her, throwing his cellphone into the nearest chair. "They'll help catch them honey."

Honey? When did her father ever called her that?

He placed both hands on her shoulders and gripped hard. He was trying to assure her but he was horrible at it.

She shook her head and shrugged out of his grip. "No, They'll experiment on me."

"Why would they do that?" Her mother rose from the couch while her brother remained seated.

Her parents looked at her with eye colors that didn't match her own and she clicked her tongue.

"I thought they were demons?" she backed away a step, she could feel her annoyance threatening to turn into anger.

The world was one big lie to her, she had heard the rumors of what the *demons* had done, the atrocities they had committed but nothing too far into detail.

She thought it was all a lie to get kids to behave themselves.

Her parents chanced a glance at each other then brought their attention back to their daughter. "Your generation has been told the basics about what those creatures did but were kept in the dark to protect you. We were told the creatures had died out." Her mothers explanation made her head ache. "I've never seen one but I've heard rumors about images of the creatures being held by the government." Her mother seemed like she was talking more to herself than she was to her daughter.

"This is fucking insane…" Sam gritted her teeth, she had to get out of there before the cops arrived.

"Watch it." her father warned her even though the swear word was the least of their worries.

She looked him in the eyes."They thought not telling us the details would protect us?" She took another step back. "Knowing more about them would have prepared us! Gargoyles? I believe it now. But demons? Isn't that farfetched? All I think of is a ghost show and just like ghosts, demons aren't real."

She said all of that but in reality, what could she believe anymore?

There could have been a ghost behind her and she wouldn't know.

It was like how she didn't believe that the creatures were kidnapping people until she came face to face with one. She had no choice but to believe in them now since she was one of them.

She chewed on her lip, why did they even call themselves gargoyles?

She hadn't seen a full transformation yet but there was no way they looked the part, the stone creatures were nothing but that: Stone.

"You wouldn't under-" her father started to explain but Sam cut him off.

"Exactly." she snarled "I would've known about them, what they did… I still don't know what they did exactly but here I am, stuck in this mess!"

All of the anger and hurt that she had felt over the past two weeks was threatening to erupt and the only thing that brought her back was the looks on her family's faces.

They were looking her like she was evil, her parents backed away while her brother retreated onto the floor in front of the couch.

"Oh no." She thought to herself, she didn't realize the pressure in her eyes had changed along with her teeth and nails. She had learned to control it with her will, but anger still sought to defy her.

"Mom…Dad…I…" she tried to reason with them.

"Mo..Monster." Her mother gasped, her blue eyes filled with tears. "They turned you into a monster."

Sam's heart sank at her mother's words but what really got her was the fact that her father was in the middle of grabbing his pocket knife.

Sam's throat felt like it was about to close from the nerves. She didn't think they would welcome her with open arms and she didn't want them to find out about her being made into a monster but that proved to be futile.

Without another look, she sprinted out of the living room into the kitchen then out the front door. She could hear their footsteps following her on the hardwood floor but they didn't have the courage to follow her out the door.

Her own family thought she was a threat.

She ran to the backyard where their beat down shed stood and she swung the large red doors open but not without the squealing hinges making her flinch.

Inside stood what she was looking for: Her motorcycle.

She hopped on it as she heard sirens in the distance and pulled on her helmet, maybe she didn't need it anymore but it was still the law.

She opened the compartment between her legs and pulled out the keys to the bike. The sirens suddenly turned off and she knew what the officers were doing, they were trying to trick her into thinking that they weren't coming. Only they didn't know that she had hearing beyond a human. She started the bike and it roared to life, and though it was loud, the sound was music to her ears. She tightened the straps on her bag then pressed on the gas and sped out of the shed onto the grass that she had no care that she was leaving marks on.

She sped onto the road in front a car who honked their horn at her reckless driving and she sped down the road the opposite way that the cops were coming.

She bypassed the direction they were coming from by taking the long way out of town. A half an hour later, she was in the middle of nowhere and far from where they would think to look for her. She thought it was a good time to get Cale's location.

Up ahead she spotted a small nature trail connected to a parking lot and figured that would a good enough place to pull over. She turned the bike off once she was in the lot and went to pull up her visor on her helmet instinctively but realized that she had never pulled it down. She sighed, it was just another thing that had changed. There was no way she would have been able to handle the air in her eyes at the speeds she was going before she had been changed.

She pulled off her helmet and shook her head to remove the feeling that the helmet left.

She hung the helmet on one of the handlebars and rolled the bike where the trees were blocking the sun so no one could see it. She pulled the key from the ignition and shoved it into her pocket as she made her way to the start of the nature trail.

It wasn't necessary to walk in but in the case that someone spotted the bike, they wouldn't be able to see her too.

As she made her way into the woods and the sun's rays turned into shadows, the air cooler, her mind started to wander: Her parents thought she was a monster and they would have given her to the government to be experimented on. She stopped and clenched her fists, she wasn't angry at them for feeling that way, she was angry that she was put into this situation in the first place.

Gargoyles and demons? Were they separate entities? Were they one in the same? What other mythical creatures were real? She found herself hoping that this was the longest dream in existence but she knew that was as far fetched as her reality.

She leaned her forehead against the nearest tree, the bark felt odd against her skin but it didn't hurt, if anything, it cooled her down.

Her mind wandered to Mina and how bad she wanted to see her and to tell her that she was not entirely okay but she was alive. She knew it would be far too dangerous because of the fact that she was being looked for and that she could very well transform on her like she had with her family. Anger hit her like a bag of bricks, she hated that she was made into a gargoyle but oddly what angered her more was the fact that she couldn't control her abilities.

She gritted her teeth and punched the tree as hard as she could, not expecting what was going to happen next: The tree split where her fist had landed and it fell between the other tree branches and they restricted it from making its way to the ground.

She jumped back and watched as the tree settled in place with eyes that looked like they were going to pop out of her head. She wasn't sure if it was the anger or the shock from what she had done that caused her to shake from head to toe.

She looked at the stump that the tree had left behind then brought her fist up to see that the impact didn't even leave a mark on her.

She closed her eyes and drew a sharp breath to try to calm herself.

What was she becoming?

Her eyes flew open and she grabbed the cell phone that Cale had given her and flipped the screen to the contacts to find the number that he had entered. Along with it was the previous owners mothers and fathers numbers along with an endless number of friends.

She wondered how the person who owned the phone was doing now as she pressed Cale's name. After five rings, a voice she recognized as Cale's answered the phone.

"…Hello?" His tone seemed uncertain, she knew he was hoping it was her.

Her hand shook from the power she had exerted when she broke the tree and she found it hard to speak.

"Hello?" He repeated.

"It's Sam." She replied shakily and she could hear him telling someone who she guessed was Emily that it was her on the phone.

"...How'd it go?" He asked when he brought his attention back to the phone.

She shook her head even though he couldn't see it. "Not good."

"I'm sorry, Sam." He apologized like it was his fault.

Sam placed her hand on her forehead then ran it down her face but left it on her mouth and squeezed. At least her nervous tick didn't change along everything else.

Cale didn't interrupt her while she calmed her nerves and she appreciated it.

She removed her hand when she was ready. "Your offer still stands, right?"

She was sure the answer would be yes even though he was apprehensive after what she had done, it was Emily who was a different story.

"Of course." He replied and gave her an address that she typed into her phone.

"We're on our way there now, I'm going to throw my phone out the window after we hang up in case they can track it."

Sam looked down at her phone, they could very well be tracking the phones right now.

"I have some extra people with us as well." Cale added suddenly and Sam blinked.

"Oh." she started to make her way back to the bike. "The more the merrier I suppose." she smiled to herself though she was surprised that her former cellmates had picked anyone up.

"Yeah, I guess you could say that." Sam could hear the smile on Cale's face but it didn't seem like a happy one.

Sam straddled her bike. "I'm leaving now, I'll see you guys soon."

"You too," Cale replied. "Stay safe." he added and she could hear the rush of air on his side as he opened the window to prepare to throw the phone out.

"You too." She muttered then clicked *end* on the touch screen.

She sighed and pulled out her wallet that she had grabbed before leaving her house. She only had her license and a fifty dollar bill. More than enough to buy a phone from the drugstore.

She slid on her helmet and started the bike, the engine rumbling to life as she turned on the map settings to the nearest drug store for the phones last hurrah before she broke it.

She placed her wallet back into her pocket and mounted the phone on the stand between the handle bars. As she pulled her helmet over her head, she slowly rolled to the road then hit the gas.

* * *

Chapter 12

It was pitch black by the time Sam pulled off the exit that her brand new phone had directed her to take and it didn't take long for her to find herself on winding backroads.

She had never been this way before and all she could think of was how thankful she was for the map feature on the phone. She jumped a few times while passing cows and other livestock, she was feeling a bit on edge and the feeling was justified. She looked in the windows of houses as she passed them and saw people watching television and eating dinner. The bright lights were welcoming and she hoped where she was heading looked the same.

The pavement turned into dirt and the potholes made her almost fall off the bike. There were no more houses, only trees and darkness. She found herself looking down at the phone to see if she was going the right way but the phone wanted her to continue straight and to her dismay, she did as she was told.

Where the hell was Cale's hideout?

She rolled down the rough road and she wanted to go faster out of unease but speed wasn't an option. She looked down one more time to check the map but found that it had stopped working due to lack of service.

"Don't panic." She tried to calm herself but flinched when she heard something rustling beside her in the woods. She pressed the gas to go faster, she wasn't usually like this.

She was always the one who was upfront in a haunted house but after what she had been through, she didn't have the same amount of courage that she once had.

She was really starting to panic as the road continued on with no end but as she turned a sharp corner, she saw lights shining through the trees in front of her…lights coming from a house.

She followed the lights and found herself on a long rocky driveway and before she knew it, the house was in front of her.

It was dark but she could tell that the building was old and the paint was chipping off in various spots. It had two floors and the window panes looked haunting.

Sam cut the loud engine and pulled off her helmet. She looked to the corner of the house where a black four door Jeep was parked.

She didn't think about it before but now she wondered where Cale had gotten a car.

Her head snapped to the front door as she heard it open with a creak. Cale stepped out and he stopped on the front porch to look at her for a moment then stepped down to meet her.

"I was starting to worry." he admitted as he stopped in front of her.

"Me too." she sighed as she looked back to the door to see Emily peaking out. She raised her hand in a half wave and Sam awkwardly returned it.

"She'll come around." Cale assured her as he took her bike by the handles and began pushing it to where the jeep was parked.

"Sure." Sam said unconfidently as she followed him.

"I didn't peg you as a biker." he laughed lightly and she smiled. "I don't consider myself one, I bought it on a whim one day and ended up getting my license." She turned to the Jeep. "How did you manage to get this?"

"It's mine, when I called my dad I asked him where it was, turns out they brought it to a lot near where we were locked up." He face fell. "My dad was paying to keep it there until he could come home, I called him and asked him to have them release it to me. I had to work for it though so the workers wouldn't recognize me. My father understandably freaked out when he got my call, he was going to come home tomorrow but I told him to stay and that I was fine."

He laid his hand on the Jeep, he looked pale from the dim light coming from the house. "I told him not to call the authorities and to act like I'm still missing, I told him to trust me and that I'll be alright."

Sam knew the last part was a lie and she also wondered how his father could be so understanding. She turned to the house. "And this?" she motioned towards it.

"This is the house I told you about." He gazed up at the old thing.

Sam's eyes moved from one end of the house to the other. Everyone who had been imprisoned had their lives changed drastically. Cale didn't expect things to play out this way and Sam bet he had hoped to move into the house when his service to the country was done. To settle down and live the rest of his days there.

That seemed so out of reach now.

Cale watched as Sam's expression grew sadder as she thought of the reaction she had gotten from her parents.

"They know." she turned to face him as he was about to comfort her and he jumped a bit.

"They know what?" He knew the answer, it just needed to be said out loud.

"That I'm a gargoyle, the government knows the gargoyles are behind the disappearances."

He locked his jaw "How the hell-"

"I guess the stories were true, only they didn't care enough to give us the details."

"What about the demons?" he blinked.

"I don't know."

They were going to treat them as a separate entity until further notice.

"And the unicorns?"

She knew he didn't say it to be funny but she snorted.

"Let's go inside so you can meet everyone and get settled in." He said after he laughed along with her.

She grabbed the phone from the mount on her bike and powered it off as the two made their way to the house. Cale held the door open for her and she stepped inside to see something different from what she had expected: Unlike the outside, the inside had clean hardwood floors that were glossy and the walls were painted gray.

"We already finished the inside." Cale explained as he removed his shoes and Sam followed suit. Once their shoes were off, the two stepped into the hall that led into a living room which had a gray carpet and the walls were the same color as the entryway.

On what looked like brand new furniture that consisted of a large sectional couch and a chair sat five people including Emily. On the floor sat three others.

Sam didn't imagine that many people when Cale had told her that he had tag alongs.

She looked around and recognized some of them: The black haired girl that she had freed but now in the light she could see teal streaks in her side bangs. The stocky football man was there as well and the chubby spiky haired man.

The room was quiet as Cale made his way over to Emily and sat on the arm of the coach.

The black haired girl shot up and made her way to Sam and she braced herself as if she was coming in for an attack. But what she did was even worse in Sam's book: She gave her a hug.

"You saved us." the girl squeezed harder and Sam felt a twinge of warmth fill her chest. She raised her right arm and patted the girl on the back. When the girl finally let go, she stood back and looked into Sam's eyes, like she was reading her.

Sam pressed her lips together and avoided her gaze.

"Hey Ari, can't you see you're making her uncomfortable?" the girl that was sitting on the floor in front of where Ari had been sitting called over with a entertained tone.

Her mousy brown hair was cut short and she wore a low cut pink shirt. She was skinny, *really* skinny, but not enough that it was a problem.

"Sorry." Ari apologized. "I'm Arianna but you can call me Ari."

"I'm Sa-" Sam started to introduce herself but Ari cut her off with a smile.

"We know who you are." Ari walked back over to sit next to the short haired girl on the floor and Sam moved to sit in the free recliner. She sat awkwardly and her back cracked painfully, the soft material was foreign compared to the hard ground that she had slept on for weeks.

She looked at the people around her, they looked so clean compared to her. They had the time to shower and change into new clothes while she hadn't.

She longed to do the same as she turned to the left where Cale and Emily sat.

She noticed that Cale looked like he had lost weight but he still held his muscle tone. He was wearing a black t-shirt and sweats while Emily also looked thinner. Her curls were still loose but she looked much better in her sweater and pajamas.

"Since staring awkwardly at each other isn't getting us anywhere, I guess we should follow Ari's lead and introduce ourselves." The spiky haired man laughed softly. "I'm Trevor." he looked comfy in his oversized attire.

Sam nodded. "Nice to meet you." She was thankful that he didn't hug her like Ari had.

Beside him sat a dark skinned boy who waved at her with muscled arms. His hair was pulled back into tight braids that hugged his scalp. "I'm Daniel and this is my twin sister, Jeannie."

His sister scoffed from beside him. "I can speak for myself."

Her shoulder length hair swayed back and forth as she gave her brother an annoyed look. The two were dressed in night clothes like everyone else, Daniel in a football team shirt and Jeannie in a tight fitting pink tank top. She looked back to Sam with a smile. "Thanks for helping in getting us out of there."

Sam nodded again.

The girl who had saved Sam from further embarrassment from Ari's hug winked at her, "I'm Kira, nice to meet ya."

Sam smiled shyly in return.

"I'm Cam." a skinny dirty blonde haired boy introduced himself before her eyes were even on him. He wore a dark green shirt with a skull on it. He looked completely uninterested and he didn't seem friendly like the others.

Sam rose a brow. "Hi."

She faced the last person to be introduced: The stocky boy she had saved with Ari and Trevor. "Dylan." he nodded towards her. "I'm sure you're tired of hearing this but thanks for getting us out of there."

"No problem." Sam's mouth quirked to the right.

Jesus that was awkward.

She looked around the room and stopped on Cale and Emily again. They had both watched her as she learned the names of her new peers.

Cale nodded as he gave her the imaginary mic to say what she wanted and she turned to face the newcomers.

She was no longer awkward as she got to her objective. "I have a simple question," she crossed her legs. "Why are you here?"

The group looked at each other, they obviously didn't expect the change in atmosphere but Sam wanted them to know her reasoning for being there. Plus they needed to know what they were getting themselves into by being with her and her former cellmates.

"I'm here because I don't have anywhere else to go." Ari was the first to answer and Sam rounded on her. "You have everywhere else to go." She uncrossed her legs and leaned forward, she couldn't believe how she was acting.

Never in her life had she been good at speaking especially in front of others. Being changed into a gargoyle had not only changed her body, but her mind. Arthur had a hand in that as well.

"If you think it's safe here, you're misguided."

Jeannie's mouth hung open. "But you and Cale saved us and not only are the gargoyles going to be looking for us, but so are the humans… How can we not be safe around you?"

"Arthur wants Sam to fight Carma," Cale answered with his eyes down. "He'll be looking for us but Sam is higher on his list because of her white eyes."

Sam's eyes rolled to look at him without moving her head. So he had told them about Carma?

Emily looked down to her hands that were cupped together so hard that her knuckles were white. Daniel shook his head and gripped his knee. "I still don't understand why your so called *friend* would join them so easily?"

"She's weak minded if you ask me." Cam looked between Sam, Cale, and Emily.

Sam could see the anger building in Cale but he fought to keep his composure.

"Carma has a...problem." He drew a breath. "She had an accident when she was fourteen, she was at our local beach when she got dizzy and almost drowned. She was rushed to the hospital and her mother told me that when she woke up she kept saying how weak she was." He began to look unsettled.

"She hasn't been the same since." Emily continued for him even though the subject was just as hard on her. "She's been in and out of mental hospitals and she was diagnosed with dissociative identity disorder." She released her hands with a suction sound and pressed them to the sofa. "By being changed into a gargoyle, I guess she got the power she always wanted and it must be the reason why the other personality to took over."

The group seemed dumbfounded and Sam's mouth was dry.

"She should've stayed in the mental ward." Cam continued with his harsh words.

"She didn't have a problem for two years until she was taken. There was no reason for her to be locked up but I guess none of us knew we were going to be changed into monsters." Cale growled through his teeth as he gave Cam a look that would intimidate a well seasoned fighter. Black fluid twirled in the corners of his eyes as he fought his transformation.

Cam remained quiet for the rest of the conversation about Carma though Sam could see the obnoxious looks he gave.

"How do we get the *real* Carma back?" Kira who had her elbows resting on her knees while enjoying the show finally sat up straight.

"I've never seen her this bad but I'm sure the Carma we know is still in there." The black liquid dissolved from Cale's eyes as he calmed but

Sam could still see the unrest in them as he looked towards the fireplace.

She gave him a sad smile, "We'll get her back." she assured then brought her attention back to the other ex-prisoners. "Arthur wants to pit Carma and I against each other to see who's the stronger white eyed gargoyle. He'll come for all of us but at this point, I think he sees me as entertainment. He already has Carma, Kellan, and Camilla so he doesn't need me." Sam clawed her nails into her palm as she felt rage rush through her again.

She was feeling that emotion a lot as of late, but she had to calm herself. "It's not safe for you here but if you go home and it goes like it did for me, you'll show your new features to your family and they'll reject you like mine did."

"You showed your family that you're a gargoyle?" Trevor gave her a look filled with disbelief.

"Not on purpose-" Her tone was harsher than she wanted it to be but she couldn't believe that he would think that she would do such a thing intentionally. "-but as I'm sure you know, even a quickened heartbeat can cause your eyes to change and your teeth to sharpen."

The group gave her looks that consisted of clenched jaws and furrowed brows and it confirmed that they knew what she was talking about.

"It's up to you to go home and see if your loved ones will accept you or stay here and risk your lives." Sam didn't really want Cale and Emily to be around her either but she knew with Carma involved, they would be thrown into the situation nonetheless.

The three of them were better off together, she knew better than to ask them to stay out of it. It was Cale's house that she was staying at anyway.

She leaned into the soft chair as she waited for the groups reply.

"There's nowhere else for me to go." Kira sat up straight and gazed at her black heeled shoes as she tapped them together. "My parents kicked me out a year ago and I know my girlfriend won't accept me now." She looked up, closed her eyes, and smiled widely. "Onto the next."

Sam couldn't believe Kira's reason to stay, she glanced at Cale and Emily and their faces matched her own.

"I'm staying too." Ari leaned forward. "I want to learn how to control these abilities and get revenge on the fuckers that ruined my life." She ruffled Kira's short hair. "I'm sure that's her reason to stay too."

Kira swatted her hand away. "Yeah, sure, whatever." she replied with annoyance but Sam caught her sideways glance at the carpet as she got lost in thought.

"I want to stay but I want Jeannie to go." Daniel looked determined as he looked between Cale and Sam then to his sister as she scoffed at him. "I'm not leaving." His sister fought him and Daniel's eyes narrowed. "It's not safe."

"Nowhere is safe." she challenged him.

The siblings gave each other looks that said that this conversation was far from over but now wasn't the time.

Trevor who had his arms crossed the entire time shook his head.

"I figured all of this when I left with you guys." his eyes set on Cale and Emily. "I knew what I was getting into when I saw the three of you meet in the middle of the cave when you got us out. You didn't say anything to each other, all you did was run but I knew from the looks on your faces that you were in it for so much more than escaping and hiding out forever." He brought his attention to Sam. "Why don't you hide? Go someplace where they would never think to find you? I understand Cale and Emily want to save their friend but what reason do you have?" His eyes drove into her soul and she hated it.

She thought about his question as she felt everyone's eyes fall on her, she wanted nothing more than to leave.

She lifted her head and leaned forward again. "Saving Carma is important to me too, I didn't know her long but she took care of me when my head was cracked open."

She saw Cale and Emily's gazes soften as they watched her explanation.

"I want revenge like Ari plus I want to stop their plans." She could feel the pressure in her eyes peak as her heart rate fastened.

"...Maybe I want to kill Arthur." the air around her changed as she felt nothing but pure hatred for the man who had ruined all of their lives and threatened the future. The group reacted to her white eyes by flinching or looking at her with awe. Cale and Emily had seen her eyes before so they didn't have much of a reaction.

She didn't bother hiding her eyes like before, she didn't care what the people seeing them would think. It showed her resolve for revenge and her will to stop whatever Arthur was planning.

Cam who had looked interested in Sam's change continued to look at her like she was a brand new toy. "I don't care about learning how to be a monster but I do want to stay, I'm sure I can be of some help." He said finally.

The pressure in Sam's eyes dissolved as she thought of what he could really be there for but she knew it would come out sooner or later.

"Do as you wish." She replied with a look that showed that she didn't trust him.

"Dylan?" Cale questioned the last to respond as if Sam's little show didn't happen. The stocky boy looked around as if he wanted to say that he was leaving but was afraid of being called a coward.

"You don't have to stay." Cale assured him. "No one will judge you for it."

Dylan replied by shaking his head with a sheepish smile, the poor guy had everyone's gaze on him while they waited for his answer. He nervously picked at the skin on his index finger. "I won't be of good use to you, all I know how to do is play football, I'm all brawn and no brains but I want to stay."

"We all started somewhere." Cale assured him again.

Sam took a look at the group, there was a lot of work to be done and they could be attacked at any moment but she couldn't allow herself to think that way.

If they were attacked this soon after escaping, it wouldn't be Arthur's doing.

As if reading her mind, Emily spoke. "How long do you guys think we have before they find us?"

"I think we have awhile." Cale answered her. "My name or my father's isn't on the owners list for this house so the cops can't find us unless my father slips up." He drew a breath and gave Sam a look that revealed that he was thinking the same thing as her and he continued. "If Arthur finds us first which I'm sure will happen, he won't show up right away."

Cam gave him a questioning look. "Why won't he?"

Sam answered for Cale. "Because he let us escape."

They figured that was a good place to end their conversation. Though Sam, Cale, and Emily continued to check if their new comrades were sure that they wanted to stay but they were met with the same answer every time.

Cale was leading her to the bathroom, he had asked Emily to take her but she didn't want to be left alone with her and he felt it rude to ask the girls he had just met to show her the way.

"I'm sorry about that." he apologized for Emily's refusal but Sam shook it off.

"I don't blame her." She watched as Cale's injured shoulder bobbed up and down as he walked in front of her.

"You didn't mean it." he said as he turned his head to look at her, the steps creaked every time they took a step and it annoyed her.

"I know but I still did it."

The two made it to the second floor where the carpet was an olive green and the walls were the same color. "I'm not mad." he assured her but she didn't want to talk about it anymore.

"W-where did everyone get their clean clothes?" It was a stupid question but she wanted to change the subject.

He turned to her as he opened the bathroom door and flipped the light on for her.

"We stopped by a small store on the way here, going to all of their houses was out of the question but so was all of them wearing my clothes."

Sam imagined stocky Dylan popping out of Cale's shirt and the girls swimming in them.

"Yeah, that's true." Sam agreed with a small chuckle.

"It was hard to be discreet in the store since it's not everyday you see dirty malnourished young adults running around, I'm sure they thought we were on drugs." Cale explained and Sam thought of her adventures at the gas station.

She had an *aha* moment as she let the backpack fall off her shoulders and she pulled her laptop out and handed it to him along with the charger and the phone she had bought.

"These can come in handy." She proclaimed as Cale looked down at the devices.

"I was thinking of how a computer would come in handy." He flipped the device around in his hands. "I even thought about sneaking into my fathers house to grab my own laptop but this will be a lot safer." he beamed.

"Don't worry," she said as she stepped into the bathroom then turned around and leaned against the frame. "I deleted my browser history."

Cale looked puzzled but snorted once he realized her intentions and Sam snickered. She obviously wasn't worried about it, she just wanted to make him laugh and he knew it.

After the two finished with their laughter, Cale placed his empty hand over his mouth.

"Thanks, Sam." his voice was muffled from his hand but she heard the gratefulness in his tone.

She knew he wasn't just talking about her getting him to laugh but the fact that she wanted to help Carma as much as he did. "I bet you're ready to get that dirt and blood off so I'll make my leave." He stepped back as he dropped his hand.

"Yeah," Sam sniffed as she looked down at herself. "I think it's about time."

Cale made his way back down the stairs and Sam backed into the bathroom and closed the door. She took in the room as she turned away from the door: It wasn't big by any means, it had barely enough room to walk between the shower, sink, and the toilet but it was cozy and warm.

She dropped her backpack on the floor and opened the shower curtain. The metal rings attaching the plastic cloth to the bar over the shower squealed as the two metals rubbed together. Inside the tub was both men's and women's shampoo and conditioner, they must have picked them up when they got their clothes.

She started to wonder why Arthur and his group didn't take their money but she answered herself quickly: His goals obviously had nothing to do with money.

She opened the wooden cabinet over the sink and the hinges squeaked louder than the curtain. she gripped at her head for a moment as a sharp pain shot through her temple but it diminished as fast as it came. She grabbed the clean towels that Cale had told her were inside the cabinet and looked into the mirror as she closed it.

The stitches in her right temple were practically hanging by a thread so she grabbed the string and yanked. It came out with no resistance and caused her no pain.

She leaned into the mirror as she examined the fresh scar. Arthur had said that it was going to leave one since it was done by a gargoyles nails and it certainly did. The stitches were overkill to her but maybe they wanted to make sure she would heal fast to not make a mess of things.

She went to touch the scar but she remembered what he had said after he told her about her injury.

"You're always going to punish yourself, aren't you?"

She sensed something from him at that time, was it sadness? No, it couldn't be, she was overthinking it.

She closed her eyes as she looked at the gray in her irises again, it wasn't noticeable unless someone really looked. She didn't bother to think of the reasoning behind it, she figured it to be another gargoyle thing.

She began pulling off her dirt covered clothes and let them fall to the floor. After she stepped into the tub and closed the curtain, she let the hot water pour onto her dirt covered skin. She looked down to see dirt running down the drain as it washed off of her.

She turned to the right and grabbed the shampoo, conditioner, and soap on the little shelf built into the tub. They smelt heavily of vanilla and it soothed her.

As she washed the soap out of her hair, she noticed all of the dry blood from the injury Arthur had inflicted on her and the one she had done to herself wash down the drain.

Her muscles ached from the water and she closed her eyes as she leaned her head forward on the wall to let the water run on her back. She drew a shaky breath and exhaled sharply, causing her to cough until her eyes watered.

When she finally composed herself, she finished with her shower and wrapped a towel around her body and another around her long hair.

The whole time she was standing in the sweltering water, she had to fight herself to not think about what was going to happen next. They had to prepare for what was going to come but the outcome was so uncertain.

How could they even compare to Arthur who was born a gargoyle? How could they teach themselves how to be gargoyles when they had no idea?

There was no way they could beat their enemies with their inexperience.

Instead of hitting something in the tub, she punched her thigh and yelped from the pain but it was nothing compared to the feeling in her heart. She had to calm herself, even if there was something to plan, she wasn't going to do it with the mindset she had now and she certainly couldn't do it by herself.

She dried her hair then let the towel that was wrapped around her middle drop to the floor. As she looked at her now clean body, she realized that like Cale and Emily, she had lost a good amount of weight.

She turned from the mirror and got dressed into gray loose fitting sweats and a band t-shirt. There was no time to think about how different she looked or her dreams that weighed on her constantly. Especially when there were things to get done in the real world.

She was crazy and she knew it, there was no reason to keep dwelling on it. Besides, insanity wasn't always a bad thing.

She brushed her hair that reached the middle of her back and getting the knots out proved to be a tedious task. When she was done, she threw her dirty clothes in the hamper like Cale had instructed and grabbed her bag and shut off the lights as she opened the door and made her way into the hallway. She could hear the group talking downstairs but didn't listen as she looked down the olive green hall past the bathroom. There were two doors on either side which she guessed were bedrooms and at the end of the hall was a large window. For some reason it caused her unease, she hated that it was far too dark to see outside, there could be something out there and she wouldn't know it. Her breath hitched as a nervous feeling rose in her chest but the smell of food filled her nose and calmed her down.

She took another glance at the window then made her way downstairs.

It turned out that Emily, Jeannie, and Ari were making food for everyone while the remainder of the group was still sitting in the living room with Cale. He was sitting in the recliner that Sam had sat in and her laptop was sitting in his lap, the screen illuminating his face.

"Find anything good?" She asked as she set her bag down at the corner of the stairs and Cale looked up from the screen as everyone else turned to meet her.

"You look better." Ari called from the kitchen and Sam turned her head a little to the left to an entryway to see Ari waving a knife.

The kitchen was easy to see from the living room, it was nice to know where everyone was. "I feel better." Sam snorted at the fact that Ari looked like a crazy serial killer.

She made her way to the empty spot on the couch across from Cale.

"I was thinking about what you said earlier so I decided to look more into it." Cale explained as he flipped the laptop around to show Sam while the others looked on.

On the screen was a large paragraph labeled *Gargoyles*, it talked about how they attacked cities and towns over twenty years ago and killed almost every human in them.

"We already knew that though." Sam noted as she read the article.

Cale shook his head as he scrolled down the page and it showed autopsy photos of mutilated bodies. Some had their throats slashed by what looked like claws, some were stabbed through the chest, and some bodies were torn apart to the extent that they were unrecognizable.

The images left a pit in the bottom of Sam's stomach and by the looks on everyone's faces, they felt the same. Cale's jaw was locked but he had obviously already seen the images so he kept his eyes away as he scrolled down to show more.

The new set of images showed the towns after the attacks: Fires, torn down buildings, and streets filled with rubble.

"They killed people for sport." Cale's voice shook and Sam looked at the image of a male that was still on top of the screen. She could see the fear etched on his face.

It was the look he must have had just before his throat was torn out. Sam's heart lurched and she turned away.

Cale saw the effect the images were having on them so he clicked off the page then turned the screen back to face him.

"It was hard to find the website but after doing some digging, I found that page." He swallowed. "It turns out there's people out there that are intrigued with the gargoyles. I thought maybe the images could be from other disasters but when I dragged the image to the search bar, it brought me back to the website." He began typing as he explained. "It says they've been shut down by the government countless times but they haven't been shut down recently, they think they're distracted by the kidnappings."

"How did they even get those images?" Cam questioned with a brow in the air.

"Supposedly it's run by an ex-government worker that got tired of the shit going on there." Cale responded as he typed then flipped the computer again.

"This was also weighing on my mind." he pointed at the screen.

It read *Demons,* "You can't just type in demons because you'll be overwhelmed with articles about the evil spirits that the devil sent from hell and how to ward them off with prayer and gems."

Sam was sure everyone in the house at one point had looked up more information on the creatures but were met with bullshit articles. The whole thing sounded stupid so everyone looked to Cale who had the answer's on Sam's laptop.

Emily, Ari, and Jeannie made their way back into the living room just in time for the explanation. It was clear they were listening from the kitchen.

Cale clicked the tab for the website they were just looking at but this time, the article read:

They call them demons but are they really?

Cale read the page for the people who were too far away to read the tiny font. "It says the creatures attacked a government building that had experimental bombs and while they were there, they said they were gargoyles. It also said that a bomb was missing from the facility after the gargoyles left but there was no event that suggested that the bomb was used."

Sam's mouth went dry and her heart raced as Cale spoke about a bomb. It reminded her of her dream and the sound of the explosion rang in her ears. The feeling of her body being torn apart flooded her mind.

"So are they separate entities?" Ari challenged.

"It says they named the creatures demons because of the way they looked and the monstrous things they did but..." Cale scrolled down the page and stopped at two side by side grayscale pictures. They were extremely blurry but they both held images of a creature: One had short horns and long wings emerged from it's back. It also had claws and teeth similar to the ones the gargoyles got. In the other picture the being had considerably longer horns and instead of long pointed nails, the thing had talons. What shocked the group the most was the glare coming from the creatures eyes. While the other creature only showed the whites of its eyes, this one's eyes were blurred completely.

The first creature was obviously a gargoyle but what the hell was the other thing?

"The guy who owns the site isn't giving a straight answer as to if demons are real but he did say they aren't the spirits you see on ghost shows." Cale ended his explanation and the group sat quietly as they took in the information.

The website, (depending on how true it was.) had helped with some of their questions but it also created more. Why didn't the government warn the newer generation about the threat even though they thought the beings were dead? Why did the older generation seem not to know anything of real value about them? The fact that they had taken down the website on many occasions was enough to answer the question though.

Cale flipped the computer back to him again and tsked, Sam and the others looked at him, waiting for him to explain what had happened.

"They just deleted it." Shock filled his voice.

"What?" Ari leaned on the back of the coach directly behind Sam.

"They just deleted the website, I'm refreshing the page over and over but it says the website is no longer available."

"Turn off the computer now." Dylan warned with panic in his tone.

Cale did just that as the fear of getting tracked hit everyone at once. Could they even do that?

They weren't taking the chance.

Cale shut the computer and set it on the stand beside him. The group sat in silence as panic got the better of them and the air around the room got warm with nerves.

The oven timer went off and made all of them jump

"Fuck!" Emily who had practically jumped out of her skin ran into the kitchen to shut the alarm off.

Sam pressed her hands together as she thought of the images of the supposed gargoyles. She had no hope for a chance to win before but after seeing the being that was thought to be a mutated gargoyle, the nonexistent hope that she had furthered into oblivion.

"We can grow wings…?" Kira asked suddenly and everyone seemed shocked that that was the first thing she would ask.

After looking at her face, they realized she was trying to change the mood. The side of her mouth tugged as she looked at their stupid faces though Sam could still feel the nerves of the small girl who sat next to her.

"How the hell do we get wings and hide them?" Daniel looked puzzled as he tried to turn to see his back and Sam thought of how Arthur nor the others seemed to have wings hiding under their shirts. Emily emerged from the kitchen with an annoyed look, waking everyone from their thoughts. "Food is done."

The group made their way to the kitchen, the smell of food filled the room and it made Sam's mouth water. The smell was noticeable in the living room as well but she was far too invested in the conversation to notice. The kitchen was spacious with an island counter in the middle and the stove and sink were placed in another counter against the wall so the person working with them would be able to see into the backyard through a window. Off to the side of the room was a table it's own space. Sam looked to the stove to see a huge pot of macaroni and cheese cooling off.

"I think that's enough for everyone." Emily said but sounded unsure.

"None of us has had anything but cold soup for weeks, eating too much will probably make us sick anyway." Jeannie noted as she grabbed a bowl from the ten placed across the counter and she scooped some of the macaroni and cheese into it and handed it to Trevor. When Sam got her bowl, she slowly took a bite and her taste buds sung from the feeling of having something of a different flavor to eat. The room filled with moans of appreciation for the food.

"I don't think I want to eat chicken noodle soup ever again." Trevor slurred his words from his mouth being full and his peers agreed in unison.

Sam gagged at the thought of the soup then found herself wondering if Arthur and the others had moved their lair and what had happened to the other escapees.

"Do you want more Sam?" Cale asked and broke her away from her thoughts.

She looked down to her empty bowl while realizing that she was already full. She looked up from the bowl and shook her head. "No, thank you."

"I guess it'll take awhile for us to get used to eating again." Cale said as he stepped forward and took Sam's bowl. He already had everyone else's bowls but Sam hadn't noticed him go around to collect them. He walked the bowls to the sink as Dylan let out a big yawn and made everyone realize how tired they were. Cale looked down to the dishes now laying in the sink. "These can wait till tomorrow."

Sam agreed, even the plan could wait till tomorrow. None of them had the mental ability to think of anything wise when they were this tired.

Cale showed everyone to their rooms, the four girls got their own rooms upstairs and the boys got their own as well. The rooms only had one bed but the girls had no problem sleeping in the same bed and since there were four rooms, they worked as two person bedrooms. It also helped that Cale had managed to find a few air mattresses.

"That was convenient." Sam had her arms crossed as she made her way down the steps behind Cale.

"We slept on them when we were too tired to go home after working all day and we still didn't have mattresses." He shrugged.

Sam rubbed her hands against her arms in an effort to get warm. "I'm fine with sleeping on the couch." She admitted as Cale brought her to a room she hadn't paid much attention to on the bottom floor. The room was only a few feet away from the front door.

"I'm fine with the couch too but one of us is going to have to take this room." He said as he opened the door: The room was large, far larger than the ones upstairs, and in the middle was a full sized bed with a navy blue blanket that matched the walls.

"You can have it." Sam said with no hesitation, she definitely felt like she didn't deserve the room, especially one all to herself while the others had to bunk together. "I'm seriously fine with the couch."

"Me too." Cale walked into the room and leaned against the door frame. "To be honest, I prefer sleeping on the couch."

She had been facing away from him as she looked at the small touches added to the room and she turned to face him."Why?"

He considered her for a moment. "I want to be in the open in case something happens, it's something I've always done even before this happened."

She exhaled and swallowed. "And I'm better off in here in case I freak out again from another dream."

"That's not-" Cale stepped towards her but she rose a hand and shook her head. "I'm not saying that because I think that's what your true intentions are, It's how I feel personally. At least in here, I'll be able to deal with my shit without hurting anyone."

Cale seemed to be at a loss for words and Sam could tell that he felt bad about the situation.

He was the one who had been injured and his shoulder was a constant reminder of what she had done and even though he seemed nervous, he never once resented her for it.

"If you truly like sleeping on the couch, go for it." She glanced into the hall behind his head where only a few feet to the right was the front door. "You like to sleep on the couch because you can jump into action while I wouldn't mind staying here in case someone shows up."

Cale turned his head to look at the wall to his left as if he could see though it into the front yard. They would be able to hear an intruder before seeing them anyway. It was one of the things Sam didn't mind about being a gargoyle.

Cale turned back to her and nodded and she looked him in the eyes. There were dark bags under them and she knew it wasn't just from the lack of sleep.

"We'll get her back." She felt like she had said this a thousand times.

"...Yeah." his eyes averted to the floor. "There's so much to do."

"And we'll do it together, all of us." Sam's eyes softened, comforting people wasn't her forte but she was slowly getting better at it.

Cale nodded again and turned to leave while grabbing the door handle but before he shut the door, he stopped.

"Thanks, Sam." He thanked softly as the door shut with a click.

Sam stood for a moment as she looked at the door and she could hear Cale walking on the wooden floor and the couch creaking as he laid down. She could also hear the mumbles of the group upstairs but she couldn't make out the words, she didn't want to.

She sat down on the edge of the bed and pulled her backpack off her shoulders which she had grabbed before everyone had decided on room arrangements. She pulled all of her clothes out and laid them out beside her as she grabbed a hair tie and pulled her hair into a bun then sighed.

Her eyes were heavy but so was her mind.

She got up and picked up her clothes, setting them on the dresser to the left and she opened the drawers to find them empty. She set the garments inside then flipped the switch to turn the lights off.

She made her way to the bed then pulled the blankets back and settled into them like a cocoon. She zoned out the voices and the creaks of bedsprings, she only focused on the sounds from outside. She couldn't help but feel proud at the fact that she had control over at least one power.

She had found out that having a motive would help with control but she was far from finding out the way to transform like Arthur had. Or even like the being's in the pictures.

She rolled to her side and nuzzled into the pillow, the soft bed was quite the upgrade from the cave ground but she was as restless as she ever was.

She peered through the darkness as she tried to relax but the thoughts of what was to come flooded her mind. She knew the others were doing the same and she found some comfort in the fact that she wasn't alone.

She exhaled sharply and closed her eyes, exhaustion was setting in and even her stressed mind couldn't stop the sleep from coming.

Chapter 13

She woke the next morning with the smell of bacon filling her nose and she blinked a few times as she rose slowly from the bed. The sleep was still in her eyes and she was trying to think whether she had a dream or not. She had a hard time remembering them as of late but was always able to hold onto bits and pieces. The events of the last few weeks must have had a toll on her dreams.

She wiped her eyes then got up to get dressed. She pulled on a pair of jeans and a t-shirt then pulled the hair tie from her hair and let the strands fall. She ran her hand through the front and pushed it out of her eyes by making it rest more to the left.

The sound of talking and dishes clattering from the kitchen made her move quicker as she made the bed and once she was done, she rushed out the door to meet everyone.

Cale, Cam, Daniel, and Dylan were sitting around the middle counter while Emily, Trevor, and Jeannie were leaning against the counter nearest the stove.

Sam looked out the window into the backyard when something caught her eye and she noticed Ari and Kira standing outside. Kira was taking a drag out of a cigarette while Ari stood there looking tired. Her long hair was in a ponytail and she picked at the ends of it as it laid over her shoulder. Sam was starting to feel embarrassed that she was the last to wake and everyone looked up as she stepped into the room.

"Sleep well?" Trevor inquired as he grabbed a bowl then made his way over to hand it to her. Inside was five pieces of bacon. "Apparently yes." She took the bowl. "Thanks." she added as he stepped away.

There was an empty chair across from Cale and she took it. Everyone had obviously already eaten and she felt awkward but took a bite. She turned her head a bit as she munched and noticed Emily looking at her with a untrusting look. Sam quickly faced forward and continued eating.

She didn't know eating was so untrustworthy.

The door slid open behind her and Sam turned in time to see Ari and Kira making their way into the house. "Morning." Ari smiled as she shut the door behind her.

"What's up?" Kira asked the group as she nodded Sam's way.

"Cale wouldn't talk about anything gargoyle related until you woke up." Daniel informed Sam as he leaned his head onto his arms.

"Oh." She replied simply.

Why would he wait for her?

The group brought their attention to Cale as he finally woke from his thoughts and he acknowledged them. He met Sam's gaze first because she was directly in front of him.

"You're a big player in Arthur's game, so I feel it's essential that you're here while we plan." He declared and everyone turned to look at her.

She wanted to reject it but he was right, only she and Carma had gotten white eyes which meant they were stronger. She had also made quite the name for herself back at the cave.

Plus there was the showdown that both Arthur and Carma were planning.

"Have you thought of anything?" she asked after a chill shot through her.

Cale looked around the table, his expression was nothing short of disappointed. "I don't have an elaborate plan that includes us trapping them or working with the government but I-"

"Why don't we try?" Jeannie interrupted and their attention changed to her.

She looked startled at everyone's looks that all understandably seemed judgemental so she explained herself. "I know we're worried about them experimenting on us but we have to get them to understand that we're on their side."

Everyone knew where she was coming from and in a perfect world the government would understand, but it could go south like how the situation with Sam's parents had gone.

"This isn't a movie where the misunderstood group shows up and magically gets their enemies to help fight their common enemy. It just doesn't work that way in the real world." Cam explained with an air of annoyance that Jeannie would suggest something so stupid. His pale eyes never left the spot on the counter that he was looking at.

"You don't need to talk to her like she's stupid, it was just a suggestion." Daniel warned and Cam shot him a look that was less than friendly.

"Stop before you start." Sam warned as she narrowed her eyes at Cam.

They couldn't fight amongst themselves, they wouldn't achieve anything if they did.

Cam glanced at Sam but didn't change his expression. She had to practice what she preached but it took all she had not to smack the look off his stupid face. The air seemed to change around her and she feigned a cough to defuse it.

"The plan I have may sound absolutely stupid but it's the only thing that might work." Cale continued with their conversation as if the small banter had never happened.

"What is it?" Emily pressed with an eyebrow perked, she obviously wasn't told anything about what he was thinking either.

"...We try to fight them." Cale almost seemed embarrassed at the simplicity of what everyone thought would be an elaborate plan.

They were silent as they considered Cale, only the birds chirping outside could be heard. Cale had said that the plan was going to sound stupid but they thought he was down playing it.

"Let me explain," Cale defended suddenly as he started to feel the judgement of his peers. "There's nothing I can think of that will give us a chance, the government will never trust us. That's just wishful thinking and believe me, I've thought of it." He leaned forward and placed his palm to the right side of his face. "There's no fooling Arthur," he looked up again and his eyes met Emily's and Sam's. "We know he's a master manipulator so it's obvious that he won't be easily fooled. He spent some time visiting our cell, visiting Sam actually..." he paused for a moment to take in some air. "And we know first hand that even in the slim chance that we can trick him, even trap him... There would be no way to hold him."

"If he's too strong to trap and too smart to out plan, how is fighting him and his cronies going to go any different?" Dylan challenged with a scowl.

Cale considered him for a moment then leaned back into his chair as he crossed his arms.

"Isn't it obvious? We train our asses off...If that's what you guys want to do?" he looked around the table, stopping on each person to see their expression. He didn't bother looking at Sam since he already knew her answer.

The remainder looked baffled as they thought of what they were going to do.

"I'll try." Emily was the first to speak, "I have the basics from what you and Sam taught me in the cell."

Cale smiled at her, he seemed proud of how far she had come from being scared out of her mind to someone who was willing to fight for what was right.

"I knew what I was signing up for when I tagged along with you," Ari who had a somewhat even expression during the conversation shrugged. "I want to learn how to fight and I feel like I owe it to you for breaking us out of there."

She turned to Sam who shook her head. "You don't owe me anything, if you were to leave I wouldn't hold it against you."

Ari smiled even though there was a tinge of something else hiding in it. "I know, it's just that I want the courage to speak up like you."

"That'll get me killed someday." Sam chuckled though she had the feeling that her words held some truth.

The girls looked at each other with smiles on their faces, even though Ari had made her feel uncomfortable at their first official meeting, Sam felt nothing but trust. It was a strange feeling since they had only just met.

"I took wrestling in high school along with football so I might be of some help." Dylan spoke up and everyone brought their attention to him. The news wasn't surprising, he definitely looked the part of a high school football player with his stocky build and he had brought it up the night before. He gulped and glanced at his hands. "Though when it comes to a real fight I don't know how good im going to be."

"If you choose to stay and help us we won't force you to fight, but if it came down to it we'll protect you to the best of our abilities." Cale assured him and even though Dylan still looked unsure, he nodded. Kira who was next to answer did an exaggerated movement towards her black haired friend.

"I'm the same as Ari, I made my choice when I got in that car with these two." she used her thumb to point at Cale and Emily with a smile on her face. "This whole situation is fucked up but so am I for wanting to stay."

"I think we all are." Emily rolled her eyes.

Daniel was next, "I want to stay and fight but I want Jean-" Before he could finish, Jeannie interrupted him as per usual.

"You want me to go home to get caught and get experimented on? Let me stay to learn how to fight and to control this power and if worse comes to worse, I'll run."

Her eyes flared as she looked up at her brother and he shook his head. "I'm not going to leave whether you tell me to or not." she added before he could speak.

"You promise to run?" he asked his sister with doubt etched on his face.

"I will." she assured and Daniel looked forward in reply. Jeannie looked elated that she had won.

"Cam?" Ari called over as he clutched his cup. He had his eyes set on the little writing on the front of the cup but everyone knew that wasn't what he was really looking at.

He raised his head first then his eyes, "I'm still sitting here, aren't I?" he challenged, his tone rough and Sam watched as his grip loosened on the cup.

He was still a mystery but she was going to figure out his reasoning before long.

It came down to Trevor who had been quiet as everyone agreed to fight. He had sweat on his brow and his skin was pasty. "I-I don't want to fight but I also don't want to leave." He breathed, his anxiety contorted his face. "I won't be safe on my own..."

"You won't be safe here." Cam grunted and gave him a look full of annoyance.

Trevor put his head down in embarrassment, "I'll try to learn how to be a gargoyle but I promise you that I'm not much of a fighter and training won't even help me."

Sam who had been watching Trevor with sympathy turned her head to Cale and Emily who she found were looking at her.

As if they could read each other's minds, they nodded to each other. Maybe spending time in the cell had helped with learning each others emotions.

Sam leaned her head back and sighed, "You are welcome here whether you want to fight or not, don't think we'd think any less of you because of it." she brought her head back down and Cale finished for her. "But when the time comes to fight and it's undoubtedly going to happen, we want you to run." he glanced at Jeannie. "And that goes for everyone."

"Don't you want to run?" Cam scorned "Don't act tough, when the going gets tough, you'll run like the rest of us." He also meant this for Sam since he glanced at her as he spoke.

Cam returned his gaze to Cale as the latter considered his question for a moment then he broke into laughter. "Of course I want to run!" he chuckled but as his quickly as his amusement had started, it dyed out and his expression got serious.

"Of course I want to run," he repeated. "But what choice do I have? I could run away right now and forget about Carma, but I can't." He lowered his gaze. "They'd come looking for me like they would the rest of you so I'd need to hide."

The way he was acting reminded Sam of the way he was last night only he was talking openly now. "They'd find me and they'd find Sam since she's a part of Arthur's plan so if we stay back and fight and it makes the smallest bit of difference, I'll be happy."

Cam looked intrigued but satisfied with Cale's answer so he brought his attention to Sam. "What Cale said poses a question," his pale blue eyes bored into her but she didn't look away. "Aside from your eyes, why is Arthur so Intrigued with you? He already has Carma, who if I remember correctly, has white eyes as well."

Sam closed her eyes finally, hiding them from Cam's pressing gaze. "My guess is as good as your's." her eyes flew open. "Maybe because I caused my fair share of trouble and that's what he wants."

she thought again of what he had said before he left the doctors room after she woke up from her spout of insanity. She hadn't told anyone about it, it wouldn't change anything anyway and it would complicate things further.

"I'm curious about what he really has planned." Cam was getting awfully chatty and Sam thought it to be a good time to find out what he wanted.

She looked at him with narrowed eyes and she could feel everyone's gaze on the two of them. "Why are you here?" she asked and raised her hand to cut him off as he was about to speak. "And don't give me a bullshit reason that you want to fight, you hardly look like someone who would willingly fight."

He huffed. "I don't know whether or not you can call this a bullshit reason but this is the truth." he leaned forward as if to make sure everyone could hear him. "In the small chance that any of you weaken Arthur, I want to be the one to make the final blow."

The group looked baffled at his explanation.

"So the same as you guys really." he added as he saw their looks.

"Why?" Emily puzzled.

"Why?!" Cam's voice rose for the first time and made everyone jump back. The sound was high pitched and it caused them all pain because of their heightened hearing.

"Isn't it obvious? He fucked up my life and your's too. Isn't that the reason why you're all here?"

"We're here because we want to stop all of them not just to have other people do all the hard work then take the credit for ourselves." Ari smacked her hand on the table and they all flinched again.

"Sorry." she apologized as she winced herself.

Cam's nose flared. "Well that's how it is for me."

A few moments had passed and the counter was pretty much cleared as most of the group went to get ready for the day. Cale, Emily, Kira, and Ari had stayed back since they like Sam had gotten ready beforehand. The bacon that Sam was eating was cold now but she nibbled on it as she realized how hungry she was.

"That was a beautiful conversation." Kira said sarcastically with a unlit cigarette sticking out of her mouth.

"Very beautiful," Emily rolled her eyes as she watched Kira roll the dangerous stick between her lips. "I don't know how you can do that."

"This?" Kira pulled the cigarette from her mouth. "Ain't going to hurt me now, only thing that can kill me are our gargoyle buddies."

"I wonder why they want to be called gargoyles?" Ari asked, her voice was muffled from having her face hidden in her arms.

"Did it say anything on the site?" Sam wondered.

"No." Cale answered, he was back on the computer looking for more information now that it was confirmed that they weren't being tracked. "I'm guessing they call themselves that because of their horns and wings."

Sam thought of Arthur's transformation and of Cale's when he had lost control. How he had gotten grayish skin as if he was turning into stone.

"Is the website back?" Sam watched as he clicked on something.

"No, but I'm sure it will be." he flipped the computer around. "It seems our assumption was right."

On the screen was a new's article titled:

A group of people that were kidnapped have been found and have been brought in for medical surveillance.

It talked about how the families were notified and more will be released when more information is known to them. Afterwards the article listed all the people who were still missing with pictures of them. They found themselves amongst the images and they noted that their bright smiles had changed to stressed and broken.

"Medical surveillance my ass." Kira hissed.

"It seems they don't want the public to know about it being gargoyles yet." Cale turned the computer back around.

"Don't you mean *demons*?" Emily said in a mocking tone.

Everyone grinned at Emily's words while Cale went onto the next article.

Sam's mouth went dry as she waited for him to finish and to tell them what had happened. "The people they found let it slip where they were being held but by the time official's got there, the place was cleaned out."

No surprise there.

"Arthur let us go, of course he'd be prepared for them to show up." Sam crossed her arms and leaned back into her chair, her long hair smacking the middle of her back as she moved.

"Why do you think he let us go?" Cale agreed with her but wanted her opinion on the matter.

"I saw him before I left the cave, he was looking straight at me but he didn't bother going after me." she chewed on her lip. "And I think he meant to give me the idea on how to control our transformations."

"Why would you think that?" Emily rounded on her and Sam couldn't help but note that that was the first time since she attacked Cale that Emily willingly talked to her.

"He said he had the *power* and the *will* to achieve his goal so I took it from there." Sam's eyes dropped to her bowl and she pretended that there was something interesting about the bacon.

"How can you be sure?" Ari who was closest to Sam was looking at her with her deep blue eyes and Sam was getting to the point of hating the color.

"I'm not." She answered. She was feeling aggravated but she couldn't blame them for wondering why he would help her learn how to control her power, maybe she was delusional.

"I agree that he purposely let us go but him indirectly telling us how to control our power is too up in the air." Cale's expression was soft as he said this, he knew how she was feeling and spared her feelings.

Sam turned to look out the sliding doors, the sun was shining but everything seemed so dark. Her heart still raced at the thought of her dream that resulted in her death along with the little boy and the three brothers. The girl she saw in her reflection still haunted her and how it was her but not at the same time.

"It doesn't matter," she turned back and her face was even. "He's our enemy either way."

The room was quiet until Emily spoke, "Do you think we can do this?"

"I don't." Cale admitted. "Teaching everyone how to fight when we're not good ourselves is going to be difficult."

"We can teach them what we know while we learn along the way." Sam assured even though she had the same doubts as Cale.

"I'm sure none of it will compare to what Arthur and his gang knows." Kira laid her head on the cold counter and huffed. "Why the hell is this happening?"

Sam sighed, she had asked herself the same question countless times.

Not long ago she was living a normal life with her parents and she was finally able to see Mina after so long just to be ripped from her again.

She could hear Daniel and Cam bickering up stairs. "Jesus Christ it's like I'm in highschool again." she rolled her eyes and got up. "If we're lucky, they won't beat the shit out of each other before we get the chance to fight who we're really supposed to."

"It'd be entertaining to watch though." Kira snickered and Sam grinned as Cale, Emily, and Ari chuckled.

"My bets are on Daniel winning." Emily said through a laugh and everyone agreed simultaneously.

There was a noise from upstairs and the laughter died out as Cale shot up and ran upstairs.

"Kick each others asses outside!" He barked and the girls who were listening downstairs started snickering again while Sam had a shit eating grin. There was no way Cam was going to swoop in to kill Arthur

The group stood in the backyard, ready for their first day of training, but most of them looked like they'd much rather be somewhere else.

Sam and Cale were standing at the front since they were the ones with the most fighting experience. They watched as Daniel and Cam glared at each other while the others looked on.

They glanced at each other.

Lucky them.

"What do you think we should do?" Cale wondered, the nerves of being in the spotlight starting to show.

She just looked at him for a second with an equal amount of nerves but looking at each other wasn't getting them anywhere.

She faced forward and exhaled, "This is where you get to kick each other's asses."

She thought of when Cale had said the same thing and had to stop herself from laughing.

"If you want to fight, do it here." she turned to Cale and gestured for him to take the lead, he had the military experience after all.

"Pair up so we can see what you already know." he instructed.

The only ones that didn't hesitate were Ari and Kira who paired together without a second thought. Daniel and Jeannie paired next but that was obvious due to them being siblings. Cam and Dylan paired even though neither looked happy about it and the size difference made it obvious that it wasn't going to be fair.

Last but not least, Emily stepped over to Trevor who was only there to feel it out.

"No." Sam pointed to the siblings. "Daniel, I want you with Cam."

Daniel's face didn't hide how unfavorable that would be for him and Cam looked displeased himself. "Why the hell would I want to pair with him?" Daniel shot.

"You wanted to fight, didn't you?" she raised a brow and everyone watched as her tone turned sarcastic.

"I do but-" Daniel stammered.

"You're not going to learn anything by fighting with your sister, you'll take it easy on her and her with you. You won't learn properly if you're going to worry about hurting the person you're fighting." She explained.

By the look on everyone's faces, they seemed to agree but the thought of hurting each other was strange. Weren't they supposed to be on the same side?

"She doesn't mean to *really* hurt each other, but you'll want to use some kind of force." Cale assured them.

"No breaking bones, maybe some bruises here and there but that's all." Sam gestured for Daniel to switch with Dylan and he hesitantly made his way over while Dylan complied immediately. Poor Jeannie watched as her brother left then looked up at Dylan, it was easy to tell that she was wondering why she was stuck with the football player.

"Start." Cale directed and they looked at him like he was a crazy person.

"Fuck it." Ari punched Kira square in the face and the crack of knuckle against cheek could be heard through the trees.

Kira had turned her head from the impact and everyone watched with shocked expressions as she staggered backwards then turned her head and gazed up Ari. She grinned as blood poured from her nose into her mouth then she pounced.

Sam blinked, she didn't mean it literally.

"Um-" Cale started but he still seemed to be confused with what had just happened to continue. "You guys get started too." He said finally as he watched the girls fight.

After being distracted by Ari and Kira, each pair started their demonstration but with much less excitement. Cale and Sam watched and noted that Dylan, while he was being gentle with Jeannie, indeed knew how to wrestle well.

Jeannie tried getting away from him but he was much too big and she found herself in the worlds gentlest head lock.

Emily showed valor even though she was sparring with Trevor who was a head taller than her. The training she had done with Sam and Cale shined through and she was able to get Trevor into a arm bar, though she was gentle about it.

Even though she had won, Trevor had been shaky so the match was for from even.

Sam turned to see Cale's reaction and sure enough, he was smiling at the progress Emily had made.

There was a loud crack that changed their line of sight: Daniel had just punched Cam in the nose and blood poured from it. He proceeded to kick his legs out from under him and Cam fell to the ground who looked up like he wanted to kill Daniel.

"Like hell you're going to be the one to kill Arthur." Daniel scoffed then walked away to stand next to his sister and Dylan.

Perhaps pairing them together wasn't such a good idea but it made a point.

"HA!" a girlish laugh rang through their ears and this time, they turned to see Ari sitting on Kira's back as the ladder laid on her belly, defeated.

Kira seemed to have no care in the world as she rested her already bruised face against her hand.

"Emily was right." she snickered and Emily swallowed as everyone aside from the four who had been in the kitchen gave her a questioning look.

"That was a shit show." Sam had her arms crossed as she spoke to Cale.

Emily made her way over and Sam was regretting that she had told them not to hold back much. She turned her head to look at the group in front of her who were talking and laughing amongst themselves aside from Cam who was sitting on the ground wiping the blood from his nose. Kira's bruised face had already started to heal, it was amazing how fast they healed due to their gargoyle blood.

"At least we know who knows what and what we can use." Cale acknowledged Sam's statement as he highfived Emily. "You did great."

"It doesn't prove much since I sparred with someone who didn't want to fight back." She brushed off Cale's praise but smiled triumphantly.

Sam raised her head to see Trevor talking with Jeannie and Daniel, a nervous smile on his face. Cale was right, they had found out what each of them knew but it also showed them how much work they had ahead of them.

Sam watched as Cale and Emily joked and pushed each other with smiles on their faces.

Her chest ached as she thought of how lonely she felt, she longed for Mina to be there but that was impossible.

Emily caught her looking and her face went flat.

Sam missed how they were in the cell, it was funny how they went from Emily falling asleep on her shoulder to her not trusting a fiber of Sam's existence.

Sam swallowed. "You did great."

Cale looked between the girls as Sam inhaled sharply then turned to the group again. "I think we should split into boys and girls for now so we can teach them the basics and so there's not as much nerves." she explained.

Ari and Kira turned as they overheard what Sam was saying.

"Sounds good to me." Ari nonchalantly made her way to Sam with Kira in tow.

After Cale had agreed and they had explained the next step to the rest, they found themselves on either end of the backyard in their gender groups. Aside from Trevor who Sam figured should be in their group due to him seeming to be more comfortable in the company of the girls.

Sam taught the girls plus Trevor the self defense moves that she knew along with the one's Cale had taught her. As she watched them give them a try, she made a mental checklist of the strong points each of them had.

Ari had a good amount of strength and the damage that she had done to Kira proved that she didn't lack in the department.

Kira on the other hand didn't leave much damage but she was quick. She was able to dodge what the others couldn't and she was able to sneak out of the headlock that Ari had tried putting her into. Jeannie was fluid in her motions and she had a good amount of strength. Emily who had already learned the moves, moved like a seasoned veteran. Trevor was quick to learn but his nerves slowed him down. Sam perfected her moves while the others practiced and when they were done, Emily directed them to take a break.

Sam was sitting on the ground with her eyes closed and she focused on the back of her eyelids as she felt the breeze hit her face and the sweet smell of pine filled her nose.

"That wasn't as eventful as the demonstrations." Kira's voice appeared as she settled beside her. Someone else sat to the right of her and she guessed it was Ari. She opened her eyes to acknowledge the girls.

"No, it wasn't..." she agreed as she remembered how their demonstration had gone."What the hell was that about anyway?" she rounded on them and Kira shrugged while Ari leaned back onto her elbows.

"You didn't want us to hold back." Ari stated.

"I didn't say to punch each others lights out." Sam huffed and the girls expressions got serious.

"After we were changed into monsters, we were both shook up." Ari's face twisted.

"That's how we became friends," Kira continued for her friend. "We leaned on each other and made a promise to ourselves that we would get revenge somehow. That's why we left with Cale and Emily. They along with you got us out of that hellhole and we knew if we stuck with you guys that we would somehow achieve our goal."

Sam closed her eyes again and when she exhaled, it came out shaky. "The odds aren't in our favor." They had so much to face, *She* had so much to face.

Carma was out to get her along with Arthur who was a far greater threat.

"We have the strength and we wanted to show you that." Ari explained and Sam blinked her eyes open.

"Hitting hard isn't going to cut it, you were sloppy and you damned well know that Arthur's men are far from that." she glanced between the two girls. "I'm glad you have the strength, you especially." she acknowledged Ari. "But remember that the moves you just learned and the ones you're going to learn combined with your strength will make you a force to be reckoned with."

When Sam was done, Ari's serious expression turned into one of understanding.

"And another thing," Sam continued. "Just because I helped in breaking you out of that cave doesn't mean I'm special in anyway. I'm sure I'm only targeted by Arthur because of my big mouth and that I have white eyes."

"I want to see them." Kira demanded suddenly and Sam jumped. "You saw them in the cave and last night."

"It was dark in the cave and it was unintentional last night." Her short hair wiggled in the breeze. "I want to see you change them while you are still in control so I can clearly see them."

Sam picked her head up to see that the boys had finished with their training and they were making their way over to join them.

"We're going to have to control our change soon so this will be a good demonstration." Ari leaned forward to meet Sam's face.

Sam wanted so badly to push this onto Cale but what would that make her? A coward.

That's what it would make her and she wasn't going to let that happen. Plus Ari was right, it would be a good demonstration.

She inhaled and exhaled as she thought of her reasoning and allowed her will to surface. She thought of Mina, her newfound allies, and the innocents she could save.

The pressure in her eyes began to build and she felt the power surging through her like it had in the cave. The power was so different when she had control over it, it felt so *free*.

Her nails extended into points and her teeth followed suit. Her ears grew into long points and they almost looked like elf ears. The pressure in her eyes peaked and Ari and Kira looked on in awe at her new look.

Cale and the others came into view and both he and Emily looked at her with curious expressions. There was no getting used to this.

The group just stood there and studied her and she imagined they were thinking about what they would look like when they finally transformed.

"That's new." Cale pointed to her ears.

She didn't notice the change so she flinched and grabbed at her right ear to find the end going into a point. She touched the left and it was the same.

Emily cocked her head, "Why would her ears wait until now to change?" she seemed to be saying this more to herself than to the others.

"Did you do anything different?" Cale asked as their looks were starting to get to her.

"No." she replied shakily and dropped her hand from her now pointed ears. "Maybe I have more control than last time."

Cale merely nodded as he thought to himself.

"We want to learn how to do that as soon as possible." Ari demanded and Sam shook her head as she got up. She let the pressure go and she was normal once again, but it didn't stop her from checking her ears to make sure.

"Learning how to fight as humans first will be better than rushing to transform." Cale explained for her.

The girls seemed disappointed but didn't push it.

Cam who had been watching from the back looked like he had just seen an amazing show and the rest seemed like they had seen a ghost.

"This isn't even a full transformation," Sam brushed the stray pieces of grass from her pants. "We saw what Arthur looks like in his partial transformation and it wasn't even the final result." The memory of Arthur's grotesque form still sent chills down her spine.

"And the picture on that website was too blurry to make out." Daniel added as he stared into space, "But from what I could see, the final result is monstrous."

"If that picture is even real." Jeannie rolled her eyes.

"I think it is." Trevor jumped in and they were startled to hear him after he had been so quiet. "If they want to be called gargoyles, they have to fit the part."

They thought about the stone creatures and the pictures of the monsters on the website along with their own transformations. So far, their transformations had gone along with the stone beings.

Sam twisted her arm to feel for a bump of any kind on her back but aside from her shoulder blades, it remained flat. After taking her arm away, she noticed that she wasn't the only one who had checked.

"We get horns too I suppose." Dylan said as he felt his forehead.

Sam glanced at Cale, he was looking at his outstretched hand as if he was holding something. His unkept hair laid in his eyes as he looked down, blocking the view of them.

"We should take a break, we've been out here for awhile." Trevor sensed the change in the people around him and Sam looked away from Cale as Emily caught her staring at him.

"Yeah." She pulled her own hair out of her eyes.

"I took cosmetology so I can cut hair." Ari spoke up and when Sam was wondering where the statement had come from, she followed her gaze to Cale who was pulling his hair out of his face. After a moment, he realized what she was getting at and he shook off his downcast mood.

"That'd be great." he accepted her offer with a small smile.

Sam sat at the counter as she rolled an apple in her hand and as she took a bite, she turned to Ari who was cutting Cale's hair.

She munched as she watched his black strands fall to the hardwood floor. They had moved a chair next the clear doors and a towel was placed over Cale's shoulders to prevent his hair from falling on him. Sam took another bite of the apple then rolled it to the next unbitten spot as she gazed into the living room where Kira, Jeannie, Daniel, and Trevor were watching the news.

They were waiting for more news on the cave but aside from the same thing that was on the computer earlier and unrelated events, there was nothing new.

Sam listened as the newscaster gave the mantle to the weatherman and she heard Kira tsk.

"They'll report about it more." Ari assured as she snipped another strand.

"That's a given." Sam got up and threw the apple's core into the garbage.

Cale had his hands cupped tightly, the anxiety he was feeling showed in his engorged veins. Sam knew it wasn't caused by Ari potentially messing up his hair.

"They wouldn't give out too much information anyway." he said as he loosened his grip when he noticed Sam looking.

She grabbed her laptop and opened it as she sat back down.

Her homescreen wallpaper flashed on: It was of Mina and herself from when they were in the 5th grade. They were holding ribbons from a field day event that they had won. Sam's wavy hair reached to the bottom of her ears and she swam in her assigned bright yellow shirt.

Mina's blonde hair reached the middle of her back and she was a hair shorter than Sam at the time. She wore a yellow shirt as well.

Sam found herself looking at it for a moment, taking in their smiles, and she thought of how innocent but ignorant they were at the time.

Not in a million years did her younger self think that she would be in this situation.

"Who's that?" Ari who had a view of the screen from where she stood asked.

"Is that your friend?" Cale guessed and Sam nodded without turning to them.

Ari looked between the two, she didn't know that Sam had sacrificed herself for her friends sake.

"You want to see her, don't you?" Cale's voice was gentle, he knew how she felt after all. Although his situation with Carma was so much worse.

"I'm sure she blames herself since I took her place." Her voice shook, she wanted to tell Mina that she had chosen this to protect her and she would do it a thousand more times.

Emily entered the room and felt the somber mood.

"You took her place?" Ari set down the scissors as she finished with Cales hair, her sight on the back of Sam's head. Sam and Emily's eyes met but Sam didn't look away this time.

"They were targeting her instead of me, I fought them off so she could get away and they took me instead."

Emily had heard the story but she listened to it like it was new to her. Maybe she had pushed it to the back of her mind after all of the things that had happened.

Cale listened with a somber look, he didn't even bother to see if Ari had done a good job with his hair. He leaned forward and rested his elbows on his knees as he watched Sam's shoulders as they moved up and down as she spoke.

"So you're telling me they didn't single you out, but you still somehow ended up being Arthur's main target?" Ari was perplexed.

Sam smiled, "That's why I said there's nothing special about me, it's a coincidence that I ended up with the stronger eyes and that he wants to test me."

"Speaking of eyes-" Daniel spoke as he entered the kitchen followed by Kira, Trevor, Dylan, and his sister. "I wonder what determines who gets what color and why is one stronger than the other?" Daniel leaned against the counter next to where Sam sat while the remainder took a seat. Kira who still wanted to watch the news found a seat that allowed her to see the television.

Sam knew they could hear their conversation but didn't think they were listening.

Even though what she had done was heroic, she didn't care to brag about it. But it was too late and the result she didn't want to happen did and she noticed that they looked at her with newfound respect.

"I'm not sure." Cale stood and Sam finally turned to look at him. His hair was shorter but not too short, the cut was enough to keep his hair out of his eyes. "He changed all of us with blood."

Sam clicked her tongue. "But was it the same type?"

She was answered with confused looks but Emily who was into this kind of stuff lit up.

"I wonder if we had to be compatible with the blood?" Her eyes stared into space as she thought. "Even though their blood is stronger, it looks the same as a humans…" She continued and Sam thought of the blood bag that had been used to change her. There seemed to be no difference between gargoyle blood and human blood.

"If they go by blood types, that means-" Jeannie stopped short as she was filled with realization.

"That means there's more full blooded gargoyles out there." Cale finished for her as he stood beside Sam. Even though she didn't want to recall it, she thought of the day she was changed into a gargoyle and something hit her. "Arthur told me the bag was filled with his blood…" Her voice drifted.

The group glanced at each other as she felt Cale shift beside her.

She rose a brow "What is it?"

"Arthur wasn't there and Archie never specified whose blood it was." Kira explained and as Sam glanced around the counter to see the rest, they confirmed that she was the only one who had Arthur with her.

A chill went through her. Was it because she was the first person?

So many questions went through her mind and from the looks she was getting, her comrades were having them too. Her mouth felt dry and she swallowed it into her throat.

"It's a coincidence." Cale spoke from beside her and she looked over her shoulder to him. His attention was on the others but when he caught her looking, his eyes moved her way.

He knew something was going on, all of them did, but to spare her feelings, he made an excuse.

Sam didn't want to hear excuses, she wanted answers.

"Why do you think he's so intrigued with me?" she rounded on the group when they were about to drop the subject. "I've given you my opinion so I want to hear your's."

They just stared at her while some turned away from her intense glare.

"Why do you think?" Her voice got deeper as she felt her unease rise. It wasn't aimed at them but the stress she felt from Arthur's game was eating at her.

"Maybe he think's you'll join him." Ari shrugged, she wasn't accusing Sam, she just wanted to let out an idea.

"Why would he make sure to be there when I was changed then? He knew nothing about me at that point aside from my recklessness." Sam placed her hand over her eyes to block out the light, it helped her think.

"Maybe that's the reason." Emily's voice rang out and Sam had to remove her hand to believe it was her but sure enough it was.

Instead of looking at Sam with her usual glare, it was replaced with pity.

Sam's heart raced, now was the time to tell them what she was hiding.

"After I calmed down from my panic attack, he spoke to me like he knew me..." she spoke more to Cale and Emily since they knew what had happened. "He said I'm still punishing myself."

"What is that supposed to mean?" Cale sat beside her so he could get a better look while everyone else besides Emily were giving each other confused looks.

"I don't know..." she wanted to run and she wanted them to stop looking at her but she needed to talk about her worries or they would only get worse.

As if on cue, Cam entered the kitchen. "The cave we were locked in is on the news." he used his thumb to point behind him and everyone dropped the conversation to rush into the living room.

The inside of the cave was showing on the screen: The place was empty of whatever the gargoyles had used but the bars were still attached to the cells. The newscaster spoke as the images of the cave continued to show. She spoke of how the cave had been *manmade,* though that was wrong, these creatures were not men.

How could any human ever make something like that without going unnoticed?

Sam noticed the makeshift doctors room but any evidence of what they were doing there was gone.

"Those who have escaped are in custody and they are being treated for wounds inflicted on them but there are many still missing."

The groups faces showed on the screen plus two that were not amongst them, a boy and a girl.

"...I've been told that this could be the work of traffickers but we will let you know as soon as we find out more." The reporter finished as the screen went back to her. She was a skinny woman in a pink blouse and she was standing outside of the cave. She looked nervous from being near the thing and they could see cops and men in black suits investigating the area behind her.

"That's bogus, how could anyone think traffickers would go as far as making a prison in a cave." Daniel huffed as he threw himself on the couch and the news changed back to the weather.

It was obvious that she was reporting fake news.

"Fake as a new pair of tits." Kira sat on the arm of the sofa beside Daniel and flicked him in the temple. He smacked her hand away but laughed all the same.

"Of course they're not going to tell people that the *demons* are the reason behind this." Cale sighed and took a seat.

Sam watched as everyone took their seats while she remained standing.

"What could humans do against gargoyles?" Ari perked up in her seat. "There's a huge power difference."

Sam recalled a dream of her supposed parents dead from some sort of an attack but she shook her head, her dreams had nothing to do with this.

Or did they?

Her heart began to race and her comrades were looking at her with a mix of worry and confusion.

"Excuse me." She slurred her words as she ran from the room then out the front door. She ran until she made it to the side of the house then collapsed on the grass as she hyperventilated and gripped her stomach. A panic attack was waiting to peak it's ugly head all day, but trying to find Arthur's reasoning and thinking of her dreams had pushed her over the edge.

She shook as she crawled to the house to lean on it, tears falling from eyes and her breaths coming out as gasps.

There was no way her dreams were connected to what was happening, Mina had spoken about past lives but there was no way.

A sob broke from her lips.

There were gargoyles and maybe even demons...Anything was possible at this point.

She bit down on her lip so hard that it bled but she didn't mind the pain, she couldn't even feel it over the pain in her chest.

Why was this happening to her?

After a few moments she had calmed for the most part but her heart was still quick.

She leaned her head against the house as she felt her nerves tingle under her skin. She had so many questions with no answers.

What was Arthur's plan? Why was he fixated on her?

Though the answer to this question could never be answered, she asked it all the same: What did her dreams mean?

She would be sure to ask Arthur when they enviably meet again.

Chapter 14

Two weeks had passed and not only did the group get better at fighting, they had also grown closer. They laughed easier and they leaned on each other, along with that, they learned more about each other. Even Daniel and Cam seemed to be getting along.

Cale and Sam had taken turns going to get the necessities such as food and clothes.

They wanted someone who had a handle on their abilities there at all times to protect the place while the other went to go get the things they needed with a few helping hands that volunteered.

Sam was sitting on the couch with the television on, she watched the screen but wasn't really seeing it. They watched the news everyday but the information never changed much.

She rested her elbow on the arm of the couch and placed her head in her palm. Ari had cut her hair a few inches so it fell a quarter of the way down her back instead of the middle. She currently had it up in a bun, a few stray pieces sticking up. She was wearing a tank top as the weather had gotten warmer but she didn't stray from her jeans.

She moved her eyes to Cale who was sitting in the sofa across from her, her laptop on his lap. There was still no luck in finding the website he had found the night they had gotten there but they held onto hope. They had to get as much information as they could about Arthur and his lackeys.

After Sam's panic attack two weeks ago, the group didn't press her anymore on the matter of Arthur's plans for her. It was definitely a contributing factor but it was the thought of her dreams that had brought her over the edge. She was still haunted with the images from her dreams but aside from that, she hadn't gotten any new ones.

The rest of the group was munching away at their breakfast in the kitchen since Cale and Sam had gotten up early to train on their own. It gave them the chance to practice while transformed or in their pre-gargoyle forms as they've decided to call it since it wasn't a full transformation. The two had already eaten their breakfast, showered, and gotten ready for the day all before the others had woken up.

"Any luck?" She asked but she knew the answer.

Cale shook his head. "None, but I'm sure he'll get the website back up." he continued with a different subject. "I did find some fighting moves we can learn though." He looked up from the screen with a smile and she returned it.

The two had sparred many times now but never tried beating each other. It wasn't hard to tell that they were almost equal when it came to fighting, in their human forms at least.

Though Sam would admit that he had an advantage over her.

They hadn't tried *really* sparring yet in their pre-gargoyle forms, but the time was fast approaching to give it a try. They were running low on time, Arthur could be knocking on their door at any moment.

"Sounds good." she sat up and Cale gave her a nod while her head jerked towards the others. They had talked about teaching the rest of the group how to change into their pre-gargoyle forms during their sparring session that morning but they weren't sure if they were ready.

"I think we should let them try it." She suggested finally as she brought her attention back to Cale.

"It won't hurt anything and it gives us the chance to try moving up with our own transformations." He agreed.

Sam smiled then looked into the kitchen that had suddenly gotten quiet as the group listened in on their conversation.

"You hear that? Get your asses outside!" They could hear the smile on Sam's face.

They excitedly got to their feet and ran to the door and Sam could hear it slide open then footsteps exiting out of it. Emily emerged at the corridor between the kitchen and the living room and met Cale and Sam as they snickered to themselves. Their comrades had been asking about learning the transformation for the past two weeks to no avail.

"Are you sure we can do this?" Emily questioned but they were sure that she was asking for herself more than she was for the others.

Cale walked past her. "I do." he said simply and left the room as he made his way outside.

Emily's eyes were down the entire time but they shot up as Sam made her way towards her. Sam glanced at her as she walked past her and she could feel her turn to follow her. They were the only relationship that hadn't mended.

Sam walked into the morning air and the sun shined on her, the start of summer was fast approaching. What a peaceful setting for what was going to be such a monstrous event.

Sam watched as her comrades stretched and sparred with each other to warm up and she found herself grinning. She was so proud of what they had learned but they, including herself, had so much to learn before they could even come close to Arthur and his group.

She made her way to Cale, "How do you wanna do this?" she asked and she was reminded of their first training lesson on their first full day there.

"Same way you taught me I suppose." he looked down at her as she watched Cam flip Daniel over his back. She had expected Daniel's reaction to be anger but he laughed as Cam helped him up. She returned her attention to Cale, "I'll let you take the lead."

He blinked. "Don't put this on me!" he whispered but it was far too loud to sound like one. Sam snickered then smiled again, "You're far better at the leadership role than I am."

"There's no leaders in this group." he pressed but looked thankful for the compliment.

"I suppose not but I'm sure they would rather listen to you over someone who's not right in the head."

He shot her a look. "We all have our problems."

She leaned forward to look at his injured shoulder. "Sure."

The group stopped what they were doing as they saw Cale and Sam standing at the forefront and Emily stood off to the side as everyone else stepped forward.

Cale took another glance at Sam then spoke, "We learned how do this by chance, Sam was smart to pick up on what Arthur was saying and used it to her advantage. We tried to use anger as a trigger but while we were strong, we had no control and without control, we had no chance." He took a breath as he remembered their laborious training in their cell. "We even tried sadness but that proved to offer a lack of control as well…" He turned to Sam a fraction as if he was handing the mantle to her, she was the one who needed to explain this part.

She gave him an acknowledging look then faced forward, "Arthur was talking about his plan and I was taunting him." She drew a breath as she closed her eyes then opened them. "He said he had the *power* and the *will* to achieve his goal and while saying this, he transformed into his gargoyle form. After he left, I realized that though he might not have not meant to do so, he gave me the answer to our problems." Her eyes narrowed as she tried choosing her words.

"We needed to use our will to transform." She looked at each of their faces as they listened intently. "It can't just be what you want to do, you can think of those things but what will really help you transform is looking into yourself and pulling the desires that you've hidden to the front of your brain." she stepped forward and her eyes changed along with her teeth, ears, and nails. She had gotten a lot faster at it.

"For example: I think of my parents, the friend that I saved, and the desire that was hidden inside me is-" she swallowed, she had realized this after she had transformed a few more times. "The small chance that things will be normal, no more anxiety attacks, and that this is all a dream."

Cale was watching her with a sad expression, she hadn't told him any of this.

The others faces mirrored his and Sam was embarrassed that she was so open about it but they had to know so they could find their own reasons.

"I think of my friends and my father." Cale began with his own. "And my deepest desire is that my birth parents were still alive."

Sam turned on her heel to face him and she was met with his sad ink filled eyes. His claws, teeth, and his pointed ears were out to play as well. They gazed at each other until his features went back to normal.

She glanced at the ground as she turned back to the group, their mouths were open from what they just heard and seen.

"Give it a try." Cale directed and the group set to work with no hesitation.

It didn't take long for some but it took a great amount of effort for the rest. Ari, Kira, Daniel, and Cam had all changed within the first few minutes of them trying while Emily, Jeannie, Trevor, and Dylan took half an hour to an hour to change, Trevor being last.

Even with him being last, Sam felt proud of him for coming so far since he had arrived there. she moved her gaze from him and looked at the group as a whole and she was met with eight pairs of pitch black eyes staring back at her. She smiled at them as Cale stepped forward and fist bumped Kira.

"Told you." he bragged and she laughed embarrassedly.

"What was your reason?!" they found the question making its way around and the person being asked always looked embarrassed and choked up while Kira stated her's freely. "A beautiful girl and I living a peaceful life together and my dad fucking off in the corner!"

The group stared at her aside from Ari who snickered with a hand over her mouth to try muffling it. Kira laughed so hard that she gripped her gut. "I love the looks on your faces!"

Once everyone knew she was joking, they all laughed along with her. They should have known she was pulling their legs.

They looked so strange with their new looks, they looked monstrous but acted so human.

Sam felt pride in that.

"This is amazing." Cam flexed his fingers, "I can feel the power going through my veins."

The rest started to do the same. "You're right." Jeannie inhaled and exhaled, a smile spreading across her face. "This really is amazing."

"I want you guys to fight now." Sam directed and their happiness turned to nervousness. "But be very careful not to hurt each other."

"Are you sure we can do this?" Ari looked to Kira who had been her main sparring partner. Unlike the first day, she didn't want to hurt her friend.

"Yes, but I want you to switch partners." Sam pointed to Ari then to Dylan, the two of them had improved the most so it was only right to have them fight. "I think the two of you will be a good match."

The two got on well but they were hesitant to partner up.

"You really think they're ready to fight in these forms? They just learned how to change." Cale asked her and she could hear the doubt in his voice.

She looked up at him for a moment, he was facing forward and his eyes were set on Emily who he feared for the most. Sam turned her head back to the others and answered. "I think they have the willpower not to hurt each other plus we've done alright."

They had started out fearful but they eased as their control got better. "Besides," she chewed on the inside of her lip. "There's no telling how much time we have left."

He tensed, he knew she was right.

"I think you and Emily should spar." she suggested and he nodded, he would be more at ease knowing that Emily wouldn't get hurt. "I'll take Ari's place." Sam made her way to Kira who perked up when she saw her new partner.

"I'm glad it's you." she admitted and Sam rose a brow.

"Why? I thought you liked everyone here?"

Kira gave her a look that suggested that she should know the answer. "Not only will I learn more because I'm with you, but you're also nice to look at." Kira explained with a mischievous grin and Sam blinked, "Uh, thanks?" she cleared her throat awkwardly but laughed afterwards.

"Aren't you going to transform?" Kira pondered and Sam woke from her embarrassed state to see that the others had already started. They were obviously taking it easy as their moves were much sloppier than they were when they were in their human forms.

Sam turned back to Kira, "I want you to come at me while I'm still human."

Kira gave her a look that could only mean that she thought she was crazy. "That wouldn't be fair." she pressed.

"I want to try this, if things get too out of hand, I'll change right away."

"Why do you even want to do this?" Kira challenged with her hands on her hips. She looked like a fairy with her short hair and small stature, her pointy ears added to the look as well.

"I have to face Arthur and you know it…" Sam's voice came out as a beg, "I need to get as strong as possible."

Kira considered her for a moment then sighed. "Fine, but promise you'll tell me if I get to be too much for you." She demanded and Sam agreed.

The girls stood across from each other, Kira in her pre-gargoyle form and Sam in her human form. Even though Kira looked much more intimidating than Sam due to the change, the height difference evened it out a bit. Sam towered over Kira and while Sam was skinny, she had curves while Kira was like a porcelain doll, easy to break.

Kira exhaled nervously, "Here goes."

The two went at each other, a punch and a kick by Kira followed by two swift dodges by Sam. Sam's heart raced, Kira was fast... Extremely fast compared to Cale.

Sam had to pay attention or she would be in a world of hurt if a punch landed while she was in her human form.

Kira stood back for a moment to see if Sam had changed her mind but when Sam remained in her fighting stance, she came at her again.

While trying to dodge Kira's attacks, Sam used her sense of hearing and found that she could hear the bones cracking in the arm or leg that Kira was going to use to attack. She used this to her advantage but it wasn't long before she could no longer keep up and had to change herself.

It was effortless, she didn't even need to think of her will as it was engraved in her mind. She blocked a elbow with her crossed arms that would have collided with her face, the force was strong enough to break a bone if she was still in her human form.

"Just in time." She thought to herself as she shook the pain out of her arms and Kira smiled that she had forced her to change. Sam smiled determinedly at her and the two continued to battle.

Dylan had Ari in a headlock but she squirmed out of it. The two shot to their feet and breathed heavily from the physical work. They set forth again until Ari came out on top when she locked Dylan in an arm bar. The force almost broke his arm but she stopped in time, she had barely tried to hurt him.

She opened her hands and looked down at them as Dylan sat up and rubbed the sweat off his brow. It was definitely strange seeing a girl much smaller than him getting the edge on him.

Jeannie and Trevor were taking it easier than the others, Trevor obviously didn't want to do this and Jeannie knew it so she raised the white flag.

"I'm not going to fight someone who doesn't want to." she sighed and slumped down onto the grass and watched the others with a longing expression until her eyes flashed and she got up to join her brother and Cam.

Daniel had an advantage over Cam with their size difference but Cam was holding his own. Cam dodged so fast that Daniel couldn't get a hold on him until his sister came over and caught Cam off guard by knocking him into her brothers punch and left them both in shock.

A three way fight ensued which resulted in Jeannie being defeated by Cam after he dodged all of her attacks which tired her out and made her easy to defeat. Daniel snuck behind Cam after his victory and pinned him to the ground only to be knocked off.

As he went down, Daniel brought his hand down onto the back of Cam's head and smashed it on the ground to stop him from getting back up. The force left a dent the size of his head.

Cale and Emily's fight was already decided as soon as they teamed up. Cale held back but he was still stronger than Emily and while she knew this would happen, she didn't mind as she would get stronger by pairing with him.

Her nails extended and Cale noticed that she fought like a cat, her nails nearly grazed him many times but all he would do was push her away instead of fighting back.

"Don't hold back!" she barked and Cale looked taken back.

He didn't expect the timid girl he knew to want to fight full force against him.

Finally he actually punched at her, but he was still holding back. She smiled as she roundhouse kicked him and it barely landed on his upper right leg. He buckled back but recovered quickly and kicked back that resulted in Emily falling to the ground with a thump.

"I'm sor-" Cale was about to help her up when she shot back up and swiped at him again but he stepped out of reach.

She chewed her lip until she got an idea.

She stretched her leg out and tripped Cale as he was backing away and was able to graze him while he was mid-fall. She left four bloody scratches near his collar bone along with rips in his dark green shirt.

He looked down at his wound as he collected himself then back to Emily with surprise.

"Sorry!" She started as she rushed towards him with regret etched on her face but Cale smiled mischievously and came at her with the intent of continuing their sparring session.

They twisted and turned as they fought until Emily tried her surprise move again but she couldn't fool him a second time.

He pulled his foot away and she tripped and the fight ended with Cale playfully stepping on her back with a proud smile as he breathed heavily.

"That was fun." he stepped off of her and offered a hand to help her up and she hesitantly took it only to pull him to the ground with her.

He landed on his hands and knees while laughing.

Emily got serious as he twisted around to sit, he was still laughing but stopped as he noticed her looking at the wounds she had caused.

"Are you ok?!" She asked nervously and he pulled his shirt away from the scratches.

"It's fine." He shook off her worry. "They're just scratch-" he stopped abruptly which raised Emily's anxiety even more.

"What is it?" she pressed as she leaned forward to see for herself.

Cale looked up to meet her gaze, he was clearly shaken. "They're already gone."

"That was awesome!" Ari knelt down and put a arm around Emily's shoulders. "You were slick as fuck!"

The already healed wounds were forgotten as a loud crack made them flinch to where Sam and Kira were fighting.

Kira was leaning against a broken tree with a grin on her face while one of her eyes was closed indicating that the hit had actually hurt. The top of the tree fell down behind her and the vibration went through the ground, knocking her to her butt.

In front of her stood Sam who had pushed her into the tree, small horns were now sprouting from her head.

Kira tried getting up as Sam made her way over to check on her. "I'm sorry, was I too rough?" she asked as she helped her.

Kira had gone back to her human form from the hit, "Nah, I told you to do it." she reached out and grabbed her hand. "You got horn's by the way." she pointed at the tiny points on Sam's head.

"I know." Sam reached up and felt the points. "It feel's weird."

Kira was surprised at her lack of emotion but shrugged, what was there to be shocked about now? She literally rammed her into a tree so hard that it broke in two.

Besides, both Sam and Cale had sprouted their horns during their early morning training, though the sensation was still taking a little getting used to.

"That's the second time I've done that." Sam lowered her arm as she studied the broken tree. "I have to learn how to control my strength."

The two girls turned to the group to be met with shocked faces.

"You just... broke that tree." Dylan blubbered.

"She almost broke my ass." Kira rubbed her tail bone but grinned at Sam.

"You have horns!" Jeannie exclaimed and Sam rose a brow as she pointed to Jeannie's ears. "And you've got pointy ears!" she mocked.

She had gotten to the point of not being surprised at the new features she had gotten as she learned to perfect her gargoyle form.

The area around where her horns had sprouted felt tight but not unbearable so she didn't mind them being there anyway, they came with the territory.

"You could've hurt her!" Emily rasped, her nostril's flared.

"She would have if that hit was any harder but she knew that." Kira assured Emily as she stretched to put an arm around Sam but she could only reach to just below her shoulders. "My back is going to be a little sore but not enough to leave a bruise."

Emily didn't look persuaded from Kira's explanation but dropped the matter.

It was true though, Sam knew what she was doing. She only allowed herself so much power and when she felt like she was going too far, she backed off. She had pushed Kira into the tree like she had when she punched the tree on the nature trail. But unlike before, she knew what to expect and knew that Kira wouldn't get hurt with the strength she used.

But inside, she feared what would have happened if she messed up and used a little more of her strength.

She was starting to panic, what if she really did hurt Kira?

She looked to Cale, he already knew what she was capable of since he was on par with her so naturally he didn't look as fazed as the others.

"I still can't believe you broke that tree..." Trevor gawked at the two halves.

"It's not the first one." Sam stated as she exhaled and the horns, ears, teeth, and nails dissolved back into her skin then her eyes returned to hazel.

Cale blinked twice and his eyes returned to his normal chocolate brown.

"How do we turn it off?" Jeannie asked nervously and Sam thought it was funny that she made it sound like she was turning off a gaming console.

The others started to look panicky, none of them wanted to look like a body-mod fool for the rest of their lives.

"Just relax and imagine the power leaving through your fingertips." Cale explained as he got up and they followed his directions and it worked fairly well aside from Ari and Cam whose nerves got the best of them but as they calmed down, they too returned to looking human.

"Let's take a break for now." Sam suggested, the early morning training and using her new abilities was starting to take a toll on her. Plus, the restless sleep she had been getting didn't help.

"I was about to suggest that." Emily claimed with an air of annoyance then looked to Cale's ripped shirt as she turned to go to the house.

As everyone trailed after her, Sam and Cale stood back.

"Why did you do that?" He pressed but he didn't sound accusing like Emily had, he was simply asking.

"I'm nowhere as strong as I want to be," she watched her friends backs as they walked away and she could see Emily watching from inside the kitchen window. "I want them to be ready for what's to come…Arthurs lackeys won't hold back like we do."

"What if-?" He began with a questioning look.

There it was, the accusing.

"What if I didn't know my own strength and hurt her?" she interrupted. "I thought about that." she looked down at a blade of grass blowing in the gentle breeze and it felt warm against her skin. "...It feels like I'm a different person when I'm using my abilities." she explained and Cale returned to his understanding expression and sighed. "Me too."

Talking to each other about the matter only made Sam realize how fast the power could corrupt them. "I feel like I'm in control but I know I'm far from it, my mind tell's me not to worry about it and to let go…I knew what I was doing but it still makes me wonder when the power will get out of control."

"We're playing a dangerous game." Cale locked his jaw and Sam nodded with a lump in her throat.

They definitely were.

Sam stood in the bathroom feeling where her horns had been, the area was still tingling and underneath she could feel small nubs. They weren't noticeable even if someone was face to face with her, only touching them gave away that they were there.

She made a noise, she thought of them as pimples only much less noticeable.

She dropped her hand and laid her palm in front of her, it was shaking from the power she had exerted. She gripped the sink and looked into the mirror: Her eyes were gradually growing grayer. Where it had started from the outer edges of her irises, the color slowly crept to her pupil. It still wasn't noticeable to the others but it ate away at her, she had originally blamed it on the change in her body and that everyone probably had it. But she had checked everyday to see if the others had the same problem only to see that she was wrong, it was just her.

Besides, if that were the case, Arthur, Kellan, Camilla, and the rest would have had their normal color engulfed by color by now.

She made a noise as she exhaled, the thought that she could have hurt Kira seemed to have worn off. At that moment she had control, though that would most likely change as she got stronger.

She exhaled sharply then turned from the mirror and her graying eyes.

She didn't know why she was starting to feel angry but she figured it was the same as a toddler with a lack of sleep. She punched her thigh to stop her nerves from going haywire and she winced but it distracted her from her thoughts, she relished in the pain.

She leaned her head back and sighed as her leg ached. There was so much...so so much on her mind to the point that her thoughts seemed jumbled.

She composed herself then made her way downstairs, her sleepy eyes weighing her down.

She thought getting out of the cave and sleeping on a soft bed would help her but it didn't, she had so much to do with so little time.

She stopped at the bottom of the stairs: Most of her peers were watching the television aside from Ari, Kira, Jeannie, and Trevor who were playing cards on the floor.

Ari looked from her hand as she heard Sam and like a chain reaction, the rest turned to her. Unlike before, Sam didn't care, she was used to having many eyes on her now.

"I'm going to lay down for a bit." she pointed to the hall that led to her borrowed bedroom.

"Want me to tell you when we have lunch?" Cale called to her as she stepped towards the hall, he had changed his ripped shirt to a clean white one.

Sam noticed that there were no bloody marks showing through the thin fabric. She hadn't seen what had happened but she knew it was done by gargoyle nails, his healing was extraordinary. The mark she still had from her self inflicted wound confirmed that, even though it had dulled it was still there while Cale's were gone completely.

"No, thank you." she waved without looking back.

She closed the door behind her and leaped on the bed then snuggled into her pillow. The blankets rubbed as she moved and the coils in the mattress creaked. The noise would have bothered her two weeks ago but she had a pretty good handle on controlling what she really wanted to hear.

She inhaled and exhaled sharply as she wrapped herself like a cocoon into the blankets. She wanted to sleep but her mind began wandering to what could happen next.

It was funny how when one was so tired, the mind was the most awake.

Her mind was no match for her heavy eyes though and after a few restless rolls, she fell asleep.

She could hear stomping, the dark around her was dense but the footprints could be heard as plain as day.

She knew she was dreaming, she had been thrown into this pitch black dream state before.

Someone touched her last time, it had felt so real.

She tensed as she prepared herself for the being to get closer, what was she going to see this time?

Stomp... Stomp... Stomp...

The door flung open along with her eyes.

"They finally caved!" Ari exclaimed with a shaking hand gripping the door handle.

Without a thought Sam shot up from the bed and followed Ari into the hall. She expanded her hearing and she could hear the newscaster talking as she followed Ari into the living room.

"We have an exclusive interview with Detective Reginald Deluca.

He has been the head of the investigation for the disappearances, he is here to tell us that traffickers are not to blame."

The usual woman spoke and a man's voice appeared as Sam and Ari entered the room.

Everyone looked Sam's way to acknowledge that she was there but quickly looked away. They knew this was coming and guessed what the officials were going to say but it had always been just that: A guess.

The detective was a rough looking man with dark skin. He had scruff on his chin which had more hair than his head. His brown eyes had bags under them but they had a serious look to them, he looked to be about fifty.

"I know the public has been told that the culprits behind the disappearances are traffickers." his tone was as rough as his appearance and Sam was sure it was due to stress. "But I am here today to confirm that the culprits are not who you've been told."

Back at the house, whoever was sitting were on the edges of their seats while the one's standing seemed to lean forward.

"We originally didn't say anything because we wanted proof and we didn't want to cause alarm unless it was completely necessary." he looked into the camera as the woman sat nervously beside him and the newsroom was completely silent. Even the usual clicks or cough's that could usually be heard in the back were gone. "I'm regretfully informing the public that the creatures that many have called demons or gargoyles have returned after twenty years and they're behind the disappearances."

Sam's heart thumped, they actually did it…they told the truth.

What was this going to mean for them?

She looked around the room to see the others reactions: They had wide eyes but kept them on the screen as if transfixed.

She gulped then returned her gaze to the television.

"We want to tell you the truth for your own good, we have found that hiding the truth will only put you into further danger as it did twenty years ago. The proof we have extracted is from the young adults we have taken into custody that escaped from the creatures." he paused and his dark eyes almost looked like they were on Sam.

"The creatures have turned the people they have kidnapped into gargoyles as I've come to call them personally. We're not sure how they achieved this but we were told the creatures blood was used."

"I-" the newscaster started but she closed her mouth as no words could come out, she looked like she had seen a ghost or something even worse… A *demon*.

"There are twelve other people that are unaccounted for but it has been confirmed that this girl-" the detective picked up a picture from the table in front of him and Sam felt sick when she saw that the picture was of her.

The photo was taken of her two months prior to all of this, it was cut from a family photo.

The others looked back at her but she only had eyes for the screen as a cold sweat dripped down her brow.

She shouldn't have gone home.

"If anyone sees this girl, it's been confirmed that she too has been turned into a gargoyle. It could be that she is in hiding or she has joined her creators. The remaining eleven might not have gotten away but we are looking for them tirelessly." The man got up then left without another word as if he didn't care that he was on live television.

Cale shut the television off, they had gotten the information they needed.

The room was quiet as they thought about what they had just heard. Sam had her hand over her mouth to stop the sick feeling. Her heart raced and the silence made her wary that the others could hear it thumping against her ribcage.

"What the hell are we going to do now?" Trevor gripped the couches fabric. Everyone was surprised that he was the first to speak but it didn't last long as the question weighed on their minds.

"We just have to continue what we've been doing." Cale said finally and even though what he said was obvious, the thought of their conditions being outed changed the game completely. "I'm going to call my dad and explain what's going on before he sees this." He got up as he pulled the phone that Sam had bought from his pocket.

She looked at the device, she felt so violated from being the center of attention on the newscast.

It was hard to believe, but her mind felt even more jumbled than before.

"You're going to tell him?" Emily asked nervously.

"There's no other way," Cale turned so they couldn't see his face. "He's going to find out anyway, it might as well be from my mouth." he walked into the kitchen and the others listened as he opened and closed the sliding door, but not before Sam caught the beep of him sending his call.

"Should we even stay here?" Cam got up. "Even though neither

Cale's nor his fathers name is listed on this house, we could still be tracked here... especially now that his father is going to know the truth."

Sam thought of the possibilities and spoke them out loud. "Someone could show up here at any moment, human or gargoyle, the human's have more of a chance to track us..." She thought of Archie's talents not only in the medical field but in finding information.

She pursed her lips. "I lied...we're fucked either way, but I still think we'll be fine here for the time being."

"Why would you say that? This is one of the most obvious places we'd be especially since we've already been here for two weeks." Daniel looked at her with judgement and she felt something creep inside her.

She leaned onto the back of the sofa.

"They think Cale and the rest of you might not have gotten away. Though the chance they're still looking for you guys is high, I'm sure I'm their main target since it's been confirmed that they know I escaped and I was changed like the others." She swallowed and exhaled. "By the way Detective Deluca talked, the people they have in custody haven't told them that Cale, Emily, and I orchestrated everyone's escape."

Everyone was quiet for a moment until Kira posed a serious question. "Do you think they're experimenting on them?"

They always thought that they would be experimented on if they were caught but the possibility was greater now that the humans knew about them.

"Yes." Sam replied quickly, "They'll want to use them to find out the gargoyles weaknesses." The answer was obvious but Sam's blood ran cold as she spoke.

It was hard to think who had it worse: Sam's group who had to fight Arthur, or the escapees who were thrown into another cell almost immediately after they were freed.

They sat in silence for what felt like hours but in reality, it might have only been ten minutes. They occasionally glanced at each other and cleared their throats.

The door in the kitchen slid open as Cale stepped back into the house and Emily hopped up to meet him.

Sam figured by how gentle Cale shut the door, that the conversation had gone well... as well as it could have gone at least.

He looked glum as he stepped in with Emily behind him, he hadn't said a word to her but his face said it all.

"I told him about my… Condition." he declared.

No one dared to ask what his father's reaction was so they just looked at him until he continued. "He said he saw the news online and said that he had a feeling that something was up… I begged him not to call the police and he said he won't because he knows what they'll do to me." he inhaled sharply. "I told him to stay where he is and that I'm fine." he fisted his hands. "He told me not do anything reckless and I promised him I wouldn't."

He lied to his father and it was obvious that he hated himself for it.

Emily placed a hand on his shoulder to assure him it was the right thing to do but while he calmed a bit from the gesture, the pain still showed on his face.

"I'm gonna go upstairs." Daniel declared with a shaking voice as he got up and his sister trotted after him.

"The situation is still the same I guess…" Ari swallowed after they watched the siblings go out of sight. "It's just as shitty as it's ever been."

Everyone aside from Ari, Cale, and Sam were asleep. Sam watched the minutes pass on the digital clock under the television but looked away after it hit 12:00 AM. The three of them sat in silence, well not in complete silence since Ari was chewing on her nails. Cale's eyes were focused on a spot on the rug that was caused by Daniel and Cam's bickering at the beginning of their stay. Daniel had pushed Cam, who was holding a glass of orange juice, and it spilt on the floor resulting in the stain.

Sam was sure he wasn't really looking at it, it was just a point to focus on as he escaped into his thoughts.

"I'm heading up." Ari shot up and gave Cale a nod while she raised a hand towards Sam who raised her own and the two gave each other a light high five.

Sam brought her gaze back to Cale who hadn't been fazed by Ari's departure as he continued to sit the way he had been.

"Cale?" She leaned forward.

"Hm?" he acknowledged her but didn't look from his spot.

"Talk about it." she demanded softly and he finally looked from the stain to meet her eyes, he looked exhausted.

"What do you mean?"

"What's bothering you."

He closed his eyes and sighed as he leaned into the chair, "I told my father that I'm a monster and he couldn't believe it. He didn't seem to be shocked that it's gargoyles though, he was around when the attacks happened twenty years ago."

Sam watched with a soft expression as he opened his eyes and explained more, "I'm sure he didn't come to terms with it but he accepted me after I explained that I haven't changed, not mentally at least. He was glad that I kept in touch with him so he'd know that I'm still myself even with this body…. I couldn't believe that he accepted me so fast so I questioned him and he said that I'm his son regardless if those monsters changed me into one of them."

How did his father accept him so quickly when Sam's parents rejected her?

His father was hiding something.

"But that's not what's bothering you?" Sam inquired, she felt almost jealous of how accepting Cale's father was towards him. She remembered her parents faces as they had found out the truth about her, it was something that had haunted her for the past two weeks.

"He told me to stay put and to not fight against the creatures and I told him I wouldn't." he gripped his jeans. "I lied to him but I'm sure he knows I'll do it anyway. He was hesitant when I wanted to join the military but he agreed…. You should of heard his voice Sam."

She let him calm a bit before she spoke, "He knows the type of person you are…But you don't have to do this." she assured him.

He didn't have to after all, Sam was Arthur's focus and she'd do her best to get Carma back.

Cale smiled not out of happiness, but from his own recklessness. "That's the problem, I want to fight them… Even if Carma wasn't with them, I'd still want to fight." he chuckled. "I feel like you're rubbing off on me."

She rose a brow as she leaned back into the sofa. "Is that a bad thing?" She was only joking of course.

His brown eyes softened finally as he continued to smile. "Of course not."

The smile went away as fast as it had came as he thought of what was really bothering him. "My only fear is that I'll die fighting the gargoyles after I promised him I wouldn't."

Sam looked at her own hands, she realized that she was unconsciously pressing them together. The chance was very high that they were going to die. They could run but they remained at the house and learned to use their new abilities to fight against their enemies.

Even Sam could run, maybe go to another country where it would be next to impossible to find her. (Though she was sure if Arthur wanted her bad enough, he'd find her.) but nonetheless, she stayed to fight.

Of course she was scared like the others.

Damn, she was scared but what kind of person would she be if she ran?

"I'd be lying if I said that it didn't weigh on me... but I'll fight anyway." She said finally and Cale nodded in agreement.

She got up from the couch with a small smile, "I'm going to sleep so I can get up in time for our usual sparring session."

He returned her smile, "It's about time you got off my bed."

It was true, she had been sitting where he slept.

She bowed her head. "I'm sorry, kind sir."

She looked up as she stepped backwards and they both allowed themselves a chuckle.

"Goodnight." Cale said as he moved to the couch and he grabbed a pillow that was resting on the floor beside it and he placed it where Sam had been sitting.

"Goodnight." she replied as she made her way to her room.

Chapter 15

Sam and Cale tiptoed as they made their way from the living room into the kitchen. The digital clock read 5:37am and outside the window was an orange hue as the sun rose again.

Cale slid the door open and allowed Sam to sneak through before shutting it gently behind himself. They weren't trying to hide their training sessions from the others but they also didn't want to wake them. They learned much more by sparring with each other and it allowed them to carry on what they had learned to the others.

The two wore loose fitting clothes as if they were going to a gym: Sweatpants and a T-shirt. The short sleeved shirts weren't practical because of the chilled morning air but they would warm up soon enough.

"I want to try the move I found yesterday." Cale told her with a yawn.

"I'm down." she stretched her legs since they were heavy with sleep.

Cale averted his eyes as he thought of how the technique was executed. "It's meant to get the person coming at you onto the ground so you can pin them." he explained.

They had learned many new ways to fight that included special punches, kicks, pinning moves, and different kinds of martial arts. Though some were more difficult than others, they managed to learn most of them.

Cale started teaching Sam the move he had found as he learned it himself. It was fairly easy to learn aside from the awkward position but that wouldn't matter in hindsight. What would really make it hard was trying to use it in action.

The two were ready to put it to the test as they stood opposite of each other, their eyes their gargoyle colors as they released a small amount of energy to practice the move.

They went at each other like they were enemies but of course they held back to a degree. Both of them waited for the right moment to use the move but the opportunity didn't hit quite yet.

Punch, kick, dodge until Sam finally found her opening to try it: Her eyes moved quickly as she watched Cale's limbs move just as fast. She ducked underneath his attack and wrapped her arms around his chest but he fought her and restricted her from continuing further. Sam didn't let go but Cale remained flat footed as the two battled with each other.

She had to let loose, she had to let more power out.

Like on command, the energy flowing through her felt more intense and she was able to pin him to the ground.

Cale struggled under her strength. "That's not a win." He joked as he still attempted to push her off but gave up after he realized that his efforts were futile.

He spread his arms on the grass in defeat and Sam released him. She sat beside where he laid and peered down at his smiling face.

He clearly wasn't upset that he had lost.

"It doesn't count anyway since you have the stronger eyes." he rolled his own as they went back to their normal color.

Sam's wavy hair brushed his chest as she looked down at him, he was looking up at the lightening sky with a calm expression. The rising sun made him squint but Sam's shadow helped a bit with the light.

"That's true." she admitted then grinned. "But it still feels good."

He chuckled. "I'll let you have that, at least we know the move works."

She leaned back onto her hands as her fingers dug into the grass. Her eyes changed back like Cale's had only her's didn't return to their normal color: The gray ring had grown wider but the hazel still had the upper hand. For now.

She sighed as she used her fingers to pull her hair behind her ears.

"Wanna go in?" Cale had gotten up as Sam focused on a cloud that looked like a dog.

She moved her head from the cloud to Cale, the thoughts he had from the night before were hidden now. He reached his hand out and she gripped it as he pulled her up.

"Wanna surprise them with breakfast?" he asked as he opened the door for her and she thanked him. Emily had been making breakfast on the occasion that they didn't eat cereal, it would be nice to make her something in return. Maybe it would help with her attitude towards Sam but she doubted it.

"Sounds good." She agreed as they stepped into the kitchen.

Cale and Sam sat at the table while the others sat at the counter while they ate the pancake breakfast that was prepared for them.

The cooks were covered in flour as they picked at their food, the two of them had ended up getting into a small food fight which Cale had won since Sam was saturated in flour. The white powder stuck to her eyelashes, making her eyes pop all the more.

"Are you twelve?" Jeannie tried a judgemental tone but she had a grin on her face.

The others looked at them with entertained expressions.

The two huligans glanced at each other and snorted at their looks.

"I think so." Cale agreed.

"I appreciate the effort but we'll need to go to the store now." Emily stated, she was uncomfortable with them going out into the public eye and the fact that Cale and Sam had used their rations for fun annoyed her a bit.

"I'm out of the running for going out." Sam sulked as she flicked a piece of bacon.

Was this what being a celebrity felt like?

"I'm a fool for going home."

"You didn't know you were going to lose control or that your parents wouldn't understand." Trevor assured her.

He was right but he was also wrong. She knew the chances of her losing control but she still went. She could've snuck in but deep down, maybe she wanted them to accept her.

"I'll go later." Cale told as he got up and shook his shirt, the powder started to fall on the already covered floor. "I'm going outside to shake this off."

"Same." Sam followed him and as she stepped out the door, she could hear the sliding of chairs on the hardwood floor. She turned her head to find everyone up and following her.

"You coming out for fresh air?" she questioned as she stepped the rest of the way through the doorway.

"We figured since you guys are sorta our teachers and you're going outside, we might as well train before you guys clean up." Cam explained with a smooth tone. He had changed, the arrogant attitude he once had was essentially gone. Though Sam was sure that it was still in there.

She looked to Cale who was ruffling the flour out of his black hair and she followed suit but she did it a bit differently by bending over and flinging her hair back while ruffling her hands through it.

"That seems like a good idea, I just wasn't sure if you wanted to start now." Cale looked clean as he stopped his swatting. "We don't know how much time we have left."

Sam stopped her cleaning and like the others, brought her gaze to Cale.

The air could be cut with a knife.

The happy times they had here were real but they were also a lie. They could joke and bond as much as they wanted but it wouldn't hide the fact that they had to fight. Sam was waiting for the day when the others finally changed their minds, to get the hell out of there and run. Honestly, She wanted them too.

Revenge wasn't worth it anymore, Sam knew that, but she wanted it all the same.

During these past two weeks, she realized that while revenge was still an option, the real reason she was going to fight was because she had no choice.

She could run and hide but her fate would meet her all the same, Arthur was her fate.

"Then we better make the time we have worth it." She advised.

"Change into your gargoyle forms and fight, I don't care who you do it with."

She stepped away as they transformed and Ari, Daniel, Cam, and Kira had retained their lesson from the day before but Emily, Jeannie, and Dylan had some difficulty.

Their eyes flashed between black and their normal color as they struggled to hold onto their power.

Trevor joined Sam and Cale as they watched.

"I'm going to sit this one out." he muttered and they nodded.

Sam knew Trevor would leave them before long and while she wanted him to leave now in case something were to happen, she didn't want to cast him away until he was ready. He was safer here at the moment.

The rest finally attained their forms and after Dylan had blamed it on stage fright, the group set to work.

"You're not joining in?" Cale wondered and Sam shook her head.

"It's getting harder to hold back, I can still feel the energy from earlier, I don't want to chance it." She felt the ache under her skin as the power fought to rise to the surface again. She turned her head to look at Cale. "I can ask you the same thing though."

"I want to see what they can do." he explained with an amused look as he noticed that there was still powder on her face. "We've taught them everything we know aside from what we tried earlier and I want to see if they remember it all." He brought his attention forward as he explained. Sam could also see the remnants of their food fight on his tan skin as she watched him speak.

She looked forward as well, the group indeed honed their freshly learned fighting moves and they used the extra strength granted to them from their transformations to their advantage.

Something was swelling in Sam's chest: She was proud.

Kira and Ari were now equally matched and the girls struggled to overcome each other. When Sam thought one was about to win, the other used a defensive move to get themselves out of it. She found herself grinning at their improvement.

Cam, Daniel, Jeannie, and Dylan were in a four-way fight.

Good, that was something that could very well happen.

Jeannie held her own against Dylan unlike how she had the first day and it was an odd sight seeing a small girl fighting on par with a football superstar. She back flipped away from him and Daniel tried coming up behind her for the attack and she kicked him in the knee.

Cam and Dylan teamed up against the siblings and they fought as if they were in a real battle.

Sam gritted her teeth as the sounds of the fight got louder. Six gargoyles sparring proved to make a good amount of noise as growl's escaped their throats.

Emily worked by herself and the three observing watched as she flicked her fingers and her nails retracted then came back as she flicked them again.

She was working on control, something that the others had no interest in.

Sam swung her head back to the four-way fight as she heard a sharper growl and a yell: Daniel had scratched his sister and by the intense look in his eyes, it was easy to see that he was losing control.

Sam and Cale stepped into the fray.

Sam grabbed Daniel's wrist as he tried to swing again and Cale stepped between him and his sister. Daniel couldn't even tell what he was doing anymore, all he was focused on was the power flowing through him.

He glared at Cale before he turned his head to see who was holding him and he tried to pull away. His teeth were sharp and his pitch black eyes caused the veins around them to pop through his skin. If Sam wasn't used to these kind of looks, she would've been intimidated.

She focused her energy into her fingers and like Emily, she urged her nails to go out with her will and the energy she allowed to come out made her body relax.

Daniel's breath hitched as her nails dug into his skin. Sam had found that pain could bring them back. After she gripped harder and he thrashed equally as hard only to cause the pain to heighten, he collapsed to the ground as he went back to his senses.

"I'm sorry." His voice shook as Sam let go.

Jeannie leaped from behind Cale and she fell to her knees in front of her brother and she grabbed ahold of his injured wrist as blood dripped from it.

"It's ok." she made sure to hide the scratches that he had made on her arm. "You didn't mean it."

The others who had watched the whole thing go down looked shaken.

"I think we need some down time." Emily advised as she came from behind Cale and he acknowledged her with a nervous smile. "Good idea." he agreed.

Sam kelt beside Daniel and Jeannie as the rest began to move away from them.

"I'm sorry I had to do that." she glanced at his wrist then back to his downcast face.

"Don't apologize, thank you for calming me down." Daniel looked at his sister with watery eyes. "I don't know what I would've done if you didn't stop me Sam."

Sam could see the complete and utter disappointment etched into his face as he looked back to her and she placed a hand on his shoulder. "I've lost control, Cale has lost control, and before long, the others will too. Don't put this all on yourself."

Even though he still looked down, his expression did lighten up a bit.

Sam squeezed his shoulder one last time before she got up.

"Since when were you good at comforting people?" Kira asked slyly.

"I try." Sam flashed an anxious grin.

The air around the group was still tense from the recent event but they were trying their best to ease it.

"I think we should have a little girl time." Kira suggested suddenly and she was met with surprised looks.

That was random, why would she want girl time? Especially after what had just happened?

"Come on, what's so bad about it? The guys can chill and talk about guy things while we talk girl stuff." Kira shrugged and Sam rose a brow.

What was she planning?

"I'm down." Ari agreed, of course she would.

She not only was practically stuck at the hip with Kira, she also had the same funny attitude that made the others squirm out of embarrassment.

"Stop with the untrusting look Samantha, you're hurting my feelings." Kira snickered.

She was definitely going to embarrass everyone.

"Fine." she agreed finally, maybe it could help with what just happened.

"I'm staying with Daniel." Jeannie told as the two got up. Daniel was laughing a bit at the thought of what Kira was planning.

"Good luck, girls." he said simply and the siblings made their way into the house and the rest of the guys followed aside from Cale who was joking with Emily about the situation she was about to be in.

They spotted Sam looking and nodded for her to come over. She looked behind her shoulder to see Kira and Ari already sitting on the grass like they were forming a circle around a campfire.

She turned back and made her way to Cale and Emily.

"I'm going to wait with them until you two are done." Emily said flatly and the two watched her go.

"I don't think she'll ever like me again." Sam stated sadly as they watched her join the other two girls.

"She will…Just give it more time." Cale assured and he looked down to meet Sam's eyes. "That didn't go the way we would have liked, huh?"

"No, but I expected something like that would happen sooner or later." She sighed. "If only we had sedatives so we wouldn't have to use pain to stop it."

"He'll be alright, we heal fast." Cale stated and Sam looked up at him and huffed. "Yeah, but not as fast as you do."

He made a noise. "I don't know why I heal so fast."

"I like that you can heal faster so I can kick your ass again." She joked and Cale laughed at the forced smug she was wearing.

"Again? It didn't even happen a first time." his smile widened.

"Sam!" Ari called over as she waved her hand impatiently as the other girls looked between her, Cale, and Sam.

"Good luck." Cale joked as he walked away and Sam desperately wanted him to save her.

She made her way to the girls and as she sat, she swallowed. "So…?"

"What's been going on between you and veggie boy?" Kira asked with a snicker and Sam rose a brow while Ari snorted and Emily blinked.

"*Who*?" Sam squinted, her tone low with confusion.

"You and Cale." Ari said matter of factly.

Sam just sat there and blinked while she tried to register what Ari had just asked. They watched as they waited for her to answer and like an alarm went off in her head, she almost choked.

She knew what they were implying.

"*Nothing*." she replied sternly when she regained her composure.

"You spend a lot of time together, don't think we don't know about your early morning training sessions." Kira reveled and Sam's face was almost as red a tomato, not from the accusation, but the fact that they had known about their training.

"How did you-" she started.

"Did you forget that our hearing is good af?" she said *as fuck* with the letters.

"You caught us but that doesn't mean we have a thing for each other… we weren't even hiding it." Sam looked to Emily since she was the closest to Cale. " He's a good friend and nothing more, besides, who could think of a relationship in a time like-" she stopped as she heard something flying through the air, almost like an intense whistle.

She gritted her teeth from the pain the noise was causing her as she shot up.

"What is it!?" Emily asked while sounding panicked and the three got up as a huge bang could be heard at the front of the house.

Without another thought, Sam ran to the source of the noise while gripping at her ears. They stung from the after effects of the noise and she flinched as her eardrums pounded.

She rounded on the front of the house as Cale and the others leapt from the front porch and the two groups met at the source of the noise:

A stone gargoyle head with jagged marks around where the neck should've been was thrown next to the house. There was paper rolled inside the beasts mouth, it's teeth pressing down on it.

Sam turned and instinctively faced the dirt path that led to the road. She focused her hearing and she could hear the distant sound of footsteps as they went the opposite way. She turned her head to see Cale, Emily, and Ari looking the same way with focus in their eyes along with fear.

There was no sense in chasing after the assailant, whoever it was, they weren't looking for a fight. They turned back to the stone, even though they didn't know who had thrown the thing, they knew who had sent it.

Arthur.

Sam bent down and with a shaking hand, pulled the paper out of it's mouth. She did it quickly as if it was a bomb about to blow if you clipped the wrong wire. She could hear the shallow breaths of the others and the crack of their joints as they moved nervously.

They knew what this meant: Arthur knew where they were hiding.

The theatrics of the delivery made sure of that but the contents of the letter and the way it was delivered made the tension worse.

Why didn't they attack them instead of writing a letter?

Sam thought of Arthur's face before she had left the cave, it was uninterested but deep inside there was a sense of accomplishment.

Sam realized that now… It confirmed that he had indeed let them go. She pulled the tape gently away from the paper to not rip the contents and she let it fall from her fingers as she stood back up, leaving the gargoyle head on the ground.

She unrolled the paper, it was written with small fancy letters as if someone from the victorian era had written it.

Sam began reading it out loud:

"I know this is your hiding place, I have known for awhile now. I know that ten of you reside there and I'm confident that some of you suspect that I let you escape.

You are correct.

I wanted you to make your petty plans whether it be for revenge or for simply finding a place to hide.

I assure you the latter won't work. I will hunt you to the ends of the earth until I get what I want.

So I am giving you a chance, a chance to come to me on your own.

What I really want is an exchange of wills."

Sam drew a breath as she took in the words, her heart pounding against it's cage. She licked her trembling lips and continued:

"I tell you this: If you do not meet me, I will hunt all of you down and slaughter you one by one while I make the others watch as they wait for their turn.

But it doesn't have to come to that… Enclosed is a map to our meeting place."

The letter ended there, he didn't even need to sign it for them to know who wrote it, it was obvious after all.

Sam pulled a smaller piece of paper away from the letter, the paper was crinkled and it tried rolling back to the way she had found it. She flipped it over to see that it was a map with an address written underneath, she read it out loud along with the date of their meeting.

Her mouth went dry as she said it out loud:

"Tomorrow."

Her arm dropped to her side, the letter still gripped between her index finger and thumb.

Cale pulled the letter from her and read it to himself while Sam leaned her head back and gazed up at the blue sky. The clouds moved as the earth spun, oh how she wished she could stop time. Maybe to make it slower so they could have more time to prepare.

She couldn't bring herself to look at the others and she zoned out what they were saying. She forced her eyes from the sky and was met with the panicked faces of her allies.

"What are we going to do?" Ari asked nervously, her face was pale along with the others who were either whispering to each other or just standing there with a blank look.

Sam had an answer but she didn't want to say it out loud, she was sure that they would figure it out on their own.

Cale handed the letter to Emily. "…I don't know."

Sam moved her eyes so she could get a look at his face: His eyes matched hers, fearful but knowing, he knew what he was going to do like she did.

"You're going, aren't you? The both of you?" Cam questioned over the panicked chatter but it stopped as they heard Cam's question. He looked between Sam and Cale like they were fools but that wasn't anything new.

"…Yes." Sam admitted but rushed to explain "Only because I have no other choice, you heard what's going to happen if we don't and believe me, he's not bluffing." She inhaled sharply. "He won't have anything to lose by killing us if we choose not to obey him-"

"We're not ready Sam." Kira interjected. "Not even close."

"I know damn it!" she gritted her teeth. "I wish we had more time, I wish we had all the time in the world but I have to go…Stay behind if you want, maybe I'll be enough until you guys get as far away from here as you can…"

"He said he'd follow us!" Daniel blurted.

"I'm going." Cale said suddenly and their sight changed to him.

Emily's jaw was locked in place as she held the letter in front of her, her eyes were on it but she wasn't looking at it, not really.

"And I think Sam would be enough for him not to go after the rest of you." Cale explained. "He's interested in her for some reason and she'll be worth far more to him than any of you, me included."

It almost sounded like a diss to the others but Sam wished those words were directed at her. She wanted Arthur to not have any interest in her at all.

"If you're not serious about whatever reason you've been here for, then leave and save yourselves." Cale added.

"We'll die either way!" Jeannie cried, her panicked voice echoed through the woods.

"Let's go inside." Ari demanded because of the noise, they didn't need to be heard, especially by the person who had delivered the letter.

They started piling into the house and as Sam followed up the stairs onto the front porch, she realized that Trevor wasn't with them. She turned to see him looking at the sky like she had been moments before. He turned to her when he noticed her watching him and the front door closed behind her as she stepped back down the stairs to meet him.

"Are you ok?" She asked and automatically regretted it, what a dumb thing to ask.

None of them were ok.

"I can't do this." his voice shook as he bowed his head out of self pity.

Sam knew this day would come, she had never expected him to fight with them, It was obvious from the start. He said himself that he couldn't fight when push came to shove.

"I know, Trevor." She placed a hand on his shaking shoulder. "Don't be sorry, I mean this in the nicest way possible, but I'd rather you not fight, I don't even want the others to go either."

He gave her a thankful look but his features still showed that he hated himself for not stepping up. "I want to help you, I really do."

"No you don't," Sam pinged his head gently. "You want to help me because I'm your friend but you don't want to fight and it honestly makes me happy you don't."

His eyes averted from her, he couldn't stand to look at her anymore.

"Why don't you hesitate? Aren't you scared?" he pressed then backed away like she would hit him for asking such a thing.

She watched a tree behind him blow in the wind, it looked so peaceful, like there was no other care in the world. But if one really thought about it, the tree was at a stand still while the wind made it sway. That's how she felt with the situation they were in, they were at a stand still with Arthur's group, they didn't have a good plan nor did they have time. They could only be forced to bend to the gargoyles will's.

Like the tree being blown in the wind.

"I'm terrified." She admitted. "I can't sleep at night and I feel like there's always a pit in my stomach." She swallowed. "Arthur'll chase me if I run but I won't, I have some questions that only he can answer."

Her tone softened as her thoughts weighed on her again.

"What...?" Trevor blinked as he finally looked her straight in the eyes and she clenched her jaw. "You can stay here while we go, I'm sure they won't bother you as long as I give myself up." she sounded conceded that she thought that Arthur held her at such a high value but she knew it was true.

"But if you want to leave, you can." she gave a small smile but it looked fake. "Maybe you'll have others joining you."

She turned on her heel and made her way to the house while Trevor stood for a moment with a dumbfounded look from her change in demeanor.

She stepped up the stairs onto the front porch with swift movements. Almost like she was floating on air, it was the complete opposite of her usual rough movements.

She seemed like a different person.

She opened the door and held it open for him but turned and gave him a confused look when she noticed that he didn't follow her.

"You coming?" she asked with her normal tone.

"Yeah..." he said with uncertainty as he made his way to her.

Chapter 16

"We're not ready!" Daniel's voice rang out as Sam and Trevor made their way down the hall into the living room where Cale, Emily, Ari, and Jeannie sat while the rest stood.

"And I've already told you that you can stay behind." Cale didn't look at him as he replied, he had his hands cupped together as his elbows rested on his knees. He looked restless and a bit annoyed at hearing Daniel's and the rest's thoughts when he was so caught up in his own.

"What were you two doing?" Cam shot at Sam and Trevor as they entered the room.

Sam would have whooped him for his attitude but chewed on her tongue to stop herself. She glanced at Trevor, she didn't want to be the one to tell them, it was up to him.

"I'm staying behind." he clenched his jaw as he expected judgement, but like with Sam, he didn't receive any.

"I'm glad." Ari smiled weakly then quickly turned away and covered her mouth, she wasn't crying but she acted as if she was hiding a sob.

"We have to decide what we're going to do." Daniel placed a hand on his sisters shoulder as he looked straight at Sam. "We're not ready," he repeated again. "You and Cale are walking to your deaths and you'd be taking us with you."

Sam considered him for a moment, she knew where he was coming from and she felt the same of course but his roundabout words annoyed her.

He didn't have to go while she and Cale had to.

"You heard Cale," she rested her foot against the couch. "You can stay."

"You read the letter Sam, he'll go after us if we don't." Jeannie told her softly as if she didn't want her to hear.

"I think that was for the dramatics, he'll be pleased enough that Cale and I will show up." Sam explained calmly.

As calm as she could at least.

"That sounds cocky." Cam rolled his eyes. "He'll come for us no matter what, we're better off leaving the country to live another day."

They wanted to leave to a foreign country but they had heard Sam when she read the letter: Arthur would follow them to the end's of the earth.

She looked at each of her comrades, they all looked so lost, their fates weighing so heavy on their minds.

"I'm going and I want you all to stay." She said finally and Cale looked at her like she was nuts.

"There's no way you're going by yourself." he shot up and made his way to her, placing both hands on her shoulders.

He furrowed his brows. "We're going to save Carma, remember? We need each others help to do that."

She gripped his left wrist with her right hand and nodded in agreement as he backed away.

"I'm going." Emily's voice rang out, she kept her head forward as she looked to Cale and Sam with determination on her face. "I want to help save Carma."

"Emily-" Cale started to protest but Emily stopped him. "No Cale," her voice had an edge to it. "I'm going and you can't stop me, I'm tired of being on the sidelines while the two of you put everything on yourselves… Carma is my friend too."

Cale's expression didn't change as he considered her words, he couldn't take this away from her, he'd be a hypocrite if he did.

"I'll protect you with my life but if things turn for the worse, I want you to run and don't look back." he demanded and she nodded.

Her face wavered from her determined expression as she thought of the inevitable battle but caught herself. She couldn't allow herself to show fear, it was time to prove herself.

Another emotion filled Sam: Sadness.

She was sad that someone as peaceful as Emily, whose goal was to help people through medicine, had to fight for her life and for the ones closest to her with violence.

"Are you suicidal!?" Daniel spat, "You'll be running to your deaths!"

Everyone turned to Daniel whose face was considerably red. Cam stood behind him with a look that indicated that he agreed with him.

Sam knew where he was coming from, he was trying to persuade them to run, he cared about them but his mind was clouded by the bad news.

While she felt for him, she also felt a twinge of annoyance from repeating herself.

From being accused of being suicidal.

Her mind filled with the dream she had about the explosion, the feeling of her body being torn apart. She had realized that it wasn't merely a dream, it was a vision.

"We're not-" Cale started.

"Then why go!?" Daniel shot.

That was it, a little of the old Sam emerged.

"Would you shut the hell up?!" she growled.

Many jumped from her outburst while Ari, Cale, Emily, and Kira locked their jaws and watched it unfold. Daniel blinked and Cam gritted his teeth, it was funny how well the two got on now.

"We'll die either way, would you rather they come to us or go to them and see what Arthur wants?" she questioned with her gaze straight forward, the boys had a hard time holding her look.

"Are you saying you'd join them if he asked?" Cam asked with a judgmental tone.

"Did I fucking say that?" she spat back."Of course I would like more time to learn but you heard the note Cam, he's coming for us whether we run or not." Her voice shook. "I choose to fight before he follows through with his threat."

"You might be gung-ho on getting yourself killed but we're not." Daniels tone had softened but what he said still felt like a punch to her.

He landed himself an annoyed look from Ari while Kira watched like she was seeing a debate unfold. The tension in the air could be cut with a knife.

"Watch it." Cale stepped forward. The gesture was intimidating since he was the tallest one there. Daniel retreated a step even though Cale would never hit him.

"Are we forcing you to stay here? To fight?" Sam asked calmly, not just to Daniel or Cam but everyone. She made sure to take a second to look in their eyes.

"I-" Cam started.

"Don't bullshit me." She warned. "Don't worry about what I'm doing, worry about yourself. If I die that's on me." She swung her arm in front of her. "Did I not tell you that I wanted you to leave if you didn't want to fight? I said you could stay for protection but that's no longer possible."

She pointed to Trevor, she didn't mean to put him on the spot but she needed him as an example. "Trevor is leaving and I don't blame him… I would too if the target on my back wasn't so big." her voice cracked and she swallowed to get the lump out of her throat.

She hoped no one had heard her voice waver but seeing their faces soften towards her indicated that they had, or it was because her words touched them, it didn't matter.

"Since I'm ready to die, I might as well do it fighting." she said finally, her voice rough."If I don't fight there won't be a chance to win, even if it's slim." She clawed her thumb into her right palm as she tried to hide the emotions she was feeling.

The room was silent as everything settled in and Sam felt like she couldn't breath. She wanted to run away, not just from Arthur, but from this room.

"We're leaving in the morning," Cale stood beside Sam now and Emily stepped forward so she was with them. "If you choose to come we'll welcome you, but if you don't we'll be happier."

"I'm going." Ari leaned her head on the back of the couch. "That shouldn't be a surprise." She gave Sam an acknowledging look. Sam already knew she was going to come with them, she was that type of person.

"…Me too." Kira who was standing by the fireplace with her arms crossed as she watched the situation unfold walked to where Ari was sitting."We're going into the unknown, I'm as ready as I'll ever be."

"I'll go." Cam said with no emotion but Sam knew he was going with his own plan.

When they thought that their volunteers were done, Daniel spoke. "I'm going but Jeannie is staying here." Sam's eyes widened for a second then went back to normal, she was surprised but she knew he'd let his pride win.

"No!" Jeannie shot up and grabbed her brothers arm. "There's no way in hell you're going! Especially if you're going to leave me here while you get killed!"

"I'll be fine." he smiled but it was obviously fake.

"Listen to your sister." Sam said simply but he ignored her. "I think Sam is right about you guys being safe if only a few of us go, I made a promise to myself, I have to go."

Tears started to form in his sister's eyes. "I can't go back to mom and dad and now you want me to lose you too?"

The rest of the group watched as Daniel consoled his sister with a hug, "I'll be fine, I promise."

The room dispersed as everyone separated to get ahold of their thoughts and Sam had made her way to the backyard to get some fresh air.

She sat on an extra fluffy patch of grass and stared at the tree she had broken. Did she have the strength? She turned her sights to the patch of grass that laid flat where she had overpowered Cale. Did she have the skill? She thought of the severed gargoyle head that they had left in the front yard.

"That was quite the speech." Cale came from behind her and she didn't even notice.

She made a mental note to make sure that she wouldn't do that tomorrow.

"How are they?" she asked as he sat beside her and he gazed at the tree as well. "They're ok, It's obvious they're scared but they're trying to act tough."

"Like us, right?" she smiled gently but her eyes gave her real emotions away.

"...Yeah." he looked down as he twirled his fingers nervously.

They sat silently for a moment and simply listened to the crickets chirp.

"It can go two ways tomorrow-" Cale broke the silence. "We manage to save Carma and get out of there or we all die." Sam did her nervous tick as he continued, "I keep running in my mind how things are gonna go and it always ends with us dead."

"What happens in between?" Sam asked as she watched a leaf blow across the yard.

"Usually the things that can go wrong…I'm afraid I'll lose control like I did in the cave." He closed his eyes. "I know it could help but there's no way I'll win without control, not to mention that I could hurt one of you in the process." He finally looked at her. "I'm afraid of the rage and I know the power thrives off of it."

She faced him. "The power is great but it's like a drug, when the high is gone, you're left with the aftermath." she turned away again and like Cale, she twirled her fingers.

"I've been keeping something from you-" she inhaled sharply and in her peripheral vision she could see Cale's head turn slightly towards her and her heart began to race.

"That night in the cave when I…attacked you, it was triggered by a dream." she swallowed, she was afraid to tell him out of fear of him thinking she was crazy. He and Emily knew a little about her dreams but not to this extent. "I had a dream or a vision of some sort… of my own death."

She felt his body shift beside her but she couldn't bring herself to look at him. All she could see was flashes of the vision: The hollow feeling, the landscape...the explosion itself.

She shivered. "I died in an explosion, I sacrificed myself but I don't know what for… There were too many pieces missing."

It was quiet as he took in what she said.

"Do you think it was a premonition or something?" he asked finally and she shook her head and gave a twisted smile."I don't even know anymore, but I can't ignore that it goes with my other dreams…It can't be a coincidence."

Silence once again.

"You must think I'm crazy." She finally came out and said it.

She closed her eyes like she was about to be hit, with the truth at least.

"I don't think you're crazy, though I believe there's a little crazy in all of us for what we're about to do." His eyes dropped to his white knuckled hands as they gripped onto each other.

"That's true." she smiled then sighed, "There's more to it though, I can't put my finger on it but I feel like Arthur might have some of the answers to my questions."

"Why would you say that?" he rounded on her, his expression confused.

She explained how Arthur had talked to her after her breakdown, the expression he had that she could vividly remember. Maybe her mind was playing tricks on her, she was out of her mind at that moment after all.

It still didn't explain why he would say that she was always going to punish herself. Her forehead crinkled as she thought. She certainly didn't imagine it. She thought of every possible reason why he would say something like that but nothing added up.

Nothing normal at least.

"I don't know." she said breathlessly, she couldn't bring herself to tell him what she thought. It was very unlikely that Arthur could have some insight for her vision like dreams.

She shook her head as if she were refreshing her mind. "I need to find out why he's doing this, but I'm sure I'll never get a straightforward answer."

"He probably won't even give you the chance to ask before he kills us." Cale said sullenly.

"That's true." She agreed.

They sat for awhile to take in the sounds of nature. The feeling of the wind blowing gently against their skin and the sun beaming through the trees.

They tried not to think about what's ahead or where they would be this time tomorrow. They would know when the time came.

When they were done enjoying their peace or whatever their clouded minds allowed them to, they got up and made their way into the house.

It was time to plan.

Sam and Cale sat side by side at the kitchen island, her laptop open in front of them. She gave him full control over it so she could watch and take in what they were studying.

It wasn't long before Emily, Kira, and Ari joined them. Their urgency to plan outdid their fear of what was to come. Emily sat beside Cale while Kira and Ari stood behind them and before long, the stomping of the others could be heard coming down the stairs as they made their way to the kitchen. Dylan, Jeannie, and Trevor watched with blank faces while standing off to the side as Cam and Daniel joined the others who were going to go on the dangerous trek.

Cale looked down at the hand written letter and the map Arthur had enclosed along with it.

He typed in the address on a site that would show them an aerial view of their meeting place.

Sam clenched her jaw and gave the screen a confused look as she saw their destination: It was an old farmhouse.

Why the hell would Arthur choose a place like that?

Cale clicked his tongue as the others stirred, "What the hell is this supposed to be?" Cam's tone was stiff as he tried to hide his nervousness but failed.

"I don't know how we can plan anything with this layout." Cale zoomed onto each part of the aerial picture while his face twisted with annoyance.

He finally zoomed on the area behind the barn: It was nothing but woodland as far as the eyes could see.

Sam's eyes wandered to the barn behind the house then to the area around the perimeter. There were no houses nearby, only trees and a dirt road that was most likely seldom driven on.

Cale continued to zoom in as if he hoped that the more he clicked, the higher the odds of something coming up that could help them.

Sam studied the condition of the buildings: The house and barn were built with the same old grayish wood. At one time it must have been a rich brown but the decades weathered it to it's current color. The barn was only twenty feet away from the house and an open field was beside it where the owners must have had their livestock.

That must have been a long time ago since the picture was taken five years ago according to the timestamp and Sam was sure the place was still deserted. An abandoned place for their meetup made sense but why this place in particular? She looked to the woods behind the barn.

"What a fantastic place for a surprise attack." She thought it to herself but the words poured out of her mouth.

"There's no way we could manage that," Ari leaned onto the back of Sam's chair. "But I'm sure that's what they're planning incase things don't go their way."

"I think they'll attack us even if things go their way." Cale brought the mouse to the search bar and deleted the current site to type in something new. He still hadn't given up hope on finding that website but what would it do for them now?

Pictures and articles on what happened years ago wouldn't help them now.

He scrolled through the search engine and when the first page failed, he went to the second then so on and do forth. He sighed and closed the search engine, letting the picture of Sam and Mina take it's place.

Sam leaned forward and closed the laptop, she couldn't look at the picture right now, it reminded her too much of the good times and it could ruin her resolve.

"Any ideas?" Jeannie asked, she had snuck close enough along with Dylan to see their meeting place while Trevor remained seated at the table with the same nervous look.

"I thought finding out what the place looked like would give us an idea on how to go about this but the landscape gives them an advantage." Cale tapped his index finger on the hard counter top.

Sam looked at the space where the laptops screen had been. As if imagining the image of their meeting place was still there. She imagined what it would be like to fight there, even though Arthur's group would have the chance for a surprise attack, the landscape looked considerably hard to fight in if one was between the trees.

Maybe they could use that to *their* advantage.

"We have to make sure that if there's a fight, we go into the woods to take them on." Sam said finally and she could feel everyone's gazes on her. She turned her head to see what they were thinking and all of them looked confused other than Ari and Cale who obviously understood where she was coming from.

"If we're in there we can use the trees to take cover if need be." Cale tapped his finger one last time before coming to a stop.

"And we can use them as weapons if need be," Ari nudged Sam's arm. "Punch them and knock them down to block their way."

Sam inhaled. "If only it could go that smoothly." As she exhaled she gave them a direction that she was going to be adamant on. "I want us to stay in a group, no splitting up even if it turns into a fight."

They didn't need to ask her reasoning behind it, it was obvious that their enemies were going to try splitting them up if it came to a fight. Which it obviously was going to.

If they stayed together, they could protect one another. There was no fighting fair in this battle, two of their group equaled one of Arthur's.

Sam's eyes drifted outside to see the sky turning orange, she didn't realize that the time had gone by so fast. She looked at the digital clock on the stove to see that it was past six.

Time was another enemy, it went too fast, especially when one had to prepare for the fight of their life.

"We might as well make dinner then go to sleep." Cale suggested and Sam chanced a look at him to see that he was looking from the window to the clock as well. "There's nothing more we can do to prepare with the time we have, we need to rest."

He was right, they didn't need clouded minds resulting from lack of sleep. Though Sam was sure none of them would sleep much tonight.

They agreed even though it was easy to tell that they all wanted to spar more. They understood the need to prepare themselves mentally just as much as they had to physically.

Sam took one bite out of the hamburger that Emily had volunteered to make for all of them as she wanted to do something to distract herself. Jeannie and Kira had helped but the three of them were distracted and burned most of the meat.

Sam swallowed her food but felt like she was going to be sick. Not from it tasting bad, but from the nervousness swelling in her belly.

After a few long moments, she closed her eyes and listened to the clatter of dishes as she sat in the living room. No one spoke, maybe they had so much to say but feared to say it.

She blinked her eyes open, her body felt heavy and a white light made her squint in the dark room. She picked her head up from the arm of the couch to see an empty living room aside from Cale who was sitting on the other end of the coach watching the television with tired eyes.

A blanket fell from her shoulders as she sat up. "I didn't fall asleep, did I?" She asked sheepishly.

"You did." Cale replied with a tired smile. "I don't blame you though, everyone else went as soon as they were done eating."

"What about you?" she gestured to the tv then rubbed her eyes, they were still heavy with sleep. "You could have woken me up if I was in your way."

She was on his *bed* after all.

He shook his head. "It's fine, It's a little comforting having someone here."

Her jaw slackened as she turned her head from Cale to the television.

"It is." She agreed.

The clock under the screen read that it was past midnight, they were to leave in five hours to meet their fate.

"Can I?" Cale asked and she brought her attention back to him to see that he was holding the remote so that it was facing the television.

She nodded, she wasn't even watching the thing and if anything, it bothered her heavy eyes. Cale pressed the button and the screen went blank, engulfing them in darkness. Her heart thumped as she remembered the vast wasteland in her dream-state.

The blanket slid more and she looked down as her eyes adjusted to the dark. She realized that it was big enough to cover the both of them but it only rested on her.

She pulled the fabric from the floor and flung it on him as he rested his head onto the arm like she had. He lifted his head, "You don't have to give me any." he assured her but she continued to feed more onto him.

"It's big enough." she finished and leaned back onto the couch like she had before.

"Thanks." he rested his head back down and stretched out more. The couch was long but even with Sam's knees to her chest, his feet still brushed hers.

"I'm sorry." he tried pulling them away from her but he was too tall.

"It's fine." she assured with a small chuckle. "It's the least of my worries."

"Yeah…" His voice drifted.

She cuddled her head into the arm while looking into the darkness that spread around the room. She could hear the creaks of the others upstairs and the old house settling. The time was shining red under the television. She closed her eyes and ignored it, though she could still see the red light through her eyes lids.

"...We can do this." Cale's voice came through the darkness but he didn't sound convinced.

Sam could feel his feet shaking against hers, it made her aware that her heart was thumping hard against her ribcage.

"I'd like to think so." she wrapped her arms around her chest as if she was comforting herself.

She didn't know how it happend, maybe it was the exhaustion from all the stress, but she fell asleep again.

Sam stood in front of the sliding doors looking out into the backyard where they had spent countless hours preparing for what was about to happen.

She knew this day would come but she had hoped that they would have more time. She also found herself lucky that Arthur even gave them the amount of time that they had.

Oddly she no longer felt nervous, she was numb to it all. Maybe that would change but she relished in the feeling for now.

She inhaled sharply as she closed her eyes and turned away from the sight before it got too hard to do so. She was dressed in a pair of jeans and a navy blue shirt, there wasn't anything that she could think of to wear that would improve her fighting skills.

She opened her eyes and brought her attention to Cale and Emily who were looking at the knives in the cutlery drawer. Emily picked a particularly sharp one up and examined its edge.

"I know our nails are just as sharp but in the small chance that I choke and can't transform, I'm going to bring some of these." she explained as she brought the knife to her pocket, careful not to place it where she would stab herself.

"Good idea." Cale agreed, his eyes looked tired but he was wide awake. He turned to Sam. "Is everyone ready?"

It was 6:00am and everyone had been up since 4:30 getting themselves physically and mentally ready. It would take them an hour to get there and their meeting time was 7:30am. They needed to hurry before Arthur sent his people to the house and slaughtered them all.

On cue the rest of the gang entered the kitchen from the living room. "We're ready." Kira pointed to her ears to let them know that she was listening.

"I'm grabbing a knife too." Ari stepped between Emily and Cale and grabbed a cleaver from the opened drawer.

"Grab me one." Kira demanded and Daniel asked for one as well. Cam seemed confident in his ability so he opted out.

Trevor, Jeannie, and Dylan were standing at the back and Sam could tell that they were just as nervous as their comrades that were going.

"I'm going." Dylan announced suddenly and everyone lifted their heads to meet him.

"You don't have-" Emily started.

"But I want to." He interrupted before she could finish, he was nervous but he had a serious air to him. Sam nodded, she wasn't going to stop him, it was his choice to make. "We need to get going."

She stepped through them and made her way to the living room then down the narrow hall leading to the front door. The others followed her silently and even though she still felt numb, she couldn't ignore the pit in the bottom of her stomach. She was sure the others had one too.

They stepped out into the orange hue of the rising sun and Trevor and Jeannie hugged and gave their well wishes to everyone.

Jeannie stayed by her brothers side with tears in her eyes. "You better come back." she demanded shakily.

"I will." he tried to muster some confidence.

"He will." Sam shot in as Trevor pulled away from her. "I'll protect him with my life so he can come back to you."

She returned her sight to Trevor. "I'm certain you'll be safe here but If we don't return by tonight I want you two to get out of here."

He nodded, his jaw was clenched and his face was pale. She clasped his shoulder then backed away. Cale walked to her with Emily in tow, it was time to go.

They agreed to leave the motorcycle behind and to take the Jeep even though it wouldn't fit all of them comfortably. Cale got into the drivers side and while Sam thought Emily would want to ride shotgun, she gave the right to Sam. She said it was because her mind was too cloudy to give directions. They had decided to leave the cellphone with Trevor and Jeannie in case they needed it. Sam jumped in the front with Cale and Emily sat in the back with Ari and kira who was sitting on Ari's lap and Dylan sat behind Cale. Daniel and Cam sat in the hatch in the back of the Jeep since they weren't too big. They got one last look at Trevor and Jeannie as Cale backed out then turned to go down the long driveway. They turned onto the main road and Sam directed Cale to go to the highway and southbound.

The majority of the ride was silent aside from the sighs and the rustles of a seat as someone moved. Sam looked out the window as the landscape flew by her, it was the first and very well could be last time she'd see it. Her breath hitched and she realized that she was gripping onto the map a little too hard. She moved her gaze from the window, she couldn't bare to look at the beautiful landscape anymore. Especially since she felt like she'd be leaving the world soon.

They were far from the highway now and drawing closer to their destination. She looked down to the map, she wasn't good at reading them but this one was pretty straight forward. As she looked with the corner of her eye, she saw Cale's hand shaking to the point that he had to bring his other hand to the steering wheel.

Her chest felt heavy as she focused more than she needed to on the map. She couldn't look at anyone right now, she didn't want to see the fear on their faces that grew stronger as they drew closer to their destination.

She swallowed to dampen her dry throat. "Turn at the next right."

Cale followed her direction and turned onto the final road leading to the farmhouse. Sam was starting to understand why Arthur had chosen this place: There were barely any passersby and it got even more secluded as they drew closer.

But she had known that already.

They drove five minutes down the road and Sam could see the farmhouse in the distance and she didn't need to tell them as she looked to Cale and saw his eyes narrow.

"That's it." Cam's voice shook as he started to choke.

Cale turned into the dirt driveway, the rocks crinkling under the tires until he came to a stop beside the house. The group just sat there taking in their surroundings, looking for any sign of movement. Cale was the first to open his door to get out and Sam followed. She stood beside a window and she looked into it as the girls got out on her side: The inside matched the out, the wallpaper was peeling and there was junk all over the floor and tables. She backed away and looked at her comrades.

"What now?" Daniel inquired but none of them knew what to do. Aside from the date, time, and place there was no direction on what they were supposed to do when they got there.

Cale glanced down at the wristwatch that he had bought during one of their runs.

"It's 7:27am."

They were only a few short minutes from their meeting time but one would think that Arthur and his group would have been there before hand.

They stood in the shaded area around the Jeep, the tree beside them creaking as a strong gust of wind hit. The final minutes ticked by and they were starting to get restless. Sam glanced at Cale who she realized was already looking at her with a wondering expression.

She was about to speak when she heard a familiar voice: "*Come into woods.*" Carma's direction sounded like a whisper.

Their eyes widened as Emily stepped closer to Cale. "Was that?!" she whispered urgently to him.

"Yes." he looked into the woods and swallowed. "...That was

definitely Carma."

"That was your friend?" Cam shot forward to meet Cale and Emily.

"Why is she telling us what to do?" Kira looked between the three former cellmates.

"It's all according to Arthur's plan." Sam started walking towards the small clearing that led to the woods.

Was the battle that Arthur wanted between Sam and Carma going to happen today?

She walked past the old barn as the rest caught up. She wanted to stop, to turn and run, but her legs kept moving on their own.

She couldn't turn back now.

Twigs snapped as they treaded through the trees, the ground was covered with leaves of orange, yellow, and brown. They didn't know where they were going, but Carma had said to go into the woods and that's what they were doing. Sam heard a noise just ahead and she stopped dead in her boots and Cale, who was beside her, did the same. It happened so fast that the others almost ran into them.

Carma stepped out from behind a particularly large oak tree, a smile spread across her face. Her blonde hair was cut to her shoulders and she looked stronger plus there was an air of confidence coming from her that could be felt even in the distance between them. She was wearing black skinny jeans and ankle high boots plus a pink long sleeved shirt. Everything except the shirt was the exact opposite of what she would wear before. This girl wasn't Carma, her second personality still had it's hold on her.

"Come closer." she chuckled as she motioned for them to come.

A red flag flashed in Sam's head but she cautiously moved forward like the rest.

They came to a stop ten feet away from her and for a moment, they just stared at each other. Carma with a small grin and Cale and Emily with anxious expressions while the others looked on nervously. Sam cocked her head to take a look at Emily and Cale: They looked like they wanted to run to Carma, to see if she was alright, to beg her to go back to normal.

But they knew better.

Sam looked away as her chest tightened at the thought of how hard it was to not help the person you cared for. She brought her attention forward again to see Carma's blue eyes on her, she was giving her a look that would make even the strongest man in the world tremble with fear.

"Why are you doing this?" Emily asked finally, her voice shaking. "T-This isn't you."

Carma's eyes rolled to her friend, "This is me Emily, no matter how bad you want to deny it, I'm what I always wanted to be." she smiled as she curled her fingers into a fist. "I always wanted to be stronger." She barely touched the tree beside her but it split in half when her fist came in contact with it.

Sam covered her ears as the tree cracked and whined as it split from it's bottom half and fell onto the branches of the trees around it.

"This is the kind of strength I've always hoped for," she brought her undamaged fist to the front of her and examined it. "And it's finally mine thanks to Arthur."

"Arthur didn't do this for you." Cale sounded like he was scolding a sibling. "He did this for himself."

Carma considered him with squinted eyes. "You're always so noble, so smart, you were always ahead of me but now our positions have changed." she cocked her head to the side as she chuckled. "You think I don't know that Arthur's using me? I don't care and I know far more about his plans than any of you do."

"Carma please!" Emily begged. "We're your friends!"

"You have the strength you wanted, there's no reason for you to be with him." Cale tried to keep his composure but it was slowly breaking as his lip trembled.

The rest watched as the three friends confronted each other, the tension causing them to move away.

"You're right that I could just leave, but Arthur offers so much more than you can imagine." Carma explained, "You can join us and see for yourself." Her blonde hair blew in the wind along with the leaves on the trees and one fell in front of her as her grin widened.

Sam gritted her teeth. "Being openly manipulated by someone is far from being a strength."

Carma's smile disappeared so fast that it was as if someone had smacked it off of her and her glare burned a hole in Sam but she held true.

"Tell me, Carma." She took a step forward, the leaves breaking under her feet. "Why are we here? Where's your manipulator?"

"You cun-" Carma growled but caught herself before she could finish the word.

Her face went emotionless as she brought her gaze to the treetops overhead for a second then back to the people in front of her. "So none of you have the intention of joining us, correct?" she asked simply, her tone girlish.

She already knew the answer.

Sam shook her head and turned to see Cale do the same with his jaw clenched.

"No... but Carma-" Emily started.

"None of you?" Carma tsked as she shook her head in fake disappointment. "That's too bad," she grinned as she looked to the treetops again. "For *you* that is."

They shot their heads up in time to see twenty people jumping from the trees above and the newcomers surrounded them.

Chapter 17

"Hello, friend!" Camilla landed in front of Sam, her eyes white and filled with joy. "I've missed you!"

Sam took a step back as she looked around. Each of her comrades were turned towards the newcomers as they circled them. She didn't know all of their faces, but she recognized the loud mouthed man that she had beaten in the cave and the woman and the man they had blindsided. In front of Cale was Kellan who turned from Cale to meet Sam's gaze, his eyes human.

"I've waited for this." A mischievous grin appeared on his face.

Her comrades started to move and her heart thumped.

"Don't attack!" she demanded with her arm out as if it could stop them. They stopped dead in their tracks but not before the gargoyle in front of them brought up a fighting stance.

"What the hell do you want? You know we're not going to join you." Sam's voice was filled with venom.

"We knew this would happen but came anyway so you might as well tell us what your master is planning." Cale directed as he didn't waver from one of the most terrifying gargoyles in front of him.

"It's simple-" Camilla licked her teeth as if they were a snack about to be devoured.

"You're here for what we promised." Carma started forward slowly then added speed. "To test our power!" She lunged at Sam and

Camilla stepped out of the way just in time for Sam to take the hit. Sam brought her arms to an *X* in front of her in time to protect her chest as Carma's foot smashed into her crossed arms. She flew back off her feet and twisted and turned as she hit tree after tree, branch after branch, until she landed on her side about fifty feet away from the others.

She could hear them yelling from where she once stood with them and she gasped as the pain in her arms seared. The parts of her body that had hit the trees on the way there screamed with pain as well. A trail of blood trailed from her nose as she laid face first on a bed of leaves.

Small moans escaped her lips as she forced her arms to prop herself up and as she did, she was met Carma's feet as she stepped into the small clearing that she had landed in.

Sam could smell pine coming from the trees that she had broken with her body as she shook her way to her feet. She almost fell over as soon as she got up.

"That's all it took for you to get like that?" Carma teased with a brow raised.

"Thanks to the fucking trees." Sam spat and out came a tooth.

She hadn't felt pain like this aside from when she was changed into a gargoyle. She cracked her neck as her body rushed to heal itself.

She would've appreciated Cale's healing right now.

She had to get back to the others, she couldn't let them face their enemies alone. She had made a promise to Jeannie and she intended to keep it.

"Nuh-uh." Carma shook her head as she stepped in front of the trail of broken trees she had made with Sam's body. She couldn't even see the others from here.

What a terrifying amount of power Carma had used.

"Cale!" Sam screamed. "Emily!"

She could hear the distant sound of battle and her heart raced.

"Please Carma, they'll kill them!" she rushed to her and grabbed ahold of her shirt. "They're your friends!" she let go and tried getting past her but Carma knocked her to the ground with a hard punch. She had one eye closed from the pain as she brought her gaze up as Carma walked closer. "You should worry about yourself." Her lips twitched into a smile.

She brought her leg up for a kick but Sam rushed to her feet and jumped back with anger filling her bones. She listened to the screams, the growls, and the sound of pain when someone got hit.

But no matter how hard she listened, she couldn't tell who it was, she wanted so badly to help her comrades. Her face twisted with anger as she looked at her opponent who was once a friend, who she hoped was still a friend.

"Finally." Carma grinned and her eyes turned white along with her veins as they popped around her eyes.

Sam allowed the pressure to overtake her and the power purred as she released some of it.

Her eyes matched Carma's and it was time to see if they matched in strength as well.

Cale took a hard blow in the stomach from Kellan as he tried running from their fight to help Emily with hers. He gritted his teeth as he ignored the pain and ducked under Kellan which proved to be hard since he had a good amount of height on him. His vision blurred as he struggled to see where Emily had gone, she was in a fight with Camilla who had a significant advantage over her. Cale was in the same predicament only he had more skill and strength.

Kellan appeared in front of him with an entertained smile and punched him square in the face and he fell to the ground. He could taste blood in his mouth as it fell from his nose.

They had been tricked, but in a way they hadn't been. They knew what they were getting into but hadn't expected it to go this way.

He could hear the loud crashes of Sam and Carma's fight a distance away, the power Carma used was amazing but he couldn't believe the anger and animosity she had behind it.

Sam took the blow but still got up to fight.

So this was the power of a white eyed gargoyle?

He turned and blocked a punch Kellan was about to land on him and Kellan smiled "You're not going to use your power?" he knocked Cale down with his other arm."Disappointing." he stepped over a branch that Sam had knocked down with her body.

"You're not using yours either, why're you holding back?" Cale pressed as he got up.

Kellan simply chuckled. "Think what you will about me but I don't want to fight you when you're not at your best. I'm a fair man and you need your power to come close to a little of mine."

It was true, Cale needed to use his power to fight but the heat of the fight made it almost impossible to concentrate on what he needed to transform.

He wished he had brought a knife like Emily and the others but it wouldn't be of much use, it would cut but they would heal right away. He needed to use his gargoyle nails, teeth, and strength.

Another bang could be heard in the distance as a tree fell and he could hear the sound of Sam's pained cry. He perked up, he wanted to help Sam, Emily, and his new found friends but he had to help himself.

"You hear that over there?" Kellan closed his eyes like he was listening to a symphony. "Who do you think will win?" he kneeled in front of Cale, the twigs breaking under his knee. "You think Carma will kill Sam or Sam will kill her?"

Kellan's devious smile made it obvious that he was trying to mess with him but Cale would be lying to himself if he said he didn't think about the girls killing each other.

The Carma he knew wouldn't kill Sam and the little hope he had that she could still overcome her second personality still burned in his heart. That part of Carma wouldn't allow who she was now to do so but he also posed the question if Sam would lose control and kill Carma.

He believed in Sam. He trusted her to bring Carma back to them if they couldn't do it themselves. Maybe she was what Carma needed, Sam's definition of weakness and strength were different than Carma's. Sam's fiery attitude would help drive the nail that was needed to bring Carma back to her senses.

Cale ignored Kellan's entertained face as he got up and Kellan did the same. There was an ache rising in his chest as the power rose within him. His heart rate quickened to a pace that he never imagined it could go. Kellan came at him again and he blocked it almost effortlessly as the black ink filled his eyes. The smell of pine needles, pollen, and broken bark on the trees around them filled his nose, almost overwhelming him.

Kellan smiled so wide that his mouth opened and he clicked his tongue. "About time."

Kellan turned up his power as well, his eyes turning white and the two went at each other.

Cale used all of the moves he had learned in basic training, the martial arts Sam had taught him, and the defensive moves he had learned on the web.

Everytime he had woken up early to spar with Sam filled his mind along with the training sessions he had with the others. He was outclassed by Kellan in every way possible but he kept fighting and his claws barely grazed him as he side swiped him.

In the corner of his eyes he saw Emily swing the knife she had brought with her at Camilla. Her sharp teeth bared and her brows furrowed together in anger but the weapon proved to be of no use as Camilla caught the blade with her mouth and it snapped between her teeth.

Emily fell back as she tried to retreat and fell over a stray branch. Camilla's high pitched laugh could be heard through the trees as she went in for an attack.

"NO!" Cale rushed forward, stepping past Kellan as he was inches away from being slashed by his dagger-like nails. It was like time had slowed down as he ran to his friend, the girl that was like a little sister to him. The girl who was always there for him and he for her.

He had his fear of losing control and it made him hold back, but now was not the time.

If he was going to save Emily, Carma, and everyone else, he had to push past his fears.

He had to become a different person.

The power coursed through his veins and the pressure in his eyes, fingertips, and ears heightened and an unfamiliar sensation emerged in his back. Just over his shoulder blades gray wings formed and spread as wide as he was tall. Almost as if the control over them was programed into him, he flapped his new limbs and they brought him between Camilla and Emily just before Camilla landed her deadly blow. He curled his wings around the front of him so they would take the hit and he gnawed at his lip as he felt the pain in his foreign limbs.

Emily's eyes were wide and her face was filled with terror from her near death experience. Her expression remained the same as she saw the man that had been her friend since they were pre-teens with wings coming from his back. She breathed heavily as she examined the rips in his shirt where the wings had sprouted through, the flesh on them was stone gray, like a gargoyle. The skin around his shoulder blades had also turned gray.

"Cale?" she squeaked over Camilla's ear-splitting laughter as the attacker backed away, removing her claws from Cale's wings as she did so.

Emily could see Camilla under Cale's wing as he pulled them away from the front of him. Camilla's movements were loose, she was like a puppet that a marinate had no control over.

"That's gold!" she giggled, "Our boy has got his wings!" she looked close to someone who belonged in an insane asylum.

Blood dripped from the claw sized wounds that Camilla had made in the middle of Cale's wings but as Emily watched, they began to heal.

The sounds of the battle around them slowed then stopped as they looked on at the new development.

Emily dared to look from Camilla and Cale to get a look at the people around them: Her friends were looking on with pale faces and blood and dirt covered their limbs.

Ari and Daniel looked the most beaten up as their shirts were stained with blood and they looked like they were having trouble staying upright.

All of them achieved their partial transformations and their black as ink eyes stared at Cale as the rest of the black eyed gargoyles on the opposing side looked on with the same shock. They obviously didn't expect one of them to be on the level of having wings.

Emily thought of the image on the website that Cale had found, he looked almost identical to the gargoyle they had caught in the picture.

Fear washed through her as she thought of the other image, which was much more terrifying.

"I have to say," Kellan came into view and Cale glared at him while the others looked on nervously. "I didn't expect you to come so far in two weeks." the noise from Sam and Carma's fight could still be heard in the background, the magnitude of it was nerve wracking.

Camilla looked in the direction that the girls were fighting with a gratifying smile, she longed to be there.

"Did I tell you to stop fighting?" Kellan wondered and his lackeys continued, catching their opponents off guard.

Kellan brought his attention back to Cale and Emily as she got shakily to her feet. She noticed the wounds on Cale's wings were only a width of a finger nail now and they closed as she watched.

"We won't even need our wings to keep up with you." Kellan gloated as Camilla made her way beside him and placed a hand on his shoulder. "A cocky attitude won't get you anywhere my friend, even though there's truth to your words." She snickered.

"Two on two sounds like fun." Kellan ignored her, he only had eyes for the fight ahead of him, it was merely a game to him and nothing more.

Emily who had enough time to concentrate now that Camilla wasn't coming at her every five seconds finally willed the power out of her. She breathed in through her nose and out of her mouth until the pressure evened into her eyes, ears, and nails.

"It does sound like fun." Cale agreed, his voice coming out as a growl. He looked down to see if Emily was ready, "I'll protect you." he assured her, his tone much softer.

She couldn't believe the creature beside her was Cale with his pitch black eyes and teeth that were so sharp that they hung from his mouth. Not to mention his gray wings and the rest of his skin had turned gray to match them. The sight had brought fear into her but she knew that looks didn't matter, he was still Cale and the fight had to go on.

She nodded and brought her gaze forward to the cocky faces of Kellan and Camilla. She flicked her nails into her fingertips then out again like she had before.

Like a storm, intense and unpredictable, the four started their fight.

Blood poured from Sam's mouth that had resulted from Carma's foot to gut attack. She wiped the thick liquid from her mouth while ignoring the ache in her insides.

She ducked from another kick and rolled on the ground over the branches and leaves then in one fluid motion, she propped up on one knee and pushed up from the ground with her other foot.

By the time she got back up, Carma was over her and preparing for another swing. Sam's eyes zoned in on her movement's. It was too easy.

She grabbed ahold of Carma's arm and pulled it behind her back as she stepped behind her. She bent it in an uncomfortable way while keeping a good grip on her other arm.

Carma thrashed and pulled so hard that Sam unintentionally dug her nails into her skin to hold on and blood dripped from the small wounds.

"Fucking bitch." Carma growled as she fell forward, bringing Sam with her.

Doing so gave her the time to get out of Sam's grip and as she rose from the ground, she kicked Sam in the stomach again, making her roll ten feet away. Sam landed against a tree but not hard enough to break it this time but it did knock the wind out of her.

She gasped as she tried rushing back to her feet but her arms gave out and she collapsed. She tasted the iron in her mouth as a fresh batch of blood came up her throat. Her white eyes were now bloodshot.

"So weak." Carma spat as she made her way to her, she had a broken branch in her hand and she looked it up and down.

Sam pulled herself up and leaned against the tree, her back screaming with displeasure from the movement.

She cared for Carma and wanted her to come to her senses but beating the shit out of her wouldn't help with that. Besides, Carma seemed like she had so much more control than her.

She watched as Carma swung the branch like it was a walking stick, the thing was wide enough to knock a grown man out if it were to fall on him, maybe even kill him.

Carma stopped and admired her handy work on Sam and she was sure that she looked like shit, she definitely felt like it. Through all of the pain Carma had caused her, a question rose: Why wasn't she going in for the kill? Arthur said that he wanted to see which one of them was stronger and he didn't say anything about killing being off limits.

The man wasn't even here to see the fight for himself, so it obviously wasn't that important to him, though Sam felt that was stupid to think.

He was here, but where?

"Am I to your liking?" Sam's voice was hoarse and the air she used to speak caused her pain.

Carma snickered, the sound was high pitched and Sam felt like she had spent too much time with Camilla.

"I would like you to look worse." she admitted as she swung the branch only to let it go then catch it again.

"Then why are you holding back?" Sam wondered.

Carma blinked, "I'm not-"

"Come on," Sam drawled. "You've been with Arthur and his group for two weeks, you should have been able to cause me more damage if you were serious."

It was true, there were so many opportunities that Carma could have landed a finishing blow. There were many times Sam thought she was going to but she only received a smaller brunt of the attack at the last second.

"I don't want to kill you right away." Carma assured her with anger and a bit of amusement. "That wouldn't be fun."

"Or maybe the real Carma is restricting you from doing so." Sam suggested and in a flash, the branch ravaged the left side of her face as Carma struck her.

The pain made her double over as she pressed her palm to her cheek but it only made the pain worse. She moaned as tears emerged from her right eye as the left already started to swell shut. The pain pounded harder with each heartbeat, she never thought she'd want the artery to stop. She groaned as something large fell in front of her and she didn't need to look to know that it was the branch.

"Does it look like the *real* Carma is stopping me?" Carma hissed.

Sam tried to reply but the pain in her jaw was excruciating, all she managed to get out was a couple of squeaky moans. She didn't want to imagine what would have happened to her if she had taken that blow as a human.

She heard a twig break in front of her and before she could think to do anything, Carma had her by the collar of her shirt. She pulled her from the ground and slammed her against the tree and Sam whined as the pain flared.

"Look at me." Carma demanded.

She didn't even realize that her un-swollen eye was closed until Carma had told her to look at her. She obliged and her right eyelid shook as she opened it. She tried to open the left but it was far too swollen to even attempt. In her right eye she could see nothing but stars until it adjusted to the light and she could feel her body already trying to heal the newest wounds.

"You look better now." Carma tightened her grip on her collar. "Let me tell you something…" She began with a snarl. "I *am* Carma." she leaned and whispered in Sam's left ear, her breath hitting her wounded cheek and it ached. Hearing was difficult from the damage the branch had caused.

Sam swallowed, she had to will herself to speak. "I-I know that you created this personality after you drowned, C-Cale told me." she inhaled sharply and her throat stung from doing so. "You thought you were weak because you couldn't save yourself. That you would have died in a worthless way if someone hadn't saved you. So you made this personality to save yourself from those thoughts." her left eye started to open as it healed further.

Carma brought her other hand up and wrapped it around Sam's throat, dropping the hand that was on her collar. She gripped hard enough to make it hard for Sam to breath but not enough to choke her. "You don't know a fucking thing." she growled, her nails digging into Sam's skin as anger coursed through her. "Cale's words are misguided, he wants to believe that I'm this sweet girl that would cower over the sight of a bug, but this is who I truly am… Not the weak girl you met in that cell."

It was true that she wasn't that weak girl, though Sam thought she wasn't weak before.

She didn't think the girl she met would be able to fight like this, to control the power given to her with ease. Sam wanted to tell her that being kind wasn't a weakness, that being the strongest wasn't necessary.

When she was about to say it, she realized how much of a hypocrite she was.

She wanted the strength to protect others, to selfishly protect herself, even though she didn't create another personality to do so. She didn't want to die, no one did, but she came here and risked her life along with the others.

"...I get it." She breathed and her eye opened more.

"What do you get?" Carma challenged harshly, her brows furrowed and her eyes narrowed.

It was odd seeing them like that due to the lack of iris and pupil.

Sam heaved as the pain in her gut caused by an earlier attack seared. "I-I get where you're coming from." her lip trembled, causing her words to slur. "We both want to protect and be protected, but sometimes you feel like the only person who can do that is yourself. I chose my path by staying with the others to learn how to fight and to hone these powers while you joined Arthur to learn how to use your power to protect yourself. But I know you're not as selfish as that…" She swallowed and her chest pounded. "Y-You're here to protect the others."

She had noticed that during their fight that Carma's eyes would twitch back to the other battle.

To check undoubtedly check on her friends.

"You're only fighting me because it's what you've been told to do." Sam finished and her voice evened slightly.

"….Even if what you say is true, you still don't think I'm *Carma*." Sarcasm didn't go well with this Carma but her twisted expression said it all. It was the face of a troubled person who wanted nothing more than to be understood.

"You are," Sam choked out as Carma's grip tightened around her throat. "You are Carma."

Her grip loosened and Sam could feel it shake as she did so.

There was an inner turmoil in Carma that was reaching its peak.

Sam brought her arm up and gently gripped her wrist. "You're Carma, even though you're different from how I met you and even though the doctors told everyone you're not, you are."

"You think you know more than trained professionals?" Carma scoffed with an entertained expression but a drop of nervous sweat fell from her brow, giving her true feelings away.

"I know that second personalities are real and they stem from the originals emotions… So in that sense, you're still Carma."

Carma's hand trembled against her skin, the hold she once had on her was nothing more than a brush of skin now. She dropped her hand to her side and backed away a step, her eyes wide with emotion and tears threatened to fall from them.

Sam's face ached as she relaxed against the tree and her eye opened a bit more.

"I can't say that I understand you completely, that would be wrong of me. But I think about how weak I am and of how I want to be stronger." She took a look at Carma's expression to see if it was ok to go on: She was looking at the ground with a glossed over look and Sam took that as an ok to keep going. "I work at it but I feel like I'm going nowhere, life feels like a road that leads down the same path no matter what you do… But I am no longer human."

"You're right." Carma's tone had changed but it was familiar, it was the same soft voice she had used when they had met in the cave.

Sam's eyes softened as she looked at the girl who had helped her in the cave, who had cared for her even though they had just met. She remembered the fear in her eyes when she found out her fate and she suddenly felt pity. Not for Carma, but for herself as she was sure that she had looked the same.

"We're not so different, you and I." Carma said softly, confirming that she and Sam were thinking the same. She gnawed on her lip as Sam looked on, waiting for what she was going to do next. Sam had the feeling that the fight was over, she had done it… The Carma she knew was back.

"Arthur is so intrigued with you…" Carma said suddenly and she looked Sam straight in the eyes and Sam's heart thumped.

Where was this going?

"He kept saying how it's fate for you and him to meet again, that I would help with his goal." Her eyes twitched. "It only took a few times training with him to realize that he wasn't interested in me, he only cared about what I could do for him… and that was to test you."

Her eyes hardened again as she stepped closer and Sam tensed. "I'm not sure what his plan is, but I'm sure of one thing-" she smacked her hand on the tree only a few inches from Sam's head and the bark cracked from the force she had used. "I realized his goal is you."

"Me?" Sams heart raced, it didn't make sense, they had only met four weeks ago. There was no way that in such a short amount of time that he would find her essential to his plan. Carma was so much more talented and she was already on his side.

Why would *she* be his goal?

"It pisses me off," Carma growled as she changed back to her savage personality.

The hand that had smashed against the tree swung and grabbed Sam by her long ponytail. She pulled her head towards the sky in an unnatural way.

"You think you're better than me." It wasn't a question, it was statement.

"N-no." Sam breathed as the roots of her hair pulled against her scalp but Carma ignored her.

"I thought I finally found someone who thinks I'm strong, that I'm worth having around, but he's more interested in a weak bitch like you." she pulled harder, the back of Sam's head scrapping against the tree.

Her hair tie broke as Carma's nails cut into it. She gritted her teeth, the pain didn't have the effect on her that it should have, it only annoyed her. A growl escaped her throat as she jumped up and wrapped her legs around Carma's waist. She allowed her body to fall to the side and Carma, who wasn't prepared for her weight, fell with her.

Carma finally let go of Sam's hair as she went to brace herself and it fell into Sam's face as she landed. She blew the locks out of the way as she jumped to her feet and rushed backwards, being careful not trip over the branch that Carma had used to hit her.

"I'll kill you-" Carma rose to her feet in an unnatural way, her limbs twisted as anger filled her.

Sam had only felt this kind of fear one other time: When Arthur showed a little of his power.

She tried to will herself to move, to get the hell out of there, but her limbs froze with fear. Carma's human features began to contort while her gargoyle features extended. The back of her shirt ripped as wings emerged from her back, the same Sam had seen in the picture that Cale had found.

"If I kill you... Arthur will be done for... His plan won't work and he'll be forced to leave Emily and Cale alone." Her words were distorted but the end of each syllable ran off of her tongue like silk.

Sam urged herself to move and she started to run as Carma kneeled to launch at her. Before she could do so however, Camilla jumped from a tree above and with her nails extended, she slashed at Carma's throat and her head fell to the ground with a thud.

Chapter 18

A blood curdling scream could be heard echoing through the trees and Sam didn't realize it belonged to her until Camilla pressed a blood stained finger to her lips, signaling for her be quiet. She popped her tongue out and licked her finger as Sam collapsed to her knees.

Laying only a few feet away from her was Carma's body. Blood was pouring from her neck where her head should have been. Her head had rolled a foot from her body until a broken branch had stopped it.

"You can't kill her." Camilla's voice was silky as she spoke to Carma's body then her eyes drifted to her head and she made her way to it.

She placed a foot on top of it as Sam wheezed, her stomach lurching as Camilla rolled it over so she could see Carma's final expression: It was still filled with hatred towards Sam.

Sam vomited and fell forward on her hands and she gripped her gut as tears formed in her eyes.

"Don't cry for her, she was just another worthless pawn." Camilla popped her fingers into her mouth while she talked, making her words slur.

"Why?!" Sam shrieked, her head shooting up and she laid her intense but traumatized gaze on Camilla. She tried not to look at Carma's body and her head that should have been attached to it, she couldn't bare to.

"Because she was going to kill you," Camilla cocked her head and smiled like what she had done was the equivalent of stopping a man from stealing an elderly woman's purse. Her pointed teeth were stained with blood as she licked them. "You should thank me."

Sam's tear filled eyes narrowed. "You killed her! She was your comrade!"

Camilla's smile disappeared and was replaced by a grimace "She didn't mean shit to me or anyone else. "she spread her arms out and it looked like she was waiting for a hug in return for saving Sam's life. "You're far more important than her, she was only a pawn to test your power." She rolled her eyes, "But *fuck* I'm disappointed in you." she cocked her head side to side and dropped her arms as she pondered to herself. "Though I guess it's acceptable since you've been training yourself while Carma had help."

Anger... No, *rage* coursed through Sam's veins, it caused her power to flare and she could no longer tell if she was shaking from the shock of Carma's demise or the power threatening to spill over.

"Why?" her voice shook like the rest of her. "Why am I so fucking important?!"

Camilla watched as Sam's anger boiled over, she didn't care much though, what could someone as weak as Sam do to someone so strong?

She took a step towards Sam and shrugged, "He doesn't tell us anything, only that you are not to be killed." She laid her left palm out and punched it with her right in realization.

"Aha!" her eyes lit up, "Maybe he wants to kill you himself!" she nodded dramatically. "Yup, that must be the only reasonable explanation for wanting someone as weak as you on our side! Saying you're important is just an excuse!"

Sam's breaths came out heavy and with each exhale, a growl escaped her lips and Camilla noticed this and her signature grin returned.

"We can ask him if you'd like!" She turned and Sam noticed she was going for Carma's head again. Sam unconsciously set her gaze onto it: Carma's eyes had returned to their human color but what was once bright blue was now gray and glossed over.

"I just want to bring this with me." she sang as she bent over and grabbed Carma's blood stained hair.

Sam began to hyperventilate, she was shaking to the point that her hands could no longer hold her up and she fell on her elbows and heaved.

She wanted revenge, she wanted to have Carma back, she wanted for this to have never happened. Her mind was in a whirlwind of thoughts and as she gazed down at the leaves under her, she realized that she wasn't really seeing them, all she saw was red.

Everything went blank and her shaking stopped, she was no longer aware of what she was doing but she could feel her body moving on it's own. She launched forward and in the next second she felt her right arm reach into something warm and wet.

A pained moan could be heard directly in front of her.

Her hand wrapped around something and the thing pulsed in her palm. She could hear the rustle of leaves as the wind blew around her and it tickled her skin as her sight slowly came back and all of her wounds healed.

She realized what had happened before her vision returned.

In front of her was Camilla, her head rolled to the side and Sam could see the glossed over look in her eyes as they stared into nothing. Blood was pouring from her mouth and she no longer had her signature smile.

Sam's eyes darted down and even though she knew what she was going to see, it didn't help with the terror she would feel: She was elbow deep in Camilla's back, her forearm and hand could be seen exiting through her chest as Sam looked over the dead woman's shoulder.

Inside her palm was Camilla's still beating heart.

She screeched as she pulled her arm out of Camilla and blood splashed on her front as she fell backwards in an attempt to get the body off of her.

It landed beside her and she looked at the hole that she had made. She squeezed her fist only to realize that the heart was still in her hand, she dropped it and it ironically fell to the ground next to Camilla's chest.

Sam whimpered as she gazed down at her arm: It was soaked with Camilla's blood. Her chest all the way down to her thighs was drenched as well. The bodily fluid was warm but cooled from the air and it made her clothing stick to her skin.

Sam struggled to catch her breath as she looked upon the death surrounding her: Carma had died by Camilla's hand and Camilla had died by Sam's. Camilla's blank face stared at the sky, the blood coming from the wound in her back began to make a puddle around her and it touched Sam's arm and she yelped as she crawled away.

She had killed someone.

Tears streamed down her face at the thought but she also imagined Carma's bright smile, the life that could have been so much more was snuffed out like a candle.

Camilla was evil, she took the life of an innocent person but she was still a living being and Sam took that from her.

Sam had hope that Carma wasn't going to kill her, that there was still a chance to change her but now that chance was gone.

She questioned herself as her mind rushed over everything.

Who was she to take someone's life? She didn't have it in her no matter how cruel Camilla was.

She thought of how gargoyles were supposed to be immortal and she turned between Camilla's heartless body and Carma's separated body.

When neither of the girls moved, Sam lost hope. She didn't think they could heal from a missing head or a heart. Arthur had said that they could die from outside sources.

The small sliver of hope that she had felt left an even emptier feeling than before. She allowed her body to fall to the ground and she rolled to her side. She couldn't look at the blue sky that the trees only showed partially, she couldn't take that Carma would never see something so beautiful again. She whimpered and her cries also doubled as yelling as she wrapped her arms around her chest.

What was Cale and Emily going to do? She imagined their devastated faces when they found out about Carma. Would they hate her? She wouldn't blame them, It was indirectly her fault that Carma was killed. If she wasn't Arthur's target, maybe her words would've continued to work and she wouldn't have been killed. Her mind cleared enough to realize that Cale and Emily had been in their own fight and they could very well be dead themselves. Camilla had been there with them but she showed up to Sam and Carma's battle instead, maybe she had killed them before she left.

Sam screamed as she covered her face with her hands but her eyes flew open when she realized that she was rubbing Camilla's blood on her face and hair.

Vomit poured from her mouth and she unconsciously picked herself up so she wouldn't choke on it. She heaved and shook as she vomited and a twig snapping close by made her jump.

She lazily brought her head up and her heart dropped as she saw Cale and Emily standing at the edge of the clearing. Cale had his arm over Emily's shoulder as she helped keep him upright. They both had so many slashes over their bodies but Sam paid no attention to that nor to the wings that were attached to Cale's back. She only cared about their faces and how they looked from seeing the horrible sight in front of them.

Their eyes were wide with terror as they looked from Camilla's body to a blood covered Sam then to their best friends body. Sam was sure that they knew even before seeing her head that the body belonged to Carma but the misery filled screams as they spotted her head confirmed that they held onto hope that it wasn't.

Their agonized screams as they ran to her body would haunt Sam for the rest of her life.

They dropped to their knees and sobbed and screamed as they held onto each other. They didn't touch her body and they couldn't bring themselves to look at her severed head which was only two feet away from them. They didn't even see Sam anymore as their tears blinded them.

Sam's lip trembled as she listened to their cries as they echoed through the woods and she forced herself to her feet and swayed out of dizziness but caught herself.

Whatever power she had when she had blacked out and killed Camilla was gone and it left her with nothing but painful remorse. She closed her eyes, she didn't want to see anything, especially the looks on her friends faces, the sound of their grief was more than enough.

It was during the loudest wail that Sam heard Arthur's voice.

"Samantha."

She opened her eyes and swung her body around to see where he was but she only made herself dizzier as Arthur was nowhere to be seen.

"I'm in the barn." He stated as if he could see her looking for him. *"Come alone."*

She could've said no and stayed with Cale and Emily but she knew there was no consoling them. If she stayed, Arthur would come to her which would undoubtedly make the situation worse, though it didn't seem possible at this point.

She swallowed the lump in her throat and glanced at her friends as they sobbed on each other, they obviously hadn't heard Arthur's direction.

"I'll go but I'm sure the others can hear you and they'll follow." She spoke out loud as if he was standing in front of her. She avoided the thought that all of her comrades could be dead.

"I'm sure they can't hear me… even though they're alive, they are distracted." He explained in his usual even tone.

A small amount of relief filled her as she thought of her friends alive and well but it was gone in an instant as she continued to hear Cale and Emily mourn over Carma's headless body.

She thought of how alive didn't always mean well.

"To your left." he directed as she looked around to see what direction the barn was in.

She didn't look back at the devastating sight behind her as she turned in the direction that Arthur had told her to go. She was sure that Cale and Emily paid no mind to her anyway.

She knew she was walking into more danger or maybe even her own death, but she kept going knowing that Arthur listened to her every step.

It took her a few moments of walking to realize that her shaking had stopped and it was replaced with something new: A sense of purpose.

She didn't know where it was coming from and she felt like it was misplaced, but the feeling kept her moving so she welcomed it with open arms.

Chapter 19

She had tripped countless times on her way to the barn from being distracted and forgetting where her feet were. She had almost fallen one more time but caught herself by landing against a tree as she approached the clearing leading to the barn. The old gray building looked even more haunting than before now that she knew who was inside.

She drew a shaky breath, her wounds were almost healed but she felt so weak. She didn't know what she was walking into or why Arthur wanted to meet her alone but she welcomed it. This way no one else would get hurt and she could finally find out what his interest in her was.

She gazed at the wooden door that led inside and she imagined Arthur looking at the opposite side, imagining her as she did him.

It was as if they could see each other even though the door blocked their way. He didn't demand for her to get moving, he allowed her to go at her own pace.

She forced herself to continue and she cut off her hearing so she could only hear the birds chirping and the rustle of leaves as she walked. She couldn't bare to hear Cale and Emily mourn over Carma.

She made it to the door and as she placed a hand on the handle, her heart began to race and a strange pressure could be felt at the bottom of her throat as her nerves screamed not go in. Her hand shook as she slid the door open, the wheel attached to the top screeching as she forced it to move and she flinched at the ear splitting sound.

The light from outside shined into the dark building but she couldn't see where Arthur was although she knew he was there.

"Close the door." his voice came from the dark and although she hesitated, she did what she was told. She wasn't afraid of the dark, she was afraid of what lurked inside.

As she pulled the door shut and her eyes adjusted to the dark, she finally saw him: He was sitting on the hay loft, his black pant clad legs dangling towards the ground, his hands pressed together as his forearms rested on his thighs. He leaned dangerously forward and Sam could barely make out his dark blue shirt. His expression was the same as it usually was: Emotionless.

Sam straightened in an act to seem braver but she knew he knew better than that.

"I'm surprised you came here without a fight." His voice was as emotionless as his expression.

If he truly was surprised, he was extremely good at hiding it.

Sam thought of how shockingly funny it was that he said that she came here without a fight. He didn't mean it that way, but Sam thought of the fight with Carma and the lack thereof with Camilla. She had came here with plenty of fight.

"There's no sense in denying you," she admitted. "It wouldn't have gotten me anywhere."

He jumped from the loft and landed to the noise of old hay rustling under his feet. Without falling off balance from the jump, he walked closer to Sam as if jumping twenty feet was child's play.

"You know I let you escape from the cave." He stopped ten feet away from her and tiny dust particles floated over his face as a ray of light coming from a crack in the door glared onto his face. He still had that emotionless look but there was something hidden there, was it anticipation?

"Yes." she kept her voice steady even though her jaw shook. "I think I knew from the moment I saw you standing there while we escaped."

"Are you wondering why?" he inquired with his head cocked

slightly.

She considered him for a moment, "I'm not." When her unexpected answer didn't seem to faze him, she continued. "I figured it was all according to how you wanted things to go. You gave me the means to escape when you told me about your *will* and *power* to achieve your goals."

He listened to her with no interruptions or movements, his eyes focused on the now dried blood around her mouth and hair. The blood pulled her strands back like it was some kind of gel. His eyes moved down to her arm: It was still soaked with Camilla's blood, it hadn't dried unlike her other bloodied parts because of how thick it was. It dripped onto the stray pieces of hay under her.

His eyes returned to her face and he met her eyes, the intensity making her uncomfortable.

"I let you escape because I wanted to see how far you could get on your own."

Sam huffed at his explanation, "I hope I met your expectations." she spat.

She knew that he had listened to her battle with Carma and had caught Camilla killing Carma and Sam killing Camilla.

Anger brewed inside her once again, not with the same intensity as before, but it was there all the same. She was sure that she wouldn't be able to black out and kill him, he was much stronger than Camilla.

The two stared at each other for a moment, waiting for the other to crack and speak first.

It was like a couple of siblings.

Finally, Arthur spoke. "In some way's you did meet my expectations, but in others you didn't." he took one step forward but nothing more. "You *killed* Camilla, one of my strongest gargoyles."

The spoken word hit her harder than thinking about it, hearing it from someone's mouth made it real.

Her eyes averted as the anger dispersed and it was replaced by remorse. Carma was killed in front of her by Camilla and though in some ways it was justified, she couldn't bring herself to think that what she did was right. She didn't even remember the act of killing, only the aftermath. Her mind wandered to Kellan who was the other strongest gargoyle that Arthur was talking about. He was the only white eyed gargoyle left on Arthur's league aside from himself.

"You're a murderer now." there was a touch of entertainment in his tone.

Sam's head shot up, her eyes narrow. "She murdered Carma, one of your own, remember? *Oh* but I'm sure that doesn't matter to you anyway since everyone on your side are just pawns."

It was almost funny how the fact that she had killed someone ate at her but as soon as Arthur called her a murderer, she had to defend herself.

His eyes moved to the right and she looked to see what had caught his attention but nothing was there aside from more darkness and hay. She brought her attention back to him and his eyes were back on her.

What was he thinking?

"I don't blame you, I would have killed her myself for what she's done." There was a touch of annoyance breaking through his usual demeanor and Sam snorted, he was using sweet words to mess with her. "I'm sure you would have." her voice filled with sarcasm. "Carma told me herself that you didn't give a damn about her unless she was going to help you."

"You're right," he agreed with no hesitation. "I only care for one person, therefore all others are pawns to me." he took another step forward and she could feel the air around him. "But I do not enjoy unnecessary death, I told my people to fight without the intent to kill."

His right hand was in a fist and shook from the force he was using to squeeze it.

Sam couldn't believe the amount of emotion he was showing, it was like his emotionless act was starting to fall. She also couldn't believe that he would tell his lackeys not to kill his enemies. She was sure he knew that there was no chance in hell of them joining him.

Sam and the others were in his way even though they were just flies. There was no sense in keeping them alive, especially if he was as bad as he tried to seem. She thought of how he had said that he only cared about one person.

Who was it?

"Why am I here?" she shot. "Camilla figured you wanted to kill me on your own but if you're so against killing, why would you do that?"

He considered her for a second then shook his head, "Let me ask you this, have you ever heard Camilla say anything remotely truthful?"

Sam thought of Camilla's exaggeration about Carma being tortured and that they'd hear her screams, but neither had happened.

"And what you're here for is simple," He focused on her. "I got a good idea of how far you've come by listening to your fight with

Carma, and the fact that you killed Camilla who's been a prodigy is quite the feat." Sam's breath hitched as she listened.

To hear that she had killed Camilla again stung even more than it did the first time and the anticipation to find out what Arthur wanted only added to the feeling.

"Finding out through them is boring, I want to find out for myself what you have learned." He boasted while smiling at the prospect of being able to do some fighting himself. His smile caused Sam more distress than the prospect of the fight. She had never seen him smile and to her, it only meant that what was about to come was sure to be bad.

She breathed. "Will you kill me?"

She didn't sound nervous and she didn't know why, her life could be at it's end but something kept her composed. Thinking about dying was worse than the act itself.

"I may or may not." he answered, his smile dying down.

Something was off about him, more than usual at least.

She looked him up and down, trying to see a nervous tick or anything that could reveal his true motives, but he stood still with his arm's to his sides and his eyes on her.

She moved her gaze to get a quick sweep of the barn so she would know her surroundings and what would help her during the fight.

"I won't run," she stated as she brought her gaze back to him. "I'll fight you."

"Do you think you have a chance?" he questioned and it surprised her, why would he ask her that? They both knew the answer.

She shook her head, "I'd be stupid to think I could."

She gave him a look that was filled with neither courage nor fear, she did look tired however. Tired of fighting, tired of death, tired of being afraid and hiding the fear with courage.

"But you know for damn sure that I won't go down without a fight." she added finally, if anything, at least her voice sounded strong.

Once again a smile appeared on Arthurs lips, he was showing more emotion in the short time that they've been in the barn than he ever had in the cave.

He closed his eyes then opened them again and the hazel had been replaced with nothing but white. He didn't bother to transform anymore than that, he didn't need to.

Sam who was still transformed remained the way she was.

Who was going to strike first? The anticipation made her feel sick.

What was his first move going to be? Was he going to go in for the kill right away? Had he lied about not wanting unnecessary death? Would her death have been necessary?

Question after question flashed through her mind, almost driving her insane until Arthur made his first move.

She wasn't prepared for the speed he had, he was in front of her in one second and the next, he was to the right of her, knocking her over.

She didn't think that he had hit her that hard, she didn't even feel the pain as she fell onto the soft bedding of hay but as she landed, her right arm seared with pain. She yelped but she couldn't milk it, she had to get up.

She willed herself to move the injured limb but all it did was shake and cause her more pain. She looked up to meet Arthur's gaze as she used her other arm to push herself up. He looked like unnecessary death was the last thing on his mind as his white eyes glowed with venom.

As Sam got to her feet, he started at her again but this time she could see his outline as he moved. Even though he was moving too fast for the human eye, Sam's gargoyle eyes slowed him down for her. She brought her uninjured arm up to block but she regretted it immediately: He had barely touched her with the back of his hand, it only looked like a gentle slap but like before, the pain set in and she stumbled from the force of the hit. Her breathing came out as pained moans and she bit her lip to try distracting herself from the pain in her arms.

So this was the power of a full blooded gargoyle? None of the made gargoyles had power like this.

She heard a growl that woke her from her thoughts and Arthur only stood a foot from her, his expression was animalistic as his breaths came out as growls.

"Ah," Sam thought to herself, *"There's the fear."*

She couldn't allow herself to freeze like she had with Carma, She had to defend herself, she couldn't go out as a coward.

They went at each other at the same time but as expected, Sam was thrown back and slid to the far end of the barn until she landed harshly against the wall. It creaked and whined as her weight fell against the old wood.

She might've blacked out for a moment because her sight had gone dark but as it came back, her ribcage felt like it was split in half. The pain in her arms felt like mosquito bites compared to the pain in her ribs. She howled and gripped at them but the pain was coming from all sides and her touch only escalated the ache. Especially in her arms that she should have known better not to move.

She could see stars as she bit her tongue and blood started to drip from the sides of her mouth. Her right arm was broken, her left was injured to the point of being useless, and now many of her ribs were broken. She didn't bother watching Arthur as he treaded through the hay to get to her, she heard his every step and knew when he was in front of her.

The physical pain was horrible but what ached more was the fact that all the training she had done with Cale and the others had amounted to nothing. She spent her last few weeks mauling over how she was going to get her revenge and to protect the world only to be beaten like she was nothing. She was an idiot, a *weak* idiot.

She leaned her head painfully back, the board creaking from the small amount of weight. Her eyes met Arthur's and she noticed that they had gotten softer. He knew the fight was over, he had won with just three hits.

It could've been done with one if he had taken it seriously.

He brought his arm to the front of him and flexed his fingers, his nails extending into points. Was he going to kill her without another word?

He must have seen the fear in her now human eyes because he dropped his arm back to his side."I can't say that I'm impressed." he shrugged and anger and fear twisted in Sam.

He didn't want to test her skill, he only wanted to show her how weak she was.

"WHY?!" she roared then gasped in the next instant from her ribs screaming as her lungs exerted a large amount of air.

"Why?" his voice was even. "You'll have to be more specific."

She couldn't make out his face since it was covered by shadow and the angle she was in made it hard to see. Her lip trembled as she dropped her head and drew a shaky breath.

"I know I wasn't chosen, all of this happened by chance." she brought her least injured arm up and placed a hand unconsciously over the scar on her temple. "But why?!" her head shot up, "Why are you doing all of this?! And why are you fixated on me more than the others?!" she blinked repeatedly to stop the tears from falling. "And why-?" her voice cracked. "Why do I feel like all of this is related to my dreams?"

Arthur's eyes flashed and he took another step towards her. She tried to crawl backwards to get away from him but she only pressed further into the wall behind her. Was he going to kill her? There was no changing her mind on joining him and he knew it, maybe he had finally realized that it was best to kill her.

Her silly questions weren't worth answering.

What would he know about her dreams anyway? The question only made her seem like a stupid girl who paid far too much attention to a made up world in her mind.

She tried to back away as he stopped inches from her, his dark silhouette towering over her.

This was it, even though she had said that she wouldn't go down without a fight, she was going to die on her ass while shaking and sniveling like a coward.

She tried to get up but she was shaking far too much to be able to control her own limbs. All of her injuries flared and she collapsed back to the ground. All she could do was sit there and hope that it was going to be quick.

She closed her eyes as he looked like he was about to strike but when the hit didn't come, she fluttered her eyes open to see that he was kneeling in front of her.

She continued to shake as their eyes met, his hazel eyes had returned but what shocked her the most was how gentle they were.

Not only that, but all of his facial features had softened as well.

Their gazes didn't break as Arthur spoke with a completely different tone than his normal, the gentleness that came with it felt nostalgic to her.

"I have an answer to all of your questions…" he paused for second as if he was contemplating what he was going to say.

Finally, he spoke the words that she had never expected to hear.

"You're my sister."

Chapter 20

There was silence as Sam took in his words and she didn't realize that she was holding her breath until her body forced her to take one. Her ribs ached but her jumbled mind distracted her from the pain.

Arthur allowed her to think about what he had said while keeping his eyes on her like he was waiting for an answer, for some kind of reaction.

Her breath hitched. "I-I'm pretty sure my parents only have two children."

She could have told him that he was crazy, that it was impossible and that there was no way that they could be related, but she couldn't muster the energy to lash out.

Arthur shook his head as he leaned on his heels. "Your current parents have two children but your parents in your past life had five."

Her heart began to race and a lump developed in her throat.

"Past life?"

She would be lying to herself if she said that she had never thought about having one. It was on her mind a lot as of late but for her enemy to come out and say that she had a past life and he was her brother was too much.

Mina had planted the seed and Arthur was going to make it grow.

"Yes," He said simply as he observed her shocked face and a small amount of sadness appeared on his features. "You were once the daughter of two full blooded gargoyles and the youngest sister of four older brothers."

The dreams that she vividly remembered were brought back to the forefront of her mind: The little boy in the one that she had repeatedly and the other three brothers that she barely remembered…and her parents... who laid dead in front of her.

"What happened to them?" her voice was hoarse as she spoke.

She didn't want to believe what he was saying and even though she asked him, she already knew the answer but asking felt like validating his claim.

"Our parents were killed by the humans." His eyes dropped as he answered.

Sam closed her eyes and her forehead scrunched up, the emotions she was feeling were threatening to explode. Not only did he answer the way she had expected, but he said how they died.

How many details or full on dreams did she not remember?

"Where are the three other brothers?" She kept her eyes shut. She could've called him a fool for thinking that she was his reincarnated sister. She could've use this opportunity to blindside him but she was strangely overcome with emotion. So many emotions that she couldn't tell which one she felt more of.

"They're… *Around*." for the first time since she had met Arthur, she could tell for sure that he was lying.

She opened her eyes and they focused on his: They were hazel just like hers. Her eyes moved from his eyes to his brown hair, it was the exact same color as hers. The more she looked, the more she saw what they had in common: Their noses were the same and their eyes weren't the same in just color but also in shape.

She dug into the darkness of her mind and slowly the images she was looking for flashed behind her eyes: She saw the oldest brother, his hair brown like his two younger siblings, his eyes hazel. The other siblings showed at the same time, they were twins with blonde hair and blue eyes. All five of them shared the same nose and eye shape.

A memory that she didn't remember seeing before popped into her mind: Her parents stood waiting for her as she ran up a hill, her mom had a grin on her face as her long wavy brown hair blowed gently in the breeze. It reached to the middle of her back and the hair above her ears was braided tightly to the sides of her head, her eyes were hazel and sharp.

Her father had blonde hair and blue eyes, he was tall and friendly looking with a wide smile on his face as he watched his daughter trot to him.

Finally, the little boy came into view.

Sam had dreams about him since she could remember. It was always the same dream of him meeting her on top of the hill. He was so gentle and kind, he followed her like a puppy.

The little boy kneeled in front of her now in the shape of the man who had kidnapped her and had turned her into a monster.

Her breath shook as she gazed at him, there was no denying it. With everything that she had seen in her dreams, and the feeling that pulled her into thinking that he had something to do with them confirmed it.

It must have been her past lives memories telling her to think that way.

Arthur was telling the truth.

Her head fell as she realized that what she had been seeing weren't dreams nor visions but memories.

"How?" she felt sick as her heart thumped in the back of her throat.

"You'll have to be more specific."

"How was I killed? How did I reincarnate? How is that even possible?"

He was silent for a moment, he didn't look like he wanted to talk about it. "...I'm sure you already know the answer."

Of course she did, it was the dream that had broken her, that made her lose her mind and her friends trust. The explosion rang in her ears and the voice she had heard before her demise echoed again, she knew who it was now: It was Arthur.

He had begged her not to do it.

"As for you being reincarnated, it's what happens to every gargoyle when they die, though it only happens once." he explained as he sat down on the hay as if he was having a comfortable conversation in an abandoned barn with a friend.

"I thought they were immortal?" She was far more interested in what he was saying than how chummy he was acting.

They could obviously be killed, Carma and Camilla were proof of that. Even the black and white eyed gargoyle that he had spoken of had died but she needed an explanation.

"We are immortal as in we do not age, we can still be killed and when we do, we reincarnate as humans... We're supposed to forget about our life as a gargoyle and live on as a human but I guess you're the exception." he chuckled softly like he couldn't believe it then continued. "You couldn't imagine my shock when I overheard you talking about your dreams with your cellmates."

The two sat in silence for a moment, she wasn't supposed to remember anything but her memories from her past life haunted her. Her eyes were still wide with shock but they snapped shut when one of her ribs cracked back into place as it healed, she winced and whimpered from the pain.

"I'm sorry." Arthur's tone was soft and filled with regret.

"If you're sorry then why did you do it?" she spat. "You captured innocent people and me, *your sister*." She used a mock tone for *sister*. "And threw us into those cells and made us live like rats while you changed us into gargoyles." her eyes narrowed. "I'm sure you're real fucking sorry."

For a second she saw the little boy from her dreams as Arthur's face dropped. Something inside her wanted to comfort him, to tell him that she was just trying to be cruel because she was mad but she mentally smacked herself.

What the hell were these feelings?

"I had to do it." his explanation woke her from her internal battle and she looked him straight in the eyes. "Why did you have to ruin our lives?" The anger rolled from her tongue with each word.

He seemed like he didn't want to tell her as his eyes drifted to the side. "I wanted to protect you-" he started and Sam was about to argue when he shot her a look and she shut right up.

"Our brothers want to kill you." He made his explanation short and sweet but it only confused her more.

"Why would they want to kill their own sister? I'm not really their sister anyway…she died already."

It was almost as if hearing Sam say that she wasn't his sister struck a nerve in Arthur or it was the fact that she had said that she was dead, but he continued all the same. "Do you remember when I told you about the strongest gargoyle?" He looked her up and down.

Of course she did, she used the fact that the strongest one died as encouragement that the gargoyles could be killed, but aside from that, it always bothered her how something so strong could be killed.

She nodded.

"There was a story about how over a hundred years ago, a black and white eyed gargoyle emerged and was stronger than the rest. There's been no reason on how they died and many thought that the story was made up to cause wonder for the younger generation of gargoyles-" He drew a breath as Sam listened intently to his story, she wanted to know more, she wanted the knowledge that Arthur had and the reasons why all of this was happening to her.

"..Until you were born that is."

She had almost missed the last part because of her scattered brain.

"*Me*?" Disbelief filled her voice as her eyes widened and her teeth chattered.

"*You*." He replied simply. "Well, your past life."

He was right, she and her past life were separate people even though they shared the same soul and looks. Sam was a white eyed gargoyle who was once human while her past life was supposedly the strongest gargoyle in existence.

"...that doesn't explain why her brothers are after me." she stammered.

"Our brothers were always jealous of you, you got more attention from our mother and father because of your power. They wanted to keep you sheltered and our brothers hated that." he closed his eyes. "They wanted to play with the humans and not in the way that children play: They wanted to torture them, destroy they're towns, and kill them but as long as our mother and father were around, they couldn't do what they wanted. When our parents were killed, they were finally able to do what they wanted… and you allowed them because you wanted revenge on the humans for killing our parents."

Sam was at a loss for words, her past lives brothers were the ones that had committed so many atrocities. They had killed innocent people and they were entertained by it.

She remembered the bodies she had seen on the website that Cale had found: The claw marks, the missing body parts, and the terrified expressions they had before they died.

She started to think of the vision she had of when she and her brothers had found their parents bodies. She remembered her three older brothers with malice etched onto their faces and Arthur kneeling beside the body of their mother with tears streaming down his childish face.

She could of sworn that she had spoken in the vision but for some strange reason, she couldn't remember what she nor what her brothers had said. Now that she tried forcing the memory to resurface, it only came back as bits and pieces.

Was it trying to protect her? Or was she protecting herself?

Arthur observed her, she was beginning to look pale. More than she was before. Her eyes were glossed over like some kind of film laid over them.

"You stopped them after you saw how vile it was. " He continued suddenly "They didn't like that but they knew better than to cross you. That's when their hatred for you developed, you were their little sister who was much stronger than them and you made it so they couldn't have their way."

"What shitty brothers…" It would have sounded like a joke but Sam's expression and tone said otherwise.

"Yeah.." Arthur agreed softly.

Her supposed past life had four brothers and the youngest who was Arthur had kidnapped her current life and turned her into a gargoyle again while the other three were homicidal and wanted her dead.

"They got what they wanted, their sister died." She leaned forward and another twinge of pain hit her but she ignored it. "I'm just a weak reincarnation, I'm not in their way like she was…So why would they go out of their way to kill someone who's clueless to everything?"

Arthur shook his head, "It's because you're clueless that you don't understand how our brothers work." he leaned forward in an intimidating way, like he was trying to express how dire it was for her to understand what he was about to say.

"They don't care that you're a different person, they want your soul to be wiped from existence. As long as you're soul lives, they will never feel like their sister is gone. You die as a gargoyle then you are reborn as a human. After that, you're done. There's no more reincarnating. You're gone for good. I checked myself to see if it was true." The urgency in his voice as he spoke made Sam want to run away and lock herself in a bunker.

She was getting how dire it was now, *she was fucked*.

"Even if you left me alone..." her voice shook. "If you had let me live my current life in peace, they still would've tried killing me?"

He nodded slowly, his eyes filled with regret. "They wouldn't have just killed you, they would have tortured you then they would have killed you slowly." He shook his head and furrowed his brows as he frowned, "That's why I did all of this, I ruined your current life and the lives of the others because I wanted you to be prepared for them to come after you... For you to have a fighting chance."

"Why do you care so much?" her tone was rough. "I'm not your sister." Her eyes were narrow with anger and Arthur didn't look shocked by her sudden attitude change.

She inclined her head to look at the rays of light shining through the roof. "Since I'm obviously no match for you, I'm nowhere ready to defend myself against your brothers." She brought her gaze back to him. "Why don't you just kill them yourself if you're so worried about your sisters soul?"

She refused to speak like she was Arthur's sister, she wasn't after all.

They might share a soul, but the girl that she used to be was something that Sam would never accept. She had allowed her brothers to kill innocent people, she was just as much to blame.

Arthur looked almost let down that Sam wouldn't accept that she was his sister, but his expression went back to emotionless for the first time since he had told her that she was his sister.

"My brothers are much stronger than I am, I wouldn't stand a chance. The only reason why they haven't killed me yet is because my weakness is entertainment to them." his tone had returned to normal as well.

Sam clenched her jaw, the situation only got worse with every question she asked.

"...I guess I'll die." she tried to get up but Arthur extended a hand, placed it on her shoulder, and pushed her back down.

"You're not going to die without a fight, right?" His eyes were determined but the rest of his face remained the same.

People always said that one's true emotions laid within the eyes.

She had told herself those words over and over again, that she wouldn't go down without a fight. But before Arthur had made his declaration, she was just going to sit there and die. She had backed down, her weakness had showed but now there was a much bigger threat than Arthur coming for her and she didn't know what she was going to do.

She still couldn't trust Arthur, he could be in cahoots with his brothers.

Maybe they weren't really after her, maybe he was lying to her so he could gain her trust and then go with his true plan.

A memory quickly flashed in her mind, she was in her old body, *her past lives body.*

The twins were in her face, their expressions were twisted with anger and their white eyes were narrow, they were covered in blood from head to toe. She stood true to herself as her brothers threateningly rounded on her. She moved her gaze to her oldest brother who was equally drenched in blood. He leaned against a wall with his arms crossed, his face filled with venom but she could see something else: He was entertained.

Arthur was telling the truth about her past lives brothers wanting to kill her, that much was true. "I dont think a fight will save me." She tried to push against his hand but he kept her in place. Her ribs and her still injured arms ached as she pushed against the ground.

"That's why I set this all up," he finally removed his hand and while Sam wanted to get up and leave, she sat there waiting for what he was going to say. "I have the people who joined me, they wanted power and in exchange, I told them they had to fight for me."

"But that's not enough, right?" she leaned forward so he could get a full view of her angry expression.

"No, it's not." he agreed while ignoring the venom in her voice. "I kidnapped the rest of you because I needed more help against our brothers."

"*Your* brothers." she corrected him. "They're not mine."

He just looked at her for a moment then continued, "The people that I kidnapped and forced into changing would never fight for me, but they could fight for you."

She blinked, "Why would they risk their lives for me? They don't even know me."

"You're wrong," Arthur shook his head. "Though their not fighting for you, the people that are here now are fighting with you. You're the one that helped them escape, I knew you'd break out and in doing so, it would give you the opportunity to get them on your side."

Sam took in his words, she was getting so much information to the point that her brain ached.

Her gaze moved to the hay covered ground then to a crack in the wall, the sun could be seen outside. The brothers could be coming for her at any moment, they could be here now.

Her heart began to race and her breath quickened.

How much time did she have left before they finally got her?

The future didn't look like much to her, all she saw was death.

She was breathless when she spoke. "How does that help me? You brought us here to *test* us and now you know there's no hope for us."

"Wrong again," Arthur wasted no time with his explanation. "If we have enough to help, there has to be a way to stop our brothers." His eyes narrowed. "Twenty against three doesn't seem fair but it is in this situation, if anything, it's not fair for us."

Sam thought of the probability of having twenty gargoyles helping her and she compared their strength with Arthur's. How could they fight against three gargoyles that were supposedly stronger than Arthur?

The whole thing seemed far fetched but it had it's good points. What bothered Sam the most was the fact that she'd be using innocent people for her own gain. She began to think of the way Arthur used his words and she realized that he had said something that stuck out to her.

"*We*?" She inquired.

"None of you know how to fight like a proper gargoyle," Arthur raised a hand when Sam was about to tell him that they didn't want to be gargoyles in the first place. "I can teach you how to fight in your gargoyle forms so you'll be ready for when they come, and I'll be there when they do."

Sam closed her eyes before he finished, what a world she lived in.

A month ago she didn't believe the demon theory, not knowing that she was going to be abducted by gargoyles who were the *demons* people spoke of.

Since she was young, she had dreams that didn't make sense and she had passed it off for so long only to find out that it was her past lives memories all along. She couldn't believe that she was going by anything that Arthur said but what he said and what she's seen was more than coincidental.

She imagined how it would be if she was unaware of her past life and the brothers got to her. How she would've felt having complete strangers having that amount of animosity towards her for a reason she didn't know.

It was the same now only she knew why they were after her: For the simple reason that her past life didn't let them have their way and their jealously.

"You want to join us?" She asked suddenly.

"Join you? No." Arthur got to his feet and Sam inclined her head to keep a good look on his face. "I want to fight with you, not only does it help you with getting rid of our brothers, but it helps me as well."

"You expect me or any of the others to trust you?" She spat.

It was true, How could any of them trust him after what he had done to them.

Especially Cale and Emily since because of Arthur, their best friend had been killed.

"No, but I expect you want to live." he took a step back. "I will give you until tomorrow afternoon to think about it, go back to where you were hiding, that is the safest place for now."

He turned to go as he stuffed his hands into his pockets and Sam was baffled by everything that had just happened and now she had to make a choice that could endanger her friends and or make them leave her.

But maybe that was for the best.

She watched him make his way to the sliding door, with each step the hay crunched under him. Sam stayed silent until he slid the door open and the ray of light that shined through blinded her.

Arthur was about to step out when one last question popped into her mind.

"...What was my name?"

He stopped in his tracks and he just stood there for a moment facing the sun. Sam wanted to see his expression but she settled for looking at his back. A strong gust of wind made the old building creak and outside a loose leaf was ripped from a tree and it began to fall until it slowed.

They both watched as it fluttered to the ground and it landed only a foot away from Arthur.

"Maya," He said finally and caught her off guard. "Your name was Maya."

He stepped through the door, crushing the leaf as he walked.

Chapter 21

Arthur had left the door open and as Sam limped out of the barn, she used the light shining from outside to guide her. Her limbs were heavy with all of the wounds and information she had just received but most of all what was to come weighed on her mind.

She would've liked to stay in the barn for just a bit longer to think about everything, to weigh her options. But even though she was terrified to do so, she knew she had to face her friends.

She limped through the door and like Arthur, she left it open.

She looked around to see if he was still there but there was no sign of him. She turned her head to the forest, she was disoriented to the point that she didn't trust her sense of direction so she turned up her hearing and she listened for any sign of her friends.

She started to panic when she didn't hear them but she could hear the rustle of movement and every so often a sigh.

She inhaled shakily as she made her way towards the noises, she couldn't tell who she was hearing or if they were all in the same place but she kept herself moving without thinking about what she was going to see.

Her mind was fuzzy and along with the sound of the others, there was a constant buzz in her ears. She couldn't believe any of this was real: They had been caught in a surprise attack although they saw it coming so the surprise of it wasn't that great. She had witnessed the death of Carma, a girl she had tried so hard to save and the death of Camilla who she had killed herself.

She closed her eyes and inhaled as she walked through the trees with no sight.

She had gone to see Arthur so she could get her answers and that's exactly what she got. It was just that she didn't expect for him to tell her that she had a past life and he was her brother. If having Arthur as a former sibling wasn't bad enough, there were three more that were after her just because they hated her past life.

She didn't see a future for herself anymore but Arthur gave her the option to take his help. She had until tomorrow to decide but she didn't know what she was going to do.

She focused on what was going on now instead.

She saw them before she made it to the clearing: Cale and Emily were sitting on the ground beside each other in silence. Their heads were bowed and she couldn't see their faces. Ari and Kira were sitting against a tree, their faces swollen and as purple as a berry. Their expressions were blank and their eyes stared glossily ahead.

Daniel was laying on the ground with his arms on either side of him, his breaths shallow and his right eye swollen shut and Sam noticed that he was missing his front teeth. Cam was sitting not too far from him with his knees to his chest and his arms wrapped around them. He had his head resting on his knees and Sam was surprised that his face was untouched but his clothing was torn with scratches underneath. Dylan was the only one who was standing but he certainly wasn't upright, he was resting on one foot more than the other and his body tilted to the right.

A part of Sam didn't believe Arthur about his order to not kill any of them but as she saw each of her comrades with only cuts and bruises, she knew he was telling the truth.

Their fates would have been sealed if the opposing side was fighting seriously.

Relief filled her until she saw the body in the middle of the clearing.

No one noticed as she crossed into the clearing until she stopped at Camilla's heartless body.

"Sam?" Cale's voice was hoarse from crying.

Sam looked down at the hole in the middle of Camilla's chest, the hole that she had made with her barehand. The blood was still wet and inside the hole it looked like tar.

"Where did you go?" Cale asked and Sam bowed her head. "I fought Arthur."

"....What happened?" Cam perked up.

"A lot." Her voice broke, she had so much to explain but she didn't know how.

"That's it? That's all you have to say?" Daniel leaned his head to look at her and winced from the movement."Did you win?"

She almost laughed, "That's a dumb question... I got the shit beat out of me."

"Then why are you still here?" Cam demanded while Daniel threw her an annoyed look for indirectly calling him stupid.

She shot Cam a look, it wasn't the time to speak about what had happened between her and Arthur. They needed to get out of this place before someone who might have noticed all of the noise showed up. The way Cam phrased his question bothered her, Cale and Emily had lost Carma, he had to be more considerate of them.

"What happened here?" Emily's voice was small and it made Sam tense.

Emily already hated Sam for what she had done to Cale and now she had failed to save Carma. Sam feared to see her angry gaze but as she turned nervously to face her, she saw something far worse than anger: Sadness. The tears had carved a trail through the dirt on her face, her brown eyes were red from crying and there were bags under them.

Sam's jaw shook as she brought her gaze to Cale who didn't look too far off from his friend. He was sitting next to a fresh pile of dirt where Carma's body had been. Sam hadn't noticed it before and she also didn't notice that Carma's severed head was gone.

They had buried her while Sam was off with Arthur, she wasn't there when they needed her.

"Sam…?" Cale brought her back to reality and she started to feel panicked.

She took a gander at all of them: They were looking her up and down, she was covered in blood after all, why wouldn't they look?

Oh how she wished that none of this had happened.

Everything was her fault.

"I-I was fighting Carma and I got her to come to her senses," she drew a shaky breath, everyone's gazes were on her and it felt like a strong pressure was pushing her down. "But she couldn't hold off her second personality and she was going to attack me…She wasn't going to kill me, I know she wasn't, but Camilla… she…" She couldn't finish and she was thankful no one asked her to, it was obvious what Camilla had done.

"What happened to Camilla?" Ari called who looked so tired. It was hard for Sam to see Ari and Kira the way they currently were. They had always tried bringing light to the situation but it was far from their minds to do so now.

Were they going to think any less of her for being a killer?

"I killed her." She answered as she looked down at her blood soaked arm.

The sight disgusted her, she had used it to kill someone, had forced it through Camilla's chest and ripped her heart out. What made it worse was that it was unintentional, she had blacked out and her body moved on it's own.

"You *killed* her?" Cam sounded baffled, it didn't sound real that she had killed someone so much stronger than her but nonetheless, Sam was still standing while Camilla laid dead on the ground.

"You killed one of the strongest gargoyles." Dylan's voice was equally filled with disbelief.

Sam closed her eyes, "I'll explain everything to you but it's far too long for us to stay here while I tell you."

There was a pause before Cale got shakily to his feet while helping Emily who was worse than him.

"Where are we going?" Kira asked as she helped Ari stay upright, Kira herself was having a difficult time staying up due to the size difference.

"If it's alright with Cale, back to his place." Sam looked to him, they both had the same expression as they gazed at each other. A frown was etched on their faces and their eyes were half lidded.

Cale nodded while averting his eyes to the pile of dirt beside him and then to Sam's blood drenched arm. What was he thinking?

Sam nervously looked away from him but caught his arms in her peripheral vision: They were covered with dirt from digging the hole with his own hands and underneath was the blood that dripped from Carma's wounds as he carried her to the grave.

"How are we going to be safe there?!" Daniel rounded on her, "Do you not remember what Arthur said!?"

Everyone stepped closer aside from Cale and Emily who seemed to not want to leave Carma's side.

"I remember everything that Arthur said and it's because of that that I say we should go to the house. For now at least until we figure out what to do next." She spoke quickly, they had to get out of there before someone else showed up and she wasn't sure if it was going to be a civilian, the authorities, or her past lives brothers.

"I used to think you were smart," Cam shot. "You just fought Arthur, you know how he is."

"I know how he is and I thought you did too." Sam's brows furrowed as she gave Cam a pointed look. "Do you think that I'd be here right now if he really wanted to kill me?"

She cocked her head to the side in a triumphant *I got you* way and Cam backed off and she was able to see the wondering faces of her comrades.

"Why would he do that?" Ari limped out of Kira's helpful grip.

"I said I would explain it to you after, Trevor and Jeannie need to hear it as well."

Ari bowed her head in an awkward nod and Kira agreed as well. Sam owed it to them, they always seemed to trust her, but she was sure the trust would be gone when she explained what had happened in the barn.

The group began to make their way towards the jeep, it was a slow trek as most of them limped and staggered into trees but they started all the same. Sam was at the edge of the clearing behind the others when she turned to see if Cale and Emily were on their way: They were standing with their backs to her, looking at the dirt that Carma laid underneath.

A strong ache went through Sam's head and she fell against the nearest tree. Cale turned his head and he spotted her while she was gripping her head. She rushed to drop it, she didn't want to ruin their goodbyes.

Cale's eyes were filled with tears but he didn't let them spill over, he gripped Emily's shoulder and she hesitantly turned away from her best friends grave. Unlike Cale, Emily allowed her tears to fall freely, she didn't give Sam the time of day as she and Cale made their way past her.

She turned and watched them go as they leaned on each other. Cale didn't look like he needed the help physically but mentally Sam was sure he did. Her eyes wandered to the holes in the back of his shirt where his wings had been, all she saw that was left of them were small lumps that were barely noticeable. Cale leaned his head onto Emily's as her shoulders quaked.

Sam breathed as she turned on her heel and made her way to where Carma was buried and she placed her blood drenched hand on the pile of dirt that was covering her.

"I'm so sorry..." it was her turn to have her eyes filled with tears. "I failed you, I could've saved you." her jaw trembled. "I promise on my life that I will protect them." Her fingers dug into the dirt as she closed her eyes, forcing the tears to spill over onto her cheeks. "I promise..." she clenched her shaking teeth and her forehead scrunched as she allowed all of the pain, anger, and sadness to rush through her.

She rose shakily to her feet, she needed to catch up with the others.

"I promise." she said one more time before she turned to go, a determined but tear stained look on her face as she walked weakly out of the clearing.

It was a depressing ride back to the house, Sam had elected to sit in the back with Ari, Kira, and Dylan so Emily could be next to Cale. It was quiet for the most part aside from the occasional groan and sniffle. Sam leaned on the door as she gazed out the window, she took in the landscape that she thought she would never see again but here she was, alive.

For now.

She was once Maya, the strongest gargoyle: Her power was a mutation between both eye colors and it gave her extraordinary power. She had allowed her brothers to kill innocents until she had enough and she forced them to stop, they couldn't cross her. Their hatred stemmed from her power. What she had done in her past life brought danger to her current.

She knew better than to deny that she had a past life, but she wouldn't accept the person that she once was and most of all she wouldn't call Arthur her brother. It was her past life that had four brothers, she only had one. The fact that she had a past life bothered her and even more the fact that she still had memories from that life.

Everything added up, that's why she believed.

The fact that Arthur gave her until the next day to make her decision to let him help her gave her some assurance that he was confident that the brothers wouldn't get her today.

But how long did she have?

They finally pulled into the driveway and as they made their way onto the dirt road Sam listened to the rocks being crushed under the tires, it reminded her of bones cracking… the sound of bone and cartilage being ripped apart as she killed Camilla.

"Sam?" Kira who was sitting on Ari's lap laid a hand on her shoulder, "Are you getting out?"

Sam blinked, she didn't realize that they had stopped. She gazed up at the house as she opened the door and leaped out. The others were giving her odd looks as they got out.

Cale and Emily were already out and heading towards the house only to be met by Jeannie and Trevor on the front porch. Jeannie ran past them and aggressively pulled her brother into a hug and almost knocked him over. Trevor stood in front of them with teary eyes and a smile on his face but it was wiped off as soon as the relief that they were alive faded and he saw the blood on them.

"They attacked us but they only caused minor injuries." Cale assured him.

"What about your friend?" Jeannie turned towards Emily and Cale as she pulled away from her brother.

The group froze and Daniel tapped his sisters shoulder and she turned to see what her brother wanted: He shook his head with a sullen look.

"I'm sorry…" Jeannie's voice drifted as she turned back to Cale and Emily.

"Let's go inside… there's a lot to talk about." Cale turned without another look back and made his way into the house. Emily who had started to cry followed close behind.

"What happened?" Trevor implored, his gaze stopped on Sam who was staring off into space again.

"It's like Cale said, they attacked us but they only gave us minor injuries." Dylan explained. Though he still looked scared from the ordeal, the relief that he was alive was also apparent. "There were so many times that I thought I was going to die…" he shivered. "But they held back at the last moment."

"I noticed that too." Ari agreed. "They could've killed us but kept us alive."

The conversation brought Sam back to her senses, she wasn't even sure what she was thinking about but she focused on Ari's words now. She was glad that they had caught on.

"What happened to Arthur's men?" She wondered, her comrades were in the same place when she had found them. Their enemies were nowhere to be seen.

"I wasn't paying much attention but I noticed that Camilla had disappeared from her fight with Cale and Emily, leaving Kellan by himself… A few minutes later Kellan raised his hand and they stopped mid fight then jumped back into the trees and left." Ari explained.

"He was telling the truth…" Sam's voice wandered.

Her ears were filled with *What's* and *What are you talking about's* as she confused them with her words.

"I'll explain everything inside," She started for the house. "Come on… Cale and Emily are waiting for us." It was time to tell them everything, she couldn't worry about what they would think of her.

Not if it was going to save them and herself.

She slid off her dirty shoes and stepped through the hall in one quick motion. She could hear Cale and Emily's soft breaths from the living room and when she walked through the corridor leading into the room, Cale looked up. He was sitting in the chair in the same leaning forward elbows on knees position he did everytime he had something on his mind. He motioned for her to sit next to Emily and although it made her uncomfortable, she did so without protest.

Even though Sam had learned all of these life changing things in such a short amount of time, she still felt like she was better off than Emily. The feeling that it was her fault still nagged at her, she was sure that it always would.

Sam didn't want to get blood on the light colored couch and even though the blood was mostly dry, she stayed on the edge of the cushion to prevent any rubbing off.

The others entered the room and sat without peeping a word, the sound of cushions creaking made the atmosphere even more tense.

"What happened?" Cale's swollen eyes were on Sam and her heart thumped. She had to keep reminding herself that she had to tell them. She took a sweep around the room, their curious faces were covered in dim light. She drew a breath then swallowed, wetting her throat.

First she started with her dreams and she described the first one with Arthur as a young boy. Next she told them about how she dreamed of the two people she felt were her parents who had been killed. She described the three older brothers then she talked about the dream she had in the cave. How she saw her own death, the realness of it, and a man's voice calling out to her not to do it. The group watched as Sam told her story, their faces were a mix of curiosity and judgement.

Ari seemed to be interested in Sam's words as she kept a strong gaze on her as she spoke.

Cale and Emily watched with no surprise as she spoke about her first dream, she had told them about it when they were locked in the cave together though she didn't give them details. Cale gave her a soft look as she spoke about her death dream.

"I remember the look on Arthur's face when he carried me out of the cell. It was pale and tense and he said that *I'm always going to punish myself* but it didn't make sense to me."

It still didn't make sense to her.

Finally she talked about her hunches, how she felt that somehow he was connected to her visions. How Arthur had explained that he let them escape the cave, how he wanted to test their power.

"Why would he test our power then let us go?" Kira pondered while flipping her hand in a confused motion.

"Why is he doing any of this in the first place?" Daniel spat.

This was it, there was no more explanation needed.

What they were about to hear was going to change everything, especially how they saw their enemies and Sam.

How was she going to phrase it without sounding insane? Was there even a way to do that?

"…I had a past life." She winged it and she was met with shocked looks, huffs, and snickers like she was joking.

"Do you mean you had an old life?" Cam snorted, "You can't tell me that's your grand explanation?"

"An old life as in I died and reincarnated." Sam allowed him to have his laugh, she would too if someone had told her the same.

She would have laughed in Arthur's face if she didn't have her dreams to back it up.

"You're crazy." Daniel shook his head and got up, "You've lost your damned mind."

Sam shrugged and she found herself looking at Cale to see what his reaction was.

The two had come to understand each other, maybe this was going to be what ruined it. Her heart raced as she caught him gazing at her, his expression unshaken and it lacked the judgement the others had and Emily didn't seem to have a reaction as well.

With her eyes glossed over, she stared at the wall across from her.

"Why do you think that?" Cale questioned her.

Sam felt like she was going to be sick, her heart was pounding against her still sore ribcage. "Arthur called me to the barn, he said he wanted to test my skill." she chewed her lip. "I lost and when I thought he was going to kill me, he told me I was his sister…my past life was at least."

They could have continued to pick on her mentality, perhaps they could have left but her words sent them into shock.

"And you believe him..?" Ari furrowed her brows, not in an angry way but in a way that showed she was curious.

"He was the little boy in my dreams and everything he said added up." she dropped her head. "I know I sound crazy for believing him but a part of me had a hunch about reincarnation, I just didn't think my enemy would be my past lives brother."

Mina was the first to bring reincarnation into the mix, if Sam ever saw her again, Mina would definitely relish in the fact that she was right.

A smile appeared on Sam's lips as she imagined her friends glee.

Oh how she wished she could see that smile again.

"If this is real, then why did he do all of this to you?" Daniel was still standing, his hands balled into fists. Sam had the feeling that the question also included him and the others.

"He wanted to make me strong so I could protect myself." She answered.

"From what?" Cale asked calmly, his brown eyes still red from crying.

He looked so broken, he couldn't see his father and his best friend was brutally murdered but he still tried to keep his composure.

"My past life had three older brothers who hated her, they wanted to kill humans and she stopped them from doing so." she conveniently left out the part where her past life had allowed her brothers to do it. "....Apparently they were jealous because she was the strongest gargoyle, the black and white eyed one."

Cale took in her words and leaned back into his chair, his eyes moved from Sam to Emily who had turned slightly towards Sam.

"You expect-" Dylan started and Sam talked over him. "They want me dead because they hated my past life, their own sister. And before you ask why they would do that since technically she's already dead, believe me, I already asked Arthur, they want their sisters soul to disappear and I need to die for that to happen."

"So you're telling me Arthur kidnapped his sister's reincarnation... though I'm not sure of how much of that I believe...And kidnapped innocent people and turned them into gargoyles just to make you stronger so you can protect yourself?" Kira drawled out, her right eye squinted in confusion.

Sam was getting tired of explaining, she wanted to go outside, to take in the fresh air and think.

"Yes and no." She replied. "He wants me to be stronger so I'll be ready for the brothers, he kidnapped people so they could rally behind me. In hindsight that was a stupid fucking thing to do."

"Well kidnapping people and turning them into monsters is hardly a good reason to get them to join his sister." Jeannie's voice shook with rage.

"So he did all of this to protect the girl that used to be his sister?" Cale gritted his teeth "No matter his reasons, the way I look at it is that he kidnapped us and turned us into monsters." his eyes narrowed "Most of all... Carma's dead because of him."

Sam felt Emily stiffen beside her.

She breathed, "It's my fault too... I should have protected her." she kept her eyes forward on the mantle that held the television. Her eyes were down with guilt and her bottom lip trembled. She brought her hand to her face and did her nervous tick.

"It's not your fault." Emily's voice called from beside her and Sam's hand stopped over her mouth. She turned a fraction towards Emily and her eyes were filled with tears again.

Emily crinkled her chin as she spoke to stop the tears from falling.

"It's not your fault Arthur pit the two of you against each other, that he took advantage of her condition."

"But-" Sam dropped her hand and Emily shook her head, stopping her. Her eyes were determined as she spoke, her chin relaxed. "And it's not your fault that he did all of this to save you… You're not his sister anymore."

The feeling of being watched made the girls feel uncomfortable but they kept their sights on each other. Sam couldn't believe it, Emily had ignored her for the past two weeks. Acted like she had hated her. Though Sam was sure the trust was still gone, the fact that Emily comforted her meant more to Sam than Emily could ever know.

Sam swallowed. "Are you saying you believe me? You don't think I'm crazy?"

"Of course I think you're crazy!" the tears fell from Emily's dark eyes as she blinked. "But I do believe you. I heard about your dreams in that damned cell. I thought about reincarnation but I didn't think it'd be real and I also didn't think gargoyles were real!"

"I don't believe this mystical bullshit." Cam was the one to stand now as Daniel slumped back into his chair, his eyes filled with shocked confusion.

"What does this mean now?" Trevor spoke for the first time since Sam made her announcement.

She met him with sad eyes then dropped her gaze. This was it, this was going to be what would make or break them. They were already falling apart at the seams as it is.

"…He wants to help me." she looked forward and forced herself to look strong. "He wants to join us so we can prepare for his brothers. He gave me until tomorrow afternoon to decide if I'm going to take his help."

Silence.

They couldn't think of anything to say. The man that destroyed their lives wanted to join them. How could anyone take that as good news?

"If he's so strong, why can't he handle them himself!?" Daniel shot up, his voice high from anger.

"Because they're stronger than he is, he can't kill them alone." Sam bowed her head more as Daniel hovered over her.

Daniel just stared at her, his eyes flaring. "I'm going outside." he spat and started towards the front door as Jeannie shot up and ran after him, the front door slamming behind them.

The remainder of the group sat in silence for a long moment.

"What have you decided?" Cale asked with an edge to his voice and she could see that his knuckles were white as he gripped his hands together.

"I'm going to take his help." she announced. "It's the only thing I can do." she continued quickly before they could react. "I still want revenge for what he did, but I need his help to get rid of the men who are trying to kill me. He told me I used to be the strongest but that power is gone, I have no other way to defend myself… They won't just kill me, they'll torture me until I die… They hated their sister that much."

They took in her words and the fear that filled them.

"You seem so sure…" Ari's voice drifted.

"I don't know much about my past life, but I know how her brothers were."

Ari almost laughed, not at Sam, but at the irony of it all. "And we thought we were fucked before!"

"I'm not asking any of you to stay with me, when I accept Arthur's help, I'll leave… There's no reason for any of you to get hurt by staying with me." Sam spoke quickly but they caught every word.

"I'm going to leave you guys alone so you can decide what you want to do." She got up and the sofa creaked as she did so, she knew they couldn't think properly with her sitting there.

She made her way to the back door to avoid Daniel and Jeannie at the front and when she got to the corridor between the living room and the kitchen, Ari stopped her.

"Do you know what your name was?"

She turned to everyone, the feeling of *deja vu* filling her.

They watched her with a mix of emotion, it was certain that they had never seen someone with a past life before, let alone one that knew their name and had siblings still alive and kicking.

"Maya." She told them. "My name was Maya."

Chapter 22

She sat in the backyard like she had the night before, the trees shielding her from the sun that shined particularly bright. She thought it strange that it was so bright when everything felt so dark. Her mouth tingled from saying her old name, almost like it had been waiting to speak it for years.

She sighed and smacked her tongue to stop the feeling while laying on her stomach. She focused on the sound of the gentle breeze rushing through the leaves and the bugs buzzing.

She didn't want to hear the others talking about her, she couldn't take thinking about what they could be saying. She folded her fingers through the grass, the green blades prickling against her palms. She could think all day about everything that had happened but it wouldn't get her anywhere. But it was so hard not to, the deaths and the revelations all weighed on her mind.

Was she making the right choice by going with Arthurs plan? The way she figured it, she'd be dead in no time if she didn't take his help.

The question still rose that if Arthur was doing this for another reason aside from helping his sisters soul. Sam had Maya's soul but she wasn't his sister. She knew she looked the same but her body was born anew, her flesh was hers. Not only that but also her mind, the memories she had from her past life shouldn't be there, but they wanted to shine through.

Did she want them to return? What would happen to her if they did?

She believed a person's memories were what made them who they are. If she somehow got her past lives memories, she was sure she'd be a different person. It felt like a bad thing to her, her past life didn't seem like a good person.

Her heart jolted at the prospect of her memories returning. She got up quickly since with her chest being on the ground, it made her heartbeat more noticeable. She itched the scar on her temple, it was getting thinner with each new day, before long it would be barley noticeable.

"Sam?" Ari surprised her and she turned so fast that she gave herself whiplash.

Ari was standing over her, her blue eyes wide with concern, her clothes had been changed and the blood was gone, leaving only the already healing bruises.

"Are you ok?" She dropped to her knees and sat down.

Sam turned her body to face her. "As ok as I could be…" She replied while keeping her head bowed, avoiding Ari's prying blue eyes.

The girls sat in silence for a moment, Sam could tell that Ari wanted to speak but didn't know what to say.

"How's it going in there?" Sam mustered enough courage to speak first.

"Well the verdict is in-" Ari used a mock tone and Sam finally looked up to meet her gaze: She had a small grin on her lips and she had an accomplished look in her eyes that she had gotten Sam to look at her. "They think you're crazy."

Sam loved Ari's brute honesty, even when it hurt.

"But we're all a little crazy." She continued and her smile widened triumphantly when she got an amused huff out of Sam.

"Especially me for wanting to stick with you..." Her voice drifted and caught Sam of guard.

"What?" Sam had a grave expression. "You don't-"

"But I want to." Ari stopped Sam's protest but the battle wasn't won.

"You'll be joining your enemy," Sam leaned forward and flung her right arm into the air. "You'll die if you stay with me!"

"That's my choice." Ari's face was serious, her usual mock tone gone."I have everywhere else to go but I want to stay here and you're not changing my mind."

"Why?"

"Because I want to."

Sam cocked her head, there had to be more to it but who was she to force the reason out of her?

Ari's blue eyes searched Sam's hazel and she blinked then looked away.

Sam furrowed her brows. "What is it?"

"Nothing." Ari smiled, it was obviously forced. "So we're still partners?" she extended her arm and opened her palm for Sam to shake.

Sam hesitantly placed her hand into hers, it was strange that they were shaking on something that could potentially lead to both of their deaths.

* * *

Ari had returned to the house what felt like hours ago and Sam didn't know why she continued to sit outside while everyone else was inside. She supposed she was just too damned scared of what they were going to say. She already knew Daniel hated her and she didn't blame him, she had betrayed his trust. It was weighing on her mind that if she had agreed to run like Daniel had wanted, Carma would still be alive.

If Arthur's intentions were to help her defeat his brothers, then maybe his letter was just a farce. He wasn't going to kill them if they didn't show up, it was just a way to get them where he wanted.

How much time had passed since they left the farmhouse? Better yet, how long was she sitting outside by herself? Every sound made her jump, a bird jumping on a branch above made her jump particularly high. Her heart had only one speed now and it didn't offer to slow down. She didn't know when the brothers would come for her, she thought that maybe since Arthur had said that he'd be back in the afternoon of the next day that she'd be safe until then but her fear overpowered her sense.

She looked up at the house, making sure to avoid the windows in case someone was looking out at her. She was going to have to leave this place tomorrow, there was no way she could stay here with Arthur while the others didn't agree with her joining him.

She laughed at the thought of *joining* Arthur. She said she never would but here she was, it was funny how life worked especially for Sam who apparently already had a life before this one.

She started to think of Ari who wanted to stay with her. Would she be ok with leaving?

Sam hoped that it would change her mind about helping her, maybe she and Arthur could leave without Ari knowing? The prospect of Arthur's plan that included people helping her was appealing but it wasn't worth it if it was going to lead to more people dying when it could be just Sam who died.

She was gazing at the sky over the house when the back door slid open and she jumped before looking at who was coming. She was beginning to annoy herself with her jumpy shit.

She blinked rapidly out of nerves as Cale made his way through the door and he paused as he took in her startled face.

"You're not going to come in?" He asked as he slid the door shut behind him.

Sam shook her head as she relaxed a bit. "I don't think anyone wants to see me right now."

He walked over and she felt jealous to see that all of his wounds had already healed, his face void of pain while she still felt an ache in her arms and ribs.

He sat down where Ari had earlier and he crossed his legs as he rested his elbows on them.

As usual, he cupped his hands together.

"If no one wants to see you, then what does that make me?"

She met his eyes, they were even redder than earlier.

"I'm sorry…" Her voice shook.

Was it ok for her to apologize? She felt like she didn't have the right to.

Apologizing wouldn't bring Carma back and it wouldn't make the situation better.

"Don't apologize, all of us knew what could happen but we took the risk." He unclasped his hands and ran his fingers through his dark hair then gripped it in frustration.

Sam tensed at his seething expression, it wasn't often that she saw him look that angry.

He dropped his hand when he noticed her. "I'm sorry." His face softened a bit.

She could still see the emotion hiding under his false calm, she was sure it matched her own.

"I-" Sam began but he cut her off.

"Was it fast?" his eyes were sad as he asked and it took her a moment to realize what he meant.

Did Carma die painlessly?

She inhaled and exhaled quickly. "…I'm sure she didn't even know it happened."

Cale gave her a shaky nod, his eyes looked like they were threatening to water over again. "Daniel and Jeannie left." His sudden change in subject caught her off guard, she wanted to act surprised but she knew their departure was coming.

Good.

She wanted them to leave, like how she wanted the others to go.

"Is that so?" She asked simply while chewing on her bottom lip.

Cale considered her for a moment and she avoided his gaze. She acted like there was a interesting blade of grass in front of her as an excuse to not look at him.

"Why do you believe him?"

Sam pulled the blade out of the ground as her hand jerked from Cale's question, she knew this was coming but she was far from prepared.

"In what way?"

"That you believe that he was your brother in a past life."

She finally met his gaze, he didn't look like he was judging her. He didn't even look like he was mad at her for making the choice to join Arthur. However, she could be wrong since his face held so many emotions to the point that it was hard to tell.

In truth she didn't know if she believed everything Arthur had said, and she didn't have a clear answer for her quickness to believe that they were once siblings.

"I just feel it in my soul." Her mouth spoke without giving her brain time to register what she was going to say.

She quickly turned from him again, she wasn't sure if he'd believe all of her mystical mumbo jumbo but learning that gargoyles were real and becoming one himself could have helped with his lack of belief. If someone had told Sam over a month ago that she'd be going through this, she would have smacked them upside the head and told them they were crazy.

"I'm going to stay by your side, Emily too." He declared suddenly.

She blinked as her head shot up, there was only one thing present on Cale's face now: Determination.

"No-" She started to fight but Cale interrupted her as the corner of his mouth tugged a bit. "Ari told me you'd try changing my mind but I'm going to stop you before you start."

Her brows furrowed in worry. "Carma was killed because Arthur set up this plan... A plan to save me and to kill his brothers." She swallowed the lump in her throat. "It's indirectly my fault that she was killed..."

Cale considered her for a moment, when had he ever seen her look so troubled? Of course he had seen her scared before, he remembered the terror on her face as she woke from her dream in their cell back in the cave. The creases in her forehead as she worked plan after plan through her mind as she sat against the caves cold wall. The fake smile she would wear when she tried to cheer Emily up, the way she didn't know how to properly be there for someone.

But through all of the hardships, she had held onto her strong presence.

Her feisty attitude had always shined through, often times getting her in trouble. Looking at her now, Cale found it hard to believe that that strong girl could ever look like this.

His heart still ached from losing Carma, it always would. He hated Arthur who had worked every string, moved every chess piece to where they were now. He exhaled to calm his anger, it wasn't her fault. Even if all of this was real, she didn't have a choice in any of it.

He met her eyes and he noticed inside the hazel ring that there were gray blotches. It started at the outer edge and it worked it's way to the middle, threatening to swallow her natural color whole.

"What?" Sam cocked her head and he averted his eyes.

"Nothing." he lied.

She rose a brow, that was the second time someone had done that to her since they got back. If there was a problem with how she looked, she wished they would tell her. There was nothing worse to her than not knowing the truth.

But as she thought about it more, she realized that she was still covered in blood.

Cale sighed and turned away from her, his eyes focused on a tree close by but the glazed over look in his eyes gave away that his mind was somewhere else.

"It's not your fault Carma died," his voice shook when he said *died*. "It took me awhile to come out here to talk to you, the reason being was that I was feeling the same as Daniel, I felt like you were betraying us." He turned to her and he looked extremely guilty. "I thought you were crazy for believing that you had a past life and Arthur was your brother and that he set all of this in motion to protect you... But after thinking about it for awhile, all I could think of was how stranger things have happened." he gave her an apologetic smile though he still looked broken.

Sam remained silent, the sound of her nervous heart pounding in her ears.

He chuckled to try hiding his emotions but failed. "I've been friends with Carma for years, it didn't take long for us to be like siblings. I lost my birth parents when I was a baby and my adoptive mother passed away from cancer, I had my adoptive father but I still felt like I lacked a family... Carma and Emily filled that void." He sniffed and wiped his eyes. "You want to know why I want to help you?" He asked as he composed himself. "I did all of this because I wanted to save Carma, I hoped that she would finally conquer her second personality." He shifted his head and looked at Sam with the emotion he was trying so hard to hide.

His face was filled with grief, anger, and regret.

Sam's jaw ached as she struggled to keep it in place, her teeth chattering slightly.

She had a strained relationship with her family but they had been there for her, she wished they had never found out about what she had become.

She came back to reality as Cale continued to speak.

"I thought that now that she's gone, I don't have a reason to stick with you… But the more I thought about it, more reasons came up as to why I *should* stay with you." It was like the gust of wind that had picked up around them had blown his previous emotions off his face.

"If what Arthur said is true, and his brothers are savages who want to attack and kill innocent people, they need to be wiped out." The rough edge in his tone surprised her, the prospect of a fight had changed him. "And if they're after you, I will help protect you." He ended his explanation and Sam shook her head so fast it looked like she had a twitch.

"There's no reason for you to put yourself in danger because of me."

"No, but it's what the Carma I knew would have wanted me to do."

They met each others eyes again and took in the others emotions. It was true, you could tell the most about a person from the look in their eyes.

She closed hers, tears stinging her eyelids as she did so. "I'm sorry-" Her jaw quaked as she lost her hold on it. "I'm so sorry…" she bit her lip to the point of blood and the pain distracted her from the shuffle of Cale getting up and his steps as he walked closer to her.

She flinched when he placed a comforting hand on her head.

"This isn't the Sam I know." He claimed and she gazed at him with tears in her eyes.

He was kneeling in front of her with a gentle smile and he removed his hand as he continued to speak. "The girl I know would say f*uck them*."

Sam chuckled and sniffed. "You're right, it's just that all of this makes me wonder what kind of fucked up story this is supposed to be?"

"That's life though, right?"

"...Yeah."

She peaked past him to the house.

"I thought Emily hated me..." Her voice drifted and she sounded like a child.

Cale laughed. "She doesn't hate you, she's just afraid of you."

Sam brought her gaze back to him, his shoulder was the only thing that didn't heal the way it should have even with his heightened healing.

He stood and Sam followed suit, it was time she reclaimed her courage.

"One more thing." Cale caught her off guard as she dusted herself off like she wasn't sitting outside with Camilla's blood covering her the entire time.

"You won't sympathize with Arthur since he was your brother?" Cale questioned and her mouth hung open.

What kind of question was that?

"He's not my brother now, I might have some memories from my past life but I have none of her emotions." She gritted her teeth, she might be accepting Arthur's help but the thought of him still made her blood boil. His plan to save her didn't matter, he had ulterior motives and she knew it. "What he did was irredeemable, If I get through this, I'll kill him."

Cale fought to hide his smile, the Sam he knew was back.

He huffed as his smile dispersed. "It's going to be hard working with the enemy."

"Another reason why I don't want you to stay with me." She tried to alter him again.

He shook his head as he turned to the house, "You're not changing my mind."

Chapter 23

"I'm staying." Kira told Sam when she got in the house but before that, she had been welcomed with silence when she and Cale made it into the living room. It seemed they were waiting for her there. She had used Cale as a shield to keep their eyes off of her, but alas, she stuck out like a sore thumb due to her still being covered in blood while they were washed up. The feeling of having someone's blood on her brought a shiver through her spine now that her mind was less distracted. The longer she had it on her, the more it reminded her that she had killed someone.

"...Ok." she replied, she was baffled that another person wanted to fling themselves into danger by staying by her side.

She wondered why but she learned from Ari and Cale to not question them.

Maybe she would have to leave without them knowing when Arthur arrived.

"No running off." Kira gave her a stink eye as she read her mind.

Sam swallowed. "I-I won't."

"You're a shitty liar." Cam called from the furthest end of the couch. "That's why I know you weren't lying about what happened between you and Arthur."

Everyone was looking at him as if he was something foreign. Sam didn't think any of the others had expected him to stay because she certainly hadn't. She thought that he would have left with Daniel and Jeannie because even though they had a rocky start, they had turned out to be friends.

Sam started to wonder where Daniel and Jeannie had gone... Obviously not home.

The worry that she was starting to feel quickly dispersed as she remembered that they were safer away from her.

"I'll be joining you too." Cam added. "And before you start asking why, you already have the answer."

That's right, he wanted revenge.

"You and everyone else." Cale muttered as he sunk into his usual spot across from Emily. She was watching Sam with swollen eyes, she had been crying, heavily too by the irritation in the whites of her eyes.

Sam gave her a shaky nod and Emily looked away and found salvage on a speck on the floor where someone had tracked in some dirt.

"I'm here therefore I'm staying." Dylan's voice was shaking. "I'll help in anyway I can, I owe you for getting me out of that cave."

"You don't owe me anything." Sam assured him. "Arthur wanted us to escape, he told me himself."

He turned from her in reply.

Kira who had jumped up for her announcement sat back down next to Ari, leaving Sam standing by herself. She looked over her little group, they were minus two but she found herself in awe that any of them had agreed to stay.

Trevor's presence surprised her the most. He sat beside Dylan and his gaze was on her. He had opted out of the last fight, what was he doing here now?

That was for another time, if they were lucky, they would have enough time to figure everything out.

"…I don't know what to say." She said finally.

"Don't say anything." Cale said as he and the others gazed at her. "We're going to try our best, if we die at least when we get upstairs we can say that we did what we could."

Upstairs?

It took Sam a moment to realize that he was talking about heaven and even though she didn't believe in it, she found herself thinking how she'd probably be banished to hell for what she had done today.

"Yes…" Her mouth twisted into a forced smile. "That's right."

She had taken some time examining her eyes before Arthur's arrival. She was standing in front of the mirror in her borrowed bedroom chewing on her fingers as they shook against her front teeth. She had her eyes clenched shut like it was going to change them back to normal, the gray had turned into a thick ring around her irises overnight.

When she had washed the blood from her skin the night before, she had checked the state of the color and it was only a few blotches. At that moment, she realized that it wasn't the blood Cale and Ari were looking at, but the abnormal color of her eyes.

The shade had been steadily weighing on her but this new development almost pushed her over the edge. It didn't help that she had nightmares of Carma's severed head falling onto the forest floor and Camilla's frozen face staring at her.

There was a point where she had heard Camilla's voice.

"You're always going to be a killer." She had said in her squeaky tone followed by her signature ear splitting laughter.

Sam opened her eyes and focused on the bags under them, she woke up more than a dozen times during the night, each time she had to stay up longer than the last to calm herself before she could fall asleep again.

She sighed and rubbed the sleep from her eyes, by doing so, she made them water, resulting in an annoying sting. She looked in her eyes again, hoping what was there before was just a trick of the eye. Alas the ring was still there and it was getting closer to completing it's mission in covering what little hazel she had left. It was strange that her predicament with her normal eye color caused her more alarm than it did when her eyes turned completely white.

She had to stop herself from punching Cale's dresser, it would surely break with the strength she had. As she stood there, fist shaking, she thought of how it wasn't only Cale's property but it was also his father's. She wondered how much longer they had until his father showed up demanding for his son to be checked out by a doctor.

Everything was measured in time, how long they had until the government found them. How long they had until Cale's father showed up. How long until Arthur got there and how long until Arthur's brothers would find their way to their reincarnated sister.

They had talked about time the night before: Sam had slumped beside Kira as Ari handed out bowls of salad. The group had eaten silently until they were done, looking up occasionally at the television. They couldn't take listening to the news, after everything that had happened that day, taking a break from gargoyle stuff was a good idea. They settled with a reality tv show that was filled with arguing women and chairs being thrown.

Cale turned the tv off with a sigh as another fight broke out.

"How much longer do you think we have until they find you?" Cale questioned Sam as he dropped the remote onto the nightstand beside him.

They as in her past lives brothers.

Her eyes rolled down as she thought about it.

She didn't know them, she saw visions of them, images so to say, but whatever she knew about them was gone.

All she could remember was that they were deadly.

"Arthur gave me until tomorrow to decide if I'm going to accept his help, so I'm guessing he thinks we have a little time left." She remembered the alarm that snuck through Arthur's even tone. "I'll have to get more insight on that."

"Another question is how long do you guys think we have until the government finds us?" Dylan leaned forward to get a better look at everyone while setting his empty bowl on the carpet in front of him.

"That can happen at anytime." Trevor rolled a cherry tomato around his bowl. "But I think they're busy experimenting on the gargoyles they already have." he stabbed the tomato with his fork and the seeds sprayed and splattered on the sides of the bowl.

Sam's heart thumped and she stared at the tomatoes guts without blinking. It reminded her of the blood spraying out of Carma's severed veins and Camilla's blood that had covered her arm and face. She could still feel her heart in her hand as it beat for the last time.

"Sam?" Cale's voice brought her back from her thoughts and she rubbed her hand to get rid of the feeling. "I'm sorry."

Emily who had only taken a few bites of her dinner watched her with swollen eyes then turned to Cale. "What about your father?"

Cale's father… It had upset Cale when he had lied to him.

Sam stopped her rubbing and gave Cale a curious look, as did everyone else.

"He could be on a plane here now for all I know but in all the years since he adopted me, we've had nothing but trust." His jaw tensed. "All we have left is each other…"

Of course he had Emily and even though he had said that Emily and Carma were like family to him, the feeling couldn't have been as strong as it was with his adoptive father.

"We can leave here after Arthur joins us if the problem emerges." He assured them. "We'll have to leave sooner or later anyway."

The conversation from the night before weighed on Sam's mind along with millions of other things. She rubbed eyes one more time and with the frustrated feeling still boiling in her chest, she turned away from the mirror. Looking at her eyes wouldn't change the fact that they were changing, it also wouldn't change the fact that Arthur and his lackeys would be there at any moment.

She and the others had made the preparations that morning, they consisted of a dozen plans in case Arthur's true intentions were revealed to be more sinister than he led on. Though Sam was certain that none of them would work, they were dealing with a full blooded gargoyle and his hand picked fighters.

She strided out of the room to find Cale followed by the others coming from the living room. They had all agreed to meet Arthur outside since staying inside the house made it more dangerous in case there was an attack. They met each others eyes, one could say that they were nervous about what was going to happen but determination mixed in with the negative emotion.

They had to take this chance, Sam did at least, the others merely joined in.

Sam stepped in front of them and turned to the right where she immediately met the front door. She grabbed the handle and walked out into the bright afternoon sun.

They didn't know what time he was going to be there, all Sam knew was that it was going to be afternoon. It could be three to four hours before he got there but Sam was sure that if the situation was that dire to him, it wouldn't take long for him to get there.

Twenty minutes had gone by according to Trevor's wristwatch, they had taken refuge on the front porch. Trevor and Emily were sitting on the two white basket chairs while Cam and Dylan sat at the top of the four steps leading to the porch. Cale sat on the second stair to the left while Sam sat to the right. She had her elbows on her knees and her hands cupped together as she rested them on her forehead, it almost looked like she was praying.

"Where is he?" Ari who was sitting to Sam's right on a flower pot grumbled.

Sam dropped her hands to get a good look at her: She was pale and her jaw was clenched.

It was the first time Sam had seen her that nervous.

"I wish he'd just get here so it'll be over and done with." Kira who was standing to the left of Sam said with a hard tone. She had her arms crossed while watching the clearing leading to the road. She was leaning against one of the beams that was holding the cover over the stairs.

The act of Arthur getting there would be over but he was going to stay with them. It was going to take awhile for everything to be done with. It was either going to end with the brothers out of the way or Sam dead.

Sam was sure it was going to be the latter.

She brought her hands back to her head, she couldn't bring herself to speak and by the silence Ari and Kira were met with, neither could the others.

They preferred to listen to their surroundings instead of talking.

They were met with the sounds of cracking branches, the rustle of leaves, and birds chirping, but no indication that someone was coming.

Sam's heart began to race, she hated the unknown.

She had bowed her head and was listening to the nervous breathing of her comrades when she noticed something mixed with the sound, *footsteps*?

Her head jerked and she dropped her arms, she could tell the others could hear it too as they jumped to their feet. She stood as she kept her gaze on the clearing and her breath hitched as Arthur suddenly appeared: His hands were in his dark pockets and the shadows casted by the tree's were hiding his face but as he walked into the clearing, the sun shined on him and revealed his usual hard expression. His hazel eyes were on the people in front of him.

Sam found herself unconsciously walking to meet him and she tried to stop herself from shaking but the effort proved to be futile.

They kept their eyes on one another as they walked and Sam could feel two of the others following but she didn't bother to see who. She wasn't going to take her eyes off of Arthur.

They came to a stop five feet away from each other, hazel meeting hazel-gray. By the look on Arthur's face, he already knew the answer to what she had decided.

The two that had followed stopped behind her and Arthur's gaze left her and landed on them instead. A small grin appearing on his lips. Sam turned to find Cale and Ari standing defensively behind her and as much as they tried to look tough, she could still see the fear on their faces. She was sure Arthur could see it too.

"What is your answer?" He asked lazily as he brought his sight back to Sam.

She swallowed, as much as she dreaded it, she had to take his help.

"…I'll work with you." she said roughly like it hurt her to even say the words.

"Good." he said simply. "And what of you?" he looked over her to the others again.

"We're sticking with Sam." Cale told him with an edge to his tone.

"It looks like you're missing two." Arthur observed, it seemed like he was saying it more to himself than he was to the people in front of him.

"The danger was too great and they didn't want to work with you." Sam said as she gave him a stone cold look.

She couldn't believe he had known how many of them there were but as she thought more of it, the surprise disappeared. Of course he would know, he was Arthur after all, the mastermind behind all of this.

Though she would admit that there were many holes in his plan.

"Where are your lackeys?" Ari's voice shook as she spoke.

"They're where they're supposed to be." Arthur answered her but kept his eyes on Sam. "They can't be trusted to be with you."

"Why's that?" Cam called from the porch, he was trying to keep his composure in front of Arthur like the others.

Arthur's jaw tightened, "I don't want what happened yesterday to be repeated."

He stepped past Sam and she turned and watched as he walked past Cale and Ari. He was still a mystery and no matter how much Sam blamed him for what had happened to Carma, she'd be lying if she said that she didn't notice him show remorse over it.

Cale and Ari turned and watched him like Sam had with confused looks on their faces.

They didn't think he cared about what had happened and it shocked them.

He stopped in front of the porch and gazed at the house. He had kept his hands in his pockets the entire time but as he noticed the group sitting on the porch get up defensively, he removed them and raised them like a pedestrian would with a police officer.

"I know we've had a rough start but I'm here to help now." he sighed as he kept his hands in the air. "I mean you no harm."

Kira who had retreated backwards on the porch furrowed her brows in a disgusted way.

"The fuck?" She swore.

Sam walked back to the porch with Cale and Ari beside her and they gave each other looks like the others would have an answer to why Arthur was acting the way he was.

Sam shrugged, her guess was as good as theirs.

"Um," Sam swallowed as she stopped beside him. "Why don't we go in the house and figure things out?"

Maybe it was dumb to invite him in, staying outside was a part of their plan but now she figured if he was going to do something he would have no problem whether it was inside or outside.

"Yes, we don't have much time." He agreed and dropped his hands.

Sam gestured for Cale and Ari to go on ahead and they glanced at her with the same dumbfounded look but moved all the same. Cale gripped Emily's shoulder who looked like she was about to be sick. He opened the door and led her in while Cam hesitantly took a step back while keeping his gaze on Arthur then turned to follow them. Dylan turned after his eyes wandered between the people around him and he was then followed by Kira, Ari, and Trevor.

Sam had been watching her friends go into the house but hadn't moved herself. She turned her head slightly and found Arthur looking at her, he was obviously waiting for her to go ahead.

She chewed on the inside of her mouth as she started up the stairs and he followed. As they got into the house, Arthur closed the door behind him, causing the hallway to darken.

Her nerves went haywire as she thought of how easy it was for him to attack her, to kill her. She took a bunch of glances over her shoulder as they made it down the hall but she only caught him walking with a straight face.

They made it to the living room where the others sat in their usual places, though it was defensively.

Sam turned to face Arthur and backed away several steps, "You can sit if you'd like."

She started to wonder what the hell she was doing? Why would she offer him to sit? He could stand for all she cared, she'd be happier if he wasn't there at all.

"I'll stand." He said as he stuffed his hands back into his pockets.

Sam's eyes wandered to them as he did so and she realized he was doing it to assure them that he wouldn't do anything. It wasn't like he was hiding a weapon in there that could do more damage than his bare hands could.

She chose to stand too but backed to the wall behind her and leaned against it. She crossed her arms in an attempt to look serious but her nerves made her look like a fool acting tough.

They all glanced between each other while Arthur stood there waiting for them to say something. Sam wondered if he expected her to treat him like he was still her brother, if so he was terribly mistaken. When the silence got to be too much, Sam figured she should be the one to say something. She was the one who needed Arthur's help after all, the others were merely along for the ride.

"What's your plan?" She was surprised that her voice no longer shook, perhaps it was because she was ready to get the answers she wanted.

"I've already told you my plan." He had been looking around the room but brought his gaze to her as he spoke. "I've thought of many ways to defeat our brothers but no well thought out plan will defeat them...They'd expect one from me and they'd be ready for it," He glanced at the ceiling. "So I went with the simplest one."

"Is kidnapping and turning people into gargoyles simple?" Cale asked icily.

"No," Arthur replied as if he didn't hear the venom in Cale's voice. "But more simple than trying to find my brothers weaknesses." His sight was back on Sam. "They don't have one anymore."

"Anymore?" Ari questioned dryly.

"My sister was their weakness, she was the only one who could stop them."

Sam felt everyone's eyes shift from Arthur to her and she shuffled her feet nervously.

"Why was she so strong?" Cale asked him and Sam felt it strange that they were talking about her but not at the same time.

Arthur looked like he was staring into space as he explained his sister's ability to Cale and the others. "She was a black and white eyed gargoyle, she had the power of both gargoyle eyes and then some. It was rumored long before she was born that there was another but that one perished as well."

He had already told her the gist of the all powerful gargoyles back at the cave but she didn't know that one of them was her at the time. "I've always wanted to ask you this since you brought it up before," she straightened. "How could something so powerful die?"

Her question seemed to have struck a chord in him and he shuffled. "There were no stories about how the first one died, only that it did." He sighed. "But with you, you had an extra ability…You could take in energy."

"How?"

He considered her for a moment like he didn't want to continue but she was forcing him. "I don't know how, but gargoyles can get extra abilities and you just so happened to have one along with being the strongest." He closed his eyes as he backed into the wall that was facing everyone and like Sam, he leaned into it and crossed his arms.

"You used this ability to take in the brunt of an explosion but like a battery, you took in too much and when you couldn't take what was left, the blast took you."

Sam brought a hand to her mouth as she started to feel sick. The nightmare still haunted her and hearing about it from another's mouth made it even more real. Arthur watched as she reacted to his words, she was getting pale and a drop of sweat ran down her brow.

"Sam?"

Her head jerked to the voice and she was met with Cale giving her a worried look.

The others watched her with both curiosity and pity and she dropped her shaking hand and drew an uneven breath. "Why?"

"Why?" Arthur sounded annoyed with her.

"Why did she do that?" She swallowed.

"Our brothers broke into a base and took a bomb that would blow an entire city off the map." He looked angry now. "You saved the city by sacrificing your own life." he turned his sight to the others as Sam grew paler still. "I know you're wondering how they did it, stole the bomb that is." his voice grew rougher with each word. "They're my brothers, it's as simple as that... You have no idea what they're capable of."

Sam moved her head a bit towards her comrades and through her flashbacks of the dream, she remembered the blurred image of the gargoyle on the website they had found the first night there.

Was it one of the brothers?

"How can we beat them?" Trevor was surprisingly the first to speak.

"I don't think there's a way to beat them." Arthur admitted. "Like I said, my sister was the only one who could beat them." he gestured towards Sam. "But as you can see, she's not as strong as she used to be."

"Why do you think she didn't get her old powers back when you changed her into a gargoyle again?" Cale leaned forward.

Arthur acknowledged him then turned to Sam as he answered. "It could have something to do with how I didn't give her nor the rest of you the full dosage of gargoyle blood."

"Full dosage?" Trevor breathed.

"Archie and I ran our tests before changing anyone," Arthur gazed upward as if he was looking at the memory. "We used someone who was long dead as a research subject. Even if the person is dead, the body can still be changed, but not brought back to life. First we tried half the dosage as a starting point and the body changed. After we tried the full dosage and even though the person was already dead, their nerves convulsed and all of their internal organs exploded." he brought his gaze down. "I can't change any of you fully and risk you dying."

"It seems you had no problem with having your people attack us." Cale shifted his eyes and the hate in his stare intimidated Sam even though it wasn't directed at her.

"I told them not to kill any of you."

"But my friend lays in the ground, DEAD from having her head cut off!" Cale shot to his feet. "By one of your people!"

Sam stepped forward, she couldn't let things fall apart now. If Arthur wanted, he'd kill all of them as easy as a spider with a fly caught in it's web. She didn't seem to be the only one to get ready as

Ari and Kira jumped up and Cam jerked forward. They glanced at Arthur who had his head cocked to the side as he observed Cale's aggressive stance.

"Do you think you can beat me?" The air around Arthur was terrifying. It was hard to believe that there were three more gargoyles out there even stronger than him.

Even more unbelievable was the fact that Sam was stronger than all of them in her past life.

"No, I don't think I can." Cale held his ground and even if he was scared, no fear whatsoever registered on his face. "But it doesn't stop me from wanting to smash your face in."

The room was silent aside from nervous breathing.

"That's good." Arthur smiled and leaned his head against the wall.

Cale blinked at Arthur's strange response and he looked at the people around him and they too were looking at the man in front of them like he was a strange creature.

Kira fell back on the sofa and it creaked from the sudden change in weight. Everyone aside from Arthur jumped from the sound.

Cale awkwardly sat in his chair but remained on the ready in case he needed to get up again. Ari remained standing but backed to the mantle under the television. She looked back and forth between Arthur and Sam who stood defensively in case the ordeal wasn't over with. But when the air around them relaxed as much as it could, she too leaned against her respective wall.

Kira began to hum to herself to calm her nerves and Emily who was sitting across from Cale looked stone faced from what had just happened. Cale looked at her with regret on his face.

Sam knew they all wanted to have a crack at Arthur but were far too weak to do so. She also knew they would wait for any opportunity for him to be distracted. What would hold them back was the fact that he was supposed to help Sam. Aside from Cam of course who seemed to not care about Sam's fate but only for his revenge.

"It's obvious that none of us like that you're here." She admitted. "But I'm sure you know that."

Arthur kept his gaze steady as if the words did nothing to him.

"I don't care, you know why I'm here and you know it's not to make friends."

"Well if you're going to be here, we need a certain amount of trust to be established." She used her index finger and her thumb to show how much trust they currently had: Her fingers were touching.

"What do you want to know?"

"You changed us by using gargoyle blood that went with our own blood type. I don't know how that works but I know that you didn't change all of us with your blood, so the question is, where did the other blood come from?"

Sam's question brought the others attention back to the conversation, they wanted to know where the blood had come from as well. They were sure of the answer but they also wanted to know the specifics of whose blood ran through their veins.

"There are ten full blooded gargoyles alive in this country aside from my brothers and myself, they chose to live their lives peacefully with the humans. I tracked them down and asked them for help but they didn't want to leave their lives." Arthur explained and Sam took a look around the room. She was sure the others were rearing to say something about Arthur not forcing the gargoyles into his plans like he had with them since she wanted to as well.

But also like her, they thought it best to keep their mouths shut.

"They did allow me to take their blood though." Arthur continued as if there was no shift in the air around him. "And to answer you about how blood types work with gargoyles, it's simple: Though gargoyles are far more superior than humans, we also have similarities. Like our base forms that appear human and the fact that we have different types of blood like humans."

"So there's some random gargoyles blood in me right now?" Ari shivered with a disgusted look on her face.

"Don't worry, gargoyles don't get diseases so there's nothing that could have been passed onto you aside from the power." Arthur assured her.

"Yeah, that helps." Dylan shook his head with a twisted smile.

"How's that work with our eye color though?" Cale asked what Sam had forgotten to.

Arthur closed his eyes as he explained, "The eye color of the gargoyle you got your blood from doesn't determine your own. There's really no telling what determines the color and what makes one stronger than the other, but I've found that it has to do with one's capability to hold the power. The blood cells react to the power and the color represents how the body contains the blood." He opened his eyes and there was nothing but white. "For example: My father was a powerful black eyed gargoyle and my mother was the only white eyed gargoyle of her time. That was until my brothers and myself were born, all of us inherited our mothers eyes." Like a switch, Arthur's pupils returned, followed by his irises. "Our mother had a difficult time controlling her power, while none of us did." He spoke to Sam like the others weren't there.

"A gargoyle is born with their transformed eyes, I can remember to this day the shock we had to find that you had both colors. We thought the story was just that, a story. But there you were, the most powerful gargoyle in existence."

Arthur chuckled as he leaned his head against the wall, "The only time I ever saw you use any of your power was when you had to put our brothers in their place, they not only hated you, they also feared you."

Everyone's eyes were back on her but she ignored the feeling this time.

"Are you disappointed that I don't have that power anymore?"

"It would be a hell of a lot easier but alas, we have to work with what we have."

"...Yeah." She thought of the power, of how much it would help her but instead of wanting it, she was strangely thankful she didn't have it.

Power ruined people, Arthur's brothers were proof of that along with every being that ever lived that had been given power over anything.

"Do you think your brothers know what you've been doing?" Trevor asked nervously, his lips quivering.

"I'm sure they know." Arthur answered. "I'm sure they've known for a long time." he furrowed his brows. "You may not remember but there's nothing like a good game to them, and that's what they think this is."

"I'm twenty years old, why would they wait so long?" Sam removed her back from the wall, the more they talked about the brothers, the more she wanted to get going.

"Something is holding them back and I'm not sure what but I know whatever it is won't stop them for much longer. I'm sure they know that I've found you, maybe that's why they're waiting, so you'll be more fun to play with."

He pushed himself off the wall with his heel, "There's no more time for questions, that can come later." He rounded on Sam and she stood tall as he stood in front of her. "I don't know how much time we have left but for what we do have, I can train all of you to be just as strong or stronger than the gargoyles you fought yesterday." he turned his head towards the others. "But that depends on you."

Sam drew a breath, "I have to take this chance."

Arthur took a step back and nodded.

The both of them watched as the others got up starting with Cale. "My mind hasn't changed," he stopped next to Sam but his eyes were on Arthur. "But in the slim chance that we do make it through this, know that I will try with every fiber of my being to make you pay for everything you've done."

Sam looked at Cale then back to Arthur, there was good size difference between the two and at first glance, one would think that Cale would have no problem with him. The only thing was that the person wouldn't know that Arthur would always have the advantage.

"Sounds good." Arthur said cooly as if Cale's threat was a joke to him.

He glanced past the corridor into the kitchen, "If you're prepared to take my help, it is time we get to work." He started for the backyard. "There's no more time to waste," He said as he left their sight. "Meet me outside if you want to learn how to fight like a *real* gargoyle."

Sam looked up at Cale as the back door slid open and Arthur stepped outside.

"This is going to be fun." she said sarcastically.

"This whole thing is fucked." Cale shook his head as Emily appeared beside him. He glanced down at her, "You don't have to learn from him, we can teach you later."

Emily shook her head and swallowed. "I need to do this." And like a machine being forced to move, she started into the kitchen ahead of them and Cale followed closely behind her, he couldn't leave her alone with Arthur.

Sam waited for the others to pass until it was just her and Trevor and she blocked him with her arm as he began to follow them out. He didn't meet her eyes as she looked into his face, he wasn't the nervous man she had met two weeks ago, he wasn't even the same person she had left yesterday to go meet Arthur.

"Trevor, I mean this in the nicest way possible… but what the hell are you doing here?" She dropped her arm.

He gave her a quick glance but looked away in the next second, he couldn't bear to look at her.

"I want to help you."

It couldn't be that simple but Sam didn't think of Trevor as the kind of person to have an ulterior motive.

"I don't want your help."

Her words seemed to hurt him and for the first time since she met him, he met her eyes.

Really met them.

"I don't care if you don't want it, you can't change the others minds and you won't be changing mine." The determination on his face made her take a step back.

What the hell was up with him?

"I'm sick of it, Sam." he brought his hands into fists. "I'm tired of being weak."

"You're no-"

"I am!" He interrupted her. "Don't bullshit me…"

She watched his fuming look and her face softened. "Where is this coming from?"

He closed his eyes and dropped his head,"I stayed behind yesterday and all I could think of was how you guys needed my help. I know I wasn't going to be of much help but I still could've been there for you."

Sam could've told him that it didn't make a difference, that he would have only put himself in danger but she knew better. He had to get this out and she wouldn't be of any help if she spoke now, it's like he said: She'd be bullshitting him.

"You all came home bloody and bruised plus Cale and Emily's friend was killed and you were forced to kill Camilla." His eyes were filled with tears as he brought his sight back to her. They weren't sad tears, they were angry tears. He was angry that he didn't do a thing. "That must've been so hard for you."

It was still hard for her.

She averted her gaze as she thought of her dreams from the night before. Her skin still felt dirty no matter how much she had scrubbed the blood away. She had scrubbed it until it was raw but of course the skin healed right away while the feeling still remained.

Her face must had showed her panic because Trevor apologized for bringing it up. "The reason why I didn't get any better when you and Cale were teaching me was because I wouldn't allow myself to learn. I knew I was weak so I knew it wouldn't matter. But Sam-" he gripped her arm. "I'm still scared as hell but I'm not going to be weak anymore."

She blinked as she took in his words and his grip slackened on her arm until he let go completely.

She gave him a small smile, "I admire that, but what I said before is still in effect: If the time comes and you get the opening to run, do it." She jokingly flicked his forehead.

She wasn't going to get the stupid idea out of his head but she wanted him to know that the opportunity to run was still there. "It's me that they really want so it should be easy." she tried to joke but the words came out wrong.

"Sam-"

"Promise me." her voice accidentally came out as a growl but she didn't have time to regret it as Trevor promised her right away that he'd run.

"Thank you." she stepped in front of him and made her way through the kitchen.

Outside the window she could see Arthur standing at one side of the yard while the others stood at the other and they were glaring at him.

"Let's hurry before the fight starts without us." She opened the door for Trevor as he trotted after her and they stepped outside to join the others.

Chapter 24

Arthur had a look on his face that confirmed that he had heard Trevor and Sam's conversation.

"What?" She asked roughly and he looked away without answering her.

He looked all of them up and down, as if sizing them up, and Sam could hear their nervous swallows and shaky breaths. She drew a deep breath herself and closed her eyes, she was nervous as well. She wondered how he was going to teach them how to fight like *real* gargoyles.

Was he like Sam and Cale who had taught the others gently? Or was he to the point?

She opened her eyes as his eyes landed on her and they met for half a second then he met the group as a whole.

"You're alright with your skills, I'll give you that." He started. "But compared to what a gargoyle should do, it's nothing more than amateur."

"Well not too long ago we were human so being gargoyles is still a little new to us." Kira said sarcastically while rolling her eyes.

Arthur paid no mind to her and continued.

"I heard everything during the battle, my hearing has gone to the point that I can imagine it as if it were happening in front of me. I know you tried but my men were too strong for you." He removed his hands from his pockets and they watched anxiously as he did so.

"You need to hone your new power, you're fighting like humans while you are so much more." he stepped closer to them. "You have heightened strength, senses, and speed. You can do what a human can't. As soon as you're done with one attack, you go right to the next with no hesitation, or it will get you killed." he cocked his head to Sam. "My parents taught me that."

Sam knew by the way he looked at her that he was implying that they had taught her past life the same. She huffed as she flipped her head forward and grabbed her hair tie from her wrist and pulled her hair out of the way.

"Now *you're* teaching us." Her hair swayed back and forth as she brought her gaze back to him. "No time to waste, right?"

Arthur smiled, amused. "Then get to it."

They didn't know how to start but they settled with their partial transformations since they could manage that much.

They looked at Arthur for approval but he merely watched them without acknowledgement. They turned to each other and without saying a word, they agreed to do what they had been doing before Arthur's revelation. They picked who they wanted to spar with: Cale with Emily, Ari with Kira, and Dylan and Trevor with Cam and Sam.

They did what Arthur directed, they were faster and they used their heightened senses along with their raw strength. They felt like they were accomplishing something until Arthur stopped them, the disappointment clear on his face.

"You picked up speed and power but you're forgetting you can do much more than that." He was standing where he had been at one second and the next he was standing in the middle of them.

They jumped from his sudden movement.

Sam had witnessed first hand how fast he was the day before and she feared the fact that he could move so quickly but she also found herself impressed.

"You." He turned his head to Cale as he walked back to where he started then turned around to face them. "You're Cale, right?"

Cale nodded with his jaw clenched, it was obvious he hated that

Arthur was speaking to him.

"Carma talked a lot about you and…Emily." He brought his attention from Cale to Emily.

More anger registered not only on Cale's face, but the rest of his body. He clenched his fists and stepped between Arthur and his friend, his black eyes narrowed. Arthur wasn't fazed by it though and he blinked like he was bored as he started speaking again. "She didn't see me as the enemy and if she wasn't killed, I'm positive she would have continued to help me." like always, when he talked about what Camilla had done, his expression changed to a mix of anger and regret.

Cale and Emily saw it but it didn't change the way they felt.

"Why are you saying this?" Cale pressed angrily.

"Because I'm sure she would have been proud that you're helping your friend."

Sam watched the encounter with worry rushing through her, the battle from yesterday ran through her mind and how Carma never attacked her with the intent to kill. She believed Carma wasn't going to kill her at the end, no matter how much fear she had felt at that moment, she was sure she would have attacked without the intent to kill.

Looking back at it now, Carma's eyes weren't that of someone going in for the kill, but of someone who was in the middle of an internal battle.

"I shouldn't have used her condition as a means to get things in motion, I'm sorry."

Arthur's words almost made them fall over, never in a million years did any of them imagine those words coming from his mouth.

"That's not going to change anything." Cale stated with rage in his tone after his initial shock and Arthur smiled at his reply.

"I didn't want it to." he took a step back to get a better look at everyone. "Go again."

It took them a moment to get going after the small altercation. They were surprised that he stopped them just for that. When they got going again however, they moved with ease. Like Arthur's words had gotten them into it.

Sam took the opportunity to fight two people at once. She was able to work with Trevor and train herself at the same time. She found herself surprised that with his new sense of meaning, Trevor was better than before. Though like Sam and the others, he needed a lot of work.

It was her first time sparring with him but Cam proved to be a good fighter, she had to hand it to him, he was a lot stronger than he looked. Dylan on the other hand matched his body and was as tough as he looked.

She used her speed and was able to subdue both boys and though it was a victory on her behalf, the credit was all due to her eyes. Having the stronger reaction or whatever the hell determined the eye color made it unfair.

When she was done, she offered to help Cam up from where she had tackled him but he got to his feet without help. Trevor who she had kept standing shook his head at Cam's foul mood from losing. They brought their attention to the other fights when they heard the commotion and by doing so, they realized that there wasn't two fights anymore but one.

Ari and Kira had joined with Cale and Emily and they weren't fighting two against two, but every man for himself. Like Sam, Trevor, Cam, and Dylan, they did what they were told: They were using their new speed to their advantage. Emily used her signature slashes and landed some scratches on Ari and Kira but she couldn't touch Cale. As she watched, Sam realized that what Arthur said wasn't simply an apology, it was a means to get Cale going.

He had seen something special in Cale and knew he needed the extra push.

Sam had seen it too, all of the things Cale had done while he was human helped him now. He had the most experience amongst the newcomers due to his time in basic training and the martial arts Sam had taught him during their time in the cave. He had even trained with Sam while the others slept.

He kept moving forward from the very beginning.

Sam thought of how much he had changed since the battle: The way he moved, the determination on his face, and the power that he used. He was much stronger but he was still holding back.

He subdued Ari and Kira by knocking them to the ground and they fell on top of each other. He kneeled on Ari who was on top to keep them down and they thrashed under him but with his other leg keeping him steady, there was no moving him.

Emily thought it would be the perfect opportunity to get the upper hand on him since he was distracted but as she came behind him, he pushed her gently down without even looking at her.

He turned his head to Arthur who had been watching the fights unfold with his arms to his side and his face set in concentration as he observed what they needed to work on along with their strong points.

As Sam brought her attention from Cale to Arthur, she noticed something hidden in his expression, it was small but it was there: He looked impressed.

Arthur gestured for them to end their fight and Cale obliged by removing his foot from Ari and helping the girls up.

"You have black eyes but you have the power of a white eye." Arthur explained, "But I get why you're so strong, like many other gargoyles, you have the *will* to fight. That's what helps you transform and keeps you going."

Cale's expression didn't falter as Arthur spoke and like Sam, he now realized why Arthur had said what he had. He was training them with things that could force their will to strengthen.

Arthur's eyes flashed as he brought his sight to Sam, she had the same even expression as Cale but her eyes narrowed when she saw the look on Arthur's face.

"Since you two are the most advanced with your power, I want you and Maya to give it a go." Arthur directed Cale as he cocked his head back to him.

It took a moment for Sam to realize what Arthur had done, the name was still foreign to her.

"Don't call me that." She growled. "You know my name and it's not that."

So much anger pulsed through her from the simple reason of being called a different name. It would have been over dramatic if anyone else had acted that way but she had her excuses.

Arthur ignored her and stepped back to give them room. "You're going to want to get out of the way." Arthur warned the others and they looked back and forth between Cale and Sam while the two kept their eyes on Arthur.

They didn't want to fight each other, they wanted to fight the man in front of them, to make him suffer. But unfortunately, neither of them had the power to do so.

When the others shuffled out of the way, it woke the two from their murderous thoughts.

Cale turned his head to look at Sam as she shifted her eyes to him. Their expressions had softened by looking at each other but the anger was still present. It made it look like it was directed at each other while neither of them wanted to fight the other with those kind of intentions.

"Don't hold back." Now everyone had their eyes on Arthur, he looked like he was looking forward to seeing the outcome of the fight. "You won't hurt each other with the amount of power you have now." he added to assure them.

Cale turned completely to Sam now, they could've denied Arthur, told him that they didn't want to do it, but how would they learn?

This was the first time the two of them were going to spar under the guidance of someone who knew what they were doing. It was going to be the first time anyone had seen them spar since Emily had watched them in the cave.

Ari and Kira had said that they had heard them but now they were going to see.

They began to circle each other, their eyes locked.

Who was going to make the first move?

As they circled they got closer and before long, they were an arms length away.

No one made a peep, as much as they tried to hide it, they were looking forward to seeing the fight.

Sam exhaled, the air coming out long and deep and she closed her mouth as she felt her sharpened teeth brush against her lips. When the pain sizzled against her skin, she made the first move and Cale stepped to the side and grabbed her arm. He tried pulling her into a lock but she twisted her body in a way that didn't look healthy and got away from him.

They usually smiled and laughed while they trained but they had more in store for them than just revenge. It was life and death. They should have been more serious before.

The air smelled of rain as they set into their fight and they used every move they had taught each other, but that proved to be a problem. They knew how each other worked and it made it difficult to get an edge.

"You're fighting like humans."

Sam looked in her peripheral vision and saw Arthur shaking his head. Her frustration only escalated from his remark.

How could a human fight like this? They were faster and stronger than any human wished to be.

"Faster!" Arthur hollered over the sound of the fight, his patience wearing thin.

They obliged and added more speed and it got harder to follow each others attacks. Sam had barely managed to block Cale's hit that would have collided with her throat. The hit was hard as it hit her arm but it was evident that he was holding back.

"Don't hold back!" Arthur saw his hesitation.

Cale's eyes shifted to him as he kept his fist on Sam's arm and his eyes softened as he brought them back to her. It was like he was asking her permission if he could stop holding back.

She nodded, they wouldn't know how strong they could be if they kept holding back and that's all they did with each other. They would never advance if they kept doing so and neither of them could afford to do that anymore. Sam had to take these chances in order to survive, but the prospect of hurting someone she cared for still haunted her.

She had hurt him before, the person who had decided to stay by her side even though the man that ruined his life was involved, she couldn't hurt him again.

The pressure in her eyes was almost unbearable as she allowed the power she was holding back to flood into her veins. Her hands shook and her heart felt like it was going to explode as it pumped like a birds wings against her ribcage.

Was she going to lose control like her past lives mother had?

But to her relief, other than the rest of her body, her mind remained stable.

Cale was reacting the same to his power only he didn't have the panicked expression Sam had.

They attacked each other again as their nails and teeth turned razor sharp. Cale's claws ran across Sam's gut and left thin cuts as she backed away from the slice.

The cuts throbbed and she found herself growling at him, maybe it was an animal instinct that gargoyles had but the fight excited her.

She lifted her eyes and she saw that Cale looked like he was enjoying it as well.

The moves that hadn't worked when they weren't trying got harder to avoid: Cale had barely gotten out of Sam's grasp as she tried to flip him on the ground.

Horns began to peak from under their skin until they formed into a point on either side of their heads. Their skin paled then turned light gray, they looked more human than the stone gargoyles, all they had was the added features aside from the wings.

"Faster!" Arthur yelled again and they obliged.

Every hit and dodge happened so fast that the onlookers had a hard time keeping up.

Sam's breath hitched as she fell to the ground, Cale had landed a particularly hard hit on her. Her ribs that were still sore from the day before ached from the newest hit. She was getting tired, and by the look of it, so was Cale as his chest pumped up and down as he tried catching his breath. They weren't used to moving at this speed and they were especially not used to the power they were using.

Sam leaped forward and she slashed at Cale's front like Emily had, her nails ripping his shirt and blood splashed as her hand moved away.

Emily tried to run to Cale but Ari stopped her and shook her head and Emily understood.

This was what they needed to do.

The two fighting gargoyles swung their arms back to continue their fight and their fists were only inches away from each others faces before Arthur grabbed ahold of their arms and stopped them.

Sam gasped for breath as she pulled out of Arthur's grip and Cale did the same and allowed himself to fall to ground as he tried to catch his breath. He sat while gripping at the stitch in his side while Sam swayed as she tried to stay upright, but after a few failed attempts, she fell to the ground as well.

"Not bad." Arthur admitted. "I could tell you were using what power you could handle but you were still holding back."

They hadn't meant to but their bodies wouldn't allow them to go further.

Against a real enemy they wouldn't have a problem though.

"You're going to be tired until you get used to the strain, but once you do, you'll find that this isn't even the tip of your power." Arthur explained. "Though there's no chance for you to be as strong as you used to be Maya." He added and Sam shot him a look, her vision was blurry but she could still make out his entertained expression. She understood why he called her Maya before: Like Cale, he wanted to get her going but now he was doing it because he simply wanted to.

"Yeah…" she didn't have the energy to argue.

"...You heal incredibly fast." Arthur sounded surprised as he turned to Cale.

Sam looked as well and the slashes she had made only moments before were gone. All that was left was the still wet blood from the wound. Sam brought her attention down to her own cuts and saw that they were still trying to heal though she had her's longer than Cale.

"I do." Cale breathed. "So what?" He leaned forward and rested his arms on his knees as he glared at Arthur.

"You shouldn't heal that fast." The words were drawn out from Arthur's surprise. "...You have an extra ability, a valuable one at that."

Cale gazed down at his chest and he pulled at his shirt, exposing his unharmed skin.

"Good." He exclaimed as he let go of the fabric. "I'll be a bigger threat then." he cocked his head up at Arthur who nodded, "It's a better ability than taking in energy."

Sam was starting to think that Arthur hated his sister as much as his brothers or he held quite a bit of animosity towards her.

"Good thing I don't have either." She shrugged as a drop of water hit the top of her head.

Suddenly the cloudy sky opened and rain poured on them.

"We're not done." Arthur stopped them before they could start for the house. "My brothers won't care about the weather when they decide to come for Maya." He stepped back and gestured for Cale and Sam to get up, "That was just an example of what you can do, so fight like you mean it." His voice was louder to accommodate with the added noise that the rain caused.

Sam and Cale looked at each other then to the others.

It was going to be a long day.

After hours of training, Arthur said they could call it quits. They were soaked to the bone even though the rain had ended an hour ago. Sweat and water made their sparring uncomfortable. The occasional cracks of thunder and the rush of rain was nice though as it covered the sound of their hits. The noise no longer bothered Sam, she was distracted by other things.

Another tree had been a victim of their training and the noise it made as it split could have been disguised as thunder.

They made their way into the house while limping. The stitch in Sam's side made her feel sick but she also felt accomplished, she had a better understanding of her power and she felt considerably stronger than before.

Her legs ached with every step and as she made her way into the living room, she collapsed on the couch next to Ari, soaked clothes and all.

There was no way they were changing when all they wanted to do was sit down.

Arthur came in last and instead of sitting with the others, he had reclaimed his spot against the wall. He crossed his arms and breathed, it looked like he was deep in thought.

Kira leaned against Ari but she pushed her away, "You feel disgusting." she spat, feeling disgusted with her friends rain soaked body.

"You're not feeling too good either sweet cheeks." Kira sighed as she leaned her head against the couch instead.

They were bruised and bloody from their lesson other than Cale who was already healing. He even looked like he was getting used to the strain on his body faster than the rest.

Sam wouldn't have felt jealous in any other situation but as her body ached, she felt the feeling was justified.

"How'd we do boss?" Kira inclined her neck to get a better look at Arthur and the rest turned to see what he was doing. They were surprised that he was so silent when he had constantly told them what they were doing wrong while sparring.

Sam thought she was going to have the words, "*Faster, stronger,* and *stop holding back.*" stuck in her head for the rest of her days.

"Alright." Arthur replied without removing his gaze from the ceiling. "I know what each of you need to work on and what you're good at." He dropped his gaze and it landed on Cale. "I know you can take a hit so that'll be good."

"Yeah… thanks." Cale replied sarcastically as he pulled his dark hair from his eyes which remained back due to how damp it was. The small bumps where his horns had been showed from the combination of sweat and water glistening off his forehead.

Sam brought a hand to her own forehead and felt the small bumps. At least they weren't noticeable upon first look and easy enough to cover with their hair.

"How does our body go back to normal after we're done with our transformations?" She called over to Arthur and his eyes moved to her.

"That's right." Dylan popped his head up as he rested on the arm of the sofa furthest away.

"I've always wondered where they go." Kira winced from the strain in her body as she turned to face Arthur.

"Everything has to do with blood." He answered simply. "As a gargoyle you have a surplus of blood cells that form your horns and wings plus it sharpens your teeth and nails. It also happens to gray your skin… it all happens because your blood cells are reacting to the power." he uncrossed his arms. "Your power comes from your blood."

"What about the bumps that are left over?" Cale questioned Arthur further, he had four bumps that spread from his head to his back, far more than the others.

Sam looked at the bumps on his head again, there was really no way to know that they were there unless you touched them. Only the glimmer from the rain made them pop now.

"It's from the excessive cells that form after you get the extra limbs for the first time. I have the cell build up on both my head and back but fortunately they're not noticeable to the human eye and ours as well unless we really focus."

"Good." Cale leaned into his chair and exhaled.

Although they weren't noticeable, it still felt odd to have small masses of cells under their skin.

They sat in silence for a few moments and everyone's breathing evened as they finally recovered from the excess physical activity.

Sam's muscles protested as she got up, a small whimper leaving her throat. The others looked at her from the sudden movement and Arthur had gone back to his thoughts so he didn't pay her any mind.

"Am I the only one who doesn't want to sit in their wet clothes all night?" She joked with an awkward smile. It was an effort to diffuse some of the tension and to her delight, she was met with words of agreement and small chuckles.

They got up with pained noises and most shook from their aching joints and muscles.

Sam started to make her way to her bedroom and as she made it to the corridor between the hall and the living room, her ears perked up as she heard someone outside. She tensed and turned towards Arthur but as she did, she found that he was already behind her. The others had heard the being outside as well by the looks on their faces.

"Calm down." Arthur told them as he glanced down at Sam's pale face then to the front door. "It's Archie."

He stepped past her and started towards the door and Sam found herself impressed that he could make out who someone was simply by the way they walked. She hated that she was impressed by him but her annoyance didn't last as she began to wonder why Archie was there.

The steps got louder and now she could hear the echo of Archie walking on the front porch. Arthur opened the door before he could knock.

"I see things have gone well." Sam could hear Archie's light voice but Arthur was much taller than him and the doorway was far too narrow for her to see past Arthur to see him.

"As well as it could be."

Sam didn't think she'd ever hear Arthur use sarcasm.

He turned and Sam and the others saw that he had a duffle bag in his hands. They tensed as they thought of what could be inside.

"It's my belongings." Arthur assured them as he walked their way and Archie followed.

"Hello, Samantha." Archie nodded towards her as he passed into the living room.

She gave him a jerky nod in return. Even though he was technically the one who had changed her into a gargoyle, she couldn't bring herself to hate him.

There was much to question when it came to Archie, he was a human helping a gargoyle, a human that seemed to agree with the kidnapping of innocent people to be turned into monsters. He had also been kind to her after she was changed into one, looking back at it now, she realized that he had known about her and her situation from the very beginning.

"Why didn't you just bring your stuff with you earlier?" Trevor asked as he moved against the wall to make room for them to walk through.

"I wasn't going to bring my stuff assuming you'd accept me." Arthur replied as he sat on the sofa closest to the television and Archie sat on the far end of the same couch.

Everyone watched as he rummaged through his bag and as his hand closed around something, he turned his head towards Archie and gave him a knowing look.

Sam couldn't see Archie's expression since he was facing the other way but she did see his head jerk a bit that Sam figured could have been a nod.

Arthur turned back to the bag and as he let go of the object, she could hear the rustle of fabric and the scrape of something harder. He zipped the bag shut and his eyes averted to the mantle as he drew in a sharp breath through his nose. "Don't worry about us, proceed with what you were doing." He said without looking at them.

Sam chewed at the inside of her mouth and jerked her head to the others who were looking between each other as if for help on what to do. Cale shrugged and started his way up the stairs, giving Sam an acknowledging look as he passed her. She felt like he was telling her that it was alright. They could hear them if they talked and further than that, they could hear every movement if they focused hard enough, they just wouldn't know who was who.

She turned to go as she returned Ari's loopy look as she went up the stairs.

She stepped down the hall, her ears felt like they were being pulled back to Arthur and Archie as she listened but they remained silent until she shut the door behind her.

"How did they do?" Archie asked and Sam wondered why he had waited for them to be out of the room to ask if they could hear every word. But after thinking about it, Sam figured it was because he was still human. Knowing they could hear didn't matter to him, it was just a human thing to wait for the person to leave the room before talking about them.

"Needs work." Arthur moved as he replied because Sam could hear the couch creak.

"....Do you think you can do this?"

Sam paused as she pulled her shirt over her head, the curiosity in Archie's voice surprised her.

It took a moment for Arthur to answer and Sam knew he was listening to see if she and the others were eavesdropping. Sam didn't hear them talking upstairs, only the rustle of clothes as they changed and she knew they were listening like she was.

"...I don't know." He answered and Sam froze as she threw her wet shirt on the floor.

She swallowed and found herself looking at the door, Arthur had sounded hopeless.

It could have been a ruse because he knew they were listening but it sounded so real.

"Then-" Archie started.

"Because I have to try." Arthur interrupted him and the conversation ended until Sam and the others returned.

They were warm and cozy in their dry clothes as they sat on the damp fabric of the couch. Emily sat in the chair where Cale had always resided while Cale had chosen to stand to give the rest the room to squeeze onto the couch away from Arthur and Archie.

Sam had also elected to stand but Ari had patted the back of the couch so she sat awkwardly on the edge with her legs placed on either side of Ari who was already squished between Kira and Trevor. As usual no one knew what to say and they sat in silence until Kira, who had a knack for it, started the conversation in a strange way.

"It's strange seeing you out of your lab coat." she pointed at Archie's attire that consisted of a white shirt and blue jeans.

She was right, it was strange.

"I thought you were the strict scientist type." She chuckled softly.

Archie looked down at his clothes while Arthur kept his eyes forward, ignoring the human like conversation.

"No," There was a faint smile on his lips. "I'm not the scientist type."

"So tell me then Arch-" Ari leaned forward and almost pulled Sam from her already unsteady seating position. She apologized as she leaned back against the couch, her hands closed around Sam's legs to help keep her upright. "Why's a young man like you working with Arthur?"

Archie's eyes went down, it looked like he was beginning to wish that he had left after giving Arthur his bag. It was funny seeing the man who had helped Arthur figure out how to change humans into gargoyles get flustered.

"I can't say I agree with everything he's done but I understand his cause." He lifted his eyes and met Sam's. "Not only are his brothers after you, but they'll also continue killing humans until they're satisfied… and by what Arthur tells me, that'll never happen."

"How'd you meet?" Trevor pressed the question more.

"…My father who was a doctor found him after his sister died." He swallowed. "My father...was a strange man. He took in Arthur when he found him on the streets, he was a young man who looked broken. Even after Arthur messed up and his eyes changed in front of him… my father still cared for him, he knew Arthur wasn't bad."

"I guess he was wrong." Cam shot Archie a venomous look.

"...I suppose so." Archie glanced at Arthur but he was still paying no mind to the conversation.

Archie looked like he was hiding something as he brought his eyes forward again. "I was five when my father welcomed Arthur into our home, my mother had died the year before so it was just the three of us." he drew a breath, "I followed in my father's footsteps in both becoming a doctor and taking care of Arthur." He cupped his hands. "But I've been in hiding since I decided to help with his plan, I know my father is looking down on me now wondering what the hell I'm doing." He smiled sadly as if it were a sick joke.

His father had died and Archie took his place. A boy of five had met a stranger that turned out to be a monster and later the two would join together to make more monsters.

It *was* a sick joke.

"How old are you?" Kira pondered Arthur, she really did seem interested in knowing.

Arthur looked younger than thirty after all and if the math was right, and Sam's past life had died twenty years ago, Archie would be twenty five now.

"Forty four." Arthur answered and everyone's eyes set on him at once. He looked nowhere near forty four physically but Sam wasn't surprised, she knew he was much older than he looked.

"...How old would your sister have been?" Kira acted like she was asking a very insensitive question.

She was in a way.

"...she would have been thirty nine." Arthur's voice cracked and in an attempt to hide it, he continued. "Our oldest brother Eli is fifty five but looks like he's in his twenties and the twins Oberon and Peyton are fifty three but look twenty." He looked at the group for the first time. "Gargoyles stop aging around twenty so if things work out the way I expect, you'll look like how you do now for the rest of your days or until you're killed."

"I guess I won't have to worry about wrinkles." Kira tried to joke but she turned her head to Sam as if she was saying sorry for asking the question.

Sam's face felt warm as she kept her eyes on Arthur as the other kept theirs on her.

"Do you guys believe I had a past life now?" she asked without leaving Arthurs gaze. "Do you need more proof?"

"If you're skeptical… I have this." Arthur reached into a pocket and pulled out a piece paper. He handed it to Archie who handed it to Dylan.

Cam, Kira, and Ari had no problem seeing the paper from where they sat and they realized that it wasn't just a piece of paper, it was a picture.

They gasped at the image and Emily got up to get a better look as Cale walked over and stood to the right of Sam who leaned forward with her hands gripped on the couch to look. Her heart thumped, it was a picture of *her*.

Of who she used to be.

She had seen the look before: Black trenchcoat, black skin tight jeans, knee high boots, and brown wavy hair that was braided to her scalp on one side.

The difference between the picture and the dream she had was the lack of blood and she had a smile on her face as she stood in front of a large building. Her eyes didn't match the mood though, they looked tired, so unbelievably tired.

"That was taken a few days before you sacrificed yourself." Arthur explained. "That was the city you died for."

The sick feeling was coming back, every time the fact that she had died came up, her body reacted before her mind did.

She could still feel the blast from the explosion, the blinding light, the millisecond worth of pain that she felt as her body was blasted into small fibers and even those were incinerated.

She knew the explosion was caused by the bomb her brothers had stolen.

Her friends looked between the picture and her while Cale kept his eyes on the picture to spare her feelings but she could feel him tense beside her.

"This has to be a joke..." Cam's voice drifted and Arthur reached to get the picture back.

"If only." he said as they handed the image back to him. He pocketed it and leaned his head against the couch as he closed his eyes, it was the first time they had seen him look tired.

It wasn't strange that he was carrying a picture of his dead sister around but what made it that way was the fact that the girl looked exactly like Sam.

She wanted to think that he had ulterior motives but seeing the way he acted when he spoke about his sister made her think that maybe he really was doing all of this for her.

But Sam wasn't his sister and he knew that, it could change him, he could leave at any moment knowing that she only shared a soul with his sister and nothing more.

The day was getting close to it's end and after a few long moments of silence, Archie got up. "Call me if you need anything." he told Arthur who nodded in reply while keeping his eyes closed.

"You're not staying?" Trevor asked as he and the others watched as Archie made his way to the hall. It wasn't like they wanted him to stay but having a human around surprisingly helped with the mood.

"I'm not needed here plus I have other things to do." He said as he made his way down the hall. "I think it's time I move my car before someone gets nosy." He opened the front door and stepped into the growing darkness. "Keep up the good work!" he called as he shut the door.

Sam got the feeling that he said that in an effort to be casual but it came out strange, awkward even.

"Does that mean we're staying here?" Cale questioned Arthur and he finally opened his eyes. "This is the safest place for the time being, when I find that it no longer is, we will move."

"What about where you were before?" Ari pressed as she brought her hand forward in a matter of fact way.

"I'm sure you don't want to stay with my other associates." Arthur brought his head up. "I'd prefer you stay away from each other for the time being."

"I'd prefer this not to be happening at all." Dylan rolled his eyes.

"Then leave." Arthur glared at him and Dylan's attitude changed to fear. "I'm here for Sam." He assured him.

"You're here because you have something to prove." Arthur stated roughly. "But I will tell you right now, you will prove nothing when it comes to my brothers… You'll prove nothing when you're dead."

No one could say anything to that.

Sam turned her head a fraction to Trevor who had essentially told her earlier that he had something to prove. This confirmed that Arthur had listened to their conversation. He wanted the dangers to be known and she was thankful for that since they wouldn't listen to her. She didn't know everything about the brothers but she knew none of her comrades stood a chance against them.

"Then this will all be for naught." Cale shot. "If we don't stand a chance, should we just let them kill Sam and let it be over with?" His sarcasm mixed with anger. "Why are we doing all of this just for her to be killed in the end?"

"I'm giving it the chance that if many of us work together, then we can fool them." Arthur answered as he cupped his hands.

"You said so yourself that your brothers can't be fooled." Emily spoke for the first time and everyone looked at her with shock from hearing her voice.

"No…they can't" Arthur stated as he realized what he had just said. "But I'm willing to take the chance to save her."

"...I'm not your sister." Sam's voice was sad, not because she was feeling sorry for Arthur, but because everything was centered around her, that people would die because of her.

Maybe it was better for her to die so everyone else could be saved.

"You're right." Arthur agreed. "But you dying isn't going to change anything." he said as if he had read her mind. "They will kill more innocent people after you're gone, they're reserving it for after they've killed you."

"What's stopping them from killing my family to get to me?" her voice shook as she got up from her uncomfortable spot on the back of the couch and sat where Archie had. She still kept her distance from Arthur and practically sat on the arm.

"They won't torture you by going for your family, they're more of a torture physically bunch." he inhaled sharply. "They enjoy trying to get into your head in different ways, they always did with me."

Sam blinked, she was somewhat assured about her family's safety but she found herself thinking about what they could have said to Arthur to mess with him. It was hard to think of him as being easy to get to.

"If there's enough of us, I believe that something can be done, maybe my full blooded comrades will change their minds one day and join us."

"Are you sure of that?" Cale asked as he sat down.

"No." Arthur admitted truthfully.

Kira began laughing, it had nothing to do with anything being funny but with the insanity of it all. "This is great." she wiped her laugh induced tears from her eyes.

The longer they sat, the more of them got up and either went to the kitchen or upstairs.

After getting something to eat, they retreated to go to bed. They were way past the point of wanting to know more about their situation, for today at least.

At the end of the night there was only Sam, Cale, Arthur, and Emily who was fast asleep.

Sam listened to Emily's even breathing so she could get through the silence. She was surprised she was even able to sleep with Arthur there but the sparring from earlier had all of them worn out. As Sam moved her eyes to Cale, she found his eyes growing heavy as he looked at the carpet.

"You don't have to babysit me." Arthur spoke for the first time since everyone else had left.

"I sleep here anyway." Cale answered roughly. "It's handy since I don't trust you." He leaned towards Emily and placed his hand on her shoulder. "Emily." he beckoned her to wake and her eyes fluttered open as she rose slowly, her mind still foggy with sleep. As she realized where she was, she froze.

"Go upstairs." Cale told her and she nodded with her jaw clenched.

"Goodnight." she said as she hopped to her feet and dashed up the stairs.

"What's your excuse?" Arthur asked Sam as he watched Emily leave from view.

"I spend a lot of time awake." Her vision was blurry. "I prefer to be outside of a dark room while being so."

She *was* tired though: Tired from sparring, tired from the new information, tired from stress, and tired from not sleeping the night before because of her nightmares.

"You never used to be afraid of the dark." Arthur twisted the handle on his bag and Sam's mouth twitched with annoyance. "I'm not afraid of the dark." she told him pointedly.

Cale watched them and he couldn't help but think of them as siblings bickering.

"You can go to sleep Sam." He assured her, he not only saw an annoyed girl, but an exhausted one. She brought her tired eyes to him and he gave her a small yet tired smile and shifted his head to her room.

She glanced at Arthur who was still sitting beside her, his head was turned slightly towards her and his hazel eyes were examining hers. He blinked and his eyes widened a fraction.

"What?" Sam asked dryly but she knew exactly what he was looking at: The gray engulfing her natural color.

"Nothing." He answered as she got to her feet.

"Goodnight." She said to Cale and ignored Arthur as she made her way to her room.

She laid awake with the lights off and she was engulfed in darkness. It always reminded her of the realm in her mind before she was thrown into one of her memories. Her heart raced but she kept the light off, it was like she was torturing herself.

She listened instead to the movements upstairs: The tosses and turns, the snores, and the soft breaths as the others slept. She brought her attention to the living room when she heard the light switch off. Cale and Arthur hadn't said a word to each other after Sam left. She imagined Cale keeping an eye on him, his expression hard as he embraced the hatred he had for the man in front of him.

She could have been worried that someone would try killing Arthur in his sleep and the help that he had offered would be gone but as she thought about it, she realized that there was no way in hell that Arthur would be caught off guard.

Especially with how weak they were in comparison.

She inhaled sharply and cuddled into the blankets as she brought her arms up and covered her chest as if she was protecting her heart.

Chapter 25

Her hand forced it's way through muscle, cartilage, and bone until it found it's victims beating target. Her fingers closed around it and as she pulled it from her victims chest, she brought the thing to the air.

As she looked at her prize, she saw darkness instead of a heart as it erupted around her.

She could hear laughter, a sound so chilling that it caused her legs to buckle and it sent a chill down her spine as the being cackled on. She covered her ears but the sound was too loud to muffle.

It was a deep laugh, maybe a man's, but perhaps something more.

Something monstrous.

As tears streamed down her cold cheeks, she questioned why it sounded so familiar, it was like hearing an old friend.

A friend that had led her into nothing.

"Stop…" she begged. "Please stop…"

Her eyes flew open as her heart pounded against her chest and she felt like she was going to be sick. She gasped and rubbed her eyes with one hand and gripped her gut with the other as she sat up. She was tired of feeling sick and tired of these damned dreams.

The laughter was still ringing in her ears as she tried to calm her breathing.

She kept her hand over her eyes as she listened to the snores and deep breathing of the others as they slept. As a distraction, she counted her comrades and realized that one of them was missing. She focused on the living room and only heard one person breathing.

She was sure Arthur was the one that was gone.

She shot up from the bed and almost fell to the floor as fatigue hit her. After a few moments of keeping herself steady against the bedframe, she pulled off her night clothes and pulled on her outfit for the day. She had rushed and put the wrong arm in a sleeve and when fixed, she realized the shirt was on backwards.

After taking a second to curse herself, she stepped into the hall and made her way into the living room. She looked first where Arthur had been the night before but she already knew he wasn't there. She brought her attention to Cale who was sleeping in the chair: He was wrapped in a blanket and his mouth was open as he breathed. She was surprised to see him still asleep but all they had done the day before made it understandable.

She was starting to feel nervous as she wondered where Arthur had gone.

Had he betrayed them?

Suddenly a soft tune began playing and she spun around as she looked for the source of the noise until she focused hard enough to realize that it was coming from the backyard.

She stepped towards the music and as the source came into view, she stopped walking and simply looked: Arthur was sitting on the grass with his eyes closed and in his hands was a small radio. It was old fashioned with a wood finish and an antenna sticking out of it.

Sam's ears perked as she listened to the song: It was an old rock jam that she recognized immediately since she had heard it on her father's radio when he'd work in the garage.

Arthur opened his eyes and turned his head to her and she flinched as he caught her.

Instead of keeping his eyes on her, he turned forward again and listened to the radio. Sam knew she had to go out now, if she walked away now she would look cowardly.

She slid the door open and stepped into the morning breeze, she hadn't looked at the time but she knew it was early by the way the birds chirped. She didn't put her shoes on so her toes touched the grass that was still damp from the rain the day before. As she approached Arthur, she noticed that he smelled of soap. They hadn't showed him around the house but he managed to find the bathroom to shower. It made her wary that he was able to move around so freely.

"What are your plans for today?" She asked over the radio.

"You know the answer." He said without opening his eyes and she glared at him, it was true that she already knew but she wanted details.

"Do you always whimper when your sleeping?" he asked her as the radio switched to another song.

Her face reddened, "You know the answer." she spat.

He opened his eyes and glanced at her as he flipped the radio off and got to his feet. "You're going to learn how to perfect your power today." He told her as he made his way to the house.

"Then why are you sitting out here listening to the radio when you could be teaching us?" She stayed where she was as he moved past her, only turning to face him as he got to the back door.

"I need to plan but I can't do that with all of you breathing down my neck." He grunted, keeping his back to her as he spoke.

Sam knew he spent a lot of time planning but by the way he acted, she knew that he had yet to find something that would work. She wanted to ask him what he had come up with even if it wouldn't work but she knew it wouldn't get her anywhere, he was good at keeping them in the dark.

"Wake your friends." He demanded. "I'm not wasting anymore time." He opened the door and stepped inside then sat down at the table while placing the radio in front of him as he moved the volume switch.

Sam made her way back in the house and glanced at his back as she passed. She blew her hair out of her face as she stepped into the living room and crouched beside Cale.

He looked so peaceful as he slept and she felt guilty that she was about to ruin it.

She poked his shoulder and his eyes slowly opened as he groaned and the chair creaked. His sleep filled eyes met hers and they widened. "I fell asleep." he said, disappointed in himself for not keeping watch like he wanted.

"You did." Sam confirmed. "It's fine though… he's waiting in the kitchen for me to wake you guys up so we can train."

"Great." He groaned as he pushed the chair down and leaned forward. He rubbed his eyes as Sam stood and made her way up the stairs to wake the others.

She was ready to learn more but she was far from ready for the pain that they would feel afterwards, it felt like she had just healed from the day before.

She went from room to room to wake everyone and they acted like kids being woken up for school. As she waited for them to get ready, she made her way to the bathroom and she splashed her face with cold water and wiped it off with a fresh towel. Ari stepped in the doorway, she was dressed in black from head to toe, the teal in her bangs the brightest color.

Sam's mind wandered to the picture Arthur had showed them and of her dream when she had seen her reflection: Her past life must have had a love for the dark shade as well.

"Another wonderful day of getting our asses kicked." Ari joked but didn't at the same time. Sam could see her true emotions in her eyes: She looked tired and nervous and Sam thought of how much she was regretting staying with her.

"It's fine." She assured Sam as she read the look on her face. "I don't regret anything."

"Sure." Sam found herself rolling her eyes, what was up with these people and their need to risk their lives? She flicked her tongue. "Let's go get our asses kicked."

They found themselves in the backyard like they had the day before and Arthur was walking around them. Sam's eyes followed his every move as she wondered what the hell he was doing.

He finally came to a stop in front of them. "It seems you all have average healing times for a normal gargoyle, aside from Cale of course."

"Lucky bastard." Cam said sarcastically and everyone turned to see his annoyed expression.

"I want to perfect what you learned yesterday and I'll join you." As Arthur spoke the words their attention was brought back to him.

"That's not fair." Dylan protested and Arthur huffed. "You think my brothers are going to be fair?"

He had a point.

"Maya, you and I will spar together." Arthur directed Sam and she inhaled sharply as anger swelled in her as he called her by his sisters name. She wanted so badly to break his face.

"If you call me that again I swear you're gonna get shanked." She warned him as she stepped forward and met his eyes.

It didn't take much, he was only an inch taller than her.

As they sparred Sam had a hard time keeping up with him. It was like when they had fought in the barn only this time he didn't attack her with such ferocity.

Unlike Arthur, Sam tried her all.

"You're far weaker than you once were." He smiled faintly as he dodged her punch with ease. "It's almost laughable."

"Fuck off." she spat and as she did so, she swung back again for another punch but Arthur caught her hand and pulled her forward only to flip her over backwards.

She landed on her back and her spine cracked.

"That right there, is *not* what to do when fighting your enemy." Arthur announced to the others as he gestured to Sam who was picking herself up from the ground. "You can't let what your enemy is saying bother you," he took a step towards Sam and pressed his foot against her back, forcing her back down. "The smallest distraction can be your downfall." he gazed down at the girl under his foot. "You never used to get distracted and you didn't use foul language to get your point across."

The others watched as Sam fought under his strength but the effort was useless. Cale and Ari both looked like they wanted to jump in to help her but knew better.

"I'm not you sister." Sam growled as she struggled and when Arthur finally stepped off, he had the expression of someone dealing with a child.

"Transform." He demanded and they did as they were told. "Wings too." he added as their eyes, nails, and teeth changed.

The problem with his request was that none of them aside from Cale had gotten their wings and they had no idea how to get them. Everyone watched as Cale closed his eyes and breathed in a long gust of air and as he did so, his wings sprouted just below his shoulders then as they extended out, they turned light gray.

Sam who hadn't changed to spar with Arthur watched with curious eyes as Cale grew his wings. She swallowed as she transformed to the same point as the others and tried to will her own wings to come out but failed.

They looked to Arthur for help after they were done getting their observations in on Cale who was beginning to feel like a science experiment.

Arthur shrugged, "This is where it gets hard." He grew his own pair of wings like it was nothing and what Sam found interesting was the fact that nothing else changed. He looked human aside from the pair of wings sprouting from his back.

"There is no set emotion or will to make your wings form, it's different for everyone." His wings shuddered then folded as they retracted into his back. What ever was left dissolved into his skin and he did it so well that the bumps that remained were as small as a finger nail.

"I got mine when I was ten when I was simply playing, it can happen at anytime."

The group glanced at each other. If it took Arthur so long, what made him think that they would be able to get theirs in the short time that they were gargoyles?

It proved to not be an easy task as they fought and tried to get their wings to come out at the same time. Sam heaved as she blocked a hit from Ari whose face was red from the physical activity.

"This shit isn't working." Ari gasped as she dropped her arms.

Sam glanced at Arthur who was watching with his hands still in his pockets, she wondered if the picture of his sister was in one of them.

"No, it's not." She sighed as she brought her attention back to Ari.

Kira tackled Ari but Ari flung her to the ground. "What the hell was that supposed to be?" Ari judged Kira as she got back up as if nothing had happened. "I just wanted to hit something." Kira gritted her teeth as she turned to Cale who was fighting with Emily, Trevor, Cam, and Dylan.

He wasn't using his wings so he kept them tucked behind him to keep them out of the way.

"Shit's not fair." Kira complained as she looked away from the fight and bowed her head.

"…Yeah." Sam agreed as her eyes wandered around their surroundings. She wasn't sure what she was looking for but her eyes stopped on the fallen trees. She blinked as an idea came to mind.

She walked past the girls and they watched with curious eyes as she touched one of the fallen trees with her boot.

She breathed as she tried to settle her nerves, she was probably going to embarrass herself but she wanted to try. If they were able to use their strength to knock them over, she figured there should be no reason why they wouldn't be able to pick them back up. Besides, she and Cale had pushed a boulder out of the way during their escape from the cave so it wasn't impossible.

She stretched her arms in front of her and knelt down like she was going to lift a weight at the gym. Only difference was that this was a full sized tree and she wasn't entirely human anymore.

She squeezed her hands under the tree, the bark digging into her skin as she started to lift.

At first it picked up a bit then fell back to the ground, almost crushing her hands in the process. She drew an unsteady breath, she couldn't lift like a human, she had to be a gargoyle.

As the thought went through her mind, she lifted again and this time the tree rose from the ground and stayed in the air. Her knees shook as her body took the weight, she felt like her arms were going to break in two.

As she pushed through the pain, her body gradually got used to it and she was able to keep the tree in the air with ease. After a full minute of holding it up, she pulled her hands back, letting the tree fall and the ground shook. Her hands still shook from the weight, or it could've been the power she had exerted. She breathed slowly to calm the feeling.

If she practiced more, she would be able to use this strength in a fight, she could do so much more than knock heavy things over, she could pick them up and use them against her enemies.

"Jesus Christ." Kira approached her from behind and observed the tree. "We can do that?" she turned to ask Arthur.

"Obviously." He answered pointedly.

As Sam turned, she realized that all eyes were on her. All of which looked like bottomless black holes. Arthur seemed to acknowledge what she had done but didn't seem impressed. Sam understood though, according to him she was so great in her past life that anything she did now looked like child's play.

"Since she can do it so can you, so get to it." he demanded and that's what they did for hours: Fight, lift, and try to get their wings to come out.

At the end none of them were able to get their wings and Sam felt frustrated as she fell into a chair at the kitchen counter. Her cheek was bruised from a hit Ari managed to land. Everyone but Cale joined her in the kitchen as he went to change out of his ripped shirt. It wouldn't be long until he ran out of shirts if he continued to keep them on when using his wings.

Sam pulled out her hair tie and her waves fell to her back as Arthur leaned against the sliding door. Emily who was the closest to Sam sensed that something wasn't right about her. She had a harder time training due to the fact that her dream was weighing on her. The laugh would ring in her ears as she fought. She had gotten distracted from it when Ari had hit her.

The bruise ached as her jaw clenched, the sound was ringing in her ears again.

Arthur watched her with crossed arms as she took in the laughter, her features were stiff and her face was pale. Sam, Emily, and Arthur ignored the others as they talked about what hits they landed and who was able to lift the tree and who couldn't.

Emily looked between Sam and Arthur, knowing that something was about to happen.

Cale returned with a fresh shirt but Sam didn't notice as her mind wandered to places she had never been. It happened so fast that her mind couldn't keep up.

"I need to start taking them off before doing that." Cale joked as he walked into the tension filled room. Arthur still had his ripped one on but he didn't pay any mind as he kept his eyes on Sam who was shaking ever so slightly.

"Sam?" Ari touched her hand as she noticed her acting strange but she flinched away.

Sam realized what she had done after the silence she was met with and her head shot up as she blinked. "What?"

"She was seeing if you were ok." Arthur told her and Sam turned her head and squinted.

"Thanks for telling me." She bowed her head as she thanked him over dramatically.

Arthur didn't react to her immaturity, he just continued to look at her until she felt uncomfortable and she brought her attention back to her friends. "I'm sorry." she sounded sincere this time.

"You're fine, Sam." Cale assured her and everyone else gave her acknowledging looks while still looking uncertain about her strange behavior.

"Do you think we'll start getting better?" Trevor called over to Arthur to help with the strange air going around the room.

"I do," Arthur finally looked away from Sam who was back to looking pale. "But even if you do get better, my brothers will still be stronger."

"You're great at setting a shitty mood." Cale spat and Arthur huffed in return but an amused smile appeared on his lips. "Even if someone could get stronger than my brothers, the fact stands that they're murderers and a being that shows no restraint when it comes to killing will always be stronger."

They got that, a loose cannon would always hold a candle over someone who held back.

Did any of them even have the courage to kill someone even if they were evil?

It proved hard for Sam since she had been haunted by Camilla since she had pulled her heart from her back.

"You should have no problem then." Sam said unconsciously and she blinked as her head shot up: They were all looking at her as if she was crazy. She turned her head slowly to Arthur and sure enough, he was giving her a death glare and she gulped.

"Elaborate on that." He demanded and she tensed.

She wasn't even sure if the words were meant for him. She felt it was more directed at herself but she felt that excuse wasn't going to work so instead she explained what she had been thinking all this time: "You can't tell me that when your brothers were killing people that you stood on the sidelines and did nothing?" Her voice shook at first but as she continued, her words got stronger. "And as much as you want to deny it, you are indirectly the reason why Carma was killed."

She thought she had him but the look on his face frightened her and she found herself sliding back into her chair. She wasn't the only one feeling the change around him as the others instinctively got out of their chairs and took a step away from him.

His voice was raw as he spoke, "Do you think your hands are clean of blood?" he uncrossed his arms and stepped towards her. "You've had to have seen something in your vision's of your past life, I can tell by all that whimpering you do in your sleep. If you don't know what you were, you're fooling yourself."

Sam's eyes glanced down as she thought of her dreams, especially the one when she saw herself for the first time: She was covered in blood.

She had ignored it, maybe it was something else… Maybe she had saved someone.

She had used every excuse in the book.

She began to think of the dream with her parents and brothers, she couldn't remember it before but as Arthur's words registered, what she had hidden to protect herself came back to the forefront of her mind: She wanted revenge on the humans, she was the first to suggest it and her three older brothers relished in the fact while Arthur looked frightened.

"Ah, you do remember." He leaned forward so their faces were inches apart. "I didn't kill one person while you and our brothers went off to get your *revenge*. You thought of it that way but our brothers had always wanted to terrorize the humans. You killed innocent people because of your own selfishness."

Sam started to shake.

She knew she wasn't Maya and that her past life shouldn't reflect who she was now.

But she had memories of her time as the full blooded gargoyle.

That had to mean something.

"And let me tell you something, *sister*." Arthur got even closer and Sam pressed a foot to the floor in case she had to move quickly, her eyes wide with fear. "You killed more than our brothers did combined, the four of you kept a kill count and you won by dozens each night." his words burned her and her heart raced as her eyes blurred.

She had so much blood on her hands… Whose was it? Was it a mothers? A fathers? Why'd she do it? Revenge on innocent people wouldn't bring her parents back and it certainly wouldn't make humans accept gargoyles.

"And you've killed in this life as well… you just can't help yourself, it's in your nature. You're always going to be a murderer." Arthur's words brought her back to reality and they stabbed her like a knife, especially the last few.

Camilla's voice had told her those exact words in her dreams, *"You're always going to be a murderer."*

Rather than the laughter, Camilla's voice now replayed over and over again, telling her what she truly was… *a murderer*.

"That's enough." Cale appeared beside Sam and he placed his arm between her and Arthur. "She's heard enough."

Arthur backed away, he had accomplished what he wanted.

Sam was completely and utterly defeated.

The room was silent but Sam wouldn't have known since her mind was doing backflips. Her shaking had escalated and she couldn't catch her breath.

"Sam?" Cale cupped her shoulder and she jumped to her feet, her eyes wide and her brows furrowed as she pulled from him and ran from the kitchen to the living room. She ran down the hall where she opened the front door and stepped into the sunlight.

She ran to her bike and tried starting it for the first time in weeks and it sputtered to life. Without bothering to put her helmet on, she wheeled the bike away from the house then straddled it.

"Sam!" Cale ran from the still opened door followed by Emily, Ari, and the rest. Their efforts to catch her were futile as she was already speeding down the driveway, the engine roaring as she forced the machine to shift quicker than it was supposed to.

Rage covered Cale's face as Arthur stepped outside and he grabbed the scruff of his shirt and lifted him in the air with ease as the others watched with pale faces. Arthur didn't seem fazed by Cale's anger but he allowed him to express it.

"You bastard!" he growled. "Why the fuck did you tell her that?!"

"She had to know." Arthur replied simply and Cale gritted his teeth as he punched him in the jaw, breaking it. Arthur stumbled backwards as Cale dropped him but he quickly set himself upright while lifting a hand to force his injured jaw back into place.

"If you truly did all of this for her, you have a fucked up way of showing it." Cale growled. "Now she's heading to God knows where."

Arthur's face was downcast and it infuriated Cale. "Look at me, you piece of shit." he demanded and Arthur lifted his eyes.

It was like his eye sockets had sunken into his head as an emotion they thought they would never see on his face appeared: Worry.

Cale ignored his look and spoke his mind. "I don't know if you're doing this for the reasons you said you were but if you are, you need to get rid of your anger towards her. You're mad that she left you and now you're taking it out on her current life."

Cale had him hook, line, and sinker.

"Cale." Emily rested a hand on his shoulder and as he turned to face her, he noticed her sad expression and his own softened as he turned back to Arthur to see his handy work.

"You're a fool." he spat.

"I am." Arthur admitted and caught them all off guard. "You're right… About everything." he laughed. "A human whose life I ruined just put me in my place."

He was met with silence. He had let the anger that his sister had left him get the better of him and he had said things that he didn't mean.

He truly did all of this for her.

He breathed, "I don't expect you to help me but I'm going to find my sister… before she gets hurt."

"Of course we're going to help you, for Sam's sake." Emily stepped ahead of Cale, she hadn't acted like she cared for Sam for weeks but was the first to volunteer. "Cale and I will go while the others stay back, if we all leave and get caught there'll be no hope."

Cale was shocked at Emily's courage while Arthur gave her a strange look, when did she get so brave?

"Is that fine with you?" Arthur called over Cale and Emily to others.

"Emily's right." Ari agreed. "I'd like to go but I should stay in case something happens."

They were nervous for their friend but what would they be able to do?

Trevor looked especially pale as he thought of how much he wanted to go save his newfound friend.

"I'll drive." Cale stated as he jumped over the stairs to get off the porch and Emily followed him as Arthur jumped over the railing and landed in front of Cale as they ran to the Jeep.

Cale had left the keys in it so he grabbed ahold of them as soon as he got in and started the vehicle. Arthur was already in the passengers seat and Emily sat in the back. Cale backed out quickly, slamming on the breaks as he shifted gears, then turned towards the dirt driveway leading to the road. When they got to the road, Arthur advised him to slow down.

"Why?" Cale questioned while keeping his eyes on the winding street, his knuckles white on the steering wheel.

"It'll be a problem if we get pulled over." Arthur stated.

"Where do you think she's going?" Emily asked as she leaned her elbows on their seats.

Arthur thought for a moment and as they got to a stop sign at the end of the road and Cale turned to look at him, his eyes suddenly widened. "Go to the freeway and head north." he directed. "And scratch what I said about slowing down, I don't know how much time we have."

Cale and Emily glanced nervously at each other in the rearview mirror before Cale turned left and pressed the gas pedal to the floor.

Sam stepped off her bike as she shut off the engine and she almost fell when her numb legs took her weight. She was stupid for leaving the safety of the house but she had acted with emotion, not with wit. Her stupidity shined bright as she gazed up at the trail leading to the cave that Arthur had used as his base.

She didn't know why she went there of all places but something had called to her as she raced down the thruway. She had gone there without any recollection.

She wiped her forehead to her chin as she thought of Arthur's words: She was a murderer not only in her past life, but in the present.

She could deny it but she and her past life were the same person, they only had different experiences.

Her teeth chattered as her nerves reacted to her thoughts.

How many innocent people did she kill during her quest for revenge?

Arthur was right, it was carrying into this life. She didn't like that she had killed Camilla, that she had blacked out and did it, but she had done it.

Who was going to be next?

There was yellow caution tapes blocking her from the bridge so she picked one up so she could duck underneath and she made her way up the stairs until she made it to the flat of the bridge. The metal clinked under her boots as she walked and she watched as car after car flew by underneath as they made their trek on the thruway.

It was a strange feeling being back there and it only got worse as she stepped off the bridge and looked up the incline that led to the cave where everything had changed.

She wasn't sure if it was fate that Arthur had found her or it was just a coincidence. All she knew was that she shouldn't be seeing her past lives memories.

She had heard about reincarnation before, how people got small glimpses at places they've never been before, of people they've never seen.

Her situation was so much more, not only did she still hold some of her memories, she also had prior family members running around.

She trekked upward, following the trail while looking for the opening that led to the cave. She had to be careful, there could be police officers or F.B.I agents wandering about. She finally found the opening and she weaved through a couple of trees to get there. She made sure to be careful not to step on any fallen twigs or trip over lose rocks as she continued upward.

As she got to the top, she wondered why she didn't feel tired, it was quite the hike up but her muscles didn't resist like they used to. Was it from all of the training she did? Or was it from her gargoyle blood?

She hid behind a tree as she looked into the clearing: At the other side was the opening of the cave, the large mound of rock was so familiar to her even though she had never seen it before. She had been blindfolded as she was led into it and she didn't dare look back when she ran from it.

Her eyes drifted downwards into the clearing and her heart thumped: There were two people facedown on the ground, their limbs twisted in odd ways.

What the hell happened?

She took a step and glanced around but there was no one around other than the two in the middle. She hesitantly walked over to them, her mind told her that it was a trap but who would have known that she would come here? In the humans minds, this place might be too hard for her to return to and there was no reason for Arthur and his gang to return as well.

She kneeled next to the people who were both men, she noticed them to be in their early thirties and as she flipped them over, their eyes stared blankly at her. They were filled with fresh tears and their expressions showed their last emotion before they had died.

They were filled with fear.

Her breath hitched and she stammered backwards as she got up but as she did so, she didn't hear the person coming from inside the cave.

"Hey!" a males voice called to her and she began to run.

It sounded familiar but she didn't know who it belonged to.

The man jumped from the caves opening to the front of her like it was nothing and he had a smile on his face as he grabbed ahold of her neck, his nails digging into her skin.

His smiling face filled with shock as he took in his catch and she felt the same emotion along with dread. She had come face to face with a man with blonde hair and blue eyes whose features matched her own.

His smile returned and it was more terrifying than before as he took in his sister's reincarnation.

Chapter 26

Sam grabbed ahold of his hand and tried prying it off but it didn't budge. Her heart raced as she realized who the man was: It was one of the twin brothers, she couldn't tell which one as she didn't have that kind of memory but she knew she was in trouble.

"There's no mistaking it..." His voice was high with excitement. "You look exactly the same..."

"I'm not-" she struggled but it only made him tighten his grip, his hold made it hard to breath but not enough to cut off her air completely.

"I saw the news… I saw you and I knew Arthur had gotten to you." He leaned closer to her face. "You're Maya, You're my sweet sister."

She was able to get out of his grip while he was distracted and she ran backwards but almost fell in the process.

She was sure if she ran he would catch her but if she stayed, she'd be killed.

Either way the outcome would be the same.

She took in the man in front of her: His blue eyes shined with glee and his mouth was opened in a wide smile. She thought of how even though she had been reincarnated, they had the same blood running through their veins. That wasn't going to save her though, blood didn't mean anything to the brothers and if they had killed her once, they'd do it again.

This was it, her stupidity was going to get her killed and their would be no reincarnating.

"Oh! Excuse my manners!" He bowed his head jerkily. "You must not remember me… I'm your brother, Oberon." He brought his head up again and he chuckled to himself. "I'm sure Arthur has told you about me."

"You're not my brother and I'm not Maya." Sam stammered. "I'm not your sister."

"But you are," he stepped towards her and sniffed the air. "You still have the same scent." his blue eyes flashed with excitement. "I can't believe the luck I have!" he started to laugh, only it wasn't a laugh, it was more of a cackle. It echoed through the trees and it sent a shiver through Sam. "I came here to see what my brother has been doing and I find you!" He closed his eyes, "*And you're all mine.*"

It confirmed that the other two brothers weren't there but the situation was just as dire. Going by what she remembered, Oberon was the most sadistic of the siblings.

Her breath hitched as her knees threatened to buckle from anxiety.

She didn't know what to do: If she ran she'd be toyed with, if she begged she would look like a fool. She wished she had never left the house, She was fool.

A fucking fool.

"Aw, don't look like that." Oberon spread his arms and his blonde hair blew in the wind. "It's a family reunion, a small one but I prefer it this way."

In the snap of a finger, he was in front of her again, his fingers twisted in her hair as he pulled her head back so she was looking into his face. He was taller than Arthur, maybe by five or six inches, and as she stared at his face she saw a little bit of Arthur and herself in his features.

"He'll be mad if I kill you but I'm getting tired of waiting." He let go of her hair as he got done glaring at her and she fell to the ground from the force but scurried back to her feet.

Who was the *he* Oberon was talking about? She wondered if it was Arthur but Oberon didn't seem like the type to care about what Arthur thought. Was it one of his brothers?

"Eli and Peyton will be mad If I kill you without giving them a turn but fate chose me to find you so I'll oblige." He smiled and his teeth extended into sharp points. "Are you going to go out with a fight or are you going to stand there and wimper while I kill you?" he cocked his head curiously.

"I'm going to die either way." She spat. "You're going to kill someone who knows nothing of why you're doing this." She was lying of course, she knew the gist of it but she still didn't know why jealousy would drive them to want to kill their sister. The person who shared their flesh and blood.

"You see," He started as he made his first strike and Sam collided with multiple trees from the force of the hit. Without even allowing her to feel the pain, he appeared in front of her again and grabbed the scruff of her shirt only to throw her back into the clearing. She smashed against the outer edge of the cave as she landed.

She gasped as the pain hit her, several of her bones were broken. Oberon was treating her like a rag doll and like a doll, she had no control.

As she tried getting up, Oberon stepped in front of her and she froze. She braced herself for another hit but he continued his explanation instead. "Mommy and Daddy-" he used a mock tone. "Always fawned over you, always told us to keep our eyes on you, the gargoyle from the tales…" he was beginning to become visibly angry as his joking came to a stop. "You knew you were stronger than us and you used that to your advantage to keep us from doing what we wanted."

"That's not my fault!" she argued and she found her voice to be muffled from the pain in her throat. Oberon's foot came crashing down on her head and she heard something crack as her head came in contact with the hard ground, the force leaving a dent the shape of her head.

She whined as she tried pulling his foot off her and in return, he began moving it in circles on her ear and it felt it was going to tear. She yelped as blood began to drip down the side of her head.

"We hated you even when you let us do what we wanted… you killed more than us. You had those fucking eyes at the end of each night… Those eyes that looked like daggers, you had them every time you denied us what we wanted." The force he used on her head increased along with his anger. She yelped as she felt her skull beginning to crack as he crushed it between his foot and the ground. Neither of them would give but Sam's skull threatened to.

She began to wimper from the pain as her arms began to go limp from trying to pull him off of her.

"Shut the fuck up." Oberon's foot left but he kicked her in her ribs in the next second and she went flying into the middle of the clearing.

The pain was stabbing as all of the ribs on the side that Oberon had kicked broke. She screamed and grabbed at them, the pain was a sign of something more than a break, something was punctured. As her breathing became labored, she realized it was a lung.

"Music to my ears…" Oberon closed his eyes as he walked to her and he took in the sounds she made. Her pained filled face gave him more satisfaction than a thousand dying humans. "I almost feel sorry that Eli and Peyton can't be here."

He kicked her gut and something erupted inside her and that something rushed up her throat and she regurgitated it onto the dirt. She could no longer see clearly but she was able to make out the color: In front of her was a puddle of red… blood.

She heaved again and with her pain filled limbs, she tried to crawl away from her attacker.

She was like a dying animal trying to make their last ditch effort for survival.

"Do you think I care that you're no longer my sister?" he pulled the back of her shirt as he spoke and brought her back to where her blood was. He smashed her face into the puddle and she choked on it.

"The fact that you are her reincarnation is enough, I'm sure Arthur has told you that we are far from kind…. Especially me." He flipped her over and pressed a hand to her broken ribs and her screams were excruciating to hear but Oberon listened to them like they were a beautiful melody. "That's what I want to hear!" he smiled and pressed harder. "More! More! More!"

She complied even though she had no control and her ribs broke further and they punctured her lungs deeper. She no longer had the air to yell and it made Oberon bored.

"I want to be honest with you," he leaned into her ear as he knelt down and straddled her middle. "When I found out that Arthur had changed you back into a gargoyle, I expected more."

Sam's eyes had turned white during Oberon's attack in an effort to speed up the healing, but the internal wounds were beginning to be too much for even her power to handle.

He glared at her half lidded eyes. "You're but a ghost of what you used to be." He wrapped his fingers around her throat. "I want to watch you die slowly then I'll bring your body to Eli and Peyton… They'll be mad but when they get over it, we'll show you to Arthur." An impressed grin appeared on his lips. "Ah," he blinked and leaned down again. "I've always wanted to ask you what it was like being blown into a million pieces?" His tone was venomous against her ear.

Her dream came back to her, the memory of death.

She could feel her body being pulled apart again, it could've been the pain she was feeling now but she could no longer tell the difference.

She screamed silently as her lungs fought for air and she wheezed as Oberon's grip tightened until she began to choke. Her legs thrashed and her eyes rolled into the back her head. She had been holding onto his wrists, trying to pull them away, but her hands were now shaking at her sides.

"I regret that I didn't get to see the light leave your eyes the first time but this will do." He explained as his grip got even tighter.

Her chest felt like it was going to explode and her gut rose up and down as she tried to salvage any air that could escape through.

"I know I should be worried about what *he* will do when he finds out that I killed you…" It seemed like he was talking more to himself than to Sam. Her hand reached up and grabbed at his face but he ignored it as he watched her's. "*He* has quite the interest in you but I don't care… this is my time and fate is smiling at me." He loosened his grip slightly then all of his strength came at once. "Everyone has interest in you!" He roared. "Interest in a worthless bitch!"

Sam could feel the cartilage in her neck being crushed and the muscles being torn. She no longer tried to breath and her eyes closed as her body began to shut down.

She was dying… *dying again.*

All of her efforts, all the plans she had made, they had amounted to nothing.

She was fated to die in both of her lives.

"OBERON!" A familiar voice roared and Oberon's grip slackened as he became distracted by the newcomer.

Sam was barely holding onto consciousness as her breaths came out as wheezes. She couldn't catch the air that she had lost as her injured lungs struggled to inflate.

"Arthur!" Oberon called gleefully and Sam flinched.

She didn't know how, but Arthur had found her and this was the moment of truth, she would know whether or not he was telling the truth about wanting to save her.

She couldn't open her swollen eyes and she could barely make out their words.

"I'm so glad you're here!" Oberon laughed. "Damn my luck is insane today!"

Arthur glared at Oberon then his eyes drifted to the girl under his brother: She was bloody and her eyes were swollen shut, her breathes were shallow and whistled as the holes in her lungs leaked air.

"This isn't the time," Arthur started, his voice shaking. "I thought you would have wanted to get a fight out of her."

He was trying to persuade Oberon to let her go so she could provide him more entertainment down the road. Arthur knew his brother well, knew what he truly wanted, knew how vile he was.

Oberon chuckled as he let go of Sam's throat and rose to his feet, settling over her.

"Do you know what I see when I look at you?" He pointed at Arthur with an amused smile. "I see a weak piece of garbage, you're always trying to think things through, always running after our little sister like you're a lost puppy." he snorted.

Arthur took Oberon's words but kept his eyes on Sam who was holding onto only a thread of consciousness. Her body was beginning to convulse as blood leaked through her insides. Half gargoyles were similar to humans in that aspect… internal bleeding wasn't good.

"If that's what you want, then I have to hurry before she dies." Arthur tried to keep his voice even but it came out as a beg. "Eli and Peyton will be angry with you for taking their chance away."

Oberon cocked his head as if Arthurs words were some kind of mathematical equation that he didn't understand. "Why does it matter? If I kill her now, it'll be out of the way and we can finally do what we want."

"She's not stopping you whether she's dead or alive." Arthur assured him. "She's weak, there's no way she can stop you."

Oberon huffed and rolled his eyes. "That's where you're wrong, brother." he pressed a foot on Sam's ribs and she screamed silently as she withered in pain.

Arthur wanted so badly to attack Oberon, to get him away from her, but it would ruin his chance to get her out of there if he could change his brothers mind.

Oberon continued, "Though she won't stop us personally, there's someone who insists we keep her alive and won't let us do what we want while she is."

"Who?" Arthur took a step. "Who's strong enough to hold you back?"

"Fuck off." Oberon answered. "Your face is annoying me, you always followed this bitch. You followed her when we killed the humans even though you didn't agree, you followed her when she stopped killing and now you changed her back into a gargoyle to save her." He cackled. "You can't tell me that you don't hold any animosity towards her for leaving you? She chose to save those pathetic humans instead of staying with you. She left you alone, don't you want revenge?"

Arthur shook his head, his expression pained. "I've hated her for what she's done, I felt like I wasn't important enough for her to stay alive. That she chose the humans over me, but at the end of the day, the fact that I missed her overwhelmed the anger and the pain that she left me with." He drew a breath as he took another step. "She's my little sister, big brothers are supposed to love and protect their sisters... not kill them out of jealousy."

Oberon's foot retreated from Sam's ribs as he listend to his brothers words.

Sam had caught them, they were phantom and echoed in her ears as her head rolled to the side but she had caught it all, he was doing all of this to protect her.

Her heart thumped in her ears as she thought of every harsh word he had ever said to her, how it had stemmed from his anger that she had left him with. As his words sunk into her mind, she realized that he had another reason for his harsh ways but she couldn't think of it anymore as her limbs went limp and her mind shut down as she lost consciousness.

"I've always hated you," Oberon growled. "We've kept you alive for our own entertainment but I've always thought of ways to kill you... There's nothing stopping me from killing this bitch and you. She's not strong enough to protect you anymore, *Artie*." He kicked Sam's body over and her limbs sprawled out in odd ways. "I can kill humans no problem because their not a fight." he pointed at the two men that he had killed prior to Sam getting there. "They're fun to kill because before they die, their true emotions show: They beg or they fight and it's entertaining. But you can only go so far with killing humans... it's too easy. Killing you and this girl would be easy but I would also get the satisfaction of doing it."

He smiled as his eyes turned white, "My patience is wearing thin brother and you know I've never had much of it." Oberon set back as he prepared to attack and Arthur braced himself.

As Oberon flung himself forward, another jumped from the woods: A man that looked exactly like the man he was stopping.

Oberon's twin, Peyton.

Oberon's face filled with shock as his twin caught him but changed back to his usual entertained expression right away.

"Brother!" he said gleefully.

"Shut up." Peyton turned from his twin to Arthur then to Sam who laid inches from his feet.

He rounded his neck back to his twin. "We let you out of our sight and this happens." he flicked Oberon's forehead and he flew backwards from the simple tap and landed against a tree. Leaves and bark fell from it as Oberon pulled himself up.

"I wasn't going to kill her Peyton, I was just going to bring her an inch of her life then torture her some more." Oberon had a hard time trying not to laugh over his lie.

"You're a horrible liar." Peyton rolled his eyes then knelt down and examined Sam. "This is our sister..." wonder filled his voice and his head shot up as he heard Arthur move anxiously.

"Don't worry Arthur, I won't kill her." he stood back up. "The terms of our contract with a certain *someone* doesn't allow us to do so until he allows us, though-" He looked down at his sisters reincarnation. "It doesn't look like she will live much longer as she is now."

Arthur shook as he looked between Sam and his brothers, he wanted to run to her, to get her out of there. He didn't even pay any mind to the fact that his brothers were working under someone, he had suspected as much.

"You can have her." Peyton assured him and as he did so, he kicked her to him: She flew through the air, her limbs limp as she fell into Arthur's arms as he jumped to catch her.

Arthur moved his hand and gently moved her face so she was facing him, her brown hair was sticking to the side of her face as she wheezed.

Arthur's head flung upward, his face filled with rage.

He was infuriated that he didn't have the ability to beat them, to avenge his sister's death and to protect the person she was now.

"Hurry… I don't think you have much time left." Peyton gestured for him to go. "With the way she is now, there's no way she'll be able to heal from this and don't take this out of kindness… we simply can't kill her yet and besides, Eli isn't here and it wouldn't be fair to him." He shot Oberon a look and his brother shrugged in return, he showed no remorse for his actions.

They knew Sam wasn't changed completely and Arthur wondered if they knew that the complete change would kill her as much as her injuries were going to.

Arthur steadied himself as he carried her and he turned to the trail to retreat. She was as light as a feather to him so he was able to go as quickly as he wanted.

Before he went down the incline, he looked over his shoulder: Peyton was standing where he was before, a smug look on his face while Oberon was waving enthusiastically goodbye.

"See you again, brother!" He called with a chuckle.

Chapter 27

Arthur sprinted to the end of the trail where he had left Cale and Emily. They had insisted on going with him but he had persuaded them that in the case that something happened only he needed to die and his hunch was right.

"What happened?!" Cale ran to meet him, his jaw shaking. Emily had fallen against a tree out of shock of seeing Sam's limp body in Arthur's arms.

"My brother happened." Arthur growled as he continued towards the bridge. "Take my phone out of my left pocket and call Archie." he demanded as they ran to the Jeep.

They didn't bother to take Sam's bike.

Emily grabbed the phone from Arthur's pocket as Cale opened the back door: Arthur laid Sam gently on the backseat and got in on the other side as Cale rushed into the drivers seat. Emily was already inside waiting for Archie to pick up the phone and when he finally answered, she jumped.

"Arthur?" Archie's voice echoed from the telephone.

"T-This is Emily." She stammered as her nerves got the best of her. "Sam's hurt…we need you."

"Put him on speaker." Arthur demanded as he stared down at Sam.

Cale had a death grip on the steering wheel as he sped down the road leading away from the mountain. Emily pushed the button to make the speaker turn on and Arthur wasted no time:

"She ran off and they found her, I was able to persuade them to let her go for now but she's not going to make it if we don't do something." He spoke quickly as panic overcame his tone.

"…I'll meet you at the house." Archie said simply and hung up, being a doctor must have taught him how to remain calm in dire situations.

Emily dropped the phone on the middle console and she turned her head and gasped as she got her first look at Sam's injuries. Arthur paid no mind to her, instead he kept his eyes on Sam to make sure she was still breathing. Her haggard breaths could be heard through the vehicle.

"How did this happen?!" Cale punched the steering wheel as he glared into the rearview mirror at Arthur. "This wouldn't have happened if you didn't push her!"

"Cale…" Emily tried to calm him, it wasn't the time to yell.

"Let him Emily, you and I both know he's right." They could hear the pain in Arthur's voice and the two looked at each other with shock. Arthur was full of surprises today, the man that had always acted like he didn't care was filled with emotion as Sam laid dying in front of him.

After everything he's done, he still cared for her. Seeing her hurt was the breaking point for his facade of hatred.

Arthur punched his knee and Cale and Emily jumped at the crack it made as the bone broke. If Arthur felt the pain, it didn't show as he continued to stare down at Sam's broken face.

When they got back to the house, Archie was already there, his black sedan parked in front of the house as he stood on the porch with the Ari, Kira, Trevor, Dylan, and Cam. They ran down to meet them as they pulled in.

"We heard what happen-" Ari began nervously but stopped when she saw Sam in Arthur's arms as he pulled her from the Jeep. Their faces were pale and they remained silent as Arthur carried her to the house. He had a slight limp from his self inflicted injury and Archie trotted beside him as Cale and Emily followed close behind.

"Put her in the bedroom." Archie directed as he opened the door for Arthur and he did as he was told. He laid her limp body on the bed and stepped back so Archie could examine her: She was becoming more pale by the second and her breaths were slower and drawn out.

Cale stood in the doorway while Emily stood behind him in the hall. They watched as Archie pressed on her chest, picked up her eyelids, and checked her pulse. He watched his wristwatch as he listened to her heart, timing how many beats per minute.

When he was done, he swallowed and gave a look that meant things weren't good.

"What can we do?" Arthur's words were hard to make out as he rounded on Archie.

Archie looked up to meet the gargoyles eyes, "You know what we can do but you also know the risk." He held his composure as he spoke.

"She could die either way?" Cale and Emily understood what Archie was suggesting, they were told the risks of being changed completely. The human body could only handle so much, Sam was part gargoyle now but her design was still human.

"She WILL die if we don't do anything." Archie answered, his voice rough.

Arthur's jaw clenched and he was almost as pale as Sam who was now beginning to make pained noises as more blood poured from her ruptured organs.

"Do it then." Cale shocked them. "If this is the only chance she has, we need to take it." he looked determined but his voice shook as he spoke.

Suddenly Sam regurgitated blood and it poured down her mouth onto her neck and chest.

"If you need blood, I got plenty." Arthur stretched his arm out and showed the purple veins popping through his skin and Archie nodded and exhaled. He opened the duffle bag he had brought with him and pulled out needles and tubing to exchange the blood.

"There's no time, I-" Archie started but Arthur sliced his arm open with a sharpened nail.

"Take it." Arthur bent his arm down as his blood began to pour from the cut and Archie quickly grabbed an I.V bag and willed the blood to pour into it.

Emily fell to her knees from the gruesome sight, it reminded her of Carma's death. There was a dying girl laying on the bed as someone split their arm open to give her the blood she needed to live. It wasn't something someone saw everyday. Cale kneeled to comfort her as he kept an eye on the scene in front of him.

"I think it's best you leave for this," Archie suggested as a drop of sweat fell down his brow. "I don't think you're going to be able to handle seeing her in a moment." Arthur's blood already almost filled the bag since he had hit a few veins. Archie handed him a cloth from his bag to hold to his wound as he closed the bag and started pulling more equipment out to start the transfusion.

Cale's jaw clenched and he hesitantly got up as he pulled Emily with him.

"Save her." He said as he turned to leave with Emily in tow, it wasn't a request but a demand.

Arthur nodded more to himself than to Cale but Cale wouldn't have seen it as he and Emily had already left out the front door to join the others outside.

Archie shoved a needle into Sam's inner arm as she began to shake like a leaf, he then proceeded to attach a tube so he could administer Arthur's blood. He turned to Arthur one last time before he flipped the switch as if he was asking him if it was ok. There was a great risk that came with what they were about to do but it was as Cale said: They had to take this chance.

Archie turned back to the bag and flipped the switch and Arthur's blood began to run down the tube into Sam's arm. At first nothing happened as the blood slowly ran through her veins but after a moment, she began to convulse and whimper as the blood ate at her insides. Her fingers twisted and her head swung back and forth as she fought it and soon the room was filled with her agonized screams. Arthur watched ruefully as the girl that was his sister but not at the same time writhed with pain. What she was doing was the sure sign of the blood doing it's job but they weren't sure how much her body could take. Maybe since she had adapted to the first half of the blood her body could take on the full thing.

They could only hope.

Arthur pressed a hand to her twitching arm with his injured one. He had to have faith in his sisters reincarnated body. It didn't matter that she was born a human in this life, she still had her strong soul.

To Arthur that had to be enough.

She growled and huffed and thrashed for several minutes until she fell limp against the blankets that were now disheveled from her thrashing. She had stopped breathing and her eyes were half lidded but she wasn't awake.

"No-" Arthur placed his hands on either side of her face. "Please…" His voice drifted as emotion filled his tone.

Sadness, regret, and anger all mixed in one.

Sadness, that it had come to this.

Regret, that he was the reason that she had ran off.

Anger, that his brothers were so vile to do this to her.

He was no different, he had abducted her and changed her into a gargoyle again. He had committed so many wrongs, he brought innocent people into this to fulfill his goal in saving her.

But in the end, all he truly wanted was his sister back and if she didn't get her memories back, she would hopefully kill him after the the slim chance that they had taken care of their brothers. That's why he had treated her so badly, to give her the reason to kill him because if his sister didn't return, there would be no reason for him to live on. If she killed him, she'd be a hero to the others and they'd stay by her side.

All of that was falling apart now… his plan based on his own selfishness.

He could have let her continue being human and watch her from afar if he had found her in a different way. He didn't know why he had settled in the town where he had found her. He had looked up records of people born nine months after she had died in her previous life like he had with his parents. He had found a lead that there was a girl that looked like his sister, there were many girls that could have fit the look but Maya had an air to her.

One that someone could never forget.

There wasn't a picture of the girl but it did say how old she was, her hair color, and her eye color. It had fit Maya's description but like any other lead, it could have been an average girl.

But till this day, Arthur remembered reading the girls name for the first time:

Samantha Knight.

Arthur's lip quivered as he removed his hands from Sam's cold face, his blood drenched arm had stained her shirt where it had rested. She was still and her skin had gotten paler, she looked like a dead person.

"Please…" Arthur gently took hold of her hand and pressed it to his forehead. "Please don't leave me again." his voice was filled with sorrow. "Don't leave me…"

The finger closest to her pulse felt something move and his head shot up as Sam gasped for air. There were no more restrictions as her lungs healed and her body relaxed as her broken bones snapped back into place. Her internal bleeding had stopped, Arthurs blood had done its job, she lived through the dose of blood that would make her into a full blooded gargoyle.

Even though she was out of the woods, her body was far too weak for her to regain consciousness so she remained asleep.

Archie who had stood back to make room for Arthur's goodbyes shot forward and pulled her arm from his hands to feel her pulse. Arthur watched with a hopeful expression and as Archie turned, he smiled at the doctors expression.

He was smiling as well.

"Don't leave me again…" Arthur's plea played over and over in the dark wastes of her mind. What kind of request was that? She couldn't control when her time was. If some higher force called her to join them, she didn't have a say, no matter how much she wanted to stay.

Oh, how she wanted to stay

She knew the emotion all too well as she had made her way to the bomb and placed her hand on it. The seconds felt like years as she waited for the explosion to take her.

She drew a breath and gazed around the void: She wasn't sure why she tried, she never saw anything before, why would she see something now?

She waited for the wandering creature but it never came, instead a fog drifted into the darkness and it was illuminated by some kind of light and it made her want to touch it even if it was against her better judgement. She reached and her hand sunk into it, her hand felt warm then it spread into her arm, up her shoulder, then to her head. As it got to her temple, the darkness disappeared and she was standing in a field, the blue sky spreading above her like a vast ocean, the grass tickled at her jeans as a gentle breeze picked up.

She was wondering where she was when she heard a child's scream behind her. She turned on her heel and was shocked with what she was met with: Her past life as a child who was no older than seven sparring with her mother. She looked exactly as she did when she was younger in her current life, her cheeks chubby and red while the rest of her was thin, her long brown hair was in a braid.

"I don't want to do this anymore!" Her squeaky voice rang between the gusts of wind, a few stray strands of her hair blowing in her face.

Her mother who Maya looked like a corbin copy of when she got older had the hair around her scalp braided. It reminded Sam of how viking women would wear their hair. She knew where Maya had gotten the look from later in her life, she really looked up to her mother.

"You can't use your power until you learn discipline." Her mother said as she held a hand to her free hair so it wouldn't get in the way as the wind picked up.

"I can use it now and I'm sure I won't have a problem!" Maya whined and her mother gave her an annoyed look. "Do you remember what happened last time?"

Maya froze and her little face fell.

Sam wondered what had happened but she was sure it had to due with a lack of control. Sam thought Arthur had said that she had no problem controlling her power, why did he lie? The question quickly dissolved as a bigger one replaced it.

How was she seeing this?

She had always been in the body of her past life in her memories so why was she standing there as if she was a separate being?

"You don't teach my brothers like you do with me…" Little Maya frowned. "Eli, Peyton, and Oberon hate me for it."

"I teach you like this because of the power you have and your brothers don't hate you." Her mother knelt down and pulled her daughters stray hairs behind her ears.

"I'm not special." Maya pouted. "I don't know why I have this power."

Her mother looked into her eyes, hazel to hazel, and gave a small smile. "I don't know why you have this power but I'm sure one day you'll know and I'll be so proud… And don't say you're not special because you are, especially to me."

When her daughter didn't perk up, she thought of something to pick up her mood. "When you have full control of your powers, I'll allow you to meet the humans."

Maya's sad gaze turned to shock then excitement, her parents had never let her go to the towns or the cities they had always stayed near. "Promise?" Her squeaky voice rang through the breeze.

"Only when you have full control."

Maya nodded repeatedly, she looked like a bobble head. "Yes!"

"Layla?" Maya's father came into view and behind him was a series of tents that Sam didn't notice before.

Her mother turned to meet her husbands gaze, he looked exactly how Sam had seen him in her memories. Her heart sped up as she thought of how much Oberon and Peyton looked like him.

"The boys require your attention." He told his wife and she got up and dusted herself off. "What did they do now?" she asked roughly.

"They insist on going to town and you know I can't stop them when they set their minds to something."

It made sense, he was the only black eyed gargoyle in the family if you didn't count Maya's single eye. Their father had no chance against any of them anymore, he used to be able to subdue them but as they learned how to fight, they got stronger than him.

"Watch your sister, Artie." Their mother ran in the direction of the tents with her husband in tow.

Sam rose a brow, who the hell was Artie?

She jumped when a young Arthur rose from the ground, the grass had hid him from her sight. He rubbed the sleep from his eyes and yawned as his sister gave him an amused look.

"Did you hear what mom promised?" she looked like she had won the biggest prize at an amusement park.

"...Yeah." Arthur got clumsily to his feet and Sam almost laughed at the difference between the boy in front of her and the man Arthur was now. Boy Arthur was tall and straggly while current Arthur had a good amount of muscle and his face was so much more serious.

"May," He started as he sat beside her and she cocked her head towards him as she laid on the ground like he had been moments before. "Why do you think they teach us how to fight?"

Maya looked at him like the question was the dumbest thing she's ever heard. "Because we were made for a higher purpose and we have to be ready." she used a mock tone.

"Ready for what?" Arthur pressed and Maya was stumped, she shrugged. "Mom and Dad said they'll tell us when we're ready."

"We'd be even more ready if we knew what was coming." Arthur was smart, he preferred to analyze everything before making a move. Maya felt like he had a point but their parents weren't dumb enough to keep them in the dark

if something bad was coming. She was young anyway, naïveté came with her age.

As she stood and watched, Sam found herself wondering what they had to be ready for: Her current enemies were her past lives brothers but they couldn't be what her parents were talking about.

She swallowed, what if other creatures were real? The demon theory was vivid and it could just be what people called the gargoyles, but the question rose in her mind: Were demons really a separate entity?

She looked back to the kids and she staggered backwards when she saw Arthur staring at her. Could he see her?

"What is it?" Maya sat up and turned to where her brother was looking but saw nothing.

He shook his head, "Just thinking." He assured her as he looked away.

The memory dissolved and Sam was flung into a new setting, they were in a campground of sorts. Around them were deserted RV's and ten cabins that were equally as empty. They were there without the owner's consent but they didn't plan on being there long.

"Here, Maya." Her mother handed her a bowl of chicken soup as she and her siblings sat around a fire. The sun was hiding behind the trees as it set and it made it look like it was far later than it was.

Sam approached the family and she noticed that Maya and Arthur had aged: Maya looked like she was thirteen or fourteen and Arthur in his late teens. She hadn't seen the other three siblings in her last memory but she knew who was who: Eli was the tallest and his brown hair shined as the fire flickered and it casted a shadow over his face. Sam noticed that he looked the same age as his parents due to their lack of aging while their children did until they were of age to stop. Peyton and Oberon sat beside each other, Peyton looked bored as he held onto his soup and glared into the orange flames. Sam wasn't sure how she was able to tell the twins apart, but the fact that Oberon had beaten her close to death was a huge indicator. His blood thirsty grin was engraved her mind.

She shivered as she stood beside Maya. So this is what they did? They moved place to place so they would go unnoticed.

Oberon snickered to himself as he flung a piece of chicken in the fire and Maya looked up from her bowl and chewed as she glared at her brother.

"What's funny?" Arthur asked innocently and he was met with a death glare.

"None of your business, weakling."

"Oberon!" Their mother chastised him as she made her way into the nearest cabin. She had stopped to face her son, her brows pushed together, and Sam thought of how she looked like her current lives mother when she got mad that she and her brother were fighting.

"Yeah yeah, I'll be nice." Oberon rolled his eyes and their mother shook her head but entered the cabin, somewhat satisfied with him.

"I was just thinking about how great it'd be if we could go to the village down the road." Oberon leaned forward so Maya and Arthur could hear, he had his normal devious smile on his face.

"Why? So you can torture people?" Maya set her empty bowl at her feet and crossed her arms.

"Yeah to be honest with ya." He shrugged and laughed. "When do you think mom and dad will let you go to town to meet the humans?"

It had been years since her mother had made the promise and she almost had full control over her power but had yet to make it to any town that they passed during their ventures.

Maya chewed her lip.

Oberon was trying to get a rise out of her and he knew how to. It ate at her everyday how her parents sheltered their children, especially her.

She hated her power, it held her back from living and it caused turmoil between she and her brothers.

"That struck a nerve, didn't it?" he snickered and she shot him a look.

"Do you want to test me?" She growled and Sam found herself backing away from her past self.

Maya's eyes were like daggers that cut into the soul of the person they landed on. Oberon sat back in his chair and Sam couldn't believe what she was seeing: He was scared of his sister.

"We don't want a repeat of what happened the last time you pissed Maya off." Peyton snickered and Oberon punched his arm.

Eli leaned forward finally and Sam got a good look at his face: The oldest son of Layla and Daniel had the perfect mixture of his mother and father. He had a small grin on his face from Oberon's embarrassment.

"Maybe one day you'll use that power of yours for something useful." he pointed at his sister and his grin grew into a full fledged smile. "Miss legendary gargoyle."

Maya's face turned beet red and Sam also felt her embarrassment like it was a phantom feeling.

"Leave her alone." Arthur tried his hand at being tough and Eli swung his head around to face his youngest brother. He looked like he was surprised that he was even there, "Oh, the weakling wants to defend his little sissy, how

sweet." he turned to the twins and they laughed in unison at their younger siblings embarrassment.

"Cut it out!" Their father stepped out of the cabin, their mother in tow. "Could we leave for five seconds without you going at each other?"

"Afraid not dad." Oberon said slyly and their father shook his head. "Well get over it and listen to us for a few minutes." The siblings perked up at the aspect of new information and Sam found her heart racing in anticipation as well.

"As you know, your mother and I worked with the humans long before you were born." their father began his explantation and Sam found herself stuck on his words: They had worked with the humans? To do what?

"But that stopped when the former head of the F.B.I died and the man that didn't agree with our existence became the new head, they've reached out for our help again and we're going to offer it."

"You want to work with those creatures?" Eli spat like they weren't monsters themselves.

"They're not creatures, their humans and they're the same as us Eli." His mother corrected him.

"No," he shook his head. "We are far more superior and they commit so many atrocities so why don't we just put them down?"

Sam glared at him and when she looked down to her past life, she noticed that she was doing the same. Arthur looked terrified as he looked between his oldest brother and his parents until he stopped on Maya to see what she thought: Her annoyed expression gave away that she didn't agree with Eli.

"Don't EVER say that." His mother rounded on him and gripped his chin to force him to look at her. "You don't know the humans like we do, you didn't fight with them."

Eli smacked his mothers hand away and Arthur gasped like it was the most horrible thing he's ever seen. The twins looked on with satisfaction as their brother spoke the words they had always wanted to speak themselves.

"You won't even tell us why you fought with them, you two are always saying that we're here for a 'higher purpose'-" He did a dance at the words. "My purpose isn't fighting with those worthless creatures."

Their mother looked hurt from her sons harsh words, she couldn't believe that she raised him to be the way he was."You'll know when I think you're ready."

"Bullshit." he shot up. "I'm done with your charade." he spat as he walked into the woods and the twins followed him while snickering to themselves.

"Can you trust them?" Maya asked as her parents watched their oldest sons leave. Sam looked away as they disappeared into the woods and she

brought her sight to the remaining four.

"I think their all talk." Her mother's gaze didn't leave her sons even though they could no longer be seen.

"No," Maya shook her head and her brown waves fell into her face. "I'm talking about the humans."

Her father stepped in front of her and knelt between her and Arthur. "We can trust them, besides, there's nothing they can do to us." he smiled reassuringly.

Sam watched the look on their fathers face as he spoke and she got the intense feeling that he was lying.

"Do they know where we are?" Arthur asked nervously, his hazel eyes wide with fear.

"Of course not." He assured his son. "I've held onto this old thing for years waiting for a call but I didn't expect it to come." He held out a damaged cell phone, it was an old style one that was bigger than their fathers hand and it surprised Sam that it still worked. "It's too old for them to track us so I haven't had a problem carrying it."

"Do they know about us?" Maya asked, 'us' as in she and her brothers.

"I haven't told them but I'm sure they suspect something."

"Hm."

"It'll be fine." Her father assured her.

No it wouldn't, Sam knew what was going to happen after this: Maya's anger and her oath of revenge that led to her murderous rampage with her brothers.

The scene dissolved again and it returned to pitch black.

She had killed so many people on her quest for revenge but something made her stop and she wanted to know what that was. She wanted to know how the humans killed her parents. She remembered their torn bodies and she felt sick. She pressed a hand to her mouth as she continued to think.

Above all, she found herself wanting to know what her parents were hiding.

The memories had raised more questions than they had answered but at the end, she was certain of one thing: Arthur was telling the truth about his plan to save her.

His words on the mountain, his pleas for her stay with him, and how his child self clung to her past life made it true. She just didn't know what she was going to do about what he's done to get her this far.

She wanted to get out of her dark dream state and return to the others, to let them know that she was alright and to tell them about her new found information.

Arthur could back her up if he was up for it, but she wasn't sure if the others would listen to him. She wasn't sure what was going on outside, but she found her hatred for Arthur to have diminished and it was replaced with understanding. She wasn't sure how to feel about it.

A bright light shined over her and it made her eyes sting. The never ending light spread before her like a trail leading to a path she was always meant to take. It coaxed her forward, her feet tingling, and like a trance had washed over her, she began walking as if she was going to find something in this vast wasteland. Suddenly she froze as if someone forced her to, the light turned off and she was thrown into darkness again.

Chapter 28

"She's waking up!" She recognized Emily's voice as her eyes slowly opened.

She blinked at the view in front of her as her eyes adjusted: She was back in her room at Cale's house, surrounded by her comrades who had big smiles on their faces aside from Cam who looked indifferent to it all. She turned on her mound of pillows and found Arthur sitting to her left. He had a gentle smile and his eyes were filled with relief.

"What-" she began but Emily, who had been to her right, knelt on the bed and wrapped her arms around her, muffling her words.

"I'm so glad…" her voice drifted and Sam could hear the crack as a sob threatened to escape. "We can't lose anyone else." She let go of Sam and leaned on her toes. "Don't run off again, you moron." She tapped Sam's shoulder with her fist.

"...I'm sorry." Sam bowed her head. Not only did her stupidity almost get her killed, but it had also hurt the people around her.

She was good at doing that in both of her lives.

"You're alive, that's all that matters." Arthur's soft tone took her by surprise, his hard ass charade was over since it proved to be detrimental.

"How though?" Sam turned towards him as Ari and kira sat on the bed, causing her to lose balance and she smacked her hand on the bed to level herself.

"Sorry." Ari patted her shoulder then pulled Emily into her who yelped and flung her limbs about in shock. Sam kept her eyes on

Arthur who was watching the girls flutter about.

"Tell me, *Artie*." She uttered slyly and Arthur looked baffled at her use of his embarrassing childhood name.

"Do you-" His voice shook and his eyes were wide.

Sam shook her head, "Not all of my memories, but I remembered a little… I remembered that you were always by my side."

Cam tsked and left the room as Sam's mushiness annoyed him and there was an awkward shuffle at Sam's change in attitude towards her past lives brother.

"Now tell me how I'm alive." She brought her attention back to Arthur after glaring at Cam's back as he left.

Arthur's surprise turned to nervousness as he tried to bring himself to tell her that she was a full on monster now. Cale stepped closer to the bed and the two turned to him.

"I told him to do it to save you." He looked guilty but proud of what he did. Sam didn't have to ask what that meant: They had changed her fully.

She turned her hand and looked at her palm, she felt different not just in mind, but in body. She didn't feel any pain from Oberon's attack nor the after effects of the transformation other than a strange buzz as the new power surged through her veins. She lifted her eyes as Cale started to look nervous and she gave him a small smile to assure him that it was ok and relief filled his face. The tension in the room eased as the others relaxed.

"I thought we couldn't be changed completely." She brought her attention back to Arthur and she jumped as she saw his still healing arm.

She knew how he got it, she was unconscious but she somehow knew what had happened.

"You can't, it worked for you but I wouldn't try it with anyone else." He moved his arm from view as he noticed her looking at his self inflicted injury.

"Hmph." She started to think of the irony of him hurting himself to save her, she had gone off and almost got herself killed.

She didn't mean to laugh but it came out anyway. "I'm always going to punish myself, right?"

Her comrades, who looked dumbfounded that she found the situation funny looked between her and Arthur.

"I didn't think you'd remember that…" He dropped his gaze.

"I do and I also know why you said it: I allowed myself to die because I wanted to repent for what I did… I punished myself."

Cale turned to Trevor and Dylan who were watching the former siblings with intrigue. He motioned for them to leave the room since he was feeling that they were intruding on a personal conversation. Emily broke out of Ari's grip and she rose from the bed and pushed her and Kira off as she also read the mood.

Everyone left the room and made their way to the living room, Cale who was last gave Sam a nod as he shut the door behind him.

Sam dropped her gaze from the door then leaned her head against the pillows. Her body was feeling fine but so much was going through her mind, as one question came to mind, another replaced it.

"You're acting strange." Arthur brought her back to reality.

She turned to him, "I wouldn't expect myself to act normal after almost dying again."

Her words stabbed him like a knife and she regretted them immediately. "I'm sorry."

He blinked, "You really are out of it if you're apologizing to me."

She really was, the girl that had left the house came back as someone else entirely. She was still Sam of course but certain things had changed for her. The actions of the people around her made that so, especially Arthur's.

"You saved me." She stated.

Arthur shook his head, "But I'm the reason you left, I put you in that situation…" he swallowed. "You almost died again because of me."

"But you saved me." She repeated. "I almost died again because of my own stupidity, I heard what you said to Oberon-" the name made her flinch. "About how a brother is supposed to love his sister, to protect her…"

"I thought you were unconscious." He looked embarrassed that she had heard his heartfelt words.

"I was after you said that."

Arthur twisted his fingers and rested his elbows on his knees, it reminded Sam of Cale's nervous sitting position.

"You're showing a lot of emotion, are you done with your hard ass act?" She questioned and Arthur shot his head up.

Ah, another emotion she wasn't used to seeing.

He huffed then smiled, "I should have known that you would see through it sooner or later."

"It was sooner I suppose." She smiled then frowned. "Seeing the memories of us when we were young made me realize that the boy you were would have never turned out the way you tried to act… Even if what happened changed you." She looked into his hazel eyes. "I know some of the anger was real though, you couldn't help but feel hurt by what your sister did...What *I* did."

Arthur clenched his jaw and averted his gaze, "Do you still hate me?"

She sighed, she couldn't tell how she felt anymore, there were so many memories that she had to jumble with. Her newest memories left her confused especially the fact that she was a different entity than her past self in them.

"I don't know how I feel anymore…" Her voice drifted. "I can't forget what you've done and that's where my problem lies and it certainly doesn't help that I feel my past lives emotions circulating with my own."

"I'm sorry…" Arthur bowed his head and he reminded her of the boy in her memories, only he was much bigger now.

As they sat in silence, a question that popped up more than the others resurfaced and she knew she couldn't wait to ask.

"How many times did our parents meet with the humans before they killed them?" It was strange talking as if they still shared the same mother and father.

As per usual, Arthur was shocked by her sudden knowledge of her past life resulting in him taking a moment to answer her.

"…They met a few times over the span of two years, they never told us what the humans wanted or what they did during their meetings, but at their fourth visit they were killed so we never found out."

"And that's where everything began." A shiver went up Sam's spine as she remembered the bodies of Maya's parents, her declaration of revenge, and what came after.

"It is," Arthur agreed and Sam cocked her head as she listened to him. "From the very start, something was meant to break." He laughed suddenly and it caught her off guard. "Our parents would always say that there was a reason for our existence but here I am, forty four years old and still unaware of what that is."

"Why do you think they never told us?" She inquired and Arthur shrugged as his expression changed to annoyed as he thought of his ignorance. "Maybe to protect us or they thought we weren't ready." he sighed as he looked down at his closed hands. "Maybe they would have told us if our brothers weren't such fuck ups."

Sam shrugged like Arthur had, there was no telling what their purpose was, especially since their parents weren't there to tell them. As her shoulders dropped from her shrug, a sharp pain went down her arm to her ribs and she flinched away from the pain as she gasped.

"You have to be careful," He warned her. "Even if you're a full blooded gargoyle, you still took a lot of damage." He pressed a hand to her arm to make her stay where she was as she fought the pain. When the pain dispersed, she glanced down at his hand and he pulled it quickly away. She didn't know why, but she found it funny that instead of his harsh attitude, he now played a hand at being a caring brother.

She leaned her head against the pillows and drew a breath, "I don't think we can beat them."

If Oberon was that strong, she could only imagine how the others were, especially together.

Arthur copied her, only he leaned his head against the hard wall. "You know how they are now, especially if you've seen them in the memories you've gotten back." He leaned his head down so he could give her a questioning look and she nodded. He brought his head forward again, "I knew you did since you never called me Artie when we were little… our brothers would pick on me with that name." His annoyance turned to a chuckle. "You used to threaten them whenever they picked on me."

"And they backed off." Sam smiled. "They were scared of Maya and I get why."

He rose a brow but she didn't want to talk about her astral projection in her own memories. How she got to see first hand the fierceness of her past life. It would only make the situation more confusing.

"When it comes to beating them, it depends on if we're prepared." Arthur went back to the problem at hand.

"I don't think we'll ever be prepared," She shook as she remembered the pain she felt as Oberon attacked her. "If *you* can't do anything, none of us can stand a chance, I certainly didn't…I didn't even have time to attack."

Arthur watched as her face paled. "I'll protect you May...Sam." He corrected himself before he got the name out. It seemed he had a hard time not calling her by the name he knew her by. It made Sam realize that though he called her by her past lives name to annoy her, he also did it out of habit.

"You can call me Maya." She declared and the shock on Arthur's face almost made her laugh.

"You don't like it though." His tone was uncertain, as if she was messing with him.

"Names don't matter." She assured him. "I am who I am."

He just stared at her for a long moment and when he finally spoke, his voice was still filled with disbelief. "You've changed."

"They say near death experiences have that effect on people." Her eyes rolled to the sun shining through the crack under the bedroom door.

After several hours and countless attempts to get her to stay still, Sam wandered into the living room. Her legs shook as she did so but she knew it had nothing to do with the injuries she had gotten from Oberon: Her body was getting used to the energy that came with being a full blooded gargoyle. She had asked Arthur what had happened to the little bit of human blood that she had left and he told her that his blood would have taken it in to strengthen itself. Even though she had the title of full blooded gargoyle now, she was still genetically human. Her genetic design was still human even with the power that she now held.

She sat on the end of the couch across from Cale's chair and Arthur and Emily who had followed her from the bedroom sat wherever there was an open spot. Cam was sitting at the far end of the couch closest to the television with his arms crossed and his eyes staring blankly forward.

Kira who was sitting beside him was giving him a side eye and Ari was twirling a piece of her teal hair between her fingers. Sam noticed that her natural light brown hair was coming in at her roots. Trevor was sitting on the floor with his legs crossed, he looked somber as he glanced at Sam.

Dylan was sitting beside Sam and he had cupped her shoulder and smiled at her as Arthur and Emily sat beside him. He looked uncomfortable having Arthur close to him but remained seated. Cale entered the room from the kitchen with Sam's computer in his hands, he had it opened and the light shining from it illuminated his face.

He acknowledged Sam with a smile as he sat in his chair.

"You still looking for that website?" Ari asked him and he glanced at her then back to the screen. "I don't know why I even try."

"Why would you when you have the encyclopedia right here?" Kira gestured towards Arthur.

"What website?" Arthur looked between the two.

"We found a site that was supposedly ran by a former F.B.I agent and they had quite a bit of information on gargoyles." Cale explained as he shut the computer in defeat. "You're right, Kira." He added afterwards.

"What kind of information?" Arthur pressed the subject.

"They had records on what towns were attacked-" Cale stopped abruptly and looked at Sam who had turned considerably pale as she thought of all the towns and cities that were attacked and the pictures of the mutilated bodies they had left in their wake. She could have killed one of the people in the pictures, maybe she had killed them all.

She couldn't believe that none of them hated her for what she had done but maybe it had to do with her not being the person who had done it.

"I can tell you later." Cale glanced at Arthur and he nodded as he caught Sam's shaken expression.

"What's up with the chummy attitudes?" Cam's voice caught them off guard like they had forgotten that he was there.

"This is chummy to you?" Ari questioned with disbelief filling her tone that he would even think that they were being chummy. "Do you see us holding hands and singing kumbaya? Maybe you want us to be at each other's throats until his brothers get here and kill us all because we were too hard headed to work together."

"I don't give a damn that his brothers are coming for her!" Cam flung his arm out and pointed at Sam who was just coming off her small anxiety attack. She normally wouldn't have flinched at the gesture but her nerves were on edge.

"The reason I stayed here was so I could kill this fucker when the time came." His arm moved from Sam to Arthur.

"We knew that," Kira rolled her eyes. "But thank you for the declaration."

"Try killing him and see what happens." Sam warned before anyone else could speak and everyone besides Arthur and Cale collectively inched away from her but she did earn herself some confused looks from them. She didn't realize what she had said nor did she try to be intimidating but that's what she had achieved. She reminded herself of Maya when she had threatened Oberon.

Cam was shocked by Sam's threat for only a second before he began his rant again. "Her attitude towards him has flipped, whether it be because she appreciates that he's done all this for her... Or that her past lives emotions are controlling her."

Maybe he had a point about Maya's emotions having something to do with her new attitude towards Arthur but it had nothing to do with control. She chose her own emotions, she didn't ask Arthur to devise his plan to save her, it got people killed and she hated it. She would always have animosity towards him but she couldn't deny that her need to kill him had gone down the drain since getting more of her memories back and hearing his words back at the mountain with Oberon.

"Do you think just because he saved me that I would forget what he's done?" She growled. "You'd have to be an idiot to think I'd ever forget but I also know that with the situation I'm in that holding onto anger isn't going to get me anywhere."

Cam rose a brow and rolled his eyes at her explanation, "What about you, Cale? Emily?" He looked between the two: Cale kept an even expression but his eyes lowered to the carpet while Emily flinched back into the sofa.

"You guys have lost the most from this monsters plan... like the rest of us, you can't meet with your parents... Your father must be worried about you Cale and I'm sure Carma would be looking down on you right now wondering why her friends joined the man who led her to her death."

Cale closed his eyes and inhaled, a small smile appearing on his lips and it sent a chill through the room. "You think you know her better than I do? Someone you never met?" His voice came out as a growl and Sam found herself retreating into the sofa like Emily.

Cam leaned back as Cale turned towards him. "No, but I know that-"

"You. Don't. Know. Shit." Cale said one word at a time, the newer having more venom than last. "If you don't like it, you're welcome to leave."

Cam didn't say another word but he also didn't leave. No one understood why he stayed nor could grasp his true intentions and when he left the livingroom to go upstairs, the room got noticeably calmer.

"Who knows the whereabouts of this house?" Arthur asked Cale after Cam left.

"My father and the two that left, Daniel and Jeannie." Cale answered but he kept his eyes on the empty stairs.

"Does your father *know*?" Arthur asked.

Does he know about your condition? He meant.

"Yes, but don't worry...he won't do anything." Cale assured him as his eyes retreated from the stairs.

"I always worry." Arthur declared.

"Do you think we should leave?" Emily asked as her eyes drifted around the room.

"Not yet, even though there's a few who know of this place, it's still the safest for the moment." Arthur sighed. "It's too dangerous to be on the move right now and I'd rather keep you away from the other gargoyles."

"How long do you think we have?" Trevor got up from his spot on the floor and sat where Cam had been.

"Give it a few more days and we'll find another place." Arthur brought his attention back to Cale. "Are you sure about your father?"

"One hundred percent."

Arthur leaned into the sofa, "A few more days." He and Sam met each others eyes. "Until then we'll continue to train here until we find out where we can go... If *you're* up to it though." he tested Sam and she smiled. "You know I am."

Archie had arrived later in the day to check on Sam. "The transformation was a complete success." He told them with relief in his tone.

The evening news played in the background as Archie finished up with the check up and joined Sam and Arthur on the couch to watch. Cale had his eyes closed as he listened to a woman talk about sports and Emily, Kira, Ari, and Dylan played cards on the floor while Trevor insisted on training alone outside while Cam remained upstairs.

"Coming up next, the dramatic turn in the kidnapping case." A man's voice declared before commercials interrupted the newscast.

Their eyes flew up, was he talking about them? It was hard to tell because kidnapping was also a norm with humans. Cale had kept his eyes closed but he perked up a bit, they had all remained silent as the commercials played then ended and the man that had spoken returned to the screen. He had gray hair that matched his gray work suit, he was sitting at a large desk with the woman that had been on many times before. She was much younger and unlike the man, she was dressed in bright colors.

"Richard Harper, the fifty seven year old father of Cale Harper who was kidnapped almost a month ago and remains missing-" Cale's eyes flew open and he flung his head towards the screen and listened with wide eyes as the newscaster continued. "He had been teaching in Japan but returned to the states to help in the efforts to find his son. After weeks of being home, the fifty seven year old was found dead in his home due to an apparent heart attack." The air in the room sank as the news took a heavy toll on those closest to Cale.

Arthur and Archie watched as Cale rose to his feet and walked towards the television as if it was calling to him.

It showed a picture of a house in a subbard type setting, in front of the house was an ambulance and police cars parked as the rescue squad and the officers walked about.

Finally it showed an older man of asian decent on screen when he was alive and well, in the picture with him was Cale who was considerably younger than he was now.

"We were told that he was adamant that our newscast with Detective Reginald Deluca about the kidnappers being the supernatural attackers from twenty years ago was a lie."

They ended the newscast and it left the people watching empty.

"Cale..?" Emily rose to her feet but stared at the screen as it changed to sports. They could see Cale's broken expression in the reflection on the screen.

"T-This can't be happening…" His voice shook with every syllable. "I have to make sure…"

"Take my phone." Arthur pulled his flip phone from his pocket and extended it to Cale who turned on his heel and grabbed it from him as he ran to the front door.

They heard the door open but it didn't shut as it was the furthest thing from Cale's mind. Emily glanced at Sam who nodded and with that, she followed him out the front door, shutting it behind herself.

Sam covered her face with her hands and brought her knees to her chest as a heavy emotion washed over her. Her hands unconsciously moved from her face to her ears as she heard the phone ringing that no one would answer and she could hear the sound of Cale letting his emotions go: He didn't cry but yelled out of anger, hurt, and pain.

They all sat in silence, their faces pale as they tried turning off their hearing. Cale's pain was becoming their's as he got louder and they could hear Emily trying to console him with no avail. Even Arthur who had been distant from the rest showed sympathy as he bowed his head and he closed his eyes.

He knew how it felt to lose someone and the aftermath.

Sam got up but wobbled as she did so.

"You-" Arthur began

"I'm fine." her voice was rough.

She made her way up the stairs and shut the bathroom door then sat on the floor. She wasn't hurt anymore, her body wasn't as frail as it used to be, but her emotions had remained the same and they weighed her down.

Cale's father had returned home and to protect his son, he had lied to the authorities.

She ran a hand through her disheveled hair and pulled at the roots. With the other hand she tried to do her nervous tick but stopped herself and flung her hand to the floor. She had almost died but had gotten another chance while Cale's father died. One life was saved while another was ripped away, there was never a middle ground.

What kind of fucked up world was this?

After a scalding shower, her muscles had loosened and her body moved easier as she descended down the stairs. Everyone was still in the living room but Cale and Emily had yet to return. She knew that it would be awhile before they would return and the silence outside indicted that the two sat in silence.

Arthur's head popped up as Sam stepped off the last stair and the others followed his gaze. Trevor had rejoined them and it was clear that he had heard the news.

"This life is wrong…" Kira murmured.

Sam could have taken that in many ways.

Before long the night came to an end as midnight struck. Archie had insisted on leaving but Arthur explained that it would be dangerous to leave the house that was supposed to be empty at a time like this. He also convinced him that his presence might help with the mood.

The others said their somber goodnights and made their way to their rooms while Sam, Arthur, and Archie remained in the living room.

"You can go if you want." Arthur assured Sam but she shook her head. "I want Cale to have the room so he can have sometime to himself."

Arthur gave her a sad look and no matter how much emotion she had seen him use, it still caught her off guard.

After several long moments she found herself dozing off but when she closed her eyes, she didn't fall asleep. Instead she listened to her thumping heart and she focused as it fell from one beat and picked up another until she could only think of the feeling in her chest.

"Things are looking bleak." Archie's voice was soft so he wouldn't wake Sam.

"I don't need you to tell me that." There was false entertainment in Arthur's tone.

Sam couldn't believe it, they both thought she was asleep and were starting a conversation with her there.

"Be honest with me Arthur," Archie's tone had gotten serious as the direness of their situation came to light. "Do you honestly think you're going to be able to save her?"

Sam's heart thumped and a pressure appeared in her ribcage along with her beating heart as if someone was pushing on it. She prayed that Arthur couldn't hear her heart quicken but she seemed to be home free as he answered Archie's question.

"You have no idea how much I want to say yes," Sam could hear the desperation in voice. "I'm not strong enough to take on my brothers and every plan I've made will fail."

"Then why do you keep trying?" Archie shook his head and rose his arm towards Sam's supposed sleeping body. "She's not your sister anymore."

Arthur chuckled but it had nothing to do with what Archie said being funny. "I get that a lot and as I recall, this isn't the first time you've said that to me. But you have to understand me Archie... You grew up with me around, you know how broken I was after I lost Maya. I don't want to save this girl because I think she's my sister, I want to save her because they share a soul." He inhaled and as he exhaled, his breath caught. "I know very well that they're not the same person, but her memories are trying to return and it gives me hope."

Sam wished she wasn't there anymore, she had originally enjoyed the prospect of hearing Arthur's thoughts but it made her depressed.

What Cam had said about her past lives emotions controlling her seemed to be true. She wouldn't have felt sympathy for Arthur before but now she felt inclined to feel bad for him since it was her past life that brought him down this path. She had turned the innocent boy she had seen in her memories into a conflicted man who ruined people's lives because of his selfish desires.

What Arthur said next made Sam's heart ache: "If she dies in this life, I don't want to go on anymore." His words were sullen as he gripped at the roots of his hair in frustration. "This world, it's people, it holds no purpose for me… I can't find the *higher purpose* that my parents talked about… I can't protect anyone from my brothers but while I'm alive, I'm going to try for her."

There was a long pause while Archie took in Arthur's words and Sam felt cold as her chest ached. Her eyes were beginning to water and the sting made her flinch, she was lucky that neither of the men were paying attention to her.

"I've done all of this for you because I care for you," Archie's face had fallen. "I helped you turn innocent people into gargoyles, I ruined everything for them. The people that chose to change were changed by the power, they turned into monsters and many people that I changed are being experimented on by the government… another was killed by Camilla who was in turn killed by her." Sam could feel their gazes on her and her face went hot. "And the people with us now are risking their lives for her," he was beginning to sound aggravated. "Tell me Arthur, after everything she's done in her past life… After how much she's hurt you and how she is now, why does she deserve your help? Why would you die for her?"

"You don't know what she's been through," Arthur defended her with no hesitation. "What she's done to make up for her wrongs, that what she did haunted her for the rest of her days..." His voice broke. "She sacrificed herself to make up for it and even now she's punishing herself and it'll never be enough for her."

Archie tsked and shook his head, an amused smile on his lips. "Don't look at me like that."

Arthur was giving him a look that could be read as '*Do you regret helping me*?'

Sam wished she could see it, wished she could walk away to try to compose herself after hearing what she just had.

"I regret all of it but I don't regret doing it for you…" Archie swallowed. "You've turned out to be a brother to me so that makes Maya my sister." He declared and there was a long pause as Arthur took in his words.

"I never thought I'd have a brother who actually cared about me." Sam could hear the smile in Arthur's voice.

"They're related by blood but they're not your brothers." Archie spat. "They don't deserve that title."

Sam hiccuped and their attention was brought to her as she pretended to nuzzle into the arm of the couch as she fake slept.

"My suicidal siblings who don't age." Archie said jokingly but frowned in the next second.

Chapter 29

She woke at her place on the couch, her head aching and her eyes burning as she opened them. She had definitely slept in an uncomfortable position but as she sat straight, her spine went back into place and the ache subsided. She was thankful for quick healing.

She gazed around the room: She was alone and she could hear the gentle breath's of her comrades upstairs. She could tell that it was morning thanks to the sun shining through the kitchen and the dim light in the hall. She didn't realize that she had fallen asleep, maybe amongst her pretending, she had actually done it.

As she got to her feet, the blanket resting on her fell to the floor and she wondered how Cale was doing.

She felt no restrictions as she made her way from the living room to the kitchen, her body had gotten used to the transformation. She was thankful that it didn't take as long as the first time.

She grabbed an apple from the jar next to the sink as a sharp pain shot through her stomach from hunger. She had refused to eat anything the day before, there was far too much on her mind for her to have an appetite. Her mouth watered around the sweet flavor as she took a bite and she noticed something in the backyard: Arthur was standing to the left looking out into the woods while Cale occupied the the other side, he was sitting on the growing grass and his face was hidden in his hands.

Sam left her unfinished apple on the table and made her way to join them.

Arthur turned towards her when he heard her approaching, he knew it was her long before she had even stepped outside no doubt.

She took in his tired expression, she felt awkward that she had heard his and Archie's conversation, had heard his true thoughts.

Her eyes wandered to Cale who didn't acknowledge that she was there. She didn't blame him, she should be the furthest thing from his mind and she preferred it that way, it would make him safer.

"Where's Archie?" She stammered.

"He went to join the other gargoyles... the half one's that is." He made sure she didn't misunderstand him.

"Why?" She pressed.

"Things can go wrong at any moment, we need to meet with them when we leave this place."

She didn't like the idea of being with the other monsters that he had created but it made sense, they needed their help whether she liked it or not.

Arthur saw her distasteful expression, "I'm not going to let them hurt any of you."

"Is that what you promised yourself before?" She met his eyes and he pulled them away from her and looked at Cale who had removed his hands from his face and was watching the two have their conversation.

He looked tired, extremely tired. The purplish bags under his eyes hinted that he hadn't slept a wink and Sam noticed that he didn't look like he had cried at all.

"I'll leave you two to your conversation," he huffed as he got up. "I'm fine with joining them if it means that they can help us-" He met Sam's eyes. "I'm going to wake up the others so we can get going on our training." His voice was dull and lacked emotion.

He was obviously holding everything in.

"Cale-" Sam stepped in front of him as he made his way to the house.

He froze but he didn't look at her, he kept his eyes over her head to avoid meeting her gaze.

"What is it?" He asked finally.

She furrowed her brows and took another step towards him and he glanced down as she pulled him into a hug.

He tensed at the suddenness of it and Sam couldn't believe it herself.

She kept her arms wrapped around him even when he didn't hug her back, her head resting on his shoulder and her eyes closed.

"I'm here." She comforted with a nervous tone.

His hands shook as he slowly brought his arms closer to her but when he was an inch from touching her, he pulled away and made his way to the house without another look.

"You tried." Arthur said from behind her as they watched Cale close the door to the house.

She pulled her hair from her face as she turned to face him. "Have I

always been shitty at comforting people?"
"Yes." He said without hesitation.
"Thought so."

As they waited for the others to join them, they began discussing what they were going to do after they left Cale's place aside from joining the other gargoyles.

"How long do you think we have until they've had enough of waiting?" She asked with her arms crossed and her eyes narrowed.

"If I know my brothers as well as I think I do, then it could be any second."

Sam could see the frustration on Arthur's face, he was stumped as to what they could do about the brothers. They were all too weak to fight them and Sam knew after Oberon's attack that even if they had numbers on their side it still wouldn't be enough.

She started thinking about the attack and the words Oberon had said to her and she remembered something she had forgotten about, something that could change everything.

"Oberon said that someone was holding them back… he said *he*… who do you think that is?"

Arthur perked up at her words but as he thought about it, he went back to his sullen mood.

"When Peyton stopped Oberon, he brought up this person but I haven't an idea who *he* is."

"Whoever it is, their stopping them from killing me." she shrugged. "For now at least." she cocked her head as Arthur's eyes became glossed over from his thoughts. "Are you sure there's no one from the past that they could be working for?"

He shook his head, "As I said I don't have a clue… what really worries me is the fact that there could be someone out there that can hold my brothers back."

They simply looked at each other and Sam knew they were thinking the same thing: The person their brothers were working for had to be strong…Unbelievably strong to hold them at bay.

Sam jumped as the back door slid open and Arthur who was facing the door seemed unfazed as he had likely seen their comrades coming. Sam hadn't bothered to listen for the newcomers to approach since she was lost in thought.

Ari yawned with sleep still in her eyes. "You look a lot better." she smiled at Sam who had turned to them.

She was surprised to see Cam amongst them but she had also suspected that he wouldn't leave, if he had it would foil his plans for revenge. Sam watched as his narrow eyes found Arthur and he gave him a look filled with hatred.

Cale was in front of Emily and he looked determined to get going with their training. Emily was giving him a worried look and as she looked away, she met Sam's eyes but quickly dropped her gaze since she didn't want anyone to see her worry.

Sam noted that she needed to talk to her later, about Cale and her sudden change towards her.

She backed away from Arthur to give the others room to see him as he directed them what to do.

"You know what to do." He waved for them to do so and they collectively did what they were told. Within seconds, Arthur was met with seven pairs of pitch black eyes and a pair of eyes as white as snow.

Their transformations were as easy as blinking an eye now, fluid and quick. Sam felt a bit odd as the new power coursed through her, her hands shook but with a few easy breaths, she was able to go back to feeling the way she had before she was transformed completely.

"Good, you've retained control." Arthur nodded towards her as he turned to walk away a few more steps. Sam couldn't help but get the feeling that he was disappointed.

The others seemed to get the same feeling as they looked towards her and she shrugged in return. Their relationship may have gotten better but she still didn't know anything about what he could be thinking.

He turned back to them and they noticed his eyes had turned white. "I want you to do what you normally do but I'm going to be in the fray for real this time." His snowy eyes fell on each of their faces. "Don't worry, I'll hold back." he assured them when he saw their nervous looks. "But my brothers won't, so this is your final chance to leave before it's too late."

When none of them moved aside from awkward glances and shuffles, he shook his head. "I'll never understand humans."

Without warning he went for Ari. She didn't have the time to dodge his attack and as his hand came in contact with her throat, her hands wrapped around his wrist. The others came to her aid as her hands tried to pry his fingers off.

Sam could tell that he was holding back as his fingers came lose without much force but it also could have had something to do with him dodging the others attacks.

There was no fighting fair, everyone went at Arthur at once and even then he held them off with ease. If anything it wasn't fair for them even though he was just one against eight.

Cale relished in the fight, it took his mind off of everything and it brought a smile to his face as he landed a hit on Arthur's jaw and broke it.

Arthur also smiled as he jumped back from Trevor and Dylan's attack, his hand on his injured jaw, pushing it back into place.

Before long amongst the pointed ears, teeth, nails, and horns, Cale's wings had appeared who had pulled off his shirt before doing so. The others looked on in awe as the grayish limbs protruded from his back. It was odd seeing the gray skin of his wings coming from his tan skin, it made them look fake.

Arthur pulled off his own shirt and like Cale, he willed his wings to come out. The rest who didn't have the ability yet watched as Arthur and Cale fought, their wings adding more speed as they flapped. Unlike in folklore, gargoyles didn't use their wings to fly, they used them to add strength to their attacks.

As Cale tried to land a kick on Arthur, the latter flapped his wings and he rose six feet from the ground and managed to dodge the hit. As he fell, he surprised Cale with a kick of his own.

Cale fell to the ground but he pushed himself up with both of his arms and a flap of his wings. Sam was beginning to feel envious that they could use their wings while she couldn't. So much that she found herself trying to urge them to come out but her efforts were proving to be futile.

The two winged gargoyles smiled as they sparred and relished in the fight. Cale who was fighting as a means to keep going and Arthur who had always fought with people much stronger than him or his monstrous subordinates.

Sam knew if he wanted, Arthur could have beaten Cale within seconds. He had used his strength on her when they were in the barn, where she had found out the reason behind her visions, where she had found out the truth about her life.

Arthur turned his head towards her as he blocked Cale's hit with his arms crossed like an *X*.

He saw her determined expression and although she didn't mean to have it, it took over her face and her eyes were sharp as they narrowed. Cale could have used the opportunity to further his attack on Arthur while he was distracted but curiosity overcame him and he turned to her as well. Arthur dropped his arms and backed away from Cale, signaling that he was done with him. The others looked between the once siblings and they saw their need to fight each other, felt the bloodlust that full blooded gargoyles instinctively had.

A growl escaped Sam's throat, she felt like an animal getting ready to pounce.

Her comrades looked at her like she was a completely different person. She had always been quick to fight, had relished in her training, but none of it compared to how she looked now.

Cale watched her with a curious expression while the others showed more fear than curiosity.

"I'm curious if you've gotten stronger?" Arthur smiled as he taunted her. "I can tell that you've developed the taste for blood." He took a step towards her. "Let's fight like we used to, Maya."

As if her old name was the signal to start, the two went at each other: It was exhilarating to let the power flow through her. She struggled with having full control, the bloodlust that Arthur was talking about threatened to take over and each hit caused her to shake. Her fingers curled and twitched as the power controlled her limbs, it directed her where to hit as if it were built into her.

"Control your breathing." Arthur demanded as he caught her clawed hand.

Her pointed teeth bared and her heavy breaths whistled through the cracks. She unlocked her jaw and did as she was told and drew a breath. The pressure on her chest loosened but a new pressure appeared in her eyes.

As Arthur was about to attack again, her eyes slowed his movements and with her renewed calm, she lifted her right leg and twisted her middle, landing a swift kick on him. He had barely managed to block the kick with his lower left arm before it landed on his side.

The force of her attack made him stagger backwards and even though he tried his best to stay upright, he fell backwards. The arm he had used to block her laid limp at his side, pain registering on his face. Even though he had blocked it, Sam's kick had still caused damage to his side as it had forced his arm into it during his block.

He brought his attention from his injuries and as he met her eyes, his widened. His mouth dropped and it hung open with shock.

Sam blinked, "What is it?"

The others couldn't see what he was looking at since Sam was facing away from them so they seemed as puzzled as she was as they took in Arthur's pale expression.

Though that could have been from the shock of seeing her knock him down.

Sam cocked her head when Arthur didn't answer, maybe he was just shocked like the others that she had managed to hurt him.

He swallowed and shook his head, "I-It's nothing," he closed his eyes as he got up, the pain from doing so showing on his face and he whimpered slightly from the pain. "I thought I saw something."

She rose a brow. "Ok?"

He gripped at his injured arm that was still swinging beside him as if it didn't have any bones.

A part of Sam felt bad for hurting him but another part of her remembered every hit he had landed on her and the sorry feeling went away.

"Spar with each other until this heals." He directed the others as he leaned against a tree.

It took them a moment to get going as they were too intrigued with what had just happened.

"You too." He did a *shoo* motion with his uninjured arm as he noticed Sam still watching him. She followed his order this time and as she joined the others, she was met with *Holy shit's* and *I can't believe you did that's*.

Arthur watched as they started sparring again and he kept a careful gaze on Sam but as she seemed to go back to herself, he dropped his eyes.

His arm ached as it rushed to heal and the bones repaired themselves. He flinched and his breath shook as he tried moving but his side ached with as much ferocity as his arm.

There was only one other time she had hurt him like this: When she still Maya, she had lost control while sparring when they were little. It ended up being the reason why their mother wouldn't let her transform until she learned discipline.

He had cried from the pain the first time since he was much younger and weaker but now even though it hurt, the pain drifted from his mind.

He had lied to her about not seeing anything.

It could have been a trick of the eye, maybe it was wishful thinking, but before she blinked, Arthur thought he saw a pitch black eye amongst the white.

Chapter 30

They trained for the remainder of the day while taking occasional breaks. Everyone had the goal to get stronger, and by the end, they felt like they had accomplished that.

Arthur had been out of it for the remainder of their training and Sam wondered if her landing a hit on him had actually bothered him that much but she knew he wasn't that kind of person.

As she gulped down a cup of water, she found him looking at her eyes again and she set the cup down and gave him a judgmental look."I'm starting to think you actually saw something."

"I didn't." He assured her roughly.

"Mhm." She rolled her eyes.

"Would you two stop bickering? My head is killing me." Kira pressed a finger to her temple and rubbed: She had gotten a swift kick to the head by Trevor who had apologized profusely afterwards.

"Let's not bring that up with Trevor around." Ari warned Kira as she practically fell into a chair, she huffed at the prospect of hearing more of Trevor's apologizing.

Trevor along with Cam had already made their way upstairs so they were in the safe zone.

Unless Trevor was listening of course.

Sam stretched her arms in front of her as Cale walked behind her to get his own drink. He had gone back to his sullen mood and he didn't say much as the others entered into conversations.

"Since we're going to be joining with our buddies soon, is there anything we should know?" Kira yawned after she asked her question.

"Keep your distance." Arthur said simply.

"Noted." Kira gave him the *ok* hand signal.

Sam felt uneasy and as she looked out the kitchen window, she saw the orange hue of the sun going down. Even though they had spent the day training, she felt like it wasn't enough.

It was never going to be enough. Especially after facing one of the monsters they were training to take down. She had believed Arthur's warnings about them, had believed her own memories, but she didn't think that it would be this bad. Past that was also the prospect of something else being out there. She had yet to tell the others as she didn't see herself making it past her brothers.

All of this would amount to nothing.

Cale sat down across from where she stood and looked at her with understanding in his eyes.

He felt the same and she knew it.

They hadn't gotten up early to train together for nothing, hadn't pushed themselves for nothing. All Sam could think of was moving forward but it was hard to do so with her past lives demons constantly haunting her.

She feigned a smile and she turned her head to meet Emily's gaze.

"Emily, can we talk for a minute?" She pointed to the front door.

Emily blinked as she wondered what Sam wanted to talk about. "Sure." She agreed and got up.

Arthur who was sitting next to her had been staring into space and as Emily got up, he woke from his daydream and his eyes wandered around the room.

Cale rose a brow at Arthur's odd behavior while Ari, Kira, and Dylan watched from the table with dumbfounded looks. None of them were used to Arthur acting the way he was, he showed a lot of emotion as of late and since Sam had knocked him down, he seemed to be zoned out.

Sam ignored him as she made her way through the house and out the front door with Emily. She listened for any hints of someone listening as they sat on the front porch and when she didn't hear any signs of curious ears, she got to the point.

"Is he going to be ok?" *he* as in Cale.

Emily turned towards the front door as if someone could burst out at any moment but when no one came, she turned back to Sam with a sullen look. "I'm sure he will be but for some reason he's holding it in and won't tell me anything."

Sam's face fell, she got the same cold shoulder from Cale earlier, only it was more understandable with her than it was with Emily.

"When-" It was hard for Emily to say what she was about to. "When we found Carma… he let it out, he allowed himself to feel the pain but now it seems he thinks he needs to keep it to himself. Maybe it has something to do with his father going the natural way, maybe he feels that his father didn't suffer like Carma did." Emily's eyes watered but she blinked the tears away. "It must have been hard for you, it must still be hard… seeing it happen then being forced to kill Camilla." She automatically regretted her words as she saw Sam's face.

"I wasn't forced…I killed her because I was furious." Her voice shook as she spoke and her breath hitched as she continued. "And to be honest, I don't even remember doing it."

"I'm sorry I wasn't there for you." Emily apologized and Sam perked up. "I was letting my fear of your strength influence me."

Sam shook her head, "I hurt Cale because I was having a panic attack, I wasn't myself and if I was you I would have felt the same." She swallowed the lump in her throat. "What made you change your mind about me?"

Emily just looked at her for a moment then faced the tree covered driveway.

"When Carma died-" her voice broke at the words. "I kept hearing her voice in my head telling me that I should stick by you… I don't know why, but her voice kept repeating it over and over until I had no choice but to do as I was told." She chuckled. "There were many times that I wanted to leave, especially after I found out about you having a past life and Arthur being your brother." She laughed now. "To be honest, I thought you were insane for believing him but as I thought about it and put your dreams into consideration, I believed it. But I still find it hard to believe even though things seem to add up."

Sam couldn't say anything, she couldn't think of any words to say. All she could think about was Mina and how she was the first to tell her about reincarnation. She still couldn't believe that she was right.

Emily sighed when Sam didn't say anything, "Even when I decided that I was going to stay by your side, I still couldn't muster the courage to make things right." She swallowed. "Until you ran off on your own and almost got killed.. I knew that was my final chance."

Sam's jaw shook. "I'm sorry… For everything."

"It's not your fault."

"But I'm still sorry."

Emily turned to her as she heard the break in her voice.

"As much as everyone wants to deny it, it's my fault." Sam smiled not because she was happy, but from the irony of it all. "I'm not the same as my past life, I don't know what drove her but in many ways, I understand her. I think getting some of her…*My* memories has brought me in that direction." She did her nervous tick. "I was a murderer, I did so many horrible things and I died to make up for it. I knew that before Arthur said anything about me killing people, I just hid it in the back of my mind to protect myself when in reality, I was only making it worse." Her hand went from her chin to her wavy hair, she had been wearing it down a lot lately. "I'm scared," she admitted finally.

"Of course you're scared-" Emily began but Sam cut her off.

"I'm not scared of what you think I am, of course I don't want to be killed by my past lives brothers but the more I think about it, the more scared I am to get my memories back." She covered her eyes. "Will I be a monster? Maya wasn't a monster when she started out but she turned into one… Maybe It'll be the same for me."

Emily caught her off guard by patting her shoulder and she flinched. "I think that since you fear being a monster that it will prevent you from becoming one." She shrugged. "Would it be so bad to have your memories back? I'm sure there's some good ones too."

If she got her memories back it would change her. Memories made a person and she would have the memories of two lives. She pictured getting the memories back of the people she had killed, how she had done it, and the aftermath that ensued.

The girls watched as the sun slowly went down under the trees, making the orange hue turn into a foggy gray as they got caught up in their thoughts. Before long they could smell food being cooked in the kitchen and the girls turned to each other as the smell made their mouths water. They just realized that they didn't eat breakfast nor lunch.

They sat and listened to the bugs chirp for another minute before they got up and joined the others in the kitchen.

After eating their dinner which was so graciously made by Ari, they sat in the kitchen and made their plan for after leaving the house.

Arthur suggested going to the safe house he had for the rest of the half gargoyles and although none of the half gargoyles currently with him wanted to do so, they agreed.

It was like Cale had said earlier, it was going to help their cause.

Before going to sleep that night, Sam had elected to stay in the living room as a feeling of dread overcame her. For some odd reason, she got the feeling that something was going to happen.

She could sense every crack of a branch as the wind blew, every creak of the house, and the snores of her comrades that were already asleep.

When she offered Cale the room he thanked her but said he'd rather stay in the living room as well. He seemed to have the same unease that she had along with the grief of losing his father.

Sam was returning to the living room from upstairs when she noticed Arthur standing at the front door looking out into the darkness through the tiny window at the top. As he sensed her watching him, he turned and made his way down the hall towards her, stopping in front of her and meeting her eyes for a second before turning away and laying on the couch.

Sam cocked her head towards Cale who had seen the whole thing and he looked as confused as she was. Arthur should have been able to notice her long before he did, there was something on his mind. They turned off the lights but left the television on a children's channel. Arthur had already fallen asleep as Sam and Cale stared blankly at the bright screen. Sam's eyes moved with the images of a talking goat as Cale seemed like he didn't see the screen at all.

Sam's eyes moved from the television as Cale moved his chair away from it, their eyes meeting accidentally and they held each others gaze for a moment before looking away.

"You know you can tell me what's on your mind." She continued with her efforts from earlier. She knew what it was like to hold everything in and the repercussions of doing so.

He smiled gently, "I know and I appreciate it, I really do." He swallowed. "Let's just focus on saving you first." He leaned the chair back and she could no longer see his face.

She sniffed as she laid down, she wanted so badly to punch something, all of this was because of her.

Every. Single. Thing.

Their blood would be on her hands if something happened to them, she would always be a killer even if she didn't do it herself.

She wished they would leave her alone to die.

She chuckled silently to herself, is this how she felt before she died the first time? Did she crave it? Did she know that she would reincarnate but still retain some of her memories?

She wasn't sure if she would ever get the answers to her questions so instead she decided to let sleep guide her into nothing.

"Maya." A voice sang her name.

Her eyes flew open and she practically bumped heads with Ari as she shot up. Ari almost fell as she dodged Sam's head but caught herself with her hand on the floor.

"What the hell?" Sam breathed and rubbed her head even though it didn't make contact.

"Arthur decided that he wants us to leave today." Cale came from the stairs with Emily in tow. "He couldn't get you up so he left it to Ari while he went outside to stand guard."

"Stand guard?" She repeated breathlessly.

"He's worried and I don't blame him." Trevor rubbed his tired eyes. "Just wish it wasn't six A.M."

Sam got to her feet and she noticed that they were holding onto bags filled with their belongings. Cale had his bag in one hand and her laptop in the other.

"I'll go get ready then." She said as she made her way to the bedroom that she had made her own for almost three weeks.

As she stepped out of the room, she was now clothed in black jeans and a T-shirt and the bag she had brought with her the day she got there was refilled with her belongings.

"Why wouldn't I get up?" She asked as she met the others in the hall, it was on her mind the whole time she packed.

"You just wouldn't." Cale answered. "I was there when Arthur tried but all you did was say your name."

"Why would I do that?" She asked herself more than the others. She thought of the voice in her head before she woke up and her eyes widened. "What name was I saying?"

"...You were saying Maya." Ari answered reluctantly.

She didn't have a chance to think about it as Arthur knocked on the door to make them get a move on and they jumped from the noise.

Sam opened her bag that still had some room in it and Cale dropped the computer in before she opened the door and stepped outside. Arthur was standing on the other side of the door to allow them to get out of the house, "Nice to see you among awake." He nodded to Sam. "...What were you dreaming about?"

She just gave him an apprehensive look.

"I'll drive since I know where we're going." Arthur turned to Cale as they made their way towards the Jeep and Cale handed him the keys.

The sun was still rising and Sam was met with the orange hue again as she waited her turn to get into the vehicle until it was down to Cale, Arthur, and herself.

"What's going on?" Cale shut the drivers side door before Arthur could get in. "You're hiding something."

Sam looked between the two as Arthur's expression got serious, "Something isn't right."

"What do you mean? Does it have something to do with you looking out the front door last night?" Sam inquired and he nodded with a locked jaw.

"I know you sense it too." Arthur gave the two of them an urgent look.

Sam swallowed as he looked up at Cale who she found had the same nervous expression.

"There's too many things leading up to something going wrong and we need to get out of here before it does-" Arthur explained but he stopped as a familiar voice interrupted him and sent chills down their spines.

"That's a good idea, brother!"

Sam turned pale and Arthur jumped in front of her as Oberon came flying from a nearby tree. He landed on his feet like a feather landing gently to the ground, his pointed smile reaching his blue eyes and he licked his lips at the sight in front of him.

"Oberon-" Arthur started.

"Shut the fuck up." Oberon rolled his eyes then snapped his fingers and on cue Peyton walked from behind the same tree his brother had jumped from.

Sam hadn't seen the other twin since she was passed out the first time but she knew who he was from her memories… Like his brother, he hadn't changed at all.

"Sister." He nodded towards Sam as he joined his brother.

Cale went for the back door on the Jeep but with lightning speed, Peyton was beside him and his hand was on his wrist, threatening to break it. Arthur had pulled Sam away from the Jeep as his brother got too close.

"Get them out of the vehicle or I'll crush it with all of them in it." Peyton warned with a smile.

"You'll kill us either way." Cale spat and Oberon's laugh boomed from behind them, "He's right!"

"Cale, what's going on?" Emily's muffled voice yelled through the window and Sam could see her terrified expression through the tinted glass.

"Do it Cale." Arthur directed him urgently.

Cale's hand shook with both frustration and nerves as he grabbed the door handle. "Get out." He demanded with an edge to his voice.

The passengers sat for a moment with wide eyes as they took in the scene outside with clarity.

"NOW." Peyton growled and they did as they were told out of fear.

To make sure that none of them would be able to get back in, Peyton kicked the vehicle to its side and the ground shook as it fell. The crunch of metal made their ears ring as they jumped away from the falling mass. Peyton rejoined his brother with a satisfied look on his face as he took in his handy work. None of them dared to run, they were smart enough not to.

"I'm glad to see you're still alive." Peyton rolled his head to his sisters reincarnation. "Surprised, but glad." He grinned as he turned to his twin."I guess you couldn't finish it."

Oberon gnawed on the inside of his mouth at his brothers effort to annoy him. "She got lucky." he assured him.

"So did I." Peyton agreed, his smile as mischievous as his brothers. "Eli and I have our chance now."

Sam trembled behind Arthur, maybe even more than the rest. She knew their power, knew what was coming. Arthur held true and kept his body in front of her as a shield. Even though she was terrified for herself, she wanted nothing more than for her friends to escape. She wished they had left when they had the chance, she was sure they were feeling the same.

"Why are you here now? I thought you couldn't kill her yet?" Arthur tried to prolong the inevitable.

"Becausssse-" Oberon stretched out the word. "We've had enough, we've waited twenty years… Almost twenty one, and we're not going to let that bastard stop us anymore." His smile grew wider as he took in his youngest brother's stone expression and his reincarnated sister's fear.

"You never used to be scared, you were cold and calculated…" He looked disappointed to see his sister in this state. "To be honest, it'll be less fun killing you without your cocky attitude being snuffed out."

"Who's the bastard?" Arthur pressed. "Why is he stopping you?"

It was almost impossible for things to be more dire but Sam was proven wrong when Arthur's question about the *bastard* annoyed the brother's. Especially Oberon who growled and gritted his teeth. The twins faces were filled with venom as they thought of the man that had held them back.

"Are we not good enough for you?" Oberon laughed and it was just as terrifying as Sam remembered. "You won't have to worry about that dear brother, you won't make it long enough to meet him."

"... It's just that I'd like to know who is strong enough to make you three into terrified bitches?"

If they weren't so terrified, the half gargoyles would have been surprised with Arthur's remark.

"I have to hand it to you Artie," Oberon's lip trembled from anger. "I would have never thought that you would have the balls to say that to me." He cracked his fingers, "Too bad you won't live long enough to do it again." his face started to change as he walked to his younger brother, "I'm going to rip her apart and make you watch."

Emily hid behind Cale while Ari and Kira pressed themselves against each other in an effort to protect themselves. A whimper escaped Trevor's lips while Dylan trembled against the bottom of the Jeep. Cam watched with a pale face, he looked like he wanted nothing more than to run as Arthur prepared himself for Oberon's attack. He wasn't as strong as his brothers, but he sure as hell was going to try.

"That'd be boring though, right brother?" Another voice rang out and everyone but the siblings looked for the source. Even Sam knew who it belonged to before their oldest brother emerged from the house. Eli shut the front door behind himself as if he lived there.

"That's the problem with you Oberon, you just don't know how not to be a greedy prick." He spat at his brother as he walked down the porch with his hands in his pockets. "That *bastard* is finally letting us do what we want, don't fuck it up." He turned towards the frightened group in front of him, his eyes scanning them from left to right until they fell on Sam.

His lips turned upright until a smile emerged. "*My sister*."

It was sick that he used a loving voice.

He stopped beside his brothers and he ran his hand through his brown hair. Oberon looked annoyed that his brother had foiled his fun but he'd have it all the same.

"So these are the kid's you kidnapped?" Eli dropped his hand as he took in the group again. "Good looking bunch, looks like they can handle a good fight...with someone on a weaker scale at least." He looked around at the empty space around them, "Where are the rest? Did your plan not go as well as you would have liked?"

Arthur didn't give him the time of day and it entertained his brother's more.

"Come on Artie, let us see our sister, I didn't get a good look at her last time… with her being covered in blood and all." Peyton snickered.

Arthur didn't move an inch.

"What the hell are you getting out of killing a girl that has nothing to do with you anymore?" Cale hissed and caught them off guard.

Even with Eli being the tallest of the siblings, Cale stood taller than him.

"I like this one." Eli chuckled then answered. "You don't know our past boy, you don't know what we went through together, If you knew the things she's done you'd think the world would be better off without her in it."

"And you're no different." Cale countered and the brothers cackled: The sound made all of them flinch, it echoed through the trees and the morning birds stopped their chirping and flew off.

"Come on Arthur, you've got to let us see our little sissy…. It's been so long!" Eli wiped a fake tear from his eye. "Calling from outside all night was rough."

Sam's eyes widened, the voices in her head weren't a part of a dream, they were the voices of her brothers.

She wasn't sure why no one else had heard them.

"If you don't move, I'll kill all of these maggots." Oberon threatened as his patience wore thin.

There were several gasps from the bloodlust that was coming from him and silent tears fell from Emily's eyes as Cale protected her like Arthur was with Sam.

Sam gritted her teeth as she stepped from behind Arthur who tried getting in front of her again. She pulled at his arm to stop him from blocking her but she didn't stray too far from him as she stood front and center.

The brothers took her in and Eli and Peyton seemed more interested than Oberon who had already had his chance.

"You look you never even died…" Peyton glowered at her.

"It's a shame her power didn't retain as well as her looks, right Artie?" Eli brought his attention to Arthur who looked like he was about to jump at any second to protect his sister. "What a good brother you are to do all of this for her." he turned back to Sam who was trying her damndest not to show any fear.

"When Oberon and Peyton came back, they told me that you're no longer a black and white eyed gargoyle." He cocked his head as he urged her to show him her eyes but she didn't do what he wanted and unlike how his brother would have reacted, he showed no anger from her denial.

"You're partially like your old self." His head went front and center. "But I still don't see why *he's* so intrigued with you, you're but a shadow of what you used to be."

"I don't know who you're talking about." She spat as her eyes narrowed, she was tired of hearing about this man and his interest in her but not of who he is.

"But *he* knows you." Peyton took a step forward as he caught the defiance on Cale's face. Oberon and Eli followed their brothers gaze and their eyes glittered with intrigue.

"You look familiar..." Oberon examined Cale. "And not because we saw you on television."

Cale had a questioning look as his head shot towards the house and the rest followed his gaze: The house was smoking and they could smell the wood beginning to burn.

"NO!" Cale shot forward but was stopped by Eli.

"It's a nice place, I'm sure you and your father worked hard on it."

Cale was staring at the burning house with a pained expression but it turned to shock as Eli's words registered in his head.

"How do you-"

Sam began shaking so hard that she had trouble standing, she hadn't known Cale's father's health... didn't know if he was able to die in such a way, but she still found it strange that he would die so suddenly.

"He was a good man, instead of begging for his own life, he begged for yours. It almost made me change my mind about killing him." Eli's grin said otherwise.

Cale leaped at Eli with his nails as sharp points but Arthur stopped him. The half blooded gargoyle was filled with rage as he turned to Arthur who didn't look too far off from the younger man.

He shook his head, "You'd die and that's exactly what your father didn't want." His arm shook as he tried to keep Cale contained.

"Cale!" Emily gasped from behind them but neither dared to turn. Silent tears fell from Cale's rage filled eyes.

"Why?" Arthur hissed as he brought his attention to his brother. "He had nothing to do with this!"

"Because I wanted to make a point," Oberon was the one to answer. "When Peyton and I happened on the two that left this place-"

Sam's heart sank, the two that had left this place...Daniel and

Jeannie.

"What did you do to them?!" Ari shrieked, her blue eyes watered over as both fear and worry washed over her.

Peyton inclined his head past the three in front of him to get a good look at her in the back.

"It was fate that we happened to walk past them while we were in town. You see, we can smell other gargoyles if they are close enough. At first we questioned them, they were good friends and didn't tell us anything until we started torturing the sister and the brother babbled. When they told us where our dear siblings were and they were no longer any use to us, we killed them."

At the sounds of the cries and wails as they found out about Daniel and Jeannie's fate, Peyton brought his hands to the air like he was face to face with a police officer.

"Don't worry, it was quick!" He exclaimed then laughed with his twin.

Eli looked satisfied as Sam's knees buckled and she fell to them.

"This is what the great Maya has turned into?!" Oberon taunted. "You disappointed me on that mountain and you're disappointing me now."

Sam kept her head down as he dissed her, "If you kill me.... Will you let them go?" her voice was barely more than a whisper but she knew they could hear her.

"No!" Arthur fumed as he continued to hold Cale back.

"It's not your choice to make," her head shot up and she took in the satisfied looks of her brothers, "I want you to let Arthur go too."

Arthur looked shocked for a moment but he continued on with his rejection of her plan. "I'm not leaving you and I'm not going to let you die!"

"I'm not going anywhere." Cale's voice was still filled with rage as he finally relaxed against Arthur's arm, though he still looked like he would jump at any moment. "I'm not leaving you."

Sam took in the tears in his eyes, he looked so tired… tired of losing people.

"W-we're in this together." Emily piped up but they could hear the tremble in her voice.

"You'll leave." Cale demanded without looking at her. "We all don't need to die today."

Why did they have to fight with her? She was worthless, she didn't need to live anymore. Why didn't they just let her die and let it be done with? Arthur had his reasons but she had been a killer in her past life and she wasn't too far from being one in this life.

Protecting her and dying for her held nothing for him.

A high pitch laugh made them flinch and they brought their attention back to the brothers. "Do you honestly think we'd let any of you leave?" Oberon snorted.

"If anything, you gave us a wonderful idea." Peyton looked between his brothers and Eli was the one to speak.

"If you can't give us a good fight, we'll just have to entertain ourselves in a different way." He walked closer to Sam and Arthur stepped in the way and the two brothers came face to face. Eli showed no fear while Arthur was tense. "She seems to have started caring for you again... and she clearly has grown a bond with these people." he brought his head down so he could get a better look at his brothers eyes. "Let's see what happens when she loses you all."

Arthur's eyes widened as Eli lifted his arms and his brothers started forward.

"NO!" Arthur tried stopping them but Eli's fist made contact with his chest and he flew ten feet into the air and fell harshly to the ground.

The others tried to run but the brothers were too quick for them.

"Stop!" Sam shrieked through the yells of her comrades. "Just kill me!" She jumped to her feet and tried to stop Oberon as he fought with Cale but he flung her to the ground.

"Make sure you pay attention little sister!" He cackled.

Eli watched his brothers with his arms crossed and his eyes wandered to Sam as his smile broadened.

Arthur came into the fray and defended Emily, Kira, and Trevor as Peyton practically snapped Kira's neck. Her little body fell to ground with a thump, her head falling to the side as if her neck had actually been broken.

Cam jumped in front of Cale and started fighting Oberon. Sam shot forward again but Eli grabbed ahold of the back of her neck and forced her back into place.

"Watch, little sister." His breath tickled her ear as he bent down to reach her. "Watch as these people die because of you."

She struggled and pulled against his grip as Oberon shoved a clawed hand through Cam's stomach and with his hand still in place, he flung his victim towards the burning building and he landed on the porch where he slid down the steps and came to a stop.

Eli's nails dug into Sam's neck as she let out a howl.

"What a sweet sound." Eli closed his eyes and smiled.

Oberon swiped Cam's blood from his hand and it splattered on Cale who tried to shake off what had just happened and continued their fight.

Arthur was able to knock Peyton to the ground but he jumped up with ease, "I have to admit, you've gotten stronger!" He chuckled. "Maybe you'll entertain us more than I thought."

Arthur pushed Trevor and Dylan behind him as Ari knelt beside Kira and protected her unconscious body.

"PLEASE JUST KILL ME!" Sam begged, tears pouring from her eyes. "LEAVE THEM ALONE!"

"You're only making us want to torture them more." Eli chuckled in her ear, "I never thought I'd hear you beg." He got closer and as he spoke, her brown waves moved from his breath. "Don't worry, you'll die when their dead…along with your beloved brother."

Her eyes flashed at his words and her body changed into it's gargoyle form: Her eyes, ears, nails, and horns changing all at once.

A growl escaped her lips as she dug her nails into the dirt and pulled against his grip. She began to drag Eli as he gripped tighter and his nails penetrated her skin.

"Woah!" He exclaimed as he dug his heels into the ground. "I didn't know that he meant that much to you in this life!"

As Arthur kept Peyton from the others, Cale fought Oberon with the ferocity of a monster as he let all of his pain and anger out on the full fledged gargoyle.

Oberon cackled as he dodged every hit, his cackle going along with a loud crack from the house as the wood began to collapse from the fire. Sam removed her claws from the dirt and brought her arms over her head and clawed Eli's wrist: Blood began pouring out as she broke a vein.

Eli didn't even flinch from the pain, he simply looked annoyed as if a fly had landed on him.

Everything went quiet aside from the crackle of the fire as Cale scratched the side of Oberon's cheek and blood gushed from it. Oberon's entertained expression turned annoyed as his eyes narrowed at Cale who felt the change in his mood.

With a slash of his hand, Oberon sent Cale flying through the air and he slid into the house, a loud snap ringing out as his spine broke.

"CALE!" Emily ran from behind Arthur as Cale rolled from the house. His eyes were closed and his mouth open as he laid unconscious. Tears streamed down Emily's cheeks and she whimpered as she collapsed to her knees beside him. In a panic she brought her hands to his throat to check for a pulse, her face fell further when she didn't feel anything and her scream was blood curdling as she figured the worst had happened.

Sam pulled out of Eli's grip as he got distracted by Emily and she rushed towards Oberon with her teeth bared. Oberon's expression lightened as he saw her coming for him. He was about to strike when Arthur jumped in the way and took it instead. Blood poured from his mouth as the hit to his gut made something inside him break.

"Arthur!" Sam shrieked as Oberon wrapped his right hand around Arthur's throat and pulled him from the ground.

Sam ran forward and tried prying Oberon's fingers from his neck as he started to gasp for air and Oberon used his left hand to fling her away and she went tumbling to the ground. Peyton who had stopped his attack on the four trembling part gargoyles turned to watch. He laughed at her weakness while Eli retained his satisfied expression.

Sam persevered and shot up again with tears in her eyes as she took in the pale faces of her friends and Cam who was still on the front steps of the porch.

"STOP!" she roared as she ran to Oberon and hit him as hard as she could but he remained grounded. "LET HIM GO!" she shrieked as a gurgling noise came from Arthur's throat. "JUST KILL ME!" she sobbed but she was only met with laughter as Oberon pushed her over again.

She felt dizzy as she pulled herself to her hands and knees, her arms buckling under her weight. She wished her old power would return, she didn't care anymore if it would change her or what it would do to her.

She had to save them no matter the cost.

"It'll all be over soon!" Peyton yelled over the screams, sobs, and the cackling of the fire.

A large part of the the house collapsed onto itself with a bang as Sam tried to will herself to get up. This was all her fault…

Her fault…

A scream brought her back to her senses and her head shot to the front of the house where Emily was crying over Cale.

"No-" She repeated the word over and over again. "Don't leave me… DON'T DIE ON ME!"

Something strange came over Sam.
It was nostalgic....It was so familiar...

So familiar...

So familiar...

So familiar...

"No Mommy!" A child screamed. "Please don't leave me Mommy!" The child wailed.

She was sure her eyes were open but she was met with nothing but darkness.
"Ah," She thought out loud. "This place again."
She punched the ground and let out a yell.
"Why!? why!? why!? why!?-" She repeated over and over until her throat ached and her eyes stung from the amount of tears they were shedding.
"WHY?!" She raged and punched the ground again and she flew backwards as she heard a sharp crack.
She leaned back on her hands and blinked at the site of the noise but it was far to dark to see anything. She closed her eyes as more tears threatened to fall. She was weak, even when she had all of the power in the world. Strength meant nothing when one could be easily influenced.
She wobbled to her feet and like a crazy person, she ran around the darkness of her mind: "LET ME OUT!" she begged as if someone could hear her.
While she was there, her friends were getting killed.
But what could she do even if she made it back to reality?

Weak.

Weak.

Weak.

Dread overcame her as her stomping echoed through the darkness even after she came to a stop.
She knelt down and screamed so loud that her lungs hurt and her head pounded.
Another crack rang out and she froze.

She slowly got to her feet and as she managed to stand up, one crack turned into clusters and she found herself covering her ears as the ground under her gave way.

She shrieked as gravity pulled her and instead of being thrown into something other than darkness, her mind filled with visions as she fell. She was seeing memories from her past life.

It started with Maya's first memory, as far back as a child could remember at least, and Sam gripped at her head as Maya's childhood filled her brain. Every happy memory with her parents and Arthur and every fight with her three older brothers. She relived Every time she had begged her parents to let her go to the town they were closest to. Every single memory up until after the scene with the fire and the announcement that their parents were going to help the humans again. Her head felt like it was going to explode as she came to a crash in a grassy field.

Her breath hitched as she brought her head up to face her new surroundings:

Unlike the memories she had received where she saw everything though Maya's eyes, she was on the outside like she had been after Oberon's attack.

She was getting a different look at the outcome of her parents deaths.

She got to her feet and hesitantly made her way to the mourning siblings. She didn't want to see it, she didn't want to see the bodies of the people who were once her parents. Especially now that she held her childhood memories as her time as Maya.

Tears streamed down her cheeks as she came closer while making sure to keep her eyes away from her past self. She yelped at the sight of the bodies, it was so much more detailed than it was the first time, it was as if a fog had lifted. The scene was so much more brutal: Her parents bodies looked like they had been dissolved by something, parts of their limbs were gone and there were gaping holes where their vital organs were hidden.

She stood closer to her mother who looked far worse than her father, naturally the humans had used more power on her since she was a greater threat than her husband.

Sam collapsed next her mother's deformed body, she was almost unrecognizable and for the first time, she understood her past lives need for revenge but she knew the repercussions of that desire. Where it would lead her.

"I want revenge." Maya growled as her tears dried out like a well.

Sam lifted her eyes from her mother's body and took in her past lives rage and as she met her eyes, she was thrown back into her old body like she had seen the memories originally. She saw through Maya's eyes as she spoke her words and felt rage engulf her whole being as she fought not to grieve.

The scene changed again and as it did, the memories in-between washed over her: Death, calamity, and horror filled her mind as she remembered every single person that she had killed along with every scream and whimper that escaped their mouths.

It was as Arthur said, she was the most savage of them all.

She was outside of her past lives body again as she landed in the next memory. She would have been confused but all of the emotions that she felt at seeing her past lives crimes filled her mind and she could think of nothing else. They were sitting around a fire again, only they all looked like young adults now and their parents were no longer there. It was night and the stars shined almost as bright as the fire.

"And then I slashed his throat!" Oberon snickered and his brothers laughed along with him with the exception of Arthur who sat away from his siblings. His eyes were on the fire as he tried to drown out his brothers disgusting conversation.

Sam kept her eyes on him to keep her mind away from the memories and as his eyes lifted towards his sister, she followed his gaze: Maya was sitting on the ground, her knees to her chest as the moon reflected in her gray eyes.

Gray? Her eyes were hazel the last time she had seen her from the outside…

Sam swallowed the lump in her throat, they had changed color like how her's currently were.

"What about you May?" Oberon woke his sister from her trance and she brought her attention from the moon to the three savages. She looked uninterested in their conversation and no emotion registered on her face as she spoke. "The same as usual."

Eli rose an interested brow. "What was your count?"

"I don't know." She kept her eyes forward but she didn't seem to see anything.

The sweet little girl that she used to be was no more, her eyes were that of a dead person. As dead as the people she had killed.

Her hair was in viking style braids, like how her mother always had hers. There were loose strands pulled out of the four braids that were attached to the right side of her scalp and there was blood splattered over her. Upon further investigation of her look, Sam realized that she was wearing her mother's trenchcoat. Which along with her pants and knee high boots, the fabric was as dark as the night around them.

"A lot more than Arthur I'm sure." Peyton looked triumphant as he began his assault on his youngest brother.

Arthur had been against the killing of innocent people from the start. Unlike his brothers who simply did it for the fun of it or his sister who did it for revenge and to prove a point. Arthur didn't speak or acknowledge his brother but they knew he had heard Peyton. His eyes lifted to the tips of the flames and Sam could now recognize him as the man she had met in the mountain side cave. He looked the same as he did in real time, the only difference was the weight of his pain showed on the Arthur Sam knew, the Arthur in front of her now lacked that though he showed a lot of sadness.

"You should really try it sometime," Oberon licked the dried blood off of his palm. "It's a rush you'll never forget."

Sam's eyes darted between the murderous brothers and Arthur who was beginning to look paler by the second. She looked to her former self who seemed like she didn't even know the conversation was happening. She had a dull look on her face and her gray eyes were glossed over as if she was in another world.

Eli watched his sister as if he knew what she was thinking about, like he knew what was about to happen.

Annoyance flashed on Oberon's face as Arthur continued to ignore him.

"You're so weak, It's disgusting to think that we have the same blood." He spat. "It sickens me to look at you." Silence filled the area around the campfire aside from the hot embers cracking.

Arthur was beginning to shake and he chewed on the inside of his mouth to stop his jaw from trembling. Maya's eyes rolled to Arthur but she maintained her uninterested expression as she took in his sadness then brought her attention back to the fire.

Sam was surprised that she didn't say anything to stop the twins attack on her brother, from what she knew, she had always defended Arthur.

"You're always going to be that scared little boy," Oberon continued his assault. "Maybe I should rip out your voice box if you don't want to use-"

"Another word and I'll rip your tongue out." Maya growled and caught the twins off guard while Eli grinned since he knew it was coming.

Oberon's eyes narrowed as he brought his attention to his sister and as he saw her piercing gray eyes, he recoiled and jerked his head away.

He knew it wasn't a threat, it was a promise.

The air around Maya felt dense to the point that Sam found it hard to breath. She found herself backing away as her former self got up and walked away from the fire. No one said another word to Arthur for the rest of the night since they knew their sister was listening.

Sam felt a jerk and she found herself back in her former body. It moved on it's own.... No, it moved as Maya once had. How she once had.

She was laying on a grassy incline, her eyes on the stars.

Her heartbeat was slow but as she continued to think about her kills for the day, it fastened. Not from the thrill, but from the guilt.

She brought a shaking hand to the sky and covered the moon that was hovering over her. So many images of the innocent people that she had killed flashed into her mind. These people didn't have anything to do with it, they were innocent but she killed them all the same.

Why was she doing this?

When she started this she felt like it was justified but she was a fool.

Who the hell would think the killing of the innocent would change anything?

How would they see your point of view by doing something so horrendous?

Her parents had been killed because the humans thought they were a threat. She knew that from the beginning, but what had she done? She confirmed their suspensions. She let her anger and grief consume her and made herself into a monster.

She remembered her mother's orb like eyes as she laid dead, her body in pieces.

She had seen so much gore, had been the cause of most if it, but nothing chilled her more than the sight of her parents.

"Thanks for that." Arthur approached and her hand dropped to the ground, it was unlike her to be caught off guard.

"Yeah…" Her voice trailed off, she and Arthur had retained their relationship and when they went out on their 'hunts', he would come along but stayed at the of edge the town.

Her older brothers thought him to be weak but Maya saw him as the gentle older brother that understood her more than anyone else. Sometimes she was jealous of him, he had kept his innocence while she became a monster, but of course she brought that upon herself.

Arthur sat beside her and she pulled herself up from the ground, they sat in silence for a long while just staring off into the night. She didn't know what to say to him, she knew he was disappointed in her, that he had his own feelings on the matter but she had heard them all before.

"You know," He caught her by surprise but she turned her head slightly to listen to what he had to say. He had a nervous look on his face like he was unsure if he should say what he was about to."...I can tell it's eating at you."

His head dropped as he feared what her reaction was going to be.

Her laughter almost made him get whiplash as his head shot up and as his gaze landed on her again, he realized that she wasn't laughing but crying as tears poured from her eyes.

"You're right." Her voice shook as she finally let everything go.

That was the first time Arthur had seen his sister cry since their parents were killed.

The scene changed again and this time she remained in her past lives body. The memories of what came after her conversation with Arthur washed through her as she made her way through the blood soaked town. She hadn't participated in her brothers 'fun' this time around but something called for her to look at the aftermath.

Maybe she was sadistic or she felt left out.

The thought of the latter made her feel sick.

She tugged at the collar of her mother's coat and covered her nose: It had been two years since her mother's demise but she could still smell her scent on the fabric, it always calmed her.

Her boots clacked against the concrete as she stepped over the body of a middle aged man, his torn out throat was obviously Oberon's handy work. Her ears rang as she heard the screams of the survivors as they ran for shelter or called for their missing loved ones. The yelps of the injured made her flinch and her heart raced as she continued towards the edge of the carnage.

She was almost out of the town when a child's whimper made her stop dead in her tracks.

"No mommy!" A little girl not much older than seven cried over her mother's body. "Don't leave me mommy!" she sobbed and shrieked. "Please mommy!"

Maya fell to her knees and the little girl jumped then screamed as she ran from her mother's body, the sight of Maya terrified her.

Maya's shoulders trembled as tears streamed down her cheeks and she collapsed to her front as her shaking became uncontrollable. She whimpered as she covered her mouth, the little girls pleas for her mother still echoing in her ears.

She had caused this, she was the one who had wanted revenge, she had allowed for this to happen.

Everything was her fault.

A blood curdling scream escaped her lips as she gripped at her aching heart.

She had broken up so many families, had seen so many children cry for their parents but the little girl crying over her mother was so familiar.

She had continued the cycle of pain with her selfish revenge. The humans had killed her parents and like how she had cried over her mother, she now saw it from the outside.

And she was the cause of it.

She remained there and sobbed until Arthur came to find her hours later.

She leaned against a tree as her brothers sparred with each other, several days had passed since her breakdown and while she didn't say much, she had nightmares to the point that not sleeping at all was the easiest option. She knew she deserved it even though she felt she deserved much more pain than that, but she also knew no matter the punishment that nothing would make up for all that she's done.

Arthur brought her a bowl of soup but she simply looked at it, "No thanks." Her voice was hoarse from the lack of speaking.

Arthur leaned against the other side of the tree to her left, he had found her that night… had seen what had broken her.

"Nothing will ever change what you've done." He admitted truthfully and more tears began to well up in her gray eyes. "But-" he slid over so he was beside her and he discarded the soup to where he had sat before. "You can stop it from happening again."

Her eyes moved to her oldest brothers who were ignoring their downcast sister and their boring brother. They had continued their killing spree without her, she had already thought about stopping them but she supposed that her lack of action had to do with her want to forget it all.

It wasn't working.

"I deserve to die." Her voice trailed off and Arthur flinched. "No you don't." He reprimanded. "I'm not going to let you."

She couldn't believe she had the strength to roll her eyes.

He saw her do so and he grabbed her shoulder and shook her.

"You're all I have left and you want to leave me?"

Of course she didn't want to leave him, especially in a shitty world like this.

She shook her head.

"You can never take back what you've done but you can stop them from killing more people." He moved his gaze from Maya to his brothers who were too caught up in their training to listen to them. "Only you can stop them."

She should have done this before, but for the first time in days, she felt a sense of purpose. That and dread as she thought of how she was going to break the news to her brothers and she also wondered how she was going to be able to stop them from doing what they wanted without having to kill them.

Oberon went flying as her fist came in contact with his face and he landed harshly to the ground next to Peyton and Eli who had already tried fighting her. They had gone out the night before and murdered two people as if she wouldn't find out, she could smell the blood on their hands even with them washed clean.

"What did I tell you?!" She growled as her black and white eyes shined with venom.

"Not to kill more people, yadda yadda." Eli rolled his eyes. His jokester attitude proved to be faulty in hiding his dismay for his sister in the weeks since she had told them that there would be no more killing.

Arthur stood behind her and the older brothers hated it.

"We thought you were stronger than this." Peyton dissed. "But now you're allowing him to sway you."

"This is my choice," Her eyes returned to gray. "This is what I want and what I want is to stop killing innocent people."

"It never stopped you before." Oberon rolled his eyes as he flicked a speck of dirt from his pants.

"No it didn't," Her voice broke as she agreed with him. "But now it is."

"You won't be able to stop us forever." Oberon threatened and Maya walked over to her brother who stood so he'd be on the same level as her.

"That's funny because I think I can." Her smile was savage and it rocked Oberon to his core. It took every fiber in his being not to strike her right then and there but he knew the effort would be worthless, she was too strong.

"The strongest gargoyle." He spat as he bowed. "What will we do?"

Every memory leading to her demise played until she was thrown to the familiar hillside. She was stomping to her brothers as she entered the memory.

"What did you do!?" she roared as she grabbed Eli by the scruff of his shirt.

"We had some fun." He snorted. "You wouldn't believe how much work it took to get this thing."

Her eyes flashed to the large object behind Oberon's head, it was gray and had red markings, she knew right away what it was: A bomb.

"How?!" She shoved Eli to the ground and he grunted as his hatred for his flashed in his eyes.

"We broke into the humans military base," Peyton placed a hand on the bomb and rubbed the smooth metal. The thing was huge: It was as long as Maya was tall and as wide as a trunk of a large tree.

"It took a bit of effort to get in and we were wary of them using the same weapons that killed our parents but after breaking in, things turned out to be

easy." He moved his gaze from their prize and as he turned to Maya, satisfaction covered his face."We were hoping to find something smaller but we were pleasantly surprised to find this."

Her eyes wandered between each of them, she knew what they were planning but for some reason she wanted to hear it from their mouths. "What are you going to do?" Her voice shook as her mouth dried.

Her brothers loved watching her composure being ripped apart and she thought of Oberon's words after she had scolded them when they had gone against her.

Eli cocked his head as he got up and dusted himself off, "We're going to kill everyone in this city and what an easy way to do it." He said matter of factly.

"No you're not." Maya growled, Arthur had gone into the city to get supplies. If Eli, Peyton, and Oberon had their way, not only would thousands of innocent people die, but Arthur would as well.

"I told you to stop killing humans!" she fumed as she rounded on Eli again, "I'll kill you for this!"

"Will you?" For the first time her brothers showed no fear at her threats. "You'd kill your own flesh and blood? What would mother and father think?" Eli used a mock tone and chuckled as his sisters face fell.

"Foolish." Oberon ridiculed as Maya stood down.

"You're wrong about us just killing the humans sister," Maya's eyes widened as Eli lifted her chin with his index finger. "This is also meant for you." He removed his finger but her head still inclined to look into his satisfied eyes. "You'll save these people, won't you? You have the power to do so… a bomb is made of energy after all and that's your extra ability."

Her breath hitched as she fell to her knees, she had said that she wanted to die but that was when death seemed so far away.

Eli kneeled in front of her, "I'd hurry and make up my mind before this baby explodes." He lifted his eyes to the bomb. "You see, the humans built it on a timer like a smaller bomb only there's no wires to clip to stop it from exploding." He chuckled and it made her flinch. "Humans are just as savage as we are."

Maya remained silent as her body began to tremble, her heart thumped in her ears and her sight blurred with anxiety. Eli leaned forward and kissed her forehead. "I guess this is goodbye." He got to his feet and the twins followed.

They knew what she was going to do, they knew her too well.

"See you in the next life." Peyton teased as he walked past her and Oberon snickered at his brothers words.

Maya didn't say a word as her brothers left her to die, she knew they were jealous of her and had even resented her. She just didn't think that they hated her to the point of devising a plan that would surely end in her demise. Unlike her empty threat of killing them, they actually meant it, they had finally found a way to get her out of their way. Of course her brothers would find a military base with explosives, nothing seemed to be far fetched when it came to them.

She could hear the ticking of the timer inside the bomb and her head shot up as she glared at the harbinger of her death. She jumped to her feet, she could move it but the explosion would still hit the city, maybe even the others surrounding it. She turned towards the city below and she could hear the sounds of cars as people drove to their jobs or did their morning errands. The sound of children playing made her heart race faster, she could feel it in the back of her throat and it made her sick.

The image of the little girl crying over her mother's body flashed in her mind along with everything she had done wrong in the past two years.

Every single life that she had snuffed out, their faces as they died, the feeling she had when she watched them do so. She was just as bad as her brothers. She didn't deserve to live.

She smiled and looked up at the sky,"Is this repentance for all I've done?"

It was fine by her.

She pulled off her mothers coat and let the fabric fall through her fingers and she didn't look back as she made her way to the bomb. As she made her death march, she thought of how gargoyles supposedly reincarnated. She had never really thought about her parents reincarnations, to her even if they shared a soul, they were no longer her parents.

Her bottom lip trembled as she stopped beside the bomb, the ticking was growing louder as it came closer to it's detonation. Maya couldn't help but think of it as a timer leading to the end of her life.

Was it a full life?

No.

Was it a good one?

Maybe in the beginning.

Did she have regrets?

eternally.

She had always wondered why she had the ability to take energy, she had found out about it by accident when her mother had asked her to change the batteries in a flashlight. No matter how hard she tried, she couldn't get the batteries to work even though they had just been taken out of a new package. After many tries, her mother had her try it on the bulb itself and the glass broke on contact.

She didn't know how to use the ability, she had practically shut it off as she found no use for it but she knew it would be enough for this. It was ironic that something she had thought was useless would help bring her to her end, if there was such a thing as fate, it was laughing at her right now.

She placed a shaking hand on the bomb and closed her eyes as she drew a breath. Her shaking stopped, her resolve was clear.

"NO!" She jumped as Arthur ran up the hill.

She couldn't bring herself to look at him so she kept her eyes closed.

"You're not doing this!" he demanded as he tried pulling her away from the bomb but she was sure footed and didn't budge.

"It's too late." her eyes opened and she took in her brothers pale face, it almost made her resolve crumble to ashes.

"No…" His voice drifted.

"I can't let these people die and even if I did leave, we'd still be caught in the blast."

Her brothers really did plan this to a T.

"Don't leave me!" he began to beg. "You're all I have!"

She whimpered as she tried to ignore her brothers pleas, she had no choice but to let him down. She was going to leave him alone in this world where he had no one aside from his murderous brothers.

The clicking quickened and she knew it was time.

She pushed Arthur and as he fell from the top of the hill, his tear stained face twisted with shock as his sister smiled sadly and closed her eyes.

"I'm sorry…."

She only heard the beginning of the explosion but nothing more as her body was torn to shreds. Every fiber turned to dust as the explosion took her and only her.

She woke with a start in the desolate dream state and after a moment of wondering where she was, she remembered what had happened and a blood curdling scream escaped her throat. There was an intense tingle going though her veins as the energy she had taken in washed though her.

She grabbed the side of her head and squeezed as the ringing of the explosion still buzzed in her ears. Tears poured from her unseeing eyes and she collapsed to her side, her chest heaved as she convulsed and saliva poured from the side of her mouth.

"I'm sorry! I'm sorry! I'm sorry!" she apologized until her throat was raw. She pounded her fist into her chest but it didn't do anything to slow her racing heart.

"WHERE AM I?" she screeched but she was met with nothing but her own echo.

Her breaths were haggard as she tried to compose herself, she knew she had died but had no idea why she had landed in a place as desolate as this.

It was dark, so damned dark.

Was this her hell?

Tears fell from her eyes as she looked into the nothing, hoping that she could see something, anything. When she continued to see nothing but darkness, she gave up hope.

Maybe this was where she would spend the rest of eternity instead of reincarnating. That's what she deserved, she deserved everything she was getting.

She jumped as she heard a footstep echo through the darkness.

"Arthur?" She asked hopefully but she knew that her power had worked and her brother was still in the world of the living.

Another step rang out and she shakily got to her feet.

"Who's there?!" she tried to extend her nails to defend herself but they wouldn't budge. Instead she was left with a feeling of dread as she prepared herself for the attacker. She knew how to fight, maybe she could take them without her power.

A million possibilities played in her head as she waited for the being, she thought maybe it was a guard that dragged sinners to hell. But instead of a creature from hell, she was faced with a small ball of light and as the ball extended, the darkness turned to pure white.

She gasped as she saw the culprit behind the footsteps: It was herself.

Only it wasn't.

The girl stared blankly at her, her hazel eyes looked like how her's used to before they had changed to gray. She just stood there with nothing but her pale skin and her wavy brown hair covering her breasts. Her right hand was reaching for Maya, her fingers curled slightly, and as Maya examined the girls unblinking eyes, she realized the thing didn't have a soul.

She swallowed, she didn't know how she knew it, but she could feel it in her own soul that the body in front of her would be her own.

She chuckled as more tears streamed down her cheeks and her laughter turned into a cackle until finally it turned into a full on sob. She grabbed the empty shells hand and it practically fell on her.

"I'm sorry!" she repeated again as her jaw trembled. She didn't know who she was talking to but she knew someone was listening. "I promise you!" she inclined her head to look at the never ending ceiling.

"I promise I won't fail you in my next life!" She gritted her teeth. "I WILL NOT FAIL!"

"I know." A man's voice echoed through the void, his tone sending warmth

through her cold soul.

She collapsed to the clear ground along with her new body as the world around her fell apart and she fell along with it.

Chapter 31

As she relived her past life, it felt like it had lasted years but in reality, it only took seconds.

Sam and Maya were no longer two sides of a coin, they were one in the same. Sam was Maya and Maya was Sam and as she woke from the past, she took in the present: She was still on her knees while her friends watched the dire scene in front of them.

Oberon was still choking the life out of her brother.

Everything slowed… the fire, the chaos, and her heart.

It all froze as she got to her feet and before Oberon knew she was there, she broke his arm and Arthur fell to the ground while gasping for breath.

"What?!" Oberon puzzled, the shock of Sam being able to injure him distracting him from the pain in his arm. Before he could do anything about it, Sam flicked him on the forehead and he went flying through the burning house into the woods behind it.

The house crashed in on itself until it was nothing more than a heap of wood and fire. Sam admired her handy work for a moment then turned to Eli and Peyton.

She had gotten her memories back from the familiar sight that had changed her in her past life and it was all thanks to them. Her heart fluttered at their expressions, the shock and fear felt as nostalgic as the scene that brought her memories back.

Cale's eyes fluttered open as Peyton took a defiant step towards his sister, his face twisted to try to hide his shock. Emily who had been crying over Cale a few seconds prior didn't notice him wake up as she watched the scene with tear stained cheeks with as much surprise as the others. Cale didn't have an idea of what was happening but as he saw Sam standing tall against her former brother, he knew something extraordinary had happened.

A growl rolled over Sam's tongue as she knocked her brother to the ground.

"What the fuck happened?!" Peyton growled as he pulled himself from the dirt.

When he was sure that she was distracted with Peyton, Oberon returned to the fray with a healed arm. He used every ounce of his power as he tried slashing her throat from behind. But his effort was futile as Sam's ears pressed to the back of her head as she sensed him. She brought her arm up and swiped his attack away.

Oberon fell to the ground from the force of her block and silent shock spread across the watchers as Sam stood with her eyes closed. When she opened them, the brothers faces turned pale at the sight of her: Her right eye remained white while the other had turned black.

Arthur shakily pulled himself up and as he took in Sam's different colored eyes, his face lit up with awe and something more: Hope.

"What is it?!" Oberon was still behind her and as pulled himself up, he stepped around her and practically fell backwards as he took in the eyes that his sister once had.

The eyes that he had always hated.

"How?!" He roared. "You shouldn't have them!"

"I shouldn't?" She rose a brow. "Oh brother, you never were the brightest."

"What?" he growled while trying to hide the shock from her calling him her brother.

"You pushed and pushed until I broke out of my cage…" She cocked her head and the bone cracked in her neck. "You see, you can only push a caged beast so far until it's had enough, and I can tell you brother, you've done just that." Her eyes rolled to Arthur but she maintained her even expression as his eyes widened and they filled with tears, he looked like his old self again.

She knew he understood what had happened but their reunion would have to wait for when this was over. "Tell me brother," She straightened her neck so she looked Oberon straight in the face. *"What will you do?"*

He turned ghost white as she taunted him with his own words.

Her mismatched eyes dissolved and they revealed two fully gray irises, the hazel was completely gone.

"There's no way you can have your memories back! Much less your power!" Peyton stammered.

"And why's that?" she flexed her fingers as a nostalgic feeling consumed her, the power warmed her veins as if it were happy to be back.

She now knew that her power had always been associated with her memories. Her acceptance of her blood stained life as Maya was needed in order for her full power to come back. She didn't know why it worked that way, but once again, she knew that it was fate having it's way with her.

She was misguided, vicious, and sinful during her time as Maya and as Sam she was filled with anxiety along with being awkward and weak. But at the end of it all, she was the same girl with different experiences and with her memories back, she was more than just Sam or Maya. The experiences from both of her lives made her wiser and much stronger not only in body but in mind.

She raised a hand and her nails grew into points then fell back into her fingertips. She wasn't messing with her power, she was giving it a feeler. It was enough to corrupt even someone with an impenetrable mind. She had been seduced by it before but with Sam's state of mind, she didn't have to worry about it.

She lifted her eyes from her hand and brought her attention to her brothers: The twins stood front and center as Eli stood where had been the entire time. They looked like they had seen a ghost or perhaps a *demon.*

"This power is where it's supposed to be." The side of her mouth twitched as she smiled.

Cale lifted himself from the ground as his back healed and Emily flinched from his movement until she turned and her face lit up with relief as she wrapped her arms around him.

"Thank God!" she cried.

"What happened?" He asked while keeping his eyes on Sam and Emily pulled away as she brought her attention back to Sam.

"...I don't know." He could hear the fear in her voice.

Sam's eyes twitched towards him, the gray rings catching him off guard and he flinched. He regretted doing so as her face fell for a second but returned to apathetic as she turned back to her brothers. At that moment, Cale knew the girl standing in front of him was no longer Sam but something more. He remembered the picture that Arthur had showed them and seeing her now, he thought of how she undeniably looked like her past self.

Like Maya.

Like Sam.

Like herself.

Oberon and Peyton stopped their gawking and nodded to each other before they went in for their attack. Sam dodged Peyton's claws and sent Oberon flying through the woods again. The sound of trees being smashed echoed through the ones that remained standing.

The growl that came from Sam's throat was nothing like before, it was more than animalistic, it was monstrous.

Peyton twisted and attacked again but this time Sam didn't dodge, she allowed his claws to pierce through her arm. She felt the pain as his nails pushed through skin and muscle. She could feel them scrapping bone but it was nothing compared to what she had felt before.

Being torn apart was far worse.

With her good arm she clasped a hand around Peyton's neck and a pained gasp left his lips as her nails curled into his windpipe.

"You'd kill me?" he breathed. "You'd kill your own brother?" the whistle of air escaping his throat was almost comical.

"You're asking me if I'd kill you?" her lip curled. "Oberon was going to kill Arthur and you killed me." She leaned forward so her lips met his ear. "But you couldn't stop there could you?" her tone was soft but venom filled every syllable. "This is happening because you pushed me."

"Please…" he began to beg but only got the word out as Sam ripped his head off from the base of his neck and threw it to the ground. Blood poured from the round body part as it bounced and some of it splashed onto Sam's front as Peyton's headless body fell like his head had.

The air around her was filled with gasps but also silence as some of her comrades couldn't muster a noise. She had killed many people and what little emotion she had for her brothers when she had failed to kill the first time was gone.

She didn't care what her parents would think of her nor what it made her. She didn't have the patience to deal with her brothers murderous ways anymore, if killing them made the world safer, then so be it.

Her eyes landed on Eli whose jaw was shaking like the rest of him. Aside from Arthur, he was the smartest. He knew he couldn't take his sister in a fight, especially with how she was now.

Sam ducked suddenly as Oberon flew towards her again, his teeth bared and a roar coming from between them.

"You fucking bitch!" He snarled. "You killed your own brother!" He looked as animalistic as his sister.

Sam rose a brow, "It's ok for you but not me?"

Oberon roared again as he used all of his strength to attack his sister:

Every punch, slash, and kick was dodged with ease as she used her senses. She could hear the change in air as a limb flew through it and the sound of Oberon's heart as he thought of a new way to kill her.

In turn she used every skill that came to her along with her memories. She was a little rusty from her body not being used to the motions, but it did the trick.

She jumped back from Oberon's next slash as she was only an inch away from having her throat ripped out. She swooped down and grabbed Peyton's head by his blonde hair and used it as a weapon against Oberon.

He took in his late brothers fearful expression that was still etched on his severed head. If Oberon felt any remorse, he didn't show it as he clawed his way through the head but before any real damage could be done, Sam pulled it away and whacked it across his head.

Oberon howled as blood splatter rained down on them and he fell to the ground. He tried getting to his feet but Sam stepped on his chest, her heel right above his heart.

For the first time ever, she saw true fear on her brothers face. All the other times were nothing compared to this, he knew she was no longer going spare him. She dropped Peyton's now unrecognizable head beside Oberon as he tried to scurry from under her.

"You did this," She began and he lifted his upper half from the ground until Sam smashed him back down, causing the dirt around him to collapse. She roared and her teeth grew into points, the sound was deafening and caused dread to rain down onto anyone who heard it.

She exhaled as her teeth went flat again. "You did this," She repeated. "I was asleep until you woke me."

Oberon began to shake and his blue eyes glimmered with fear at the girl standing over him.

"You could have done what you wanted, you could have let me live as a human and none of this would have happened."

"Please-" He begged like his twin. "You're my sister…"

"The sister you killed then tried to kill again."

His face fell, "Please…"

"Don't worry," She removed her gaze from his face and looked at a tree that stood close to them. "You'll reincarnate."

Her foot collapsed through his chest and he screamed as the skin, muscle, and bone broke. As he laid dying, the scream grew softer until it was nothing more than air escaping his lungs.

She removed her foot and as she kept her eyes away from his body, she turned to the others. Arthur had gotten out of the way during the fight and he was watching with the same expression as everyone else. They were filled with shock and fear, they even flinched when she looked at them. Eli took a step back as she brought her attention to only him.

"Those damned eyes!" he rasped.

It was her dagger like eyes that had haunted him and his brothers everyday, even after her demise. She took a step towards him and he flinched.

"Tell whoever you're working for that Maya is back." She demanded and his mouth dropped as surprise overtook him and he tried to catch his breath.

"Go before I change my mind." She threatened and with no hesitation, he ran through the woods only chancing one look back as he made his escape.

She needed him alive, she needed him to pass on her message.

There was someone out there that could hold even the likes of her brothers at bay and it made her uneasy. None of them knew what the higher purpose that their parents had talked about was but she knew she would find out soon as a threat even bigger than her brothers loomed on her.

She dropped to her knees, the high was over and everything hit her at once: Her memories that had returned along with her power. The people that she had killed, her own death and the realm she was thrown into before she moved to her next life.

Further more, what she had just done and what was coming next.

She bit her lip and drew blood as a sob escaped her mouth and her shoulders shook. Her wavy brown hair fell into her face and it hid her tears from the others.

None of them knew what to do, they had just watched her get her memories back, had witnessed her kill two of her brothers and let one go to spread the news to some unknown person. As soon as they realized she was crying, they not only felt fear but pity towards her.

Arthur was the one to approach her and he knelt beside her. "Maya…?" He said the name like he was making sure it was really her.

She wrapped her arms around him in reply and after a pause, he returned the hug. Sam's forehead rested on his shoulder as she cried into his shirt.

Every regret poured out of her all at once but with Arthur there, her regrets of leaving him and forgetting him made her lose it the most.

She thought of how he had lived the last twenty years alone. How it had changed him and forced him to commit so many wrongs.

She had never wanted that for him.

"I'm sorry," She sobbed. "I'm so sorry…"

Tears welled up in Arthur's eyes as his sister apologized over and over.

"I'm s...orr..y." Her words were incoherent as her sobs consumed her ability to speak.

Arthur tightened his grip around her, he didn't need to say anything, she understood by the gesture that it was alright now.

Chapter 32

How could anyone expect anything to be normal after what happened?

After Sam's dramatic reentry into the world as both of her lives combined, they had picked themselves up and tried to get rid of as much evidence as they could. It proved to be an uneasy task as Cale had to witness the house he had worked so hard on with his father turn to ash while Arthur threw the corpses of his twin brothers into the rubble.

He didn't say a word as he tossed Oberon into the fire and Sam watched with next to no emotion as her brothers body fell into the fire and cinders flew into the air. Her swollen eyes fell to Cam's burning body and his glossy eyes met hers: She didn't like him much, she'd be lying if she said she did, but as his skin burned to muscle, she had to turn away.

"Let's go." Cale had taken one last look at the burning structure before turning to the Jeep which had been flipped back over by Sam. The side that it had fallen on was dented and scratched but it was still in working order.

They didn't know where they were going anymore, meeting with the other gargoyles in the state they were now would only make things worse. They also didn't need their help anymore, not yet at least.

They had found themselves camped out in a wooded area hours later, Archie had provided tents for them after Arthur's call for help. He had arrived hours after the group got there and he had Kellan in tow who had noticed the change in Sam, her now gray eyes bored into him as he stared at her. The blood of her brothers still covered her and the foot she had used to stomp away Oberon's life was drenched in his dried blood.

Arthur had stepped in front of her to stop Kellan's curious gaze and his eyes flashed to Archie who had already heard what happened. The two men gave each other looks of understanding and after saying goodbye, Archie left with the violent gargoyle.

A few days had passed and they were about to find another place to stay. The others had somewhat remained the same towards Sam but when she wasn't looking, they would look at her with fear and sometimes wonder.

Wonder that she had defeated her brothers.

Wonder that she had gotten her memories back.

Wonder that she now held two lives within her and wonder that she knew that something that was an even greater threat than her brothers was on it's way.

None of them talked about how she had gotten her memories back, they were kind enough not to ask and she appreciated it. Maybe one day, when the time was right, she would tell them about the wrongs she had committed in her past life and the event that had changed her. But she felt like that day would never come.

Who could ever be open about anything if they had done what she had?

They packed their camp and decided who was going to carry what since they had ditched the Jeep and needed to walk to their next destination.

Emily handed Arthur's bag to Sam with a smile, "You know you can talk to me, right?"

"I know." Sam returned her smile. "Thank you, Emily."

She was sure that Emily would go back to hating her after seeing what she had done but she had remained the same towards her.

Sam turned to Arthur and Cale who were in a conversation away from the others. She dropped her gaze and Emily startled her as she placed a hand on her back and gave a push.

Sam blinked back at her as she nodded towards the men.

Sam hadn't talked much with them since they had gotten to their camp aside from occasional small talk. She didn't know what to say and neither did they.

She and Arthur hadn't had a proper conversation as brother and sister in twenty years. Plus she was close with Cale when she was just Sam and it made it difficult for her to make the effort to talk since she was worried that he was disappointed in what she had become.

Besides, she was no longer just Sam and Cale knew that and Arthur also had to live with the fact that she was no longer just Maya.

She sighed and with Arthur's bag in her hand, she made her way to them and she listened in on what they were talking about:

"None of you have to stay with us," Arthur told Cale. "I've caused you all enough pain… especially you."

Sam stopped in her tracks and swallowed, she was definitely nervous about where their conversation was going to go. She was lucky with not being forced to choose between Arthur and her friends and she wasn't even sure what she would do if they split up.

She couldn't leave Arthur alone anymore, the pain of what she had done to him still left a pit in her chest and it ached even now.

Cale lifted his head from his tent, the red fabric falling through his fingers as he shoved it into it's carrying bag. "You want to show remorse now that your brothers are out of the way and your sister is back?" He challenged and the full blooded gargoyle shook his head then frowned at the younger man.

"I've always been remorseful." He assured Cale.

"But your selfishness was worth more than your remorse."

The men remained silent for a long moment as the others rustled and talked behind them. Neither of them knew Sam was listening.

Cale sighed. "I can assure you nothing has changed…I'm staying."

Arthur looked baffled at his words, "Why would you stay with someone who destroyed everything for you?"

Cale's eyes dropped to his hands that were still holding the tent. "Because there's something out there, right?" He brought his gaze back to Arthur. "I plan on helping this world like my father always had." He took a step towards him, "And I choose to believe in Sam."

He turned to leave and was met with her standing only feet away. He didn't look embarrassed that she had heard his declaration, maybe he was mustering up the courage to say it to her anyway.

His brown eyes met her gray as he made his way to her. The old Sam would have acted awkwardly, would have sputtered and flinched but with how she was now, she stood there and waited to see what he was going to do.

She was undeniably like how she used to be, she was like Maya.

She looked into his face as he stopped in front of her, she wasn't the only one had changed: He stood taller even though he was tall before, his face was more determined but there was also a softness in his eyes as he gazed down at her. He caught her off guard with his soft smile and she noticed that under the smile, he still looked sad.

She was even more shocked at what he did next: He pulled her into a hug. Unlike last time where he was the one to hesitate, it was Sam's turn to do so.

"That's for last time," he said as he pulled away. "And I want you to know that the same stands for you."

She had to think about what he was talking about for a moment until she remembered what she had said when she had hugged him. *That she was there for him.*

She returned his smile, "And mine still stands."

No matter the changes, she was still the girl he knew and her feelings hadn't changed.

"I know." He smiled again, a little bit of relief hidden within.

He turned to Arthur who was watching them then he turned back to Sam and he gave her a look that he understood that the siblings needed to talk.

"I have my problems with him but since he's your brother, I will respect that. Just know that I will never like him." He stated and she nodded. "I understand…believe me, I do."

Arthur had committed so many wrongs in his quest to protect his sister, a part of her who was still Sam still resented him for what he had done.

Cale gave her another look then walked past her to join the others.

"We might survive this." She joked but Arthur didn't find it funny, she was definitely back to acting like Sam.

"You finally want to talk?" he pondered and she gave him a confused look. "I could ask you the same thing?" It was true that neither of them had made the effort to talk to each other, all they had was the breakdown she had right after she had killed the twins.

She inhaled and closed her eyes and like a switch, she opened her newly gray eyes and her expression was much more serious."We really do need to talk."

Arthurs jaw was stiff as he nodded, it was like he was nervous about what she was going to say.

She pointed at a clearing in the woods that led to a small ledge and they made their way to the spot silently aside from the twigs and rocks that were being crushed under their feet.

As they stepped into the clearing the sun shined on them and it took a second for their eyes to adjust to something other than the dim light of the woods.

She looked down the incline but unlike in her memories, this one didn't lead to some beautiful sight, it led to more dirt and rocks.

She sat down on the edge and patted a particularly large rock beside her to get Arthur to sit with her.

He sat and they both looked into the sky.

"I'm sorry… For everything." She started and Arthur dropped his gaze as his sister spoke with her eyes on the clouds over head. "For all of my faults and wrongdoings….That are far too many to count." She finally looked at him when a pair of birds flew out of view. "And most of all, I'm sorry for leaving you."

Arthur was silent for a moment as he took in her words and when he finally spoke, it sounded like the tone he had always used when they were younger: Soft and understanding.

"I was so lost after you died, I didn't have anything to live for and I got to the point that I tried ending myself."

She held her breath as he spoke, her bottom lip trembling when he talked about killing himself. He was supposed to be her happy brother who was peaceful and loving and she had ruined it.

"That's when Archie's father found me…" He continued on with his downcast eyes. "That's when he found out that I was a gargoyle, my body was healing itself and he walked in as it was." His smile shocked Sam due to the mood being so somber. "He freaked out at first but when I didn't do anything and he saw how broken I was…He picked me up from the ground and patched up my wound… from that moment on, he treated me like a son." His hazel eyes that had matched her's just days before met her gray. "It took me a few years to get comfortable enough to tell him about you. I kept thinking that you were out there somewhere and I needed someone to help me find you… and as you know, that responsibility went to Archie."

"Our brother." Sam said and Arthur blinked. "He was more of a brother to you than Eli, Oberon, or Peyton."

"Did you-?" He questioned and she nodded. "I heard every word."

He chuckled and she smiled, it felt good to see him laugh.

His smile disappeared after a few seconds and he got serious.

"I resented you for choosing the humans over me, I get why you did it but I was so lonely without you…" He closed his eyes and inhaled to calm himself.

"I can tell you were resentful." she rubbed the side of her head that he had injured the day they had met in the cave.

He chuckled, "I feel bad for that now, you always had courage but what you did that night was stupid."

She remembered what she had done to land her the hit, she thought of it as the spit heard around the world.

"...yeah." she rubbed her head awkwardly as she laughed with him.

"Why did you let Eli live?" Arthur caught her off guard with the serious question after they had shared so much laughter.

Her face was flat as she met his eyes again, "I need him to deliver my message."

"To the man he's working for?"

"I'm not sure if it's a man." She turned towards the sun and allowed it's light to blind her. "I'm positive this being is something more."

They both thought of how the being had been able to stop their brothers from killing her. It was a feat that the being was able to stop them from doing what they wanted.

"Why do you think he stopped them from killing me?" She pondered.

Her question was hard to answer without knowing who the being was, but one thing was certain: Whoever it was, they knew who she was and of her power. "There's something coming…I feel it in my soul." Her voice shook.

Arthur shared her fearful expression. "Is this going to be our higher purpose?"

She found herself smiling at his question "Maybe so, but I have my own thoughts on that." She exclaimed and Arthur rose a brow. "When I died I didn't just reincarnate, I also had a vision."

"A vision?" Arthur puzzled.

"I call it that but I'm not entirely sure what it really was." She shook her head, what she had seen before she had reincarnated still lingered in her mind, there was no way that it was simply a vision. Most of all, the voice that answered her before she moved on still echoed in her ears.

"I will not fail." she whispered and the voice echoed again, "*I know.*"

The darkness she was met with when she got her memories back was so much more than some kind of void in her mind. It was spiritual and held a higher meaning.

Arthur only got more confused from her strange behavior and when she realized what she was doing, she shook it off and got back to the matter at hand.

"In my…" She had to think of the right word but she settled for the word she had used to describe it before."Vision… I saw myself as Sam and the first thing that came to mind was how I failed my purpose in life, it was then that I realized what that was."

She turned her body so she was facing her brother. "The stone gargoyles on top of churches and other buildings are grotesque and frightening but why are they really there?"

Arthur thought about it for a moment.

"To guard the building…" His expression gave her the hint that he understood what she was getting at.

"Precisely, gargoyles aren't meant to be horrible creatures that kill and maim, We're meant to be guardians."

Arthur's face was set in realization as his sisters words sunk in, it made so much sense to him. He huffed then smiled at the strangeness of it all. "I can't believe that I never thought about that."

"Maybe you're not as smart as you think you are." She dissed but snickered after so he would know that it was just a joke.

As they sat and laughed, they undeniably looked like siblings not only in their similar looks, but in personality.

"You know I treated you the way I did not because I resented you, but for the reason that if you didn't get your memories back, I wanted you to kill me after our brothers were dealt with." His words made her go pale and she shook her head.

"You're a fool." Her eyes narrowed at her brothers stupidity.

He smiled, "I guess I am."

"You are," She agreed. "But you're also my brother."

It'd been years since she had seen his happy face and her words were what made it so now.

He opened his arms and she wrapped hers around him.

"We'll conquer what's coming Maya, I know we can." His breath hit her hair as he spoke.

"...Yeah." She inhaled sharply and nuzzled her head into her brothers shoulder.

Hearing her name reminded her of what she had to do now.

"Whoever knows me as Sam can continue calling me that but for now on, I want to be referred to as Maya by all others."

Arthur pulled away from her but kept his hands on her shoulders.

"What?" he seemed wholeheartedly confused.

"I need what the name gives me, It's not Sam who was born the legendary gargoyle and it's certainly not Sam whose name is known by who's coming… With this name, they know I've returned and I'm ready for them." In reality she wasn't ready, there was no telling how strong this new entity was going to be.

She felt like she was throwing her human name away like it was fodder.

"...I understand." Arthur knew the pain it caused her. "You are who you are, names don't matter." he smiled gently. "It took me a long time to learn that."

She turned away from him and lifted her eyes to the sun again, there was no telling what was going to happen in the future. She didn't know what their new enemies plans were or if they were going to survive the new threat, everything seemed so uncertain.

"Hand me my bag." Arthur demanded as he reached for it.

Sam's head shot down to the thing, she had forgotten that she had it. She handed it to him and he shuffled through it's insides and after a few seconds, he pulled out some sort of black fabric and as he unfolded it, her heart thumped: It was the trenchcoat she and her mother had shared. There were burn marks on it from the parts of the explosion that she couldn't contain.

He handed it to her and her hand shook as the fabric touched her skin.

"You kept this old thing?" She patted down the wrinkles that had been caused from being in the bag for so long.

"Why wouldn't I? It was yours and our mothers."

She didn't bother to look at him, she only had eyes for the coat. It didn't smell like her mother anymore, the scent had been replaced by the smell of fire.

She handed it back to him, "Can you hang onto it for a bit longer?" She kept her eyes away from Arthur as he took it back. "Of course."

Along with thinking about the coat, she thought of the other thing that he had carried around with him for all these years.

"Do you remember where you took that picture?" She pondered as she finally looked at him.

He blinked in confusion but it quickly came to him: The picture of her in front of the large building that he had taken days before her life as Maya had ended.

He pulled the image from his pocket and handed it to her. She didn't get a good look at it before due to her being hardheaded but now she took the image in and with it, she thought of the day it had been taken.

It was the first time she had gone to a town without the intent to kill. She came as a guest and took in the buildings that the humans had built from the ground up. It had amazed her at what they could do with what little they had.

"I remember everything." Arthur said finally as he watched her take in the picture.

He had offered to take the picture with a disposable camera they had bought at a drugstore.

She had tried smiling for the picture but the weight of her sins had pulled her down, especially after seeing how innocent the humans were. She never gave them the chance, she was only focused on her revenge.

Revenge.

Even her death wouldn't make up for what she's done and she found herself thinking that maybe that was the reason why she reincarnated with her memories intact.

She would never be able to fix what she had done but she was brought into this new life for retribution and she was going to take it with open arms.

She wasn't going to allow herself to fail this time.

"*I know.*" the voice echoed again.

End part one.

Part two

Chapter 33

Eli made his way up the large hill that led to his destination. The night around him was dark and damp as he took in the smell of rain that had stopped moments before. It was an odd smell, it bothered his senses and brought him back to the days that he had spent in the tent with his family as they waited out the storm inside. Through the nostalgic smell he also caught the scent of who he was heading towards. It was a smell as odd as the rain's lingering scent but as this smell filled his nostrils, it made him want to puke: It was the smell of their natural enemies that he and his brothers had joined.

Though they didn't have much of a choice.

He stepped further up the incline until he saw what he was looking for: On the other side of a small divot was a light shining in the shape of a large hole sticking out of the side of the earth. As Eli made his way to the cave-like structure, he was reminded of what his youngest brother had done and what it had resulted in.

The last time Eli had met with this *man,* he had been with his twin brothers, Peyton and Oberon. But now he was returning alone and it was all thanks to his sister.

"Tell whoever you're working for that Maya is back." She had said and the words echoed in Eli's mind as if she was standing beside him.

The memory of his brothers deaths plagued his mind and made his limbs heavy. He couldn't say that he loved them but he was rather fond of their presence. They helped feed his need for destruction. He twisted his fingers into his palms as anger filled his bones, he hated his sister and would try to end her worthless existence as long as he had air to breath.

The only thing that had kept his mind at ease was the fact that she had spared him to pass her message to his *boss.*

It infuriated him at first, it felt like she was pitying him, that he wasn't a big enough threat to her while his younger brothers were. Though that may be true, the thought didn't weigh on him much as he remembered that he would be the one to see her death.

He smiled as he thought of his sisters ignorance. The *person* he was working for wasn't a person, but the embodiment of evil.

He was only ten feet away from the cave when the smell of the creatures inside began to be too much for his nose. He breathed in through his mouth to stop the smell from dulling his senses. It wasn't a nasty smell, not along the lines of manure or other dirty smells but it was something entirely different. It actually wasn't much of smell really, it was like a strong warmth entering your nose and it burned at your nostrils. According to the creatures inside, gargoyle's had their own scents as well and that was how they had found them:

He and his brothers were still on a high that the death of their sister had caused when the creatures found them. She was finally out of their way and neither she nor their parents had the ability to stop them anymore.

How could they? They were dead.

It was several days after Maya had died and they were finally going to attack their next city when the creatures stopped them.

They looked human to a point but they were so much more: The first one was the most distinguishable with long white hair that reached the middle of his back. He was clad in a black coat and pants as dark as night. He was pale against his clothes and his lips were red as if he had just finished a delicious meal that had consisted of blood. His eyes were the most frightening as they looked like bottomless orbs that were void of any color.

The second looked like an older man with grayed hair stretching into a pony tail and his beard and mustache combination was as equally as gray. His eyes were as dark as the firsts but there were red and purple viens popping through the whites of his eyes. He looked like he had been crying. He was clothed in a robe that a monk would have worn.

The last was a lean man with milky skin and eyes even more bottomless than the first's. His hair was as dark as his eyes and it framed his scalp as waves. He was wearing a long coat with a collar that reached his chin. He looked young compared to the others, maybe the ripe age of twenty, and the brothers thought he looked the most human of the three.

"What the fuck do you want?" Oberon being the way he was spoke first as the three newcomers smiled with anticipation at the three gargoyles.

"Watch your tone, gargoyle." The white haired man warned but smiled.

The bothers looked to each other with shock: How did they know what they were?

"HA!" The white haired creature exclaimed as his smile widened. "We know what you are simply by your smell."

"Smell?" Peyton's eyes narrowed. "The same could be said for you."

The creature chuckled and looked at the two standing with him: The older man looked tired as he looked on at the gargoyles while the dark haired man simply stared into the brothers eyes as they looked on with disgust. Oberon took one threatening step to the white haired one and the creature's smile didn't disperse as the threat did nothing to scare him.

"Get out of here before I lose my patience." Oberon growled as he looked into the creatures face, he was tall and Oberon had to stand on his toes to meet the beings eyes.

"I'll stay here." The being snorted in reply as his white hair blew in the gentle breeze. His eyes looked into Oberon's skin, saw all of his emotions, knew his weaknesses.

Oberon swung at him but the being disappeared. Oberon blinked as he looked for his prey but he was faced with nothing but the two onlookers that the other had left behind.

"Behind you!" Peyton warned his twin but before Oberon had the time to

turn, the white haired man had him by the back of his neck. The being pushed the gargoyle down as he thrashed against the untiring hands of his captor. Peyton shot forward to help his brother but the look on the older creatures face made him freeze.

What the hell was this? The brothers were strong, strong enough to handle anyone now that their sister was out of the way. Now that she was gone, these creatures showed themselves to bring them back down the chain.

Eli watched as Oberon struggled against the being and Peyton who struggled in his own way as he fought his fear. Through the noise Oberon was causing as he tried to get away and the laughter of the white haired being, Eli found his eyes drifting to the black haired man.

When his eyes fell on him, he realized that he was already looking at him, his black eyes unblinking as he watched the oldest gargoyle.

"Enough, Azazel." His voice rang as he spoke, his tone was soft like silk but it caused more fear than it would have if it had been rough.

The white haired being named Azazel did as he was told and let go of Oberon's neck while his smile remained. The brothers could have attacked, could have ran, but they found themselves mesmerized with the fact that the small more frail looking man had told the taller more frightening one what to do.

He turned his head to his associates then back to the brothers and as his did so, he brought his lower arms into the air like he was about to show something off. Gravity fell on them and the brothers fell to their knees then to their stomachs as the heat filled air pushed them down. With each new push, the heat grew stronger and it was getting harder to bear. Azazel laughed at the sight of the brothers struggling to get up but what ever the black haired man was doing was too much for them. They were pushed down like rodents set in a trap and the feeling infuriated them.

Who the hell was this man?

As Eli wondered, the air let go and he was able to pull himself to at least his knees. His breath hitched as he took in the cooling air and it took him a moment of glaring at the man in front of him to realize that he was shaking. Eli had felt something coming from the being but had ignored it since he felt the white haired one was the bigger threat. Now he realized the feeling that he had gotten from the black haired man was far more sinister.

As Eli looked onto the beings even expression, he saw what he really was: Deadly.

This being wasn't human, he was more of a monster than Eli and his brothers could ever wish to be. Even their sister would be shaking in her boots if she was with them now.

He looked normal, weak even, but the air coming from this being was nothing like Eli had ever felt before.

He was the embodiment of evil.

"I know this is hard for you, being put in your place after trying so hard to get out." The beings smile was as terrifying as his power. "I understand, believe me."

"What the fuck are you…?" Oberon managed between his teeth.

The being rounded his head towards the twin, his black eyes shining in the sunlight. Through the glare, Oberon could see something shining in them… red?

"To know what I am you must know what these two are." He rolled his head to the two standing beside him. "Aamon," he started with the older man. "What are you?"

The old man who had been looking on with what seemed like no interest glanced at the younger man then set his sight back on the brothers as he explained.

"Malevolent, wicked, infernal…" He craned his head to the blue sky. "We are demons."

No one made a sound after the old mans announcement.

The laughter of the demon named Azazel rang through the air and carried down with the breeze, sending a chill down the gargoyles spines.

"Demons…?" Eli's voice drifted at the end of the demons cackle. "You're just a myth."

"That's sad for you to say since you have two standing in front of you now." Azazel ran his pale hand through his even paler hair. "Though it may be hard to believe since we're wearing our human forms for you."

Human forms?

"Two?" Peyton questioned as his voice shook, he brought his blues eyes to the black haired one and the being smiled.

"I'm known by many names," He declared. "The ruler of demons… Satan…The devil… But I prefer Lucifer."

"Y-You're lying…" Oberon stammered, there was no way that in front of them stood the harbringer of death, evil personified. The being that had been banished from heaven by God himself for speaking out, for wanting too much power.

How could he be real? Especially in front of them now with the body of a human?

"Am I?" There was a touch of entertainment in his tone as he brought a hand to the air to stop his white haired demon from laughing at the brothers ignorance. "That's wishful thinking on your part."

His black irises expanded into the whites of his eyes and the once irises turned as bright as flame while the pupil remained black. The demons eyes changed as well but they differed from their leaders, instead of the flamed irises, they turned blood red and the pupil turned into an animalistic slit. Like their leader, the white of their eyes had turned black as well.

Through the shock Oberon tried his hand at another attack while his brothers knew better. With a simple blink of his eyes, the devil forced the air to push down on the gargoyle again while the others felt nothing. Oberon groaned as he struggled against the rugged ground, his face smashing against a point of a rock and blood poured from where it pierced his cheek.

"…What do you want?" Eli's jaw shook as he watched his brother spit out the blood that was pouring into his mouth.

Lucifer moved his eyes from Oberon and cocked his head as they landed on Eli. The grin that spread across the devil's lips made the gargoyle flinch.

"Your sister." His voice was as sweet as honey as he spoke of her but like his usual tone, there was a certain amount of bloodlust hidden within.

Their sister?

What did the evil incarnate want with their sister? She was the strongest gargoyle but what could she do for him? Their sister, the girl that had always gotten the attention they craved. The girl that had gotten in their way but now she was finally gone…

"…She's dead." Peyton's voice drifted as fear filled him.

"I'm aware." The devil's voice showed no surprise at Peytons declaration. "But you and I both know that she will return."

"What do you want with her?" Eli's voice was gruff and it sounded as if he cared for his sister's well being but it was far from the case. Eli felt the aggravation of being under the foot of yet another being stronger than him.

"Everything." Lucifer's voice was like a purr as he licked his lips and his eyes returned to bottomless as he craned his head. "You will do as I say from now on." He declared. "You will wait to kill your sisters reincarnation until I give you the ok to do so." He leaned back slightly. "And you won't attack anymore cities."

Eli's eyes narrowed while the twins brows furrowed, how did he know they wanted to kill her again?

"You're not going to stop us." Oberon's head twitched up from the blood soaked rock. "We'll kill her."

Azazel kneeled in front of him and he flinched, it was odd for Eli to see his brother frightened by anyone aside from his sister. "You're a tough one, aren't you?" Azazel lifted his chin as Lucifer let go of his hold on him.

His calculated power was terrifying.

As Oberon tried to get up after the powers release, the whited haired demon pushed him down again and as his cheek fell onto the rock again, the blood splashed onto Azazel's face and the demon took a lick with his long tongue.

"Disgusting." The demon scrunched his pale face.

"They are our natural enemies." The demon named Aamon told. "Of course their taste would be as bad as their smell."

"What are you planning?" Oberon sputtered as Azazel still held him to the ground. "You have all of this power… the world could be yours… our sister was alive just days ago, why didn't you do this sooner?"

Lucifer sighed as he stepped closer, "It is not yet time."

Like his demon, his knelt but made sure he was was on the same level as the brothers. The old demon remained back with a smile on his wrinkled lips. "But in your sisters next life, everything will come to pass."

"Why our sister?" Eli leaned closer to Lucifer's face, his black eyes looked like they had an ocean swimming in them, an ocean of shadows. His hair that was equally as dark swayed with the wind as it picked up. If the demon of demons didn't show his power, one would have never guessed what he truly was.

Lucifer smirked as he licked his dagger like canines, "Your sister and I have a bond like no other, one that transcends lifetimes." It was his turn to laugh and Eli fell backwards as the cackle carried into the air around them. He turned to his brothers, he was sure they shared the same expression and sure enough, as he saw them, their faces were filled with dread.

Back in current time Eli's footsteps echoed as he walked down the long tunnel that led to Lucifer. He had to duck to stop his head from hitting the rock over head. It had taken him days to get there and he had to use the human's flight system to do so. Lucifer had taken refuge in many places to accommodate his plans and now it just so happened to be in Ireland.

Lucifer had always made sure to let the brothers know where he was. Eli was sure that it had nothing to do with him wanting their help but to keep tabs on who he really wanted: Their sister.

As he made it through the last of tunnel, he bent down and squeezed himself through the small opening that led to a large cavern. The cavern was well lit and as he stepped inside, the demons sitting in the corner paid him no mind. They were far too focused on the bones and blood that were left of the people they had brought back.

Demons were torturous creatures, they thrived off of killing much like Eli and the twins and even Maya had. But even with their similarities, they were different as well. The demons did more than just attack and kill the humans, they were able to possess them.

Eli thought that it was all a lie, he had heard about the demons, had heard the rumors the humans had started, but he never thought in all of the years he's been alive that he would be face to face with them, let alone Lucifer himself.

All of the rumors were true, but so much more. The demons fought with the humans, possessed them, killed them, even laid with them not out of love but out of the simple reason of being entertained by them.

Eli had only seen them in their human forms, Peyton had called them their *fooling forms* and Eli was thankful for the fact. While he and the other gargoyles could change but retain some of their human looks, he was told that the demons could change completely.

He'd rather not know what they looked like.

He brought his gaze around the cave: There were pools of blood and just as many piles of bones. The white calcium made objects still had some blood and muscle on them but the one in Azazel's hand as he gnawed on it was as white as his hair. Azazel's black eyes rolled to the demon that was sitting beside him as he chewed.

The demon's name was Cain. He was a quiet demon, he didn't speak much and unlike the other demons who relished in what they did, he seemed like he was uninterested, maybe even sad.

Eli knew better though, each of the demons had their quirks but they all enjoyed what they did. The quiet demon as the brothers would call him had an old style hairdo that consisted of brown curls and a weak beard of the same color. He was skinny but had a good amount of muscle and like how he felt when he had first met Lucifer, Eli knew that there was so much more to the demon than he let on.

The demons were sitting on a mound of rock and the lanterns light flickered off their pale faces. Azazel wore a long black coat and jeans while Cain wore a white dress shirt and slacks. His eyes looked from the puddle of blood in front of him and he met the gargoyles eyes and Azazel followed his gaze. He spit the bone from his mouth and it fell to ground with a clang.

"Hello gargoyle!" He exclaimed as Cain remained silent.

Eli ignored the demon, there were many times that Azazel had put them in their place, especially Oberon. When Eli saw him, he would be reminded of his own weakness, it was hard for someone that was otherwise strong to be treated like fodder.

"How'd it go?" A silk filled voice rang from feet away and Eli brought his attention to Lucifer who was sitting on his own mound of rock, his back leaning against the rock wall.

Lucifer could change his form, could make himself look how he wanted. One day he would be a young man with blonde hair and blue eyes and another he would be a brown haired man with a good amount of bulk. Today he was back to the black haired gentleman that he had worn the day Eli had met him. Eli knew this form was his favorite, he wore it more often than not and he seemed to savor in the look. Lucifer still had that air about him, it was the kind of air that was far too warm and dense for one to be able to breath. His demons had the same air but not to the same extent.

Lucifer rolled a femur through his fingers as he cocked his head while he waited for Eli's answer but the latter didn't know where to start.

"...She killed Peyton and Oberon." Eli's shaking voice echoed through the cave as he answered the entity.

There was silence as Lucifer and the two demons took in the news. Eli's eyes averted to the two sitting in the corner: Cain's eyes remained uninterested while Azazel's grin was as wide as his face and the fangs that stuck over his lips blended in with his skin. Eli swung his head back to Satan as he heard the beginning of a snort that erupted into laughter seconds later.

As if the act that his master was doing so gave him permission, Azazel started with his own booming laughter and Eli found himself shaking from the hellish creatures laughter as it echoed through the caves hollow shell. They looked so human but their laughter sounded like two formidable beast's fighting. It was much easier to pretend to look human than it was to sound like one.

Lucifer's laughter died out suddenly and his gleeful expression was replaced with a steady one, his eyes like daggers. Azazel knew better than to go on longer than his master and went silent.

"...And what else?" His voice was steady again.

Eli tried to not feel annoyed at Lucifer's lack of emotion, "She let me live so I could deliver a message." Lucifer looked on with impatience and Eli quickly got on with it. "She said to tell who I'm working for that Maya is back."

Lucifer's face changed again as his lips turned upright into a grin, he chuckled softly to himself as if he was thinking of an old friend.

When he spoke again, his tone was high with enthusiasm.

"While that is good news, I'm waiting on someone else's return."

Eli lowered his head, he had delivered the news not because his sister had told him to, but because he wanted Satan to act, to bring Maya to an end. But now that the news had been delivered, Lucifer acted like he had won a bet.

"You sent us after her knowing that she'd kill us?" He growled unintentionally.

Lucifer cocked his head and narrowed his eyes, "Of course I knew this would happen, you fool." There was an air of entertainment hidden under his annoyance. "I kept you away from her because she's needed for what I want… but after I found out what your impeccable brother did, I knew this was my chance." He rolled the femur over again. "I knew your youngest brother would save her and in doing so, he gave her the means to get her memories and power back." His smile extended into his pale cheeks. "I just needed you boys to give her the extra push."

"You were ok with us dying as long as it got you what you wanted?!" Eli snapped. "After all we've done for you!?"

The air changed and Eli regretted his words immediately, he couldn't breath as the heat hit him and he heaved to get some kind of relief.

"You think I couldn't have done any of this without your help?" Lucifer pondered and cocked his head. "The help of gargoyles? Our natural enemy?" He snickered as he rose a brow at the gargoyle in front of him. "A weak one at that." His smiled dispersed. "You bring me this good news and you try to ruin my mood with your whining."

His eyes grew darker as the annoyance registered loud and clear on his face.

"You're annoying me," He said simply as he waved Eli away. "Leave before I change my mind and finish what your sister started."

"Until next time, gargoyle." Azazel waved with a happy smile while Cain kept his eyes on the puddle of blood. Azazel chewed on his victims flesh like bubblegum as he kept up with his exaggerated wave.

Eli swallowed his heart as it raced at the back of his throat and he turned to the caves exit. As he walked, he felt pressure on his back that was caused by the demon's gazes on him.

The sound of Lucifer throwing the femur to the ground echoed through the cave and to Azazel's delight, Eli jumped from the noise. Eli had only felt fear on very few occasions: When his sister had returned and when he met with the devil.

He continued walking down the low tunnel as a growl came from behind him and he was certain it was Lucifer's pet getting it's dinner that it's master so graciously threw to the ground.

He stepped into the night as the beast dragged it's large feet to the location of the bone and his ears pressed to the back of his head as the beast chewed the bone to splinters between it's sharp teeth.

Chapter 34

It had been 4 months since her memories returned and since she had made the declaration that she would be referred to as Maya by everyone aside from those who already knew her as Sam.

In the past 4 months the group had moved from place to place by stolen car only for them to abandon it to walk the rest of the way to their destination. The places consisted of abandoned houses, wooded areas, and empty camps.

They had arrived at their current abandoned campground two weeks prior and although they would have moved to another location long before now, they seemed to be partial towards the place since it had exactly what they needed: Large cabins that consisted of a small living room, a bedroom, and a bathroom.

The area was always shaded and kept cool in the fall heat. Oddly what Maya had liked the most about the place was that they were close to Washington D.C.

No matter where they had gone, they brought a police scanner in case they could hear any sign of their impending threat finally making their move. In doing so they ended up spending their time fighting smaller crimes that consisted of robberies and kidnappings.

Washington was at an all time high.

Fighting crime didn't help with the guilt that she forever had, but in doing so, it kept her distracted from what she had done. She felt like it helped keep her mind steady as she prepared for what was to come.

It was dangerous work, especially now that they were in Washington where the police officers were always out and there was a fair share of undercover detectives. Maya didn't mind the threat of the humans at this point, all she worried about was the creatures that she was about to meet. When she had made her *declaration of war,* she had imagined that Eli would tell her enemy that she was back and they wouldn't waste anytime. But here she was, 4 months later, and still running like the wanted person that she was.

She hadn't seen Mina in so long but thought of her everyday, she wondered if she had gone back to college. It was that time of year but she also wondered if what had happened ruined her.

She certainly hoped not.

She didn't want her friend to be as ruined as her, but it gave her some solace that she would never be as monstrous as she was. Maya, no *Sam* had made sure of that when she took her place.

This was where she was always meant to be, Maya was right where she belonged.

It was fate.

She sat on the cool ground as she watched Cale spar with Trevor, the frail boy she once knew was gone and he had been replaced by someone stronger. Aside from that, it was easy to see that he had shed some pounds. It was a hot day as they neared the middle of October and while Cale had taken his shirt off, Trevor opted out.

Sweat dropped from Cale's brow and chest, instead of losing weight, Cale had gained it, though it wasn't in fat but in muscle.

Maya averted her gaze as they fought each other in their human forms and looked down at the unbitten apple that rested in her right hand. She began to raise the fruit to her mouth when her body froze and her eyes widened as unfamiliar voices echoed in her mind:

"Eat it." A silky voice demanded.

* * *

"I can't..." A girlish voice replied.

"He doesn't love you... If he did, he wouldn't keep this from you."

"He said I can't..."

"You won't die, you will become like him."

"Sam... Sam... SAM!"

She blinked as she woke from her daze.

"I swear you day dream more and more lately." Ari pressed a hand to her hip and she rose a brow at Maya's puzzled face.

Like the others, Ari had changed in the past four months: She had lost weight and gained it back in muscle. Her once long black hair only reached to the bottom of her chin but it retained it's color. Only now the teal in her bangs was accompanied by purple. Her fashion hadn't changed much as she still wore all black to match her hair color.

"Lot's to dream about..." Maya's voice drifted as she moved her gaze from Ari to the apple that had fallen slightly from her hand.

It was true that she had been daydreaming a lot, she was beginning to hear voices and she would black out during the phenomenon. They were always filled with a silky voiced man but she had yet to see him. Most of the words made no sense to her and she wondered how they were significant to their situation. She understood her visions before when she was getting her memories back, they were to be expected, but now that she had her memories back, there was no reason for her to hear voices.

Her eyes lifted to Cale and Trevor who didn't notice her sink into her delusion.

"Hey Trev!" She called and he narrowly dodged Cale as his eyes moved to her. "Catch!" She demanded as she threw the apple at a speed invisible to the human eye but with him not being human anymore, Trevor was able to catch it.

He placed the fruit in his other hand as he shook the one he had caught it with, "Ow." He groaned.

Maya smiled. "Nice catch."

He scrunched his face but smiled. "Thanks but it'll be nice if you hold back next time."

She rose a brow. "I did."

"You know she can throw harder than that, did you forget about all the times that she beat us at baseball?" Cale brought his eyes to Maya then to Trevor. "I think it's unfair."

"It has nothing to do with strength," Maya smirked. "It has everything to do with skill."

"We'll find out later, won't we?" Cale met her eyes, his voice filled with playful competition.

"We shall." She said as she got to her feet.

"Ya'll wanna do some training?" Kira came from behind and Maya turned to face her as she stopped next to Ari.

Kira's hair had done the opposite of Ari's, it had grown to the bottom of her chin and she kept it in a braid. Some of the strands that hadn't grown to the proper length popped out in odd places. Her arms crossed over her graphic tee as she rose a brow. "This'll be good practice for baseball later." She smirked as she met Maya's eyes.

Maya had been lucky, her comrades remained beside her and much to her surprise, they had grown closer. She had asked them many times why they remained with her, it had been four months and their threat had yet to show themselves.

It was true that the humans were after them, but there had to be some way to hide from them without staying with the girl that endangered them.

"Sounds good to me." She nodded in agreement. "It'll be a nice warm up for when I kick your asses later."

Kira and Ari snorted in unison as Maya turned and joined the boys.

Before they started, Arthur, Emily, and Dylan joined them.

Arthur and Dylan were shirtless as well as they made their way to the others. They had spent the afternoon at the playground utilizing the jungle gym and the other childish contraptions that turned out to be good for strength training.

Arthur had remained the same as he already had a good amount of muscle and he had kept his hair style the same like Cale had. The only difference was his emotions, unlike before when he was always on the defense and thinking about the threat of his brothers, he enjoyed his time with his comrades and relished in the fact that his sister had returned not only in body but in mind.

Dylan also held the same amount of muscle since he was already toned from his football days, his brown hair had become scruffy and he had grown a mustache and a beard.

Emily had Ari cut her hair to her shoulders but with her curls, her hair reached to the middle of her neck. She had improved the most aside from Trevor when it came to fighting. She wasn't only more muscular, she had also gained more confidence.

The three returned almost on cue to join the others in their training and Maya was sure that they had listened to them about their want to do so.

"You guys are still going on about how I beat you at baseball?" Arthur questioned and the area was filled with groans.

Arthur met his sisters eyes, the eyes that had matched his own four months prior but had changed to stone gray. Maya had changed a lot since her days as just Sam: Her wavy hair had returned to being braided into her viking style hairdos. Today she had decided to wear the braids on either side of her scalp while the hair in the middle trailed down the back of her head. Her hair had grown longer and reached the middle her back which was clad in a lilic shirt that hugged her figure. The self-inflicted scar on her right temple had gone completely as the months had gone by and her skin had grown paler than it already was.

"Well let's get this done so we can find out who's going to beat who at baseball." She flicked her brothers forehead before she turned to the others as they all positioned themselves in a large circle around Trevor, Cale, and Maya.

As they fought, their improved skills shined though and unlike four months ago, they were all almost equal in their skills. Cale still had an edge on the others while Maya and Arthur still had unfair advantages. But nonetheless, the half blooded gargoyles were able to keep up the the full blooded ones and even landed a few hits. After awhile many of them gave up including Kira, Ari, and Emily who had decided to start dinner in Emily's cabin. Arthur had left the fight and simply watched from where his sister had sat as she and Cale practiced their paired attacks.

The two still practiced together, Maya didn't think having her old power back was enough and she truly enjoyed learning what Cale had to teach.

They watched as Trevor and Dylan fought at the line of trees at the opening of the woods.

"Now's a good time to try it." Cale brought his gaze back to Maya as he looked down into her face.

She looked up to meet his eyes, "Lets try it like we're in an actual battle." She backed away a step as she crossed her arms behind her back and grinned as she glanced between Cale and the two fighting at the tree line.

Cale chuckled as he watched her playful smile as she backed all the way to the tree line opposite of the other two.

She inhaled sharply as she set herself up to run, she allowed the pressure in her eyes to build and when she placed them on Cale, he was met with a left black eye and a right white eye. Cale allowed his eyes to change to black and nodded to her when he was ready.

Her eyes blurred as she moved them to the area around Cale, she imagined people fighting, the sound of battle, and the nervous air that came with it.

She relished in it all.

She started off and as she ran, she weaved through the imaginary fighters and made her way to Cale who had turned the other way so he could sense her coming as if he was distracted by a fight. She reached her arm out as she approached him and his darted out and grabbed hers.

She felt like a fly as he lifted her and threw her through the air towards Trevor and Dylan.

Trevor turned his head to her as he heard the change in the breeze but it was too late and she was landing on him, her arm's outstretched so she could pin him to the ground.

"I think your new move works." Trevor smiled up at her after the initial shock wore off.

"I think it does." Maya agreed as she got up and highfived Dylan as he raised his arm to do so, the pressure in her eyes dispersing.

It had taken the others awhile to get used to her mismatched eyes but after awhile, they did. Though sometimes Maya would catch them looking at one more than the other as if they were wondering which one was more noticeable.

"Yes!" Cale exclaimed as he jogged over to them and the two highfived each other in a job well done.

"You guys love showing off." Arthur called from his spot and they turned to him.

"I noticed that." Trevor rolled his eyes to Cale and Maya and rose a brow as he watched the two snicker with each other.

It had also taken awhile for them to get used to Arthur's presence and especially his new outlook on life. But as the months went on, they found themselves talking casually to him, though the things he had done were far from forgotten. They had to act civil in a time like this.

Especially since he was Maya's brother.

"Dinners done!" Ari called from Emily's cabin and they turned to see her through the small window in the kitchen. "Let's go you fucking hooligans." She rolled her eyes playfully as she disappeared from view.

Arthur got up and made his way to the cabin while Trevor and Dylan followed behind him. Arthur turned to them before they went into the cabin and told them how they should find a new move to mess with his sister and Cale the next time they sparred. The two men agreed but still felt awkward with accepting the help of the man who was once their enemy.

Cale and Maya hadn't noticed that they were being left behind as Cale told a story to Maya of the time he had face planted during active duty. She laughed at his clumsiness as she imagined the fall.

"I never expected you to be so ungraceful." She chuckled as she looked up at his equally entertained face.

"Neither did I." He awkwardly rubbed the back of his head.

"Emily said to stop your flirting and get in here!" Ari who had stepped out of the cabin called while looking annoyed. She smiled as she glanced at the small window that Emily had peeped through at the sound of Ari's words.

"I did not!" She yelled nervously, her face beet red and Cale and Maya didn't have time to be annoyed at Ari's remark as they laughed at Emily's embarrassment and the sound of Kira's loud snort coming from the kitchen.

They made sure to always have dinner together, eating alone was lonely and they didn't have a television at their new dwelling.

The table barely fit all of them and Arthur who sat beside his sister practically shared a chair with her.

"You guys really out did yourselves with this." Trevor smiled over his plate of steak, potatoes, and broccoli.

They hadn't eaten anything more than cup soup and cereal most days and when they finally had the chance to get meat, they couldn't pass up the chance.

"It has nothing to do with us, our bodies are just used to shit." Kira chomped on a large piece and chewed until she leaned her head back and moaned dramatically from the taste.

Maya watched as she sat across from her and she found herself smiling at Emily who was sitting on the other side of Cale. Emily had a knack for seasonings and made sure that she had picked up some along with the steak.

"It tasted just like how it would at home." Dylan set his fork down as he got done and Maya felt Arthur twitch beside her.

Now that his brothers were out of the way and Maya was safe, Arthur started to feel more and more regret at what he had done. Maya knew the feeling all too well and she hated that her brother felt the same. She could say it a million times and it still wouldn't be enough, but she always wished better for him, but alas, their choices would haunt them for the rest of their lives.

Lives that would last as long as eternity if they made it through the new threat.

Maya nudged him to tell him not to dwell on it.

What a hypocrite she was, who was she to tell someone not to dwell on their sins when that's all she ever did?

"Do you ever think about going home?" Arthur's voice rang from beside her and surprise filled the room as silverware clanged onto plates.

Maya turned to her brother who didn't look sad or regretful, he looked like he simply wanted to know. He glanced at his sister then back to the surprised group and Maya did the same.

"...Of course we do." Ari's voice drifted. "We all have families to go to but we choose not to..." Ari realized what she had said when it was too late and she gave Cale a guilty look but he waved it off.

"I know what you meant, my adoptive mother died a long time ago and my birth parents died when I was just a baby so I don't remember much... It's my adoptive father that's still fresh in my mind... But I know he'd be proud of what I'm doing." He smiled gently but Maya knew it was for show.

Cale had felt his fair share of grief and it had taken awhile for him to be open again. But after awhile, he started to act like himself again. Though once in awhile he would wander off by himself and let the grief hit him.

Arthur's eyes had dropped like Maya's had, the siblings were somewhat the cause of Cale's father's death. It was Maya's existence that brought calamity upon them and it was Arthur who had brought them into this mess.

The room was silent as they all thought of how things used to be, how it should've been.

Maya found herself wondering what life would have been like if she had never attacked the humans and sacrificed herself to save them. She also wondered what it would have been like if she had never gotten her memories back and remained only as Sam.

Trevor awkwardly cleared his throat, "W-who want's to play baseball?" He asked as he tried to lighten the mood. He was met with silence but after a moment, the others agreed. They obviously needed something to do to get their minds off their thoughts. Friendly competition would be enough to do so.

For now at least.

Emily volunteered to stay back and wash the dishes but Ari told her that she would do them.

"You coming?" Arthur asked Maya as she watched Ari retrieve the dishes with a sullen look on her face.

"Maybe after… I'm going to help Ari first." She gave him a small smile. "Go show them what I see in you."

He furrowed his brows as his eyes relaxed. Maya always told him to act the same way with the others as he did with her. He wasn't a monster to Maya, he used to be when she was Sam but her memories had changed her. She remembered her fear of getting her memories back, the fear that she would change. Indeed she had but not in the way she had feared. It was only that she had the memories of the people that she had killed.

The little girl that cried over her mother still played in her mind and she found herself wondering what the girl looked like now. She had to be close to her thirties by now, if she was even still alive. Arthur clasped her shoulder as he saw the worry in her eyes.

"Don't." He told her and she met his eyes, even though they no longer matched in color, they still matched in shape and expression. Arthur always worried that her need to die for what she had done would come back. When he looked in her eyes he would sometimes see the young woman who would have done anything to make up for it

She brought her arm to his and clasped his wrist, "I'm fine." She assured him.

After Arthur had left, she made her way to Ari who was busy washing away in the small kitchen.

It was exactly that: Small. It could only fit three people inside, it was old fashioned looking as the side by side stove and sink looked to be on the older side. The porcelain white had many stains from years of use. A gentle breeze blew though the window that was placed in front of the sink and the baby blue curtains blew inwards.

"Need help?" Maya tapped her index finger on the wooden door even though she was sure that Ari already knew she was there.

"I always need help." She joked as she dropped a plate into the hot water.

Maya smiled softly as she made her way to the sink and grabbed a dry towel from the clip hanging over it. She kneaded the fabric through her fingers as she waited for Ari to finish the first dish and when she handed it to her, she set work. The fabric squeaked against the plate and it sent a shiver down their spines as their ear drums flinched.

"I'm surprised you volunteered to do this instead of playing ball." Maya didn't mean to make it sound like she was lazy. It was just that the black haired girl didn't seem too big into doing housework unless she was with someone else.

"I can be the housewife type if I want to be." Ari joked but Maya knew better.

There was something bothering her.

"Does this have to do with our dinner conversation?" Maya asked, her words careful.

Outside the window they could hear the yells of the others as one of them got a strike. The girls eyes looked out the window even though they couldn't see the game from where the cabin stood.

"It could be." Ari said simply as she handed Maya another plate.

"I'm sorry." Was all Maya could choke out.

"I don't think you should be sorry." Ari kept her eyes on the next plate as she scrubbed.

Maya stopped drying her plate and leaned it against the sink and it clattered against the already dried one. "I think I do need to be sorry, you know I'm the reason why this is happening to you and the others." She kept her eyes on Ari's jaw as she spoke, her bangs were covering her blue eyes so Maya couldn't see her reaction. "What's more, I've accepted the man who did this to you."

Maya had changed from her days as Sam, she would have been awkward about the conversation, would have kept her eyes away from Ari. With her memories back, she acted more like she had as Maya. She had an air of confidence as she walked while when she was just Sam, she would slump and flinch at the smallest inconvenience.

The negative was that the past twenty years of having visions turned into full blown memory. Her heart constantly beat a tick faster than it used to. She was just as on edge as Arthur, only she wasn't worried about her suicidal tendencies like he was. Her mind was more focused on what was going to happen when the true threat finally showed themselves.

She wondered if she was going to become a monster again.

Why would she be worried about that? She already was one.

"I guess this happened for a reason," Ari finally turned to face Maya and their eyes met. Her brows were furrowed in a determined kind of way as her blue eyes narrowed. "The longer I've been here and the more you talk about this *New threat* that's coming, the more I believe that I'm here for a reason."

Maya clenched her teeth as she held Ari's gaze, there was no way she actually believed that. "Life doesn't work that way." She shook her head and lowered her eyes to her hands that always had a slight shake to them.

"Why not?" Ari shot and Maya brought her gaze back to the confident girl in front of her. She looked disappointed in Maya's words and her eyes narrowed further. "You're an example of how life leads you to where you need to be."

"Oh yeah?" Maya smiled and it wasn't an amused one, she almost looked insane. "Tell me the reason why I killed innocent people? Tell me how that was planned? How I was meant to do so?"

She backed down as she exhaled sharply after she realized what she was doing but to her surprise, Ari didn't stagger backwards or act frightened. It was the opposite, her eyes had lightened as she took in Maya's face which had paled more than it already was.

"You died and came back, and most of all, you got your memories back while others don't. If that's not fate then I don't know what is."

For the first time since her memories returned, Maya lowered herself. It was that word again, the word that flashed in her minds eye everyday: *Fate.*

Ari continued when Maya didn't speak, "You're not who you used to be, you are Samantha Knight, a human and you are also Maya, the legendary gargoyle."

She placed a gentle had on Maya's shoulder and she lifted her chin, "I'm not sure what's so legendary about me." She gave an awkward smile and Ari chuckled softly. "Well I guess we'll have to find out."

Another jeer rang from outside and Ari's hand left her shoulder and in doing so, she dropped the plate that she was still holding with the other into the soapy sink.

"Screw this, the dishes can wait." She grabbed the towel from Maya's hand and wiped her's dry. "Let's go show them how to play."

Maya grinned as Ari pulled her along.

Later that night, they had listened to the police scanner and when a burglary incident was reported the group jumped into action. They had taken turns going on their trips aside from Maya, Arthur, and Cale who insisted on going anytime a problem emerged.

Arthur most likely only went because of Maya while Cale still had his fathers wish in his mind: To make the world a better place.

The three were accompanied by Ari and Kira on this run who had allowed Emily, Trevor, and Dylan to go on the last few.

The five said their *See you laters* to the three staying behind who told them to be careful. It was a risk but they did it nonetheless and the feeling of the upcoming thrill always filled their bones with pride.

Maybe it was the gargoyle in them making them feel that way.

Gargoyles had their knack for danger and the group proved it.

The five made their way to the vehicle they had stolen before they came here, they kept it hidden in a lot that sat in-between the trees with other damaged cars. The white car had plenty of rust and the seats inside were ripped, the yellow cushion inside fell out and stuck on them as they sat. They had tried hot-wiring the other cars but they were far from working order as many had flat tires and parts of the engines were missing.

Arthur jumped in the drivers seat while Cale sat in the passengers side, Maya had chosen to sit between Ari and Kira in the back. As Arthur started the car, the inside lights shined on them and illuminated their faces until the light turned off and they were covered in darkness again.

With the help of the police scanner, they had found where the criminal who was fleeing with a black sadan was going and they used the back roads to get to the impending meeting place.

While Cale, Ari, and Kira monitored the sidewalks, Maya and Arthur stood on top of a large building as they listened to the sound of sirens growing closer.

Maya who was clad in a black shirt and skinny jeans that were covered halfway by knee high boots stood with one foot on the edge of the building while the other kept her steady.

Arthur wore an equal amount of black as he kneeled beside her, the only light on them was the orange hue of the street lamps below. Maya kept an eye on Cale, Ari, and Kira who were standing in front of a night club acting as if they were patrons taking a break from the party.

"I feel like I'm with a neighborhood watch." Arthur said flatly and Maya grinned at her brothers words. "We pretty much are a neighborhood watch."

"A watch with a lot more skill." He added as he looked down to the street to see the party-goers walking the sidewalks and when Cale met his eyes, he looked away. "I still don't understand why any of them are still here."

"Maybe it's the blood you gave them, they have a knack for danger like us."

"A knack for it will be of no use when the real danger arrives… you said so yourself."

Maya rolled her eyes downwards as she thought of her own words, the one's she had spoken to Eli: *"Tell whoever you're working for that Maya is back."*

She inhaled sharply as the sound of sirens blared in her ears and her head turned to the speeding sedan with the police on it's tail as it turned down the street. The sirens would have hurt their ears four months ago with their lack of control but now it sounded like it would for a human.

Cale, Ari, and Kira turned their heads upwards as Maya brought her other foot to the edge and she nodded to them to let them know that this was her's. She was the only gargoyle the world knew was freely walking the streets and she planned on keeping it that way.

It was funny that in her past life she had done this very thing, only before it was for an entirely different reason. As she waited for the car to be where she needed it to be, the images of her past lives atrocities flashed in her eyes and her heart raced.

She wasn't here for that.

She was no longer Maya, the gargoyle that had killed and ripped families apart.

Samantha Knight would never allow that to happen again and that's who she was: Samantha Knight and Maya Fletcher. With her two mindsets together, she would never go back to the way she was.

She hoped so at least.

The car was halfway down the street now and the red and blue police lights shined on her and Arthur as he stood with her. She waited for the police cars to fall back and when they did, she stepped off the building and allowed her body to drop fifty feet until her wings emerged from her back, ripping holes in her shirt, and she landed gently in front of the car. She stretched her hand out and the large vehicle collided with it.

She only felt the pain in her fingers as the hood scrunched up with a ear deafening screech. As the four police cars stopped, their tires squealed against the pavement and one even hit the back of the sedan, pushing the car and Maya back.

She dropped her throbbing arm and dissolved her wings into her shoulder blades as she backed away. She could hear Arthur from the roof top telling her to get out of there before the police got out but she ignored him. She turned to Cale, Ari, and Kira as they tried their best to fit in with the surprised civilans. Cale was having a hard time and she was sure that he and Arthur shared the same look. She took a look at the shocked criminal as he woke after hitting his head on the steering wheel: He was a middle aged man with black hair and blood was dripping over his eyes from his head injury as he met her black and white eyes.

She dropped her head and allowed her unbraided hair to cover her face, the cool fall air making her breath come out as vapor as the police ran out of their cars and pointed their guns at her. While doing so, they ordered another cop to pull the criminal from his totaled car.

"Put your hands up!" A familiar voice rang out and Maya looked between the gaps in her hair to see Detective Reginald Deluca in a full black suit, a white tie falling over his chest. He had a gun pointed straight at her and she lowered her head.

"What brings you here, detective?" She asked the man that she had seen on the newscast about gargoyles four months prior. She didn't need to look up again to know that he was he shocked.

"I was called here because of the reports of *people* catching criminals for us." His voice shook a bit.

She brought her hands to the air, she knew what they had been doing wouldn't go unnoticed.

But that was the plan.

"Maya!" Arthur growled for her to get her ass out of there.

"You're here to help and so am I." She said as she ignored her brother.

"I saw what you did girl..." The detective's voice shook as the other officers guns clicked against their fingers. "...You're not human."

"You're right," She brought her eyes up again to see that he was joined by a younger version of himself, his son no doubt.

They shared the same dark skintone and faded hair cut, though the detective was balding. The son didn't look as nervous as the other officers but he didn't have the confidence his father had. He was lower than his father in rank but he wore a suit that confirmed his superiority over the other officers.

She backed away and she could hear the clatter of guns being cocked.

She turned and ran down the alley, gunfire ringing behind her as she did so. She climbed up the side of the building she had jumped from and when she made it to the top and Arthur was gone, she knew where he had gone.

She ran to the other side of the roof that led to the back lot they had parked in. The sounds from the people below rang around her as the officers ran down the empty alley only to be met with a dead end.

She stopped at the edge of the building and sure enough the car's headlights were on and she scaled the side of the building to get down. Cale had left the passenger side door open for her and he sat in the back. She jumped in and they sped out of the lot and down the road opposite the police. Maya could still see the red and blue lights flashing in the side view mirror as they left.

"What the fuck was that?!" Arthur growled as Maya rolled her fingers, they had already healed from stopping the car.

"You could have been killed!" Cale's voice shook from both anger and relief.

She looked into the rearview mirror to the three in the back. She already knew how Cale felt about her little show but when she saw the fear on Ari and Kira's faces, she looked away and met her brothers angry gaze instead.

"I was delivering another message." She admitted.

"What?" Kira who was sitting between Cale and Ari leaned on Arthur and Maya's seats. "To your brother's boss?"

Arthur turned his head from the road to his sister as he turned onto one that was free of other cars. She had scared them with her stupid behavior, especially Arthur who feared for her everyday. She had to deliver her message but her heart lurched at the thought of the fear she had caused them.

"I won't do it again." She assured them. "I delivered both of my messages: To the person our brothers were working for and to the humans… that we're not what we used to be."

"It's going to take a hell of a lot more than that for them to trust us." Arthur turned back to the dark road and Kira sat back down.

Maya listened to their calming breaths as they sat in silence for a moment.

"I know." She agreed finally with a hitch in her tone.

Chapter 35

Eli was sitting in a run down tavern drinking scotch that would do nothing to him since alcohol didn't have an effect on gargoyles. The building was old, the white paint on the walls and ceiling were chipping off at places and Eli thought he saw a couple chips fall into someones drink. The table that he resided at was in the far corner but he had a good view of the people sitting at the bar. The bar stools turned with a squeak every time someone moved and it annoyed him.

It had been four months since he had delivered his sisters message to Lucifer but he had done nothing and remained in Ireland that was thousands of miles away from Maya. It infuriated Eli that she still breathed and much more that she was likely living happily with their weak brother.

The occasional demon would come to keep tabs on him but they were small fries compared to Lucifer's high ranked demons. The creatures were made of shadow and if he wasn't paying attention, he would have missed them. Since Eli had met Lucifer twenty years ago, he had learned many things: The demons were as ferocious as they were described to be and many of the well known demons in literature were real.

He found himself wondering since Lucifer was real that there shouldn't be a reason why God couldn't be. The two came hand in hand after all, it was God who banished Satan from Heaven and in doing so, he brought the world to the mercy of a tyrant.

If God was an all powerful being, why did he allow the devil to roam free on earth to mold his plan? He also found himself wondering why he never struck down he and his siblings to stop them from attacking innocent people.

Question after question rose within him: Why were gargoyles real? Did God really make all living creatures? Why did he allow them to sin? Maybe he wasn't the all powerful being that people made him out to be.

It infuriated Eli that there were beings stronger than himself but the only bright side to it all was that Maya had no idea what was coming and it filled him with glee.

Maybe Lucifer would allow him to watch when her life was snuffed out for the second time. The look in her eyes as she died would make the wait worth it, he wasn't able to see it the first time and it was something he had regretted for a long time.

Those dagger like eyes haunted him no matter the color, they could've been the color they had inherited from their mother. They could have been gray which they had changed to. Even more so, the colors that had changed the direction of his life the day she was born: Black and white.

He gripped his glass of scotch and his nails extended, leaving long cuts in the glass. He was tired of waiting, he wanted her to pay, not only for killing his brothers, but for simply existing.

Peyton and Oberon had to have been conceived by now and their reincarnations would be born humans. Eli thought of putting them out of their misery but that was impossible, there was no way to find them now.

He had to hand it to Arthur… he truly was smart.

He had found his sister, made her into a gargoyle again and saved her from Oberon's attack.

He thought of Lucifer's words from four months ago and how he had planned on everything happening the way it had. He had played the brothers as if they were puppets.

The glass shattered against his clawed fingers and as he looked upon the patrons, he found them staring at him. All he had to do was glare at them and they carried on with what they were doing before his outburst. He was about to go back to his thoughts when he saw a shadow at the other side of the room. It was far too dark to be a normal shadow, it was pitch black and the edges were dense lines. Eli knew who it was as soon as the shadow dispersed and from it stepped a man.

Though the being wasn't a man, it was a demon.

Abraxas.

This demon terrified Eli as much as Azazel, perhaps more: His hair was as white as snow and it was cut short to frame his scalp. His skin was paler than milk like the other demons but his eyes lacked the black irises that the others had, instead they were pink.

More terrifying than his looks were his abilities: He could use shadows to transfer himself to wherever he wanted but if he threw anyone else in them, they would be swallowed then spit up as a corpse. Abraxas was a torturous heathen, he got off on the screams of the person suffering from his abilities. He would even result to human tactics and would rip the nails off his victims fingers and toes, plus he would pull the teeth from their mouths.

Anything that related to the pain of another creature sent him into a frenzy and he would have to hold himself back from killing them too early and spoiling his fun.

The creature currently had a dark hood over his head as he walked confidently to the gargoyle. The hood covered his unnatural looks but Eli could see him perfectly. The demons pink eyes were smooth and unblinking, his mouth in a tiny grin as he sat across from the gargoyle.

"Gargoyle." He nodded to him as he reached for a piece of the shattered glass, the smell of booze filling the demons nose. His voice was drawn out and sounded like a hiss.

"Demon." Eli was annoyed that he had allowed his voice to shake.

The demon looked around the bar, his neck moving in an odd way, and his eyeballs shifted in their sockets. "What are you doing in a place like this?" He asked as he brought his attention back to Eli, his grin turning into a full on smile.

"I have to pass time while I wait for your boss." Eli answered with his eyes on the shard of glass between the demons long fingers.

"You pass time by spending it with the beings you hate?"

Eli's eyes rolled up as he heard Abraxas' words. All of the demons were the same, they would take any chance they could to mess with their prey. But Eli wasn't their prey, he was with them by Lucifers will. He knew he was being used but it would be worth it in the end when he finally saw the end of his sister.

"You no longer need to pass time," Abraxas got up from his chair, the legs sliding against the wooden floor. "Our master has called for you."

Eli shot up and his chair squeaked like Abraxas' had and it hit the wall behind him.

This was it.

"Let's go." The demon turned to go but not before stopping to make Eli go ahead of him.

Eli made his way out the front door and after a moment, he realized the demon wasn't following him. He turned on his heel as the once lit tavern filled with shadow and the twenty people inside were engulfed in it. The humans screamed and gasped with pain as Eli ran backwards away from the shadow. As he turned his head down the narrow street, he realized that bodies lined the buildings, their eyes lacking their pupils and their pale faces were contorted into screams.

Eli's shock filled face turned back to the tavern as Abraxas stepped out of the dense shadow where the door should have been. His hood was down now, his face exposed. The killing had added some color to his cheeks and Eli was sure it was from the thrill.

"Let's go." The demon said again and Eli followed him as he walked down the street lined with corpses.

* * *

Lucifer still resided in his hillside cave and the narrow hall that led to him smelt of rotting flesh and Eli had to hold his breath. He hated the smell of corpses, especially the excretion as their organs shut down. Eli could even smell the fear that the demons victims had felt. Even with the smell, Lucifer must have had the demons clean the mess since there were no bodies as Eli walked inside.

Eli thought of the darkness that came with death, did they really die just to be met with eternal darkness? When gargoyle's reincarnated, did they see an afterlife before they moved to their next life? His mind wandered to the humans he had killed and the patrons at the bar whose lives were just snuffed out by Abraxas' shadow.

He even thought of sister, who had faced death already. He wondered if she had seen something, her memories were back after all. With any luck, she would be back to whatever she had seen if there had been anything at all.

He brought his head up and was met with four of Lucifers strongest demons. They were standing in front of him with grins on their pale faces.

Azazel stood the tallest and he looked as proud as can be. "Hello, Gargoyle!" He sang.

Cain stood with his dark eyes as downcast as ever, his mouth shaped into a frown as he paid no mind to the newcomer.

Aamon stood in his old human form, wrapped in his robe.

Astaroth was a female demon that Eli had met before, her long red hair fell to the middle of her back and her eyes were as dark as the other demons but her pupil had a red tint that never went away. Unlike the other demons who wore a good amount of black and showed almost none of their pale skin, she wore a black corset with a good amount of cleavage showing.

Eli still wondered what her power was.

"It's been awhile… *Eli.*" Her voice was smooth as she spoke, almost seductive. "But as I've been told, you've been busy…" She smiled and licked her dagger-like canines. "As have I."

She was the only demon who didn't call him Gargoyle.

Eli didn't bother to say anything as Abraxas approached the other demons with his shadow swirling at his feet.

"What am I here for?" Eli asked finally as Astaroth gleamed at Abraxas before the demon turned to face Eli like the others.

Eli had never seen the demons in one place at the same time and even now not all of them were present. Only Lucifers elite five were present which was a feat in itself.

Eli's eyes wandered from the demons to where Satan had sat four months ago but the being was no where to be seen.

"Do not worry gargoyle, he will be here soon." Azazel's smirk widened as he stepped closer to the gargoyle. "You're going to love it."

As if on cue Lucifer came walking in from the narrow hall and Eli took in the devils favorite form: Black wavy hair, pale skin, and black eyes that stared forward as if into nothing. His lips were shaped into a smile before he had even spotted Eli standing in front of him. He made his way to the mound of rock where he had sat four months ago. Only this time, he didn't sit, he stood in front of it.

"It's been awhile, my monstrous friend." His silky voice echoed though the opening. "But I bring good news," He brought a hand through his dark hair as his face lit up with excitement. "The war is about to begin."

Eli's heart jolted at the declaration, the last time he had been here Lucifer had threatened him but now the being looked on with glee as he took in the gargoyle.

"Why after so long?" Eli didn't mean to question him but the words slipped out.

Unlike last time, Lucifer didn't get angry from the question, the opposite happened instead.

His smile widened.

"Because there wasn't enough calamity at that time."

Calamity?

The look on Eli's face must have indicated that he needed an explanation because Lucifer started to explain: "For my plan to work, the world must be plunged into darkness. Throughout the ages, I have been the cause of war, famine, and sin and in doing so my will has spread across the world." He cocked his head to his demons. "These five have been very busy spreading my will across the world. The oil crises, the fight between religions, nuclear weapons, the lower end wars, and even the world wars are the work of my demons and myself. Even now my other demons are going by my will. My very existence brings calamity to this world and finally the amount needed for everything to go my way is almost at hand."

He closed his dark eyes and inhaled deeply, he looked at ease, excited even. "The greatest war of them all is fast approaching and I'm so very excited for the outcome…" He chuckled. "Even your sister is rearing to go."

As the words escaped his smiling lips, he tossed a phone that he had grabbed from his dark pockets to Eli who caught it in his right hand. The touch screen phone had a picture of a girl standing in a busy street, her brown wavy hair hiding her face while the rest was braided against her scalp. Her laced up boots reached her knees as they blended in with her dark pants and her equally dark shirt. Her hands were in the air as police officers pointed their guns at her and in front of her was the smashed front of a large car.

There was no doubt this girl was his sister, she had regained her signature look.

Only she was missing one thing: Their mothers coat.

"She want's my attention." Lucifer's voice drifted as he chuckled on.

Eli brought his head up from the phone and met Lucifers gaze. He could feel the excitement radiating off the demons behind him and the hair on the back of his neck stood up. He had always asked Lucifer what his fascination with his sister was but he had never gotten a straight answer. It could have been because she was the strongest gargoyle but Eli knew better. Lucifer acted as if he knew his sister. When he talked about her, Eli noticed how he would hold a tone that one would use if they were talking about an old friend.

"What's your fascination with my sister?" Eli asked again with the possibility that he'd get the run around again.

Lucifer brought his gaze to the empty spot beside Eli as if he was looking at someone, and when he brought his eyes back to him, he looked like he had seen a happy memory.

"Your sister and I go back to a time when she was known as *Anna*."

The named rolled off of his tongue and Eli found himself taking a step back. "Anna?" He breathed, this couldn't be what he thought it was. "There's no way…"

"There's many ways," Lucifer stepped close to accommodate with the step Eli had taken back. "Look into that small brain of yours…look past the delusion that your sister was lucky to have gotten her power." He took another step. "Your sister had a life before she was Maya, a life that I snuffed out."

Eli shook as Lucifer leaned into him, his warm breath hitting his ear.

"I haven't told you what my plans are yet… people are taught that there is a heaven and a hell but they are misinformed."

For the first time since he had stepped into the cave, his smiled disappeared and it was replaced with a snarl. "When God banished me from heaven and casted me to this planet, he didn't expect for me to dwell on it's resources. To use his human pawns as my own, to make this world mine." He stepped away from the gargoyle as his smile returned. "There is no hell under our feet," He licked the bottom set of his pointed teeth. "*This* is hell."

He wandered between his demons and they smiled as he walked by aside from Cain who had simply looked up to meet his masters gaze.

"Fighting is hell, losing is hell, breathing is hell, and loving is hell. Every living creatures existence is hell and that's what this world is going to be: *Hell*."

He brought his feet to the front of Eli again. "This world will be all that I've envisioned and your sister will help me." He shrugged. "She just doesn't know it yet."

He turned to his demons again as Eli's face turned pale with shock. "The final faze of our plan can be started." He nodded towards his demons. "Every holy building and monument around the world will be destroyed and I leave it to you." He brought his hand to Astaroth and Aamon. "You will direct the other demons around the world to do so while you three-" He brought his gaze to Azazel, Abraxas, and Cain. "Will come with me and the gargoyle."

Eli's head shot up as he heard the mention of him and Lucifer smiled at his shock. "Don't you want to see your sister again?"

Eli nodded and for the first time, he smiled along with the demons as they looked as rearing to go as their master.

"I hope I'll get the chance to meet her like my predecessor had." Astaroth's girlish voice rang out as she stepped to Eli and placed a hand on his shoulder and he flinched at the touch.

"You will." Lucifer assured her as he stepped away from the group and when he spoke again, it was to neither his demons nor to Eli but to someone who wasn't there.

"I can't wait to see you again, *my sweet Anna.*"

Chapter 36

They were sitting in Kira's cabin with beer bottles in their hands. It had been several days since Maya had made her display of courage to get her message across and all seemed calm.

Kira and Ari had gone out on the last food run with Arthur's money but they had not only brought back food, but also a twenty pack of beer. Arthur didn't get annoyed with their lack of responsibility with his money, he owed it to them and so much more.

"I don't give a fuck if I'm under twenty one, I'm a gargoyle and I'm drinking the damn beer." Emily had exclaimed after Kira had joked with her about being too young.

It made Maya think of how her birthday was coming up, the day she was born as Sam was only three days off from when she born as Maya. It was strange how it worked that way but even stranger was the thought that she had made it longer in this life than she had in her last.

It made her think about how much time she could have left in this one.

"Hmph." Ari shook her head, disappointed. "No matter how much we drink, we can't seem to get drunk."

"And to think I was a lightweight." Kira tossed her bottle to their growing collection of empties.

Maya knew gargoyles couldn't get drunk, she had tried it in her past life to no avail so she simply drank and tasted the bitterness of the brew.

Arthur had only downed one bottle and the empty glass was still in his hand. He had a funny look on his face that Maya knew was a sure sign that he felt bad for their inability to get drunk. Though at the same time, he thought it was funny that they tried so hard to do so. Like

Maya, he didn't want to ruin it for them so he kept to himself and let them believe that their tolerence had heightened.

Cale had his bottle rested on his knee as he smiled at Emily's first reaction to the drink and Maya found herself smiling at him and the rest one by one.

Even with everything going on and everything yet to come, she'd be lying if she said that she didn't enjoy the times they had during their travels. They had all bonded in ways many couldn't. Being kidnapped, changed into gargoyles, and having to learn how to use their newfound abilities because of the threat of Maya's brothers had done the trick.

They had witnessed her getting her memories back and they saw her at her lowest as she took in those memories. They saw her kill her own brothers and send one away to tell a new enemy about her awakening.

"I think we should go out." Kira woke her from her thoughts.

"Go out?" Cale rose a brow. "You guys were already out."

"I don't mean it that way." Kira's eyes met Maya's as she looked up. "I mean we should go to a bar or something."

She was met with silence and the air around her would have made her feel stupid if she cared.

Ari looked from her to the rest, "I agree with her."

Arthur shook his head, "It's too dangerous." His smile had disappeared and it was replaced with a grimace as he looked between the two girls and his sister.

"Of course it is, especially after what your sister did the other day." Ari admitted. "But I don't see it being that big of deal since no one knows what we look like. They know what Sam looked like four months ago but she's changed so I don't think they'll recognize her."

"It's not happening and I don't want to catch you going out either. You're not going to risk your lives just because you want to party." Arthur shot up and made his way out of the cabin but before he stepped from the door, Kira made him freeze. "You're the one who put us here, don't act like you care about us now."

He stood back for a moment then with a twitch of his head, he walked himself the rest of the way out.

"I'm sorry." Kira brought her attention back to Maya who brought a hand to the air to assure her it was ok. She and the others had every right to be mad at Arthur. She inhaled as she uncrossed her legs and leaned forward. She placed her empty bottle onto the small lightstand to her right and she could feel all their eyes on her.

"It doesn't bother me that you guys still hate him, what else can I expect? I would still hate him too if I didn't get my memories back but I did and he's my brother." She made sure to meet each of their eyes. "I'm not one to judge, I killed innocent people so I'm far from innocent myself."

"That was your past life." Cale assured her. "You're not who you used to be."

Maya turned so she was facing him, "I'm my past life and I'm also Sam." She smiled sadly. "We are one in the same."

Cale shook his head, "I don't believe that."

"I do."

The others watched as the two looked at each other, it was like they were the only ones in the room.

"What do you think?" Kira asked after clearing her throat.

Maya knew Kira was trying to get her away from her thoughts before her self loathing started again.

"Arthur's right, It's too dangerous." She said as she moved her gaze from Cale.

"If I remember correctly, you put yourself in danger just the other night." Kira smirked and Maya's mouth went into a straight line. "And you did when you had your brother run to the guy he's working for."

"That's not the same thing." Emily defended but it didn't work and instead of Kira, Ari spoke now: "You told me that in your past life that you always wanted to live amongst the humans. To be friends with them…To experience what they did and now's your chance."

More silence.

"I think you've forgotten that I've lived as a human for the past twenty years." Maya shook her head as she leaned into the sofa again.

"Yes but you didn't have your memories back yet, you said so yourself that you and Maya are one in the same… you even want people to call you Maya because of the exposure." Ari had her hook line and sinker and Maya found herself getting annoyed with how well she could read her.

"Which that's dangerous too." Kira said slyly about her name choice.

"….Theres no way Arthur would let me go after the stunt I pulled the other day… I'd be stupid if I went anyway."

"Mhm that's the point." Kira nodded.

Maya rose a brow.

"It's the fact that it's stupid that they won't expect you to do it. Come on! how many brown haired girls go to a bar?"

A lot.

"How many of them have gray eyes?" Maya clapped her hands together.

"They didn't see your eyes."

"You can wear my clothes for good measure." Ari shot in and Maya's eyes drifted to the lavender pants and the light blue shirt Ari was wearing. It was definitely a big change from Maya's usual black attire but even she had some color, just the other day she was wearing purple herself.

"What do you guys think?" Maya asked the others who had only watched as the girls tried to convince her.

She was met with looks that could only mean that they didn't know what to say.

"...I think it's too dangerous." Emily's voice drifted and Maya nodded.

It certainly was.

"...But I think we can handle a night out." Emily continued and Maya almost fell from shock. She looked around to see Cale and Dylan looking the same while Trevor, Ari, and Kira all had pleased expressions. Maya couldn't believe Trevor was going along with this, let alone Emily.

"Four versus three." Kira smirked as she faced Maya.

"Four versus four," Cale corrected her. "Arthur is against this too."

Kira's eyes narrowed and she crossed her arms but when Dylan spoke, she smiled.

"I'm willing to go." He seemed nervous.

"See!" Ari exclaimed as she brought her hand forward. "They want to go, you know it's not that bad when a stick in the mud like Emily wants to go."

"Hey..." Emily's voice drifted.

"But-" Maya started but Cale interrupted her. "I'm going if Emily goes and Arthur will go if you go. He's knows he won't be able to stop you so he'll tag along."

Maya inhaled sharply as defeat filled her. "...Fine."

"Sweet!" Kira shot up. "We'll go tonight."

Maya's face felt warm as she got up and left the cabin without another word.

"I'll come to get you so you can try my clothes!" Ari called from behind her as she stepped into the sunlight and shut the screen door behind her.

Maya sat in the living room in Ari's cabin while she rummaged through the drawers in her bedroom to find an outfit for her to wear. Maya thought of Arthur's reaction when she told him they were going and after promising him more than a dozen times that she wasn't going to pull anything, he finally agreed. Even as Sam she had never gone to a bar, but Ari was right, she did want to experience this.

"You're taking too long and it's kind of worrying me." She laughed as she turned to face Ari's room. She could see her back and hair as she pulled one article of clothing out of the drawer after another.

"I'm not going to make you look bad." She called from the room.

"That's not what I'm worried about." Maya admitted, she was far more worried about how much skin she was going to try to have her show.

"You're fine." She said as she slammed one the drawers shut and she stepped out of her room and handed Maya her clothes for the night: A black long sleeved shirt with the fabric twisted into vines along the collar that would reach to the base of her neck. The pants were the same lavender that Ari had on earlier.

Maya had to admit, she was pleasantly surprised. "I believe you now." She laughed as Ari handed her the clothes.

"Yeah yeah." Ari rolled her eyes and jumped as there was a knock on the door. "Who is it?" She sang and Cale's voice called from the other side.

"Oh yeah… the shirt I stitched up for him." Ari turned to the little back porch that only her cabin had. "Can you let him in?" She called back as she jogged out of the room.

Maya got up, the old couch creaking, and when she opened the door, she motioned for him to come in. "Getting the shirt that Trevor slashed the other day?" She asked as she stepped out of the way.

"Yeah," He stepped into the cabin and stopped at the couch where he turned to face her. "It's better to use our personal tailor than to keep buying shirts."

"That certainly does make sense." She agreed as Ari returned with a freshly sewn shirt. She was certainly talented not in just cutting hair, but in sewing and designing clothes. She handed the dark green shirt to Cale and he looked to where the slashes were, they were barely noticeable now.

"Thank you." He said as another knock on the front door rang out but instead of waiting to be let in like Cale had, Kira barged in after only knocking once.

"Sup?" She nodded towards Maya and Cale then rounded on Ari. "Can you come back to my cabin quick?"

"Why?" Ari asked in a mock tone.

"The fuck you asking me *why* for? let's go!" She grabbed her friends hand and pulled her from the cabin leaving Cale and Maya alone.

"I wonder what that was about?" Cale asked with a brow rose as he pulled his dirty shirt over his head to put on the fixed one.

Maya didn't worry about Kira's reason to barge in as her eyes found Cale's injured shoulder. Even with his heightened healing, it was the only part of him that didn't heal correctly.

"Sam…" his voice drifted as he caught her looking. "Don't worry about it."

"I can't help it." Her jaw clenched. "You're just another on the long list of people I've hurt."

His eyes softened as he dropped his old shirt on the couch. "You're a different person now."

"So that's your reason for sticking with me?"

He shook his head, "You've changed, people learn, they adapt, they become better. You've had two lives and you still have time to make it right."

"That's what everyone tells me but if you knew the things I've done, you'd know that I'll never be able to make it right. What you saw with my brothers was just the tip of the iceberg, they were evil but the people I killed weren't." She dropped her gaze and crossed her arms as a shiver went down her spine.

"I know what you did, I know it was you but you're not who you used to be." Cale flinched as he saw her face fall further. He stepped closer to comfort her but Ari ran through the still opened door and interrupted.

Her eyes flashed between the two: Cale who was shirtless and Maya who was red from her thoughts.

"What did I miss?" She asked while out of breath.

They stepped down the sidewalk that led to the bar while their eyes planted on the place where Maya had stopped the burglar just nights before. There were still pieces of the front of the car on the road and a few cops stood around the area as if she'd come back.

Maya wondered where Deluca and his son were now, were they looking for her? What were they planning? She thought of the gargoyles that they had in custody, how they were experimenting on them and could've found a way to injure them to the point of death… like they had with her parents.

She thought of the two sets of parents that she had, the two that were dead and the two that were alive in her current life. Did they worry about her? Did they still love her?

She had thought about it before but now wasn't the time, she agreed to go out and have a good time and that's what she was going to do.

With security checking at the front and the police still wandering around, they chose to turn into the alley Maya had made her escape into and snuck to the side door. It was locked and the handle wouldn't budge for a human but they weren't human and as Kira twisted it, the handle broke from the door. After she placed it back in the hole to make it look like it hadn't been broken.

"It seems like you've had some prior experience…" Trevor who had been getting cold feet as soon as they got to town joked.

"I do… only I didn't have inhuman strength before." Kira said as she opened the door for them.

They all took a glance at each other and Maya held Arthur's gaze a bit longer than the others. They were all dressed like they always were aside from Maya who had ditched her black jeans. It seemed like they would blend in with the other partygoers but she still had a bad feeling that she'd be recognized. But it was like Kira had said, there were many girls that had brown hair. She had ditched the braids for the night to blend in more, the viking hairstyle would make her too noticeable.

Arthur gave her a look and it reminded her of when he had acted emotionless towards her when she didn't have her memories. She knew now that the look meant that he was nervous or deep in thought.

As the door opened, the sound of the blasting music inside became clear. They were lucky that they had learned to control their hearing or their eardrums would have been in a world of hurt as they stepped inside. The bar was currently filled with a rap song with a heavy beat and it sounded like a horror movie in song form. The bass shook the ground as they walked. The side door led to the bathrooms that laid in a dimly lit hall and with a sharp turn, they saw multicolored lights flashing. The bass grew louder as they met the dance floor and on it was at least fifty people and it strangely made them feel better since they'd fit in with the crowd.

The partygoers bounced and danced to the beat, some of the dance moves were far from appropriate but none of the group paid any mind to it as they had all seen it before.

Maybe some of them had done the same moves.

Maya's eyes headed to Kira and as she did so, she realized that the others were looking at her as well.

"What?" Kira rose a brow when she noticed them looking at her and Ari erupted into laughter as she grabbed her hand.

"Let's go!" She pulled her to the dance floor where they started thumping to the music.

Maya looked between her brother and the others then back to Ari and Kira dancing with the other partygoers. As just Sam she would have never jumped on the dance floor but as both Sam and Maya, she didn't think of being embarrassed by her lack of dance skills so she turned and like Ari, she grabbed ahold of Emily's hand who looked visibly nervous and pulled her as the others watched. The music changed to a remix of an old popular song as they stopped beside Ari and Kira who looked gleeful as they danced. Maya started moving and skipped to Emily and took her arms as if they were dancing to a messy salsa song.

Before long, a large smile appeared on Emily's lips and she laughed at how bad they were dancing.

They deserved this, they had no idea how much longer they had until everything fell apart. The music, the crowd, even the strange smells of the people around them were welcome. It made them feel human for the first time since they had been changed.

They didn't know how much longer they'd be together like this.

Before long they were joined by Trevor who linked arms with them and danced along with them. The people dancing around them ignored them since they looked the same as everyone else aside from Ari who jumped on Maya's back and hooted. Maya who was particularly strong almost fell, not from Ari's weight, but from laughter.

Ari and Kira were right, she needed to experience this.

She chanced a glance to where she had left Arthur, Cale, and Dylan to find that they were leaning against a wall as people danced in front of them. Arthur had a straight face as he watched them enjoy themselves while Cale and Dylan said something to each other then laughed.

Maya smiled at them, especially at Arthur, she didn't want to force him to join her and the others. She knew he wasn't the type to go out to a place like this, she was just thankful he was there in the first place. She turned back to the others as Dylan pushed himself off the wall and was met with a drunk girl with long blonde hair and green eyes, her outfit was far from classy but she didn't care as she pulled him to the dance floor near Maya and the others.

Arthur and Cale continued to watch them from the wall and Arthur glanced at Cale who he was surprised still stood with him.

"You're not going to dance?" Arthur asked him over the music and the younger man shook his head. "I'm not much of a dancer."

"Neither am I." Arthur admitted as he crossed his arms. "But it seems like they're having fun."

Cale kept his eyes forward and watched as Maya and Emily continued to dance together. He could hear their laughter over the music. He smiled at their happiness, both girls had been through so much and he hadn't seen Emily smile like that since before they were taken.

"You've lost the most since this began…" Arthurs eyes bored into him and caught him off guard. "But you choose to stay with us, why?"

His eyes met Arthur's then rolled back to the sight in front of him: Maya was twisting Emily in a circle then the two girls joined hands and practically fell when they stepped on each others feet.

What *was* keeping him there?

Of course he wanted to help protect the world from the impending threat but he didn't need to do that by staying with Maya and Arthur.

Or did he?

He kept his eyes on Maya as her smile widened and she laughed at her own clumsiness. Even though there were many differences in how she acted and looked compared to before, she was still the girl that gave them courage when they needed it most. She was still the girl they had all bonded with. She also just so happened to be the girl who had a past life who had committed many wrongs, who had died to make up for it. Who was born again only to have dreams of her past life until she was caught by her past lives brother and turned into a gargoyle again. She had trained to defeat the man who had ruined her life, she fought to save Carma, she made the difficult choice to join Arthur after she learned of her other brothers who wanted her dead. It all led to her getting her memories back and killing her twin brothers while letting her oldest brother go. She had made so many difficult decisions and they all knew that she would have to make more before long.

They all had too.

He was so deep in thought that he didn't notice Kira making her way to them.

"Would you two stop being so serious and dance like everyone else?" She poked both of the men on their foreheads and she had to go to her toes to do so.

Arthur gently smacked her hand away, "I'm good."

Kira didn't seem to mind that Arthur had rejected her, instead she turned to Cale and grabbed his hand. "Come on," she said while pulling him away from the wall. "Your girl is out there."

"Who's that supposed to be?" He yelled awkwardly over the music as the small girl pulled him to Maya and Emily as the girls danced and they turned to give Cale bright smiles as he finally joined them.

Arthur watched as Maya said something to Cale and the two laughed.

His eyes dropped, he had been against going to the bar but after seeing them like this, he knew it was for the best. None of them knew what was going to happen next, they deserved this moment of happiness while they still had it in their grasp.

A chill went up his spine and his head shot up, his eyes meeting Maya's who he knew had felt the same thing.

The other gargoyles and the partygoers didn't seem to notice it so the two played it off as a coincidence but they knew it wasn't.

A smell began to fill the air, it wasn't dirty, maybe it was sweet, warm even. It filled their nostrils until they couldn't take anymore but as fast as the smell came, it was gone.

Chapter 37

Maya woke with a start the next morning and her heart raced at the sound of the police scanner she had left on from the night before.

She rubbed her eyes as she turned it off and she pulled herself up from the bed. Her hands shook as she pulled her hair out of her face.

The chill that ran down both Arthur's and her spines still laid waste to her mind while the smell still lingered in her nose. She couldn't lay a hand on what the smell was, but it felt familiar to her. Though in memory, she felt like she had never picked up on the scent before.

She flipped on the light switch and for the millionth time, she thought about how thankful she was that Dylan had found out how to turn the breaker on to get the power to work. Though she hoped whoever owned the campground didn't notice a change in their power bill.

The sunshine coming from the windows in the small living room was far from enough for her to get a good look in the mirror as she settled in front of the it. With a quick brush through her brown waves, she weaved four large braids to the right side of her scalp as her loose hair fell to the left. Her gray eyes almost looked silver but it could have been a trick of the light.

They shot downwards to her now still hands, her human nails had grown long enough to cover the tops of her pale fingers. She inhaled sharply as she backed away from the mirror and pulled out her clothes for the day: A black top and skinny jeans. She turned to the small chair at the side of the room and gazed at the shirt that Ari had let her borrow. She had enjoyed wearing it and she found herself loving the vine patterned fabric around the collar. She almost didn't want to return it. She pulled on her clothes and took the police scanner. It had been quiet the past few days and even during their outing the night before.

As she stepped out of the room, she turned the scanner on low volume. She'd be able to hear it if something of significance was announced even at the lowest setting.

Her cabin was the exact same as the others only she chose the one closest to the tree line. She stepped her way to the front door that was placed to the right of the bedroom. She pulled on her knee high boots and laced them up. She found the boots to be easier to fight in, at least for her, she was sure the others would disagree.

She was about to open the door to leave when she heard someone approaching from the other side. Her eyes shot downwards as she listened to the way they stepped and how they breathed. Though it was more difficult than usual with the music still pounding in her ears from night before, she was able to make out that it was Arthur.

She opened the door before he had the chance to knock and like his sister, he had listened and knew she was already at the door. They met each others eyes as she moved the door out of the way and they knew they were thinking the same thing: Something was coming.

They weren't sure how they knew and although they felt that going on a feeling and a smell was far confirmation, they trusted their guts.

This had to be it.

"Do you think it's the man our brothers were with?" Arthur asked then clenched his jaw.

"I'm not sure." She answered as she stepped outside and closed the door.

They hadn't seen any events on a large scale since they only had a police scanner for their current area. Maya got the feeling that they were missing something by not having access to any kind of world news.

She stepped down the one stair that led out of her cabin and was met with the cool fall air. It didn't get cold there as it did in New York but Washington still managed to get a good chill.

"I'm not even sure who or *what* our brother works for." She said and as she stopped in front of him, his eyes shifted to the ground as he shook his head. "...Whatever it is, I'm sure you're strong enough to take it on."

She could have felt pride at her brothers words but she couldn't help but feel that they were wrong. She thought he was smarter than that. She was the strongest gargoyle, she should be able to handle anything, but they didn't know what their enemies were. Maybe he was wishful thinking.

He saw the look on her face as he brought his eyes up again and they softened. "We can handle this together."

The feeling of dread was telling them otherwise but they stopped talking about the matter as Trevor popped out from Emily's cabin and he stopped as he spotted them and called for them to join everyone for breakfast.

"You still have that thing on?" Dylan asked about the police scanner after they were done eating their eggs.

Maya had the scanner on the entire time they ate and even though it was on low volume, it was still easy to hear due to their heightened hearing.

"I want to be prepared." She said simply as she flipped the volume lower, the static was getting to be too much as they waited for an announcement.

"Prepared for what?" Emily pondered as she poked at the scanner and the static paused for a second. It made Maya think of her old ability, if she had touched the scanner before, it would have malfunctioned, but as she touched any kind of technology now, it remained unfazed. The ability she once had was gone and she was thankful.

"....Prepared for what's coming." She answered finally.

The room went silent and Arthur's eyes that were already on her narrowed.

"Do you think *they're* coming?" Cale leaned forward where he sat on the couch and he placed his elbows on his knees.

"I still don't know who *they* are and I don't know... I just feel like something's coming."

They all glanced at each other, she had said the same thing four months ago and here they were... still waiting.

"I feel it too and I didn't before." Arthur defended. "Whoever's coming will be here soon and it's not going to be another four months."

A collective chill went up the half gargoyles spines, they could feel the apprehension in the full blooded gargoyles and the unease spread to them.

"That's why you've been listening to that thing since we got back last night?" Cale shot upwards as the feeling made him want to get moving.

"...Yes." Maya admitted.

"Do you think they'll show up on the scanner?" Emily who was sitting beside Maya leaned closer to the scanner and tapped it again.

"Definitely." Maya brought her eyes from the scanner and looked around the room at her now visibly nervous comrades. "I know whoever's coming is going to call me to meet them."

"Will you go?" Dylan's voice was higher than usual.

"Yes." She replied with no hesitation and she could feel Arthur's leg stiffen under the table.

Through the silence, her ears perked up and her hand shot unconsciously forward to turn up the dial on the scanner:

"Dispatch, we have a report of a suspicious man near Lafayette square. The suspect has a dark hood covering his face and hands in his pockets. The callers have said that he has been harassing people on the streets and may have robbed three of them."

The scanner went back to it's beeping and fuzz until a males voice came across:

"Responding."

The groups eyes met again.

"Do you think...?" Arthur tapped his nervous fingers on the table.

Maya's eyes found his and her brows furrowed, it very well could be but it could also be a false alarm. She felt like the being they were waiting for would have a dramatic entrance and this could very well be a bout of crime that Washington normally had.

Maya started to think about it and as she did, she realized that her enemy would try to fool her. They didn't need a dramatic introduction to get her attention, they knew she'd come nonetheless.

Her heart lurched, she had to go just in case and as they saw her jerky movement, the others flew upwards.

"You're not going." Maya told them as she stepped to the front door and Arthur followed.

"We're all going." Ari jogged past Arthur and grabbed Maya's shoulder, pulling her back. "We're going." She said again, her voice stern.

Maya's jaw shook as she took in their nervous but determined faces. "You know the condition if I let you go.

"We know the deal." Trevor shook his head at her worry.

The condition was the same as it always had been: To run if things got bad.

"You're strong," Dylan smiled. "If it's the people we've been waiting for, I'm sure you have more than enough strength to stop them."

Maya couldn't think the way they did, she had to take into consideration that this being was strong enough to hold all three of her brothers back. She had dealt with the twins with ease and could have with Eli but she could feel it in her soul that what they were about to happen upon was going to be the hardest thing she had ever faced.

"…Yeah." She said with uncertainty as she turned and stepped out the door.

Lafayette square was just that: A square. It was overcrowded and stuffy as tourists took pictures of the many monuments that Washington had. Maya didn't bother covering her face in fear that the police would confuse her with the man clad in black. It had taken awhile for them to get there and they felt like it was a false alarm since they had yet to see the assailant. Maybe the police had already caught the man but they noticed the officers still walking around as they talked on their radios so the gargoyles listened in.

"Suspect has yet to be found."

Maya found herself wondering if Detective Deluca would show up. She was sure he would, especially now that he knew she would come out if there was crime.

Maybe this was a set up by the humans.

Her eyes wandered nervously but no one including the officers paid no mind to the gargoyle's. They luckily fit in with the tourists and students on their school trips. Cale who was the tallest stepped in front of Maya as the officers got closer and as they walked by, he stepped away.

"Thanks." She said as she stepped beside him and he nodded.

"It might just be a creepy guy." Kira blew her bangs out of her face as she crossed her arms with a huff. They had spent 30 minutes of searching and the heat was beginning to get to them and dulled their senses.

"...Yeah." Maya agreed and she could feel relief fill her bones.

Maybe she and Arthur were overreacting, their senses could had gone haywire from the loud music the night before. The smell could have been a type of perfume and the chill from the setting.

She truly believed it was an overreaction until the smell filled her nose again and she turned back and forth to look for the source. She turned on her heel to find Arthur who had been standing behind her, a stone expression on his face as he stared straight ahead.

She gave him a confused look as she turned away and found what he was looking at: The hooded man was walking away from them towards a bunch of buildings.

The others noticed him as well as they followed her gaze and before they could say anything, Maya was running after the man and Arthur followed close behind. Maya weaved through the masses of people and while doing so, she tried her best not to lose sight of the man. As she pushed herself through the biggest group, and after being called various names for her rude behavior, she noticed the man turning slightly to face her. The smell grew stronger the closer she got and she held her breath as she began to taste it her mouth.

She kept her eyes on the building that he had turned into as she continued to run. It had red shingles while the one beside it had blue. It was easy to tell where he had gone and she would have thought he was stupid if she didn't know he had lurred her there.

She stopped abruptly before she turned down the alley between the buildings that the man had gone into and she turned to see the others still dealing with the crowds.

Good, she had to do this alone.

The alley was cool and dark compared to the streets due to a canopy covering the top. Her feet echoed as she stepped further, it was longer than she had anticipated and she had yet to see the hooded man. She knew he was there, she knew even with her dark clothes that he could see her as she approached him.

When she heard a noise in front of her, she reached her right arm out and grabbed the man by his hood.

She could see him now but still couldn't make out his face: He was tall so she had to stand tall to grab him. She pulled him down to his knees and she kneeled in front of him.

"Who are you?" As she questioned him, she accidentally breathed in through her nose and the smell made her gasp.

He could see the discomfort on her face and the being cocked his head, as he did so, a ray of light shined where his mouth was: She could see that he was smiling now, his teeth were sharper than a knives point. Maya's eyes shot up from his mouth to his eyes and what she saw shook her: The middle of his eyes were glowing crimson.

As she jumped, he moved his arm, his sharp nails rushing to her gut.

To get away, Maya entended her wings and flew backwards as she pushed off the ground.

She slid to a stop on her right knee while her left boot remained planted on the ground, the sunlight shined on her as she returned to the front of the building.

Blood dropped from her torso as she felt a twinge of pain and she chanced a glance away from the alley to look at her wounds. There were three deep scratches across her rip cage and they strayed down her stomach. She felt uneasy at the thought that if she had been a fraction slower, her guts would have been on the blacktop.

The sound of people gasping filled the air and she tuned to where she came from: The civilians she had passed moments before were looking at her like she was a monster as they took in her gray wings which had ripped through her shirt. Arthur and the rest had paused for a moment as they took in her shocked expression but they began running again, knowing that something had forced her to use her wings in public. As they got closer, they saw the blood running down her front from her wounds.

Her eyes flashed as she brought them back to the alley and she rushed to her feet before she was met with the creature again. He had appeared in front of her as if he had teleported and he had ditched his hood. Maya could take in her enemy now: He had long white hair and skin paler than paper. His lips were red as if he had a delicious drink of blood before he had lurred her in. His smile was filled with over fifty dagger-like teeth and his eyes were black aside from his irises that shined like a flame.

She tried dodging his hit but he swept his hand by her as his smile widened and with barely a touch, she was thrown into the clearing past her comrades and in front of the crowd.

She could hear the police officers yelling between the screams and gasps of the people around her as they ran the opposite way. With her teeth bared, she looked between her comrades who had split down the middle to get out of her way as she was thrown.

The creature stood with a wide grin and he licked his teeth as he watched her. Her comrades looked at her with both shock and fear before they turned to the creature who had gotten the upper hand on her. Arthur kept his eyes on her as his jaw clenched and his skin grew almost as pale as the white haired creatures.

This was it.

Maya jumped to her feet as ten police officers pointed their guns at her.

"Stay where you are!" One of them yelled but she paid no mind to them, she only had eyes for the white haired man in front of her. He had caught her off guard, whatever he was he certainly was strong and she would have to fight seriously.

Though she had to hold back due to her *condition.*

She began to run to the assailant as she used her wings to cover herself from the bullets. They stung as they ripped through her extra limbs but the rest of her was unfazed. She ran with blood pouring from both her front and wings and before she made it to the being, he was in front of her again and this time she was ready.

A growl escaped her throat as the two began their hand to hand combat. The being moved with ease and used every move Maya could imagine, moves that she had seen in old movies and in army boot camp videos. He knew it all and the smile on his face only proved it as the thrill he felt from the fight filled his veins.

He laid a hit against the side of her neck and though the bone cracked, she shot forward again and continued their fight.

The being's high pitched cackle filled the air, the sound and smell coming from him sent Maya's nerves on edge but she held true as she threw herself backwards and snapped her bone back into place with a quick hit of her hand.

The others began to help starting with Arthur and Cale but as she watched, Maya saw a shadow moving at their feet and from it a man almost identical to the one she was fighting emerged. This being had short white hair and his skin was as pale as his allies.

"No butting in." The creature cocked his head at Arthur and Cale as they froze just before they fell into the shadow. Their faces filled with apprehension and their mouths hung open slightly as they took in the being. Emily and Trevor screamed as Dylan found himself cowering backwards and Ari and Kira took two steps back.

The being turned to face Maya and her eyes widened as she saw his irises which were pink and his pupils were slits.

"They won't be bothering us anymore." He nodded behind her, his smooth tone filling her ears. She brought her attention to where the cops once stood and she found their bodies piled on the ground. The bodies of some of the on lookers could be seen in the distance as well. They were mangled and were in odd positions, their eyes wide and their mouths opened as blood poured from them. Pressure built in Maya's eyes as she took in the senseless killing, the type of killing that she had done in her past. The pink eyed man smiled at her as she turned back to him.

"Oh!" He exclaimed. "It's the eyes I've heard so much about!"

She looked between the white haired beings and she squared up as the longer haired one stepped closer to her. "It's definitely her, no one has ever been able to take my hits as well as she has, not even her brother's."

Maya clenched her teeth as her eyes narrowed.

"You have fun with the weaker ones while I play with her some more, *Abraxas*." The long haired creature's jaw cracked as he moved it.

Arthur prepared himself as Maya met his eyes, these were the beings Eli, Peyton, and Oberon were working for but the question still rose: Who was the *he* that they had spoken of?

She backed flipped as the long haired one came at her again, her already bloody wings taking the brunt of the hit and blood splattered onto the attackers pale skin. She used her extra limbs to swat him away and within the next second, she used the same speed he had with her and she roundhouse kicked him across the face.

He went flying into the building he had hid beside while Maya turned to help the others as they fought with the short haired one named Abraxas. Arthur and Cale were having trouble with the creature and like the long haired one, he had a smile on his lips. The others tried to help but they had to dodge the shadows that rose from their feet.

What kind of power did this creature have?

Maya was about to attack the creature from behind when the long haired one appeared before her again and she flew backwards. She was met a smile even wider than before and his eyes were filled with glee.

"HAHAHAHA!" He cackled and the gargoyles flinched at the sound. "That was much more than your brothers could have ever hoped to do to me!" His eyes smiled as he talked with his teeth instead of his mouth.

That hit should have killed him, it should have snapped his neck in half.

Not only was she the first to take his hits, but he was also a first for her.

What the hell were they?

More police officers ran into the square, the tourists had ran far from the area and Maya could hear more sirens in the distance.

This was going to be a problem.

She gritted her teeth as she swung her head to the ten men who had stopped at the bodies of their colleagues. She took in their pale faces as they looked up from the dead then to the creatures in front of them.

"Get out of here!" She screeched. "RUN!"

"They won't have time." Abraxas cocked his head as the shadow at his feet wiggled then expanded. As if following a trail, the thing narrowed as it rushed to the officers and Maya and the others watched with dread as the shadow reached them then expanded at their feet.

The creature was right, they didn't have time to run. With silent screams etched onto their faces, they fell inside the shadow like how the creature had stepped out of it. Within seconds, they came flying out again, their bodies mangled and torn as they landed harshly to the ground.

The gargoyles mouths hung open, at any moment the being could do the same to them.

"You're used to being the strongest and it shows." The long haired one chuckled. "Don't look so shocked at the sight of worthless souls being taken…I've been told you used to do the same."

Maya shook as she turned to the being with anger swelling inside her and her teeth extended into points like the creatures they were fighting though they weren't as sharp.

The creature took one step closer as a breeze picked up and their striking white hair blew with it. The different monsters went at each other and for the first time since she had killed her bothers, Maya fought with ferocity and aimed to kill. The creature had gotten many life ending hits from her but as he went down, his smile remained.

Anytime she had gone for his heart, he had dodged her with ease.

The being named Abraxas stood as if transfixed with their fight but Arthur attacked him and he was forced to bring his attention back the weaker gargoyles. He could have killed them with his shadow but kept them alive.

Why was he holding back?

Maya tried going to the others again as the creature swatted Emily to the ground but the one she was fighting stood in her way again and she growled.

"You're everything I was promised!" The being grabbed ahold of her chin, her breath hitching from the iron like smell coming from it's mouth. "You smell better than your brothers." He leaned down and whispered as his long tongue protruded from his mouth.

"*Enough.*" A voice filled with silk filled the air and the creature pulled away from her with a hint of disappointment.

She would have attacked him while he was distracted but she followed his gaze as he turned to the monument of the 7th president riding a horse in the middle of the square.

From behind the statue stepped the source of the voice, his black curls bobbing over his pale face as he walked. He was clad in a black coat and jeans, a smile on his lips as he spotted Maya.

She looked into his eyes and her heart thumped as she took in the black orbs that rested in the middle of the white. Her hands shook as she felt the air change as he walked closer until they were ten feet apart.

Behind him walked a slightly taller man, he looked old fashioned with his brown curls and a light beard on his chin. He was clad in a white dress shirt and black slacks. His dark eyes remained down as he followed the man in front of him.

"Hello, *Anna*." The black haired man purred and suddenly Maya and the other gargoyles were forced to the ground as an intense pressure fell on them.

They heaved as they tried to push themselves from their stomachs but the air grew denser still, making it harder to breath. Maya shook as she narrowed her eyes at the pain in her head. She forced her neck to turn to the others who seemed to be having a harder time than she was as she was the only one who wasn't flat on the ground. She instead rested on her knees as the bones pressed into the concrete.

The pressure in her eyes grew stronger as she turned back to the black haired man and the white haired creatures walked away from their prey to the newcomer, their smiles still wide. The brown haired one looked out of place among his black clad allies.

The black haired man snickered as he looked down at her, "You've gotten stronger my dear..." He grinned. "I only got you to your knees this time."

"Who are you?" She spat breathlessly as gravity pushed on her.

This was *him*.

This was the man her brothers had worked for.

As fast as the pressure had came, it dulled, but not enough for them to get up. Maya remained planted on her knees while the others joined her in the position, their pained gasps filling the air as they did so. Maya struggled against what was left of the pressure but couldn't move anymore.

"You don't remember me?" The man faked his disappointment, the silk in his voice made him sound insane. "I guess that's to be expected after dying two times."

Two times?

Maya's heart raced as the man grew serious, his black hair blowing in the breeze. "You knew me by a different name back then, but I'll tell you my real name from the start this time: My name is *Lucifer*."

Lucifer? As in the devil?

Fearful confusion filled the air as the gargoyles looked on at the creatures in front of them.

Maya turned to Cale and Arthur who were to her left, they were both wide eyed and their jaws hung slack. She turned back to the creatures but her eyes landed on the black haired one first, it was like there was a pull between them... there was no way that this was the devil...he looked so...*human.*

"I'd be lying if I said I wasn't disappointed, *Anna*." He smiled at her confusion. "Although it's understandable that you don't remember, it still hurts." He rose his arms like he was some kind of display. "I'm even wearing the form I took when I met you."

She turned her head to see who he was talking to but found no one aside from her comrades. As she brought her gaze back to him, his eyes were still on her.

Her voice shook now as she spoke, "I'm not the one you're looking for.... I'm not Anna."

"Of course not." He agreed. "But you once were and you very well could be again."

Her heart thumped and she couldn't breath as she thought of the possibility of having another life before she was Maya.

It wasn't possible, was it?

No...

It couldn't be...

But it was.

This couldn't be real, this had to be a dream...There was no way the being that even Maya and Arthur were told about when they were younger was standing in front of them now.

Lucifer, the being who was banished from heaven after he demanded too much power from God. The deity threw him to earth as punishment and unknowingly brought chaos to the world and it's unsuspecting civilians.

Another question rose: If the devil was supposedly in front of them now, did that mean that God was real as well?

When you thought of one, you would think of the other.

They came hand in hand.

Light and darkness.

"Oh! Where are my manners?" Lucifer turned his head to the white haired creatures beside him. "I got so caught up in our reunion that I forgot to introduce *my demons.*"

They all felt sick as Lucifer pointed first to the long haired demon, "This is Azazel." He declared and the first demon nodded with a smile.

Lucifer then pointed to the short haired one, "Abraxas." The second demon stood still as his master introduced him, his pink eyes wandering over the gargoyles faces, taking them in.

"And lastly, Cain." Lucifer finished his introductions with the brown haired demon who continued to keep his eyes down as if the creatures in front of him were boring to him.

"There are more of my elite demons in other places doing my bidding." Lucifer continued. "There's also the thousands of lower class demons...and the one's in limbo that are yet to be freed.... Plus the new ones waiting for my call."

"This is a joke..." Arthur's shaking voice came from behind Maya but her eyes remained on the man who called himself Lucifer.

"I wish it was, *brother*." A familiar voice filled the air and from behind the statue walked their oldest brother, Eli. "It took me awhile to believe it too, but it's true that who's standing in front of you now is Lucifer and his demons." He turned his hazel eyes to Maya as she moved her gray ones from Lucifer. "I delivered your message, little sister."

"Look at this family reunion!" Azazel snickered. "It's too bad she killed the twins…this would have been even more interesting!"

"This is who you're working for?" Maya's defiant voice came out over Azazel's cackle. "You'll always be someone's bitch."

Eli shot forward but Azazel appeared beside him and stopped him with an outstretched arm. The demon watched as the gargoyles eyes filled with bloodlust and he snorted as he turned to Maya then to Lucifer.

"I understand why you like her!" He exclaimed as he dropped his arm from Eli.

"What the hell do you want?" Maya ignored both her brother and the demon as she turned back to Lucifer.

He chuckled as he looked from her eyes to the sky above him.

"I've lived in this world since the beginning of time, so it's not surprising that I've read human literature." He brought his dark eyes back to her and she could feel the pull between them strengthen. "The villain always tells their enemies what they're planning and gives them the means to beat them…*how stupid*." He licked his teeth as he gleamed at her, his eyes growing darker as his expression changed to something more sinister. "But I will tell you that it will be *hell on earth*."

Eli's footsteps echoed and broke the tension in the air.

"I'm surprised to see you still with my siblings." His voice filled Maya's ears and through the shock of Lucifer's declaration, she turned to find her oldest brother kneeling in front of Cale, the ladder looking on with narrowed eyes. "It's their fault I killed your father… they're as much to blame as I am."

"I fail to see how it was your sisters fault." Cale snarled as he tried to hide the grief he felt at the mention of his father. "I however see a weak fucker who was always jealous of his sister." He looked into the stronger gargoyles eyes with venom. "It must have made you feel tough, killing someone weaker than you, since you could have never done so with your sister."

"You fucki-" Eli spat as he began to pull his arm back to slash Cale's throat.

Maya struggled to get up as she tried to stop her brother and the air around her filled with whimpers but like before, Azazel stopped him.

The gargoyle looked at the demon as he tried pulling his wrist out of his grip but the demon seemed to have no problem holding him back.

"You're annoying me." Lucifer said the same words he had four months ago. "They can't die yet… I told you this and you still choose to defy me."

The gargoyles watched as Azazel turned to his master and the other demons. Abraxas was looking on expectantly while Cain kept his gaze down.

"Peyton and Oberon were the same." Lucifer brought his narrowed eyes to Maya. "I can see why you killed them, *Anna.* I've thought about killing them for a long time but I've kept them alive…and they did their job well."

There was that name again, the mention of it sent a chill down Maya's spine.

"If you killed them…" his voice drifted as he turned to Azazel and Eli, the gargoyles face twisted in fear as he knew what was about to happen. "…then you won't mind if I kill this one, *right*?"

Lucifer's words were confirmation for Azazel and a millisecond after Lucifer finished his last word, Eli's head went flying off his body as the demon slashed his throat.

His body fell in front of Cale who jumped while his head flew back and landed next to Abraxas. The short haired demon knelt and lifted it by it's brown hair, blood pouring from the bottom, and the demon grinned at the puddle on the ground.

Azazel stepped away from the body as Cale tried moving away from it with no avail. The demon admired his handy work as he walked backwards until he stood beside Maya.

He turned his head to her and examined her unfazed expression while the others watched Eli's blood pour from his now separate body parts.

Maya knew Emily and Cale would be the most fazed by the death, not by who it was, but how it was done: Carma had met her fate this way by Camilla while Maya had watched.

Though this time she didn't feel the blind rage she did last time.

She felt nothing.

It had happened so fast that Eli didn't even feel the slash while she had felt every rip and tear as she took in the explosion they had so carefully prepared for her.

She was just as savage as she ever was: She killed two of her own brothers and watched with no emotion as another was killed.

She almost fell back as the pressure pushing on her disappeared completely and she turned to the others: They were still trying to get up as the pressure continued to hold them down, their eyes filled with either tears or shock.

Arthur's eyes were on her, his jaw clenched tight, he didn't seemed fazed by his brothers demise either but the two of them knew what could happen next: One of their own could be killed.

Lucifer's words that declared that they couldn't be killed yet were hard to believe.

"You've certainly changed, *Anna*." Lucifer's voice made her turn back to him as she shakily got to her feet.

Fear filled her core as she looked up at the devil as he spoke with his dark eyes on her.

"You fought many demons in your past…I'm curious if your skill in fighting them has changed." His dark hair blew out of his eyes and Maya watched as they lit up with excitement.

For the first time, Cain's eyes lifted from the ground and he watched as Maya turned with a sharp exhale to Azazel who Lucifer had nodded to.

Chapter 38

Maya fell to the ground beside Arthur as Azazel attacked her and her brother tried reaching for her but Lucifer strengthened the gravity around him and he was pushed down so he wouldn't interfere. Lucifer's control over his ability was terrifying, at anytime he could squash any of them like a bug.

Maya took a good look at her brother as he struggled and shook her head to stop him from doing so. He was only causing himself more damage by trying to move.

She got to her feet and rubbed the blood from her mouth, when they fought moments before, Azazel hadn't moved like this. It was apparent that he was holding back before and the ache in her face confirmed it.

"This is underwhelming." Azazel appeared behind her and she turned, her fist colliding with his face and although he was knocked backwards a couple feet, he didn't seem to be fazed.

Maya didn't waste any time in running at him and the two fought with valor but even with her power as the black and white eyed gargoyle, she couldn't best the demon. Her chest heaved as she began to tire while the demon didn't break a sweat.

This couldn't be it… she couldn't use her full power now... it would…

"It's just another thing amongst many others that she's forgotten." Lucifer called and Maya's eyes flashed to him, her feet instinctively turned to him and she began to walk in his direction with a snarl on her lips. Her black and white eyes as sharp as a daggers edge.

Lucifer who had been watching from his spot in front of the statue with the other two demons had a face like he was watching a movie but as she approached him, his mouth turned into a grin.

Azazel appeared in front of her and she swatted him with her clawed fingers but he caught them with his own. She pulled her hand out of his rough grip and broke her own fingers as she ducked around him. With the same speed Azazel had been using with her, she tried going for Lucifer again.

A sharp pain erupted in her heel and she fell forward onto her front as the pain seared and the yells and gasps of her comrades filled her ears.

She should have been able to dodge Azazel's attack and she should have been able to hear it coming but the demon had upped his speed again. While he knelt down, he had slashed with his claws and cut open the achilles heel on her right foot. Blood spurted onto his nails and the ground as she fell and she bit her tongue to hold back her scream as the pain hit. Her foot practically swung from her ankle as she tried pulling herself up and her weight made the hanging muscle collapse.

"Maya!" Arthur called out with rage and desperation as he saw his sister fall.

"Sam!" The others called and through the tears building in her eyes from the pain, she could see Arthur and Cale trying to crawl to her.

"She has many names." Abraxas knelt to get a good look as her face as she struggled to get up. "It must get confusing."

"Get away from her!" Arthur roared and Lucifer gestured to him. "Don't worry, she won't be killed…not today at least, she's too important." He titled his head as he watched her try to grab Abraxas but she fell down as the demon moved away.

It was hard to believe that she wasn't going to die today. She was powerful in her own right, but the demons were something else and she had no idea how to fight them. Worse was that, Lucifer had said that this was only the tip of the iceberg.

There was no beating them.

Her eyes twitched to Lucifer as she forced herself to her feet but most of her weight went to her left leg as the tendons, muscles, and skin rushed to heal in that order in her right.

She would have to use her full power against them in order to cause any damage and even then, she was sure that these weren't even their real forms.

Even more devastating was the fact that she was certain that Lucifer was stronger than his demons. Much, much, stronger. His display of power was enough to prove it.

He also knew her while she didn't know him.

He had every advantage over her.

"You're something else." Azazel cackled and Maya's eyes found him again. "I can't wait for you to evolve further… All of you." He turned his head to the others. "This will be everything you promised and more, my master." He bowed his head to Lucifer and Cain's eyes rolled to the demon and Maya who stood lazily in front of him.

Azazel began walking to her with a hop in his step and Maya tried limping away only for her ankle to give out. No matter how hard she tried, she couldn't stay standing and she finally fell to her knees and her comrades screamed for her to get up. The girl they thought was stronger than anyone was being completely and utterly beaten.

Arthur's nails dug into the pavement as he crawled through Lucifer's power.

"You're the most fun I've ever had," Azazel praised her as she inclined her head to see his face. She tried to crawl backwards to get away from him but she slid on Eli's body and fell on the corpse. Cale who was still struggling next to the body reached for her with desperation etched on his face.

"I can't wait to play with you more." Azazel gave a toothy smile as he brought his clawed hand behind him and Maya prepared for the slash.

Lucifer had to be lying, there was no way they would keep her alive.

She had died already, the feeling didn't bother her. She was even prepared to die again if it meant that it would make things right.

She remembered the words she had uttered in the realm in her mind:

"I will not fail."

The sound of everyone yelling for her filled her ears and the air rushed as Azazel's arm flung forward. She ignored the sounds around her as her eyes fixated on his claws that were about to slash her throat.

She had to fight, she had to….

But death wanted her soul so badly.

But death didn't come for her nor did Azazel's attack.

Instead a man stood between them in a white trenchcoat that reached his ankles. His hair as bright as the sun and his eyes as blue as the sky. In his hands was a sword, it's silver edge gleaming as the sun shined on it and Azazel's nails clinked against the blade as it stopped the demons attack. No one saw him coming nor did they see the five that had appeared in front of the other gargoyles as they protected them. They were all clad in the same white coats as the man that stood between Maya and Azazel.

They had swords in their hands and some with daggers at the ready. Maya couldn't get a good look at them as her head shot to where Lucifer stood: With him was another white coated man with his sword at the devils throat who was smiling as his hand rested on the hilt before it could cut his skin. Cain took a step back as his uninterested eyes fell back to the ground.

The man who had attacked Lucifer was identical to the one who was protecting Maya. His short blonde hair blew in the breeze and his blue eyes focused on his enemy.

"It's been a long time, *Venandi.*" Lucifer met the newcomers eyes as he pushed the sword away, his voice high with excitement.

With that the people known as the Venandi started their assault on the smiling demons and unlike Maya, they went for only one vital area: *The demons hearts*.

Lucifer kicked the one in front of him away and he bowed his head to Maya as Arthur and the others ran to her as his hold on them released.

"Until next time, *my sweet Anna*." He purred as he stepped into Abraxas' shadow that had appeared in front of him with Cain's hand on his shoulder.

Azazel who had been pushed back by the man who stopped his attack back flipped away before the man could shove his sword through his heart.

Abraxas was fighting the five that had protected the other gargoyles but jumped into the shadow at his feet and it moved to Azazel where Abraxas' hand reached through the ground and grabbed his comrades legs, pulling him into the shadow with him.

"Goodbye." The demon waved with his fingers as he sang the word, his white hair was the last to be seen as he sunk completely into the shadow.

Cale had reached for Maya's hand and pulled her up as the demons escaped. He helped her stay up right as she hopped with her uninjured leg.

They and the others ran from the white coats who even though they had protected them, could still be enemies in it for their own agenda.

The man who had attacked Lucifer watched as they ran, his sword at his side as his comrades walked to him. The gargoyles ran to the outer edge of the square but when they got there, they were met with a line of bodies and Abraxas' shadow was swirling around their twisted limbs.

They had wondered why no one else had came aside from a few officers and this answered it.

Abraxas was crowd control.

Maya's heart sank as they stepped over the bodies and even though she couldn't see the faces of the others since they were in front of her and Cale, she knew they were terrified.

She turned her head to Cale so she wouldn't see the corpses and she found him looking forward to try avoiding them as well, his jaw set in a line and his eyes were wide with fear and anger. Arthur who remained behind them in case they were followed took in the bodies with a saddened face, he had always hated death…now more than ever.

Abraxas' boundary had led all the way to their stolen car, it was clear that the demons wanted them to escape.

As they rushed to the car, the question rose of how the people known as the Venandi had made their way in with the shadow blocking them.

They squeezed in the car and as Arthur started driving, the shadow dispersed so they could get out of the parking lot. As they turned to take a final look at the scene, the shadow disappeared completely and all that was left of it was the corpses of it's victims.

The car was silent until they were to the safety of the highway after Arthur had taken every side road incase they passed the police on the main ones.

"This can't be real…" Emily's voice shook as she gripped onto the hair against her scalp and Maya was reminded of her fear in their cave prison over four months ago. "I know things were crazy, but the devil?"

Maya met Arthur's eyes in the rear view mirror as she sat with Emily, Trevor, Ari, and Kira who was sitting on Ari's lap. Cale who had helped her inside sat next to the window beside her.

The devil, demons, a group of people called *The Venandi,* and a woman named Anna.

All of it weighed on Maya's mind, especially of how Lucifer spoke to her like he had known her. Of how she had another life, a life when she was known as the woman named Anna.

She had seen her oldest brothers death, met her greatest enemy, and learned something about herself that could change everything. She knew the others were thinking the same, especially Arthur who watched her with an odd look.

She couldn't think more of it as she turned around while feeling her heel snap back into place and as she did, she spotted a black SUV hot on their tail. The others followed her gaze and they realized it was the people in the white coats following them. Behind the first SUV was another and with their strong eyesights, they could see more of the coats in the second vehicle.

"We've got company." Ari's teeth chattered as she leaned her elbow on the back of her seat.

Maya met the eyes of the driver in the first vehicle and she recognized him as the man who had attacked Lucifer. His eyes bored into her but she didn't look away as a voice in her head told her to meet them and she knew it wasn't some kind of premonition: It was her own voice.

"Stop in the rest area." She demanded as she turned in her seat.

"What!?" Ari, Kira, and Dylan said collectively but she didn't pay them any mind.

"We need to meet with them," She met their eyes. "They saved us and they fought the demons a hell of a lot better than I did."

They lowered their eyes and Maya softened her gaze.

"It's about time you realized that I'm not invincible." She turned between Emily, Cale, and Trevor. "What do you think?"

"I have to agree with you." Cale who was far too tall to be sitting in the back leaned against the seat as he breathed in slow to calm himself. "They saved us."

"I agree as well." Emily swallowed. "What else can we do?" Her frightened face met Maya's and Trevor simply nodded even though Maya figured he was about to wet himself.

"Arthur…?" She asked finally and not only did she look into the mirror to meet his eyes, but so did the others. He dropped his eyes from the mirror and kept them on the road.

"Better to meet with them now instead of letting them follow us to our hideout."

When they approached the rest area, they pulled off, and so did the Venandi.

They were lucky the small pull off was empty for the time being and the shade the trees provided covered their car. Cale, Arthur, Emily, and

Maya were already out as the cars parked behind them and when the rest of the gargoyles were out, they stood together as they waited for their pursuers to get out.

Maya could stand on her injured leg now but limped as she stepped closer.

The drivers side of the first car opened and like a chain reaction, so did the rest. The five that had stood against Abraxas came from the first car along with the two blonde haired men. From the second came another seven people of many ages, races, and gender, their white coats billowing behind them. The one that caught their eyes the most was a pale man who kept his eyes closed and his eyelids were covered with pink scars, his brown hair framing his head. A dark skinned girl helped him walk as they approached Maya and the others. She looked the same age as the gargoyles and she seemed too innocent to be fighting demons.

The gargoyles stood defensively as they stopped in front of them, the blonde haired men front and center.

"Gargoyles." The man that had attacked Lucifer said in a thick accent that they figured to be British as he bowed his head as if the gargoyles were royalty and the others joined in.

Kira rose a brow and like the others, she turned to Maya and gave her a confused look like she would have an answer to the newcomers strange behavior.

"T-that's not necessary." Maya waved her hands awkwardly and they picked their heads up to take in the looks on the gargoyles faces.

The man who had bowed first was surely the leader of the group and he kept his eyes on Maya. His blue eyes made her uncomfortable so she dropped her gaze.

"Who are you?" She asked simply and she was sure the answer couldn't be worse than hearing that the devil and his demons were real.

"We are the Venandi." The man who had protected her from Azazel declared, his accent as thick as the other man's. "It translates to *hunter* in latin but to make it easier for you, we are demon hunters. " There was no need to question them, the demonstration had been made, they certainly knew how to fight demons.

The demons that people thought were gargoyles were separate entities.

"And you are gargoyles, warriors made by God." The leader declared and broke them out of their thoughts.

Maya blinked rapidly as she glanced at the others shocked expressions.

"Warriors of God?" Arthur shot in, his mind on what Maya had told him four months ago about gargoyles being guardians.

The man turned to Arthur as the other Venandi watched, "Gargoyles were made by God to defend the world from Lucifer's demons. They were sent by God to protect the universe from the darkness being cast by Lucifer's shadow."

Shadow.

The power that Abraxas had, the power they had pushed past.

"How were you able to get past that demons shadow?" Cale questioned. "The people who touched it died…but you were able to get through it to help us."

"Holy water." The man who protected Maya spoke again. "*Real* holy water, blessed by the leader of the Venandi… My brother, Alvertos." He turned his head to his slightly taller brother.

"We are, in a way, people sent by God to fight demons. The Venandi and gargoyles have fought together in the past." His eyes wandered across the group in front of him again. "But you have lost your way."

"There's no way we were made by God when we've done so much wrong." Maya spat, the probability of her being made by God who was supposed to be light itself infuriated her.

Why would someone as damned as her be made by someone who was supposed to be all good? She had her reasons for not believing in him: War, sickness, famine, death.

So much suffering had been felt by countless people and he even let the devil run around to do what he wanted. "I killed innocent people for revenge and my brother turned these people into gargoyles. If what you say is true, then my friends weren't made by God to fight… they were caught up in it."

"As Arley said," the leader known as Alvertos pointed to the other blonde man. "You have lost your way… No one is without sin, not even God himself." He met Maya's narrowed eyes. "It has been a long time since the demons last showed themselves and you have forgotten your purpose and how to fight them. It should be built into you, even the gargoyles that were once human. The years have dulled you, made you oblivious to your meaning. But this will be as it was over a hundred years ago: The black and whited eyed gargoyle will lead the other gargoyles against the demons…With the help of the Venandi this time."

Maya'a mouth went dry at the mention of the black and white eyed gargoyle, of which she currently was.

Lucifer had called her Anna, had treated her as if she was an entirely different person.

Was it possible that she was also the gargoyle from over a hundred years ago?

She felt pressure on her again and she jumped from thinking that Lucifer had returned. She turned her head to the man to the left of Alvertos, his eyes that had been closed were now open and Maya swallowed at the sight: His pupils and irises were gone and they were replaced by a light blue sack. The rest of his eyes were filled with red veins. He couldn't see her, but his eyes were on her all the same, as if he could see right into her.

The Venandi saw her apprehensive look, "This is Donato, he's a seer."

"A *seer?*" Ari's voice almost came out as a groan.

"He can see visions that God has decided to project onto him, that's the reason why we're here, that we were able to find you." Alvertos' blue eyes scanned the group. "Donato had a vision of the square and of the demons, of Lucifer himself, and-" He pointed to Maya. "You."

To add to these strange events, there was now a man that received visions from God himself. The man who was still staring at her with his unseeing eyes and sending a chill through her body.

"Can he stop staring at me?" the words rushed out of her mouth.

"It feels like he can see you, doesn't it?" Arley turned to Donato. "It's because he can, not with his eyes of course… he was blinded by his own father for having visions, he thought it was unnatural. He can't see you with his eyes but he has seen you in his visions, he has seen your eyes, has seen what you have done and will do."

"So you know what she's done?" Arthur pressed. "You know gargoyles aren't beings to be adored?"

"We know what she's done, Donato has seen it all." Arley nodded to the blind man to give him permission to speak.

"She has killed countless people as she's said. Until she saw something that changed her-" His voice was soft and his accent was as thick as the other mens and Maya found herself transfixed on it. "The sight of a little girl crying over her mothers body, it reminded her of her own sorrow and after seeing it, she was sent into a state of depression. She desperately wants to make up for what she's done." His eyes met hers and she unconsciously took a step back. "She knew and still knows there is nothing that will make up for it, she chose death to save countless people but she also chose it to end her own suffering… She reincarnated as a human, something that she had always wanted to be. She got her memories back at the sight of seeing her friends the same way the child and her mother were." His eyes flashed to Cale and Emily and they blinked at the man then moved their gaze to Maya. "…And at the sight of her brother having the life choked out of him. She dealt with the twins and sent the third away to deliver her message." After meeting Arthur's eyes, he turned back to Maya. "She will not fail this time."

She stopped breathing at his words. He knew everything he shouldn't, had told them the reason why her memories came back when she hadn't even told them herself.

He knew everything and what's more, he knew the words that echoed in her mind since she had gotten her memories back:

"I will not fail."

The being that had replied to her words echoed through her ears and her jaw clenched after she finally allowed herself to breath. Emily startled her as she placed a soft hand on her back to calm her. She turned to see her comrades looking at her with worried but confused looks.

She turned back to the sightless man, "Do you know what came after I said those words?"

He nodded, *"I know."*

She swallowed as the words hit her, her eyes falling first to the ground then back to the blind Venandi. "I wish I could say this isn't possible but with everything I've seen…with the way that fate has played it's hand… I believe you." Her eyes narrowed. "But I don't believe God is the one who orchestrated this, to me, he is just as guilty as I or Lucifer himself."

"I accept that." Alvertos nodded while the other Venandi scowled at her words. "You will learn soon enough." He stepped to her, "You were made in his image, there must be a reason why he made you do what you have."

A twinge of annoyance rushed through her and she was about to rebute when Alvertos changed the subject, "We would like to see your eyes."

They were obviously looking at them now, but their human eyes weren't what they wanted, it was their *gargoyle* eyes.

Maya turned her head slightly to Arthur and their eyes met. He nodded and as he did so, his eyes turned white. The others followed nervously and theirs turned pitch black.

Maya turned to the Venandi and took in their expressions as they watched her comrades eyes change. This generation had yet to see an actual gargoyle by the looks on their faces, but they didn't show fear at the beings, they had fought with the demons who were much more terrifying.

They were filled with wonder, wonder that they were faced with the supposed creatures created by God. The creatures born to defeat the demons, though none of them knew how.

Their eyes finally went to Maya's who had yet to change. Donato's prying gaze set on her like he could actually see them.

She allowed the pressure to build and the Venandi's faces lit up: Her right eye shined white while her left darkened to black.

They tried bowing again but she grabbed Alvertos' arm and pulled him back up. She wasn't sure if she was allowed to do that, but the Venandi didn't seem to mind.

"Theres no need for that." She said as she let him go. "I'm not something you should be bowing to."

They simply looked at her and when she felt uncomfortable, she turned her eyes back to normal. What a strange group of people, they were like the people who came to the door and preached to you.

"We apologize, we've been told of your existence by the Venandi before us." The dark skinned girl who had helped Donato spoke as she stepped closer to her blind companion. She turned to Alvertos and Arley as if asking if was ok to say what she wanted and they nodded.

"Go ahead, Arabella." Alvertos smiled.

Maya flipped her eyes between the four who stood in front of the rest of the Venandi. "I'm not the gargoyle your ancestors knew, that one is long dead and was unfortunately replaced by me."

Her eyes widened suddenly.

But Anna could have been.

Her heart lurched and she could feel it in her throat when she spoke. "Did your predecessors speak of anyone by the name of Anna?"

The other gargoyles turned to her, they also wondered who Anna was.

She lowered her gaze, did the woman named Anna have anything to do with her? Lucifer had spoken as if they were the same person after all. Maya couldn't think of how it was possible for her have another life before she was born as Maya. Gargoyles only reincarnated once, or at least that's what she had been told.

The four turned to give each other strange looks, "We apologize but no." Alvertos bowed his head. "Our ancestors never met the black and white eyed gargoyle from that time, they only heard stories from the gargoyles."

Maya lowered her eyes.

"We also apologize that we were a bit late." Alvertos pointed to Maya's severed heal that was still gradually healing. He then moved his eyes to the bruises and marks on the others who were already healing, of course Cale's already had. "Before now we've only fought lower class demons, these were Lucifer's elites."

"You've killed some?" Emily asked shakily.

"Only lower tier demons, Lucifer and his higher ranked demons haven't shown themselves in awhile but we know of their abilities from the Venandi who have faced them."

The sound of sirens on the highway woke them and they looked between the trees to see multicolored lights flying in the direction of the square.

Maya was sure that the police were already taking in the carnage.

How many lives had been lost?

Her face twitched as her jaw locked. The gargoyles would be blamed for it, all of the witnesses to prove otherwise were killed by the demons.

They had to get back to their safe place.

"What do you plan on doing?" Cale asked the Venandi as he felt the same unease.

"We plan on helping you fight Lucifer and his demons. We know what they are planning and we hope that you can also help us." Alvertos explained then turned to Maya. "He will come for you if you don't go to him."

Him as in Lucifer.

He wouldn't have to worry about her not coming to him, as long as he was around she would try to stop him. There was something about him that called to her, the visions she had been having over the past four months were a warning. She had them for a reason.

"I need to talk to my friends." She stood tall as her ankle finally healed completely and Alvertos nodded.

She and the others walked to the front of their car.

"You know what we have to do, right?" She asked as the others turned to her, her eyes still on the Venandi as they watched them talk.

"What else can we do?" Cale lowered his head so he could meet her eyes. "They saved us from the demons." He flinched at the word. "It's hard to believe the stories are real."

Emily frowned, "We thought gargoyles were the tip of the iceberg."

"We didn't know we would have to face them." Trevor leaned into the circle they had formed. "I say we have them come with us to teach us how to fight them, maybe it'll jog your memories on how to fight them." He furrowed his brows at Maya and Arthur. "Maybe the blood flowing through us will teach us how to fight them too. We are half gargoyles but there shouldn't be a reason why we can't."

"I'd rather you leave at this point." Maya shot in and although the idea looked better now that they knew who they were facing, they still gave her annoyed looks.

"We're not."

Maya could hear the unease in Ari's voice, she had talked about fate and now it was falling down on her. They seemed like they wanted to leave after what had just happened. Even Maya wished that she could run but not only did she not have a choice, but she also had her need to make up for what she had done.

"I will not fail…" She whispered and she was met with the confused looks of her comrades, Arthur especially.

Detective Deluca kneeled next to a puddle of blood next to the Andrew Jackson equestrian statue. The monument also had blood splatter over it and Deluca found himself examining it as the coroners carried the last few bodies out of the scene.

They had counted up to 75 dead and none of them had external injuries aside from a few broken bones that wouldn't have resulted in death. They had trails of blood coming from their eyes, noses, mouths, and ears.

Deluca had seen death before, when he first started as an officer over twenty years ago, the gargoyles were on the rise. These bodies looked nothing like how the victims looked at that time.

The gargoyles had been sloppy, had made sure the humans knew it was them. The bodies now looked as if they had been attacked by something entirely different. His mind went to the girl he had seen the other night, her face had been covered but by description, he knew who she was:

Samantha Knight.

A girl that was once human but had been changed into a gargoyle.

He swallowed as he remembered an image of one of the gargoyles they had managed to get on a surveillance camera almost twenty one years ago.

Samantha Knight and the gargoyle from back then looked exactly the same.

How was that possible?

He didn't know what kind of power gargoyles had and what they were able to do with them. All he knew was that they were murderous creatures that had no soul. The humans that had been turned into gargoyles that they had caught still whined and begged to be let go, but their *doctor* would never allow that to happen. He would never want to lose his research subjects. Deluca thought of the plump man in his lab coat, his mustache practically covering his mouth and his head shined as his hair receded.

The man disgusted Deluca.

"Detective Deluca?" He turned his head to his son's voice and was met with the man who shared his name.

"You can call me dad." He huffed as he pulled himself up.

Detective Reginald Deluca Jr. had been in the police force for five years before he moved up the ranks to detective along with his father. Though it would take him a long time to get where his father currently was. His father called him Reggie so the others wouldn't confuse the two of them.

"...what do you think happened here?" The lack of fear in his son's voice didn't bother him. He had seen his fair share of graphic scenes but never on this scale.

It had been a long time since Deluca had seen this much death and as he looked into his sons face, he could see the fear in his dark eyes.

"We can blame it on terrorists and that's most likely what they'll release to the public... but in reality with everything that's going on, it seems the gargoyles are back to their old ways."

His son's eyes dropped at his words but he didn't seem surprised. "Do you think that girl from the other night has anything to do with this?"

Deluca took in his sons worry, he couldn't help but think that he was the exact replica of himself from when he was his age.

The problem was that he was just as naive.

"She's not a girl." His voice drifted as he corrected his son. "She's a monster."

They pulled into the long drive that led to the cabins and directed the Venandi to park amongst the old cars, though the large SUV's wouldn't fit in with the junk. With the amount of people with them now, they'll have to move to a new place within a few weeks.

That's if they even had a few weeks left.

As they stepped out and were met with the 14 Venandi, all of them in white coats, Maya noticed they also wore white gloves. The gargoyles awkwardly led the way to the cabins, they still had their fear of letting the Venandi come with them but what other choice did they have? They would have been dead if it weren't for them although they figured the demons would have kept Maya alive for the simple reason that Lucifer was transfixed on her.

She thought of the slash across the throat she would have gotten if Arley didn't get there in time. Was Azazel really going to kill her?

They made it to the intersection of the cabins and they stopped and turned to the hunters. Maya felt comfortable enough now that they were in the safety of their temporary home to ask what they knew about the demons.

How to fight them.

Their plans.

And how to kill them.

"We'll start with what their planning." Alvertos removed his gloves and the gargoyles had to listen closely to understand what he was saying due to his accent. "There is no telling what Lucifer wants to do, but we have been making a pattern of the demons attacks." He pocketed his gloves and the others did the same. They looked like robots. "The demons have been destroying holy churches and monuments."

The gargoyle's minds went to what Lucifer had said about it being hell on earth.

"He said it'll be hell on earth." Emily sounded like she was about to be sick. "Do the attacks on these holy places have anything to do with it?"

The blonde men took in her words and Arley was the one to speak. "He must be getting anything that has to due with God out of the way. Getting rid of things that are holy will only bring unrest to the people who support our savior and his power will be void from the world."

"He's been waiting a long time for this, there's been ample time to strike especially after the first black and white eyed gargoyle died. We believe he needs war and calamity to make his plan work. He is the reason for any wrong thing in this world, it is his power that does so." Alvertos explained further.

It would have been difficult to believe but it made perfect sense. Now that they knew that Satan himself was real, all of the bad things that had be fallen upon the earth made sense. He caused turmoil in humans, he could play with their minds, as he had played with Maya's.

Even now, his words played over and over in her mind.

"What can we do?" Cale took initiative and Maya side eyed him, he was good at being a leader.

"Most of the holy places have been destroyed but we have more Venandi stationed at the remaining places to protect them while we are here to stop the demons from destroying the one's in this area. As the leader and my brother in second command, we have taken the top eleven fighters with us. With the help of Donato, we knew Lucifer and his demons would be here and you as well."

"Why do you think he appeared where we are?" Maya asked roughly though she knew the answer.

"You." Donato said simply. "I haven't seen the reason yet aside from the fact that you are the strongest gargoyle but there is another reason why he is so transfixed on you."

"...Can gargoyles have more than two lives?" She asked suddenly and she was met with curious looks again.

"There's no way to tell for sure but you are an exception, gargoyles aren't supposed to get their memories back after they've reincarnated." Arley explained and changed the subject back to the matter at hand as Maya's heart raced at his words. "We can only teach you so much before Donato has another vision and we have to fight the demons again. But what we can tell you without showing you is that there is one vital spot that you *must* hit to kill them," he pressed a hand to his chest. "Their heart."

"That's it?" Kira sounded shocked as she turned to Maya as if she was surprised that she couldn't have done something as simple as that.

"It's easier said than done."Arley sounded annoyed. "You've fought them and you've seen how they move... what's more, there is a risk to the person attacking the heart." He dropped his eyes to his now gloveless hands then brought them up again. "Demon blood will eat alive the person who get's it on them, we have yet to see what it does to a gargoyle but it has killed many of our own kind. It's a tar like substance and it doesn't look like normal blood, it's pitch black."

Maya took in the information along with the others, it certainly was a problem and she was nervous to find out what the blood could do to them.

What's more, her mind kept moving to the day of Carma's death. She had killed Camilla by ripping her heart from her chest when she had blacked out.

Her mouth felt dry as she wondered if it was her instincts, only they were directed at the wrong being. She looked down at her now shaking hands and thought of her parent's words: That they had a higher purpose.

She almost laughed at the irony of it all: *This* was their higher purpose. Their parents simply didn't want them to know how terrifying their enemy would be.

A slight buzz started ringing in her ears and she turned to go, she had heard enough. Arthur could tell them where they would be staying.

"I have a police scanner so we'll listen to that while you wait for your seer." She addressed them as she walked then bit her lip. "...I need a moment alone." She said as she stepped through her friends.

"We can get through this, Maya." Donato called and she stopped, she hadn't told them her name but she knew right away that he knew it from his visions. "We have to believe in God's will, we will speak with him and ask for guidance."

Maya's feet planted as she felt their eyes on her back. "God has never spoken to me," She started as she began to walk again. "But the spirits have."

The buzzing had gone to her brain as she stepped into her cabin and shut the door behind her. She knew they had to prepare but she couldn't let them see her this way.

Her neck was beginning to twitch and she brought her fingers to her temples as she stepped to the coffee table in front of the couch.

She had left the scanner on the table and she reached to turn it on. As she did so, the buzzing in her head became too much to handle and instead of her fingers, she used her hands to press as hard as she could to ease the pain.

"No!" A voice that sounded like her own echoed in her buzzing ears.

The pain in her head sharpened and she couldn't breath, it felt as if someone was holding her underwater.

"STOP!" She screamed along with the voice in her head and she collapsed harshly to the floor.

Chapter 39

She woke with a start and the first thing she saw were the stars in her eyes. Her head pounded and she gasped for breath, the smell of mildew on the carpet filling her noise as she pulled herself up. As her vision cleared, she saw that the side of the coffee table had cracked. She must have hit it as she fell and by the feeling in her head, the body part must have been what broke it.

She groaned as she pulled herself onto the couch and rubbed at her temple where her scar had been, there was no blood so the table didn't break skin from the fall. With the worry of having hurt herself gone, she began thinking about what had just happened.

Her own scream had filled her ears and she could still feel the buzzing in both her brain and ear drums, though it had gone down considerably. Her throat still felt restricted and she had to take a few deep breaths to catch her breath.

She rubbed her nose as she thought of what had just happened in Lafayette square and the knowledge she had just received from the Venandi.

Lucifer and his demons were real, gargoyles were born to fight them, and there were humans trained to fight the demons with the gargoyles.

Her hand dropped to her leg and she felt a cool draft on her skin where her wings had popped through her shirt. Her eyes lowered to her hands as she twisted her fingers together, it had been a long time since she had an episode like that.

She thought the visions were over aside from the occasional voice and flash of a face that she didn't understand.

She didn't worry about them before but now that she knew Lucifer had a fascination with her and that he called her by a different name, the episode chilled her.

Gargoyles can only have two lives.

One as a gargoyle and one as a human.

But she was an exception.

No, it wasn't possible.

It had to be a freak thing that she had gotten her memories back, that her two lives became one. She never had visions of a past life when she was simply Maya.

Her heart thumped as she thought of Lucifer's face: His pale skin, his black wavy hair, his black bottomless eyes. Another chill blew through her as she remembered the air that he had around him. The smile on his lips as he saw her, the excitement in his voice.

He was a manipulator, she knew the voices she had heard the other day were of him and Eve. She had heard the story of Adam and Eve, of how God placed them in the Garden of Eden and told them they could eat anything aside from the fruit on the forbidden tree.

Lucifer had turned himself into a serpent and tempted Eve to eat the forbidden apple, she was weak minded and the temptation was too great, with one bite, she cursed mankind.

Lucifer could very well be manipulating Maya now to put her on edge, to move her mind from what she had to do: *Stop him.*

She couldn't think of that now, she couldn't think of another life and she would have to try to keep her visions at bay. If she returned to how she was before she had gotten her memories back, she would certainly cause problems on the battlefield.

She furrowed her brows, she only *hoped* Lucifer's words were simply a manipulation.

A knock on the door made her wake from her thoughts and she turned to it. All of her friends were there starting with Arthur.

As she got up to open the door, she thought of how she couldn't make out the steps of the demons as they fought, how she couldn't sense Azazel aside from his smell.

She opened the door and without looking at them, she stepped out of the way so they could come in.

"We've certainly found ourselves in quite the mess." Arthur said as he stepped past her. "I've lodged the Venandi in the empty cabins on the other side of the camp."

Maya nodded and she flinched as she noticed him looking at the cracks on the coffee table. Cale's eyes were also down and the two men met each others eyes before looking her.

She desperately hoped she didn't have a mark on her head.

"What happened?" Arthur pressed with his hazel eyes sinking into her.

"Nothing." Her voice was rough, she started to wonder how long she was out for if Arthur was able to get the Venandi settled in.

He dropped his eyes back to the table as the others sat down while Cale's dark eyes were still on Maya as he continued to stand.

Arthur sat where she had a moment ago and Emily joined him as Maya shut the door.

"We need to speak before we start working with the Venandi." Arthur said finally after Maya sat on the arm of the couch beside him. "We almost died today…"

"We wouldn't have today," Maya spoke before she realized what she was saying. She looked around nervously but as she took in their curious faces, she said *fuck it* and continued on. "You saw the way he acted when Eli tried attacking me and tried killing Cale…" She met Cale's dark eyes and she could see the apprehension in them. "This is a game and we're his players, many have played through the centuries but they have all lost."

"You seem like you're able to read him well." Kira leaned forward and the couch's old hinges creaked. "You just met him."

She inhaled sharply, "Did I though?"

"Hell on earth…." Dylan's voice cracked with disbelief.

"We'll have to deal with the humans too," Maya shot in, thankful that the subject had been changed. "We're going to be blamed for what happened today and they'll be looking for us." She thought of detective Deluca and his son, she'd be seeing them again soon no doubt. "But they should be easy to maneuver around."

"What if they have what killed your parents?" Trevor asked nervously and he seemed to regret his question right away but Maya shook her head while Arthur didn't seem fazed at all.

"We're speaking of our survival right now, it's a good question to ask." Arthur assured him. "We'll keep the scanner on while the Venandi use their seer…" His voice drifted as he was still baffled that there was someone who could see visions given to him by God.

"…We'll have to learn from the Venandi how to fight them, if we learn, we may be able to cause some kind of damage. We have to talk to them about our plan of attack and where they think the demons will attack next."

"I don't want to find out what happens if the demons blood get's on us." Kira shivered. "We're half breeds unlike you two, it may affect us like humans."

"I don't think so," Arthur shook his head. "Your bodies are more gargoyle than human."

"Hopefully we'll be able to turn on our built in instructions on how to fight them." Maya turned her head to her brother, her tone sarcastic. "That God so *graciously* gave us."

"Can you imagine….?" Kira's voice was hoarse as she looked down to her knees with sad eyes. "We're going to fight demons to try to save the world…I wonder what my abusive fuck of a dad would think of me now?"

A suffocating air filled the room at Kira's words, she usually joked about the pain her father had caused her but they knew better. She covered her pain and loneliness with jokes, but this time she let them feel her emotion.

"Fuck what he thinks." Ari placed a hand on her shoulder and smiled gently.

"…Do you know what we have to do next?" Arthur asked and his face filled with apprehension at what the others reactions were going to be. "We'll need the help of the other gargoyles that are with Archie."

The room was silent as they thought of the others joining them but the reaction Arthur thought he was going to get didn't happen.

"We just accepted people that we don't even know, I don't see why we can't get the other gargoyles to help us." Cale leaned forward and placed his elbows on his knees and fisted his hands as he sat on the coffee table. "But will they even come when they find out what we're up against?"

The number of gargoyles with Archie had gone down in the past four months. With the brothers dealt with and their bosses sister back, they didn't see a reason to stay.

They weren't kidnapped like the gargoyles here and the ones in custody, even the two that ran remained free and were still in hiding.

Maya didn't mind the aspect of the other gargoyles joining them but her mind went to Kellan and her eyes narrowed. She was definitely going to regret having him around even though he was the most powerful of the others. To her, he was a pain in the ass.

They knew they would have to join with the other gargoyles sooner or later, they just didn't know it would be under these circumstances.

Who would have ever thought that Maya and Arthur's brothers were working for the devil.

The thought was almost laughable.

"We'll have to see." Arthur said finally.

As they left the cabin to meet with the Venandi, Maya stopped Ari and as she turned to face her, she looked confused.

"I need to ask a favor." Maya pulled at the back of her shirt where her wings had ripped through. "I know as of now that only Arthur, Cale, and I can use our wings but in the chance that any of you get them, can you make something so we don't rip our shirts?"

It wasn't a good time to ask for such a thing but maybe it would help with the nerves Ari felt.

Ari rose a brow as she walked around Maya then stopped at the front of her again.

"Maybe just take the top of the back out… where the shoulder blades are?" Maya's voice drifted as she started to feel nervous at what Ari was thinking. The outfits weren't necessary, they could deal with ripped shirts.

"I'm on it." Ari gave a small smile.

The Venandi had their own cabins but they were stationed in one as the gargoyles made their way inside. The added eight gargoyles to the fourteen Venandi made for a tight squeeze.

Arthur came in last since he was on the phone with Archie and Maya met his eyes as the others awkwardly made their way to the demon hunters.

"They'll be here tomorrow afternoon." He stated as he placed the old flip phone back in his pocket. "Let's hope nothing else happens before then." Maya said as she joined the others.

"The rest of the gargoyles are joining you?" Arabella asked who was sitting on the couch, her white coat was off now and showed a tight white long sleeved shirt that had a strap going across her chest with knives sticking out. They were all safely covered and Maya sniffed as she picked up on something, she wasn't the only one who did as the others scrunched their noses.

"You must be smelling the sage." A pale boy that was sitting next to her smiled at them as he pulled some of the plant like substance out of his own arsenal.

"I'm Micheal." he said as he wrapped it around a knife then placed it back inside its casing.

The other Venandi along with Alvertos and Arely watched from the chairs placed around a table, they had obviously moved it there telling by it's odd placement.

A girl with blonde hair and cold blue eyes watched the gargoyles while a boy with black hair and a scar running down one of his brown eyes drew a long sigh. An older man with a good amount of scruff was the oldest one there.

They were the only one's that Maya really looked at. Aside from the leaders along with Donato, Arabella, and Micheal, the other venandi didn't seem to care much about telling the gargoyles their names and

Maya wasn't hurt by it. She didn't care about their names, she didn't even care if they were going to be friendly. They needed to work together to fight the demons. That was the only reason they were together.

Donato who was sitting beside Alvertos kept his eyes on Maya and she had to fight the Sam in her to stop herself from saying something.

"I'm Maya." She smiled at Micheal instead and she turned to the others who stood around the room.

"I'm Emily" Emily sounded nervous as the Venandi's eyes landed on her.

"Kira." Kira nodded towards them.

"My name is Ari." Ari told as she sat on the back of the couch, her legs beside Micheal.

"Dylan." Even with his tough form, Dylan looked like a mouse under everyone's gaze.

"I'm Trevor." Trevor blinked to them as he finished pretending that he looking out a window.

"Arthur." Arthur crossed his arms and leaned against the wall closest to Maya.

Last but not least, Cale told them his name.

The Venandi were silent for a moment as they took Cale in, he was the only one who didn't have any marks left from the demons attack.

"You heal fast." Alvertos tapped his fingers on the table.

"I get that a lot." Cale said as he leaned against the wall opposite of Arthur. He didn't sound annoyed nor did he sound like he was taking a compliment, he just seemed indifferent to hearing the words for what felt like the 100th time.

"Gargoyles can get extra abilities and that's Cale's." Arthur explained but the Venandi kept their eyes on Cale who was starting to get restless under their prying eyes.

"You have Native American blood flowing through you, yes?" Alvertos questioned him and Cale blinked, confused by the question.

What did it have to do with healing fast?

"I've been told a few things about my birth parents and I've only seen a few pictures, but my father was half Native American while my mother was European, so I suppose I'm less than half."

The Venandi took in the information and as Alvertos looked into Cales' eyes, he explained why Cale took the transformation so well. Why he healed better than the others and why he thrived off the power.

"Native American's are very spiritual people, they can feel the earth and it's energy in their bones and it courses through their veins. The blood of a gargoyle is spiritual as is but with your Native blood, it hightens your abilities. The bloods mix perfectly."

Cale tightened his jaw at the news and his comrades watched as his eyes wandered downward.

Maya frowned at the look on his face, talking about his birth parents was hard enough but now he just learned that it was thanks to his fathers linage that he was protected.

When Maya spoke, she did so with the intention of getting her question answered but also to get their attention off of Cale so he could think in peace.

"Do you have an explanation as to why a gargoyle would have the power to take in energy?"

Arthurs head practically snapped in her direction and he swallowed. The Venandi cocked their heads at her question while the other gargoyles looked on curiously.

"We have never heard of a gargoyle with that kind of power… who had it?" Arley asked with furrowed brows.

"She did." Donato's soft voice rang out and their eyes flew between the two. "That's how she died, she used the power and sacrificed herself to save the city her brothers were going to destroy. Only their real plan was for her to die."

"And they achieved their goal." Maya said simply as she looked into Donato's injured eyes.

Her death no longer fazed her the way it used to, she embraced it even. Her heart thumped and her eyes lowered to her chest…she would do it again. "And now my brothers are gone and my enemy is the embodiment of evil."

"With your…Er…ability…" Kira started as she sat in front of Ari and beside Micheal who turned red as her arm touched his. "Can you see the outcome of this?" She reached her arm out to Donato but quickly brought it down as she remembered that he couldn't see.

Donato turned to the sound of her voice and simply looked at her with his unblinking eyes until he dropped his gaze and turned to the window to the left of Arthur. The sun shined through and illuminated the dim floor.

"I haven't seen the outcome but I've been told this:" he turned his head so he was facing the group again. *"The hand of God will bring about the end of the world but will also save it."*

The gargoyles were taken back by the prophecy but the Venandi all seemed to have heard it before.

"The hand of God?" Maya, who in neither of her lives had been religious, had no idea what the thing was.

Was it a literal hand? She thought of a severed hand that crawled around on its fingers.

"It's the bible." Kira interjected before any of the Venandi could speak and she had to explain herself as she was met with the shocked looks of her comrades who were surprised that she would know such a thing. "My father used to cram it down my throat."

"How is a book going to end the world but save it?" Dylan almost laughed at the craziness of it all. "Should we go buy one now?"

"That's all I know." Donato dropped his eyes again. "It's all God will tell me."

Donato's words only posed more questions but what did they expect? How could anyone know the outcome of this situation? Who would know who was going to make it through to the end? If any of them would make it through?

If Lucifer wanted the end of the world, then it was surely in his grasp.

Maya chewed on the inside of her lip as she thought of what the end of the world would look like. "When do you think they'll strike next?"

"Lucifer hasn't shown himself in over 100 years and the first thing he did was call out to you. He knew you were going after criminals, he knew you would come and when you did, he took the opportunity to test you…I have a feeling he counts on you to come the next time he strikes and it leads me to believe that he will give you time to prepare." Alvertos explained, his blue orbs narrowing.

"Why the hell would he wait for us to prepare?" Trevor stepped closer. "He has his plan… Why would he wait?"

"You saw it today… we apologize but we watched before stepping in and we saw what happened," Arely smacked his hand on the table. "Lucifer has his fascination with the black and whited eyed gargoyle… he *wants* her." He pointed to Maya with his hand still on the table and she took a step back. "I don't know what their relationship is other than the fact that she is the strongest gargoyle, of course he'd want to *play* with her because of the fact that she is." Arley stood as his words struck a fire in him.

"But who is Anna?" Emily pressed the name like Maya had. "He called her Anna and the demon's talked to Lucifer about how she lived up to their expectations."

"As we said, we do not know." Donato was the one to speak. "A third life could be a possibility but it's been said that Lucifer is a manipulator. He manipulated Eve in the garden of Eden, he temps people into war and murder. He could very well be tempting her into something more."

"You won't have to worry about that." Maya spat as she turned to walk out of the cabin, she had heard enough. Especially at the mention of Eve whose voice rang in her head.

She had heard the devils manipulation. This was not the same.

"If it's ok with you, we can better prepare ourselves tomorrow." She said as she turned to face them at the door and the others who had gotten up to follow her stepped out of the way.

Alvertos and Arley nodded. "We understand, this is a lot to take in."

Maya rolled her eyes as she walked away.

It certainly was.

They were standing near the car graveyard the next day as they waited for the other gargoyles to arrive. Archie had called a half an hour earlier and had said that they were a short distance away. The fear that something would happen filled their minds but that was the least of Maya's worries as she stood with bags under her eyes from tossing and turning all night.

She couldn't say that she had any dreams, instead she had flashes of gold appear in her mind and it woke her every time with a jump of her heart.

She would rub her eyes to stop the color from coming back to no avail. She finally drew the line at the 20th time and remained awake.

And so she stood there with her new pair of knee high boots that she had bought along with others as a spare. Azazel's attack had ruined the other pair and had also left a nasty scar where the wound had healed.

She turned to Arthur who was in a deep talk with Alvertos and the other Venandi, they had ditched their coats for now and wore black half sleeved shirts with their weapons at their sides. Crosses were placed over their chests by silver chains. Donato sat on a hood of one of the junk cars with Arabella and Micheal.

"Are you ok?" Cale stepped beside her as the others talked amongst themselves at another car. Emily had asked her the same thing that morning, she had come to check on her but Maya wouldn't say what was on her mind. She had been semi open with them about getting her memories back but now the visions and the flashes of color made her feel unnatural.

As if she was ever natural.

"I'm ok." She answered. "Couldn't sleep much last night."

"Neither could I." Cale kept his eyes on the rusted Cadillac closest to them. "What happened yesterday and what's to come filled my mind."

Aside from the flashes of gold, Maya had also thought about Lucifer and his demons. Especially the looks on their victims faces that had fallen to Abraxas' shadow.

"Welcome to the beginning of the end." Cale's voice drifted as he turned from the car to Maya.

"Aren't you glad we're spending it together?" She knew it wasn't the time to joke but she smiled anyway and Cale returned it.

"Yeah." He chuckled a bit. "Us, the demon hunters, and the people who were once our enemies."

"What a turn of events." Maya shook her head with a smile as she turned to the long driveway.

The crunching of rocks filled the air and brought everyone back to reality as a silver van entered the long drive. When Archie parked the car, no one went to greet the newcomers, they waited to meet them in the middle.

Their numbers certainly did diminish. What used to be over twenty was only ten. There were some faces that Maya recognized while some she didn't.

She recognized the man and woman that Cale and she had attacked when they broke out of the cave. She met Cale's eyes as he spotted them and they gave each other awkward looks. They hoped they didn't hold a grudge.

Archie walked to Arthur and the two hugged, "It's been awhile." Arthur said as he let go of the man who was like a brother to him.

"I wish it was under different circumstances but we knew this would come." Archie brought his attention to the Venandi that were standing around Arthur.

"This is the Venandi." Arthur paused for a moment. "They're demon hunters."

"Nice to meet you." Alvertos bowed his head and the rest did as well. The three that were sitting on the car had gotten up and with the help of Arabella, Donato stood with the others.

Maya turned her attention back to the other gargoyles and when she started to wonder where he was, Kellan came into view as he stepped out of the van with his usual cocky smile.

"Look who it is," He exclaimed as he saw her. "Batshit crazy."

To his dismay, she didn't say anything.

"You're not fun anymore." He sulked but his voice was filled with more sarcasm than disappointment.

The Venandi and the others watched with curious expressions as they waited for Maya's reply.

Kellan stopped in front of her and her eyes lifted to meet his as she spoke. "Do you remember what I said to you all that time ago in the cave?"

Since he cocked his head, the answer was obviously no.

"I said you should be wary of quiet people."

He grinned and she did as well, there was animosity in their eyes but something else: They were entertained.

"We need to get to work." Alvertos called and they turned to the man.

While Maya nodded, Kellan looked to Cale who was still standing beside her.

"Still alive and kicking?" He taunted and Cale smiled.

"Perhaps neither of us will be soon." He said simply as he followed Maya who was following the rest as they went with the Venandi to the small picnic area.

Alvertos stood with Arley as they took in the new warriors along with the old. The Venandi stood at one side while Maya and her crew were in the middle and Kellan and his gang were at the opposite side as they sat on the picnic tables.

"Are we really going against the devil?" The woman Cale had knocked out back in the cave asked before the two Venandi could start. The disbelief could be heard in her voice, her long blonde hair swept across her arms as the wind picked up.

"If you do not believe, you will soon enough." Alvertos said calmly and the girl swallowed as the other gargoyles that had recently arrived made nervous movements.

"I wouldn't have believed it either if I wasn't there yesterday." Kira's voice echoed around the area. "I wish it was just a nightmare."

"It is one, only it's real life." Emily added as she sat down on top of the picnic table that Cale and Maya were at.

"It'll be worse than a nightmare if we don't stop them." Donato called from the group of Venandi and all of their heads shot to him. "We must plan and we must teach you how to unlock your abilities."

"How do you even know how to teach us?" Ari furrowed her brows. "You're not gargoyles."

Alvertos and Arley considered her for a moment. "We do not know but-" Alvertos turned to Donato who finished the sentence for him. "But God knows."

The area went silent at the absurdness of it all. Yes Lucifer was real, they had seen his power and his demons. If he was real, then so should God.

To Maya, even if he was real, he was doing his job poorly. She closed her eyes, poorly like how she had done her job. To protect, to save, and to be able to fight demons. She had failed at them all.

"They can't be that strong." Kellan's voice shot and Maya's eyes narrowed.

"They are." Arley shared in Maya's emotion.

"Eight gargoyles couldn't do anything to them?" A mousy haired gargoyle asked.

"I couldn't do anything." Maya's voice was low as she rolled a rock with her foot but her eyes flashed when she heard Kellan snort.

"Now to the problem at hand," Alvertos got their attention again. "Lucifer's goal is to destroy all of the holy places around the world." He crossed his arms and the muscle popped through the fabric. "This is just a guess, but we believe he is doing so to cause the collapse of people who worship God. With his will being destroyed, Lucifer's will be the one to take it's place. We believe he waited to do this now because he needed to build up enough energy to set his plan into motion. He has caused war and any other disaster that has befell on us. He thrives from calamity and it gives him strength."

"What happens after he destroys all of the holy places?" The man Maya had knocked out asked, he did a good job at hiding his fear.

"I'm not sure if that's the last of his plans, but I'm certain it will lead to the end of the world." For the first time, Alvertos sounded nervous.

"The hand of God will bring about the end of the world but will also save it." Donato shot in. "The hand of god will be the final nail to bring the end… we'll just have to find out what that is."

"Yeah cause I know it's not the Bible even though it's caused enough shit already." Kira groaned as she exaggerated her head falling onto the picnic table.

"Have you seen anything that tells you when they'll strike next?" Maya asked Donato quickly to ease the anger Kira had caused the Venandi as she dissed their religion.

"Tomorrow at the latest." He answered with an expression that made his eyes seem all the more unnatural. "And I have a feeling more demons are going to enter the fray."

"Will Lucifer fight himself?" Kellan pondered with a smile, he was obviously looking forward to a fight.

"He doesn't need to." Alvertos answered for Donato. "His demons are more than enough to handle what he wants to get done." His eyes flashed to Maya but they darted away. "He's not only in it for the outcome, he's also in it for the game. He won't fight until someone is worthy of his attention."

"He's saving himself for someone." Donato added.

Apprehension and fear could be felt in the air, and for the first time, Maya wondered why they were even going to try. There was no way they could stop Lucifer and his demons.

Maya thought of Lucifer's face and it made her feel something that she hadn't felt since she had gotten her memories back: *Dread*.

"Look at all of you." Kellan spat, his blonde eyebrows furrowed. "You look like you're getting ready for your own funerals."

"You didn't fight them." Arthur who sat beside Ari on the jungle gym said with an air of annoyance at his former subordinate. "If you're only here for a fight, I assure you you'll end up dead."

Kellan gave him a look filled with venom, "You're going to fight with the thought that you're going to die, fight with the intent that you're going to win!" He rounded on Maya. "I thought you of all people would agree."

"You didn't fight them." She repeated Arthur's words as she kept her eyes forward to avoid him.

"I've heard of your power, I've been told that you died and came back, you got both your power and memories back." He stepped in front of her now so she was forced to look at him. "Show me that power."

She blinked, "What's that going to do?"

His blue eyes set on her gray. "If the demons are as strong as you say they are, and even you, the strongest gargoyle can't fight them, I at least want a taste of what I'm dealing with." He backed away from her with his arms spread, tempting her to fight.

The others watched with wide eyes and Maya closed her own as she stood.

"You want a demonstration or you just wanna fight me?" She opened her eyes and they were now black and white.

Kellan grinned as the gargoyles that hadn't seen her mismatched eyes gasped.

"A little bit of both." He admitted as his eyes turned white. The same color she had four months ago before she had gotten her memories back.

"I'm not how I used to be." She warned him.

"I know." His smile widened as he backed further away so they'd be out of the way of the others.

No one stopped them, it would be a good lesson for the new fighters of the power the demons had and it also demonstrated the kind of power Maya had.

She was no longer Samantha Knight, the human nor was she Samantha Knight, the white eyed gargoyle. She was Samantha Knight and Maya Fletcher, the last name that her father had chosen for their family.

Though she was more Maya than Sam now.

"Well," Maya extended her arms at her sides like Kellan had. "Let's show you what you're dealing with." She fisted her right hand and went for him.

Kellan, thinking he was smart as he dodged her hit, walked right into her fist as she took a simple step in the direction he tried going. Their legs almost twisted together as she moved so fast that he had no time to dodge.

She used enough strength to knock him down but not enough to cause damage. Blood bursted from his nose as his ass collided with the ground. Maya growled as she stepped back and Kellan tried getting up with a blood soaked smile but Maya's fist collided with the ground and it rocked like a small earthquake and he lost his grip and fell back down.

She got the reaction she wanted out of him: His eyes were wide with shock that their power gap had grown that much.

"I'm holding back." She stated as she knelt in front of him. "I was holding back when I killed my own brothers." Her eyes fell. "And to be honest, I was holding back when I was fighting the demons." She swallowed as she turned to Arthur who had known her secret from the start. "I can't use the power that I used to have."

They all looked on with shock from the sudden news.

"Although I'm a full blooded gargoyle again, and my power is essentially back, my body is still modeled after a human. It can't contain my full power… If I use it, I'll die from the strain." She had found out after her fight with her brothers. She was weak for a few days afterwards and she had heart palpitations. She had gotten over it quickly because she didn't fully tap into her power, but if she had, she would certainly be dead.

She turned from her brother who she had told after it had happened. That's why he feared for their new enemies arrival, it meant that Maya would surely sacrifice herself to try to help the world.

She would do so without hesitation if it led to it.

"That's just a taste of the power that the demons have and we only fought two of them." She said as she got up. "We'll use the Venandi's help to learn how to fight them so we can unlock our instincts." She turned and was met with the shocked faces of everyone including her comrades who had become her close friends.

They looked like they had seen a ghost, she had kept her inability to use her full power from them after all.

She turned to Alvertos as she watched their shock turn to worry. "Shall we begin?"

Detective Deluca's shoes echoed down the long hallway. It was void of any color aside from white and the lights would cause anyone to squint. His son Reggie followed on his heels and his feet echoed along with his fathers. They were in a government building that had no name nor reason released to the public. It had been put into place eight months ago, it was a building designed to collect information against their enemies: The gargoyles.

Deluca and his son were on their way to meet a man that was far from a person he enjoyed being around.

He found himself wondering what kind of asinine thing the doctor would tell him today.

"You don't look excited, Detective." Reggie walked beside him now, his joke filled with nerves.

"I hate when they have me meet with him."

They as in the higher ups.

A scream echoed through a white door with a window in the middle of the hall and the men stopped dead in their tracks. This was where they kept the humans turned into gargoyles, and this was where the

Doctor did his experiments. The halls smelled of iodine soap from his *research*.

Deluca took in his sons sad eyes, he disagreed with what they were doing to them.

Who wouldn't? they didn't have a choice. They were kidnapped and changed into monsters.

"Let's go." He directed his son and they continued down the hall.

At the end of the hall stood a door much larger than the others and Deluca tapped on it with his fingers and a raspy voice called from the other side. "Come in."

With a creak, Deluca opened the door and was met with a room that was impossibly more white than the hall. There was a large wooden table in the middle with six chairs placed around it and a man was sitting at the table by himself, his eyes on a large screen in the corner of the room.

Clarke was a strange man and many weren't able to stay around him long without feeling uneasy. He was around the age of 70 and his grayed hairs made sure everyone knew so.

His mustache almost covered his mouth and it popped up as he acknowledged the father son duo as they entered the room.

"You've been called to see me?" His smile was barely noticeable under his graying mustache.

"Unfortunately so." Deluca admitted truthfully.

Clarke chuckled as he picked up a pair of glasses from a pile of papers that sat in front of him. He turned back to the screen and Deluca and Reggie looked with him. They had picked up surveillance from the square and on the screen was the girl they had seen just days before. Her brown hair was out of her face now to show that it was indeed Samantha Knight. From her back were gray wings the size of her body, her sharp teeth bared as she kneeled down and her eyes black and white.

"I've never seen that eye color mutation before." Clarke tapped his finger excitedly on the table while Deluca narrowed his eyes and Reggie held his breath at the sight of the girl on the screen.

"I've heard the stories of how the government used to work with the gargoyles until an *event* happened." Deluca got the doctors attention and he leaned his head against the back of the chair. His eyes rolled to the picture again as it changed. Now it was on a group of seven, the man standing at the front had white eyes while the rest had black. They seemed like they were looking at something with fear in their eyes.

Nothing else could be seen in the pictures.

"It's unfortunate that we didn't get it on video." Clarke pouted. "Of all the days for it to freeze."

"Why did you have us called here?" Deluca shot as he got tired of the doctors whining.

"Because~" The doctor sang. "It seems our gargoyle friends are back to their old ways and you need something to fight them with since you can't kill them with a good ol' bullet."

"What is it?" Reggie was the one to ask.

Clarkes smiled widened. "What are gargoyles made out of?"

That was quite the question. The one's on the screen? Flesh. The beings on and in front of buildings? Stone.

"How do you melt stone?" He asked suddenly and Deluca's eyes widened. "Hydrofluoric acid."

"Precisely." Clarke snapped his fingers. "It was how I killed the two that still wanted to work with us and it's how I would have killed the four that attacked our cities if I could have gotten to them."

"They're not stone though." Reggie stepped forward as he furrowed his brows.

"It dissolves their skin and blood cells to the point that they can't regenerate anymore."

Deluca turned to his son who didn't look too excited about the doctors discovery. He turned from his son's angered expression and glared at Clarke as he asked the question he knew his son was about to ask. "Are you using the acid on your *experiments*?"

Clarke simply looked at him with a brow in the air, "I would like to, but alas I cannot lose my precious research subjects…I know it works, no need to test."

Deluca felt his son stiffen beside him as he gritted his teeth.

Messed up motherfucker.

After a few moments of silence, Clarke spoke again. "That girl is the same one who attacked over 20 years ago."

"That's not possible." Deluca spat as he pointed at the screen as it went back to her. "That is Samantha Knight, the girl that was taken along with the others… she was human and even if she was the gargoyle that you speak of, she'd be over 40 years old."

He had seen the pictures of the gargoyle from over twenty years ago, he's seen the similarities between the two girls, but there was no way that they could be the same person.

"You're wrong, detective." Clarke said with an air of defiance.

"*What*?" Deluca took another step and the doctor smiled. "I know the gargoyles better than you, I worked with them after all." He pointed at the screen as the picture flipped again and Samantha Knight was back to her human form. "From the surveillance over 20 years ago-" He turned from the screen and flipped over a picture laying in front of him: In it stood the same girl, her hair the same color and it was pulled into the same braids. She was clad in a black trenchcoat and knee high boots, she was looking straight into the camera and they could make out the blood splatter on her face.

Her gray eyes were like daggers.

Deluca took in the picture that he had seen before as the doctor continued to talk. "The two gargoyles that survived after our partnership were fools, they thought we trusted them but who could ever trust a monster?" He chuckled and it sounded like fingers scratching a chalk board. "They told us how they didn't age past the age of twenty and they could only die by unnatural causes. If they did die, they would reincarnate." He smiled at the two and their shocked faces met his. "The two that lived were a couple and you know what that means-" He snorted. "They bred!"

Reggie didn't know why he felt offended that he spoke of the gargoyles as if they were livestock.

The doctor continued, "I have a reason to believe that the four that attacked the cities are their offspring…They attacked us because they wanted revenge for killing their parents." His smile widened. "That girl was killed somehow and reincarnated."

"That's not possible," Reggie spat. "There's no such thing as reincarnation and even it was, how in the hell did she get her memories back?"

Deluca placed a hand on his sons shoulder and he turned to his father with a sorry expression.

"Anything is possible, my dear boy." Clarke said as if he didn't feel threatened by the young man. "If you've seen half the things I have, then you would surely believe."

"What have you seen?" Deluca asked for his son.

"You will soon find out." Clarke swiped the picture from him. "I can't wait to see what my old friends produced." He said almost lovingly as he examined the picture of the girl. "She looks just like her mother."

With that Reggie had enough and turned to go, his father not bothering to stop him.

"Yeah," Reggie thought to himself as he gritted his teeth. *"So you can experiment on them."*

Chapter 40

On the side of a hill sat Lucifer, his bottomless eyes closed as he took in the cool air. Night was beginning to fall and with it the end of the day.

He had seen his old friend again, he had seen *his sweet Anna.*

He had been around since the beginning of time, his fall from heaven had not changed him much. If anything, he relished in being able to do what he wanted. He did however hate how God wanted power all to himself. Only God had the right to relish in his own power. Only God deserved the honor of being the strongest.

Lucifer wanted more, he felt he had every right to have the same love and glory that his brother had. God was selfish, he wanted the power all to himself.

He felt it to be his birthright.

Lucifer's punishment was to be cast onto earth.

That was God's mistake.

God was a fool.

The humans had been told for centuries that there was a heaven and a hell. You live your life without sin and you go to heaven. If you live your life with sin you go to hell to spend entirety in flames.

What a lie that was.

There was a heaven but there is no hell.

Yet.

Lucifer opened his eyes and smiled at the world around him: *This* was going to be his hell.

The clear blue sky would be as red as blood. The oceans pull as strong as a typhoon. The rain would be acid. The air so hot that one could barely breath. The screams of the humans as his demons tortured them filled his ears.

He pictured Anna's heart in his hand, her warm blood dripping through his fingers as her body laid at his feet, her gray eyes wide with shock.

A chill went up his spine at the memory: The look on her face as he killed her. The shock that filled her eyes, the noise she made as her lung's took their last breath of air. Her already pale face whitening further, her shoulder length wavy brown hair stuck to her blood soaked face as the liquid poured from her mouth.

She had certainly changed in both looks and mind but to Lucifer she was the same.

Two more lives meant nothing to him.

He knew she would come back after he killed her, and so she did.

The news of gargoyles killing innocent humans fell upon his ears many years after he had killed her. It was quite the turn of events, who would have thought that God's warriors would do the opposite of what they were made for. The gargoyles were a fallen species but he knew Anna was so much more, she was his promised opponent.

And yet she wasn't ready.

And so he found himself looking at the city in the distance during Anna's third life. This was his hell, his *soon* to be hell.

The humans had always thrown around the phrase that *living was hell*. Or that *they lived in hell*. Lucifer cocked his head, when he was done modeling this world in his image, they would wish they had never uttered such words. They would be thankful for the life they had.

Humans were weak in both body and mind, it allowed Lucifers influence to take over them so his plan could come into effect. He needed as much calamity and sin as he could take for earth to become his hell.

The time was coming, with every place that God had influence on being destroyed, and the faith the humans had in him being questioned, Lucifers will filled the world.

God knew of Lucifers plan and sent warriors down to stop him but they had all failed.

With each kill, Lucifer sent a message to his brother, a message that said that someone *holy* could never stop him.

No one could ever stop him.

He could only be stopped by God's own hands.

God sent Anna into the fray and she was different from the others.

A chill went through him and he gripped onto his knee as he laughed.

"This is our fate Anna!" He called to the woman though she wasn't near. He sensed her however, knew she wasn't far away and knew she felt the same pull he did.

"Master." Cain's even tone came from behind him and as Lucifer snapped his finger, the demon stepped beside him.

Cain was a quiet demon who had chosen not to fight on many occasions. Lucifer knew it was because this demon was like himself: He wanted someone worthy of him.

Cain wasn't always a demon, not in the way Azazel or the other demons had always been. He had been human, a human made by God, but he had been betrayed by the holy being.

His power was the best amongst Lucifer's demons, not for it's ferocity, but for it's use.

"What is it?" Lucifer asked his favorite demon.

"When will *we* attack again?" Cain's eyes were down as they always were and when Lucifer got up, they remained so.

"*We* as in Azazel and Abraxas?" Lucifer asked to be more precise and Cain nodded.

Lucifer looked into his bottomless eyes that matched his own.

"There will be more demons joining us this time." He faced forward again and his smile returned. "Yesterday was just a refresher for my dear friend, the Venandi showing up only added to the fun." He ran a pale hand through his favorite forms black hair. "This will be everything I wanted and more."

"How do you know she won't run?"

Lucifer would have gotten annoyed at the question if it was anyone aside from Cain.

"She won't run," Lucifer thought of her expression from the day before as she tried pushing past Azazel to get to him. The ferocity, the simple need to fight him. The want that filled her eyes was forever engraved in his mind along with the look she had when he had killed her. He had spent over 100 years with that look stamped into his mind.

"She desires me in more ways than one." He chuckled.

No matter the names she went by, she was still his *sweet Anna*.

Chapter 41

Maya sat down on the couch in Ari's cabin after their training with the Venandi. They had all made the decision to have a meeting with only the original group and Maya knew exactly where this was going.

It definitely wasn't going to be about the moves the Venandi had just taught them.

"Were you ever going to tell us?" The annoyance could be heard loud and clear in Ari's voice as she shut the door behind her and joined the others as they sat. Their eyes were on Maya but they glanced at Arthur who stood in the corner as they knew that he had known all along.

"I didn't want you to worry." Maya said gently, she was currently feeling a little weak from the power she had used to fight Kellan.

"Well you've certainly haven't made us do that before." Kira said sarcastically as she smiled crazily.

"If everything goes well, I won't have to-" She started but Emily interrupted her. "Promise you won't use your full power."

Maya met her tear filled eyes. "...That's not something I can promise." Her voice lingered as she moved her gaze to the others one by one until they landed on Cale who was looking at her with the same sad eyes he had when he had lost his father.

She swallowed and found salvation in the floral print on the carpet below.

"You've always made us promise to run if things went south and now I want you to promise us that you won't use your full power." Emily urged further and Maya brought her eyes to her again.

"You would rather the world come to an end? She didn't mean to sound annoyed but it came out that way. Her eyes shot to Arthur who she knew was enjoying being backed up by the others for the first time.

"You died once because you wanted to make up for what you've done…" The tears finally fell from Emily's dark eyes and Maya flinched. "You're the same as you were back then… you'll die to make things right and I hate it." She pounded a fist down on her knee as she gritted her teeth. "At this point I'd rather you die at the hands of another than your own." She chuckled but not because it was funny. "That sounds fucked up."

Maya hadn't necessarily died from her own hand the first time but Emily had a point: She had walked into deaths arms. She had wanted it.

"Promise us." Emily said again as she regained her composure. "Now."

Maya's breath hitched as she bowed her head. "…I promise."

Lies.

"Why does the power bother her but it doesn't bother us?" Kira asked through the tension, her eyes curious but nervous. "We're genetically human too."

"You don't have the power Maya does," Arthur answered. "You're genetically human but the amount of blood that I gave you and the power you have doesn't take a toll on your body."

His eyes twitched to Maya then back to Kira and the rest. "The blood given to you and the power you have equal each other out while Maya has too much power and not enough of a gargoyle base."

The room was silent until Ari spoke. "I'm glad that's over with since you don't need to dwell on something like that on your birthday."

Maya blinked and crinkled her forehead as she turned to Arthur who was obviously the culprit in telling them because she hadn't.

He rolled his eyes away from her and a small smile appeared on his lips.

"It's one of them." She said as she turned awkwardly back to the others. "My first lives, my birthday for this life is only a few days away."

It was still strange for them to hear her talk about her lives being separate. To them she was still Sam while she was Maya to Arthur and the Venandi. She had chosen Maya over Sam but she knew it was only in name.

Her chest felt cold as she thought of another name that she could have been called: *Anna.*

"Even though I would like to celebrate on the day your current body was born, I feel now is the best time." Ari shot up as the others watched her. "And I can't wait to give you your gift from all of us."

The sudden change from their previous conversation was bad enough but now not only was her birthday brought up but there was also a present.

"I…You…" She stammered. "You guys didn't need to get me anything."

"Don't worry, we didn't spend much." Cale assured her as he watched Ari reenter the room with black fabric folded over her hands and Maya gave her a confused look as she handed it to her.

The soft fabric felt familiar and before she unfolded it to see what it was, she looked up to meet everyones eyes as they waited to see her reaction.

She gave Arthur a knowing look then turned back to her present and unfolded it: It was her old trench coat, the one she had inherited from her mother. She had left it behind when she sacrificed herself in the explosion and later had Arthur hang onto it for her while she sorted herself out. It was only right that it was given to her again.

It was refurbished completely, where the bits of the explosion that she couldn't contain had seared it, it was now fresh and new.

The buttons that had fallen off were replaced with brand new silver ones and at the top where the collar was were two gargoyles on either side. Their mouths were opened in a growl, their eyes narrowed with rage.

She closed her eyes as tears began to fill them and she inhaled sharply, there was no longer any scent of the explosion nor of her mother.

She cleared her throat as she opened her eyes, she had managed to hold the tears back. "I don't know what to say… thank you."

She was met with relieved smiles. "Arthur gave it to me a few weeks ago and asked me fix it up so it can be given to you as a birthday present." She turned with a grin to him as he looked down as if he wasn't listening. "He suggested that we all pitch in ideas of what you would like so the gift would be from all of us."

"So sweet of him to include us." Kira gushed with a monotone.

"Thank you." Maya repeated as she caressed the side of one of the gargoyles faces, it was a nice touch.

"I have something else for you but this one you asked for." Ari turned again and she made her way to a pile of black clothes that she had on the windowsill. "I was only able to get us girls done because I had the material handy." She said as she picked them up and she handed one to Emily, Kira, and Maya.

Emily unfolded hers and from the back Maya could see that it was a shirt with a cut out that would reach to the bottom of their shoulder blades. She flipped it around to get a look at the back and Maya noticed that it had a floral design at the collar like the shirt she had borrowed from Ari the other night. She didn't know Ari had owned that many shirts with the design.

She brought her eyes to her own to see that it had the same design as the shirt she had borrowed the other night only it had different fabric, it was almost elastic.

"This was your idea?" Emily asked Maya and she looked up, not bothering to look at the back of her own shirt. "It was but I can tell Ari had fun with it." She grinned.

"You have no idea." Ari turned as if she was trying to hide something and Maya rose a brow.

"I'll get yours done later."Ari assured the guys.

"I don't need one." Arthur said as he watched Kira flip hers around. "If I don't want to rip my shirt, I'll just take it off."

"Same for me." Cale nodded. "Thanks though."

"In the chance I get them it's easier for me to have a ripped shirt since-" Dylan pointed at his chest. "You know."

They obviously knew, the men didn't need to worry about it as much as the girls.

"And I don't see mine coming anytime soon so it's fine." Trevor said lastly with a smile. "I just want to live through this." His smile turned upside down. "I want all of us to live through this."

As everyone fell silent, Maya's eyes fell to her coat and she rubbed her fingers along the fabric until she found one of the gargoyles heads. She looked into the eyes engraved in the silver then their teeth carved into points. It was almost laughable that the strongest gargoyle, the one that could help the most, couldn't use their full power.

She *could* use it of course but it would lead to her death. There was no telling the power would even be enough to stop Lucifer and his demons. She had to wait to use it, she made her promise but she'll certainly break it.

When the time was right, she would certainly use it.

She didn't fear death but she swallowed at the thought. She had died once already and she'd do it again.

She was a gargoyle, one of the supposed warriors of God, and even though she had her doubts, it was time she acted like one.

She wasn't going to fail this time.

A man in a white dress shirt walked to her, his face twisted with rage and his brown hair swayed in front of his venomous eyes. Her short hair fell into her eyes as the man leaned down and grabbed her by her brown locks. She screamed as he pulled the roots and slammed her head against the wall.

"YOU THINK YOU CAN FOOL ME?!" He roared. "YOU CRAZY WHORE!" He slammed her head into the wall again and again until blood poured from it.

"Anna!" A girls voice called for her and she opened her eyes as the man got distracted by the newcomer. She could barely see past the stars in her eyes but she could make out the outline of her friend in her white dress.

A dress a woman would wear in the 1800's.

Her eyes fell to her own dress and she blinked to keep herself awake as she fell to the ground when the man let her go. He made his way to her friend and she watched as his outline jumped onto her.

Her friends screams filled her ears along with the laughter of the man…

A pressure began to build in her eyes…

She was brought back to reality as she almost fell to the floor. Her chest felt like it was being stepped on as she took in what she had just seen…What she had just felt… What she had just heard.

Anna.

There was that name again.

Her teeth chattered as she thought of the vision. It was the next day and as she stood in front of the mirror, she had blacked out again. She clenched her eyes shut to avoid looking at herself, the shirt Ari made her had almost slipped out of her hands. She held tightly onto the dresser and curled the fabric around her fingers to steady herself.

Her breath shook as she forced herself to open her eyes to get a move on. The visions weren't going to consume her like they had the first time.

The situation was much more dire this time.

She pulled her T-shirt off and with her eyes closed again, she pulled on the shirt that Ari had graciously made for her.

It hugged her frame but stretched to accommodate her curves, the long sleeves reached down to her wrists and the vine like collar curled down to the top of her chest.

She blinked as she felt something wrong with the shirt. She was getting far too much air on her back where it should have been covered.

She flipped her arm around and felt for the fabric at the bottom of her back but she was met with skin instead. She turned on her heel and twisted her neck to the mirror so she could see what she dealing with and her jaw dropped: The cut out reached to the bottom of her back, just above her waist. She knew Ari had planned this as she took in the top which was being held up by the collar that was attached to the long sleeves.

Her face turned red as she flipped around so she was facing the mirror from the front again. With the look that consisted of black skinny jeans and the top, she really did look like she was wearing a battle suit. The only problem was the back.

She gritted her teeth as she stomped out of her room to the living room where she pulled the front door open.

"Arianna Amethyst Fay!" She hollered so loud that Ari would know that she was annoyed.

"I'm in trouble." Maya heard her from the playground and she could also hear Kira's snicker as Ari got up from the swing set and her footsteps grew closer until she came into view.

"What is this?" Maya asked with an edge to her tone.

"It's the shirt you wanted." She said simply as she stepped into the cabin and Maya shut the door behind her. "I didn't say that I wanted it cut to my ass." She whispered since she was sure the other gargoyles were listening. "You didn't do the others like mine." She looked at the much smaller cut out on Ari's back as she wore her own.

"Just wear your coat over it." She shrugged as she took in her handy work. "I like it to be honest, the side braids and your all black attire makes you look badass." She placed a cracker in her mouth that she had carried in with her. "I think the knee high boots will be a wicked touch as well." She added as she smacked on the salty crisp.

"Why?" Maya asked nervously as Ari licked the salt the cracker had left on her index finger.

"Have you seen your wing span?" She questioned with a brow in the air. "I wasn't sure how big of a cut out you needed, so I decided to do the whole thing."

"How am I supposed to fight in this?" Maya pulled onto the stretchy fabric and it slapped back into place, her face still as red as a tomato.

"Don't worry," Ari assured her as she watched her flinch. "I made it so it wouldn't fall out of place." Maya gave her a look and she snickered. "It's just your back, lighten up."

"I could smack you." Maya's threat held no promise.

"You could, but who would sew your clothes from now on?" Ari shrugged as she made her way back to the door and stepped outside.

A few minutes later Maya joined the rest at the playground with her newly refurbished trench coat hiding her revealing shirt. Whoever had seen the picture Arthur had carried around of her looked at her without blinking and the Venandi looked on with confused expressions.

"What?" Maya asked, confused with their reaction.

"You look exactly like you did back then."Arthur was the one to speak as he was the one who seemed the most fazed by her look.

"I thought I always looked like this." She shrugged.

"Not like *this*."

He was right, four braids hugged the right side of her scalp while the loose hair rested on the left. Her black skinny jeans, black knee high boots, and finally her mothers trenchcoat. She looked the exact same as she did when she would go out with her brothers and do the unimaginable.

But this wasn't like before, she was going to protect the people she had once sought to attack.

This look used to mean death and carnage, but now it was going to mean life and hope.

She had to tell herself that.

"It's different this time." She said as she turned to Donato, ready to change the subject. "Where do you think Lucifer and his demons will attack first?"

His clear eyes met hers, "Theres three places that I've seen: The Washington Monument, The Lincoln Memorial, and The Jefferson memorial."

"Why would they attack those places?" Cale asked with his brows drawing together in confusion. "How are they religious?"

"There's bible verses carved into the blocks." Alvertos answered. "Theres more places around here that are the same but I'm sure Lucifer will leave them to his lower ranked demons." He looked at the unlikely crowd around him. "He'll surely send his higher ranked demons to the most known places... and where he thinks we'll show ourselves."

They thought of the power Azazel and Abraxas had. The power that Lucifer had showed and the power that the demon Cain could be hiding.

The nerves started to set in for the group of gargoyles who had seen the demons and Lucifer first hand. Their fear was apparent on their faces as the other gargoyles watched with their jaws tight and the Venandi gave them looks of understanding.

"You simply have to remember what we taught you yesterday." Arley assured them. "Remember what we said: Go for the lower ranked demons for now."

"That's if there are lower ranked demons." Cale shook his head as he attempted to hide his nerves. "It was only Lucifer and his higher ranked demons last time."

"It's as we said, he wanted an introduction." Alvertos narrowed his eyes as he thought of the devil's game. "Now it's time to work."

"Well," Kellan piped in, though he had somewhat learned his lesson, he was still rearing to go. "Instead of fearing the unknown, let's get a move on."

They were standing under the pillars inside the Lincoln memorial since it gave them cover from prying eyes. Kira had suggested that Maya should wear a wig to better her disguise, so on their way to the monuments Kira ran into a halloween store and bought a long blonde wig. It reached to the bottom of her back and they were shocked at how well it fit.

They had split into teams: Some of Archie's gargoyles had gone off with some of the Venandi to the Washington monument. Archie had remained back at the cabins since he would be of no use in a fight. The other gargoyles and the remaining Venandi had gone to the Jefferson Memorial.

Maya and the rest of the gargoyles that had already faced the demons had decided to stay together and Arely, Alvertos, Arabella, Micheal, and Donato had elected to join them.

The seer came with them not because he was good at fighting, but due to his visions being of some help.

As tourists walked by to take a look at the 19 foot tall statue of Abraham Lincoln, they looked instead at the gargoyles and the Venandi as they stood together. The Venandi in their long white coats that hid their weapons and Maya with her long blonde wig and all black attire made them stand out like a sore thumb.

They were surprised people were still coming here after what had happened the other day but they supposed the government was keeping it quiet.

Maya's eyes wandered over the Bible verses that the Venandi had told them were etched into the monument. They spoke of God's will and power.

As Maya read the verses that happened to be over the family of tourists, she noticed them looking at her with judgemental faces.

"Oh my God!" Kira skipped to her comrades from where she and Ari stood at the wall opposite of them. "I love your costumes! Is there a halloween party tonight?"

Maya's lips twitched as she almost laughed at Kira's over exaggerated voice as it echoed through the pillars. She turned her head as Kira ran to Alvertos and he tried his best to act along as Arabella and Micheal snickered at their leaders horrible acting.

Cale had a grin on his face as he leaned on the pillar beside Maya, his arms crossed over his black shirt. Emily who was standing beside him had turned her head so no one could see her holding back her laughter. Dylan and Trevor had small smiles on their faces and even Arthur looked entertained even though his eyes still wandered in case there was any sign of the demons.

To make it even more convincing, Kira pulled a disposable camera from her pocket and asked for pictures of them. She took a few with the Venandi then she moved to Maya, Cale, and Emily who she forced to squeeze together.

Emily played along and rested her arm against Cale's back and Maya did the same as the two brought their arms around each other like Emily had. Maya's just above Emily's and Cale's arms rested on the girls shoulders. He looked lopsided since Maya was much taller than Emily.

The camera snapped and the flash went off at the same time as the tourists camera who were taking pictures of Lincoln's statue. Maya's eyes blurred from the light and everything froze as she picked up a familiar scent. Her smile wore off as she looked to the others and they had the same nervous expression as they too smelt the sweet but deadly scent.

Arthur shot from his pillar as Cale and Maya removed their arms and stood in the middle of the memorial. They twisted and turned so they could see the source until their eyes landed on Donato who started convulsing.

"THEY'RE HERE!" His words slurred as he yelled while Micheal and Arabella stood to protect him.

"Get out of here!" Ari screamed at the tourists and they gave her dirty looks.

"GET OUT!" Arthur roared and they ran from the monument with no hesitation.

Maya's breath hitched as she noticed a shadow behind one of the tourists that she supposed was the father of the group. She ran after him as she noticed it starting to swirl at his moving feet as he trotted down the stairs. She caught up to him and pushed him out of the way as Abraxas pulled himself from the shadow and instead of grabbing the man like he had planned, he grabbed Maya by the ankle that Azazel had already damaged.

He almost pulled her into the shadow but as he noticed it was her, he threw her down the stairs where she rolled down until she landed on one of the children. The boy shrieked as she pulled herself off of him.

"RUN!" She growled as she got up and her wig fell to the ground, revealing her brown hair.

"We got lucky!" Abraxas chuckled at her anger. "I was about to pull you down!"

His shadow blew past her as he aimed for the family again and she jumped in front of it.

"You'll have to kill me." She said as it stopped inches from her toes.

The demons smile widened as he turned to the others who were on their way to help her and he willed his shadow to get in their way and they were forced to stop.

"Don't worry," Azazel's voice rang out and they looked up to find him jumping from the top of the monument, his long white hair flying around him. He faced the group still in the monument with crazed eyes, "We brought you some friends to play with this time."

Glowing red eyes appeared from the darkness of the memorial and the dark masses had the outlines of humans as they stepped from the shadows. Maya had heard of shadow creatures from when she used to watch ghost shows but not in a million years did she think she would ever come face to face with not only one, but 70 as they finished stepping out and surrounded her comrades.

The hair on the back of her neck stood and she turned from the two demons and the shadow creatures as they approached her friends and she spotted him in the distance:

Lucifer.

He was standing on the other side of the large pool of water that the humans had placed in front of the memorial. Cain was standing beside him with his uninterested eyes on her as his master smiled.

"Good to see you again." He licked his lips as if she was a snack. "I knew you'd come."

Maya growled as she turned away from him, he wasn't going to fight, he was only there to watch. She had to focus on the demons in front of her, and as she brought her eyes to the two higher ranked demons, she saw the others start their battle with the shadow creatures.

She inhaled sharply as she unbuttoned her coat and let it fall from her shoulders, the gargoyle clasps clinking as they hit the concrete.

She heard a whistle from behind her and she knew it was Lucifer reacting to her backless outfit. She ignored him as the cells moved in the bumps on her shoulders and her wings sprouted until they were the length of her body.

Azazel cackled as his smile widened to the point of spreading across the entirety of his face.

Maya narrowed her eyes as she took one step forward… *only one.* She breathed as she shook her arms and hopped up and down.

"What are you doing?' Abraxas cocked his head as Azazel cackled on.

The nerves worked through her and her heart slowed, "Doing what I'm told." She answered as with a flap of her wings and a push of her legs, she flew past them.

As she thought, Abraxas was forced to move his shadow in fear of her getting sucked into it.

She was far too important after all, and with the demons being forced not to kill her, she was able to join the fray against the shadow creatures. The Venandi had told them to fight the lower class demons first and that's what she was going to do.

She landed beside Cale who fought with one of the creatures with his nails and teeth extended, his wings ripped through his shirt. His narrowed eyes were as dark as the being he was fighting. With each hit or swipe of his nails, the creature would disperse as if it were a gas then came back again as a solid and attacked.

Maya remembered their training with the Venandi as she fought her own shadow creature. They had warned them about the creatures but they never imagined them being like this. Alvertos had told them to strike when the creatures did, it was the only time they were solid.

But it wasn't that easy, the creatures moved fast and with the gargoyles inexperience, they found themselves unable to land a hit while the shadow demons did.

"Feel it in your veins!" The Venandi had yelled countless times as they trained the day before.

They had to *feel* the power. They had to believe in their reason for being made in the first place. They weren't creatures that were made to kill, they were guardians.

Maya had said so herself.

Training with the Venandi brought them back to when they were learning to control their transformations. They had to use their resolve as their reason for learning the transformation to make it work.

This was essentially the same.

Maya's shadow demon came back for it's attack as she and Cale were pushed from each other as more of the creatures began to appear around them.

It came to the point where not one of the thirteen fighters had less than five demons fighting them at once. The Venandi had five more creatures on them than the gargoyles as they fought together and they were taking down the creatures while the gargoyles couldn't.

Alvertos had explained that their swords were made of a mix of steel and silver, the blades were dipped in water that he had blessed, the hilts were made of meteorite. The holy water was enough for the demons to turn to dust as it ate away at their forms.

Maya's eyes darted to the higher ranked demons below and she was glad they were only watching. She knew they were enjoying the show.

Her attention returned to the demons she was fighting and instead of dodging the next hit, she turned away from the shadows as she noticed Cale facing her. His demon turning it's back to her. They were 15 feet apart but she knew it would be enough. She turned back to her own fight as a demon hit her arms that she had crossed over her chest. The hit sent her flying into the air and she flapped her wings to push herself back to Cale.

She reached her right arm out and he looked up from his fight with a grin as he grabbed her arm and spun her around. As he did so, she swiped at the demons that were attacking him and she managed to get them as they materialized.

They weren't like the higher ranked demons so destroying their hearts wasn't necessary.

That's if these things even had hearts.

The gargoyles didn't need holy water or a fancy blade to kill the creatures.

Like the Venandi had said: They were *made* to kill demons.

Cale flung her back to her own demons as the ones she had destroyed fell as dust to his feet. Maya's demons tried attacking her as she was about to land but they miscalculated and she killed them too. They were strong yes, but they clearly weren't bright. Their red eyes flickered off as they fell around her, leaving dust on her black boots.

"Freeze!" A familiar voice rang out as she turned to fight more demons but instead she was met with Deluca walking up the stairs along with fifty more officers including his son. Their guns were pointed at them and the shadow creatures.

Maya's eyes shot to where Lucifer and Cain had been standing but they were gone along with Azazel and Abraxas.

The officers froze as they laid their eyes on the creatures that the gargoyles and the Venandi were fighting.

"What the hell…?" They could hear one of the officers ask with a shaky breath.

Suddenly all of the shadow demons disappeared, leaving the gargoyles and the Venandi alone with the officers.

Maya met Deluca's eyes. "We're not doing what you think we are." She raised her hands to show them that she meant no harm and the others did the same aside from the Venandi and Arthur who looked for the demons.

"There's no way we can trust you." Deluca's deep voice echoed through the memorial as he took another step but raised a hand to make the other officers stand down.

"I don't deserve trust after what I've done, but we're not your enemies…not anymore." Maya swallowed, she couldn't let this turn into a fight but she wasn't going to wait for the demons to return either.

A nervous shuffle carried through her comrades to the officers and Maya's gaze moved to Deluca's son who flinched at her black and white eyes.

"*You're* our enemy." Deluca caught her attention and she turned back to him.

"She's right." A new voice echoed and Maya felt someone behind her and as she turned, she was met with a red haired woman with the same eyes as the demons.

"The gargoyles aren't your enemies." The newcomer smiled as Maya tried attacking her but she caught her hand in her palm. "*We are.*"

The shadow demons returned along with Azazel and Abraxas, surrounding Gargoyle, Venandi, and Officer alike.

Chapter 42

Gunshots filled the air but Abraxas' shadow rose from the ground and the bullets flew into it instead of the gargoyles and the demons where they were aimed.

A thump echoed through the memorial and as Maya pulled her hand from the female demon, she saw Dylan hit the ground. He hadn't been in Abraxas' perimeter and a bullet found him. His screams filled the air and Trevor dropped beside him to examine the wound: He was hit in the chest but no where vital so he should heal.

Wrong.

Instead of healing, the skin peeled away then caved into muscle, bone, and foam as the substance ate away at his flesh.

It only took a few seconds for him to die as his chest caved in on itself and he looked to have been split diagonally from his lower body. Trevor yelled for him as his blood began to pour down the steps. The others faces filled with shock at the scene and the demons watched with an air of entertainment.

Maya and Arthur had seen this type of death before: When their parents were killed.

The humans had put something in the bullets, something that could kill gargoyles.

Maya's jaw shook as she turned to the red haired demon and she was met with a sharp toothed smile.

"Was that your friend?" She chuckled and through her anger, Maya tried going for her heart as the gargoyles and the Venandi started to fight the shadow creatures. Azazel and Abraxas had joined they fray, the ladder using his shadow to keep the bullets away from the rest of the gargoyles.

He was protecting them…?

The officers tried relentlessly to get through the shadow and their forms could be seen through the dark haze as they attempted to do so.

They couldn't mourn Dylan, as much as they wanted to they couldn't. The loss of their friend didn't break their will to fight, it made them fight with the ferocity of what they were: Monsters.

If it weren't for the demons, Dylan would still be alive, if it weren't for the demons, they wouldn't have to fight at all.

Another ear shattering scream filled the air and they saw that Micheal had stopped fighting and Azazel had disappeared. The young man stood with his head bowed and none of the shadow creatures approached him.

"Micheal!" Arabella who was still protecting Donato screamed for him. They should have left Donato behind no matter what his use was. She couldn't help Micheal and as she met his eyes, they were the color of a demons: Black and red.

"NO!" She screeched and Micheal laughed, only it wasn't Micheal, it was Azazel.

"I'm your friend!" He said in Micheal's voice. "You won't kill me!"

Arely roared and pierced his sword through the man's heart with no hesitation and in doing so Azazel appeared in his own body again, watching with a grin as the body he had just possessed fell with a thud.

Micheal who had returned momentarily gasped for breath.

"T..thank…You." He said to his master with his last exhale and Arely locked his jaw as he picked up the dead man's sword and fought with it along with his own.

Tears fell from Arabella's eyes as she fought on, her sobs could be heard over Azazel's cackle as he dodged all of Arely's attacks.

Abraxas went for Arthur and Cale and the two looked like they were dancing as they dodged Abraxas' shadow until he stopped using his power and back flipped over the two men. He passed through his own shadow that was blocking the officers from coming in.

They shot at him but he didn't bother to dodge, the bullets flew through him and his tar-like blood fell from his wounds but they healed right away as they didn't get his heart.

His right arm blocked one of the bullets just before it hit his chest, his pink eyes filled with delight as the shaking officer nearest to him planted his feet. He licked his teeth as the black blood slid down his arm into his hand. He brought it to his mouth and licked his palm before balling it into a fist.

"*Burn.*" He demanded as he flicked the blood onto the officers face and the man screamed in agony while gripping at his burning scalp as his face caved in until only his skull remained.

He collapsed on the stairs with his body still intact and his blank eyes dissolved into their sockets. During his fun, Abraxas' shadow had shielded him from the pesky bullets that felt like bug bites to him. Many officers ran after seeing the devastating sight but Deluca, his son, and twenty others remained.

"Leave!" Deluca demanded his son but the young man shook his head as Abraxas went for another officer whose courage disappeared and he ran with a scream until the demons shadow caught him and it swallowed him whole.

Reggie watched the terror unfold but he didn't let the fear show on his face, only a drop of sweat fell from his brow. They didn't know what these creatures were but there was no way he was going to run and leave his father behind.

His eyes shot to Maya who had just been thrown to the bottom of the stairs by the red haired demon. She rolled into the large hole leading to the underground of the memorial and the red haired creature jumped in after her with a girlish laugh.

"I'm going after them, you stay here for back up." His father demanded as he watched the two women. His eyes wandered over his remaining officers, they were shooting the white haired creature but it's shadow was still protecting it.

Cale and Arthur jumped from the stairs and began fighting Abraxas to get him away from the officers. Arthur jumped in front of one of them before Abraxas could splatter his blood on the shaking man. It got on Arthur instead and he groaned from the pain as the blood began eating away at his face. He wiped it but it still continued to burn and he fell to his knees as his body tried to heal the wounds.

"Go to the water!" Cale directed him to go to the pool of water placed in front of the memorial as he pushed Abraxas away.

The father and son watched with shock as the gargoyles defended them but Deluca didn't wait anymore as he ran to where Maya and the female demon had gone.

"Stay!" He advised his son as he descended the stairs into the hole.

When Maya had fallen into the pit, she had rushed to her feet but before she could jump back to the others, the red haired demon had jumped in with her.

So instead she turned for the locked door behind her and kicked it in. She willed her wings back into her shoulder blades as she ran inside the tunnel-like underground. It was at least ten degrees cooler than it was outside and as she breathed, her breath came out as vapor.

It took a moment for her eyes to adjust to the dim lights that were placed overhead and through the light, she could make out the graffiti on the stone pillars: One of a donkey and another of woman who looked to be a flapper smoking a cigarette. At the end of the long tunnel was pitch black and she was thankful for the lights, though it could also be a curse since she could be seen easier.

Could demons see in the dark? She wasn't sure.

She wanted to hide behind one of the pillars but she knew the demon could smell her out. The smell of mold mixed in with the smell of the demons and there was also a constant echo as someone moved above. She hid behind one of the pillars anyway as she heard the demons footsteps echo through the tunnel.

"Hellooo." The demons smooth voice sang. "I was told you were a fighter but here you are, hiding from me."

Maya held her breath, she needed the element of surprise and she'd be lucky if she got it.

"I didn't think I'd be able to meet you since Lucifer sent me off with Aamon to deal with the monuments overseas." She explained as her feet echoed through the tunnel and with each step, Maya's heart leapt. "But I got my jobs done fast so I could get here to see you."

The demon stopped as the sound of water dripping filled her ears.

"Oh! Where are my manners?" She said after a moment. "I'm

Astaroth." She announced with a chuckle. "No need to tell me who you are… I've heard a lot about you, *Anna*."

Maya shuffled at the name and Astaroth snorted.

"Though I've been told you go by different names now." She began walking again. "Is it Maya or Samantha?"

She was only a few feet away now and Maya was about to jump from behind the pillar to attack when another set of feet echoed into the tunnel.

Astaroth's feet stopped moving and Maya froze.

Was it Arthur?

No.

Cale?

No.

Another demon?

Her breath hitched as she thought of fighting two demons at once but as she listened, she picked up on the steps. There was a slight limp that could have been caused by an old injury and she had noticed it before: The newcomer was Detective Deluca.

"A human?" Astaroth cocked her head and Deluca's gun clicked.

"Don't move."

The demons girlish cackle filled the tunnel and it even carried outside. "That won't hurt me human, it may kill a gargoyle but it won't kill a demon."

"*Demon*?" Deluca's voice shook. "I heard you could be real but you've been passed off as gargoyles… Maybe you're really a gargoyle trying to help your friends."

Maya heard a loud smack that bounced off the walls as the demon clapped her hands together. In her head she begged for the detective to leave, he was going to die because he was too hardheaded to do so.

"It's an insult to be compared to gargoyles," Astaroth snapped her fingers. "You seem new to the supernatural so maybe you don't know that the gargoyles used to work with the humans to fight us demons… I'm sure your government covered it up and that's the reason why they killed the last two gargoyles remaining from the alliance."

Maya's knees almost buckled as she heard the mention of her parents. After all this time she finally knew what they had done with the humans.

This truly was their higher purpose.

"I'm not going to say it again," Deluca threatened as he ignored the demons words. "Don't move."

"What are you going to do?" Astaroth growled but not from anger, it sounded like she was holding back a laugh.

A gun shot filled the air and Maya practically leapt out of her skin as she heard Deluca make a pained noise and it echoed as he was slammed into a wall.

She prepared herself to jump out but something told her to wait and her body shook as she held herself back.

Deluca began pulling himself up and a trail of blood ran down the side of his mouth.

He groaned as he got to his feet. "Y-you're a monster…" His voice echoed and the demon grinned. "Do you honestly think that I see that as a bad thing?" She recoiled back as she was about to land her finishing blow.

Right into Deluca's heart.

Maya jumped from behind her pillar and with the speed of her full power, she stepped in front of Deluca and took the hit for him. She bit her lip to hide the pained noise that rushed up her throat like vomit but her gasp from exerting too much power couldn't be held back and she paled as her heart thumped.

The attack had pierced through her shoulder, just above her heart. A groan finally escaped her lips as the pain reached all the way down her arm into her fingertips.

"You fool!" The demon squeaked. "I'm not supposed to kill you!"

A trail of blood dripped down the demons arm and it dropped onto the cool stone under them. Maya chuckled at the fear in the demons eyes, she hadn't expected to see any of them with that kind of expression.

"Demon skag." She spat, the pain in her shoulder didn't bother her as much as the power that she had used eating away at her insides. "What happens if you kill me?"

Deluca had fallen from the force the demon had used to plunge her nails into Maya's flesh and he crawled from behind the two monsters and watched with wide eyes as Maya grabbed ahold of the demons wrist so she couldn't remove her nails from her shoulder. In the next instant, she forced her head forward, a loud crack filling the underground as she head butted the demon.

Astaroth staggered backwards from the hit, bringing Maya with her, and they met each others eyes.

Black to black and white.

"What happens if you kill me?" Maya asked again with venom. "WHAT HAPPENS IF YOU KILL ME!?" She roared when she didn't get an answer and the demon tried stepping away but Maya's grip was too tight. "Will Lucifer kill you!?" Maya cocked her head as her heart raced, the power almost bringing her into insanity.

"Kill me!" She demanded. "KILL ME!" Her forehead was almost touching Astaroth's and she could feel her heart beating against her skin from the headbutt.

The demon's fearful expression changed to delight and Maya growled.

"This is the reason why Lucifer's so obsessed with you!" She caressed the side of Maya's cheek with the back of her cold fingers. "You're a fucking peach! You don't fear death!"

A roar from outside caught their attention and Astaroth gave her one last smile before removing her nails from her shoulder as Maya's grip loosened. "See you later…" The demon backed into the shadows and disappeared from sight.

Maya collapsed to her knees as her body could no longer remain standing. She inhaled sharply as she turned her head to the detective who was watching her with curious eyes.

"Get out of here." She demanded breathlessly and when he didn't move, she yelled. "Get out!"

She heaved from the air she had just exerted and she gripped at her side.

Deluca got to his feet, his face twisted with both shock and fear as he looked down at her. "Why should I?"

Her heart and breathing finally slowed but she was far too weak to stand. "Because something's about to happen and you don't need to be down here with me."

"…You're not leaving?" He asked.

"I can't." She said simply, she could hardly move after all. "Now go."

He watched her as he backed out of the door as if she was going to attack him if he turned around, but as he left from sight, she could hear his feet as he ran to the officers and his son.

She couldn't hear the battle above anymore and she was getting worried so she tried getting up. As she stood, she felt dizzy and found herself unable to move. Her body needed more time to heal.

A ear deafening crack rang from above her and her head shot up as the ground shook.

"Maya!" Arthur's voice called from outside the door until she saw him rushing through it with the others.

All of her friends and the Venandi jumped inside as another crash rang out and the sun shining through the door was blocked after the memorial fell in on itself.

They grouped together as the sounds of the memorial crashing down consumed their eardrums until it finally came to a stop after what felt like an eternity.

They were lucky the weight of the stone above didn't cave in the ceiling of the underground and as they opened their eyes, they realized they were blocked inside.

Arthur who had jumped over Maya to protect her in her weakened state got up and walked to where the door had been. There wasn't even room between the rocks for the sun to shine through.

"What happened out there?" She asked as she looked to Emily and Cale who had sat beside her. Their faces were covered in sweat, dust, and their own blood.

"Abraxas took the memorial down with his shadow." Cale swallowed. "We managed to get out of the way before he covered it with his shadow and when he removed it, the building started to crumble."

"He roared before he did it so he could warn the other demons." Arthur turned back to them and through the light of the lanterns, she could see burn marks on his face and they were already blistering. He saw the look in her eyes and turned away again. "I got demon blood on me."

Her mouth hung open as she took in the damage it had done.

"At least we know you won't dissolve like humans do." Alvertos said as he leaned against a wall and slid down to sit alongside the other Venandi. "But I'm sure if Abraxas had splattered more, you would have."

The gargoyles took in the scratches on the Venandi's faces, Arabella's face was soaked with tears and even now she choked back her sobs while Donato bowed his head. Arely who had killed his own comrade had his mouth set in a thin line.

They had lost Micheal like how the gargoyles had lost Dylan, and now that they were trapped inside the tunnel under the now destroyed memorial, the grief set in.

"Why did you have to kill him?" Kira's question to Arley would have been harsh if it wasn't a serious one.

Arely didn't meet her eyes as he explained, "Once someone is possessed by a demon, the hold can never be broken even if the demon leaves the hosts body." He flinched as he thought of Micheal's possession. "It's presence would always be there and it would bring the host's inner turmoils to the surface..." His jaw shook. "It would have been worse since it was Azazel who possessed him."

Arabella covered her eyes and a sob escaped her lips and to try calming her, Donato rested his head on her shoulder.

"I see the government has found a way to kill you." Alvertos changed the subject to the gargoyles.

"It was the same thing that killed our parents." Arthur stated as he leaned against his own wall. "Whoever found the way to do us in must be quite the bright person."

Maya started to get up but she felt woozy and as she tried to walk, she almost fell but caught herself.

"Did you tap into your power?" Emily asked roughly and Maya stopped moving. "I had to use it to save the detective, but don't worry, I made sure not to use too much of it."

"We saw the detective running out as we were running in." Ari told her and Maya perked up.

"Did he make it?" She asked as her heart jerked.

"His son ran to him and helped him away so I'm sure he did."

Relief filled her but dread quickly replaced the feeling "...And the demons?"

They had succeeded in destroying the memorial.

"We don't know." Alvertos was the one to answer. "But I know they're still out there and the other Venandi and gargoyles could be facing them now along with the humans."

Maya stepped to where the door used to be and rested her head on the cool rock. "We could get out of here now but I think we should wait to heal and rest up before going out." She turned and leaned her back against the rock. She couldn't fight right now, she would only get in the way. "None of us are in the shape to fight."

The other's agreed.

They weren't sure how much time had passed but they knew it had been more than an hour. Ari, Kira, and Trevor were leaning on each other as they slept after they had cried themselves into it over Dylan.

Arthur was sitting alone as he rested his face on the wall to cool his burns.

Maya's eyes found Arabella and Donato who had retreated to the far back of the tunnel. She made her way to them and knelt down.

Arabella looked at her with sad eyes. "When we left England I knew not all of us would make it but I guess I wasn't prepared enough."

"A week ago I had no idea who my enemies were," Maya leaned closer. "I bet you can imagine my surprise at finding out that my enemy is Lucifer."

Her eyes rolled to the blank stare on Donato's face.

"We failed in saving this monument, but we won't fail in avenging the people we lost." She wished she could believe her own words.

She placed her hand over Arabella's and squeezed, "Stay strong." She smiled gently as she got up and walked past Alvertos and Arley who were sleeping and Arthur who she noticed had fallen asleep as well.

She spotted Emily laying on the ground, her head resting on her shoe like a pillow. Beside her was Cale sitting with his knees to his chest, his arms resting on them as he leaned against the stone wall. Aside from Maya, he was the only gargoyle still awake. She stopped in front of him and his dark eyes met hers.

"Can I sit?" She asked and he patted the ground beside him as an answer.

She knelt down then turned as she leaned her naked back on the rock and a chill went up her spine. She thought of her coat and hoped it didn't get lost under the rubble.

"This is familiar." Cale spoke and she turned to him.

It really did feel familiar, it was like the time they were locked in the cave together when Arthur was their enemy and the demons and Lucifer were the least of their worries.

"You were panicking from the storm so Emily and I sat with you."

Maya smiled, her fingers twisting together. "It feels like it was so long ago." She breathed. "Centuries even."

Cale rested his head against the wall. "Even when you were scared to death, you still wanted to make sure that Emily and I were comfortable." She could hear the smile in his voice and she thought about her offer to him about resting his head on her shoulder.

They had been awkward with each other at that time, but now there was nothing but trust.

"The offer still stands." She assured him. "Like how I'm always here if you need me."

"I know." He admitted. "I don't see much of a future anymore but you keep on going and I look up to you for that but you also scare the hell out of me."

She turned to face him and their eyes met. "Why?" She asked softly.

"Because you're willing to give up everything if it means making up for what you've done. You can't use your power but I know one day you'll have to."

"I've already died once." She said simply as she dropped her eyes.

"And you're ok if you do again?" He asked and she flinched.

She didn't fear death, not at all. She walked into his arms willingly but something pulled her away. If the being was real, he surely hated the gargoyles for their immortality and reincarnation. Especially Maya who seemingly reincarnated two times already.

Outside of her thoughts, she pulled her back from the wall as the rock started to irritate her.

"I can see why you got mad at Ari." He chuckled as she rubbed the marks the rock had left on her back.

"She's a wiseass." She smiled as she pulled her hands away from her back and this time she leaned where the fabric was over her skin. Her arm touched Cale's and the heat that formed between them was welcome against their cold skin.

"We have a fight waiting for us when we get out of here." She said as she watched his arm fall between them so they could share more warmth.

"...Yeah." He agreed as she rested her head on his shoulder and his head rested on top of her braids.

Maya could smell the soap he used against his shirt and the cool smell soothed her nerves as she closed her eyes. Cale could smell her berry shampoo in her hair and it reminded him of a warm sunny day.

Even with being trapped in an underground tunnel, unbeknownst to them what could be going on above them, they fell asleep as they appreciated their final peaceful moment.

Chapter 43

They picked rock after rock from the opening, some the size of boulders, and when Cale pushed the largest out of the way, the sun shined on them. They were able to climb the rest of the rocks to get out. It was easier to see their wounds in the sun and although Arthur's had healed, there were pink scars where Abraxas' blood had splattered on his face.

The wound Astaroth had made on Maya's shoulder was still trying to heal and she knew it would leave a scar as nasty as the one Azazel had left on her heel.

"Maya." Arabella called and Maya turned to see her pointing at her trenchcoat where it had been neatly folded and placed on one of the pillars that had fallen.

Maya stepped to it and rested her hand upon the fabric before she picked it up. She knew right away who had left it there for her: Lucifer.

Her hand tingled as if he was still holding it.

"We have to help the others." Alvertos stated as she pulled her coat from the ground, they could hear his bones cracking as he moved, his fights from hours ago still took their toll on him.

They hadn't healed much but they couldn't hide under the rubble forever.

They took in what was once the Lincoln memorial: It looked like it was never there aside from the lower half of Abrahams body that remained where it had been while the upper half laid on the ground beside it. Under the rubble laid their comrades bodies along with the officers. Maya forced her gaze from it and looked around for any sign of the demons or the police that still lived.

Maybe they were gone or she thought so at least until she saw Abraxas' shadow wrapped into a barrier around the perimeter in the distance.

They were still here.

"The Washington Monument is closer so we should go there first." They looked to Arley who had spoken then to the pointed monument that was still standing.

It's mismatched stone stood in the sunlight, it's pointed top hidden by the suns glare. They took in the height and Maya remembered her days as Sam in school, how she had learned that the monument was made with two different stones since the original ran out. She never thought that one day she would defend it and she never thought she would see the Lincoln memorial fall.

They had failed at this monument but they had to save the other two.

She didn't understand at first why the demons hadn't taken down the remaining two while they were underground but on second thought, she understood completely why they hadn't: They were waiting for her.

"How are we going to fight in that?" Ari stopped beside Maya as her deep blue eyes gazed at it, they were slightly squinted from the sun after being in the dim light of the tunnel for so long.

"Anyway we can." Cale said as he walked past them and they followed.

It was suspiciously silent as they approached the monument and even with their hearing the gargoyles couldn't make out anything odd. If Maya remembered correctly, this was the place that Kellan and his group had gone to. They could smell the demons in the air and they knew they were being watched from afar.

Why were they waiting? Their prey had brought themselves to the mercy of their attackers but the beasts had yet to arrive.

"We have to split up." Alvertos looked over the large pool of water that laid between the two monuments.

"How should we split up boss?" Kira asked as her eyes twitched back and forth anxiously.

"I'm not leaving my sister." Arthur stated and the rest of the gargoyles looked at her as if splitting from her would be the most terrible thing.

They didn't trust her after all, at any moment she could use her full power and sacrifice herself. They didn't have worry about that though, something told her now wasn't the time.

"We'll go to the Jefferson monument." Arley meant *we'll* as in the Venandi. "I have confidence you'll be able to handle it here."

They nodded to the Venandi in agreement.

"Good luck!" Arabella called as she ran with her hand on Donato's back.

They turned from the four Venandi when they were at the middle of the pool of water.

"We need to split as well," Maya flipped her eyes between them. "Few of us out here and a few inside." She looked at the door that led into the monument. "I think those of us who have wings should go inside while the others stay out here in case we need to jump out." She turned to Arthur. "But you need to stay out here and help them."

She wasn't surprised when he shook his head. "You're not going without me."

She gave him an annoyed look and gripped his shoulders. "I promise you that I won't use my power…I *promise*."

"It's a good thing I'm here." Kellan walked into view from behind a tree and he looked the worst they had ever seen him. "You're right," He let out a shaky sigh. "The demons are strong." His eyes darted to the monument. "Especially the one who calls himself Azazel."

"What happened!?" Arthur asked as they met with him.

"We heard the commotion at the memorial you guys were at and we were about to help you when the shadow creatures attacked us. Before we knew it, your memorial went down and the higher ranked demons joined in." His eyes met Maya's. "The sun's going down and I have a feeling that's what they've been waiting for." He gritted his teeth. "The demon that controls shadows needs a power boost from using it so much earlier, he's going to use the setting sun to his advantage."

"And that means the shadow creatures are going to be stronger too." Trevor added and Kellan nodded.

"I've been knocked out over there for I don't know how long," he pointed at a line of trees where he came from. "But before I lost it, I saw some officers going inside along with our Venandi."

Maya swallowed, "How many?"

"Five officers, five Venandi, and I don't know where the other gargoyles went."

Maya pondered what they were going to do and when she came up with a plan, she knew it was going to be hard to get by the others, especially Arthur.

"Kellan and I will go inside while you guys stay out here so the shadow demons don't come in."

"We can't split up." Cale was the one to speak first and she met his gaze. "We're not going to, we'll be in the monument and if things go south, I'll jump… I swear."

"Only lies come out of your mouth." Arthur spat.

"Don't worry boss." Kellan wrapped an arm around Maya's shoulder. "I'll push her out of a window if I need to."

Maya glared at Kellan as they stepped into the monument but she quickly set to the task at hand. She was thankful the others had let her go along with her plan, but as she looked inside the monument, she wondered why they were even trying to fight in there.

The lights weren't on and she knew they wouldn't work even if they found a switch, maybe it was for the best as she spotted the bodies of tourists laying on the floor. She closed her eyes and her heart fell.

"You've seen this sight before, lets go." Kellan grabbed her arm and pulled her to the stairs since the elevator didn't work. She pulled her arm out of his grip and he almost fell backwards. "You're pretty good at failing as of late." He said as he steadied himself. "It was your monument that fell first."

"Fuck off."

Her Sam was showing.

"Theres the girl I know." He snickered then froze along with Maya who also heard the commotion outside. They ran to one of the windows placed in the stairway to see their comrades surrounded by the shadow creatures.

Kellan and Trevor were right about the sunset strengthening the creatures: They had darkened so much that they were no longer see through and their eyes glowed brighter than before.

The gargoyles below had their teeth bared and their eyes were their respective colors.

As if the shadow creatures knew Maya and Kellan were watching, several turned and met them standing in the window. Maya's heart lurched as they disappeared and she knew they were on their way.

A yell from upstairs made their heads shoot upwards but in the next moment, the shadow creatures were around them.

"You go on ahead, I've got them." Kellan said as he attacked the one standing in Maya's way.

She ran with no hesitation but she felt a lump in her throat at the thought of leaving him behind. They've never gotten along but that's just who she was. She felt even worse that the others were fighting below without her help.

After what felt like 20 flights of stairs, she came to a stop at one of the small rooms that the tourists could look out of. She found several officers and tourists dead with their eyes staring blankly at her inside. Upon taking another step, she noticed that some of her own kind were amongst the dead: The man and woman Cale and she had attacked back in the cave.

Their fingers were intertwined as they took their final breaths.

She clicked her tongue in frustration as she continued up the stairs but it didn't take long for her to find the culprit behind all the death: Up another flight stood Abraxas, his pale form glowing as the sun's orange light shined on him through a window on the flat. His shadow extended onto the flight of stairs behind him as he waited for her.

"I could smell you from a mile away." He smiled and she noticed blood on his pointed teeth.

Human blood.

As she stepped onto the flat with him, her eyes flew to the corner where Deluca laid shaking on the ground, blood pouring from his mouth. His son laid unconscious on the other side of him.

"I was just having some fun." Abraxas stepped in front of them as Deluca's eyes met Maya's.

"What did you do, you bastard?" She growled as her fist's shook.

He cocked his head as he licked his blood soaked teeth, "You see *Anna*," he said the name with an air of seduction. "I have a *hobby* as you humans call it."

He leaned to the detective who tried crawling away but the demon grabbed ahold of one of his teeth as his foot smashed onto the man's leg to hold him in place.

"I love torturing people." He declared as he pulled the tooth from Deluca's mouth and the man screamed with agony.

Maya rushed to the demon as anger swelled in her chest and the demon backed away from the detective.

Maya knelt and checked on the detectives wounds but as he met her eyes, he shook his head. "My son…"

Her eyes wandered to the young man and she listened for a heartbeat, she sighed with relief at the thumping in his chest and she turned back to Deluca and nodded.

Relief filled his face for only a second as he looked past Maya to the demon who had caused their injuries. Maya turned to face Abraxas and her eyes narrowed as his hand fell to his inner thigh as if he was going to pleasure himself.

"I wonder what it would be like to torture you..." His voice wandered as excitement filled his tone. Maya didn't know how demon anatomy worked, but as she watched above his hand, she could tell that thinking about her torture filled him with pleasure. "It's too bad Lucifer won't let us do anything to you..."

"What does he want with me?" She questioned as she got to her feet, her eyes shooting backwards to Deluca.

She had saved him once already and now he laid dying after being tortured by a demon. Abraxas' pink eyes lit up as he saw the sadness on her face. "Don't worry, you'll find out soon."

Maya felt a tug on her boot as she started forward to fight the demon and she turned to Deluca again. "Save...my...son."

Her eyes fell to his son and her face fell further.

"I'm going to save you both." She assured him.

"I'm not letting you do that." The demon chuckled as his shadow extended.

"*Watch me.*" She mouthed as she stared at the window.

She wasn't going to use her wings for this, she didn't need to, they'd just be in the way.

She pushed her feet against the ground and the demon grinned as he prepared for her worthless attack. But instead of going for the demon, she twisted her body and grabbed ahold of Deluca's son by the collar of his shirt. She dragged his body with ease to the window but the demon stood in her way. Her eyes changed and a desperate breath escaped her mouth before a roar crawled up her throat. The window shattered at the ear deafening noise and as the demon tried blocking her, she threw the man's unconscious body from the now broken window. If her roar wasn't enough to signal her comrades, she yelled. "CATCH HIM!"

In a rage, Abraxas grabbed the back of her head and smashed it against the stone windowsill. Through the stars in her eyes, she saw Arthur with his wings extended as he caught Deluca's son in midair. The others watched with shocked expressions as they fought the shadow creatures. Their eyes moved from the injured man in Arthur's arms to the window he had been thrown from but before they could see her, Abraxas picked her up by the back of her neck and threw her against the wall next to Deluca, his weakening eyes meeting her's.

She nodded to let him know that his son was safe and his dark orbs filled with relief once again.

"I wasn't done playing with that." The demon growled as he knelt in front of her, his pink eyes narrowed into pink slits. "I'll make sure you provide me with a replacement."

"Play with yourself." She snarled.

He cackled in reply as his eyes darted to Deluca who was desperately trying to get up. The demon got to his feet and backed away from the two as Maya helped the detective.

"We'll play a game." He said as the shadow extended around his feet. "I'm going to give you one minute." He brought his index finger to the air. "If neither of you are out in that time frame, I will destroy this place with you in it." His shadow began running along the wall until the end of it went out of sight as it twisted up and down the staircase. He stepped into his shadow and as he sank down, a smug look appeared on his face. "By the way," He licked the bloody finger he was still holding up, his tone smooth like white wine. "The minute already started."

Before the demon was even gone, Maya grabbed ahold of Deluca and began pulling him to the window. A trail of blood at his dragging feet as it poured for his mouth.

She wheezed and she started to feel dizzy as the power she had used to break the window slowed her down, each time she used it, the more it deteriorated her body.

Her breath hitched as the two of them fell to the ground.

"Gar..goy..le." Deluca mumbled against the ground until he found the strength to pull himself up. "Save… yourself."

"No." She said roughly as she grabbed him by his shoulders and continued to pull.

She had never cursed her body as much as she did now and she swore as her arms gave out and he fell from them again, but this time he caught himself on her shoulders.

"You're different than before… Samantha Knight." He placed a shaking hand on the side of her face. "…Miss Fletcher."

She felt like she was going to be sick as she collapsed backwards onto the windowsill.

"Tell my son…what you did…you have to kill… the demons…"

"Tell him yourself!" She yelled as she pulled him with her.

"I won't." He smiled at her desperate expression. "Tell-" he choked on his own blood. "Tell him…I love him."

Those were the detectives last words as the flat turned pitch black and he pushed her from the window. She screamed for him as her hand reached out but it was too late, the shadow had consumed him.

She bit her lip to the point of drawing blood as her wings erupted from her back and she smoothed her landing as a loud crack filled the air. She watched as the two stones that held the monument together split then cracked into millions of pieces as it fell.

"Sam!" Cale and Emily ran to her and helped her get away from the monument's falling debris.

The ground shook as they joined the others, Kellan was amongst them and the shadow creatures were gone. Kellan had likely ran out when he saw the shadow wrapping around the wall. Arthur had Deluca's son thrown over his shoulder and he met his sisters eyes as another crack filled the air.

They turned on their heels and watched as the Venandi and the gargoyles that had been stationed at the Jefferson memorial ran from it as it came crashing down along with the Washington Monument. The two groups ran beside the body of water to meet in the middle. Alvertos and Arely's eyes were filled with anger while the others were filled with fear.

As they were about to meet, they were blocked by Abraxas, Astaroth, Azazel, and finally Lucifer with Cain in tow as they stepped from Abraxas' shadow.

The devil smirked at the sight of the broken crew, his dark waves blowing out of his bottomless eyes as they landed on Maya.

"Checkmate, *Anna*." His silky voice was filled with satisfaction and in the next second he and his demons disappeared back into Abraxas' shadow.

The sun had gone down by the time they got to their cars. They were silent as the feeling of being completely and utterly defeated filled them. They had left Deluca's son on the edge of the battle zone where someone could get to him quickly. The demons were gone for now, more officers would be there soon. Reginald Deluca Jr. was the lone survivor of the humans who had remained behind. The demons powers were truly a force to be reckoned with, a power that sent fear into the gargoyles souls.

Fear was inevitable with an enemy like this.

Like last time, they walked through the garden of bodies that the demons had left behind.

With each new corpse Maya's heart fell further into her chest until it felt like it was in her stomach.

* * *

They had lost again.

She had lost again.

She thought of Deluca who was now dead, it was her fault, everything was.

Aside from Alvertos, Arley, Arabella, and Donato, only seven Venandi remained from the group they had brought with them from England. One of the survivors told them how Azazel had taunted them about the other Venandi who protected the monuments across the world.

How they were all killed.

Alvertos said they could call on more but how many more did they have?

Maya had elected to drive and as she took ahold of the steering wheel, her knuckles turned white as she gripped tightly in frustration. The bright lights of the Venandi's SUV filled their car as they followed them back to the camp. They had parked far away from the monuments so their cars blended in with the others that drove down the dark roads.

The drive was silent for the time it took to get back and the silence continued as they made their way to their cabins.

The moon was the only thing that lit their paths.

Chapter 44

Hopelessness was the same as dread in many ways but with the two emotions being separate, it was clear the gargoyles and the Venandi were currently feeling both. The loss of Dylan had hit the gargoyles like a rock, their comrade that had been with them since the very beginning died in such an agonizing way. He suffered before he died and death was the only release for him at that point. They had lost some of the other gargoyles and only five remained from Arthur's old guard including Kellan.

Archie had stitched up and treated the Venandi's wounds while the gargoyles allowed their healing abilities do it's job.

Maya leaned her head against the chain holding the swing she was currently sitting in at the playground, her mind had been on Deluca's sacrifice since the night before and she didn't have a second of sleep. He had told her to tell his son that she had saved him, that he loved him.

Her lip trembled as she rubbed her head on the cool chain and it clinked as she swung a bit. She placed her hands on the chains and gripped hard until they dug into her skin.

Deluca's son should be awake by now, he would also know of his fathers demise.

She had failed.

She failed in saving the detective due to her bodies weakness, she had also failed in saving the monuments.

She had failed in protecting everything.

"I will not fail." She whispered to herself.

"I know."

Oh how she wished that she could find the source of the voice so she could strangle him.

"We can sit around and think about our failures all day but we need to plan what we're going to do next." Arley said finally in their fifth silent minute since they had met at the playground.

The gargoyles eyes met the Venandi's where they sat together at a picnic table. The blonde haired girl, the older man, and some of the younger Venandi had lived to see another day.

"How many more of you can you get to come?" Archie asked as he sat down beside Arthur at their own table.

"The Venandi come from all over the world but when I called upon them before all of this began, only 20% of them heeded my call." Alvertos explained. "... The ones I stationed at the other monuments have been killed."

"So zero?" Kira's glossed over eyes rolled to them as she leaned her chin on the table where she sat with Ari and Trevor.

"I know of forty that can help us." Alvertos assured her and she snorted. "Only forty? The end of the world is sure to happen with those numbers! All we need now is the hand of God to fuck everything up."

Maya's eyes moved to Donato who didn't react to Kira's words about the hand.

"I can get a call out to the full blooded gargoyles that I'm in contact with." Arthur bowed his head. "But there's only 10 of them and I'm not sure if they'll want to fight." He lifted his head and his hazel eyes met his comrades, the marks that had yet to heal on his face shined against the sunlight.

"You'd think they would since their chummy lives would be destroyed by the end of the world." Ari spat as her eyes narrowed.

The swing beside Maya creaked and their eyes went to Emily who swung back and forth.

"It's worth a try." She told Arthur with a sullen tone and he nodded with his mouth in a thin line. Now more than ever, he regretted bringing them into this.

"Tell my son…what you did…." Deluca's voice echoed in Maya's ears as if the man was still alive.

Arley's fist colliding with his table woke her from her thoughts and she practically jumped, whilst most of the others actually did.

"If Lucifer wanted us dead, we would be rotting in the dirt right now." He spat. "He's playing with us, we're not enough for him to take seriously."

"We need more people to help us…" for the first time, Alvertos' thick accent fell as the severity of their situation worsened. "But I don't know if even that will be enough." His eyes roamed to Maya and her heart thumped as she guessed what he was thinking.

He wished she could use her power… She knew he was thinking it because she wished for the same thing.

"Tell my son…what you did…"

She coughed as she choked on her own saliva, she knew what she had to do but it was as Alvertos had said: More warriors might not be enough. Her mouth felt cold as she made sure to meet the eyes of her comrades. "We need the humans help."

She was met with silence then disbelief.

"Did you see how they were slaughtered?" Arley furrowed his brows as he looked at her like she was insane. She certainly did feel crazy for suggesting it but she had her reasons.

"Did you see how their bullets damaged Abraxas?" She questioned as she let go of the chains and leaned forward, the bar above creaking from her weight. "If they had managed to get his heart, he would have been done for."

"What ever substance was in those bullets can kill us but I don't think that's what hurt Abraxas." Cale who was sitting on the other side of Maya added as realization hit him. "I saw one of the bullets on the ground covered in Abraxas' blood…there was steam coming off of it and underneath-" His eyes met Maya's. "Silver."

When one would think of silver being used on the supernatural, they would think of werewolves, maybe even vampires. They looked to the Venandi for validation.

"Silver has been used in exorcisms for centuries, even our weapons are made with some of it's material."

"That proves we need their help." Trevor stood as the news hit him.

"But how are we going to get them to join us?" Kellan asked realistically. "As we all know, this one and her brothers made sure a long time ago that they could never trust us." He pointed at Maya and she hid her hurt under a glare.

"Watch your mouth." Arthur warned him with a snarl and Kellen grinned.

"You too, you kidnapped these innocent humans and changed them into your kind, there's no way they'll ever trust us and-"

"I'll go talk to them." Maya interrupted.

"Theres no way in hell I'm letting you do that." Arthur didn't even think about it. "You know what they're capable of, they killed our parents… or did you forget?"

"I'll never forget." Her eyes narrowed. "But I need to push that aside and deal with the real problem and that's Lucifer."

"I agree with your brother on this one." Cale shot in and her eyes fell as she turned to him.

"You're too important to be the one to go." Alvertos agreed. "We'll deal with the demons with what we can get of Venandi and gargoyles." He stood. "I'm going to make the calls."

Maya's eyes fell to her cupped hands, her idea had been rejected.

When she looked up again, she was met with Arthur who was watching her with narrowed eyes and she nodded that she agreed.

She dropped her eyes to her knee high boots and her hand wandered to the gargoyle clasp on her coat. She ran her fingers on the smooth metal and as her eyes found Donato, she realized he was looking at her. Not really *looking* at her, but she knew he could see something.

"Tell my son…What you did…"

Donato's eyes left her's and she understood what she had to do, she was going to talk to the detectives son. In doing so she was going to put herself in a great amount of danger, but she was willing to make the sacrifice.

She bit her lip to hide her smile, an insane one.

What was another sacrifice on her behalf?

She had done it before.

She waited until she was sure the others were asleep that night and she gently closed her cabin door behind her and with her hearing, she listened to the even breathing of the others as they slept. She had to be quick before any of them woke up but she knew there was one that was already waiting for her: Donato.

The demons had given them a day of rest but they could attack again at any moment.

"Checkmate, Anna." Lucifer's voice sent a chill up her spine, the look in his eyes as he spoke to her was cemented into her memory.

He wouldn't do anything without her being there and she wasn't sure how, but she had a feeling that he knew what she was going to do.

He was keeping her alive for something and it was for more than his own enjoyment.

She walked up the two stairs that led to Donato's cabin and without a knock, she opened the door and stepped in. He was sitting on the couch with his blank eyes on the fire place.

"No one heard you?" He asked softly as his blank eyes landed on her.

"No." She shook her head as if he could see her doing so.

She was surprised none of the Venandi stayed with him due to his condition but she was thankful for it. "You know what I'm going to do, don't you?" She asked as she sat beside him.

"Of course I do," He placed his gaze on the hearth over the fire place. "I don't need to see to know."

"And you're okay with it?"

"You're going to give yourself to the people who killed your parents and caused you to go into a downward spiral." He shrugged. "I'm neither okay with you going nor am I against it." His words were harder to make out as his accent thickened the more he spoke.

He turned to her at the sound of the couch creaking as she moved.

"What you're about to do is extremely dangerous considering what happened to your parents." His clear eyes bored into her. "You must be determined to see Lucifer defeated."

"I'm not doing it because I'm a supposed warrior of God…" her voice drifted as her eyes caught a candle flicker on the window sill.

"You want to make up for what you've done." Donato finished for her and her eyes fell to her lap where her fingers twisted together.

"Dying once wasn't enough for you?" He asked emotionlessly and her jaw shook.

That's if she had died only once, there was the possibility that she had lived and died before she was born as Maya.

She didn't answer him as she was consumed with her thoughts but when the quiet began to be too much, she finally spoke.

"If it's so dangerous, why are you letting me go? Have you seen something?"

His gaze dropped slightly, "The only thing that I can see are hints of our future and that the hand of God will bring about the end of the world…but will also save it." He leaned his head back and looked up at the ceiling. "Our lord has told me that much."

Donato's premonitions would have annoyed her if she didn't have her own. She inhaled sharply as she prepared herself to ask a more than inconsiderate question.

"Why did your father blind you?" She regretted it as soon as the words poured out of her mouth but he didn't look offended.

"My father was an abusive man." His frown deepened as he blinked. "He would beat my mother for the simple reason that a meal was cooked wrong."

For the first time, Maya was able to hear sadness in his tone as the emotion filled him.

"My mother left and never came back…I don't blame her, but not too long after, I started getting visions of Lucifer. How he tempted Eve, how he was the cause of every bad thing that fell on the human race since the beginning of time." He smiled gently but it wasn't from happiness. "I was ten and was stupid enough to bring my visions to my fathers attention." He closed his eyes. "He blinded me with antifreeze so I wouldn't be able to see them anymore, so I wouldn't be insane like my mother."

For the first time in four months, Maya did the nervous tick that she had as Sam. Her hand fell from her forehead to her chin where it remained for a moment.

How could anyone do that to their own child? How could anyone do anything like that to another person in general?

The last question only reminded her of how much of a hypocrite she was.

She had done terrible things in a different way.

"H-How did you get away?" She asked shakily as she dropped her hand from her chin.

"Alvertos found me," Donato looked straight forward. "After my father blinded me, I was sent to live in foster care… People heard the reason why my father did what he had but they thought he was the crazy one. Alvertos heard the stories and he adopted me so I could join the Venandi." He sighed. "The Venandi have been killing demons for hundreds of years, they come from all over the world but the sector with Alvertos is the main branch." He turned to her again. "His and Arley's ancestors have been the leaders of the Venandi since the very beginning… They know demons aren't merely the creatures they have been made out to be in religion, they know Lucifer resides in hell but not the hell the humans have learned about, *This* is Lucifers hell."

"This is?" Maya remembered what Lucifer had said about it being hell on earth.

"Have you ever heard anyone say that this world is hell?" Donato asked calmly.

She did and in many occasions, she had been the one to say it.

"That's his plan, this will be his hell since there is no other. He can't have heaven nor God's position so he's going to make the world he was banished to his own. God has known about this since Lucifer's fall from heaven and he made the gargoyles to fight his demons… He also made the Venandi to do the same and to help the gargoyles in their efforts."

Maya inhaled sharply. "Why do you think he made you a seer?"

"God works in mysterious ways." He said simply. "Maybe he sent me to help you."

Maya shook her head. "Did God find it necessary to have you blinded for your ability?"

He didn't answer.

She had never believed in God and now it was like she was forced to do so due to Lucifer's existence. People acted like God was a powerful being that could control the way one's life could go. She gritted her teeth at the thought. If that was so, then why did people die of disease? Of cancer? How could he have designed bodies to turn on themselves? Why did he allow murder? War? Famine? He was powerful, but he couldn't handle Lucifer himself so he sent others down to earth to do so. In reality it was his fault that Lucifer was running wild on earth. He had banished him here instead of dealing with him properly.

Another question came to mind: Why did he allow her to kill innocent people for her worthless revenge?

"He's going to know what you're doing." Donato woke her from her thoughts and she looked at him, his clear eyes were on her again.

He meant Lucifer of course, she and Lucifer were connected in some odd way and she knew even though she had always been told that gargoyles only reincarnated once, that she was Anna.

In some shape or form, she was the woman Lucifer had known.

"I know…" Her voice broke. "He can't leave *Anna* alone."

"I have yet to see anything on why he calls you that name." Donato assured her.

"You don't have to," She said as she got up. "You and I both know that we'll find out soon."

She made her way to the door and rested her hand on the handle.

"Tell them what I'm doing and that I'm sorry." She swallowed as she turned to him. "Tell them to wait and to trust me."

Donato nodded silently as his unseeing eyes found the fireplace again.

As she was about to leave, his voice stopped her. "Be careful." He warned. "If something happens to you, this will all be for naught."

"Of course." She thought to herself as she walked into the darkness outside, the chirping of the crickets her only salvation.

Reginald Deluca Jr. sat alone at the table in the room where he and his father had met with the man he liked to call the *Mad scientist*. His head throbbed but his heart hurt more. He was the only survivor of the squad that had gone to stop the gargoyles but instead they were met with more than that: Creatures who called themselves demons.

As he sat with his eyes swollen from the tears he had shed from the loss of his father, he thought of how Clarke had said that they would find out why they had worked with the gargoyles.

With all of the grief that filled him, he still remained where he needed to be. Where he could make a difference. He had been transferred months prior to his fathers team, they were a team whose purpose was to hunt gargoyles, to find out what they could do about them. The creatures had killed countless people over twenty years ago but before they had committed their terrible crimes, they had worked with the humans to fight demons.

Demons…

Even now the thought terrified Reggie, the thought of the gargoyles alone were enough to make a man lose his mind but he had faced the demons now. To him they were more frightening than even the gargoyles.

He ran his hands over short hair and squeezed his fingers against his scalp, the hair prickling his skin. He remembered his father being tortured by the demon with pink eyes and short white hair. How he had tried saving his father only to be knocked out, but before he had lost consciousness, he had seen the female gargoyle as she ran up the stairs of the Washington monument. Her eyes were filled with anger as they landed on the demon and they widened as she saw him and his father. He had lost it after that but even now he felt the air rushing past him as if he was falling.

His father died and he didn't know how, he could have died by the hands of the demon or he could have been killed by the gargoyle.

No, the gargoyle didn't do it… the demon did.

In just one day Reggie's life had been shattered, similar to how the three monuments had fallen.

How the monuments around the world had fallen.

All places related to religion… to God.

What were the demons planning?

He exhaled sharply at the thought of the beings that one would hear about on ghost shows and folklore. He had heard of shadow creatures when his friends had talked about their experiences in wooded areas. Reggie never thought he would see not only one, but over seventy. He thought of how the creatures were fighting the gargoyles and how the gargoyles fought the more monstrous demons. It was clear the creatures were enemies.

The door opened and Reggie dropped his hands from his head as Clarke and the director walked in. The man was as old as Clarke but he looked much more welcoming. His silver hair that had usually been slicked back was a mess and it rested against his dark scalp. His suit was disheveled and his dark eyes had large bags under them.

"I'm sorry about your father." He said as he rested his hand on Reggie's shoulder. "He was an outstanding man."

"Thank you, sir." Reggie nodded slightly as the two men sat at the table with him.

Clarke had found a seat beside him and he found himself rolling away from the man.

"I've been told everything you reported." The director tapped his fingers on the table. "I didn't think it would ever come to this."

"You knew the entire time." Reggie couldn't hide the annoyance in his voice. "That there were more than just gargoyles out there."

"We thought the demons were dealt with." The director removed his hands from the table. "The gargoyles of that time helped us make sure of that."

"And you betrayed them."

Reggie had to watch his tongue but there was much more on his mind than offending the old men. "Don't you wish you didn't do it now? Instead of killing the ones you worked with and experimenting on the gargoyles we have now, we should-" he stopped himself before saying anything else.

"I understand your anger young man, your father and the rest of the people that we lost were great fighters." Clarkes voice only annoyed Reggie further, especially this early in the morning.

On the screen above where it played the surveillance camera at the front of the building the time read 6:00 am.

"You will be pleased to know that we are placing you in charge of the group we have just trained, most of them you know from your own classes." The director leaned forward and intertwined his wrinkling fingers.

The new trainees had already told Reggie of their promotion but half of them had left after hearing what had happened at the monuments. Who remained were mostly the people who had been training for the gargoyles their whole lives.

It was no longer just the gargoyles, they had a new enemy: The demons.

They were new to Reggie at least.

The newcomers were loyal to Reggie's father and now that he was dead, their loyalty went to Reggie. The other groups would treat him and his newbies as pawns when the time came. They were the people who had fought with the gargoyles over 40 years ago only to betray them.

Reggie's eyes fell to the black polished gun that laid on the table in front of him and beside it was a case of the hydrochloric acid bullets.

"We have our ways to get rid of both creatures." Clarke smiled his nasty smile. "That's why I've been working so tirelessly with the gargoyles that we have."

Bullshit, he was just having *fun* with them.

"Sir." A woman's voice came over the radio in the directors pocket. *"We have a problem up front."*

Their heads shot to the screen and at the camera stood the female gargoyle known as Samantha Knight. She had ditched her all black attire and wore a lilac shirt and jeans while her knee high boots were replaced with sneakers. She would have looked like an average woman if they didn't know what she truly was. Her long wavy brown hair wasn't braided to the side of her head and it blew in the morning breeze, her eyes were sharp as they stared forward.

Reggie's eyes widened as the director shot to his feet and ran from the room. Reggie continued to watch the screen with a lump in his throat as the guards pushed her roughly to the ground and put her wrists in handcuffs.

It was stupid really, it was obvious the restraints wouldn't work but she didn't break them, she didn't even fight back.

What would she gain from doing this? Why wasn't she fighting back?

Reggie's eyes moved from the screen as the guards pulled her from the camera and they landed on Clarke whose eyes smiled along with his mouth, an excited chuckle escaping through his yellow teeth.

Chapter 45

Cain was a quiet demon, perhaps too quiet. Who could ever know what the creature was thinking? What he was going to do? He was no average demon, he didn't relish in the kill like the others, he didn't jump on the chance to torture and maim.

But he was the strongest.

As he walked up the incline of the hillside that the demons resided on, his mind was blank. His bottomless eyes laid on each blade of grass that he crushed as he walked. The other demons were behind him, now joined by Aamon. They knew better than to talk to Cain, they had tried taunting him one time, had said that he was weak for not using his powers. That's when the other demons got a taste of Cain's power, a power even they couldn't break out of.

They never bothered him again.

He stepped over the first body, it was a man around the age of 30 and Cain looked to the man's chest: There was a fist sized hole between his ribcage and his heart was gone.

The other demons laughed and gawked at the body, even poked at it like it was some strange object. Cain continued onwards and with each step there was another body always the same as the last: A hole in their chest, their heart gone.

Finally he was met with Lucifer who was surrounded by 20 more bodies. The Devil's foot was on a shaking girl as she tried throwing him off. She laid flat on her back and her legs attempted to push him off but she failed, Lucifer's strength was too much for her. Cain took in the girls looks: She had brown hair that reached the top of her ears, it laid more to the left than to the right, her narrowed eyes were hazel. Cain recognized her valiant expression, it was similar to the look Lucifer's sweet Anna had when she tried going for the devil after she had met him for the first time in this life. Cain knew why Lucifer played with this girl more than he had with the others: She looked just like Samantha Knight…like Maya fletcher.

His fascination with Anna transcended lifetimes.

"Let me go!" She growled but fear could still be heard in her voice as she twisted her head to the dead that laid beside her, her defiant facade was beginning to break.

"...Please." She began to beg as she looked into Lucifer's obsidian eyes that held no emotion.

It was like he was bored.

"Please don't kill me!" Her voice cracked as he leaned forward and placed a finger just above her breasts and trailed it over her heart.

"PLEASE!" Desperation filled her voice but in the next second a pained gasp escaped her lips and the air leaked from her lungs as Lucifer forced his hand through her chest and wrapped his fingers around her heart. The artery continued to beat even after the girl lost consciousness, it tickled against Lucifer's palm as he pulled it from her chest. The tubes attached to it flung blood onto the girls face as they broke.

Lucifer stepped off his last victim and sat down on a stump as the heart came to a stop in his hand and after looking at it for a moment, he brought his attention to his demons.

A smile appeared on his lips. "It'll never be as good as it was with her." Disappointment mixed with his typical silky tone. "They can never get the look right... they act tough in the beginning but they always end up begging... *she* never did."

"The girl has gone to the humans." Aamon's rasp filled the hillside and Lucifer's dark eyes rolled to him. "Why do you tell me as if I don't know? I know what she's planning as I know that she will not allow herself to die until she faces me." He chuckled with a gleaming smile. "She's broken out of an institution before, she can do it again."

Cain's eyes wandered to the city miles away, where the black and white eyed gargoyle currently was.

"We haven't done anything in days..." Azazel whined. Unlike Cain, Azazel was a demon that thrived off of carnage.

"Patience." Lucifer said smoothly. "You'll get to play with the gargoyles again soon."

Cain's eyes moved back to his master as Lucifer brought his attention to him.

"You'll get to play soon..." Lucifer's voice drifted as his grin turned into a full on smile. "You'll get to play with your master's favorite toy."

The human's base was a secret building disguised as a medical supply building. Maya had found the place by following a police car and after she lost them, she used her senses to pick up the scents of the gargoyles that were imprisoned there. It was hard as she picked up another smell that resonated in the building.

She found herself locked in a cell that was void of any color other than white. She had allowed them to take her, had let them pull her into the building that smelled of sanitizing soap. She had even allowed them to cuff her even though she didn't understand why since she could break them in a second.

The cell was placed deep in the building along with twenty more. They ran on both sides of the hall on the other side of a white door with a window and Maya was placed in the first cell to the left as one would walk in. She didn't see the other prisoners but she could hear them, the sounds were familiar, she had heard them in the cave Arthur had locked them in.

So this was where they had been locked up?

Where they were being tortured.

This was where she was going to experience what they had and she had willingly brought herself into this situation.

The guards had thrown her in there and they hadn't been back in hours, hours that she could have broken out not only herself but the other gargoyles as well.

But she wasn't there for that, she had another objective: Deluca's son.

The room had a small bed and a toilet along with a sink, the gargoyles were held in by a clear glass-like substance at the front and even though it looked weak, the substance would have no problem keeping in a gargoyle that had no control over their power.

As Maya sat on the cold floor, the saline type soap filled her nose and made her feel sick. A deep inhale made her eyes water as they moved to the cell across from her where one of the gargoyles laid under the covers on their bed, they had been there since she arrived.

"Hello?" Her voice echoed through the air holes in the glass and the gargoyle flinched. "It's okay." She assured them. "I'm one of you."

The person got up and she was met with a scrawny boy, his hair dirty blonde and it reached his shoulders, he also had a mustache and beard combo. He was wearing a white jumpsuit over his scrawny form. His blue eyes were dull and there were bags as purple as grapes under them. They lit up at the sight of her and Maya rose a brow as he recognized her as the girl who had saved him and the rest back when Arthur was still their enemy.

"Y-you're the girl that spat in that gargoyles face…the one that saved us." His voice cracked at every word from it's lack of use before now. "I-I came in with you that day."

She blinked as she remembered the boy that had begged as they were being dragged up the mountainside to Arthur's lair.

The boy's mouth turned into a small smile, "You can get us out of here… None of us know how to use our powers but I think you might be strong enough."

He had no idea how strong she was, the bad thing was that he had no idea that she had joined their enemy. Had found things out about herself and was fighting against beings more terrifying than any gargoyle.

"I will when the time is right." She assured him and his face fell. "Why not now? Why are you here?"

"To get the help of some of these humans."

The boys face contorted into a judgmental look, "No one here will join you, I've heard them talk about *demons* but they must be talking about us… they experiment on us, feed us twice a day, and-"

"The demons are a separate entity." She interrupted him. "And beating them is worth everything I'm about to go through."

The boy shook his head, "No… you need to get us out of here now…" His teeth began to chatter. "The doctor-"

He was cut short as the door opened and in stepped the seven guards who had thrown her in her cell and an older man with a determined look on his face as he kept his hands in his suit pockets. Another man stepped in who had a lab coat on that covered his stocky build. His mustache practically covered his mouth but Maya could tell that he was smiling at the sight of her.

She found the gargoyles eyes across from her and she knew this man was the doctor he was talking about. She would have to be wary of him.

Something caught her eye and she flung her head back to the entrance as Deluca's son stepped inside, his tired eyes meeting hers and she frowned.

He had just lost his father. The man she had failed to save.

"Hello, gargoyle." The first old man said with a rough voice, he was a tired looking man, his dark skin beginning to wrinkle. "I know the other gargoyles that were kidnapped are working with you but you're here alone, why?"

She didn't answer.

The man shook his head, he knew he wasn't going to get her to speak, knew she wasn't like the rest.

"You know this young man I'm guessing?" He said as he turned his attention to Deluca's son. "This is Reginald Deluca Jr. You are acquainted with his now late father as I've been told."

Her heart thumped at the mention of him being called *late* and his son locked his jaw at the word.

"You don't need to worry about my name." The old man shrugged. "But I'm sure you'll like to know the name of this man beside me." He turned his attention to the grinning man in the lab coat and Maya followed, her eyes narrowing.

"This is Clarke, you will be spending a lot of time with him."

Clarkes smile widened so much that she could see the whole thing under his mustache and Reggie's eyes flipped uneasily to him.

Maya got to her feet and the cuffs clinked against her wrists as she walked to the clear screen holding her in, coming face to face with Clarke. She pulled against the cuffs and they broke apart instantly. They all jumped aside from Reggie who watched with a locked jaw and Clarke who leaned his head against the glass and made an excited noise as he did so. "Nice to meet you, Samantha Knight."

She nodded with a defiant look.

Seconds after she allowed herself to be pulled out of the cell, the guards were anxious as they did so since they clearly feared her.

They brought her to a room that was as white as the rest of the place with a hospital bed in the middle. There were tools along the white cabinets and on the other side of the room Maya noticed there was a large window that she knew was a viewing room.

She could see the director, a bunch of other man, a few women, and Reggie as they sat in the chairs placed as if they were in a concert venue. The hospital room was the stage and Maya was the entertainment.

She didn't show any fear as the doctor told the guards to force her to the bed where they strapped her arms and legs down. It was funny how much force they used to push her down while she acted like a rag doll and let her limbs go limp.

The straps were triple wrapped with a strong leather and after they were done adjusting them to her wrists and ankles, they wrapped chains that were attached to the floor around them for good measure. She continued not to fight, she had to deal with this in order to talk to Deluca's son, *Reggie* as she had decided to call him.

She brought her gaze to the doctor as the guards left the room and as she met his eyes, her pulse quickened. He leaned down so he was only inches from her face. "You look just like your mother." His raspy voice made her limbs pull against the restraints.

She looked just like her mother? He had to be talking about her mother who had given birth to her in this life, maybe he had spoken to her.

He shook his head as if he knew what she was thinking. "I love the look on your face, I'm talking about your past lives mother... *Layla.*" He sang her mothers name and her eyes widened.

"How do you know my mother?" She asked roughly and the doctor chuckled.

"You even sound like her." He closed his eyes. "Ah, it's been a long time since I've heard Layla's voice but looking at you now, it's as if she's been reborn." He pressed a wrinkling finger to her forehead. "You're just as reckless as your parents for coming here willingly."

She leaned into his face as he removed his finger and their foreheads almost touched, "Answer my question." She growled.

His breath smelt like antifreeze mixed with cleaning solution and she had to fight not to recoil.

He smiled then pulled away from her and she watched as he circled her as if he was a lion testing his prey. Her mind flashed to when Arthur had done the same thing when he had changed her back into a gargoyle.

"Your parents and I go way back... they and many other gargoyles worked with us to fight against our common enemy... *The demons.*"

She watched as he removed a machine from a drawer and he placed it on a stand with wheels then rolled it to her.

She had always known that her parents had worked with the humans but they had never told her why. Now she knew they were protecting their children from the truth but in reality they had made them unprepared.

"The director at that time treated the gargoyles like friends, he had used them but cared for them. Your father and mother met each other fighting the demons with us. Your mother couldn't control her power since she was the only white eyed gargoyle left after the demons had killed the rest... she had no way to learn how to control her power." He pulled out two rods that were attached to the machine. "Only a fool would be blind to the relationship your parents were forming and when all was said and done and the demons were out of the way, the two ran off together and bred."

He turned to her so fast that she almost flinched. "The gargoyles that you killed with, were they your brothers?" Her silence was a yes to him. "Where are they now?"

"They're dead." She said simply and she purposely left Arthur out so they wouldn't go looking for him. She wondered how Clarke knew that they could reincarnate but she didn't think too much of it since he likely had heard it straight from a gargoyles mouth. The gargoyles only knew they reincarnated because of the feeling that filled them and the proof of their reincarnated comrades.

Maya wondered why they reincarnated and had no memory of their past lives but she had reattained her's.

"That's too bad." The doctors face fell slightly. "You must be devastated to have reincarnated with your memory intact and your family ripped from you."

She held no sadness for her brothers, she felt nothing when she had witnessed Eli being killed by Azazel and the doctor didn't know that she had killed two herself.

What a monster she was.

"There were surveillance cameras where you and your siblings attacked." He said as he turned back to his machine. "Their eyes were white like your mother's and yours," He wheeled the machine the rest of the way to her and stopped it beside her head. "Are a mixture of your mother's and father's, why?"

Why indeed.

There was no known reason why she had the mutation, God had supposedly made her that way but why only her?

"I want to see them." The doctor woke her from her thoughts and her eyes widened when she realized what the machine was.

The thing was silver with many wires coming from it, a nob caught her eye with three different levels: The lowest green, medium was yellow, and the highest was red.

He was going to electrocute her.

The doctor picked up the rods and turned on the machine and as it started, a buzz rang around the room, causing Maya to flinch. She fought against the restraints for the first time but she had to stop herself. She turned to the viewing room and her eyes met Reggies, he looked like he was about to be sick and she swallowed as she looked away, he wasn't the only one.

She wasn't weak, what was a little electricity compared to having her body ripped apart?

No fear.

She felt no fear.

She couldn't fear.

Her mind was going haywire and her hands began to shake.

"Don't fear. Don't fear. Don't fear. Don't-" She thought frantically to herself but Clarke interrupted.

"Don't worry about your teeth, beautiful." The doctor touched the two rods together and a spark came out.

Maya flinched at the noise and her heart raced to the point of hurting, her ribs the only thing holding the erratic organ in.

"I've done plenty of experiments… they'll grow back." He finished then pushed the prods to her temples.

If it wasn't a padded bed, she surely would have smashed the back of her head in. The shock touched her brain's every cell and it felt like the organ was going to explode. She growled from the pain as her teeth chattered until she gritted them so hard that blood began to pour from her gums.

The doctor's laugh filled her ears and her changed eyes found him as he blocked her view of the ceiling.

"Look at them!" He exclaimed at the sight of her mismatched eyes and he pushed her head over so the people in the viewing room could see. "The perfect combination of her mother and father!" He gleamed as he pulled his head away.

With her heart pounding in her ears, Maya watched as he turned the dile up to the highest setting and she couldn't hide her pain anymore as a scream escaped her mouth as the power hit her stronger than before. As she felt the shock surge though her every cell, she thought of Lucifer:

His devilish smile that looked so human and his charcoal eyes as they laid on her.

Her teeth began to chip as she pressed them together in an attempt to ease the pain. Her limbs pounded against the bed and the chains and straps holding her down began to tear. She could break them but couldn't let herself.

She had to take the pain, she needed to talk to Deluca's son…she needed his help.

As another volt hit her brain, her vision blanked and the flash of gold that she had seen in her dreams filled her eyes instead. A gasp escaped her lips as she chewed on her now bleeding lip, the sound of the doctors laughter dulling as her ears rang.

Another flash appeared and it panned out so she could get a look at the gold object:

It was a treasure chest of sorts, it's brilliant color shining against the sun and long rods of the same color were attached to either side. On top were two winged beings facing each other as if in prayer. There were four men dressed in white cloaks keeping the gold chest in the air by the rods. There were others walking alongside them as the desert sky darkened and a roll of thunder filled Maya's ears. The tan skinned people looked around nervously and started talking in a language she didn't understand.

As more electricity hit her from the machine, a bolt of lighting came down and struck a man who was holding the chest. He fell violently to the ground as his body became a crisp. The screams of the people around him echoed through the desert as the other men who had been carrying the chest fell as the electricity surged through them as well.

The electricity stopped and Maya fell back to the bed but even with it gone, there was a still a buzz in her aching brain. Her nerves screamed as a constant tingle surged through her aching limbs.

What did she just see?

"You handled that a lot better than the others." Clarke's voice crept up beside her and he leaned his chin on the bed, his eyes wandering to the scar that peaked through her shirt.

"What's this?" He picked up her shirt slightly to get a better look as her chest heaved up and down as she tried to catch her breath. The scar was in the shape of three claws, the middle claw had gone deeper than the others. The skin that had grown back was a deep shade of pink.

The adrenaline was wearing off and her gums were starting to ache, she had to spit blood from her mouth to prevent from choking on it.

"There's only one way to leave a scar on a gargoyle-" Clarke looked up from the scar that Astaroth had caused and looked to the people in the viewing room and Maya's eyes twitched to follow his gaze.

"The nails of their own kind or a demon."

Most of the people in the room looked like they were enjoying her pain while there was a small amount that looked sick from the sight of the suffering girl and Reggie was one of them.

Her eyes were still wide from the pain and the vision she had. She shook from the electricity plus she could feel herself fighting to not break out of her restraints… to not kill the man beside her and every person in the viewing room.

Why was she feeling bloodlust like this?

She could have simply punched the doctor in the chest and that would've been enough to rupture every vital organ in the area, she also saw herself ripping out his throat. The thought gave her great pleasure.

She felt like she was going to be sick as she realized what she was thinking, she wasn't who she used to be, she wasn't…

Was she?

She forced herself to ease against the bed as the doctor rounded on her again, "Look at those pretty white teeth all broken up, give it the rest of the day and they'll be back to normal." He smiled as he rolled the machine away with a push of his hand. She could hear the clank of it hitting something but the doctor only had eyes for her.

"Don't worry, I won't be using that for the rest of the day so your pearly whites can heal." He leaned beside her again and whispered in her ear. "Why are you here? Why would you willingly subject yourself to this?"

Her eyes rolled to the ceiling as she ignored him.

She had to stop herself from spitting the blood that poured from her mouth in his face. It didn't get her far when she had done it with Arthur. Maybe the doctor would like it, he seemed the type.

"Are you still looking for revenge? I know that's the reason why you killed all those innocent people."

Her heart lurched as more blood dripped from her aching mouth and when she spoke, her voice was hoarse and air whistled between her broken teeth. "I'm finishing what my parents started."

No, what the *demons* started.

"Now," the doctor smiled as he turned to rummage through one of the drawers and he brought out a scalpel. It's edge shined in the florescent light as he twisted it between his index and middle fingers. "Let's see how well you hold up compared to the other gargoyles."

She wasn't sure how long she had been tortured by the doctor but it had felt like days. The minutes felt like hours as he cut into the skin on her arms, legs, and stomach. He never cut too deep, he knew how far he could go before the gargoyles couldn't take anymore, he wouldn't take that risk with Maya.

She was far too valuable of a subject.

She leaned her tired body against the back wall of her cell and closed her eyes after the guards had brought her back. They had practically dragged her back inside. This experience taught her that her body would not only suffer from using her power, but from her healing as well.

Her breath shook as she thought of the vision she had when the electricity hit her brain cells.

What was the golden treasure chest? Where were the people carrying it? *Who* were they?

Her jaw shook at the image of the man's charred body as it fell from the chest and the others who fell with him.

Her weak limbs fell around her as she nuzzled her forehead to the cool wall, her eyes wandering to the boy in the cell across from her who watched her tired form.

He didn't bother speaking to her, his point had been proven.

Her eyes fluttered shut again, this had to be worth it…It had to be…

She remembered when she had turned to Reggie as the doctor cut into her arm, it had hurt of course but it was nothing she hadn't experienced before.

The young man's face was contorted into something she couldn't make out. Did he agree with what was happening to her?

The skin that had healed over the cuts stung from the twenty times the doctor had cut into her. She shuddered as her eyes began to feel heavy, she had been up for over 24 hours and most of it was spent being tortured. The doctors coat consumed her mind as it was the only thing she had seen for hours.

The fuzz in her brain made her lose consciousness and she dreamed of a man with a white long sleeved shirt. His black suspenders holding up his pants of the same color.

He had brown hair and sharp brown eyes that were now blank. It was the man she had seen in her vision before, the one who had smashed her head repeatedly into a wall.

He was dead now, his body laying against an old style radiator, his head bent against his shoulder in an odd way from the bone being snapped in half. Blood began to trickle down his nostrils as his orb like eyes laid upon her. Everything had gone black when she done it.

Was this what it was like to kill a man?

She didn't feel guilty nor did she regret what she had done. She was indifferent to it.

Did she want to kill him? No.

Did he deserve it? Hell yes.

Her chattering teeth could be heard over the sound of the doctors, nurses, and guards as they ran to see what the commotion had been. It felt like justice that the man who had tortured and beat them for his own pleasure was dead by her hand.

They had begged for their beatings to stop.

He had begged not to die.

Mercy? What was that?

Such a thing didn't exist in a world like this.

It was as if she was moving in slow motion as she jerked her head to the other body that laid amongst the man's. The girl was no older than twenty, all she had were those short years before her life was so savagely taken from her. Her neck was broken as well, tears still in her blue eyes. Her blonde hair tangled against the white floor.

Why did he have to kill her?

Her existence was like a light to Anna but it had been snuffed out, leaving her in darkness. The girl was all she had in this place. She was the only thing that kept her going in these cold walls.

She didn't have time to mourn, she had to flee or her friends sacrifice would be in vain. She turned the opposite way of the echoes of feet and her own feet ran as fast as they could as she sprinted down the hall, hopefully to her escape.

Maya opened her eyes as her heart thumped her awake and as they adjusted to the fluorescent light, She realized someone was standing at the glass in front of her cell.

His dark eyes were filled with turmoil and grief as he looked upon her.

Reginald Deluca Jr.

Chapter 46

Reggie had left the viewing room as Clarke cut into Samantha Knight's arm for what felt like the hundredth time. The gargoyle didn't seem like she felt any pain but as the blade trailed up her arm, splitting her flesh as it did so, Reggie could see her eyes twitch and her hands ball into fists.

As he got up from his seat, none of the other group leaders or the director tore their eyes from what was happing in the makeshift hospital room. Reggie should have been the same, he should have watched and enjoyed that the gargoyle who had killed countless people suffered as she had made her victims suffer.

But he couldn't do it.

He stepped out of the room and closed the door behind him, his back leaning against the wall beside the heavy door as he looked to the ceiling.

The gargoyle could get out of her restraints at anytime, he had seen the chains threatening to break along with the leather straps.

He dropped his gaze and pushed himself off the wall, his footsteps echoing through the empty hall. He would never get used to the bright lights in the building that they had built specifically to house the gargoyles. He thought of the night he had seen Samantha Knight in person, how she had stopped a car moving at full speed with one arm and showed no pain after the fact.

This girl… this *beast* could break out of here at anytime. She was holding herself back as the doctor played with her and most importantly she had saved his father.

His father had told him what she had done, how she had jumped in the way as the female demon went in for the kill. How she had told him to get out of the underground of the Lincoln memorial while he still had the chance.

Ever since Reggie had woken up on the lawn between the wreckage of the monuments, he wondered how he had gotten from the highest point of the Washington monument to the safety of the ground. He wondered what had happened after the arrival Samantha Knight.

A shiver went up his spine at the thought of the pink eyed demon.

Demon.

What kind of world was this?

Not only were there gargoyles, but there were also demons and the embodiment of darkness, the maker of the demons: Lucifer.

This couldn't be real but no matter how hard one pinched themselves, there was no waking up.

A reality where humans once worked with the gargoyles to fight the demons only for what was left of the gargoyles after the battle to be killed. For the gargoyles killed to leave behind children who would seek revenge for their parents deaths.

Reggie swallowed, for one of them to be killed and reincarnated into a human only to be made into a gargoyle again.

"Reg!" A familiar voice rang through the hall and he lifted his head to meet Lucas, a man the same age as him with brilliant blonde hair and blue eyes. His skin was pale and he stood a head taller than Reggie. His suit matched Reggie's all the way down to the black tie.

"Oh, I'm sorry!" Lucas mused as he approached. "I should be calling you *boss* now."

"I'd rather you not." Reggie smiled only for it to turn into a frown again.

Lucas looked down at his sullen friend, "You don't have to be here you know, you just lost your father."

Reggie shook his head, "I have to be here." He met Lucas' blue eyes. "He would have wanted me to keep going… he would have wanted me to do anything I could to get rid of the demons."

The taller of the two rose a brow the same color as his hair, "Not the gargoyles?" He didn't sound like was was judging Reggie's choice of words, but it was still a good question to ask.

"They're not the problem, not anymore." Reggie admitted and when he thought Lucas would laugh in his face, the opposite happened.

"Anyone with a brain can see that." Lucas said as he looked past Reggie. "I heard Samantha Knight came here freely…I'm guessing the doctor has her now?"

Reggie nodded as he tightened his jaw.

"It's too bad she's a gargoyle…" Lucas sighed. "She's a fine one."

His eyes fell to Reggie again and he furrowed his brows. "What are you planning?"

Reggie had ignored Lucas' comment about the female gargoyles looks as his mind filled with what he had to do next. "I don't know." He met his friends eyes again. "But my mind keeps bringing me to what my father would have done."

"And that is?"

Reggie gave him a look that could only mean he should know what that was going to be.

"I agree with you." Lucas sighed again and dramatically fell onto the wall beside him while crossing his arms. "I've never been on board with what they've been doing here, these creatures aren't monsters. They were once human and this was forced upon them." He turned his head to the room where Maya was and Reggie watched as his face fell. "And I'm sure she and the other gargoyles aren't the one's that used to attack us, they've changed."

Reggie was shocked at Lucas' willingness, he was sure he didn't know that Samantha Knight was one of the gargoyles that had attacked them, had killed them.

Perhaps it was better to keep it that way for now.

"The rest of the team agrees." Lucas woke him from his thoughts and he looked up as he almost fell from the shock. It shocked him that they were willing to betray everything they've worked for to join him.

"If I end up doing this, it won't be safe, we could die and theres no way we'll be enough to help with their cause."

Lucas snickered. "What would my parents think of their son joining the creatures that were once their enemies?"

Lucas' parents had both been on the police force when the gargoyles were attacking cities.

"Why are you willing to do something so stupid? especially after what just happened?" Reggie pressed with an air of nervousness.

Was this a ploy and Lucas was really going to tell the higher up's his plan?

Lucas looked him dead in the eyes, "My grandfather died months ago and I was the person he wanted to talk to before he died. He told me he fought against the demons with the gargoyles and he told me that he'd do it again." He narrowed his eyes. "He told me they were coming again, the demons. He was sure of it since the gargoyles were making their comeback. He never told my parents, he left it to me so I kept quiet about it until now."

Reggie remembered Lucas' grandfather, how he had met him when his father had introduced the older gentleman. The man never seemed proud of what was going on there.

"If you choose to do it, I'll be behind you." Lucas assured him. "But find out soon before they really mess that girl up." His eyes landed on the door where the doctor was having his *fun*.

Several hours after the gargoyle had been brought back to her cage, Reggie made his way down the hall to where the gargoyles were kept. He had decided to speak to her before he made his final decision. The doctor had his fun for the day and Reggie was sure he and the director were planning what they were going to do next.

The guards would allow him to go anywhere he wanted due to his status, even in the hall where the gargoyles were. Before doing so however, he made sure to make the camera's malfunction so their conversation wouldn't be heard.

What were they going to talk about?

He wasn't even sure where to start.

He had used the hours since she was brought back to her cell to think, but this wasn't a decision to make on thoughts alone. He needed to hear her side, to hear her plan and more importantly, to find out what had happened to his father.

He scanned his card as one of the guards wandered down the hall in the opposite direction. The door unlocked with a click, he had to hurry before they noticed the cameras weren't working.

Maya stood to meet Reggie, she felt refreshed after getting some sleep and the strain was gone. She made it part of the way but stopped in the middle of the cell as she saw the apprehension on his face. Her eyes wandered to the boy in the cell behind him, he had peaked his head up from the bed to get a better look.

"I don't think we've officially met aside from ways less than ideal." She said as she brought her eyes back to Reggie and she saw his jaw tighten.

"This is where you belong." He tested and she frowned, she could hear a hint of a bluff in his voice.

"Do you honestly think you can keep me in here?" She said as she pressed a finger to the wall. "If I wanted, I could simply ping this wall and it would come crashing down…. But I haven't."

She wouldn't be able to do it without any repercussions though.

Reggies eyes widened at her words but they went back to normal right away. "Why haven't you?" He asked with his voice shaking.

Maya narrowed her eyes.

"I willingly got myself locked in here, I've suffered your mad scientists experiments so you'd realize that my comrades and I aren't the problem, the demons are."

"You and your kind killed innocent people-" Reggie started but Maya interrupted. "I know very well that I'm a murderer." Her voice broke at the last word. She inhaled sharply then continued as Reggie watched on. "Your father was a smart man-"

"Don't talk about my father you *monster*." He growled and for the first time, his soft eyes narrowed and she could feel the venom coming from him through the glass.

She kept her eyes on his as she allowed him to calm.

"Do you know how it feels to die and to be reincarnated?" This was the first time she had spoken about her reentry into the world with a human other than Archie. "To have no recollection of what you did in your past life… to have dreams about your past that were too vague to understand… to be hunted by your past lives brothers due to the simple fact that they were jealous of their sister's power?"

"I don't care-" Reggie began but Maya kept going.

"I died because I wanted repentance for what I've done." She had to stop to calm her pulse.

Talking about what she had done always brought her back to the state of mind that she tried so hard to ignore. Death called for her and she was willing to answer.

"I've chosen to fight for the humans that are still alive, even though I know that it'll never be enough to make up for it all."

"I get it." Reggie shocked her but she knew what was about to come next, something she knew she would have to tell him.

"How did my father die?" He asked and his voice cut off at the end, he tried to hide it, but she could see his eyes water from the emotion.

She swallowed, "Your father died protecting me… he pushed me out of the monument's window before Abraxas' shadow could consume us both." She was sure that Abraxas wouldn't have let it go that far though, she was Lucifer's play thing after all. There would have been quite the punishment for killing his masters favorite toy. "He had me save you and he saved me."

Reggie dropped his gaze, "You saved him at the Lincoln memorial, he told me you did."

"I did." She said softly as she made her way to the glass and pressed a hand gently to it.

It was cool against her palm but she could feel the warmth of Reggie's breath on the other side.

He lifted his eyes, first to Maya's gray orbs then to her palm resting between them.

He lifted his hand and met hers, it was quite bigger than her own and now that she stood level with him, she found herself looking up slightly to meet his eyes.

"Join me and get revenge for your father." She said the words no louder than a whisper. "We're not your enemies, Lucifer and his demons are."

Even through the glass she could feel his hand flinch, "He's real?"

Maya dropped her hand, her gray eyes falling to the white floor. "He is."

The demons caused her fear but Lucifer caused more than just fear, she felt empty, she felt weak, and what scared her the most was an emotion that made no sense: Longing.

Out of everything she could feel, why did she long to fight Lucifer? To be brought face to face with him?

"What time is it?" She asked suddenly and Reggie brought his wrist up so he could look at his watch. "It's 2:30 Am." He answered causally.

"I'm going to give you three hours to decide what you're going to do and if you can get anyone else to join you." She looked straight into his eyes. "I'll be breaking out at that time and I expect you to meet me at the edge of the property." She pointed at his wristwatch. "Leave that here."

"Maybe we can wait a few more days…to better prepare…" he stammered.

She shook her head and she looked like she had a twitch due to how she did it. "I'm not going to let that motherfucker torture me more than he already has." She chewed on her lip. "Lucifer isn't going to wait on me much longer before he decides to end the world without me."

Who was she kidding? Of course he would want her there, he needed her, she just didn't know why.

"The end of the world…?" The detective narrowed his eyes. He was finding out what they were dealing with, what he was about to jump into.

"This world," Maya motioned as if they could see the world in her tiny cell. "Is only a mold for Lucifer's ideal landscape… his *hell.*"

At her words Reggie undid the strap keeping his watch to his wrist and placed it on the floor so she'd be able to see it at an angle. She thought the news would have changed his mind but it seemed to ignite a fire in him.

"I hope you don't make me regret this." He said as he stepped back.

"Me too." She admitted.

There was no telling if their little alliance would even work.

But before that, Maya had to get out of there.

It had been almost three hours since she had talked to Reggie and her eyes lifted from the watch to the boy across from her. For the first time since Reggie left, he had gotten up from his bed and sat at the glass like Maya had since the young detective left. He didn't say anything, he knew the cameras were on again. Maya wouldn't lie that she was nervous Reggie would betray her but she had to take the chance. If she hadn't at least tried, coming here would have been for naught.

She had hoped the doctor wouldn't get the early morning urge to experiment on her but she'd been lucky.

Her eyes met the boy across from her and his eyes twitched to the cell beside her. She took that as a sign that her neighbor was aware of what was going on.

Her eyes twitched to the cell next to the boy and for the first time she saw the person locked inside: A short girl with a bob hair cut and like the boy across from Maya, she wore a white jumpsuit. She was glad she wasn't forced to change into one.

She looked down at her now bloody lilac shirt and jeans and she found herself missing her battle attire. The bobbed girl's eyes met her's then Maya rolled them to the camera that was placed to the right of her at the top corner of the hall. It provided her with a good blindspot so she could pass her direction to the others.

Her heart began to thump as the minutes went by and she got up from her spot and faced the opposite way of the camera.

She met their eyes as she mouthed each word slowly, *"Tell. them. to. stand. at. the. front."*

She was glad when they nodded meaning they understood.

With her hearing she listened for the gargoyles to move out of the way one by one as she watched them mouth her direction to each other. When they were all moved and the two she could see looked back to her, she closed her eyes as she backed away from the front.

She placed her index finger on the wall that separated her from her neighbor. With the strength she was about to use, all of the walls that were separating them would come crashing down.

As she had told Reggie, she could break out of here with a ping of her finger.

And so she did.

As her index finger hit the wall it went crashing backwards and as it did so, it flew back to the others and knocked them down with it. Some of the gargoyles couldn't help themselves and screamed at the crashing rock but Maya paid no mind, she had to get them out of there.

As the stone settled she motioned for them to run through the holes to her cell.

She kicked through the clear casing holding her in her cell and after jumping to the boy's cell, she did the same. With the same ferocity she had used to knock her side down, she destroyed the walls on his side. When she was done, she was surrounded by half blooded gargoyles.

A guard opened the door as they were about to speak to her but she was ready and put him in a sleeper hold as another came in behind him. The one fell to the ground and Maya set to work as guard after guard made their way in. She was surprised that none of them used the guns that had killed Dylan but she was happy they didn't. With all of the guards down, she directed the other gargoyles to run ahead of her so she could cover the back.

"Anyone who knows how to fight get in the front!" She hollered over the alarms that were now going off. The sound sent her on edge as her adrenaline reached it's peak.

As they made their way to the door that led to their freedom, which was easier than they had imagined, Maya ran to the front and punched it out of the way. The heavy steel door flew twenty feet away and landed harshly on the concrete in the orange haze of the rising sun.

She allowed the gargoyles to run ahead of her as she kept an eye out for more guards.

After the last person ran past her, deja vu filled her. It was like the time Arthur had let them escape from the cave.

The humans were letting them go…

She didn't give herself time to think about it as she ran behind the rest. She found the dirty blonde haired boy standing in the middle of the parking lot, waiting for her as the others continued to run to their freedom.

"Where are you going now?" He asked as he started running as she caught up with him.

"To my friends, I came here to see if I could get help from a human and I hope I've achieved that." Their voices bounced as their bodies did.

"…I'm going with you." He stated and she side eyed him.

What a change since she had met him on the way to their mountain side prison.

"I don't have time to teach you how to be a gargoyle." She said simply as she turned to see if anyone was following them. "But come if you want."

He nodded but came to a stop as Maya, who was still looking over her shoulder, ran past him but stopped as well as she noticed him behind her.

She rose a brow as she turned her head to see what he was looking at and her heart stopped.

Standing only a few feet away from her was her childhood friend, the girl she had protected almost five months ago from the same fate as the gargoyles she had just freed.

The girl that unknowingly led Maya… No, *Sam* to her fate.

Mina.

Chapter 47

Mina's eyes filled with tears at the sight of the girl who had saved her from this fate, who had taken her place, who was her best friend.

Her blonde hair had grown considerably but it was clear that she didn't take care of it so it was knotted in several places. There were bags under her once painted eyes, she was pale, and her pink lips were quivering into a smile. Her jeans were tattered and her navy blue jacket had dust covering it.

"Sam…" her voice drifted and Maya's heart thumped.

Mina had been her best friend since the beginning of this life, she was her closest friend when no one had bothered to understand her. She had never judged her for her dreams, she had even tried to find the reason why she had them. She was the first to suggest reincarnation.

The boy Maya had just saved stepped forward and caught Maya's attention. His eyes met hers and in the next second he ran after the others to leave the girls alone.

After the shock of seeing her friend after so long wore off, reality set in and Maya began to walk past her.

She had to get out of there before the humans changed their minds about letting them escape. What's more she had to get Mina out of there. She couldn't stay here nor could she stay with Maya.

Mina grabbed her arm as she passed and instead of pulling out of her grip, Maya turned to her friend. "What are you doing here Mina? How did you find this place?"

She didn't mean to sound so cold.

"I-I never thought I'd see you again…" The tears finally fell from Mina's eyes and they rolled down her cheeks to the ground. "I heard what happened to you," She loosened her shaky grip and faced Maya completely. She looked into her gray eyes and shuddered at the change, she had known her when her eyes were hazel.

"I've always thought about you… I didn't care that you were changed into one of them, I knew it wouldn't change you… you're still Samantha Knight… My best friend."

Maya took two steps away as she pulled her arm gently out of Mina's grip and looked into her tear stained face. She looked so tired, her once makeup covered face was empty of all it's color.

Mina's eyes dropped to the blood on Maya's clothing then to the scar popping out of her collar.

Her eyes filled with fresh tears at the sight. "What've you been doing…?"

"I've always been a gargoyle." Maya's voice drifted as she took another step back. "I'm a monster and I *have* changed."

She changed her eyes to her mismatched gargoyle one's and Mina jumped but her fear quickly changed to awe.

Maya shook her head. "You were right about my dreams…the boy I saw…the things I never saw in this life…" She swallowed.

She didn't want to tell Mina in fear that she would think she was crazy, but at this point, what difference would it make?

"I was reincarnated." Her voice was small as she finally mustered the courage.

Mina's eyes widened and she seemed to turn paler than she already was. "There's no way-"

"It's true." Maya interrupted. "And do you know what I did in my past life?"

She didn't want to ruin Mina's image of her but she also had to get her away from her.

"I killed innocent people." It was almost laughable at how nonchalant she was at announcing it.

Mina shook her head and Maya could hear her heart hammering in her chest. "You didn't…"

"Do you want me to describe it to you?" Maya snarled. "I'm one of the monsters from the scary stories our parents used to tell us… the stories that we didn't believe." Instead of withdrawing this time, she stepped closer to Mina. "You blame yourself for this happening to me but this is fate… it led me here and brought my memories back from my past life." She narrowed her eyes. "It also led me to my enemy… the hardest one I've ever faced."

"I've seen what's been going on!" Mina stammered. "I know you're fighting what's out there! They can blame you for what's going on but I know it's not you!" She grabbed ahold of Maya's shoulders and shook her. "You don't have to sacrifice yourself! You don't owe the world a thing!"

Maya pulled away from her and Mina fell backwards.

"You have no idea what I owe this world." She turned away from her friend. "Live your life for me, don't blame yourself for what I'm going through…it's fate."

Mina fell to her knees as tears poured down her cheeks and blocked her vision. She wasn't going to chase after Maya, she knew she wouldn't be able to stop her.

"Don't die!" She begged like it was something Maya could control. "Live!"

Maya turned off her hearing as she tried ignoring her friends pleas and she began her walk to where she and Reggie were set to meet.

She wished she could live a life with Mina like she used to but it was fate. Her heart felt heavy as she heard her friends sobs behind her and she wondered how Mina had even found this place. Maya had found the building thanks to following the officers and her senses, but there was no way Mina could have found this place. Even if the humans had broadcasted her capture they would never let the world know her location.

Her body began to feel heavy from not only the power, but from the fog in her mind.

She kept shuffling on until she found Reggie at the edge of the property where she had told him to be. Seven others were standing with him near a black car parked at the end of a tree line. The boy gargoyle was standing along with them and the humans were side eyeing him, they were clearly nervous with what they were doing.

Maya practically fell into Reggie as her knees buckled and he grabbed her elbows to help her stay up right but she quickly pulled away.

"Are you ok?" He asked awkwardly as the others looked on nervously, some of the humans looked like they thought she was attacking him.

"I'm fine." Her voice shook. "It comes with the power."

Of course she was physically compromised but also emotionally after her talk with Mina.

Her eyes dropped to the large duffle bags hanging from a blonde haired man's shoulders while another brown haired man who was far shorter and stockier than the other held onto two more.

"Plenty of weapons." The blonde haired one flashed an awkward smile. "I'm Lucas."

Aside from the two men, there was a short girl with sun colored hair. Her eyes light blue with a hint of hazel. Two more girls with brown hair, one to her shoulders and the other to her waist though it was tied back into a braid. There were two more men, one looked to be in his late teens with his young face, but his green eyes were narrowed like a hunters. The last man was stocky and at his waist was an arsenal of guns.

Maya felt apprehensive just looking at them, the image of Dylan's dissolving body filled her mind along with her parents.

"Let's get going." Reggie advised, waking Maya from her thoughts and they all squeezed into the car. Maya sat in the front to show Reggie where to go.

As they pulled out of the parking lot, she looked to see if anyone was following them but no one was there aside from the sound of the alarm still going off in the building.

They passed where Maya had parked the car she had taken from the cabins and it was gone.

Her eyes landed on the people behind her, they looked uncomfortable especially the one's who had to sit on another's lap. The gargoyle boy looked like he didn't belong as the humans wore fancy suits while he remained in his white jumpsuit.

She gave them an awkward nod as they met her eyes then faced forward as she told Reggie where to go for the rest of the ride.

Mina wobbly pulled herself to her feet, her eyes swollen with tears. She had blamed herself for everything that had happened to her best friend but she had never thought that Sam would embrace her power as a gargoyle.

She was her friend but she was also not.

Mina chewed on her lip, Sam was Sam and she was her friend. She couldn't believe she was right about Sam's dreams, but even with what Sam had told her, there was no way her friend was a murderer. Reincarnation was farfetched, but with how skeptical Sam was, she still admitted it.

Sam believed it.

It was hard to believe the girl who had always protected the weak, who had taken her place on that fateful night was once a killer.

If she was, she had changed. Sam was no killer but her past life could have been.

She must hate herself for it, for something that happened a lifetime ago.

Mina thought of the enemy Sam had spoken of and wondered who it could be. They had to be terrifying to cause such an uneasy feeling in her friend.

As she began to make her way to her car, someone appeared behind her and before she could run, the person grabbed ahold of her and covered her mouth to hide her scream.

The thing that had grabbed her wasn't a person at all, it was a demon.

Astaroth's bright red hair fell on Mina's shoulder as she leaned into her ear.

"What a beautiful reunion." She whispered with a smile that showed her pointed teeth, her hand covering Mina's blood curdling scream until the girl passed out from the lack of air.

The others met Maya and the newcomers as they walked up the long drive to the cabins. Either they had heard them pulling in or they had not slept at all. Maya who was leading the way was met with their shocked and relieved faces and her eyes found Donato who stood with the other venandi. He stared at her with his milky eyes and nodded at a job well done.

Kellan's face was smug as he stood with the remaining gargoyles that came with him and Archie. Maya had found Archie's gentle face as Arthur caught her in his arms.

As he held onto her, the others stopped around them and out of respect, remained silent as the siblings had their moment.

"I could strangle you for being so reckless." He growled but smiled.

"That would defeat the purpose." She smiled gently.

He pulled away and walked past her to Reggie who was standing close behind her as if she was the only one he could trust. Reggie looked into Arthur's face as the other humans stood defensively. Arthur was shorter than him but he was much more intimidating.

The gargoyle extended a hand and the other humans flinched while Reggie remained grounded. With slight hesitation, the detective extended his own hand and shook Arthur's.

"Glad to see you here and well," Arthur nodded. "You didn't look too good when my sister threw you from the monument and I caught you."

Reggie looked between the siblings as Maya turned to them.

"You threw me from the building?" He asked awkwardly, his eyes wide.

"Your father wanted me to save you and that was the only way I could do it." She turned away with a frown, she couldn't take the look on his face. "He wanted me to tell you something," her voice shook. "He said he loves you."

She heard the catch of air in Reggie's throat as he took in his fathers last words and she swallowed. She was still filled with self hatred that she couldn't save his father.

She was quickly distracted from the feeling as she was met with Ari,

Kira, and Trevor as they pulled her into a group hug.

"You fucking fool." Ari said as she pulled away, a relieved smile on her face that matched the others. Maya gave them an apologetic smile as she looked from them and found Emily walking to her.

She walked to meet Emily in the middle and she reminded her so much of Mina who she had just left behind to protect.

Emily tugged around her middle to pull her into a hug like the others had and she balled her fist as she brought it to the side of her head.

"I wish I could hit you for being so stupid." her teeth chattered as she gently bumped Maya's head with her fist.

"I wouldn't be mad if you did." Maya chuckled as she leaned into the hug.

She was certainly good at hurting everyone who cared for her and she would gladly take the well deserved punch with no complaints.

Emily let her go, leaving Maya to the person who hadn't hugged her yet.

Cale.

He stood there for a moment with an expression she couldn't read but as he closed the gap between them, he lifted her into a hug. Only her toes touched the ground as he wrapped his arms around her back. She wrapped her arms around him as she rested her chin on his shoulder, their cheeks touching. His eyes closed as he picked up on the scent of the cleaner that had filled the prison, it had settled into her hair and clothes.

He had seen the blood on her shirt, saw that she had grown paler than before.

He pulled her tighter to him, his fingers twisting into her wavy hair.

"You really are a fool." He said against her exposed ear, his voice filled with both relief and worry.

"I'm sorry." She nuzzled into his neck, the smell of his cool smelling soap soothing her nose from the smell of the hospital cleaner.

The day had turned to rain and they found themselves inside one of the larger cabins so they could plan. Like they had with the Venandi, they had shown the humans where they could stay and many had to bunk together due to running out of cabins.

It was strange: Gargoyles, the Venandi, and humans together to fight their common enemy.

Maya felt pride that her parents would have been proud.

She sat in an arm chair, her four viking braids had returned after she had washed the blood from her skin. Her battle suit had returned as well in case something happened. Her trenchcoat was on to cover her exposed back for the time being.

The human named Lucas was showing off the weapons he had snatched from the experimental center, he had explained that the bullets were in-coated in hydrochloric acid. It was poetic that they could meet their ends the same as their stone counterparts.

The gargoyles thought of how Dylan's body had dissolved from the acid and Maya's heart raced at the thought of him withering in pain as his body burned. Her parents had met the same fate.

"I'm sure my grandfather worked with your parents at one point." Lucas sat across from Maya and Arthur who stood beside her chair. "He didn't think what happened to your parents was right and I'm putting aside what you did so we can fight the real threat together."

What they did as in killing innocent people for revenge. Maya had explained her story so he knew what she had done.

"Is this even going to be enough?" Reggie who was standing against a wall to the left of Maya with his arms crossed questioned. "I was able to get seven of my people to come with us and this gargoyle." He nodded to the boy who had declared that his name was Jared.

He was sitting with Ari, Kira, and Trevor at the coach as the three welcomed him with open arms. "Lucas managed to grab over seventy weapons but you saw what happened when the demons attacked the monuments. It didn't matter how many of us there were or how many weapons we had."

"By the sounds of it, the gargoyles and the humans who worked together managed ok." Alvertos piped up and they all turned to where he was sitting with the rest of the Venandi at a table. "God will open his arms and pull us into his embrace."

He was met with strange looks aside from the Venandi who understood his banter. "He will give us the strength to fight this threat and we will prevail."

"Yeah, sure." Kira said with a mocking tone as she flicked a speck of dust from her pants.

Maya turned to Reggie to find that he was already looking at her, he had a brow up and his mouth was in a line as if he was trying to stop himself from saying something.

She lifted her eyes to the ceiling to let him know that this was a normal thing for the Venandi.

The short blonde haired girl that came along with Reggie nervously stepped forward, "I came here with Deluca to set everything aside and fight for the world…" her voice broke. "But what happens if we fail?"

Maya was surprised Reggie didn't tell them what she had told him but as she watched his face fall flat, she knew he had. Perhaps they wanted to hear it from the mouth's of the people they were joining.

"Hell on earth." Donato answered before anyone else could. "And since you're new here, I am known as a seer. I can see visions of what's to come and since I was younger the prophecy *The hand of God will bring about the end of the world but will also save it* has played over and over in my mind." He turned to Maya. "If things go according to that, the world will surely end and Lucifer's plan will be realized… but the hand will save the world."

The shock that a seer was real didn't last long, the detectives sat along with gargoyles and warriors that fought for God all to face the same enemy. Seeing a seer was nothing in comparison to what they had faced and what they were going to.

"How does the hand bring the end?" Lucas turned to the blind man, his face had paled at Donato's words.

"I can't see how." Donato answered roughly.

"Is there anyone still alive that fought the demons back then?" Cale's voice rang out and they faced him. He was sitting on the arm of the couch beside Emily, his expression was strong and filled with determination. "There was a website that I found almost five months ago, it had pictures of gargoyles and what I think was a demon. The man who made the site was adamant on releasing the truth."

Maya's eyes widened a fraction, she had forgotten about the website.

"…I think I know who you're talking about." Realization filled Reggie's face and he spoke quickly. "The higher up's sent my father to go have a talk with him and he had me tag along, he was warned that if he kept the site up, he would be arrested for tampering."

"His name?" Arthur pressed.

"Paul Ash." Reggie answered as he met Cale's eyes. "He doesn't live too far from here."

All of the gargoyles in Maya's group met each others eyes, it had been days since the last demon attack and Maya knew Lucifer was biding his time. Meeting Paul Ash could be the answer to what they could do against the demons.

He had to know something… *anything*.

What could he know that the Venandi didn't? The warriors trained specifically to kill demons?

It was still worth a try to find out.

A chill went up her spine, she knew Lucifer was well aware of what she had done and what she doing. There was a connection between the two, the visions confirmed it along with the memories of her potential past life as Anna.

A life she and Lucifer had known each other.

With her enemy on her mind and the desperate need to defeat him, she nodded to the others.

Chapter 48

They made their way down the wet highway in the Venandi's SUV's, the wind shield wipers on the highest setting due to the rain coming down as buckets. All of the people who came with them barely fit into both cars. They had left Kellan, Archie, and the other gargoyles back at the cabins, there was no need for them to come.

They had also left Jared who had no control over his power. He had left with Maya for the refuge she would provide at the cabins, not to fight and investigate the demons.

All of the Venandi and the humans came with Maya and the six other gargoyles. They were a little on edge with leaving Kellan behind to guard their sanctuary, but Archie would keep things in check. Kellan respected only one person and that was Archie.

Reggie sat in front with Alvertos so he could give him directions, they all thought it to be wise to leave Reggie's car amongst the car graveyard since their getaway was still fresh.

Two of the human newcomers sat in the second row of seats, the man named Lucas and the small nervous girl. Arthur sat amongst the two of them and they side eyed him as he looked out the window at the cars speeding by.

To finish the car Donato, Maya, Cale, and Emily sat in the third row and although they were squished together, they made it work.

"By the looks of where you've been staying, you haven't seen what's been reported about the religious monuments being destroyed." Reggie began from the front. "They blamed it on terrorists and I believed it until I met you guys…I thought it was you until I met the demons at the Lincoln memorial, the higher up's have been lying to us for so many years."

"For centuries all of the wars and turmoil in the world has been caused by Lucifer's influence." Alvertos explained without removing his eyes from the foggy road. "He needed strife and pain to start his plan and now he needs God out of the way to finish it."

The humans remained silent as they took in the information.

"S-so everything that has happened up until now has been Lucifer's influence?" The nervous girl stammered.

"You can leave anytime you want, Tori." Lucas assured her though he had become visibly paler himself.

"No one knows Lucifer's true power or form, though many have known the power of his demons."Alvertos added flatly as if to heighten their fear.

Maya and the others had a taste of Lucifer's power when they had first met the embodiment of evil. Even now they could feel the heat that had pressed down onto them, causing them to collapse to the ground. With the haze around them they couldn't breath and their senses dulled.

How could they defeat someone that could cause that kind of damage with just their mind?

Maya found herself thinking of the words Lucifer had spoken to her, how he had only *gotten her to her knees* that time. It could only mean that there had been time before, a time where she had gone all the way down and remained there.

"The monuments have been nothing to get rid of for the demons." Lucas' voice drifted and woke Maya from her thoughts. "Not only that, but they have obliterated all of the human forces and your people-" he motioned for Alvertos and Donato.

"His final target will be the most holy city in the world." Donato shot in, his snowy eyes on the blonde haired man. "Jerusalem." He declared and the group stiffened. "Jesus preached and was crucified there, not only does Christianity have a place there, but also Judaism and Islam."

Emily inhaled sharply before she spoke. "Will we have to go there?"

"Not yet." Donato said flatly and Maya moved her gaze from the blind man to meet Cale and Emily's confused looks.

They could never understand him, his visions had changed him along with his fathers abuse. He had never been normal, his visions had taken that right from him.

It was similar to how everyone in the car along with him and the car behind him had changed, even the gargoyles that Maya had saved from the research center. No one had a chance at being normal anymore.

"I've made the calls to the full blooded gargoyles but I have yet to receive an answer." Arthur changed the subject.

The shock of finding out that there were more full blooded gargoyles out there didn't last long for the humans.

"Did you leave a message?" The girl they now knew was named Tori asked nervously from beside him.

"As good as I could get when the gargoyles in question are in hiding." He turned to meet the three younger gargoyles, two that were half blooded and Maya who was full blooded but still genetically human. "They've seen what's been happening and I'm sure they know it's the demons. They never told me about them I'm sure to honor our parents wishes, but they surely knew of the demons. If they want to help, they'll know where to go."

"But the possibility is low." Cale didn't need to ask if it was, he knew.

"Can you blame them for not wanting to fight?" Arthur asked softly as he turned back to the front again. Lucas and Tori caught the look on his face as he realized what he had said.

The resentment was still present for what Arthur had done. He had given the full blooded gargoyles a choice when his brothers were still a problem and kidnapped innocent people instead.

Maya's eyes twitched to Cale and Emily, she had flinched at what Arthur said, had wished he hadn't said it at all. The two half blooded gargoyles were looking at the back of Arthurs head, Emily with a locked jaw and Cale with narrowed eyes.

"This could be a lost cause." Reggie changed the subject again as he and the others felt the tension spread inside the car. "Paul Ash was a smart man back in his day but the last time I saw him he wasn't in his right mind." He looked into the rearview mirror to look at all of the people behind him. "After everything he's seen, it's not surprising."

"Why did he keep launching the website even though he could have been arrested?" Cale leaned forward and almost brought Maya with him because of the tight squeeze, he apologized and she shook her head to let him know it was ok.

"Many of the men and women who fought with the gargoyles and lived were known to sympathize with them though the higher up's tried to cover it up." Lucas answered for Reggie. "My grandfather seemed like he did… he never told my dad or my grandmother about his time with the gargoyles but he told me about you before he died." His eyes met his human comrades. "Paul Ash is likely the same."

"He didn't just sympathize with gargoyles, it seemed like he wanted the information to get out." Emily piped in.

The pictures from Paul Ash's website flashed in Maya's mind and she tried straying from the bodies of their victims. Instead she thought of the blurred pictures that Paul Ash had posted, one of the pictures had been undeniably a gargoyle and now that Maya had her memories back, she knew even through the blur that the picture was of Oberon.

Perhaps the government had snapped the picture when he, Peyton, and Eli had gone to steal the bomb that would end her life. She knew the second picture wasn't her kind. The first thing that came to mind was how the forms the demons were currently using were all for show.

A fooling form one could say.

Was it possible the picture of the creature with long curved horns, wings, and glowing eyes was one of the demons?

Of course it was.

Maya swallowed, the demon that had been caught on camera knew the camera was there but allowed the picture to be taken.

Why? Which demon was it?

Another question popped into her mind, one that made her heart race faster: Would she be able to take on the demons in their true forms without her full power?

She already knew the answer and her body would surely break down. The God of death would have her again, his aim wouldn't be in vain. He wouldn't stop until her soul rested permanently in his rotted hands. She would willingly give it to him though, it was her fate. If it was repentance for what she's done, she would gladly walk into the depths of hell and meet Lucifer face to face.

But this world is hell and this is where she was going to die.

For the third time.

All she could see as she pictured her end was Lucifer: His smiling face, crazed and entertained. His black hair falling into his glowing red eyes as he leaned to meet hers, a pain seared in her chest where her heart should have been.

"Sam?"

"Maya?"

She blinked as Cale, Emily, and Arthur called her respective names. She didn't realize that she had lost sight of reality.

"Are you ok?" Cale asked gently as she found herself surrounded by worried and confused faces.

She nodded, not realizing that her face had paled to the color of paper.

"Are you sure?" Arthur pressed with a look that indicated her answer wasn't good enough.

Their prying eyes were on her but she could only see what was on the other side of the windshield: There stood a house that looked as if it had been built in the Victorian era.

They had made it to Paul Ash's house, how long did it take for them to get there? How long was she lost in her thoughts?

"Certain." She assured flatly as some of the color in her face returned and she turned to Cale. "I'm more focused on what Paul Ash has to show us."

Their eyes met and he nodded, he had been the one to find the website and had continued to look for it until they had to dump her computer a few months back.

It was time to meet the man behind the site.

Oh the information he could have for them.

They got out of the car and met the others who had already gotten out. The old victorian house had white paint chips falling off of it, many of which fell into the large leafless trees around it. There were no other houses around, the closest was a half a mile down the long drive.

Their feet crushed the gravel underneath as they stepped to the house. Reggie and Lucas at the front so Paul Ash wouldn't freak out at the group of supernatural beings and Gods warriors in their white trenchcoats. Reggie knocked gently on the silver door and waited a moment but no one came. He knocked again, harder this time, but Paul Ash didn't answer.

He pressed his ear against the door as he heard something inside.

"There's a piano playing." He informed them in less than a whisper.

The gargoyles glanced at each other, they had already heard it but thought it was a track on a disk. Maybe it was.

Reggie stepped away from the door and in the next second he lifted his foot and kicked it open. The notion to not frighten the old man had gone out the window.

As the door swung open, they took a look inside: The house was messy, extremely messy, there was clutter on the floors and the cabinet that stood directly in view of the open door. A foul smell drifted from inside and the gargoyles who took the brunt of it twitched their noses.

Kira slapped a hand over her face as she let out an exasperated sound. The detectives and the Venandi looked at the gargoyles as if they were making a big deal out of it.

Reggie turned and met everyones eyes until they landed on Maya's as if asking if they should go in and she nodded.

He turned back to the house and stepped inside, careful not to make too much noise since they were breaking and entering. The others followed behind him and as they walked through the dimly lit house, they tried their best to miss the mess on the carpeted floor. They couldn't even tell what color it was due to it being covered with papers, plates, and old style toys. The walls were baby blue and it made the room dim from the lack of windows.

"Police!" Reggie called out. "Is anyone here?" He thought his authority would lure Paul out but no one answered and they all stopped so they could hear if someone was moving.

"It didn't look like this before…" Reggie looked dumbfounded as he moved his gaze over the clutter. "This place was pristine when I came here with my father…"

"Maybe he finally lost his mind." Lucas whispered. "I'm surprised they didn't commit him to a mental hospital."

Reggie ignored him as he lifted his eyes to a door that was locked with a padlock attached to the handle. Maya had found it before he did and she knew it had to have something worth hiding if it had been locked to such measures, especially in one's own home.

She was about to make her way to break the lock when Cale walked past her and beat her to it. He grabbed ahold of the large object and pulled it from the handle with ease, the handle and a part of the door falling to the growing garbage heap on the floor.

Cale let the lock fall from his hand as he reached for the hole he had made in the door and pulled it open, pushing a bunch of junk out of the way as he did so.

He stepped over the junk without bothering to see what was inside first and Maya followed close behind with Arthur and the Venandi in tow. It was wise for the seasoned fighters to go in first in case something went south.

As they stepped in, they found themselves in a room larger than they had imagined, not only that, but it was cleaner and lit by large lights overhead.

There were notebooks and binders on four tables that were placed at each wall and on the walls were pictures, pictures that sent chills down the gargoyles spines.

They were close up images of the bodies of dead gargoyles, their bodies splayed out in strange positions and they were covered in blood. They found themselves looking at the images, transfixed on the dead gargoyles.

They were human now after their reincarnations, maybe in their seventies or perhaps they had died again. Maya found the image of Oberon that had been posted on Paul's website hanging directly in front of them and she turned to see Arthur's reaction. He had yet to see the image and a small amount of shock filled his face but he quickly shook it off.

Maya moved her attention back to the wall where beside the picture of Oberon was the picture of the demon. It was blurred further due to the size of the image but they could still make out the curved horns, the pointed wings, and it's blurred eyes.

The humans recoiled while the Venandi looked on with awe, the gargoyles minus Arthur who had already seen the images looked on with stone expressions. Standing there wasn't going to make the pictures less blurry nor would it give them their answers. What could on the other hand was the notebooks and binders surrounding them.

They all set to work, the binders outnumbered the amount of them there and as they flipped though them, their arms touched from the lack of room.

They were mostly met with more images of the bodies of deceased gargoyles but as Maya reached the end of her own binder she came across a picture that made her flipping come to a stop.

It was the only picture that had living gargoyles and some of them she recognized from the pictures of the dead.

Her heart thumped at the people standing front and center: Her mother and father.

None of the gargoyles were smiling and neither were her parents, her mothers braided hair reached to her waist and she wore the signature trenchcoat and knee high boot combo that her daughter would inherit. Her father stood beside his future wife, awkward but motivated. His blonde hair was long and almost fell into his eyes. The image was black and white so it had been taken a long time ago, it had a military feel to it.

She counted each of the gargoyles including her parents and when she was done, she found it hard to believe that there was thirty full blooded gargoyles that had worked with the humans, perhaps more.

Her eyes dropped to her shaking hand, everyone aside from her parents had died fighting the demons. All full blooded.

How could the half blooded gargoyles ever hope to beat the demons if the full blooded gargoyles couldn't?

The gargoyles of that age had fought the demon fodder, not the real deal. The gargoyles of this age were in even more danger. They had to destroy the demons hearts but the creatures would never give them the chance, they were too fast and too powerful.

Maya thought of her full power and the use it could be in this fight. She had never used it. She never needed to. What she used of it now would send her body into a fit and she always wondered when the right time would be to use it.

She turned her head to Arthur who was looking through a binder to the left of her and the sound of the others going through their own binders filled her ears. Paper rubbing together, the flip of a page, a rip as their fingers pulled too hard.

She hadn't realized that Arthur had stopped looking at his own and his eyes were locked on the picture of his parents and the other gargoyles. She didn't interrupt him from his thoughts, he had never allowed himself to grieve their parents deaths due to him being caught up in what Maya and his brothers were doing.

Maya could see that he was trying his best to hold everything back. Their parents deaths had broken them, had sent Maya down a road that she should have never gone on, had made Arthur lose his innocence in order to bring her back to him.

She furrowed her brows as she looked past her brother to see Cale gazing down at a page in his own binder. The hand that held up the previous page shook and his mouth was open as shock filled him.

Maya blinked as her jaw locked.

He had to have found something interesting.

She stepped back from her own binder and Arthur settled there instead to get a better look at the picture.

Maya stopped beside Cale and looked into his face: He looked distraught, she hadn't seen him this way since he had found out about his father's death.

"What is it?" She asked softly and the others stopped their browsing and turned to see what was going on.

Maya couldn't see the page he was looking at due to him holding the one before it in the way. When he didn't answer and kept his dark eyes on the binder, she leaned to take a look.

It was a list of names but what were they for?

She read each of them and as she did, her heart began to race. She counted to twenty on the one page and there had to be thirty more pages all filled with names. As she realized what the names were, she felt like she was going to be sick and her knees buckled but she managed to catch herself on the table with her shaking arms.

It was a list of people she and her brothers had killed, it was like the names were calling out to her. They begged for her to let them live.

Her jerky movement made Cale acknowledge her, his eyes meeting her's and she couldn't explain the look in them, the only word that came to mind was resentment.

His hand let go of the previous page and with his index finger, he pointed to two names that were side by side.

Kalf Ward and *Taya Ward.*

Maya's eyes fell to the names and she began to shake as she realized what she had done.

"...You killed my parents." Cale's rough voice filled the room as she dragged her gaze from the paper to his wide eyes, fear filling her own.

There was no time to be shocked by what they had just learned as Azazel, Astaroth, and Abraxas stepped through one of the shadows and Azazel's cackle filled the house.

Chapter 49

They were no where near prepared for the demons entrance, they weren't even sure how they knew of this place. But as Azazel grabbed Ari by her hair and her scream filled the house along with his laughter, they jumped to action.

The Venandi were the first to jump but Abraxas stopped them and with a swipe of claws, he threw his back blood on them after clawing his own hand.

They had barely covered their faces in time with their covered arms. The blood steamed on their white jackets and they had to pull them off. Maya and Arthur helped the Venandi while Cale, Emily, Kira, and Trevor ran to help Ari who remained in Azazel's grip.

The demon threw her over their heads into the hall where she landed with a crash into the heap of garbage and the demon leapt over them to meet her there.

They ran after him while Arthur and Maya remained with the Venandi and the humans who were being rounded up by Astaroth.

"Go help the other gargoyles!" Alvertos' monotone voice filled the room as he yelled to Arely and in the next second he brought his sword up and blocked Abraxas' blood with his blade. The silver gleaming in the florescent light.

Arley nodded and did what he was told with no hesitation, dodging Abraxas' shadow on the way out.

Reggie and the others had terrified looks as they pulled their guns out, but they realized they couldn't use them with the gargoyles in such close proximity.

As Maya noticed their trouble, she left Abraxas to Arthur and the Venandi as she ran to help them. Her arm blocked the female demons attack before it hit Tori whose screech caused the gargoyles to flinch as it hit their eardrums.

"You've been busy." The demon mused in her girlish voice.

"As have you." Maya spat as she returned the attack but Astaroth dodged it with ease.

"What makes you think these humans will be enough to help you?" The demon cocked her head as her smile widened.

"I don't think anything," Maya replied as she stepped between the demon and the humans. The sound of the fights around her setting her on edge, her eyes twitching to Arthur and the Venandi who were trying their best to dodge Abraxas' attacks.

"I *know* I have to beat you at any cost." Maya narrowed her eyes.

"The only thing you're willing to risk is your own life." Astaroth chuckled.

Azazel seemed to only have eyes for Cale as they fought him six to one.

"You are filled with turmoil, anger, and hurt." The demon's voice was filled with honey as he teased and he allowed Cale to push him to the wall.

Cale's dark eyes narrowed as his claws went for the demons heart but Azazel ducked and slapped Cale to the floor.

"I wonder who all of that anger is aimed towards?" Azazel's eyes flashed to the room where Maya and Arthur fought and Cale's twitched the same way as Arely made his own crack at the demon.

Through the door Maya could be seen fighting the red haired demon while Arthur fought Abraxas, neither of them seemed to be getting the upper hand on the demons.

"Are you ok?" Emily came from behind Cale as the others jumped to help Arely.

"I'm fine." He assured her as he got back to his feet but the answer wasn't good enough for Emily, she had heard what happened between him and Maya, knew what it was doing to him.

"Come on boy!" Azazel back flipped over the other fighters to meet Cale again, he moved as if there was no such thing as gravity. "I want to see that anger!"

The sound of the piano track only caused Cale to be more on edge. "Where's Paul Ash?" He questioned as he approached the demon and Azazel closed his eyes as he dodged every hit the others tried to land.

"Dead." He replied simply with a grin.

Cale chewed the inside of his mouth as he went for the white haired demon.

How did the demons know where they were going? How did they know they would want to talk to Paul Ash?

Azazel's grin widened then he was gone, they looked around, dumbfounded on where the demon had gone. Arely looked suspicious, he knew what the demons could do.

Cale brought his attention to the room where Maya and the others were fighting to see if he had joined the other demons but his eyes landed on Maya instead.

Her hand was wrapped around Astaroth's throat and the demon's was around her's.

He met Maya's narrowed mismatched eyes and her pointed teeth, she was struggling against the demons pull while the demon laughed at the gargoyles inability to use her power.

Maya was the one who sent death upon his birth parents. Maybe she wasn't the one who had killed them, but she had a hand in it. He would have lived a normal life it weren't for her. He would have had a life with both parents. Would have had a family.

The girl he had met in the cave who had a past life destroyed everything for him.

It was her fault…

Her fault.

"Let's see where all that anger is stemmed from." Azazel's voice rang from behind him and before he could turn, a cold air entered him and a yell escaped his lungs as the cold filled them.

His mind went blank as the demons hold took him, he turned to Emily and the others who yelled for him but he was no longer Cale.

His dark eyes had been replaced by Azazel's bottomless black, the demon was wearing his body like a new pair a clothes.

The look on his comrades faces caused the demon unfathomable excitement.

"Now," Azazel's voice mixed with Cale's filled the room as he spoke. "Who will put this poor boy out of his misery?"

Emily let out a whimper as the other gargoyles stood frozen with shock, they knew what this meant.

Arley ran past Emily with no hesitation, his holy water sword ready to cut off Cale's head.

"NO!" Emily used all of the strength she had and jumped between her friends body and Arley's blade. The Venandi's blue eyes widened as he came to a stop, the blade only a few inches away from Emily's throat.

Trevor, Ari, and Kira had launched to help Emily but stopped as Arely pulled a knife from his belt and turned it towards them.

"It's not wise to attack me." He warned them as he kept his eyes on Emily and the demon inside Cale's body. "Move aside, gargoyle." He warned. "Your friend is gone."

Emily's voice shook. "You're not killing him…" Tears streamed down her cheeks and they glimmered in the dull light.

Azazel cackled from behind them and it sent a chill through them due to the combined voices. The demon didn't bother to strike, he simply stood back and enjoyed the show.

"Final warning." Arley pulled the sword back to ready his strike.

Even though she flinched and whimpered, Emily didn't move. The three gargoyles that stood behind the Venandi were ready to stop him. Their sharp teeth biting their lips, a trail of blood coming from Ari's.

Arley gritted his teeth as conflict filled him but he knew what had to be done and he plunged the blade forward.

With the strength he used, it would go through both Emily and Cale, killing them both with ease. But before that could happen, a hand closed around Arley's wrist with the strength that could have broken the man's bone if he had moved another inch.

Emily's tear stained eyes filled with relief at the sight of the person who had stopped Arley.

The Venandi lifted his head and his eyes met Maya's mismatched. Her teeth were sharp points and smalls horns were popping out of her head. She had left the fight with Astaroth to stop the death of her friends. Her eyes narrowed and for the first time she saw fear on Arley's face.

"What do you think you're doing?" She growled and the Venandi recoiled as she let go of his wrist and he rubbed it as he stepped away.

"The boy has been possessed." He stated with a shaky voice.

Maya turned her head and looked past Emily to Cale, his eyes had turned to Azazel's color. His expression was something one would never see on his face. A look of pure evil. Her eyes widened and her heart raced as she took in the man who she had bonded with.

The man whose life she had destroyed.

"Don't worry *Anna,* I wasn't gonna let him kill the boy." Azazel chirped and in almost a blur, he stepped out of Cale's body and it collapsed to the floor into a heap of garbage.

Emily jumped down to catch him.

Azazel became solid again as he looked down at Cale's body then to

Maya who still looked on with shock. "I was just having some fun with him," He gleamed. "And after seeing what's going on in his mind, there's no way I can let him die yet." He grinned with his own mouth now.

"May the games continue." His voice had the same amount of silk as his master's.

He disappeared again.

A scream from inside the other room made her rush back inside, she had left the humans with Arthur since he and the Venandi had pushed back Abraxas. Now she realized it was just a ploy on the demons part. They wanted to distract her and she had fallen for it.

Reggie stood in the way of the other humans who cowered behind him as Astaroth approached them, her nails extended into points.

"Abraxas was disappointed he couldn't have more fun with you and your father." She licked her lips seductively as she took another confident step towards him. "Maybe I will get to play."

The demon lifted her eyes to meet Maya as Abraxas got ahold of Arthur's throat and lifted him into the air. The sight brought Maya back to when she had gotten her memories back, how Oberon had done the same thing. Once again she saw her brother having the life choked out of him. Abraxas' shadow formed around the Venandi and trapped them in a corner so they couldn't interfere.

They were going to make her choose.

"Choose." Sure enough, Abraxas said the word as he turned to her and Arthur struggled against his grip. "Your precious brother who went through hell to find you," He turned to Reggie, his gleeful expression was borderline insane. "Or this *human*."

Maya could have done it, she could have saved both of them, but her body was already feeling the effects of using so much of her power. She didn't know how they knew it, but the demons were using her lack of power to their advantage.

She could only save one.

Astaroth began to press down on Reggie as he clenched his teeth so they wouldn't hear his screams.

"No!" Arabella tried desperately to find a way to get out of Abraxas' shadow cage. They couldn't even jump over it, the shadow would swallow them as they went over. She and the other Venandi looked on with fearful eyes, their mouths in snarls.

Maya was willing to risk it all, she was going to save both, but the dizziness hit her and she fell to her knees. Azazel snickered at her sorry state as he stepped in front of her and knelt down. "Look at what the strongest gargoyle has become! So disappointing!"

"The human!" Arthur mustered enough air to yell. "He won't kill me! Choose the human!"

Maya's head shot up and she looked past Azazel's pale face that laid only a few inches from her own.

"The human!" Arthur yelled one more time, the end of the last word failing as he lost his breath.

Maya heaved as she pushed Azazel out of the way and ran to Reggie who was getting choked by Astaroth. Her sharp nails were digging into his skin, causing blood to pour from the pricks. Maya gritted her teeth as she thought of her decision: Arthur had told her to do it and that he wouldn't be killed, but she didn't trust him.

He had made the choice to sacrifice himself so they wouldn't lose the humans help.

As Maya approached the demon, she vanished and Reggie fell against Lucas as he gasped for breath. Maya turned to Abraxas as she heard something large fall to the floor and found Arthur unconscious. Her eyes widened as her breath hitched and in the next second her knees buckled. Abraxas picked up her brother's unconscious body by the back of his shirt and carried him as the other two demons joined him.

"Don't worry," the shadow demon assured her. "He won't die in the shadow as long as I have a hold on him." His shadow swirled around them and they began to sink into it.

Maya rushed to her feet and ran as fast she could but it was too late.

She would have gone into the shadow to save him but as she reached for her brothers hand, the shadow disappeared completely as did Arthur and the demons.

She collapsed to the floor as not only the haze of using her power washed over her, but the desperation to save her brother.

And her failure to do so.

"I told you that you would give me a replacement." Abraxas' voice filled the room even though he was gone and Maya's heart thumped.

Abraxas was a torturous bastard and she had taken away his *toy*. She unwillingly did give him a replacement, his new plaything was her brother.

The shadow blocking the Venandi dispersed and they practically fell from it while the humans began to shuffle as the air in the room returned to normal and Reggie stood, his eyes on Maya's shaking back.

Maya got to her feet as Arely and the others reentered the room but her eyes remained where Arthur and the demons had disappeared. Someone stepped beside her as the rest of the room remained silent and she looked to see that it was Cale.

His eyes had darkened and there were bags under them, his brows were pushed together and his mouth was clenched shut. He was looking at her with an expression she never thought she'd see directed at her: His face was filled with hatred.

They knew the taste of defeat very well, it was sour and it left them empty. They had tasted it so many times that one would think the taste would have dulled.

But this was a new taste, a taste so bitter that their mouths hung open to ease their burning taste buds. They had lost one of their own to the clutches of a torturous demon and Maya had to explain it to Archie whose face dropped.

Another one of them had been possessed by Azazel but had lived due to Emily's and Maya's protection.

The Venandi had had their eyes on Cale the whole ride home, especially Arley who had the chance to kill him but lost it. Maya had decided to ride in the front seat while Cale sat in the far back with Emily and the others.

She was the reason Cale didn't have a family, it was her fault that his father had been killed due to her brothers trying to get to her. His birth parents more so, she was the one who led the raids on the cities and towns. She didn't stop her brothers and she had even killed the humans herself.

It was as Arthur had said, she had the highest kill count.

She wasn't sure if she was the one who had killed his parents, she never killed anyone who she thought had young children.

How fucking noble of her.

Maybe it was towards the end of her life when she had quit killing, Cale was two years older than her current life after all.

The thought didn't make her feel better, she was just as guilty as her brothers due to her inability to stop them. No, it wasn't an inability, she had chosen not to stop them.

She had been told to forget about what she had done in her past life but it always bothered her, it ate her alive. Her sins came back to haunt her in the form of Cale, the man who she had met in the cave, the man who had always been there for her. Who understood her when she didn't understand herself.

She felt sick the entire way home with not only Cale and his parents on her mind, but Arthur as well who could be already living up to Abraxas' promise of being his plaything.

They achieved nothing by going to Paul Ash's house, they only managed to get their asses handed to them again.

"He gave himself up so you could save the detectives son?" Archie asked her when they were back at the cabins and she nodded with her teeth pressed together.

Archie watched as her pale face turned paler and he placed his hands on her shoulders as the others made their way to the large cabin to figure out what they were going to do next.

The rain was still hammering down on them, their clothes drenched.

"You know what you did in your past life, you lived it again by getting your memories back, but you know you're no longer that girl." Archie assured her as his voice cracked, the rain poured down on them and it set the mood.

Maya moved her eyes from the short man to Emily and Cale who were the last to go in the cabin behind the others. Emily was looking at Cale with a nervous expression and her wide eyes moved back to Maya for a second before she followed him inside.

It could have been Azazel's possession but Maya knew better, Cale's anger was justified and Archie knew it.

"Would you have thought the same if it were your father?" She asked matter of factly as her eyes fell and Archie recoiled.

"Don't-" He began but she pulled away from him and began to walk to the cabin alone.

She could barely hear him walking behind her due to the rain coming down harder. She was soaked by the time she joined the others who lifted their heads as she walked in with Archie in tow. They had been silent before they joined them, Maya supposed it was due to the defeat that they had added to their growing list.

She looked to her friends who sat together on the couch, their faces were filled with so many emotions but they didn't look mad or disappointed at finding out what she had done.

It was Cale who looked away from her with an air of annoyance, it was her mistakes that damaged him the most.

She inhaled sharply as she sat in the chair across from them, her tired legs practically thanking her as she sat down and the pressure in them dispersed. The power was becoming more and more unbearable, even the simplest transformation made her weak.

Archie stood beside her as the others continued to look on.

The silence was welcome at first but after awhile, it became almost unbearable.

Alvertos was the one to break it, "They knew where we were going, chances are they know where we are now."

"It's Lucifer's game." Donato said casually. "He wanted the events that transpired today to happen, he wanted to take the black and white eyed gargoyles brother, everything is for her."

"Did you see any of this happen beforehand?" Kira asked, clearly annoyed. "If you didn't, your power is awfully useless."

"I don't choose what I see." Donato ignored her diss.

"Was Azazel's possession over that boy a part of Lucifers plan?" Arely spat as he turned to Cale who kept his gaze away from the others. "His hold is still on him, right now Azazel is in his head telling him he should kill us all!" He gripped the hilt of his sword and the other Venandi followed suit aside from Alvertos who rose a hand and shook his head. The gargoyles and the humans stood at the ready even though the Venandi had stopped.

"We will not kill him my brother, the gargoyles will never allow it and we need them as much as they need us." He moved his gaze between Maya and the others as they sat back down slowly, their eyes on Cale who hadn't even flinched "...But I assure you that when the other Venandi join us, they will show no hesitation in killing this man."

"I'd like to see them try." Emily's eyes narrowed until she met Maya's gaze and they fell, she knew Maya would have her back but she looked so close to breaking.

"What we plan to do is simple," Alvertos continued on as if the previous conversation didn't happen. "We wait for the demons to call us."

Maya perked up from the Venandi's plan but not in a good way, "You're telling me we're going to let my brother get tortured by that bastard?"

Her voice was rough, the roughest it's ever been, and they had to do a double take to make sure it was indeed Maya who was speaking.

"I don't know why you chose me..." Reggie's voice drifted and Maya's head snapped to him. "Your brother is more valuable than me... he can make a difference while I can't."

"You can." She leaned forward in her chair to get a better look at him as he stood away from her with the other humans. "I saved you at the monument not only because your father told me to, but because I wanted to." Reggies eyes softened but the worry was still there.

Maya leaned back into her chair, "I can't let Abraxas torture him…" her voice broke and Reggie's face turned back to fear as he thought of the torture he and his father had gone through with the demon. He knew first hand how wretched the demon was.

"We don't even know where they are." Arely was beginning to look more and more annoyed with her. "You have a connection with Lucifer even though you don't like to admit it. You can't tell where he is while he can tell where you are."

"I don't care, I'll make it work to save him!" She gripped onto the sides of her chair, her heart racing. "He's done everything for me… I can't allow him to be tortured while I sit around and-"

"Don't worry, we'll save your brother." Cale snapped and everyone practically cracked their necks to face him. The bags under his eyes had deepened and his irises were almost black as his eyes narrowed. "What's left of your murderous family will return to you."

"Cale!" Emily grabbed his arm and like a switch had been hit, Cale's eyes widened and they returned to their normal color as he realized what he had just said.

They all looked on with shock, even Kellan who would have otherwise found the event entertaining.

Maya's jaw shook and she could feel a large lump develop in her throat.

"I-It's ok, Emily." She got to her feet and almost fell as her legs gave out but Archie caught her. They all looked on with shock but none of them knew what to do. Cale watched as his mind rushed through so many different thoughts, his legs shaking as Maya pushed away from Archie, her hair covering her gray eyes.

"I-I'm fine." She assured shakily.

She wasn't.

She stepped quickly out of the cabin into the rain where she ran through the puddles. The water soaking her boots and by the time she got to her cabin, they were sopping wet.

With little to no strength, she shut the door behind her as she stepped inside and pulled her boots off without untying them first.

She had a blank stare as she wobbled to the coach only to collapse on the floor in front of it, her elbows and knees took the brunt of the fall but she didn't feel the pain. She could only feel it in her heart.

The regret.

The grief.

A monster was all she was ever going to be, in her past life, and in this one as well.

She was as bad as Lucifer, the being she tried so hard to fight.

Tears began to stream down her cheeks and they wouldn't stop, they fell to the floor and a sob escaped her lips. Her heart felt like it was going to burst through her chest and she wouldn't mind if it did.

Why couldn't she have stayed dead? Why did fate bring her memories back? What was her purpose?

The only way to ease the pain in her chest was to scream, and as her breath caught on a sob, she screamed again. The tears blinding her as they fell endlessly from her gray eyes.

Her arms and legs collapsed from underneath her and she screamed into the cold floor, her tears touching her lips and she could taste the salt in them. Her breath caught again and she whimpered as she wrapped her arms around her chest to ease the pressure but it was to no avail and she began to sob louder than before.

All of her wrong doings replayed in her mind and her wailing grew louder.

Back in the large cabin, the others remained.

The gargoyles could hear Maya's cries as clear as day even through the heavy rain. Their eyes were wide and their jaws locked.

The Venandi and the detectives could also hear her but not to the same extent. They remained silent and their eyes stared into nothing as they listened.

Emily had her hand over her eyes as she fought not to cry herself, she had never heard Maya this distraught.

Cale sat with his head down as her cries filled his ears, his hands twisted together so tightly that his veins popped out. His entire body shook as his teeth pressed together, his eyes filled with regret.

Chapter 50

Maya's cabin was filled with the sound of the police scanner. The constant buzz, beeps, and the voices of the officers filling her ears.

It had been on continuously for two days as she waited for any sign of the demons, her battle suit on and ready for when they finally showed themselves.

She laid on the coach facing the scanner, her heavy eyes on it's dark edges and the red lights that flashed. She had barely slept two hours in the past two days, it wasn't that she couldn't sleep, she wouldn't allow herself.

When the demons finally called her, she would go with no hesitation, she would proudly give herself to save Arthur.

Arthur…

Her older brother who loved her unconditionally, even when she forced him to give up his innocence. He was being tortured right now, she was sure of it. They would keep him alive to play with her but torture wasn't out of the question. The thought of Arthur screaming from the pain filled her mind and she whimpered into the couch, her body beginning to shake.

Why were they waiting so long? Why couldn't they have taken her instead?

She wished their positions were switched, she would gladly be tortured, she deserved it after all.

A knock on the door brought her back to her senses and her eyes flipped to the noise. It wasn't like her to not notice someone coming but she had been distracted as of late.

"…Come in." She said, her voice hoarse.

Emily opened the door and before she stepped in, she paused to take in her sullen friend.

Emily and the others came to visit her many times over the past two days since she never left the cabin. She would assure them she was alright and they needn't worry but they came by with the same worried expression each time.

Emily closed the door behind her and the snap made Maya flinch.

On edge was an understatement.

"You need to eat something." Emily demanded as she set an apple on the table in front of her and made her way to the other end of the couch to sit.

Maya moved her feet out of the way so she could do so, her eyes on the apple the entire time but she didn't get the urge to eat it.

She only thought of the devils influence on Eve and how it caused the fall of mankind. His whispers echoed through her ears and set her on edge.

Emily dropped her gaze from the weary gargoyle. "You know we're all worried about you, even the Venandi and the detectives."

"Hm." Was all Maya could muster as she hid the lower half of her face under her arm.

"Even Cale is worried… he regrets what he said…it was Azazel that forced him to say it." Emily's voice shook as if she was wandering in uncharted territory.

Maya covered more of her face, Cale was the only one who hadn't come to see her. They hadn't seen each other since he lost it on her, since she had broken down.

Maybe it was because of Azazel's influence but Maya knew better, it was his true feelings, the possession only amplified them. She knew Cale hadn't come by because he didn't want to hurt her again but she was also sure he didn't want to see her face. The face of the girl who was the reason why his birth parents were dead.

"Sam, please." Emily's voice broke as she noticed Maya turn to the color of a ghost. "You need to sleep, you need to eat…you need to take care of yourself."

"*Why*?" The way Maya said the word sounded as if what Emily said was stupid, that someone like her shouldn't take care of herself… that she deserved to suffer.

"How do you expect to fight the demons and save Arthur if you have no strength?" Emily tested. "Arthur wouldn't want you to act like this."

"…Yeah."

Emily shook her head as she got up and grabbed the police scanner. "You think no one cares about you and you deserve this but you're wrong!" Her eyes filled with tears. "You're not your past life! You're not *Maya*!"

Maya's eyes rolled up to meet hers, "I *am* Maya, I chose the name over my current one."

"That doesn't matter!" Emily knelt in front of her, her face filled with sadness but it was also stern. "You can be called Maya as much as you want but you're not the same girl." She placed a hand on her's. "Names don't matter, it's who you are."

"Hm." Maya repeated again and Emily got up with the scanner in tow, "I'm bringing this with me."

At that Maya finally got up. "No! I need that!" She begged.

"I'll listen to it." Emily assured her as she opened the front door and stepped out."Now get some sleep."

Although her intentions were good, Emily left her with nothing but her own thoughts.

Hours had gone by but it didn't matter to her since she had lost her sense of time.

She looked out the window to see that it was dark, the sun had left for the time being. Her heart raced as she continued to lay on the coach and although Emily had demanded it, she couldn't sleep. It was hard to even close her eyes since under her eyelids was nothing but darkness.

She couldn't handle the dark, it reminded her of the void in her mind so she laid with all the lights on until morning.

A knock on the door roused her from her thoughts first thing in the morning. As usual someone had come to check on her. She was sure it was going to be one of her friends again but she hoped it was going to be Emily coming back with the police scanner.

After she told them to come in, the door opened and closed as they entered. She peeped over the arm of the couch and was met with Reggie.

For the first time in hours, she sat up as he walked to her, his eyes on the empty space at the end of the couch. She nodded to let him know that it was ok to sit.

He sat beside her and Maya crossed her legs, her sad eyes meeting his and he gave a small smile.

"Kira is right, you do look like shit." His attempt to make her smile was futile and he knew it. "Don't beat yourself up."

"Would you not?" She questioned with a brow in the air. "I told you what I've done, you've seen the records… the people I've killed."

"You were reborn-"

"Bullshit." She narrowed her eyes but her aggression wasn't aimed towards him. "I'm still the monstrous bitch I was all those year's ago."

He furrowed his brows. "You honestly believe that?" He leaned closer to her, "You turned your life around, you died to make up for what you've done...You were born again and even with your memories back, you fight for what's right, you saved my father and you saved me."

"Two right's versus hundreds of wrongs." She dropped her tired eyes to her entwined hands and squeezed them, the veins popping out as she did so. "I broke apart so many families," She shuddered. "I'm the reason why so many kids grew up without parents, I'm the reason why Cale has no family to go home to." Her lips quivered and she instinctively brought her hand up to cover her eyes.

Cale's face when he had snapped at her still filled her mind, how angry he looked.

He hated her.

Reggie watched as her hand shook and his frown deepened.

"I haven't known you long and I admit when I first saw you, I thought you were a monster." He kept going when she didn't remove her hand from her eyes. "I thought you were my enemy and so did my father, but everything changed when you saved him from the female demon...he told me and he couldn't believe it, I couldn't either. How could something that was once our enemy, something that used to kill innocent people have changed so much to the point of saving an old man like my father?"

Maya's hand dropped an inch until it fell all the way down her face to her lap.

Her eyes were wet but the tears didn't fall, she focused instead on what Reggie was saying.

"We chased after the demons when they went into the Washington monument..." He exhaled sharply, the memory of what happened in there still haunted him. "That's where we met Abraxas and that's the last time I saw my father... when I woke up, he was gone." He met her eyes and she swallowed. "I know you tried saving him but you had no strength from saving me...I realized that after I watched you choose between me and your brother." He placed a hand on her trembling one. "You saved me twice now, even at the expense of your brother."

"...He told me to." She stated shakily.

"Stop making yourself out to be this horrible person." He shot and she flinched. "My father sacrificed his life because he saw something in you." It was his turn for his eyes to fill with tears. "He lived for me, my mother died years ago and it broke him but I was his reason to live. He must have really believed in you… a *monster*." He tightened his grip on her hand. "I don't like seeing you like this, my father believed in you and you can't let him down."

She opened her mouth but closed it, her jaw shaking as she thought of what she could say after hearing everything Reggie had said.

The door slammed open and it hit the wall, making the two jump to their feet. In the doorway stood Emily with the police scanner in her trembling hands. Behind her were the others running between cabins to tell the Venandi, the humans, and the other gargoyles what was happening.

"It's them." Emily exclaimed while out of breath. "It's the demons."

"She's the reason you don't have a family…" A voice echoed through his head. *"You wouldn't be suffering if it weren't for her."*

Cale woke with a start, it had been the first time in almost three days that he had slept more than a wink. He rose from the couch and sighed, his eyes had bags under them the color of a ripened grape. His eyes had gotten darker and it was thanks to Azazel's possession.

He got to his feet and wandered to the window at the far end of the living room. The sun was shining now, it was quite the change from the past two days of rain. He listened to the birds chirp and watched as the suns rays shined onto the changing leaves.

"It's her fault." Azazel's voice snuck up from behind him and he turned on his heel to find the room empty. His breath caught as he gripped the side of his head. *"If it weren't for her, you'd have a family."* The demons voice echoed again. *"She's a monster."*

"GET OUT OF MY HEAD!" Cale brought a fist to his head and pounded against it but no matter the pain he inflicted on himself, Azazel's voice still remained.

The demon laughed at his failed attempt at subduing him.

Maya came to his mind as he calmed, he remembered the look on her face as he said the words he didn't mean. How she had gone to her cabin and cried for hours afterwards. Even now her wails filled his ears and the guilt he felt became unbearable. He had wanted so badly to tell her that he didn't mean it, that she was no longer the girl that had killed people for revenge.

"Or is she?" Azazel mused and Cale shook his head with a pained expression as he fought the thoughts running through his head.

She was the reason his parents died, he wasn't even sure if it was her or one of her brothers who had done it. But it didn't matter who had done it, Maya was still the cause.

It was hard to believe that just days before he was worried out of his mind for her.

The relief he had felt as he pulled her into his arms, her berry shampoo had been replaced by the smell of iodine. Her smile along with her hazel eyes that had turned gray and the way they lit up when she was happy flashed into his mind. He had seen that look directed at him so many times but that was broken now.

The fiery girl he had met in the cave all those months ago didn't have a hand in his parents deaths, that was her past life.

But she had gotten her memories back from that life, a life of violence and solitude.

She had chosen to call herself Maya and to leave her new name behind. Maya was the name she had chosen to take since it would give her more exposure. The name her enemies knew her by, but as of late, it seemed they called her by a completely different name: *Anna.*

Who was Anna?

Did she have another past life that she didn't know about? Did she have dreams of this one like she had with the last?

She told no one even if she did and he didn't blame her.

He had been locked up with her, had broken out of their prison together, he had trained and fought with her. They had formed a bond, a friendship where they understood each other just by looking at one another.

He wondered what he looked like when he had lost it on her but the look on her face afterwards gave him an idea.

Her wide eyes as they began to fill with tears, her mouth in a thin line as she got shakily to her feet. Everything had changed between them because of their trip to Paul Ash's house. They thought they would learn something of importance but it only pulled them apart.

"She deserves it." Azazel's silky voice appeared again and sent his hair on end. *"Her brother deserves it."*

Arthur had destroyed Cale's life just as much as his sister had, maybe even more. He had kidnapped him and turned him into a monster and in doing so he brought upon the death of his father. Both siblings had indirectly killed his family.

Sam's smile flashed in his head again.
No, it was Maya's.
But perhaps it was Anna's.
He fell to his knees and as he did, he pounded on the side of his head again. Everything he was seeing was due to Azazel's possession. Everything on his mind was amplified and the demon took all of his pain and anger and used it against him. He could hear the muffled sound of the demons laughter in his ears and it sent a chill up his spine.
"GET OUT!" Her roared.
Three days of this had been more than enough and a thought came to his mind that he never thought would: He wished Emily and Maya had let Arley kill him.
"Cale!" His head shot to the source of the voice and he was met with Trevor pushing the front door open. The man's eyes filled with shock at seeing Cale on the ground, his fist to his head.
He inhaled sharply as he composed himself and got to the point of why he was there.
"The demons!"

Cale ran with Trevor to the playground where everyone was meeting. They were the last to arrive and when they joined the others, Cale was met with apprehensive looks. The Venandi's hands twitched as if they wanted nothing more than to plunge their swords into his chest.
Emily made her way to him as Trevor joined Ari and Kira, her sad eyes meeting his for a moment then they twitched to her right. He followed her gaze and as his eyes landed on who she was looking at, he froze.
Maya stood across from Archie who had his hands on her shoulders, she had her backless suit on with her black skinny jean and knee high boot combo. She looked gaunt, her face paler than usual, the dark circles under her eyes made it look like they were sinking in.
Archie leaned his head against her's and she continued to look uninterested as he assured her that it would be alright.
She and Cale both knew he was lying.
As he pulled away from her, she nodded and her eyes twitched to where Emily and Cale stood, her mouth falling open as her eyes widened then she turned away.

"Let's go." She demanded with a hoarse voice.

The others followed her while Cale and Emily stood back. Ari, Kira and Trevor flashed them nervous looks as they walked past them.

"Neither of you look fit to fight." Emily looked up to meet his bloodshot eyes. "I heard you talking to yourself… to the demon."

Cale kept his eyes on Maya's back as she walked away, her side braids were gone and she wore her hair completely down. It was a tangled mess and as she bowed her head, some of it pulled away from her back and he could see her back bone sticking out of her pale skin. She had already lost weight.

It was Emily's turn to follow his gaze and as she did, her face fell further. "I don't know how much more she can take." Her voice shook. "She hates herself."

Cale's heart lurched at Emily's words and as he began to walk after the others, he clenched his fists.

"She deserves it." Azazel's voice appeared again.

Chapter 51

Three days ago.

A man's pained screams filled the warehouse, the sound vibrated off the buildings hollow shell and fell back on him and his torturer. The demons cackle echoed more than the gargoyles screams, he had never had this much fun.

Arthur's head fell against his chest, knocking the air out of his lungs and blood poured from his toothless mouth.

"You're something else, you know that?" Abraxas mused, his eyes lit like a flame. "Humans break so easily but you hold up like steel." He grabbed Arthur by his brown hair and pulled his head back to the point of it touching the back of the chair he was chained to.

The strength Arthur had to break the chains was gone due to the demons torture and his body rushing to heal. Even in the darkness of the warehouse, one would be able to see the holes in his gums where his teeth should've been. Blood poured down his chin onto his neck and chest. Arthur's eyes were barely open and his hands shook against the chair, his breaths coming out as heaves.

"I can't wait for your sister to get a look at you." Abraxas licked his blood soaked hand after he flung Arthur's last tooth into the pile with the others. "Do you think she'll let it all go?" He whispered in Arthur's ear and the gargoyle shuttered. "She'll die, won't she?"

He let go of his head and it fell back down to his chest, fresh blood splattering on the floor. "We can't have that." The demon sang.

"Abraxas." Lucifer's voice echoed along with the gargoyles pained gasps and the demon turned to meet his master with his favorite demon in tow: Cain.

Lucifer stopped in front of Arthur's shaking body and knelt down to get a better look at Abraxas' handy work. "Make sure you don't kill him." He demanded with his silky voice as he stood. "Anna can't die by her own hand… she can only die by mine."

"Are you saying I wouldn't be able to kill her if she uses her power?" Abraxas cocked his head and Lucifer's bottomless eyes smiled along with his mouth. "You wouldn't be able to handle her."

The demon scowled at his master's diss.

"Besides," Lucifer turned his head to Cain. "I promised this one that he could play with her, and unlike the rest of you, he will do it right."

Cain's eyes met his master's and he nodded.

"There's a right way to play with her?" Azazel stepped through the warehouse's shadow.

"There is." Lucifer acknowledged the newcomer with a nod. "It's not too far off from what you're doing with your new toy."

Azazel's smile widened, "The boy has a lot of anger and guilt…all directed at him-" he pointed to Arthur who still had his head down as he listened. "And your sweet Anna." His eyes flashed as he brought his sight back to his master. "I'm jealous though… why does Cain get to play with her?"

"I asked nicely." Cain spoke for the first time in ages to the other demons, his voice was deep and had a rang to it.

The white haired demons looked at the one that looked less frightening than them but they knew better. His outside appearance had nothing to do with his power, he was a monster even to the other demons.

"Astaroth and Aamon already know their task for this game and remember-" Lucifer looked between his demons. "A game this fight will be." He brought his hand in front of him and wiggled his long and pale fingers. "Kill who you want but *don't* touch Anna." He moved his gaze to Cain.

"Don't worry," The demon assured his master and for the first time, he smiled and exposed his pointed teeth. "I won't need to."

Lucifer opened his mouth and what escaped sent even his demons on edge. His laughter filled the warehouse and bounced off the ceiling fifty feet above them. Arthur's heart raced at the sound while the white haired demon's simply watched as their master cackled.

Cain's expression went back to stone cold.

Now

The abandoned warehouses were twenty minutes south from the cabins and forty minutes south of D.C. Emily had explained what the police had announced over the scanner, that there had been an explosion at a site with six large warehouses.

"Are you sure it's the demons?" Ari turned and asked Emily as they sat in the SUV.

"It's been reported that it's *us* that caused the explosion… they saw horned creatures walking around." Emily explained as she looked ahead to Maya who sat in the front with Arely. Her head bowed so she couldn't see her face.

Her gaze switched to Cale who sat beside her, his eyes on the windshield. She knew he was having an internal battle, a battle with Azazel. Every so often his eyes would twitch to Maya but they would quickly move away.

The Venandi had told them the only way they could stop Azazel's possession was to kill the demon, but it seemed so out of reach. How could any of them hope to kill the creature? He would never give them the chance to take his heart.

Maya's current state didn't have to do with a possession like Cale, it was her own demons she had to face. She had faced them before but it had aways been a stalemate until now. It seemed like the demons were taking over and it wouldn't be long before she became one herself.

They came to a stop down the road from the warehouses and decided to walk the rest of the way. It was a long road that was surrounded by large trees on either side, the echoes of sirens could be heard in the distance and a large cloud of smoke rolled over the trees ahead of them.

Maya opened the door before the vehicle even came to a stop and stepped out, she no longer walked with a hitch, her determination to save her brother took care of it for her.

The others rushed out of the car to follow her and the rest of the Venandi, the detectives, and the gargoyles from the other cars exited them to follow.

All of them were there aside from Archie, Donato, and Jared. None of them would be of use and they would only be in the way.

Maya walked front and center, her strides were long but the way she moved didn't match the way she looked and felt. The only thing that kept her going was the thought of saving Arthur. No one bothered to talk to her, to tell her to slow down, they knew their efforts would be futile.

Cale's eyes landed on Maya's back as she walked, his heart thumping in his ears and Azazel's voice echoed along with each beat. His eyes moved from her as the smoke from the explosion grew closer and he could see the warehouse that had been set ablaze. There was another beside it and four more behind it and they were all connected by small enclosed bridges. As they took in the gothic buildings, they saw the graffiti on the warehouse that had been set on fire break apart, it's colors mixed with the flame and made a rainbow.

The chain link fence that had prevented anyone from entering the perimeter was knocked down at the front. It's *warning* and *no entry* signs were crushed against the ground and the fence.

What set them further on edge was the fact that although there were police cars and fire trucks in front of the burning building, there was no sign of the police or the firefighters. Maya knew what she was going to see before she got there and was prepared to see the bodies of the men and women who had reported to the scene.

Their bodies were bent and broken, blood pouring from their nostrils, mouths, and ears. Their opened eyes were wide with shock and inside them she could see the shadows that had killed them swirling in their irises.

Maya shook as she gritted her teeth, the sound of the bones rubbing together filled her ears along with the sirens of the other officers and firefighters on their way.

There would be many more bodies soon.

There were gasps and screams as the humans came upon the bodies. Maya didn't blame them, they had yet to see Abraxas' handy work and the initial shock was enough to bring a seasoned medical examiner to his knees in shock.

"Hello!" A familiar voice called and Maya brought her gaze back to the burning building and the others followed. They were fifty feet away from its burning shell but they could still feel the heat on their faces and they could even smell the demons through the fire's scent.

Their eyes fell to the red haired demon as she walked from the flames.

"I knew you'd come." She gleamed as she placed her black combat boot on the body of man that laid in her way. She rolled the back of her foot on his head then kicked him out of the way.

Once again, the air was filled with gasps.

None of them had the time to say anything to the female demon as another walked from the flames. This was an older looking demon, his long hair gray and his skin milky. His silver beard reached his chest that was covered by a black monks robe. He looked like he needed to be escorted to the nearest nursing home.

"You haven't been properly introduced to Aamon, but today my dear friend gets to play." Astaroth giggled as she cocked her head to the other demon but his face remained focused on the beings in front of him, his eyes landing on Maya after he had gotten a good look at the rest.

The click of the human's guns filled the air as they aimed them at the creatures but they waited to save their ammo for the perfect opportunity.

Kellan walked past the human's and the Venandi who also stood ready for an attack. His tall form stopping beside Maya and her eyes twitched to him to find a grin on his face. "Where's the shadow demon and the pretty boy?"

Astaroth snorted, "*Pretty boy!?*" She wiped her eyes. "I can't wait to tell Azazel that one!"

"They're both having their *fun*." Aamon answered over Astaroth's high pitched laugher.

The way he said it made it sound like the demons were off playing some kind of video game and not torturing weaker creatures.

But what they were doing was *fun*, it was in their nature to get off on another's suffering.

Maya's eyes widened and her hands began to shake as she curled them into fists.

Fun?

It was *fun* torturing her brother? It was *fun* making the last of her family suffer?

Astaroth's smile widened though her laughter had stopped.

"Don't worry," she stepped away from the opening beside the burning building that led to the other warehouses. "We're not going to stop you, our master wants you to find your brother… he's merciful after all."

With no hesitation Maya began to walk, the thought of the demons trying to fool her didn't bother her, all she wanted was to save Arthur. To see his face light up as he saw her, like it always had.

The others began to follow her, her closest friends, Kellan's gargoyles, the Venandi, and the humans. But as Cale, who was the last of the original crew crossed into the opening, a black mass closed the others off so they couldn't enter.

Maya turned and was met with the backs of the others who had made it through as they watched Kellan and the other gargoyles recoil as the shadow blocked them.

"No." Astaroth shook her head and Maya's snapped to her. "Only you six can go…The rest-" She turned as Alvertos and Arley came within feet of slashing her head off but she back flipped out of the way. "Will play with us."

On cue the shadow creatures began to step out of the shadow blocking them from Maya and the rest. They watched as the lower ranked demons did their flimsy walks to their prey.

"Go!" Alvertos yelled over the sound of gun fire as the humans began to shoot and the growls of gargoyles mixed in as they slashed at the creatures. "We got this!"

Maya chewed on her lip but as she met Reggie's eyes through the light haze of the shadow, she turned and began to run with the others in tow. The look on Reggie's face had given her the *ok* to go, but she still hated that she had to leave them. She was always forced to choose.

The warehouses were built side by side but between them was like a maze. They must have housed at one time equipment to make all kinds of goods, Maya guessed it had to do with weapons of war.

They listened for any sign of another demon but they could only hear the sound of the burning building behind them and their own feet crashing against the cracked blacktop. Maya stopped abruptly between the beginning of the third and fourth warehouses, something caught her eye in the fire of the first and as she turned to see what it was, she was met with a flash of white.

Azazel's long white hair fell around him as he landed in front of them, his black boots landing with a smack. His eyes gleamed as they landed on the gargoyles, especially on Cale and Maya.

"It's been three long days." He gleamed as he tidied his black jacket over his slacks of the same color. "But I've kept myself distracted."

He grinned at Cale as the man took a step towards the demon so he was front and center, his dark eyes filled with more hatred than any of them had ever seen. The demon looked on with his grin still intact, as a matter of fact, it only grew wider.

He had been in Cale's mind continuously for days, the two had a connection perhaps even stronger than Maya's and Lucifer's.

Azazel sighed as the fire crackled behind him, illuminating his pale form in orange. They watched as he pried his dark eyes from Cale and they landed on Maya instead. His smile turned devious. "The sound of the gargoyles screams were not enough for me."

Maya froze as her eyes widened, her jaw loosened and her mouth hung slack. An emotion rushed through her that she hadn't felt in a lifetime, not since her time as Maya, the girl who had killed for revenge. As the demon continued, the emotion worsened.

"Abraxas is a torturous fool but he's my brother." the demon chuckled. "I wouldn't be as messy as he is though."

A growl filled the air that could be heard over the intense blaze of the burning warehouse. Azazel blinked as he took in the girl in front of him, she was looking at him with the ferocity of a beast. Her black and white eyes were sharper than an edge of a blade. The eyes her brothers had always hated, had even envied and especially feared.

"*Where's my brother?*" She snarled as her sharp teeth fell over her lips, blood falling down her chin as one of them caught her bottom lip.

Kira and Ari had been standing beside her but they stepped

nervously away, their eyes wide with shock. They had heard stories of her ferocity but had always dismissed it. They saw her as Sam, the human who fought for them, but looking at her now broke that illusion.

They feared her.

Trevor and Emily looked on, their legs shaking while they held their breaths. Cale, who had turned his head slightly to take her in, looked on with wide eyes.

The demon made a noise filled with delight and they brought their attention back to him.

"He's in the last warehouse to the left! You better hurry! Abraxas might have gone too far already."

She growled again, she found it hard to fight the urge to slash the demons throat, to watch the blood pour from the artery. The demons chose to give up their spiritual forms so they could fool the humans, but it weakened them. Powers intact or not, they left themselves open by using physical forms. Maya wanted to see the regret fill Azazel's eyes as she ripped the heart from his chest, his black blood running through her fingers as she took away his chance at life.

But she had to go, she had to save Arthur. Abraxas was the demon she truly wanted to face.

And so she, Emily, Ari, Kira, and Trevor turned to go but they quickly realized Cale wasn't following them and they turned to find him still facing the demon.

Maya's eyes landed on his back and she took in his uneven breaths as his shoulders lifted with his chest. Her heart thumped as she watched his strong form stand tall against the demon.

"He'll only let you go if I stay behind." He declared and Azazel grinned.

"He's right." The demons eyes remained on Cale's. "This boy and I have some unfinished business to attend to."

Emily didn't look like she wanted to go but she knew this was a fight he would have to have alone. With her eyes down, she turned away from her friend and began to walk away, there would be no begging for him not to do it, she knew there was no stopping him.

As the others followed her, they walked past Maya whose eyes not only had returned to normal, but they had also softened to the point of sadness.

"Cale!" She called to him and he jumped at the sound of her voice.

His head turned to her again and she could see the corner of his eye right eye, the eyes that had always brought her comfort. The eyes that now looked at her like she was a monster.

"Be careful." She demanded with desperation in her tone and in the next second she turned to join the others who had stopped to watch.

As they ran, she chanced a glance back at his broad shoulders and she noticed that they had steadied. It did nothing to help with her worry though, he was facing one of Lucifer's strongest demons, there was no way to beat him.

She would have to hurry and save Arthur so she could return to help. Her heart filled with even more worry as she continued to run down the long alley.

Cale's heart thumped at Maya's words and as he brought his attention back to Azazel, he realized the demon was watching Maya as she ran.

"She's quite the woman." Azazel licked his lips with his too long tongue. "If Lucifer gave me permission, I would gladly-"

"*Shut your mouth.*" Cale snarled before he could finish and the demon looked on with an entertained expression and continued on. "After spending all this time in your head, I know your true feelings… The feelings you have yet to realize yourself. I can read you like a book… I don't blame you for feeling the way you do though, even with all she's done, she's-"

"I've had enough of your mouth." Cale interrupted him again, his eyes narrowed as they turned pitch black. Anger flowed through his veins and it boiled the blood that had been given to him over four months ago. It sent power through him, the power of a gargoyle. "I'm going to rip your tongue out."

The demon cackled but it was cut off as Cale grabbed ahold of his throat but he slapped his hand away as he jumped back, his sharp teeth protruding from his mouth.

"You think you can beat me?" He cocked his head and licked his lips but this time he left his tongue out. "I know your mind! I know your weaknesses!" He spread his arms apart as Cale looked on.

"YOU COULDN'T KILL ME EVEN IF GOD STRUCK ME DOWN WHERE I STOOD!" Within the next second, he was gone but Cale knew his game and turned around as the demon appeared behind him.

Shock appeared on the demons face for only a second before he went in for a punch that Cale blocked with his arms. Both of the limbs broke on contact but they healed as fast as they snapped. The pain Cale had felt from the breaks remained on his face as long the demons shock had.

Azazel stood back with narrowed eyes as he took in the look on Cale's face, he couldn't make out what his expression meant but he had an entryway into his mind. He used his possession over the man and when he realized what he was thinking, the demon froze.

"You're right," Cale lifted his head and met Azazel's eyes. "You've been in my mind but I've also been in yours." He kept his expression cold as he spoke out loud what the demon had discovered from entering his mind. "You're cocky and It'll be your downfall."

Azazel laughed, the prospect of this boy being his downfall was hilarious to the demon. How could a gargoyle that was once human kill him? How could he ever wish to?

Cale had left his even gaze on the demon as he allowed him to get his laugh in and as he stopped, Azazel reached his hand out and his fingers were inches from Cale's eyes.

"I don't know about *my* downfall," He snickered. "But I do look forward to how much you can entertain me."

Cale's bloodshot eyes lowered as Azazel's hold on him tightened, the fact the demon was closer made the connection all the more stronger. He swatted his arm away and the demon grinned, "You can't defy me no matter how hard you try."

"I'd like to see if I can." Cale steadied his mind as a drop of sweat dripped down his brow.

"I do too." The fire from behind reflected off of Azazel's long white hair along with his sharp teeth. "It'll only make your death sweeter."

As soon as the demon finished his words, he had appeared directly in front of Cale again, his hand on his throat, throwing him into the air away from the burning building and he landed against another warehouse. He slid to the ground into the water filled potholes that had been filled due to the last three days of rain.

With a twitch of his fingers, Cale's nails grew into points and he dragged them along the pavement to bring himself back to his feet. He didn't have time to prepare for Azazel's next attack and he fell back to the ground with the demon on top of him. Azazel's hand closed around the top of his scalp as he pushed his head into the concrete so hard it made a small crater.

The demons claws dug into his skin as he struggled through the stars in his eyes. Azazel knelt beside him, his knee in his gut as Cale tried pulling his head from the ground to no avail.

The demon was far too powerful.

"It's almost laughable." Azazel said as he brought a sharp nail to his sharper teeth and tapped it against them like he was picking a piece of food out of them. "That you thought you could best me, especially with how weak you are." He sighed as Cale growled against the ground, the gargoyles strength almost throwing him off balance.

"I would have rather played with Anna, or is it Maya? Sam?" Azazel snorted. "Doesn't matter, the soul is the same."

Cale's arm extended so fast towards Azazel's heart that even the demon was caught off guard. He flipped himself backwards off the gargoyle and with his hand now removed from his head, Cale pulled himself up and kelt as the demon landed 15 feet away.

The wide alleyway between the two warehouses would be more than enough room to fight, but it would have to be close combat. The two dark buildings set a shadow over the two of them as they glared at each other, Cale's mind becoming hazy again as the demon worked at connecting to his thoughts.

"The Venandi have told you how to kill us I suppose..." Azazel's voice trailed. "I can assure you boy, there is no way you can get to my heart."

He smirked as Cale jumped, his wings ripping the back of his shirt and with the same speed the demon had used, he managed to land a hit.

Azazel leaned his head back so he didn't get the full brunt of Cale's attack but as he grabbed ahold of the gargoyles arm, practically snapping his wrist as he did so, he brought his pale face back up to meet Cale's and his nose was bent all the way to his cheek from the punch.

His eyes narrowed in annoyance, "You bastard-" He growled as he brought his free hand up and snapped it back into place. "I'm going to make you suffer until you beg for death's salvation..."

Cale didn't listen to the demons threat as he pulled his arm from his grip and it snapped as the demon didn't let go but it was what he had planned on.

Azazel went flying into the air as Cale's severed wrist wobbled out of his long fingers. He brought his feet to the side of the warehouse like he was a cat, standing as if gravity was nothing but a word.

Cale was there within seconds and he jumped from the ground, his gray wings giving him the extra push to get him where he needed.

The demons black eyes met his as they came face to face and almost as if time moved slower, Cale's dagger like nails went for Azazel's chest again but as expected, the demon twisted and let his body fall back to the ground to avoid it.

Cale landed in front of him and like they were humans, they fought with punches and kicks.

It was hard for Cale to keep up with Azazel, he knew martial arts throughout the ages, the tactics that men had used in war. There was no way he could match the demons strength or knowledge in battle, but Azazel had unknowingly given him the means to do so.

He could see into Cale's mind, could see what he was thinking, and what was eating away at him so he could use it against him. But with Azazel's possession, Cale had also connected with the demon. Before the possession, he could never read the demons movements.

What he had been taught by the Venandi could never help with this battle along with what he had trained to do with Maya.

He gritted his teeth as Azazel smashed him into the side of one of the warehouses and as bricks fell around him, be grabbed one as it neared his hand and smashed it against the demons head. Azazel snickered at how absurd he thought the brick looked as it broke into tiny pieces against his scalp. Cale allowed his body to fall and with a swipe of his nails, he broke the demons skin and black blood ran from his chest.

Azazel's head snapped to the five long welts on his chest and before Cale could do more damage, he punched him away.

He landed some feet away from the agitated demon and his right ear rang where he had struck him. Cale watched while out a breath as Azazel lifted his head from his wounds, his black pupils and irises had overtaken the rest of his eyes and they matched Cale's until his irises turned blood red and his pupil reappeared as a black slit.

"*You got lucky*." Anger made his voice shake and more black blood fell from his chest and landed on the ground in front of him.

Cale's hand shook from the bit of the demons blood that had gotten on him. His fingers burned, the skin turning to blisters. The pain was almost unbearable.

"I got lucky?" He tried to keep his voice calm. "I just fought with you as an equal and you call that lucky?"

"*Equal?*" The demons eyes narrowed at the word.

Being equal to a gargoyle was a disgrace but being equal to a human turned gargoyle was incomprehensible.

"I wouldn't be able to fight as I am right now if you hadn't possessed me." Cale got to his feet after he tried washing the tar like blood from his fingers in a puddle but the burning remained. "You're in my mind and I'm in yours." his eyes narrowed and they looked as terrifying as Azazel's.

The two creatures mirrored each other perfectly all the way down to their venomous expressions. It was as if their emotions were feeding off of the others.

The haze in Cale's mind opened and he was met with so many voices that it almost brought him to his knees. Their voices filled his ears... *their screams*... their desperate tones as they begged for their lives.

His eyes widened as he noticed a ripple in the demons skin, his form changing. The demons eyes sunk into his head and the area around them hollowed out, leaving a shadow around them. His skin paled further and matched his hair which was pulled back into his scalp as dark gray horns began to protrude from his skull. They were long and curved in the middle, the ends reaching into sharp points.

The picture Paul Ash had posted came to Cale's mind but he didn't have time to dwell on it as a growl escaped the demons mouth as his teeth sharpened further. His ears fell down his head and went off the sides as points, his nose widened and it turned to slits in the middle of his face. His hair slicked back and fell like a shaw around his broadening shoulders. The skin around his mouth ripped and his teeth spread all the way up his cheeks. As he finished his transformation, his hollowed eyes landed on Cale, his irises shining like a blood moon.

"I'll kill you..." the monsters voice was raspy with a hint of the tone Azazel had always used. *"I'll rip you apart... I'll bath in your entrails."*

Cale froze as fear filled his very core, Azazel's true form could only be described as what nightmares were made of. The way his ears hung down, his nose like an animals, it was almost as if he was modeled after a goat.

Cale had heard of how satanists would sacrifice animals to Lucifer. Was this how the demon was made? modeled after what the humans sacrificed?

The voices and screams of the innocent became louder and Cale unconsciously brought his hands to his ears as if it would muffle the noise.

The voices in his head stopped and the screams echoed off in the distance, all he could hear now was the sound of the demon roaring.

His hair stood and his heart raced, it begged to be anywhere but there.

With more speed than before, the demon was in front of him again, his grotesque nails at his throat and Cale had barely dodged it as he jumped backwards and the nails scraped the top of his chest. Air escaped Cale's gritted teeth as the pain hit him, Azazel's nails had become stronger along with the rest of him.

Unlike before, Cale couldn't read the demons thoughts, he could only hear the distant buzz of the voices of Azazel's victims through the ages. They were telling him to run, to save himself. None of this was worth eternal damnation in Azazel's pot of souls.

There was nothing he could do…

Nothing…

He was going to die…

"Help me…Help me… Help me…" The voices begged him as he backed away from the demon who cocked his head curiously at his shaking form.

"It's my fault!" A despair filled voice replaced the others and he froze as he recognized the woman's voice.

"Be careful." Her voice echoed again, soft this time and filled with worry.

He closed his eyes as the demon came at him again, he was too fast to dodge this time. His leg snapped as Azazel kicked in his knee, the bones severed completely from each other and he let out an excruciating yell.

As he began to fall, the demons nails found his chest again, piercing him. Blood poured from the wound as his nails exited his skin.

Cale's eyes met the demons as his long mouth curled into a sharp toothed smile.

Everything went dark and Cale fell.

Chapter 52

Maya, Emily, Kira, Ari, and Trevor ran amongst the other warehouses as the one they were running to loomed in the distance.

Maya's eyes never left the building as she approached it but she knew like herself that Emily and the others were regretting leaving Cale behind.

No matter what had happened between them, she would always care about him. She could hear the sound of his and Azazel's battle behind her and it made her hair stand on edge. She wanted to run back to help him but she was like Emily, she knew it was a fight he needed to have alone. She would have to hurry, she wasn't sure if she could beat Abraxas without using her untapped power but she would if she had to. She would have to kill him to save Arthur so she could help Cale, she had to push past the symptoms caused by using her power.

The words she had said to Cale rang in her ears.

"Be careful."

It was all she could muster and she was disappointed that she couldn't say more, it seemed her awkwardness had returned.

"Sam!"

Maya almost ran into the shadow that appeared in front of her but she came to a halt as Emily's hand caught her wrist and pulled her back. She was too distracted and had almost stepped into Abraxas' trap. The long shadow blocked the length between the final warehouses, making it impossible for them to get through.

Maya chewed her lip and she could taste the blood from when she had pierced it a moment ago.

When she was about to take the risk and walk through the shadow, shadow creatures stepped through the dark mass. More than twenty circled around them and as they prepared to fight, the creatures glided past Maya and Emily who stood at the front and blocked the other three instead. As they did, the shadow they had came from disappeared so the women could continue.

Ari, Kira, and Trevor met Maya and Emily with the same amount of confusion as the two girls had as they looked back. One of the shadows turned and it's glowing eyes met Maya's and she strangely understood what it wanted.

"They'll only let us go." Her hand unconsciously gestured too Emily.

"Why?" Trevor asked as one of the creatures closed in on him and he inched away nervously.

"I'm not sure…" Maya's voice drifted, maybe Abraxas wanted them out of the way so he could fight her one on one but if that were the case, why did they allow Emily to come too?

"Just go." Ari's eyes filled with ink. "If that's what they want, we'll give it to them."

Kira gave them a nervous grin as a drop of sweat ran down her cheek, "We can handle this, go save your brother." Her expression turned serious, "You both better come back-" Her eyes met Maya's along with Trevor's and Ari's who had turned from the creatures at Kira's words. "Practice what you preach and be careful."

Maya's heart thumped as she took one step back, her eyes landing on Emily who had already turned towards her, ready to go. Maya brought her gaze forward again and nodded before she turned along with Emily and continued to run down the rest of the path that led to Arthur.

The shadow returned after it let the girl's go through.

Maya knew they cared for her, knew how upset they would be if she made the choice to sacrifice herself but she had to focus on the world.

If it meant that her life had to end to save the world she would gladly do it, they would be upset but the pain would ease as they realized why she had done it.

They finally turned the corner to the last warehouse and they were met with a light pole with claw marks on it in front of an opened door. The demons had a knack for the theatrics but Maya supposed it was justified so she would know exactly where she was supposed to go.

She looked up at the many windows on the side of the building, they were far too dirty to see through and she could smell dust and mold coming from inside the building.

"You don't have to go with me…to be honest, I'd prefer you not to." She tried to change Emily's mind but the girl narrowed her fearful eyes. "Too bad, I'm going."

"It's too danger-" Maya tried to protest but Emily shot her a look. "Shut up."

Maya sighed and her breath shook as her heart began to race, she feared what she was going to see on the other side of the door. An image of Arthur's broken body flashed into her mind and she covered her mouth as she felt sick.

There was no time to waste, she was going to save her brother.

"Stay close to me." She directed Emily as she stepped to the door and touched the rusted handle to push it the rest of the way open. The squeal of the rusted hinges made her lose her temper and she snapped the door off so fast that it fell with a crash.

She didn't care if the demon knew she was coming, all she saw was red and the image of Abraxas' broken body at her feet sent a delighted shiver up her spine.

She was becoming more monstrous by the second.

It was extremely dim inside the warehouse but as they stepped inside, they realized that it was a long hallway of sorts. There were doors on either side that led to offices and an old lunch room where the workers had once eaten. A cold air rushed to them, hitting them in the face.

Maya knew as she stepped through the hall, her feet echoing along with Emily's, that the area the air was coming from was where Arthur would be.

She couldn't run to him, she had to be prepared for a trap, so as she walked past multicolored graffiti, her anxiety worsened.

Emily gently pulled on her long sleeve with her index finger and thumb to not only comfort Maya but herself as the air got colder and the long hall ended at another door.

Maya's shaking hand reached for it right away, it was a push style door and it opened far easier than the one now on the ground at the front of the warehouse.

The fear of what she was about to find escalated as she stepped inside the bone chilling room, it was as wide as the warehouse itself and the walls reached 50 feet to the ceiling. Along the walls was more graffiti, some of pictures and others of sayings and bible verses. The middle was filled with old equipment that Maya didn't recognize, they were far too outdated.

They looked through the dim lighting, their eyes squinting through the haze, and as panic filled them, their breaths hitched and it came out as clouds from their mouths.

Through the mist they spotted his outline chained to a chair with his head bowed.

Arthur.

Maya didn't care if it was a trap or that Abraxas could step out of a shadow at any second. All she wanted was her brother safe and sound, to see his gentle eyes and smile.

She ran so fast that Emily had a hard time keeping up and as she approached him, she slid to a stop in front of him, knelt down, and gently lifted his head.

There was fresh blood dripping from his forehead and mouth which was open as he drew shaky breaths. His brown hair covered his closed eyes that had bags as big as Maya's under them. The chains that were wrapped around him were large, they looked like the kind loggers would use to attach to their skidders for better traction on rough terrain. They were thick but Arthur should have been able to break them.

Maya swallowed as her jaw quivered, Abraxas had pushed his body so hard that he couldn't use his power, his weak appearance confirmed it.

Her heart raced as his eyes slowly opened but as he realized that someone was with him, he began to thrash and pull against the chains. They rattled against his body and pulled at his already raw skin. His efforts to get free were only injuring him more.

"Arthur." She said softly but he continued to shake and groan.

The lump in her throat grew bigger as she thought of what he had gone through to get him to this point. Her eyes moved to Emily who had backed away a few steps, her eyes wide as Arthur started to hyperventilate.

Maya brought her hands gently to his cheeks, "Arthur…" As she said his name again, his body began to calm. "Brother." She stroked the side of his face with her thumb and he stopped completely, his eyes meeting her's and relief filled them.

"Maya…" his hoarse voice drifted and she smiled gently.

"Did you think I'd leave you here?" Her eyes threatened to fill with tears as she leaned to hug him. "You gave me a taste of my own medicine…" she cleared her throat to hide a sob.

She had worried him when she went off alone to recruit the humans, he had cried when she left him all those years ago, had tried ending himself. She only had a taste of how he had felt throughout his years alone.

As she hugged him, he rested his head against her shoulder, leaving a puddle of blood on her.

Emily worked at the chains and one by one, she was able to break the links until they fell from his body. The chains rattled to the ground and the noise bounced off the warehouse walls.

Maya pulled away from him and placed her hands on his cheeks again. "I'm sorry…" she closed her eyes.

"It's not your fault." His voice was barely more than a whisper, his throat was irritated from screaming during his torture.

"Everything is." she furrowed her brows as she kissed his forehead, "You're safe now."

Emily came to help as Maya lifted his weak body from the chair and he almost fell but the girls kept him steady as they started to walk.

Emily smiled at him although she looked like she wanted to scream. "I'm glad you're ok."

Arthur seemed surprised that she of all people would be glad, but it seemed to help with his morale.

"It's…not…safe…Maya." He brought his attention back to his sister as they continued to step through the warehouse, the sound of footsteps and feet dragging filling the air.

"I know." Maya's voice was rough. "I know Abraxas is here."

She wanted to fight him, she wanted to break every bone in his body and make him scream the way he had made her brother. The way he had with Deluca and Reggie. He was going to suffer and she was going to make sure of it.

"No…" Arthur continued with his whimper of a voice. "Not Abraxas."

Suddenly the air around them became even colder, their breaths denser, and they found themselves at a standstill as the shadows in front of them started to move.

From the light shining through a window, a dark mass began to move along the square patches until the demon known as Cain walked out of the shadow, his blank eyes on Maya and his face as smooth as stone.

They looked into the shadow to find any sign of Lucifer since the demon had always followed his master like a puppy but he seemed to be alone.

"You two may leave, but she-" his announced as his gaze remained on Maya. "Must stay."

It was the first time Maya had heard him speak, it sounded like he was from another time. His deep voice was smooth but it held a bit of an accent.

"I-" Emily spoke as Arthur opened his mouth but neither of them could get anything to come out. The demon had them paralyzed with fear.

"You'll let them go if I stay?" Maya asked the demon that she knew nothing about and he nodded. His curly brown hair was illuminated against the sun's gleam and in the light he looked more like a ghost than a demon.

"We're not-" Emily started as Arthur's face paled further but he couldn't seem to muster any words to say. His look alone told her that he didn't want to leave her there.

"Just go." She said as she kept her eyes on the demon, he didn't look like much to her with his black coat that almost matched her mother's trenchcoat. His pants were the same color and his boots as well, he was even the same height as her.

She started to think that aside from his bottomless eyes, one would think he was her older brother. Even though he didn't look like much, she knew better than to underestimate him. Lucifer had him by his side at all times for a reason and now he stood before her, *alone*.

Arthur and Emily kept their eyes on her as she pulled her arm away from Arthur and positioned herself in front of the demon.

"Go." She said again, her voice stern and with a gulp, Emily began to pull Arthur out of the warehouse who had no strength to reject.

The gargoyle and the demon simply looked at each other as if sizing each other up until Emily and Arthur were out of the large opening.

"I thought I'd find Abraxas here." Her voice was rough as she spoke the demons name. "Unless you're a torturous bastard like he is?"

"I am not." Cain blinked for the first time since he laid his eyes on her. "Not in the way Abraxas is at least."

Maya raised a brow, his voice was far different from the other demons. He wasn't cocky, there was no silk, and he lacked emotion.

"Then why are you here?" She pressed as the silence went on. "I've never seen you away from your master's side, you must be his loyal servant through and through."

"I serve myself and what I think is right." He stepped towards her. "I live with my goals in mind and what I have to do to ensure that they happen."

Maya made an exasperated noise, "You serve Lucifer because you're a demon, you want what he does and that's hell on earth."

At her words, the demon cocked his head. "That's a funny thing coming from you, a warrior of God who strayed so far off track that one would think that she was a demon herself." He rolled his neck and his head almost touched his shoulder. "You should also want what your master does but you did the exact opposite."

Her heart lurched at his words and she knew her reaction was exactly what he wanted. "I have no master-" Her eyes narrowed. "Especially God."

The side of the demon's mouth twitched as he evened his neck. "Good," he took another step and it almost closed the gap between them. "I'll teach you what it's like to have one."

She didn't have time to wonder what he meant as her body froze, it wasn't from fear or because she willed it to, it had nothing to do with what *she* wanted. She tried to move but all she could manage to do was shake as she fought against the pressure.

"By all means, fight it." Cain was in front of her now, his index finger on her chin as he looked into her gray orbs. "It'll only weaken you." The smell of his rotting breath filled her nose and she felt sick, his power was almost the same as Lucifer's.

His finger trailed down her chin then to her neck, her eyes watching him as he did so. His hand closed around her throat but he didn't use enough strength to cut off her air. Instead he cocked his head again and she was forced to the ground.

She fell with a thump to her knees and she looked up at him with a shocked expression, he didn't push her down physically, but he had wanted it and her body had complied.

Her own arms began to move upwards and her fight to stop them was futile as her hands wrapped around her own throat. They squeezed so hard that she couldn't breath.

They vibrated against her skin as she tried pulling them away, her lungs screaming for air. As she was about to pass out from the lack of air, Cain willed her hands to release her airway and she gasped as stars filled her eyes. Her chest heaved up and down as she tried to make up for the air she had lost and she collapsed the rest of the way to the ground.

Cain brought his foot to her ribs and pressed down, making it hard to breath again.

"I am the embodiment of mankind's temptation." He declared as he leaned into her and his eyes met her's again. "Every sin or false move… I can make it my own."

He pressed down with his heel and she felt a rib snap. She cried out from the pain but her body didn't flinch, instead it remained planted where Cain forced it to be.

"I can make you move to my will but so much more-" He stepped off of her and this time he went for her right leg.

"You will see all of your sin's and you will reflect on them." He knelt beside her leg and picked it up with both hands. "But first, I will break you."

At the second to last word he snapped her leg and she screamed only for it to be muffled by his hand. "I don't need anyone coming to help you." He said as he stood back up, "This is something you must learn alone."

She groaned with tears in her eyes as his influence pulled away from her and her instincts kicked in, she had to run… this was a power she couldn't fight.

She tried getting up but he had snapped her leg in two and it dangled as she fell back to the ground. Her nails planted into the ground as she began to crawl away, gasping as she pulled against the break in her leg and the tears in her eyes spilled over.

"This is the strongest gargoyle? How disappointing." He said with little to no emotion as he followed her. "Perhaps you are already broken and simply need to reflect…. To admit."

Maya was at a wall now and as she tried using it as leverage to get up, she collapsed again but it was at no fault of her leg, it was Cain pushing her down with his power.

Her body went numb as it filled with his influence, her good leg felt like jelly. Her back laid against the cold wall as she faced the demon with fearful eyes.

"Are you familiar with the story of Adam and Eve?" He questioned as his dark eyes laid upon her pale face and he watched it grow paler from his question.

Of course she knew the story of the first people, you didn't need to be religious to know.

God made Adam from dust and Eve from Adam's rib so he could have a companion. The two walked naked though the Garden of Eden until the serpent tempted Eve into eating an apple from the forbidden tree. The serpent was truly Lucifer in disguise doing what he did best, fooling people. Maya knew how tempting Lucifer could be, she had heard the exchange between him and Eve.

She shook against the wall as the demon stepped closer, his feet gliding on the ground as if he was walking on air.

"Of course you do, everyone does." His deep voice exclaimed. "I'm talking about what happened after… with their children. "

Maya's breath hitched as she met the demons eyes, she had never paid much attention to any story that had to do with religion. But it was obvious they had children since the two were the ones who were supposedly the start of mankind.

Her eyes followed his mouth as it continued to move, "Their oldest children to be exact." His dark eyes glowed against the dim light of the warehouse. "Two son's named *Cain* and Abel."

Her eyes widened at the first born's name and as she looked into Cain's eyes, she understood what he was getting at and she listened as he continued on, almost mesmerized by his words.

"Cain and Abel made offerings to God but our lord took preference to Abel's offering over his brothers and Cain, out of anger and jealousy, killed his own brother by bashing a stone into his skull." His dark eyes lifted to the wall over Maya's head as if he was reimagining the scene.

"As punishment, God banished Cain from the settled land to live alone in solitude, but it didn't end there." His eyes flashed as they lifted higher still. "Cain's house collapsed during a storm, killing him, the house was made from the stone he had used to kill his brother." His eyes fell back to Maya who had continued to watch him with wide eyes.

"I am Cain, son of Adam and Eve... my offering of fruit farmed by my own hands wasn't good enough for our lord while my brothers held more value. It angered me so I killed him. After my living punishment God banished me back to earth to live eternally in solitude." His eyes narrowed and the air around him changed, the cool air turning warm. "That's when I met Lucifer and became a demon. I was banished here as a lonely spirit while the other demons were once angels who had joined Lucifer by choice."

She would have found it hard to believe that the oldest son of Adam and Eve was in front of her if Lucifer himself didn't exist. Anything could be real at this point and it wouldn't shock her.

His eyes bored into her's as the pressure she would feel before they changed to their gargoyle color filled them and sure enough they changed to black and white.

He was able to force the blood in her veins to change her eye color.

What kind of power was this? How could someone have the power to control even the blood in someone's veins?

"I am the embodiment of Man's temptation-" he repeated but furthered his words. "I am their truth even when they have yet to realize it themselves, I know the truth to their lies and their deepest desires… and you are no different."

Maya gasped as she was thrown into darkness, a darkness she had been in countless times: The void in her mind.

She tried getting to her feet but she found herself unable to move as if she was still in reality. As she struggled, she heard footsteps approaching her and even though she couldn't even see an inch in front of her, she knew who it was.

Cain.

She could feel him as he knelt in front of her, his rotting breath hitting her again but the smell of the rest of him was different, he smelt of fresh fruit and farmland.

"Any being that holds the blood of Adam and Eve can fall victim to my power." He declared as his voice echoed through the void. "Gargoyles are not human, but they were modeled after humans so a small amount of their blood flows through them… especially you, who was once human, who still genetically is." She knew he was looking into her eyes even though she couldn't see him. "I can even use my power on the other demons if I try hard enough, Adam and Eve were made by God after all, we are all related in someway."

Her teeth pressed together so hard that they practically broke as his power took ahold of her again.

It didn't force her to move like before or pressed her to the ground, it instead caused the darkness around her to lessen and she was met with a city. It's tall buildings towering over her as she remained on her knees. The sunlight illuminated her shaking form and her eyes squinted at the skyscrapers. Cain stood behind her with his hands in his pockets as he took in the city along with her, his expression dull as if he was uninterested.

For some reason Maya felt like she knew this place, the long building beside her had mail cars parked in it's lot and the tall building to her right had a bench with two women talking on their cellphones. Her eyes moved along the people walking around as they went on with their day, many of them were in suits as they commuted to and from work. None of them paid any mind to Maya nor to Cain as neither of them were truly there.

As her eyes landed on the tallest building directly in front of her, she spotted something that almost made her fall backwards: At the front door at the top of a small stairway stood Eli, his brown hair prickling in the wind, his hazel eyes filled with excitement.

Beside him were the twins who not only shared in their looks, but also in their devious smiles. Their teeth reached their blue eyes as they watched the people moving in front of them and as their eyes moved to what was behind them, Maya's heart practically stopped.

The brothers made room for their sister and the Maya from that time stepped through and positioned herself between them, Eli to her right and the twins to her left.

She was fashioned in her mothers trenchcoat and her black skinny jeans, her boots reaching her kneecaps.

The current Maya who remained on her knees watched along with the demon as her other self took in the crowd as her brothers had.

Unlike her brothers she didn't look excited, she looked like she wanted to get what they were about to do over with. She began to walk to a man who was arguing with a women, the two were bantering on a grassy patch between the three main buildings, unaware of the girl approaching them. She stopped beside them and after the man got in a yell, they spotted her.

"What?" The man's dark eyebrows furrowed as his blue eyes narrowed at her.

The women looked on as Maya's expression remained emotionless and no one was prepared for what was going to happen next.

Current Maya watched as her past lives right arm swung back and it all came back to her: This was the first city she and her brothers had attacked, the angry man was her first victim.

Her past lives hand found the man's throat as she swung her arm forward, the woman's screams filling the square as she pulled against Maya's arm in an attempt to get it off of him.

The onlookers began to yell and run to the man's aid but a loud snap filled the air as Maya snapped his neck and his gasps for air came to an end as his head rolled back.

She let go of his broken neck and the woman fell to her knees beside him as he fell roughly to the ground.

Maya's opened hand remained where the man's neck had been, her body frozen as if she was trying to come to terms with what she had just done. The other civilians ran to subdue her only for her brothers to jump in and they began their own attack.

Their sisters arm fell back to her side as she ignored them and her eyes fell to the weeping woman, her tearful eyes meeting Maya's as she lifted her head from her dead lover.

The woman was her second kill.

Current Maya watched with wide eyes as her past life extended her nails into claws as they found the women's throat and she fell with a dramatic thump next to her beloved as a puddle of blood pooled around them.

Past Maya's eyes twitched and her lips shook as she took in the couple.

Current Maya remembered how she felt at that moment, the fear of what she had just done and what it would do to her.

Taking a life was no easy feat, unbeknownst to her brothers.

Current Maya watched with her mouth open, her heart thumping in her ears and throat.

This was Cain's power, he had said that she needed to reflect, to admit.

She was going to do just that. She was going to reflect on every sin she had ever committed as she watched them with the demons help.

Chapter 53

Cale was only eight when he ran from the school bus and flung himself into his adoptive fathers arms with tears in his eyes. His shock filled father watched as the boy pulled away, the kids remaining inside the bus were yelling as they played along with their peers. He knelt in front of his son and placed his hands on his shoulders.

"What's wrong?" He ruffled his dark hair to calm him, it wasn't often that he would find his son in distress. Something must have happened.

"D-Danny said there were monsters…" his little voice shook as he spoke.

"Monsters?" His father questioned, his hand still on Cale's head to comfort him.

"His brother told him there used to be monsters that killed people." Eight year old Cale explained with a sniffle after each word and his father had to listen closely to understand what he was saying.

His father swallowed at his son's words, he knew the cause of his parents deaths.

They had died by the hands of these monsters.

The names of the victims that were killed by the creatures were top secret, people talked of the creatures now and then… had even called them demons, but many thought it to be a hoax. They believed terrorists attacked the cities instead of the supernatural beings but his father knew better.

"Don't listen to that banter," he rustled his son's hair again. "That's something someone made up to make kids obey their parents."

He made a funny face and the boy laughed but as soon as the smile had appeared, it was gone, his little voice shaking again. "But what if they are real? the monsters?"

He considered Cale for a moment and he looked into his dark eyes that didn't match his own along with his hair and skin. They were of equal height as he knelt in front of him.

Even with the conversation they were having, he couldn't help but think about how his son was going to grow much taller than him.

He had seen pictures of his birth parents: His father was tall with tan skin, his eyes dark, and his hair darker. He was half Native American while his wife was European, her eyes hazel and her hair blonde. It was easy to see that Cale took after his father more than his mother but you could still see her features in his face. His eyes that always looked gentle were her's along with the shape of his nose.

His eyes fell to Cale's and he thought of how his parents had met their end.

He didn't plan to tell his son but perhaps when he was older he would tell him that he had worked with the monsters that his friends older brother was talking about.

But they weren't demons nor were they monsters to his father, they were gargoyles.

They weren't monstrous, nor were they murderers. They were as human as the people they worked with, aside from the fact that they sprouted horns from their heads and wings from their backs. He had fought the real demons alongside the gargoyles.

His mind went to the female gargoyle who had different eyes than the rest... Layla was her name.

The gargoyle had saved him countless times. To him, she could never be a monster.

"There's monsters all over the world," He said finally as he dropped his hands to his knees. "But do you know what I've learned about monsters?"

Cale waited silently for his father to continue, his eyes still filled with tears.

"Monsters are created by other monsters and on and on it goes..." His father dropped his eyes for the first time and thought of how he had happened upon his son. How he had met him after the boy had been picked up after the gargoyles had attacked his town.

He was only a toddler when he had lost his parents.

He was still in shock at what the gargoyles had done, it wasn't in their nature to kill innocent people.

He had been dismissed from the force after the demon's were 'dealt' with and when he got the call about the attacks, he wondered what had set his former comrades off.

The real demons were shadowy creatures, some even had forms that looked similar to humans but you could tell something was off about them. They came to power by doing what the gargoyles had done, by attacking innocent people. To this day he remembered the shock of finding out about the supernatural beings and the even greater shock he felt at meeting the gargoyles.

The gargoyles and the humans had willingly come together to fight the demons, the gargoyles were the one's who outed their identities and pushed for the humans to work with them to defeat their shared enemy.

"And another thing I've learned..." he met his sons eyes. "Is that they can change their ways... they can be good again, your mother taught me that."

His wife had died years prior from a sickness that took many people: Cancer.

Cale was all he had left and he was going to protect him from the truth of the monsters he spoke of until he was ready to know.

Cale blinked at his father as he took in his words, a small smile appearing on his lips as he understood what his father was getting at. He was a smart boy after all, he took after his father.

"Dad…" Cale's voice drifted, it was much deeper now since it had grown along with his body.

He was now twenty and at the age where he had to decide what he wanted to do with his life.

His father lifted his head from his laptop as he sat at the kitchen table and met his sons determined but nervous face.

"What is it?" He asked as he closed the laptop.

"You know I've been thinking about it for awhile," Cale's voice started to show his nerves. "And since you're going to Japan to teach," He looked like he was preparing to be lectured as he dropped his eyes from his father. "I've decided I'm going to join the military." He said the word 'military' as if it was uncharted territory.

His father rose a brow at his son's nervousness, "What about Carma and Emily? What are they doing?"

"Obviously not joining the military." Cale smiled and gave a small chuckle. "Emily's going to college and Carma is going to school to be a nurse, but you already knew that."

"It's going to be a long tough road to follow." His father declared and Cale nodded. "I know, but it's what I want…I want to help people like you always have."

"I've helped people by being a teacher and you're going to help by fighting bad guys?"

"I suppose." Cale pulled a chair out and sat across from his aging father, his hair was beginning to gray and his pale skin wrinkling. "I can't do it the way you have but I'll be happy to help in my own way."

"…it's not as easy as that." His father said truthfully. "People in the military have to do things they don't want to. It's not just patrolling and saving people…they have to kill to make that happen."

"…I know." Cale dropped his eyes to his entwined hands. "Do you think I'll be become a monster?"

Monster.

That word again.

His father brought his eyes to his sons and as Cale sensed his father's on his, he looked up from his hands.

"Of course I don't think you'll become a monster." His father smiled. "There's no way you could."

Cale returned his smile and his father spoke again. "Do you remember what I said to you all those years ago?"

Cale rose a brow, he remembered a lot of what his father had told him as any child would, but he had to be more specific.

His father chuckled at his confused look, "It was the time you ran off the school bus afraid of the monsters your friend told you about."

Cale's eyes dropped again as he tried to remember, "I do remember, vividly though."

"So what did I say?" His father pressed.

"That a monster can create another?"

"And what else?"

Cale was at a loss for words, how much of a conversation could an eight year old hold onto?

"I said a monster can change, that they can redeem themselves."

Cale's eyes lit up as he remembered his father's words from that time, his hands let go of each other and he laid them flat on the table. "You're saying someone can change no matter the circumstance, no matter how horrible they were or what they did?"

"Yes I am, and perhaps depending on the circumstance... they can redeem themselves and even if their actions are irredeemable, they can still do what is right."

"Why are you telling me this?" Cale asked his father with a look on his face that could only mean he thought the topic was unrelated to joining the military.

"Because you need to know." His father replied simply. "I used to be in the military, but not in the way you're going to be...I used to work with 'monsters' and they were far from being my enemies."

Monsters that were once good only to be turned into what their names described them to be by the actions of someone else. Of course there was no excuse, a strong minded being wouldn't be swayed so easily. There needed to be a punishment.

But what would this world be without monsters?

A good place.

That was the problem, this world would never be good. Lucifer had made sure of that.

Light and darkness, Good and evil.

Balance.

That's how the world worked.

Cruel, but oh so beautiful.

"...What?" Was all Cale managed to choke out at his fathers roundabout words.

"Maybe I'll tell you one day or you'll find out for yourself." His father smiled as he flicked his sons right hand, his fingernails hitting the wooden table with a scrape."I could tell you what I've done in the past but you need to

find out the rest for yourself, but today you'll learn neither."

At that time his fathers words left him more confused than assured but years later, and after everything he had been though, he would find that his father had made perfect sense.

Now was the time as he fought as one of the monsters his father had worked with, against one of the monsters his father had gone against.

Cale's injured body laid on the ground as he came to, the back of his head pounding from hitting the blacktop. The wound on his chest seared and he tried hiding the pain as he attempted to feign death.

He could hear the demon rustling above him and he tried to will his heart to slow so the demon couldn't see it pounding in his pulse. The thumping in his ears made him think the demon already knew he was alive. The demons hearing was as good as, or maybe better than a gargoyles.

Even in his act, he was alive, his racing heart made sure he knew. Azazel's nails didn't pierce deep enough.

Through his amazement at being alive, he thought of what happened before he had lost consciousness. A voice had echoed in his ears, Maya's voice.

What she had told him before she left to save her brother had echoed in his ears, *"Be careful."*

Her voice had given him the strength to move back during Azazel's attack to lessen the wound which would have surely killed him.

She had saved him.

Maya had saved him even without her being there.

The voices in his head started their conversations again, the memories of his father no longer protecting him. It was only a matter of time before the demon realized he was alive, but through the fear he thought of why those memories came back to him now of all times.

He tried not to flinch as he felt the demon lean over his face and his scent filled his nose, his long white hair falling around him like a cage. It would be too soon to see Azazel's transformed state again but he had to continue this fight, before it was too late.

His father's words had given him the strength to keep going, and with it he realized something that explained his fathers willingness to accept him when he had told him that he had been changed into a gargoyle.

His father had worked with the gargoyles along with the other humans.

His father had fought with the gargoyles, had talked with them, and had bonded with them.

It was all to take down what Cale and the others were fighting now.

His eyes flew open and he was met with Azazel's black eyes, the demon had gone back to his human fooling form. Shock only registered in the demons eyes for a second as one of Cale's hands wrapped around his throat and the other went for his already healed chest from the wound Cale had inflicted on him.

Azazel grabbed the hand that was going for his chest and snapped it at the wrist. Cale winced but he didn't pay attention to the pain as Azazel brought his hand to his throat and picked him up from the ground only to slam his head back into the blacktop.

He blacked out for a second as the pain hit him but he could feel his body being lifted again, his air being cut off from the demons grip on his throat and his back screaming with pain as Azazel slammed him against the side of the warehouse to their left.

"Fucking halfbreed!" The demons voice was filled with rage as his grip tightened around Cale's throat. *"Why won't you die?!"*

Cale started to gasp for air as his throat began to close in on him, the cartilage and muscle being crushed excruciating slow.

Though the pain, his vision came back.

He could see Azazel's smiling face through the stars in his eyes and the demon began to laugh at the gargoyles suffering and a trail of blood began to drip from Cale's mouth as he tightened his grip. Cale kept his eyes closed enough to fool the demon into thinking he was only a gasping mess as he choked the life out of him. His need for air was real as his lungs screamed for salvation, but he wasn't dead yet.

Not yet.

Though one of them would be soon.

Through his half closed eyes, he could see the demons mouth wide open as he cackled on.

An idea filled Cale's brain as he looked into the pitch black tunnel that was the demons throat.

Azazel would never let him get to his heart, *Through his chest at least.*

Cale's unbroken hand began to shake at his side as he allowed another gasp that sounded more brutal than the rest pour from his mouth. The noise made Azazel's mouth open wider as glee filled his features.

With all the strength he had left, Cale forced his hand up and shoved it into the demons mouth.

Cale's feet hit the ground again with Azazel no longer having his hand around his throat as he tried pulling the gargoyles arm out of his own. The demons eyes were wide with shock and they were bloodshot. Cale's wings smashed into the warehouse so he could stay in place as he pushed his arm further down the demons throat.

Azazel gagged and fought against him but with the strain in his throat, he couldn't seem to think nor could he dematerialize.

Cale's hand all the way to his elbow began to sting as he ripped through cartilage and bone and the black blood touched him.

He gritted his teeth as he pressed further down until his whole arm was down the demons throat, the thickest part of his shoulder ripping the skin away from the demons mouth, making more room for him to reacher deeper.

He didn't know how much more he could take as his wings shook against the demons force and his feet began to drag along the ground. But as he felt around with his hand, he realized he was at the demons ribcage and he found the beating organ.

He grabbed ahold of it and he pulled it out of it's chamber into the demons throat then out of his mouth. The tubes connecting the organ to his body tore and his black blood splattered on the ground. Azazel fell with a smack to the ground at Cale's feet. He shook against the pale concrete that wasn't too far off from the demons skin color. He stopped moving suddenly but Cale knew it wasn't over.

He took the still beating heart and held in front of his face, ignoring the excruciating sting in his fingers that flowed all the way up his shoulder. The demons black blood flowed down the raw skin of his arm.

He couldn't see what color the organ really was, but as he took it in, it looked like a normal human heart. He pricked his sharp nails into it and squeezed, the blood splattering around him as he dropped it and the destroyed organ rolled to the ground looking like a crushed black tomato until it began to decay and turned into dust. Beside it was Azazel's tongue that had been ripped from his mouth along with his heart, that too turned to dust.

Cale watched as Azazel's body collapsed in on itself until there was no sign of the demon aside from ash, it looked like he had been cremated.

Cale fell to his knees and the extra limbs on his back dispersed. The pain of the demons teeth as he bit into him and the broken bones along with his toxic blood as it burned filled him.

He crawled to the nearest puddle and used the water to wash it off of him, his hands shaking as he scrubbed. Even with the blood gone, he could still feel the sting and it left burn marks along his arm similar to how it had on Arthur's face.

He pulled himself from the puddle and laid flat on his back, his eyes finding the sun as half of the largest star peaked over the top of one of the warehouses. His broken bones snapped back together but the pain still remained. The wound on his chest began to heal but as he watched the skin sew back together, he knew it would leave a scar.

His healing was good but not enough to withstand a demons nails or blood, the marks on his arm and chest would be a constant reminder of what had happened, of what he had done.

He had killed a demon.

He heaved as his wounds seared and his head turned to Azazel's ashes, a part of him worrying that the demon would rise again. He was in no shape to fight with the state he was in now.

But he was assured that the demon was truly gone due to his head being free from the demons whispers. Even with everything going on around him and the pain he felt, he could only think of one thing: How clear his mind was.

Now that the demons hold was gone, Cale could hear his own thoughts loud and clear and he knew that even with his wounds, he needed to go help the others.

His broken bones would heal the rest of the way and the sting where Azazel's blood had been would diminish.

He inhaled sharply and pulled himself up, groaning as he rested his head against the cool stone of one of the warehouses. He began to pull himself along the warehouse and as he did so, it got easier to walk, his need to help his friends willed him forward.

The wind picked up and behind him Azazel's remains blew away until there was nothing left of the demon.

What was once one of God's angels returned to what it was originally: Nothing.

Chapter 54

Maya lurched as she and Cain reentered reality from another one of her blood-filled memories. She choked as she dry heaved due to the fact that she hadn't eaten anything in days, her stomach gave her nothing to throw up.

"That was a nasty one." Cain's voice was even as usual, even with what he had just seen.

"You let that man bleed out, leaving him to watch as your brothers killed his wife." His dark eyes watched as Maya pushed herself off the ground only to fall and she landed against the wall again.

"I-I didn't know that-" She stammered, her eyes filled with tears from what she had just seen and from her dry heaves.

"You didn't know your brothers would come to kill her even with you knowing their nature?" Cain questioned as he cocked his head, his bottomless eyes squinting through the darkness.

"I-" She gagged on the thought and she flung her hands to her face to cover her mouth.

She had relived so many of her victims deaths that she had lost count. The only thing she didn't lose sight of was the look in their eyes as they died. They had always been on her as she watched them die.

Blue.

Hazel.

Brown.

Green.

They had all begged, fought, and screamed but it didn't matter to her, all that mattered was her revenge.

"You seem like you've had enough." The demon admitted with his cool voice. "But even though you're reflecting on what you've done, you have yet to admit your greatest sin."

He knelt in front of her, his elbows on his knees as he stared into her tear stained black and white eyes. Her tears were red instead of clear.

She was beginning to bleed from her eyes.

She wheezed as she tried pulling herself from the wall but failed and fell back into it again. She looked into the demons eyes and as she focused on them, her head fell to her chest and she was forced back into one of her memories with the demon in tow.

Instead of how he had normally brought her to her memories from the very beginning, he brought her instead to the middle of it, right after she had killed a man by slitting his throat.

His body convulsed as blood poured from his severed artery and Maya watched her past self as she stepped over him, her feet planted on either side of him as he laid flat on his back.

"Do you see it?" Cain asked from behind her, a chill running up her spine as she remained planted on her knees.

Her eyes didn't leave her past self as the girl bent forward and leaned into the man's face. From the side current Maya and the demon watched from her pastselves hair was braided to her scalp and they were able to see the look on her face while her loose hair covered the other side.

"Do you see what I see?" The demon coaxed. "Will you admit to the feeling that you have hidden from even yourself?"

Maya began to shake as her eyes zoned in on her own on face, the face that was once her's. Her heart began to race as tears streamed down her cheeks, realization hitting her like a train.

Where her body made of flesh laid in reality, the tears fell as well.

Tears of blood.

She could see it, she could see what the demon could, she could see what she had hidden for so many years, for a lifetime.

As she watched her past self, she saw the look that was once her own: Her eyes were filled with delight and her mouth twisted into a crazed smile as she watched the light leave her victims eyes.

She remembered the chill, the feeling of being intoxicated. It was like a drug and in that moment, she felt nothing but the thrill of the kill.

She was another step closer to avenging her parents.

She would kill more humans until they learned that the gargoyles weren't beings to be trifled with and she was the most ruthless of them all.

She screamed herself back to reality and it echoed off the warehouses hollow shell until Cain forced her to shut her mouth.

"Don't lie to me nor to yourself." He got to his feet and stood over her like she had with the man in her memory. "How did you really feel about killing people?"

Her voice shook as the words poured out of her mouth like vomit.

"I *liked* it." More red tears rushed from her eyes as her teeth began to chatter. "I *enjoyed* it… I *relished* in it."

"What did you like about it?" He eased her on and she whimpered. "T-The light leaving their eyes…The look on their faces….The shock…. The adrenaline…" She clenched her eyes shut and a fresh batch of blood ran down her cheeks.

"And you're lying to your friends? Why?"

The change in subject made her eyes fly open.

"…I can't use my power or I'll die." Her voice softened as her frown deepened. "I was made into a full blooded gargoyle again but my body is still genetically human, when I use my power, my body breaks down." Her lip quivered. "I can feel the strain when I use my power… my body is decaying."

The demon made her meet his eyes but he didn't use his power to do so, he used his hand and lifted her chin.

"They made me promise that I wouldn't use my full power but I lied…Of course I'll use it."

"You're ok with dying again?" He asked softly and she nodded.

He dropped his hand from her chin and removed the other from his pocket, his eyes narrowed. "You came to me broken, you're not that confident girl that I saw for the first time in Lafayette square. You're not the same girl who fought to get to Lucifer, what happened?"

"I'm the reason why my friend doesn't have a family… my revenge for my parents took his away from him." Her voice broke and she tried dropping her gaze but Cain used his power this time to force her chin up. "I don't even know if I was the one who did it…it's eating away at me… but whether I did it or not, it's still my fault." She swallowed the non existent vomit in her throat.

Cain forced her into another memory, this one fresh in her mind since it was the morning before she and her brothers had sat around the campfire. The night her brothers bragged about their kills… the night she had changed her mind about killing the humans.

It was a small town and she had forgotten why they had chosen it, perhaps Oberon had gotten bored on their way to a larger one and she agreed to attack the town along with them.

Her past life stood in the backyard of someone's house, her feet were placed beside a swing set and along with the large swings was also one for a baby.

Maya remembered how she had felt looking at the swing as she watched herself. She had been depressed for days before she had ended up there and seeing the swing only sent her further into the depths of her emotions.

She brought her blood drenched hand to one of the chains that held the baby swing and felt the cool metal against her warm fingers.

She had never been on one, her parents had kept her and her brothers away from the humans and in doing so they had kept them away from any of the humans parks.

She closed her sad eyes as she fought the urge to sit down and take a swing on one of the larger ones.

Along with the screams around her as her brothers had their '*fun*', she heard a gasp and her head shot to the light green house attached to the backyard.

At the back door stood a man with tan skin, his eyes brown and his hair black. He was tall and dressed in a suit, a red tie around his neck since he had just gotten home from work. His eyes were wide and his mouth hung open as his wife appeared behind him. She was the same height as Maya and her blonde hair reached the middle of her back, her hazel eyes wide like her husband's.

Current Maya and Cain had seen them before her past self had and she didn't bother to look at the expression that she had once worn, all she could to do was look at the two in front of her.

Her past self began to run, the commotion waking current Maya from her thoughts and she watched as she jumped over the picket fence and joined her brothers a few houses over.

"Get inside." The man pulled his wife inside the house after he had jumped in front of her from Maya's sudden movement and a baby began to cry inside.

Maya and Cain watched as the man closed the door and locked it from inside.

"These are your friends parents." Cain declared and she turned her head to meet his gaze. His eyes were on the back door but when she turned to him, he turned his gaze to her.

"How do you…?" She stammered.

"Because I know." He said simply. "You never killed people that you knew had children but your brothers didn't care." His eyes narrowed. "You're right though, it is your fault either way."

They were back in the darkness of the warehouse again and Maya's eyes filled with fresh tears.

"You're a monster." Cain said over her broken sobs. "You will never not be a monster."

His power pressed down on her again and she shook as she tried getting out of it.

"You and Lucifer were made for each other and that is why he aims for you." Cain continued his mental attack.

She groaned against his power, she couldn't breath and it felt like her lungs were going to explode but at the mention of Lucifer, a fire sparked inside her and she gritted her teeth.

"*No*." She spat and the demon cocked his head as he watched her black and white eyes narrow.

"*No*?" He mocked. "Am I wrong that you once lived a life with Lucifer?" His questioning tone didn't sound right coming from his mouth. "That even now, in your third life, you still live by his example?"

"*No*." The fire seared inside of her and her voice came out rough as she fought against his power and for the first time since he showed her his ability, she began to move with her own will.

The demons eyes lit up as he watched her move, by tapping into her power, she was able to break out of his.

She couldn't move anymore from breaking out of his hold and from the toll her own power took on her body.

"I-I'm not that person anymore." she heaved but at the last few words, her voice came out as a growl. "I'm going to make up for everything I've done by stopping Lucifer, even if it *kills* me."

Cain was silent for a moment as he took in her words and Maya almost gasped as he smiled, his teeth smooth like a humans.

"That's good," His voice was calm. "But I'd like for you to get rid of the notion that you have to die to do so."

He began to pull off his coat and it slipped to the ground behind him, revealing the pale skin of his chest and stomach. The deep lines and muscles that framed him were covered with scars. "You are the only being aside from Lucifer who has gotten out of my power." At the shock in her eyes, he answered the question that rose within her. "He wanted to test my power and made me use it on him."

"You-" He brought his hand up and reached for her as she looked at his claws with fear in her eyes. "-Are a monster, don't ever forget that... *use it to your advantage*."

His power pressed on her again but she couldn't break free this time due to the use of her power before. Her body couldn't handle the energy twice, it wouldn't allow her to.

She was forced against the wall and her hands laid flat against the cold warehouse floor as Cain stepped closer to her while bringing his outstretched hand to his own chest.

"I hope you live through this, I really do." His voice drifted before his hand ripped through his chest and he didn't even flinch as his claws tore through his own skin and his rib cage until he found his beating heart.

Maya watched with terrified eyes as she began to struggle against his power, it had lessened a bit from his self inflicted injury but she remained planted on the ground.

Her heart thumped as her mouth opened of it's own accord and her wide eyes watched as he pulled his heart from his chest and the organ was drenched in the tar like blood that it pumped.

His body began to shake but he had enough strength to take another step and as his body fell in front of her, he pushed his heart into her mouth.

The tar like blood that covered the organ burned her mouth and throat as it dripped down into it and she screeched from the excruciating pain. It only got worse as he squeezed the organ and it popped in her mouth, the blood pouring down her throat into her chest.

Her eyes burned as they watered from the pain and through the tears, she could see Cain's dark eyes losing their light as his lifeline bursted in her mouth.

Her insides burned and she screamed against his hand, the limb muffling the sound until it fell from her mouth along with what was left of his heart. As the demon went crashing to the ground, he turned into dust and with his power gone, Maya fell forward and puked.

The black tar poured from her mouth as she heaved but the burn remained, on the contrary it worsened as it burned her on it's way up.

Cain had accomplished what he had wanted before his death, whatever that was.

She cried as the pain seared and she gripped at her stomach and chest as she fell to the ground next to her vomit. She moaned as she felt the liquid moving inside her as if it were a living thing and a whimper escaped her lips as it devoured her heart and her other organs.

Her breaths came out as groans as she pulled herself up, her limbs shaking as she used the wall as leverage to stay upright. The pain eased as she began to walk, the ache of moving distracting her, but she could still feel the blood moving though her.

Her mind was clouding and her vision blurred as she eased herself through the door out of the large room and made her way through the hall to the exit.

She had to get out of there, she had to get away from the ashes that Cain's body left behind. From the memories he had showed her. From the room that she had reflected on her sins in.

From her vomit, the blood, the pain.

Through the pain in her body and the haze in her mind, she only had one objective: To find her friends.

As she wobbled from the warehouse, her breaths came out shallow, her lungs not getting their fill of air so she breathed quickly to make up for it. Through the burning in her mouth she could still taste Cain's blood on the buds in her tongue. It tasted like iron like normal blood but it also tasted like how it looked, like tar.

With a touch of venom.

Her limbs began to ache with every move and she found refuge against the light pole in front of the warehouse entrance.

"*Maya*...?" Arthur's weak voice brought her head to her left and she was met with Emily rounding the corner at the end of the warehouse with her brothers arms still wrapped around her shoulders.

Maya groaned as she positioned herself towards them.

"You did it?" Emily asked with fear filling her tone and she froze only a few feet away as she saw the black blood that covered Maya's mouth and jaw along with the red trails of blood that had fallen from her eyes.

Arthur's eyes widened from the look of his sister but he couldn't go to her, he was far too weak to do so.

"Yeah..." Maya choked out the answer to Emily's question. "He's... dead."

He had ended himself but not before forcing his still beating heart into her mouth.

Emily and Arthur observed her look and she knew she looked horrible with her gray bloodshot eyes and the two types of blood that covered her face.

She positioned herself so she wasn't standing on the leg that Cain had broken but something hit her gut from the inside and she almost fell.

"I'm....fine." she assured breathlessly as their eyes widened with worry but Arthur knew better and didn't believe her words.

"Guys!"

Ari, Trevor, and Kira emerged from the long path that connected to the rest of the warehouses and caught the three off guard.

The three newcomers stopped dead in their tracks as they saw Maya and she fell further down the pole as she took in their shocked expressions.

"What happened to the shadow creatures?" Emily asked them but her eyes were still on Maya.

"...We killed most of them." Ari side eyed Maya while she answered and the other two didn't try to hide their eyes from the sick looking girl. "But the rest disappeared a few minutes ago."

The three of them looked beaten with their bruises and slashes but their injuries were nothing to worry about.

"Sam... are you ok?" Trevor asked as Maya slipped even more, the sound of the pole squeaking against her damp skin filling the air. She didn't answer him as she tried picking herself up and changed the subject.

"Cale," She wheezed. "Is he ok?"

They dropped their eyes and the answer was clear, they didn't know.

Emily locked her jaw as it trembled, the sound of her teeth chattering could be heard along with the gurgling in Maya's stomach.

Something crawled up Maya's throat and she reached back and clawed her fingers into the pole to keep herself upright. Her eyes moved to Arthur who she noticed was trying to get to her but he had no strength to do so from Abraxas' torture. Emily gripped tighter onto him so he couldn't get away and she met Maya's eyes.

"I'll be fine... Worry about yourself..." She thought to herself.

"Are you ok?" A familiar voice filled the air and their heads spun to the source: Coming from the main aisle was Cale, he was limping as he made his way to them and his chest was covered in blood from a wound that was still healing.

There were outlines of hands around his throat but they were already healing while the burn marks on his right arm shined bright against the sun.

"Cale!" Kira and Trevor ran to him to help but he shook his head with a small smile.

"I'm ok." He met Emily's eyes who wanted so badly to run to him but she had Arthur to care for.

"You won?" She asked with a hitch in tone and even with how unbelievable it was, she already knew the answer.

"...I guess." He answered and his eyes moved to Maya who was

filled with relief at the sight of him.
He did it… he killed Azazel…he killed a demon.

He did it…

He did…

He…

"I hope you live through this, I really do."

Cain's voice echoed in her ears as her thoughts began to fray. She felt like she had a fever and the blood gurgling at the back of her throat began to trail out of the sides of her mouth and it fell to the ground in front of her.

She unconsciously swallowed it back down but it came up again and this time it poured from her mouth. She dropped her gaze but she couldn't see anything, only darkness.

As she brought her eyes back up, she couldn't see nor hear her comrades as they yelled for her.

Her body began convulsing and her nails left the post as she fell forward, the screams of her friends filling the air as she collapsed and her mind went to nothing.

Chapter 55

Cale limped down the long alley that led to the warehouse Azazel had told the others to go.

He felt so free with Azazel's voice no longer pestering him but he still felt worried that the demon had lied and brought his friends to a trap.

The way he had acted the last few days filled his mind, how he had treated Sam. Learning what she had done had filled him with anger and resentment but he knew she was no longer the girl she used to be.

The memories of his father filled his mind and he thought of the state of the world.

Who could ever think that this world would live in peace? It was wishful thinking.

What mattered was how you lived your days, you make mistakes but that was life. You could regret what you've done for the rest of your days but what would that do?

Nothing.

Depending on what you did, there would be repentance.

One way or another, you would get what was owed to you.

But a life of solitude and death wasn't the answer.

There had to be a reason why Sam reincarnated with her memories destined to come back. As much as she believed it, she wasn't the girl she once was. She sacrificed herself, she was prepared for death to take her, to make her soul his.

She knew there was nothing she could do to change what she had done and she chose death. Her current life wasn't the one who had done terrible things, it was her past life. Her memories had returned and now she was fighting the mistakes she had made in another life.

Samantha Knight had gotten her memories back from her past life and the power that came with them. The girl whose soul was destined for something out of her control.

This life wasn't that of a killer gargoyle, this life was meant to fulfill that destiny.

To end it all.

This girl wasn't her past lives mistakes.

He wanted so badly to apologize to her. He was cruel to her, he had listened as she cried because of his words. Azazel's influence had made the feelings that were already there heighten. What could have been resolved had gone down a path that it didn't need to go down.

He needed to talk to Sam.

He needed to see her.

He could hear his friends talking ahead and as he rounded the corner of the warehouse, he was met with all of them together.

Ari, Kira, and Trevor stood sideways as he approached them and Emily stood with Arthur's arm around her shoulders as she kept him upright.

His heart jumped as he took in Arthur's looks: His mouth was covered in blood and his skin was pasty. He looked like he had been through the wringer. His worried eyes were planted on someone leaning against a light pole and Cale followed his gaze to see the outline of a brown haired girl.

Maya.

"Are you ok?" He called and their heads shot to him.

"Cale!" Kira and Trevor ran to him, theirs faces filled with relief as they tried to help him but he assured them he was ok.

He met Emily's eyes, they were wide with tears and she seemed to light up at the sight of him. He knew if she didn't have Arthur, she would have ran to him.

"You won?" There was a hitch in her tone and even with how unbelievable it was, she knew the answer by the look on his face.

"...I guess." Was all he managed to say as his eyes landed on Maya.

She looked relieved at the sight of him but he found himself frozen as he took in what was under the emotion: Her eyes were dull and bloodshot with large bags under them, she was as pale as paper and her all black outfit made her look worse.

What chilled him to the bone was the fact that there was demon blood covering her chin and as her mouth shook, he could see her teeth stained with it. He could still feel the pain from the blood that had been on his arm, the blood that had left a scar on Arthur's face.

The vile blood was on her face, in her mouth.

Eating away at her insides.

He watched as the black tar began to trail from the sides of her mouth like two tiny streams.

"*Sam*?" He called to her as a cold chill ran through his spine and he took a step towards her.

They looked on as she swallowed hard but in the next second the black blood began to pour from her mouth, making a puddle in front of her.

She dropped her head to look at it and when she looked up, her eyes were glossed over as if a film had set over them.

"SAM!"

"MAYA!"

They called for her as Arthur tried pulling away from Emily to help his sister but it was too late: As she began to convulse, her eyes rolled into the back of her head and she collapsed harshly to the ground.

The pain Cale felt as he lunged on his injured leg was nothing as the desperate need to help her filled him and he caught her in his arms as he yelled her name.

He turned her limp body around as she landed face first into his arms and he ignored his screaming knee as he kelt on the ground and the others surrounded him.

Their shock and fear only got worse as they saw Maya's face: Her eyes were halfway open but she was unconscious, the black blood was dripping out of her eyes like tears. They watched with dread as it began to stream out of her nose along with her mouth.

"Maya!" Arthur almost fell forward as he tried getting to her. "My sister!" He wheezed as his desperation took a toll on his already injured body and Emily caught him with Trevor coming to help.

"We need to get her out of here!" Ari screamed as her eyes began to fill with tears along with Kira, Trevor, and Emily who watched as Maya began to shake in Cale's arms. Her lips shaking along with her eyelids.

Through their tears Trevor and Emily had to subdue Arthur as he howled at the sight of his dying sister.

While swallowing the lump in his throat, Cale twisted his shaking arms tighter around her and pulled her to his chest as he stood. Her legs dangled over his arm and her head laid limp against his chest. He ignored the break in his leg and the pain from the burns on his arm as he began to run and the others followed. Ari had taken Arthur and his feet dragged along the ground as she ran after them.

Cale's eyes fell to Maya's blank face as he ran to the entrance of the warehouses, the first that had been set ablaze by the demons had almost fallen completely to the ground.

He met her half lidded eyes and pain shot through his chest. He couldn't lose her… he couldn't let things end this way. He blinked his tears away and focused instead on getting her out of there, to safety.

Archie had to know something, one of the Venandi… anybody. He could hear Arthur begging for his sister and although he resented him for everything he had done, Cale's heart ached at the thought of him losing his sister again.

He pulled her tighter to his chest as he came upon the opening at the front lot. He had to dodge the hot cinders that came from the fallen warehouse as he ran through the now shadowless path and was met with the Venandi and Reggie's crew standing in front of Kellan and the other gargoyles to shield them from the hazardous bullets.

They were positioned for a fight as they faced the police officers that had responded to the call that the gargoyles were attacking.

The demons were no where to be seen.

The officers who had their guns pointed at the Venandi and the others paled as they took in the bloody forms of Cale and Maya.

The Venandi, Reggie's crew, and Kellan's gargoyles turned to what the officers were looking at as the others joined Cale and their eyes filled with shock at the sight of the gargoyles. The Venandi's eyes fell to Maya and their shock filled eyes were replaced with desperation at the sight of the dying gargoyle who was a pivotal part in their fight against Lucifer.

Alvertos backed to Cale and brought his sword to the ready as the officers guns clicked.

Reggie and his crew brought their guns to the men and women who were once their comrades. "Please!" He begged after he turned from Maya, his forehead scrunched with nerves. "They're not your enemies! If we let her die it will be the end for all of us!"

"We can't…" A tall man with his brown hair in a bun exclaimed, his voice shaking. "We could never join these monsters…you betrayed us."

"I'm not going to let you hold them here while the girl dies."Arley walked between Reggie and his group and the other humans, his sword in his right hand.

Some of the other Venandi followed him while the rest stayed back to guard the gargoyles along with Alvertos.

"Are you going to kill innocent people to get to the gargoyles?" Arley pressed with his blue eyes narrowed, his voice cold. "I don't think you have the courage."

Cale and the rest watched as the officers recoiled but kept their guns pointed at them. As Cale watched, he noticed that there were several people missing from their group and as he realized who they were, the two SUV's they had come here with came pulling up and squealed to a stop. The second almost hitting the first as they did so.

Arabella stepped out of the passengers side of the first, she was clad in her white coat and her sword at the ready.

"Let's go!" She met Cale's eyes and he started to run along with the others.

As the officers brought their guns to the gargoyles, Arely and his Venandi stood in their way.

"They'll save us you fools!" He warned as he pointed his sword to the bun man. "But they can't if you kill them!" He spat as his eyes twitched to his brother who stood at the first SUV.

Reggie and the other humans got in the second along with the other Venandi and the gargoyles. Alvertos watched as his brother and the Venandi who had decided to stay with him pointed their swords at the humans.

"Go brother-" Arely called over his shoulder to him as he brought his gaze back to the officers. "We'll be fine…you need to focus on the black and white eyed gargoyle."

The Venandi that surrounded Arely gave Alvertos small smiles as they nodded.

The pain of leaving them behind still showed on Alvertos' face as he jumped into the passenger's side beside Arabella. They sped down the road, the sound of gunfire behind them as they sped off.

"What happened to her?!" Alvertos turned as Arabella moved out of the way.

Lucas glanced in the rearview mirror at the gargoyles as he drove, they were wounded and bloody and three of them were worse than the others.

Cale had placed Maya gently onto the seats of the second row and her head laid on his lap. The blood that was dripping out of her eyes, mouth, and nose had gotten on his shirt from carrying her and it stung his skin.

No one answered, they didn't know what had happened between her and Cain.

"She ingested demon blood…" Alvertos' voice drifted as realization filled his eyes and he watched as more blood poured from her mouth and she grew paler still.

More of the demon blood dropped onto Cale and he winced. His heart began to race as he thought of the pain that Maya must be feeling, he had only gotten it on his skin while she had swallowed it.

Alvertos swallowed and Arabella looked on as Arthur who tried pulling himself against the back seat to see his sister fell as his arms gave out. The three other gargoyles pulled him up and Emily pushed him to the seat but they watched with terrified eyes as even more blood gurgled up Maya's throat.

"How did this happen?!" Alvertos yelled louder this time and they jumped.

Lucas almost swerved off the road.

"S-She fought Cain." Emily's voice shook as she struggled not to cry.

She blamed herself for what had happened since she had left Maya to fight alone.

"Cain?" They could hear the alarm in Alvertos' voice as Arabella turned to stone.

"What?!" Kira pulled herself against the seat in front of her and she fell backwards as the sight of Maya made her feel sick. She covered her mouth as tears began to fall from her eyes and she found solace in looking out the window to the landscape speeding by.

"...Cain is Lucifer's favorite demon." His blue eyes met theirs. "There's a reason why he is."

"She killed him." Emily shot in nervously. "She said she did."

"Did she say it in those words?" Arabella pressed and Emily's eyes widened. "S-she just said that he was dead."

Alvertos punched the side of the door with anger written all over his face, "We were careless." He spat and Lucas who had listened on without saying a word piped up for the first time.

"Do you think she's going to die?" His eyes found the rearview mirror again and he watched as the gargoyles stiffened.

Alvertos dropped his gaze but they rolled back to Maya in the second row.

"Demon blood is deadly to humans while it burns away at a gargoyles skin," His eyes found Arthur's scarred face and Cale's arm as the blisters the blood had left healed and pinkish skin began to form. "It's eating away at her insides as we speak... I don't think your doctor can save her." His eyes met Arthur's and the gargoyles face filled with pain. Not from his torture, but from the prospect of losing his sister again.

Cale's gaze had never left Maya's shaking form during the others conversation. He watched as her gray eyes rolled back into her head and her lids fell over them. Her breathing was beginning to shallow and it whistled through the car along with the chatter of her teeth.

His heart dropped, he couldn't listen to Alvertos' words. She had survived so much already. She had to make it through this. The last thing he had said to her made her cry, it had broken her. It couldn't end this way.

It couldn't.

"Archie!" Alvertos yelled as they got out of the cars and Maya was in Cale's arms again.

The doctor came running along with Jared and Donato who the former helped down the stairs of Archie's cabin. Archie's eyes widened at the sight of Arthur and Maya who was in far worse shape than her older brother. He watched as her head rolled to the side and the black blood came pouring from her mouth to the ground.

"Help her!" Arthur gasped as he almost fell to his knees but once again, Emily was there to catch him along with the others.

Archie directed them to her cabin which was the closest to where they stood as he tried to hide the panic in his voice.

As they got there, Cale laid her gently on her bed where she shook against her blankets and demon blood began to stain them as it continued to pour from her mouth. He stood back as Archie came into the room as the others stood around the bed and watched as the doctor set to work. Reggie and the other detectives stood in the living room while the Venandi stood outside along with Kellan and the other gargoyles, waiting for any news as Alvertos watched with the others.

Archie checked her pulse, opened her eyes, and listened to the gurgling in her stomach along with her strangled breaths. He checked her pulse again for good measure only to do it one more time as if he had done it wrong the first few times.

Each time, his face would fill with panic.

"What is it?!" Arthur breathed against the wall as he struggled to stay up, the panic he felt making him weaker than he already was.

"Someone grab him a chair." Archie directed but his eyes didn't leave Maya.

"Archie?" Cale woke the man from his thoughts as Reggie brought a chair for Arthur and remained in the doorway as he watched with wide eyes as Archie turned to them, his face sullen. "I don't know what to do..."

"What...?" Arthur wheezed as his weak hand gripped the arm of the chair. "What do you mean you don't know what to do!?"

The others looked on with either their hands over their mouths or with denial written on their faces. Cale shook as he watched Maya groan and another clot of blood slipped from her mouth.

"I don't know how to help her... there's no way to flush it out of her, I don't know how to work with demon blood-" he swallowed as he met Arthur's eyes. "It's too late."

"No it's not." Arthur shot up and when Reggie tried to catch him, he slipped through his hands and fell to his knees. His vision blurred as his body fought against his wishes to help his dying sister.

"I know how you feel." Archie closed his eyes and gritted his teeth in frustration at his inability to do anything. "I told you before that she's like a sister to me."

"...I don't think you do." Arthur dropped his eyes and they all watched as he closed them. "She can't die again..."

"That's up to her." Reggie said suddenly and their eyes met his. "Isn't that right, doc?"

Through his worry for the girl he had left everything for to join, he looked confident.

"That's right," Archie agreed and his voice broke as he turned back to Arthur. "You know your sister, you know she won't allow herself to die until she makes up for what she's done." He stepped to Arthur, knelt down, and placed a hand on his shoulder. He hid his unsure expression with a fake smile as Arthur inclined his head with tear filled eyes.

"When she get's better, do you think it'll be wise to let her see you this way?" He gave the man who was like a brother to him a wider smile. A human and a monster.

"We have to let the blood run it's course and in the meantime, I need to help you so you can be here for her when she wakes up."

Arthur brought his eyes to Maya's shaking form and furrowed his brows.

After a few moments of unbearable silence aside from Maya's groaning, Arthur finally nodded. Though they could all tell that it took everything he had to agree.

Archie and Reggie helped him back into the chair so Archie could check him out while his tired eyes remained on Maya.

Cale placed a hand on her forehead and he could feel how hot she was, she was far too hot to be safe. There was sweat dripping from her forehead and he thought of how the blood was burning her insides, her organs being disintegrated.

"She won't allow herself to die until she *makes up for what she's done."* Archie had said.

All the times she had shown regret for what she had done filled his mind along with the time Arthur had announced that she had killed more people than her brothers before she had gotten her memories back. She had stormed out with tears in her eyes, the news broke her and it almost led her to her death.

Cale thought of the words he had spoken to her the night he had found out that she was the cause of his parents deaths. How she had gone to cry for hours. He had heard the desperation in her sobs, the sadness, the regret, and in her screams he could hear her self-hatred and pain.

He swallowed as he lowered his gaze to her pale face, she already looked like she was dead.

He turned away from her and faced the wall next to the bedframe as he choked back a sob. He couldn't cry now, he deserved to keep it all in like she had for so long. He could blame it on Azazel's possession as much as he wanted, but it was his own words that he had spoken. She could die with his last words to her being that she was a murderer.

The very thing that she had fought so hard to make up for.

Several hours had passed and night had fallen upon them. After Alvertos' constant prayers, he and the other Venandi including Arabella went to their cabins.

Kellan who had came in to check on Maya's condition along with the other gargoyles left with pale faces an hour ago from the sight of the withering girl. The humans had left as well aside from Reggie and Lucas who sat along with Ari, Trevor, and Kira along the front of the room.

Arthur and Archie sat to Maya's left while Emily sat beside Cale who had found refuge to her right. They watched as she continued to shake and the blood continued to ooze from her nose. It had stopped coming from her mouth and eyes and Archie explained how it was due to her bodies rejection of the blood and it was forcing it to come out.

Archie had prescribed rest for Arthur's condition, his body had been starved of rest for three days due to Abraxas' torture and as he sat, his head fell to his chest as his exhaustion caught up to him.

"I think it's time to go to sleep." Archie placed a hand on his shoulder but Arthur shook his head as the others watched with their own tired eyes.

Not only did the fights tire them but the stress did as well, not one of them had left Maya's side since they had gotten back to the cabins.

Arthur's bloodshot eyes lifted to Maya who was now under the blankets, the tar like blood had been wiped from her face and Archie got up, grabbed a towel, and while making sure it was thick enough so it wouldn't get on him, he wiped the fresh blood from under her nose.

"All of you need rest." He said as he threw the towel in the garbage.

"I'm not leaving her alone." Arthur stated roughly and Archie shook his head. "You need to feel better yourself, do you think she can heal while she's worrying about you?"

"Don't speak to me like I'm a child, I have a lot of years on you." Arthur lazily rolled his eyes.

"He's right." Cale's voice rang out and they turned to look at him while his eyes remained on Maya. "You need to rest so she doesn't beat herself up when she wakes up."

His own words filled him with false hope but he was going to do what it took to make Arthur rest for Maya's sake. "It broke her that she let you get taken, the state you're in now will be a reminder that she failed."

Arthur's eyes landed on Maya's shaking face. "I can't leave her-"

"I'll stay with her." Cale finally turned from her and met Arthur's eyes.

From Arthur locking Cale in his cave prison, turning him into a gargoyle, and bringing him and the others into his families problems, Cale had every reason to hate the man but Arthur seemed to trust him. Even with knowing the truth about his birth parents and the anger and hurt it had caused him along Azazel's possession, Cale would never hurt Arthur.

It would only hurt Maya and he didn't want that, he couldn't hurt her more than he already had.

"Come on." Emily got to her feet and made her way to Arthur and together she and Archie helped him from the chair. To their surprise, he didn't fight them.

As she left the room behind everyone else who had all taken their final glances at Maya, Emily turned and her eyes met Cale's.

She knew he needed this time with her, she could see the hurt on his face as he looked at her, how he locked his jaw as he tried to hide his emotions.

She gave him a sad smile as she left but he couldn't bring himself to return it. He watched her leave the room with Arthur and Archie in front of her and he waited for the front door to shut before he brought his attention back to Maya.

Her wavy hair was scattered over the white pillow and her eyes were pressed tightly together from the pain she was in. Small whimpers escaped her lips as she continued to shake under the blanket. Her arms had been placed outside so Archie could check her pulse and Cale noticed her fingers twitching.

There were blisters where the blood had dripped from her mouth, nose, and eyes.

The pain and regret hit Cale like a train and his heart began to race. It felt like no matter how hard it pumped, it wouldn't be able to fill the emptiness inside him.

"Sam…" His voice shook as he placed his hand on hers, it shook from his own grief along with her twitching fingers.

"I'm sorry." He swallowed the lump in his throat. "I'm sorry." He repeated as the tears finally began to fall from his dark eyes. "I'm sorry." He repeated for a third time but no matter how many times he said it, it felt like it wouldn't be enough.

It wouldn't be enough until she smiled at him like she used to.

The memory of her bright smile came to mind and he gritted his teeth.

Would he ever see her like that again? With her wavy brown hair blowing in the gentle breeze, her gray eyes filled with joy as they smiled along with her mouth.

He remembered the look on her face before he had hugged her when she came back from her mission to get the humans to join them. How her eyes had lit up at the sight of him, but it had all changed when he found out the truth about his birth parents.

Now instead of her happy face, all he could think of was how she looked after he had lost it on her.

He thought of the gentle gaze that she had given him when she had told him to be careful before he fought Azazel. The relieved look as she saw him after their fights.

The memory of her falling violently to the ground in front of the warehouse, her blank eyes remaining open as her body convulsed against his.

More tears fell and they landed on her arm as he leaned over her. He wanted nothing more than to see her smile again but he may have lost that chance forever.

He placed his free hand over his mouth to cover the sob that threatened to come out but removed it in the next second.

He wasn't going to hide his grief.

His blurred eyes met her face again and his heart thumped, he couldn't imagine a future without her, she could save them all.

Although at this point, he didn't think of Lucifer's plan, he only thought of Maya.

Azazel had known it, the demon had said that he knew the feelings that Cale hadn't realized he had himself.

He knew them know though.

His grip tightened on her hand as his fingers entwined with hers then he leaned forward and placed his other hand on her cheek, pulling a lose strand of hair from her face.

He loves her.

The early morning sun shined upon Arthur and Archie as they made their way to Maya's cabin. Arthur looked better, his skin tone had almost gone back to normal but his eyes were still heavy as he rushed to be by his sisters side.

Archie walked beside him and he looked as nervous as the gargoyle to see the state that Maya was in, he prepared himself for the worst but Cale had stayed with her and if something had happened, he would have gone to the doctor.

They opened the front door and without bothering to close it, they went to her room but stopped at the doorway as they took in what was inside:

Maya had stopped shaking, her eyelids relaxed and her breaths steady. The blisters the blood had caused on her face were gone and left brand new skin. The blood hadn't even left scars like it had with Arthur's face and Cale's arm.

Their eyes fell to Cale who sat where they had left him, he was asleep with his head resting on the bed beside Maya.

His fingers entwined with hers.

His eyes opened and the two watched as he brought his head up, the sleep disappearing from his brain, and he realized they were there.

Shock filled his face as he pulled his hand from Maya's and he turned from the men to her relaxed face, relief quickly replacing his embarrassment.

Without a word on how they had found the two, Archie walked forward and lifted Maya's arm to check her pulse. He closed his eyes as he listened while Cale and Arthur remained silent so he could hear. The minutes that ticked by were agony until he blinked his eyes open and as he turned to Arthur, his face was filled two emotions: Shock and relief.

"What is it?" Arthur stepped forward as Cale looked on with wide eyes.

"She seems stable but her heart is extremely slow." Archie's finger remained on her pulse, her heart budging his finger. "I can only count four beats per minute."

"What does that mean...?" Cale asked shakily as he watched her breath.

"....I don't know." He furrowed his brows. "I don't know what demon blood can do to someone if it's ingested but everything else seems normal to me."

He brought a hand to her forehead and felt her temperature. "Her temp is normal, her breathing has calmed, and the blood has stopped coming from her mouth, nose, and eyes." He chewed his lip. "There aren't even marks where the blood was on her face." His eyes flashed to the scars running along Cale's arm and the ones on Arthurs face.

"She's going to be ok?" Emily asked from the doorway and the men turned to find her and the rest of the group standing in the doorway. The humans, the other gargoyles, and the Venandi stood in the living room behind them.

"I'd like to say yes, but we won't know for sure until she wakes up." Archie frowned as he met Arthur's gaze. "I don't want to get anyone's hopes up."

Cale inhaled sharply as he took in her relaxed face, she looked so much better than she had the night before.

She had to wake up.

"We should let her rest." Alvertos piped up from the living room and they turned to see his blue eyes filled with worry, though they knew it wasn't directed only at Maya's state.

Donato's blank stare also looked desperate.

They found refuge in the living room while they left Maya to rest in her bedroom. Some sat while most stood. Arthur, Cale, Emily, and Archie chose to remain close to Maya's room in case something happened.

Alvertos waited for everyone to settle before he spoke.

"Even with everything going on, we need to talk about what our next move is." he moved his gaze over the humans and gargoyles. "The demons disappeared mid-fight and you showed up as the officers pointed their guns at us."

"It was only a game to the demons and Lucifer allowed it to happen," Donato began as his blank eyes met Cale's. "But after this, there will be no more playing." His voice was rough at the declaration. "Two of his demons were killed and he's going to raise hell because of it."

Cale had yet to tell anyone how he had managed to kill Azazel, but he was sure the others were the reason why the Venandi knew about his triumph over the demon.

"He was going to do that anyway." Kira said matter of factly, her puffy eyes narrow.

"More so than before." Donato replied simply.

Alvertos brought his attention to Arthur. "Have you heard from the full blooded gargoyles?"

"I haven't, but they'll know where to go when the times comes…I'm positive they're biding their time."

Alvertos and the other Venandi seemed somewhat pleased with his answer, "The entirety of the Venandi will be here in four days time." The leader declared in his thick accent. "They are trying to gather a few at a time since coming here all at once will bring attention to this place."

The gargoyles and detectives seemed pleased with Alvertos declaration.

"I wish I could get more people to help." Reggie's voice drifted as he looked on at the small group that he had managed to get.

"You will be enough," Alvertos assured him. "You did well against the demons yesterday… some of you almost got their hearts with your bullets."

"But the body parts we did get healed right away," Tori spoke up and her voice didn't shake, she stood tall. "They heal so much faster than the gargoyles." Her eyes moved to the other creatures. "Sorry."

Kellan rose a brow but he didn't look insulted.

"No offense taken," Ari shook her head and gave a small smile. "Did you forget we were once human too?"

"We don't know how long we have until Lucifer goes for his final target-" Alvertos lifted his eyes as he changed the subject. "*Jerusalem*." His gaze landed to the opened door where Maya was asleep. "We need her to be ready."

The gargoyles that were close to the legendary gargoyle seemed to take offense at his words, their eyes either narrowing or their brows furrowing. Even Reggie seemed to take his words harshly, Maya was the one his father had entrusted this world to.

"You only care about my sisters power." Arthur was the first to speak, his tone rough.

"True." Alvertos agreed, he didn't even bother to hide his true motives. "She would be of no importance if it weren't for her power."

The air in the cabin changed at the Venandi's words and Arthur, whose anger overflowed from the remark, stood in a threatening manner.

Cale stepped beside him with the same amount of anger flowing through him.

"She can't use her power." He spat. "It'll kill her if she does."

"She knows that." Donato shot in. "She's prepared to take the risk no matter how many promises she's made you."

"Why do you care?" The blonde haired female Venandi asked with her eyes on Cale. "You hated her just days ago for killing your parents."

Cale froze and his jaw shook as every eye in the room landed on him. He couldn't bring himself to say anything so Arthur said something for him.

"That was the demons possession and now it's gone, the demon is dead thanks to him and no thanks to you."

"Azazel's possession amplified those feelings! He felt them himself!" The girl rounded on Arthur. "Maybe he didn't kill the demon and it's still inside him!" She grabbed the hilt of her sword that rested in her holster and the other Venandi aside from Arabella, Alvertos, and Donato did as well.

The gargoyles and humans ran to guard Cale with Kellan front and center since he was rearing to fight. Even Jared who couldn't use his power came to help.

"Fuck off you blonde whore!" Kira spat. "Cale killed that demon, we can tell because we know him while you don't know shit!" She snarled as she stepped beside Kellan. "Without Sam you and your demons hunters wouldn't be shit."

Ari placed her hand on her friends shoulder to defuse the tension as they took in the Venandi's expressions that had turned aggressive. "Kira, I think you should calm-"

"Suck my left nut! I ain't calming down!" She turned her now ink filled eyes to Alvertos. "What are you going to do? Force her to wake up? You bunch of touchholes."

"Enough." Alvertos spat as his Venandi began to lunge at the gargoyles and they stopped without question. They knew better than to disobey him.

After making sure that his Venandi had calmed, Alvertos brought his attention back to the group in front of him. "I only hope she is awake and ready within the next four days."

"Lucifer will wait for her but not for long." Donato announced and the group turned to him, the air in the cabin had yet to calm and it showed on their faces. "He wants her in Jerusalem so he can have his final battle with her."

Maya's sleeping form could be seen from where the blindman stood and his unseeing eyes laid upon her as he continued. *"The hand of God will bring about the end of the world but will also save it."* He repeated the prophecy that they had heard many times before and when he was done, he turned to walk away and Arabella nervously grabbed his hand to help him out of the cabin.

"Let us know when she wakes." Alvertos demanded as he turned to follow the rest of the Venandi who already started out the cabin. They made sure to give the gargoyles venomous looks before doing so. "My brother and the others sacrificed themselves so she could live, I expect her to make up for it." Alvertos gave a smile and a nod as he left the cabin without another word, leaving the group of gargoyles and humans in both shock and anger.

Hours had gone by and Maya had yet to wake. People had come and gone but Arthur, Cale, Emily, Ari, Kira, and Trevor hadn't.

Archie had gone back and forth to help with the small injuries on the detectives and the Venandi.

They watched as Maya slept, six chairs around her bed. Arthur to her left, Cale where he had sat before, Emily beside him, and the other three at the foot of the bed.

"The Venandi are bastards." Reggie's voice surprised them as he stepped into the room. The lack of sleep and their distracted thoughts prevented them from being alert.

The detectives son leaned against the doorway as Lucas and Tori appeared behind him.

"I get where they're coming from, but they seem to forget that she's just as alive as the rest of us."

"You're right..." Arthur's voice drifted and he swallowed. "And the Venandi are right as well."

He was met with confused looks aside from Emily and Cale who understood what he meant.

"She knows she'll have to use her full power and she's prepared to." They could see the pain on Arthur's face as he spoke the truth that he had tried so hard to ignore.

The thought made Cale sick and he could only guess how Arthur felt since he had already seen her sacrifice herself to save an entire city from being blown off the map.

Her energy absorption power was still a mystery, why did she only have the ability in her past life? Why did she have the power in the first place?

"She's never going to stop regretting what she did in her past life," Arthur continued and Cale watched as he spoke. "She'll never back down from what'll help ease the pain she feels." His eyes fell on his sister's pale face. "She'll always be ready to die."

Arthur's words filled them with dread as they laid their eyes on Maya's sleeping form and Cale's heart thumped as the empty feeling took ahold of his chest again.

No one could speak, the lumps in their throats prevented them from doing so. They remained silent and the only sound that filled the room was Maya's breathing.

Cale's eyes fell to her knee high boots that Emily had placed at the end of the bed, they were covered in dust and there were scuff marks where the material had been rubbed.

He needed her to wake up, he needed her to be ok.

This couldn't be it, they needed more time.

Movement from the bed made his eyes shoot up and like the rest, he watched as Maya's eyes fluttered open, revealing her gray eyes.

Chapter 56

His dark eyes were on her now, it was like looking into two black holes. His dark hair that came as waves around his scalp shined against the stars. His toothy smile spread across his face as she looked on with shock.

Sam…ue…l…

Another figure, his eyes as bright as the sun. His shining form was like the sun itself.

"I will not fail." She told him.

"I know." He replied.

I will not.

I will.

As her eyes opened, she felt a tug at her throat and she began to cough uncontrollably. Her eyes watered and her throat seared as she irritated the already sore skin.

She couldn't see who lifted her from the bed to help her sit up to get the coughing to stop. A cool liquid entered her mouth as she felt something plastic touch her lips.

"Maya!" She heard her brothers voice.

"Sam!" She heard her other name being called.

"I'll go get Archie!" Trevor's voice filled her ears as her coughing died down and the tears that had formed in her eyes fell.

Without the tears clouding her eyes, she could see the people around her: She was surrounded by her friends aside from Trevor who had gone to get Archie. Even Reggie, Lucas, and Tori were among them.

She wasn't able to get a good look at everyone as Arthur wrapped his arms around her and pulled her into a hug. Her hands shook as she realized that they had all made it back from the warehouses, Arthur was safe.

As she returned his hug with shaking hands, her throat ached as she tried to let them know she was ok. But she remembered what had happened to her as the words she tried to find fell in her throat. Cain had forced his blood down her throat and her insides ached at the memory and she winced as the pain seared inside her intestines.

"Maya." Arthur pulled away from her and there were tears in his eyes as he looked into her confused ones. "You scared the fuck out of us."

"I'm…sorry…" her voice was hoarse and it was hard to get the words out.

Arthur helped her lean back against the pillows as he rested them against the headboard so she could sit up. She was weak, *extremely weak,* and she could barely manage to move her arms or legs.

She could hear the commotion at the front door as Archie came running in with Trevor, Alvertos, Arabella, and Donato in tow.

"Maya." Archie said with a smile before picking up her arm and placing a finger to her pulse. She watched as he furrowed his brows then met her eyes. "Do you feel odd?"

"Tired…Sore…" She choked and she found that the more she talked, the more irritated her throat became and it was forced to heal by doing so.

"What is it?" Arthur pressed as the doctor blinked. "Her heart at rest is four beats per minute." His eyes remained on Maya's as she took in the information about her own body. "If she were human, she would be dead with this heartbeat."

"It's a good thing she's not human." Alvertos said as he stepped the rest of the way into the room and the detectives gave him annoyed looks as he pushed past them.

For the first time, Maya looked around the room and took in the faces of the people who surrounded her.

They looked so relieved to see her amongst the living as she was met with smiles aside from Donato and Alvertos who were all business.

"Jesus Christ Sam," Kira exhaled sharply through her teeth as Ari smiled between the two girls, her blue eyes softening. "You're gonna force me to take out my life insurance policy."

Through the guilt of worrying the people she cared the most for, Maya found herself letting out a chuckle. Though it burned and caught in her throat.

She continued to look through the group and met each of their faces and as she got to Emily, she found her smile was the biggest of them all. She looked like she was about to jump to hug her but held herself back so she wouldn't hurt her.

"You must love scaring us." She chuckled as she tried to stifle a sob and Maya's frown deepened.

"I-" She was about to apologize when her eyes landed on Cale who was sitting next to his best friend. His gentle eyes were on her and her's widened.

He was alive.

She didn't know how he did it, but he was triumphant over Azazel.

The demons possession was over.

As she looked into his relieved eyes, reality hit her: The possession was over but the fact still remained that she was the cause of his parents deaths.

Her breath hitched and Cale's eyes matched hers as he took in her frightened face. All she could think of was how she had seen his parents moments before they had died. How she could have saved them by stopping her brothers.

"Don't lie to me nor to yourself." Cain's voice echoed in her ears.

"I liked it." Her voice replied in her head and outside her body began to shake as a whimper escaped her lips.

"I didn't...." She stammered as her breath hitched, her eyes filling with tears. *"I didn't..."*

"Cale." Emily got up as Cale looked on, his face filled with both shock and despair as Emily blocked him from Maya's view.

Arthur sat on the bed with his sister and forced her to look at him. "It's ok." He assured her. "You're ok... *breath*."

Archie checked her pulse again as her brother tried to calm her, he felt as her heart remained in it's slow state when it should've been racing.

Cale got up from his chair and backed away as they tried to ease her, he was the one who had caused her to panic. One look at him had frightened her into a panic attack and it was his fault.

He gritted his teeth as he passed the others who moved out of the way as they took in his pained expression. He ran from the front door where he fell against his own cabin that stood next to Maya's. He covered his eyes as they started to sting, his teeth chattering as Maya's frightened eyes burned into his mind.

He felt like a monster.

After a few moments Trevor came out and sat beside him but Cale couldn't move his hand from his eyes, he didn't want anyone to see how they looked.

"She calmed down, Emily and Arthur have it under control." Trevor assured him and Cale gave a jerky nod.

Trevor watched as he chewed on his lip. "She still feels bad about what happened between you two, she's not afraid of you."

"It's my fault..." Cale's voice shook. "She is afraid of me."

"I'm telling you she's not." Trevor's soft voice came out rough as he tried to get his point across. "It's the situation, not you."

"...I was so cruel to her." Cale finally removed his hand from his eyes and Trevor blinked at the tears in them, he had never seen the man cry, he had always hidden his emotions.

"…it was the possess-" Trevor started but Cale interrupted. "They were my own words Trevor, Azazel only amplified them."

"That's the point."

Cale watched as Trevor sighed "You're allowed to feel emotion you know? You just found out the truth about your parents and it hit you hard…" he turned his head slightly towards him. "How do you feel about it now?"

The answer came easy, "Sam wasn't the cause… it was who she used to be."

Monsters can change.

"Exactly," Trevor brought his gaze forward again. "She died and reincarnated." He smacked his lips as if saying what he just had was strange.

It certainly was, but so were their lives.

"She just so happened to get those memories back and her two lives combined, she's no longer Maya the killer or Sam who was locked in that cave with us." He smiled a bit. "We've all changed…especially her."

Trevor had spoken everything Cale was thinking and he brought his head down as his eyes landed on a small pebble at his feet.

"Talk to her when she feels better, tell her everything, especially how you feel about her." Trevor's words brought Cale's attention back to him and Trevor smiled at his nervous eyes.

"I think you oafs are the only ones who haven't realized it." He chuckled as Cale only got more embarrassed. "It was pretty obvious."

As fast as Trevor's entertained smile had appeared, it was gone and his eyes fell to the pebble Cale had been looking at.

"We could be dead in a few days," His gleeful tone was also gone and Cale met his eyes as he turned to him. Trevor's brown eyes didn't seem to have fear in them, they were determined. "Don't wait until it's too late."

Cale turned to his own hands, his fingers were twisted together and his knuckles were white from the strong grip.

How could anyone die without regrets? It wasn't possible.

But Cale was going to try.

"What happened?" Alvertos asked hours later as darkness fell on them again.

Maya had remained in bed all day aside from the occasional help from Emily, Ari, or Kira to go wash up and such. She felt like deadweight and she hated it.

"You have to ask her now?" Arthur gave the Venandi an annoyed look along with Emily, Archie, and Reggie who had remained in the room while the others had gone to get some rest. Donato stood in the corner as he let his leader talk for him. Maya could tell her friends and the Venandi were at odds with each other, the way they focused on one another as their eyes met, how they talked. Something had happened while she was out.

"It's fine…" Her voice came out easier now.

She had so much on her mind, Cain's mental torture had taken a lot out of her along with the blood he had forced down her throat. There was no way she could have lived, but here she was, alive.

Her heart beat was much too slow but she lived.

The blood had scarred her brother and killed any human who had gotten it on their skin. Even if the blood didn't kill her, there was no reason why the power her body had used to heal her didn't.

For the entire day, her mind had been filled by the hurt on Cale's face as she panicked at the sight of him. She had hurt him again.

Her eyes rolled to meet Alvertos' hard gaze, he had waited for her to feel a bit better before he asked the hard questions she gave him that. She had said that it was fine, but the thought of what happened in the warehouse made her slow heart leap.

"I expected Abraxas but Cain was there," She began with a deep breath as she turned to Emily, she was sure that she had told them that much. "He said Emily and Arthur could leave if I stayed and I agreed." Her eyes twitched between the two and she noticed by the looks on their faces that the story was going to be hard for them.

"…His power was terrifying." Her voice broke and she swallowed the fear. "All he had to do was look at me and my body would move to his will. He forced my body to freeze as he used his other ability to make me look at my own sins and-" She paused for a moment as she tried to hide the memories of the people she had killed. Her head down so she couldn't see the the others reactions. "He made me admit how I really felt…about certain things."

She couldn't admit that she had enjoyed killing. She had done so to herself and to the demon back at the warehouse.

Alvertos' blue eyes bored into her as if he was telling her go on, he knew there was more to the story and Maya's voice shook as she went on. "Cain wasn't a normal demon...he's the first born son of Adam and Eve," her declaration made their eyes widen with shock. "After he killed his brother, God wanted to punish him. After he was banished, he was killed by the same stone he had used to kill his brother. God sent him back to earth to suffer with his own shame but Lucifer found him instead. Cain was the embodiment of mankind's sin, he could control any being with the blood of Adam and Eve flowing through their viens and he could control the other demons if he wanted." She lifted her head as the memory replayed in her eyes. "I managed to break out of his hold but the restriction my power has on my body prevented me from doing so for long."

The look on Cain's face as she broke out of his power was still etched into her mind.

"How did you kill him if you couldn't use your power?" Reggie asked softly, his voice filled with intrigue.

The thought of what came next made Maya's insides burn.

"...I didn't." She admitted. "He killed himself by ripping out his own heart and..." Her breath hitched and Emily leaned forward to place a comforting hand on her shoulder. "He shoved it in my mouth and forced me to swallow his blood."

The room was silent as they took in what she said.

"Why would he kill himself just to kill you? He was Lucifer's favorite demon... he would never order him to kill himself...he would never order him to kill you." Alvertos took a step closer as he spoke in high speed as if his words were running a marathon. "Why?"

"He said he hoped that I would live through it." Her eyes rolled to Donato who she knew understood what was going on but his blank eyes held no emotion as they laid on her.

"As soon as I broke out of his power I said that I was going to fight Lucifer no matter the cost and his whole demeanor changed." She currently felt no fear at the memories of the warehouse, her mind was filled with so many questions instead. "For some unknown reason, he wanted me to swallow his blood and he hoped that I would live."

"That doesn't make sense." Alvertos dropped his gaze for a second then he turned to Donato who shook his head.

"I cannot tell you why he did it, I don't even know why she would need demon blood or how she even survived it." His blank eyes turned from his master and landed on Maya again. "It should have killed her."

As if hit by something, Maya suddenly felt faint and she fell further into the pillows.

"I think it's time for bed." Archie stood and motioned for everyone to go. "She's still healing and won't be ready to fight if you continue to bother her."

He shot a look at Alvertos who turned without another word and helped Donato from the room but not before chancing a look at Maya whose eyes began to shut.

"I'll stay with her." Arthur said as he turned from his dozing sister to the others. "I'm healed now so I'm allowed to." He gave Archie a cocky smile and the young man shook his head as he returned it.

"Sure you are." He replied sarcastically.

By the time they left the room, Maya had fallen asleep and Arthur leaned his head against the back of his chair.

"You should be in bed." Maya's voice was the first thing Arthur heard when he woke up in the morning. As he came to, he noticed she was looking better than she had the day before.

It was her emotions that remained questionable.

"Don't worry about me." He rolled his eyes as he sat up. "I was tortured while you almost died."

Maya dropped her eyes to her fingers that were entwined in her blankets. The color she had gotten back in her face disappeared as she thought of what had happened to her brother, hearing it from his mouth made it worse.

She was also sick of feeling like death, she had been so close to dying for the second time.

Perhaps the third.

"You'd think I'd be numb to death since I've already died but it still stings." She didn't mean to chuckle but it escaped her lips before she could catch it.

Arthur's jaw shook as he clenched his teeth, "Why do you say things like that?"

She took in his sad expression and she blinked to keep her tears at bay. "It just comes out…"

What a horrible explanation.

"How would you feel if our roles were reversed and you heard me say something like that?"

"…I'm sorry." She managed to choke out.

"Don't worry about it." He turned away as he fought his own tears from coming.

"I worry about it everyday," She admitted, her eyes on her brothers trembling chin. "I feel the guilt every hour, every minute, and every second." She twitched her fingers and she noticed that they no longer shook as she moved them. "The only thing that keeps me going is what I have to do to make up for it all… for what I've done…for leaving you."

He shuffled beside her and she brought her attention back to him, his face was pale as he gave her a cold look.

She smiled gently to reassure him, "I'm not how I used to be, I'm going to try everything in my power to not to leave you again…if I can help it."

He didn't trust her.

She snorted in a messed up kind of way, "Look at us." She exclaimed with a deep breath. "Were we born to suffer and to make others suffer as well?" She closed her eyes. "The people I killed in my past life…the people that have died because of me in this one."

She thought of Jeannie, Daniel, and Cam who were killed by her brothers and of Dylan who was killed by one of the hydrochloric acid bullets. She even thought of Detective Deluca whose death was undeniably her fault.

Finally she thought of Carma who was so undeniably like herself.

The siblings met each others eyes, "I've been thinking about fate my entire life…both of my lives-" She admitted as she looked into his hazel eyes, the color her's had been before their change to gray. "Even more so now that we both know that I had another life."

"*Anna.*" Arthur said the name that had been weighing on them all since they had first met Lucifer. The name didn't sound right coming from her brother, *Maya* was the only name that made sense coming from him.

"…A life you and Lucifer knew each other." He said what everyone already knew.

Maya pursed her lips, "It would seem so…"

She thought of Cain's words and that she may have been in league with the devil.

"I didn't think it was possible, but with how everything is going, it's believable that I had another life before I was Maya. I was associated with Lucifer… I could've-"

"Don't." Arthur stopped her, his expression rough. "Don't do that to yourself… don't add this to the long list of things you already hate yourself for."

She moved her line of sight to the doorway, at any moment the others would be coming to visit her.

"He talks to me as if we had some sort of bond, he calls me his *Sweet Anna*." Her eyes met Arthur's and he could see the dread in them. "He's my past, present, and future."

They were her words but she didn't think before she had spoken them, it was as if the words were meant to come from her mouth.

"...And you'll do what you have to to save the world?" Arthur asked with his sad eyes.

She couldn't bring herself to answer him but she didn't need to, he already knew the answer.

Hours had passed and people had come and gone and aside from her slow heart rate, Maya felt completely normal after ingesting Cain's blood.

She wondered constantly why he did what he had, it wasn't to kill her, he said so himself, he wanted her to live through it.

But it posed a serious question: What was his ulterior motive?

She was able to think a lot about it as she spent some time alone to shower and she felt refreshed as she put on a fresh pair of clothes that consisted of jeans and a teal shirt.

The Venandi had called for a meeting and they chose her cabin since she wasn't ready to go outside as of yet. Not because she was still ill, her mind wasn't ready to face the world.

Not yet.

They settled into her living room but someone was missing: Cale.

Maya's heart dropped that he may have chosen to stay away from her because of her reaction to seeing him after she had woken up. Maybe he didn't want to see the person who was the reason why he had lost out on a life with his birth parents.

"We leave for Jerusalem in three days time if we're including today." Alvertos got right to the point, his eyes landing on every person in the room one at a time. "More Venandi will begin to join us tomorrow and more will come the day we leave...Lucifer will be ready for us and we must be ready for him."

"What makes you think he will wait for us?" Reggie asked as he stood with his group. "He has everything he needs to finish his plan."

Alvertos considered him but Donato was the one to answer, "You haven't met him yet, you don't know that Lucifer won't do anything until the black and white eyed gargoyle is there."

They looked into his damaged eyes as if they could see what he was thinking.

"Why does he need her?" Lucas looked between the seer and Maya with a confused but apathetic look on his face.

"I don't know." Donato answered truthfully, "But since he showed himself for the first time, she has always been present. He's attached to her whether it be for her power or something more."

"He's sure to be pissed at her for killing his favorite demon." Arabella piped up from the corner of the room and Maya met her eyes.

"I didn't kill Cain, he killed himself."

The other Venandi had obviously heard Maya's story from Alvertos and Donato but they didn't seem to trust her.

"Why would he kill himself just to kill you? The story of him being the son of Adam and Eve seems far fetched." The same girl that had threatened Cale tested her.

"He was the embodiment of mankind's sins and he made me realize mine... If he was still alive, he could've made you realize yours." Maya said calmly and the girl gritted her teeth.

"I haven't sinned." She claimed with narrowed eyes and Maya glared into them, her gray eyes were like stones.

"No one is without sin no matter how holy one claims to be, it's in the way you think, the way you move...Even God can't say he's never sinned."

Her eyes moved to Alvertos as the girl's expression became infuriated. "He didn't want me to die but he killed himself with the intention of making me swallow his blood." She swallowed as her mind went back to the tar-like taste, how it burned going down. "I don't know why he did it, or what he thought it would accomplish, but he didn't want to kill me."

"Are you saying he wasn't really working for Lucifer?" Ari asked from beside her, her blue eyes pressing into her.

"I'm not saying that at all...maybe it was Lucifer's plan." Her eyes set on the table where her head had cracked it, the vision of her past life coming back to her.

She remembered the sharp pain in her head as the man smashed her head repeatedly into a wall. She remembered the dream she had in her cell when she was trying to recruit Reggie and the other humans. The man who had beaten her laid dead on a radiator, his neck snapped.

The blonde haired girl she had cared so much for was also dead.

Her mind went to Mina who she had left at the research facility and she wondered if she had made it home ok.

She lifted her eyes to find Kellan's on her, he didn't look like he was judging her nor did he have his usual smug look. He looked curious, worried even.

As she turned from him, she found that the others had their eyes on her as well.

"Perhaps it's best we end this for now," Alvertos pried his eyes off Maya then moved them to Arthur instead. "Have you told the other gargoyles where we're going?"

"The messages have been delivered." Arthur said simply and the Venandi nodded as he pushed himself off the wall.

"What would Lucifer do if we didn't show up in Jerusalem?" Kira called before he and the other Venandi could leave.

"He would drag us there." Alvertos answered without turning to her.

"We need a plan." Reggie who had been taught to always plan ahead due to his line of work announced.

"There is no plan that can surprise Lucifer." Donato told as he held onto Arabella's arm as she helped him up. "God has his plan and we shall follow it."

"Mother fuck-" Kira began to exclaim her annoyance with the Venandi's talk of God but Ari interrupted her.

"Kira." She said simply and Kira stopped mid-curse.

"I'm sure you'll be ready to make up for my brothers and the other Venandi's sacrifice." Alvertos smiled at Maya.

She had heard of how Arely and the others had stopped the officers so she could get to safety back at the warehouses. It was strange to her that Alvertos would even think that she wouldn't fight. Whether it be to make up for what his brother had done or for nothing at all, she would go to fight Lucifer. It was in her genetic code to want to fight him.

"See you tomorrow." Alvertos called back as he walked out of the cabin with the other Venandi in tow. Donato and Arabella were the last to leave and as Arabella helped him with his direction, Donato turned one more time to Maya before he left through the doorway.

"Memories from your other life?" Kira asked suddenly as they shut the door and Maya brought her eyes to her.

"You had the same look in your eyes when you were getting your memories back before." Kira went on after she made sure talking about it wouldn't bother her.

"...What did you see?" Emily asked while Maya rested her elbows on her knees as she sat on the couch.

"A mental asylum."

Her words brought shock with them.

"A mental asylum?" Reggie's voice filled with disbelief, he and the other humans were still new to her past life dilemmas.

The other gargoyles seemed as startled as the humans since they hadn't witnessed them either.

"I'm not gonna lie," Kellan's usual smug look had returned and it oddly made Maya feel better. "A mental asylum sounds right for you."

Until he finished the rest of his sentence that is.

"An old time one... perhaps in the 1800's." She swallowed as she ignored him.

"Are you saying you lived in the 1800's?" One of the humans asked as she looked on with wide eyes, Maya remembered that the others had called her Sabrina.

She dropped her eyes to her trembling hands. "I'm not sure."

They dropped the subject after that.

After a bit of visiting the others began to make their leave as the sun fell. The girls had offered to stay with Maya while Arthur who she was sure would have offered to stay didn't bother to ask. She wanted to be alone and he knew it.

"I'll be here in the morning to check on you." Emily told her as she pulled out of their hug. "But if you need anything, don't hesitate to come to my cabin."

"Thanks." Maya smiled gently and she watched as everyone walked to their cabins.

She met Arthur's eyes and she kept her smile so he would be assured that she'd be ok alone.

When they were gone Maya walked to the coach but stopped and looked at the small table again, frowning as emptiness swallowed her heart.

She practically fell on the couch and like before, she laid with her limbs curled around her as she looked absentmindedly at the table.

She had known her own sins but had denied them for so long. She had indeed enjoyed the thrill of killing but that had changed.

She brought a hand to her hair and ran her fingers through the long strands, it felt odd to not have her braids but she couldn't bring herself to do them.

Her braids not only helped to keep her hair out of the way while she fought, they also made her feel like a warrior. The vikings had worn their braids as such and she was no different. They also reminded her of her mother.

She didn't feel like a warrior anymore and she also didn't want to think of her dead but reincarnated mother.

Her mind wandered to Cale who was on her mind more often than not, his smile…his laugh… Even the anger he had directed at her. Even more the look he had on his face as he left her cabin because his presence had reminded her of what she had done and she panicked.

He had looked so hurt.

Nothing was ever going to change the fact that she was a monster, even in the smallest of ways she would always show that she was one.

The love of her brother and her friends would never be enough to change how she felt about herself.

The people she had killed flashed into her mind and she couldn't even count them all, maybe she was too afraid to do so. The memory of Cale's parents was clear, she forced herself to see them, she needed to see them alive as they should have been now if it weren't for her.

She could have saved them.

She could have ended it all.

Cain was right about her, she had no room to talk about the cruelty of the demons when she was just as cruel.

Lucifer needed her but why? Had she been in league with him in the past? Was she always a monster? Was a monster all that she was ever going to be?

She pressed her eyes against her arm and chewed her lip, all of the thoughts going through her head were threatening to make her break down again.

Her eyes opened hours later but she remained on the couch even as the minutes ticked by.

She hadn't realized that she had fallen asleep, perhaps her body was making up for the days she had been awake with her thoughts. The only light in the room caused a dim shine through the living room as the darkness outside filled the cabin. Her too slow heart pumped in her ears and instead of being alarmed at it's lack of beats, she listened to it as if it was the only salvation she had.

A knock on the front door made her jump, the sound of her heart had distracted her from hearing the visitor approach the cabin.

She got up and the old wires under the cushion's creaked at the loss of her weight. It had to be Emily or Arthur checking on her, they worried too much.

Another knock filled her ears as she stepped towards the door and with her mind still distracted, she didn't notice that it was neither Arthur nor Emily on the other side.

She swung the door open with her dull eyes ready to meet her brother or her friend, but they widened with shock as they landed on the person she didn't expect to see.

On the other side of the door stood Cale, his gentle eyes on her as the moonlight illuminated his face.

Chapter 57

"Can I come in?" He asked softly and after realizing that she had been standing there holding her breath, Maya nodded awkwardly and stepped back so he could enter.

He stepped into the dim light of the cabin and walked past her with his eyes down so he wouldn't meet her's.

Maya listened as his footsteps echoed off the hardwood floor while Cale listened as the door shut with a creak. Maya's heart raced as she turned to him, so many things rushed through her mind: Why was he there? What was he going to say? Was this going to be the end of what they had built together?

He stood next to the couch, his dark eyes on her as she stepped closer but kept her distance.

"How're you feeling?" He sounded as nervous as Maya looked.

"…I'm ok." She answered without meeting his eyes.

"Emily told me what happened between you and Cain." His voice drifted and she peaked through the stands of hair that had fallen into her face to see that his gaze was still on her.

"Of course she did."

They remained silent for a moment, the air dense with their emotions.

When Cale spoke, it was as if his voice was a knife and it cut the air in half. "We need to talk about what happened between us."

Maya swallowed. "…I suppose we do."

She knew this was coming but feared it all the same, this could very well be the end of them…the end of something she had grown to love.

"I don't know where to start," He let out a sad chuckle and Maya finally looked at him, his brows were furrowed and his mouth was in a deep frown. Now that she was looking at him, she couldn't take her eyes off of him. "But I'll start off with what I need to say," He looked into her eyes. "I'm sorry."

He was sorry? For what? She was the wrong one, she was the monster.

"You don't need to apologize." She assured him breathlessly as she jerkily shook her head and when she stopped, she realized that his frown had deepened and his eyes frowned along with it.

"No," He said simply. "I do."

Maya watched his careful gaze, the sincerity in his eyes…he honestly thought he was the one in the wrong.

"I'm the one who killed innocent people," She began with an air of annoyance though it wasn't directed at him."I'm the one who broke up families…orphaned children…" her eyes started to water. "I took everything from you…"

He listened to her words, how they cracked at the last and he shook his head. "You're not-"

"Don't bullshit me," Her teeth chattered as her face twisted into a snarl. "Don't be like everyone else and say that I've changed." She narrowed her tear filled eyes as Cale watched with wide ones. "Emily told you what happened between Cain and I?" She questioned shakily. "Then you must know what his power was…Do you know what he made me admit to myself? Do you know how much of a monster I really am!?"

Her voice broke and the tears spilt over and rolled down her cheeks, "I liked it!" She sobbed. "I enjoyed killing people!"

She brought a trembling hand to her mouth as she watched his reaction through her tears. His expression didn't change but she noticed that he had flinched at her words.

"It didn't last long," She admitted as she removed her hand from her mouth. "But I enjoyed it all the same."

The image of her standing over her victim filled her mind, she remembered the relish on her face as she took in the the dying man. She could still hear the gurgles that came from his mouth as he choked on his own blood. Without warning, the image switched to the memory of Cale's parents. His father who he had undeniably taken after and his beautiful mother with her hazel eyes and hair as bright as the sun.

"....I wasn't the one who did it." She said finally and Cale blinked at her words.

"I saw them..." She continued as fresh tears fell from her face to her feet. "I let them go because they had you." She shook her head. "No, I had enough of killing by that time...I wouldn't have done it anyway." She gritted her chattering teeth but the combination didn't work. "But it doesn't matter, it's still my fault!" She gripped at the fabric over her chest as her too slow heart ached at the thought.

Cale took a jerky step towards her but she flinched away and the hand that reached for her fell back to his side. He wanted to reassure her, to tell her that she really had changed.

"I've been a hypocrite..." He began as he watched her tremble. "Whenever you've had your doubts, I assured you that you were no longer the person you once were...." His heart raced as he prepared his words, he had to say the right thing. "I can blame it on Azazel's influence but I can't hide the fact that for a moment," He drew a sharp breath. "I *hated* you."

Maya almost fell as she backed away, her knees buckling at the word.

Hate.

She wanted to be loved, she wanted to make everything right, but that was an impossible wish.

"Don't go..." Cale's voice trailed as he reached for her but she pulled away from him, her tear stained eyes wide with grief.

She couldn't be here anymore, she didn't care if she lived or died and she wished that death had kept her soul the first time she had died.

If she had remained dead after her time as Anna, it would have prevented so much devastation, so much chaos. Her lives only brought pain to the people around her and she had tried so hard to break that cycle as Sam but she could never hide from who she truly was.

If she truly was God's warrior, it had to be a sick joke.

"Sam!" Cale called to her as she turned to the front door. "Sam!" He called again as she ignored him, his voice shaking.

She couldn't look at him and much more, she couldn't take hearing his voice. Even now she continued to hurt him when she wanted nothing more than to see his smile directed at her again, his eyes gleaming at the look of her.

She wanted it back, she wanted to go back to the days they would joke and laugh. She wanted to go back to the day she had returned from the gargoyle research facility, to when he pulled her into his arms.

She managed to twist her shaking fingers around the door handle when she froze at what came from Cale's mouth. *"Maya!"*

His hand found her empty one, his fingers twisting with hers.

Maya turned and she was met with a face that matched her own, tears were in his eyes and he looked devastated.

Her lips quivered as she took him in and his dark eyes smoothed as he finally got her to look at him. He had never called her Maya, he had met her when she was Sam, the girl who had been kidnapped along with him, the girl he was thrown into a cell with, changed into a gargoyle with.

They had fought through so many obstacles together, all to see another day.

When he found out about her past life, no matter how far fetched it was, he didn't leave her, he remained by her side and continued to fight with her.

Who would have ever thought that she was the one who had turned his life upside down.

Fate had brought them together but there was no telling why.

"You're no longer the girl who did terrible things because something terrible happened to you." He began and she was surprised to hear his voice so strong. "You were reborn as Samantha Knight and fate chose to bring your past lives memories back. You choose to be called Maya not because of what the name gives you, but because you still see yourself as the person who did those terrible things." His thumb ran over the top of her hand that he was holding as if he was trying to soothe her. "You are Sam and Maya combined but you're not the Maya you used to be... You're *not* a monster."

"I'm-" She began to protest but he interrupted her. "Everyone is a monster in someway, their thoughts.. their actions... some more than others, but do you know what my father taught me?"

His father, the man who had raised him after his parents were killed.

"He told me monsters can change, that they can redeem themselves... he know's because he worked with the gargoyles and perhaps he knew your parents."

The news made her already slow heart skip a beat, his father had worked with her parents?

"It's not that easy to change..." Her voice drifted.

"But *you* have." He said simply as they met each others eyes and she noticed tears were threatening to spill out of his.

"I knew you changed and I've told you all this time that you have but as soon as I found out about my parents..." His voice broke and he swallowed.

"Azazel's possession made my thoughts worse but after I killed him and my mind was clear..." His voice steadied again as if was reliving the fresh feeling of his mind being empty of the demon's voice all over again. "Almost losing you made me realize something," He placed his free hand on her cheek and instead of flinching she leaned into his touch. His skin was warm and comforting, this was the touch she had missed the most, the one that she had needed.

"I can't live without you." He finished finally and her eyes widened at his words, her hand falling from the door handle as she turned completely to him.

The two simply looked at each other for a moment, their hearts pounding in their throats as he wiped a tear from her cheek and they leaned into each other.

Living is so hard when you don't have someone to share it with and Maya didn't want to be alone, neither of them did.

She stood tall while Cale lowered his head to meet her's, their eyes never leaving the others.

There was no telling who went in first, perhaps they did at the same time, but their lips crashed all the same. It was slow at first as they simply felt each other but as they went on, their hunger for each other overwhelmed them.

Cale's arms wrapped around Maya's back as he pulled her closer and she wrapped her own around his shoulders to oblige.

After a long moment, the two reluctantly pulled away from each other to catch their breaths, leaving a trail of saliva between them.

Their breaths were heavy and as they continued to look into each others eyes, they realized their tears had been replaced with something entirely different.

Their lips connected again and as they kissed, they began to shuffle to her room, almost tripping over each others feet as they did so.

Maya clung to him as he lowered her on the bed and he leaned on top of her, placing one hand on her cheek while the other intertwined with hers. The feeling of their lips moving together and the twists of their tongues as they collided sent them both into a haze. They moaned against each others lips and when Cale pulled away, Maya's face was beet red and through the dim light, she was relieved to see his was the same.

They couldn't believe what was happening.

Cale's breath hitched as Maya sat up, his legs pinning her to the bed, and he swallowed as a more than awkward question came out of his mouth. "Have you ever…?"

It took her a moment to realize what he was asking and when she did, her face turned impossibly more red.

"No." She chewed on her lip and her eyes fell so she wouldn't meet his gaze. "In neither of my lives…you?"

Of course she never did anything like this, she had always thought that there were more important things to do. The same could be said for her time as Sam and it didn't help that she had never met anyone like Cale, had never felt for someone the way she did for him.

She was starting to feel embarrassed at her own inexperience but as relief filled Cale's eyes, she finally met his gaze and she blinked.

"I haven't." He answered as awkwardly as she had.

She was so sure that he had done it before but perhaps he was the same as she was, there were other things to do.

He chuckled from the look on her face.

"What?" She asked nervously.

Fighting demons felt more real than this.

He smiled as he ran a gentle hand through her long hair and he leaned into her again, their foreheads touching as they peered through the dim light into each others eyes.

They kissed gently as they rose from the bed and with each others help, they began removing their clothes. They kissed between each piece of clothing as the fabric fell to the floor until only their undergarments remained.

Maya pressed her hand to the scar Azazel had left on his chest, it was only inches from his heart. It was the only wound that hadn't completely healed aside from the burn marks on his arm from the demon blood.

He also had the shoulder that she had injured during her insane frenzy almost five months ago.

She stepped closer until there was no room left between them, her eyes on his injured shoulder while he watched her. She leaned in and pressed her lips to his warm skin, kissing the injury all the while sliding her hand down his chest to his stomach where her fingers found ridges of muscle. Goosebumps formed on his skin from her wandering fingers and the feeling of her lips trailing from his shoulder to his neck. His fingers slid up the ridge of her back until he found her bra and he stopped as his fingers found the clasps.

She pulled away and met his eyes, he was looking at her as if he was asking permission and she nodded.

He undid the clasps and she allowed the fabric to fall from her shoulders to the floor.

His breath hitched as he took in her curves. "You're beautiful."

Maya's heart thumped at the compliment, she had been called beautiful before but the implications had been different.

Cale meant it.

He swallowed as he leaned forward and pressed his lips to her chest, directly over the scar Astaroth had left. He trailed down between her breasts and she shuddered, a small moan escaping her lips as he found one of her nipples. His tongue circled around it while he worked at the other with his free hand. Her moans deepened and her back arched, her legs were beginning to feel like jelly.

Meeting each other in the mountainside cave had been the beginning, they were two young adults that didn't know what was going to happen to them. That they were going to be turned into creatures supposedly made by God to fight Lucifer and his demons.

They didn't know at that time that she had a past life and that her brothers were aiming for her head. They didn't know their true enemy would be the embodiment of evil.

They trained, fought, and thrived together but the months they spent with each other felt more like years and did much more than teach them how to fight together.

Maya's legs fell from underneath her and she landed on the bed with Cale in tow, the two bouncing as the mattress adjusted to their weight.

Cale didn't miss a beat as he continued to explore her body, her back arching off the bed as he moved down her front, planting kisses along her toned belly all the way down to her black laced underwear.

"Cale…" Her shaking voice trailed and he brought his face back to her's, their lust filled eyes meeting until Cale leaned down and their lips met again.

They wrapped their arms tightly around each other as if it was possible to get closer. Their kiss deepened, their tongues twisting together, and soft groans escaped their lips as they continued their assault on each others mouths.

Cale's toned chest rested against her soft breasts, their hearts mixed together, and at this moment it felt like Maya's heart was at it's normal pace.

The normal pace for a human heart was a race for Maya's.

Even with all of the other emotions that they felt, their need for each other out weighed them all. They knew these feelings were present for months but it took almost losing each other to make them realize how strong they were.

The need to have their arms around each other, the feeling of his warm skin against her cool. Their mixed smells, the hitch in their breaths as their kiss deepened.

Oh God, they needed each other.

Death was closing in on them and Maya already had one foot in the grave, but it didn't matter. Nothing mattered other than where they were right now.

There needn't be any regrets.

Her right hand rested on the groove of his injured shoulder and she felt it shift as he moved his hand down her stomach, eliciting goosebumps along the way. A whimper escaped her lips as he slipped his hand through the fabric of her underwear.

She gasped against his lips as she pulled him closer, her fingers trembling as his set to work. Her strangled moans filled the room as they fell against Cale's lips and before long she was seeing stars.

Their glazed over eyes met as they pulled apart and she moaned his name. He pulled his hand away and she found herself reaching down and pulling at his boxers, the fabric slipping through her shaking fingers. He pulled away from her and sat on his lower legs as he pulled the fabric down for her.

Modesty had gone out the window as their need for each other filled them completely and Maya sat up and lifted her bottom from the bed so she could remove her own underwear, the fabric falling to the floor from her ankles.

Their lust filled eyes explored each others naked bodies, all of their freckles, moles, and scars.

Cale positioned himself on top of her again, his elbows resting beside her while she moved her legs out of the way. She could feel him against her and it sent a shiver down her spine.

He brought his hand to her's and their fingers intertwined as their mouths connected again, a groan leaving Cale's throat as he rubbed against her.

He pulled away as their lust became too much and waiting seemed impossible. They examined each others eyes before he reached down and positioned himself at her entrance. She tensed as she prepared herself but he didn't move, he only brought his forehead to her's.

Their eyes were filled with want and their feelings for each other as they met again, a drop of sweat falling from their brows as their warm breaths hit their faces.

"Can I?" He breathed as he brought his free hand to her cheek and she kissed him in reply.

With the answer clear, he began to push into her and she gasped, Cale's lips unable to muffle the sound.

Cale clenched his teeth at the feeling of her around him, air escaping through them as he exhaled sharply.

Maya whimpered from the pain, she had been told that it would hurt but this feeling was unlike any pain she had felt before.

Cale stopped midway as her nails dug into the top of his hand, her knuckles white as she tried to ease the pain.

"...Are you ok?" He asked breathlessly as he caressed her cheek, his smooth skin comforting her.

Her eyes had clenched shut but they fluttered open from the sound of his voice, she looked into his face as he gazed at her with worried eyes. He ran his fingers through her hair and the gesture calmed her.

"I'm...ok." She assured although the pain could be heard in her voice. She breathed deeply as she tried to get used to the feeling of him inside of her.

"We can stop." He pressed his forehead back to hers. "I don't want to hurt you."

"No," she rubbed her fingers over the marks her nails had left on his hand. "If I can handle everything else, this should be fine."

Her words seemed to sadden him and she regretted them immediately so she wrapped her arms around his neck and forced him down, their lips smashing together. They both moaned as she moved her core and he moved further inside of her.

The pain was easing as she knew it would due to the fact that she was a gargoyle, she could only imagine how it would feel if she was still human.

There were only a few occasions that she'd been thankful for being a gargoyle and now was one of them.

She pulled away, their breaths heavy as they tried to catch them.

"Keep going." She directed with a smile and he kept his eyes on hers, the ferocity in them making his worry disappear.

"Keep your eyes on mine." He demanded softly and he started to push into her again.

She groaned as she fought to do as she was told but as he continued, she found solace in his dark eyes.

"You can press your nails into me." He assured her as she fought to not claw him and when her nails found his back, the pain didn't seem to bother him.

He would heal right away anyway.

He pulled out a bit and as his mouth fell on hers, he thrusted the rest of the way inside her.

She moaned so loud that anyone around could hear but that was the furthest thing from her mind. Cale who had moaned in unison with her gasped as he took in the feeling of her around him. He didn't move again as he waited for her to adjust to him and they kissed as she did so.

When he pulled away and their lust filled eyes met, it was more than enough to assure him that she was ready. He began to pull out then thrusted into her again, Maya's strangled moan filling the room while Cale groaned. Pleasure rushed through them as Maya's already healing body adjusted to him completely and he repeated the action over and over again.

Her body moved on it's own as she rocked her hips in unison with his thrusts, the bed creaking and the room filling with their moans. They planted salty kisses on each other's necks and shoulders as they groaned into damp skin and as they wrapped their arms tighter around each other, a strange pressure started to build inside of them and they stopped moving.

Maya looked into Cale's eyes and she was met with pitch black while he was met with her black and white eyes.

They were shocked at first but it quickly turned into laughter as Cale snorted.

The room filled with the sound of their soft chuckles as they held tightly onto each other, their smiling faces only an inch apart.

The sun shined through the windows but it was still dark in Maya's bedroom. The birds chirps from outside mixed with their even breaths as they slept, their naked bodies wrapped in the blankets as they laid beside each other. Maya's head rested against Cale's chest and as he breathed, it rose up and down with him as he inhaled and exhaled.

A noise made his eyes open slowly until there was a knock on the door and he shot up as he caught Maya's head so she wouldn't fall on the bed.

"Sam!" Emily called from the front door as she knocked again and Cale's eyes widened.

Maya's had opened when Cale had caught her and she looked up at him with tired eyes but blinked when she saw the look on his face.

"Emily's here!" He whispered frantically and Maya jumped from the bed as Cale did the same. Their eyes landed on each others naked bodies and reality hit them of how this was going to look. It was exactly how it looked but they would rather their friend not know what they had spent their night doing.

They pulled their clothes on while Emily called for her again.

"Damn it!" Maya cursed to herself, she had forgotten that Emily had said that she was going to check on her.

Her heart raced as she pulled on a shirt that she found on the floor.

"I'll be right there!" She called and as she realized the shirt was too big, she looked down to see that she was wearing Cale's shirt that had blended in with her own on the dark floor.

She looked up with wide eyes and found that Cale already had his eyes on her and it was clear that he enjoyed the view by the look on his face.

"I'm coming in!" Emily began opening the door and the two rushed to get their clothes on.

Cale only managed to get his pants on while Maya had just managed to pull her underwear on under his shirt. The sound of Emily stepping into the cabin filled their ears and before they could do anything, she was at the doorway. Her eyes were wide as she saw Maya who was swimming in Cale's shirt and Cale who stood with only his pants on.

"Uh…" Was all Emily managed to get out as she took in their embarrassed faces, neither of them knew what to say.

"…I'm sorry." She pointed with her thumb to the front door as she let out an awkward chuckle and began to back away. "I'm glad to see you guys getting along again!" She called and they stepped to the door and watched as she jogged out the front door.

It took them 20 minutes after Emily's departure to meet the rest outside, they were far too embarrassed to go out even after being dressed.

"Should we go separately?" Cale pondered as they stepped to the front door.

He was dressed in his clothes from the day before while Maya had changed into her usual all black attire. Though she was sure that he would have loved to see her stay in his shirt.

"I don't think it matters." She sighed as she laced her knee high boots. "Everyone probably knows by now." She met his eyes and smiled at his embarrassment. "Screw it."

He sighed softly as she got to her feet and he placed a hand on her viking braids.

Her warrior look had made a comeback.

He leaned down with a smile and she ran her hand along his shoulder as she kissed him. They enjoyed their last blissful moment before they had to talk about their fate and the enemy that waited for them in Jerusalem.

It was hard to believe that they were at odds with each other just days before, that Cale had the fight of his life with a demon and Maya had almost died after facing her own.

But it had brought them closer, closer than they've ever been.

They walked side by side to the playground where the others stood waiting for them and they were met with curious eyes as they noticed the change between the two.

Emily, Ari, Kira, and Trevor had smug looks and Arthur seemed to know as well. He had seen Cale holding her hand when her fate was still foggy, he saw the way they acted together. Only a fool wouldn't know that the two would end up together.

Though as all big brothers were, he seemed apprehensive.

"You look better." Kellan walked to meet them and his eyes fell on Maya.

"As good as someone could feel after reliving all of the shitty things they've done and having demon blood shoved down their throat." She replied as Kellan's smug face moved to Cale. He rose a brow, his eyes blinking and his lips pursing as he nodded. The look on his face was almost funny.

"You're a lucky fuck." He exclaimed as he turned away from the two and they blinked.

"Let's get planning on what we're going to do in Jerusalem." Alvertos called and they turned to meet him as he and the other Venandi sat around the picnic tables. They weren't fazed by the new development, they were all business.

"Let's." Maya met Alvertos' eyes and he could see the change in them, a small grin appeared on his lips.

With a her new mindset, she would no longer deny her connection with Lucifer, she accepted that she had shared a past life with him. It didn't matter what she had done back then, she knew what she was going to do now:

fight him.

"First we'll talk about Jerusalem's landscape." Alvertos started as he pulled out a multicolored map and they all circled around the table. As Donato had said the night before, there was no good plan to make that Lucifer wouldn't be able to see through.

But they needed to know the landscape of their foreign battleground.

"There's many buildings that have been there for hundreds of years, there's many hills and roads that connect around the city and this-" he pointed at a spot on the map. "Is The Temple Mount." He turned his body to meet the people surrounding him. "It was built by King Solomon until it was destroyed and later rebuilt, it is one of the most religious places in the world. People come from all over no matter what religion they practice to pray there."

"Lucifer is sure to start his crusade there." Donato who sat across from Alvertos declared. "It will be the beginning of the end."

A nervous shuffle ran through the group and for the first time, Maya understood Donato's prophecy. She didn't know how, but she could feel in every inch of her mind that the temple was going to be where their battle would begin.

"This," Alvertos began again and their eyes moved back to the map. "Is where the Church of the Holy Sepulchre lies, it's also called the Church of the Resurrection."

Maya swallowed as her body tensed, she knew the word resurrection all too well.

"This place," Her eyes stared blankly at the map and an old stone building flashed through her mind. *"This place is going to change everything."*

"These places will be the most significant to Lucifer, especially the church due to Jesuses influence. He was crucified and resurrected in that area and his tomb is supposedly there." Alvertos met Maya's gaze. "And we know Lucifer is one to use theatrics and this place will be perfect for that." His eyes fell back to the map like he was imaging the building like Maya was, his jaw set tightly. "It will be a shame to see them destroyed but he saved the best for last. "

"Our biggest obstacle will be the demons." Arthur shot in from behind Maya. "And we don't know how Lucifer will bring the end of the world after they destroy the holy places there. Theres no way just destroying significant places will be enough to make this world his."

"Indeed they will be." Alvertos agreed about the demons. "But in someway, we do know how Lucifer will bring the end… it's everything in between that we don't know."

That was right, they knew *The Hand of God* would bring the end of the world.

But would also save it.

"We only have three top tier demons left so our chances have gone up." Alvertos added and he was met with confused looks.

"How can you say our chances are better if the world's going to end anyway?" Lucas shook his head as Kira who stood beside him nodded.

"Because it can be saved after the fact." Donato's even voice filled their ears and they took in the blank stare that seemed to stretch onto all of them.

"Let's focus on the demons since they will be our biggest obstacles." Alvertos said with a pleased look from his underlings answer. "All of the demons serve a purpose in some shape or form, you already know this but it's much deeper than that." He lifted a finger. "Azazel was known as the scapegoat-"

"That makes sense," Cale interrupted and they brought their attention to where he stood beside Maya. "His true form resembled a goat."

The Venandi's eyes widened. "...You saw Azazel's true from?"

"I did." He inhaled sharply as he remembered the demons terrifying form. "I almost died when he used it and I would have been dead if he didn't change back."

"How *did* you kill him?" The blonde haired female Venandi asked and it seemed she was genuinely curious this time unlike the other day when she thought the demons possession was still on him.

"I shoved my arm down his throat all the way to his chest and pulled out his heart and tongue." he narrowed his eyes as they flashed to his scarred arm. "Like I promised him I would."

He was met with swallows and amazed gasps from the Venandi.

Maya turned and met his eyes until they dragged down to the scar under his shirt and they filled with relief that he had lived. They fell to his arm and she thought of the way he had killed the demon, how desperate he must have been to use such a difficult way to kill him.

Cale caught her looking and reached for her hand and no one noticed since Arthur blocked the way.

Alvertos blinked as he continued, "Astaroth is confusing since her name doesn't match who she actually is."

"What do you mean?" Ari furrowed her brows as her voice became high pitched with nerves.

"Astaroth is described as a male, she or *he* is the head of the hierarchy of fallen angels." Arabella answered for Alvertos, "Though I have a hunch that she may not be the Astaroth that we know of."

They didn't have time to ponder about the female demon as Alvertos went on, "Abraxas is the biggest problem aside from Lucifer himself since his shadow can kill us all in an instant."

Reggie shuffled at Abraxas' description, he had his memories of the demons monstrous power and his personal hatred for what he had done.

"Aamon is known to command a legion of demons but we have yet to see what they are, we'll need to be wary of his power as it unknown." Alvertos explained the next demon with no pause.

"He didn't even use his power on us at the warehouses," Arabella chewed on her bottom lip. "But I'm sure he'll use it when we meet him in Jerusalem."

"...And finally even though he is dead, we must talk about Cain who was Lucifer's favorite demon." Alvertos' hard voice filled Maya's ears, the mention of Cain brought her back to the mental and physical pain the demon had put her through.

"Cain had always been a mystery, we've only seen him on occasion and he never fought until-" The groups eyes fell on Maya as she kept her gaze on the Venandi's leader. "The black and white eyed gargoyle fought him and in doing so, she found out that he is the first born son of Adam and Eve. His power was to expose the sins of his victims and to control their bodies, he died by his own hand but not before making her ingest his blood." He tapped his fingers on the table, "We're not sure as to why he sacrificed his own life to do so."

"I wish I knew." Maya swallowed down the taste of tar that had crept into her mouth, her slow heartbeat echoing in her ears.

Alvertos went silent as he dropped his gaze and his worry seemed to stretch to the other Venandi.

"What is it?" Reggie asked roughly as their silence sent him on edge.

"I know the end of the world will bring devastation but-" Alvertos lifted his head and they were shocked to see fear on his face. "It will also bring more demons with it." He declared and a chill ran through the group at the news. "Demon's who have been exorcised will be freed and new one's will rise."

Maya inclined her head and met the blue sky and the sun that shined in it. To protect this world, she *had* to stop Lucifer.

"Don't fear." She told herself. *"Push forward, like a gargoyle."*

The day was spent preparing for their departure, they learned about Jerusalem's landscape and they discussed how the Venandi were going to carry their weapons on the plane that they had announced they had booked. Alvertos replied that they needn't worry about it which made the gargoyles and the humans even more on edge but before long they were meeting the new Venandi as they arrived and their minds went elsewhere.

"I've heard so much about you, about all of your lives." The leader of the new group that consisted of ten Venandi bowed his head as Maya introduced herself to him.

He was an old man, his hair gray and his skin dull but he wasn't old enough to quit fighting.

"Theres no telling whether or not the first black and white eyed gargoyle was me." She said truthfully, "I have no memory of that life."

"I'm glad to fight with you nonetheless." He smiled and as she met with the other newcomers, she received the same awe that she had gotten when the first group of Venandi had joined her and the other gargoyles.

Another group of Venandi arrived hours later, twelve more of them entering the fray.

"This is it." Arthur said as he sat with the group that started it all, their minds filled with the memory of Dylan who was killed by the hands of a human with a poisoned bullet. Of Daniel, Jeannie, and Cam who had lost their lives by the siblings brothers.

Emily and Cale thought of Carma: Her long blonde hair and her shining eyes. They would always remember her as the girl who was like a sister to them.

They sat at the edge of the woods as the Venandi talked and the humans went through their guns while the other gargoyles conversed with Archie.

"It is…" Emily's voice drifted. "This is the end."

"No," Ari assured her as she leaned on the nervous girls shoulder. "It's just the beginning."

Maya met her brothers eyes, this was going to be the toughest battle they had ever fought.

It had started with her being a human with strange dreams who had been kidnapped and made into something more. She later realized the meaning behind her dreams and that her past lives brothers were after her. Looking back on it all, she would have never thought that any of that would lead to where she was now.

It had all led to Lucifer.

They remained silent until Maya smiled as she huffed. "For old times sake, I'm going to do this even though I already know the answer." They gave her confused looks as her lip twitched. "Do you want to run?"

It would have been odd to laugh but after what they had been through, with everything that was about to happen, they deserved the laughter.

"You're such a little shit." Arthur smirked as he reached over and rustled her hair.

"You're only an inch taller though." She gently smacked his hand away and she chuckled along with the others until her face fell. "I love you all."

Her words had caught them off guard and brought them to silence.

"Thank you for staying with me... I wouldn't have made it without you."

Arthur's eyes softened as she placed her hand on his, her own eyes meeting the others as she turned to each of them until they landed on Emily and Cale who sat beside each other.

It had started with four but only the three of them remained, thinking of Carma gave her courage although they didn't know each other long.

She was going to fight for what Carma would have wanted, she was going to fight for her past lives parents who wanted something better. She was going to fight for Mina who she had sacrificed everything for.

She had lost so much but had gained more back: Her memories, her brother, her newfound friends, and a brand new understanding.

With how life was, she would learn much more. You never stopped learning and you never stopped growing.

Oh, the things she will learn.

It was all going to happen in Jerusalem.

They had all gone back to their cabins though many had decided to spend the night together since being alone seemed impossible right now. They were leaving for Jerusalem in the morning where they would meet the rest of the Venandi who were already there.

They were also going to meet with Lucifer and his demons for the last time, there was no more fighting and leaving. It was going to end there, in the holiest place in the world. The place Lucifer had decided to meet his *sweet Anna* for the last time.

Their fate was set, all they had to do was face it.

Cale's cabin had been taken over by Venandi but he welcomed it as he stayed with Maya in her's. His right hand was in her left as they sat on the couch, their eyes on their twisted fingers as they thought of what was going to happen next.

"Where do you think you would have been if none of this was happening?" Cale asked softly as she rested her head on his shoulder, her hair falling onto him.

"I don't know." She admitted. "It's sad to say but all I can think of is how I've always fought and it feels like I always will." She straightened her fingers then brought them back to his. "You?"

"Maybe I would have stayed in the military."

"Do you wish you were still there?" She pondered and she could feel him shake his head. "I'm here but I'm not angry about it, I'm fighting for what's right even though I would have never thought that the devil himself would be the enemy."

Maya huffed, "I know…"

His hand tightened a bit and she could feel him strain against her, "Are you going to use your full power?"

She could hear the pain in his voice and she knew he wasn't the only one worried about her willingness to die.

"…I don't know." She answered truthfully but she wasn't finished. "But I'll do everything I can not to, I want to live on and find a different way to make up for what I've done…if that's possible."

She meant it, she wanted to live with Cale and the others and she didn't want to leave Arthur alone. Not again.

She was prepared to do what she needed but she would try her best not to go down that path. She remembered Cale's words of how he couldn't live without her, even now they made her slow heart skip a beat.

"You don't know how happy that makes me." He said as his voice filled with relief and her heart thumped as she removed her head from his shoulder and met his eyes that were filled with an equal amount of relief.

She let go of his hand and their fingers brushed as she got up from the couch, her eyes on his as she turned into him and brought her body down onto his lap and straddled him.

At first he looked at her with surprise, but it quickly turned into desire as he noticed the look in her eyes. Their lips touched and they began to kiss each other slowly, savoring the feeling.

Maya's hands laid on his shoulders while his trailed up her back and he fisted them into her long hair. His lips began trailing down her cheek and he pulled her hair out of the way so he could get to her neck. A shiver went up Maya's spine as she felt his tongue against her pulse and a squeak escaped her lips.

Cale pulled away at the sound and he was met with Maya's embarrassed face which was as red as a strawberry. A smile spread across his lips and Maya huffed as she returned it and the two broke into laughter but as they finished, their eyes locked again and so did their lips.

They weren't gentle this time, they were rough.

She brought her hands to his cheeks while he trailed his fingers down her back to her bottom where he squeezed. Maya began rolling her hips and she rubbed against his groin.

His lips quivered as small grunts escaped his mouth and after having enough, he got up from the couch and walked to the bedroom, his hands holding her to him while her legs wrapped around his waist.

He laid her down on the bed and leaned on top of her as they continued their lip lock until he got up and began to undress.

Maya pulled off her shirt and her bra came with it, next she reached down to her pants and pulled them and her underwear off in one motion and kicked them off the bed.

Cale didn't get as far as Maya, he stood with only his boxers on as he gawked at her instead. Her eyes rolled down to the bulge under the fabric and she stretched her leg out and ran her toes along it, causing a loud groan to escape his mouth.

She removed her foot and he looked down to find a mischievous smile on her lips. A grin appeared on his own as he pulled his boxers down and leaned on top of her.

Their faces met again and their arms wrapped around each other as she moved her legs to accommodate him and unlike last time there was no pain as he thrusted into her.

They moaned against each others mouths as their lust filled eyes remained locked. Maya's ankles rested against his thighs as he thrusted into her again and again and she returned the favor by rocking her hips with his.

As she started to lose herself and her legs began to give out, Cale reached down and grabbed her left thigh, his shaking hand keeping the limb out of his way.

Their hot breaths hit each others faces and before long, stars began to form in their eyes. Maya's toes curled into the mattress as she came close to the edge and by the look on Cale's face, he was as well.

She placed her hands on either side of her head, the back of them resting on the pillow and Cale placed his in her's, their fingers intertwining and their milky eyes locking.

There was no Lucifer nor were there demons, it was only the two of them. They were too wrapped up in the present to focus on the future. The present was clear while the future was filled with monsters and death.

Death was waiting for the souls that he would claim from the battle and he was ready, *oh so ready* to take what was rightfully his.

* * *

Fate was upon them.

Lucifer's bottomless eyes laid on the Church of the Holy Sepulchre, the building made of bricks and history. He stood at the backside of it but still the tourists wandered around him, all trying to get a look at the place Jesus had shown his power.

Where God left his influence.

It was the same at the Temple Mount, people came from all over to cast their prayers onto the two toned building with its gold dome.

His eyes fell on a child with his parents who used their phones to take pictures of the Church. The little boy met his eyes and burst into tears, his parents turned and showed the same fear but not as dramatic.

"This is it, Anna." He thought to himself. *"This is where we'll meet for the last time."*

His eyes moved to the lanterns that were lit even in the sunshine and he grinned, a grin with teeth too sharp to be human.

This world will live in fire and blood will be it's oceans and the moon.

"Lucifer." Astaroth's feminine voice came from behind him and he turned to see the last of his strongest demons.

Astaroth, Aamon, and Abraxas.

Azazel had died by the hands of a half blooded gargoyle while Cain was killed by his sweet Anna.

No, there was no way she could have killed him. Cain was his favorite for a reason, his power would have been too much for her to handle in her weakened state.

He inhaled and smiled, *"No matter."* He said to himself then spoke to the rest out loud. "Many more to come."

"Are you sure everyone we need here will show?" Astaroth asked with a seductive tone.

"I've done my preparations," His dark eyes focused on the square in front of the church. "My influence has filled them and they have no choice but to show themselves." He closed his eyes as his smile widened. "Anna will be so surprised."

He opened his eyes again and they wandered over the tourists and the civilians around him, his ears focusing on the other humans as they explored the city.

"Abraxas." He said simply and the shadow demon grinned, an

excited breath leaving his mouth.
"Of course."

Death smiled.

Chapter 58

Arley was cuffed to a table in an interrogation room, his narrowed eyes on the two sided window where he knew the officers were watching him.

He and the other Venandi had been arrested by their own will, Alvertos had his own plans while Arely had his.

The door opened and an older man dressed in a suit stepped in and behind him walked another, this one clad in a lab coat.

"Who are you?" The first man asked as he sat across from Arely while the other stood behind him, he looked like he was hiding a grin under his mustache and his eyes were foggy. "You are in league with the gargoyles, why?"

"Same reason why some of your people left to join the gargoyles," Arely answered right away. "To fight the demons."

"The gargoyles are our enemies-" The director began and Arely slammed his hands on the table, the cuffs around his wrists clanking harshly as they hit the metal table along with his palms. "You keep spouting shit," He growled. "Will you continue to let your pride cloud your mind until this world ends? You'll be the first to die when Lucifer achieves his plan."

"I don't believe the devil is real." The director's voice shook.

"Why wouldn't he be?" The doctor smiled and Arely rose a brow at the charismatic man.

He didn't look right, he almost looked possessed but he looked like the kind of man that thrived for knowledge and would want to go anyway. "Theres monsters everywhere, why can't the greatest monster of them all be real?"

"That is the point!" The cuffs pulled against Arely's wrists as he jerked again. "Instead of focusing your time on fighting the gargoyles, you have to help them! You have to let us go so we can fight against the demons!" His blue eyes shined against the dim lighting, it was almost as if they were glowing. "I promise the end will happen and you'll have yourselves to blame when Lucifer makes you his slaves and the demons use you as their playthings."

The doctor rested his hand on the director's shoulder and the man looked up at him.

"I think we should do as he says." He revealed a toothy smile. "The world is about to end, might as well spend it having a little fun."

"I don't-" The old man swallowed but in the next instant his blood poured onto the table in front of Arley and some spurted on his face.

Arely watched with wide eyes as the doctor pulled his scalpel out of the man's throat and in the next second, he handed Arely a cloth to clean himself with.

"Sorry about that." He said as the director's body fell to the floor where he gasped as he bled out. "I'm usually a clean cut." He grinned as Arely narrowed his blue eyes.

"So," The old man removed a key from his pocket and Arely watched as he undid his cuffs and he rubbed his wrists as he stood, his eyes never leaving the doctor and the scalpel in his hand. "Where are the gargoyles and the demons going to play?"

After a thirteen hour flight they had landed in Israel. The Venandi had their aresanal of blades and the detectives had their guns but even with the laws about weapons being on planes no one bothered them. The humans never bothered to have them step through the metal detector's nor checked them over and as Maya stepped off the plane, she knew something wasn't right.

They knew they were going to Jerusalem, they knew they were going to fight the demons there. Her heart thumped at the thought of the doctor, his smiling face as he cut into her skin, how he set the shock to it's highest setting and brought it to her head and sent her body into convulsions.

She watched as the Venandi and the detectives walked to multiple cars, the Venandi that were already there were picking them up.

This was far more than just the humans making a plan, this had to be Lucifer's doing.

So this is why Alvertos had told them not to worry about their plans for the flight, he knew something was going on.

"You know what's happening, don't you?" She asked as the gargoyles surrounded her.

"Of course." Arthur's voice rang out from directly beside her and his eyes landed on the Venandi as they stepped into the cars.

When Alvertos turned to see why they weren't following, they followed him to the cars.

"You know the humans will be here too." Maya who sat in the back seat with Arthur, Cale, and Emily said to Alvertos who sat up front with the driver.

"Of course I do." He turned to face her. "That would explain their behavior at the airport."

"Why wouldn't they have just attacked us there and be done with it?" Emily pondered and Alvertos smiled.

"They are being influenced by Lucifer, but you know that already."

"He wants them here?" Cale leaned forward and Maya met his eyes.

"He wants this battle to be great but I know there is another reason why he wants them here," He leaned his head back. "Although the reason itself isn't known yet."

He turned back around.

"The city has been empty since yesterday." The driver announced suddenly and they knew right away what had happened there. "No one has been able to get inside, whoever has tried has been killed by a shadow."

Abraxas.

They remained silent for the rest of the ride to the city.

The highway that led to Jerusalem was filled with hills and the houses that stood were old fashioned and historic. Inside they were surrounded by a city that looked like it was taken right out of a history textbook. At the entrance of the city was indeed a shadow, one of Abraxas' barriers.

As soon as they stepped to it the mass opened and closed again behind them. They had tried their best to ignore the bodies of the people who had tried to enter the city: Men in police suits, civilians, and tourists. But ignoring the carnage proved to be impossible when they stepped inside the city and they were met with countless bodies.

Men, women, and children all killed by Abraxas.

They walked through the devastation to a two toned building with intricate markings and a dome top that shined gold.

Maya blinked as she stepped to it and the flash of gold that she had seen so many times appeared again along with the treasure chest.

"Are you ok?" Cale asked and she looked around to find that she had stopped on the last stair that led to The Temple Dome and she was surrounded by the gargoyles and the detectives who waited for her. Donato and Arabella were the only Venandi who stayed back.

"I'm fine."

"Are you sure he's going to be here?" Kira asked as she looked up at the dome with apprehension on her face.

"He will be." Donato answered.

"He already is." Maya's strong voice echoed. "I can feel it."

Her mother's trenchcoat blew in the breeze and underneath was her backless battle suit. Her hair in it's signature side braid.

The others had their own black trenchcoats on as well, before they had left the cabins, Ari and Kira had handed them to each of the gargoyles including Reggie and his group.

"So you don't have to worry about demon blood getting on you as much." Ari had said as they gave her questioning looks. "I wish you could see the work I've put into them but the cuts on my fingers already healed."

The coats didn't have the design Maya's had, nor did they have the gargoyle clasps, but it was easy to see the work Ari had put into them.

Maya had always known that when Ari ran off on her own before all this happened that she was up to something and now she knew that she was getting fabric. She would always be thankful for Ari.

"You look like your in league with us now." Alvertos had said as he watched them pull the coats on.

"Yes, but we're not Venandi." Ari had turned to face him. "We are gargoyles."

"And we're just simple humans." Reggie smiled at Lucas while Maya and Arthur smiled at each other.

The half blooded gargoyles had come a long way since their pained screams in the cave when they were changed into gargoyles. They were so much more than monsters.

They were guardians, protectors, warriors of God.

They accepted who they were now.

The gargoyles that once served as Arthur's guard had even smiled along with them. Kellan's smug face wasn't gone but it was friendlier, welcoming even.

They said their goodbyes to Archie who they had forced to remain behind and the gargoyle named Jared that Maya had saved from the research center.

And so they stood in front of the temple dome, the Venandi in their white coats and the gargoyles and the detectives in black. Their eyes on the area around them and on the dome itself.

Their eyes roamed over the pillars and the shadows that casted around them, they couldn't tell if it was Abraxas or the setting sun causing them. It was a bad idea to be here at Abraxas' strongest but it didn't matter, the result would be the same either way.

They didn't say a word as the orange hue covered them and what they expected happened: Abraxas' shadow wrapped around the length of the dome all the way to the stairs so they couldn't escape.

But they didn't run, they stood and waited for the demon to show himself. When he did he wasn't alone, he stepped out of the opening of the dome and on either side of him was Astaroth and Aamon. There was a nervous shuffle amongst the fifty Venandi, detectives, and gargoyles. Maya could feel Arthur stiffen as his eyes laid on the demon who had tortured him and they narrowed as Abraxas smiled at him.

The Venandi brought their swords to the ready position while the detectives pulled their guns from their holsters and cocked them.

"You people are so easy." A silky voice echoed through the dome and a chill ran through the fray.

From where the demons came walked Lucifer in his usual form, he was clad in a black dress shirt and pants with a smile on his pale face. It looked like he was dressed for a formal occasion.

It was strange not seeing Cain at his side.

"I knew Anna couldn't stay away but the rest of you had a choice." His eyes landed on Maya and she looked on with an even expression.

"We don't have a choice." Alvertos pointed his sword at him and Lucifer practically pried his eyes off of Maya.

"Oh?" Lucifer cocked his head. "Let me guess, you don't have a choice because you have to save the world?" He used a mock tone and snorted. "Fools."

Abraxas and Astaroth smiled at their leaders words while Aamon's eyes wandered over the group in front of him, he was sizing them up like had at the warehouses.

"Do you think you can stop me?" Lucifer chuckled with disbelief in his tone. "I know your little group is smarter than that, The Venandi have been around for hundreds of years and I know how your ancestors worked so therefore I know you."

Lucifer's eyes found the group as a whole, his irises looked impossibly darker and his smile stretched as he lifted his arms, "And so I welcome you to the end."

Suddenly all of them aside from Maya and Cale were forced to the ground by Lucifer's power and they struggled to pull themselves up.

Maya and Cale watched as their comrades struggled and their

pained faces as it pressed onto their bones. Reggie and the other detectives had never witnessed Lucifer's power before now and they looked like they were about to be sick and some really did throw up as their insides pushed together.

"You two," Lucifer brought their attention back to him and his expression had gone flat. His bottomless eyes rolled to Cale then back to Maya. "Azazel lost due to his own stupidity, I understand this...but *you-*" they could hear the venom in his voice as his eyes narrowed.

"You killed my strongest demon." His words came out as a growl and the air around him changed.

Maya's slow heart began to race and even though he was much weaker than her, Cale stepped protectively in front of her.

Lucifer's anger left his features as his face lit up with understanding.

"Oh?" He brought a pale hand to his dark hair and pulled the strands out of his eyes. "I see what's going on here." A low chuckle rolled off his tongue and the demons that stood with him seemed to understand as well. "So tell me boy," He grinned. "Does she hold onto you like she did with me?"

Maya's eyes widened and Cale backed closer to her.

No.

There was no way...no way...

"Come on! answer me!" Lucifer taunted as he cackled on. "I'd like to know if even that has changed!"

In a flash Lucifer was in front of her, pushing Cale out of the way while his other hand grabbed the bottom of her chin. In the next instant they were where he stood at the temple and he slammed Maya against one of the pillars."You may not remember but *I* do." He licked his lips as she struggled against him, his long fingers caressing the side of her neck as he leaned forward and took in her scent. "You smell of him...*My brother...Your creator."*

God.

His tongue left his mouth as he leaned further into her and he licked her from her shoulder to the base of her chin, a chill running up her spine as it glided over her skin, leaving a trail of saliva in it's wake.

"*His* blood runs through your veins." He smacked his lips as he met her eyes and a scream escaped her lips as a flash of memory filled her mind:

Lucifer's body on her's...their lips connected...her hands on his shirtless back.

Cale pushed Lucifer away but he had allowed it to happen, it was easy to tell since he had a grin on his face.

"Come on!" He exclaimed cockily. "It wasn't that bad!"

"Look at me." Cale brought his hands to either side of Maya's face and she looked at him with terrified eyes. He looked taken back with the look, he had never seen her with that kind of fear.

He quickly grabbed her and they fell together to the ground with the others as Abraxas' shadow wrapped around the pillar she had been against.

The pressure on the others diminished and they were left gasping as they tried pulling themselves from the ground.

"Now-" With a grin Lucifer turned his head to Aamon and the older demon looked at him with an uninterested expression. "Let's give this unlikely group something to do."

Maya got shakily to her feet along with Cale and they stood front and center as the others stood with them. Aamon took a step froward and as he did, he removed his cloak, exposing what looked to be symbols carved into his arms and torso.

Aamon, the head of the army.

The symbols began to glow and as they did, a flash of red light filled the onlookers eyes and when it was gone, it was replaced by the still forms of zombified looking creatures.

Their jaws hung open, exposing their razor sharp teeth that were already dripping with blood. Their skin was pale, almost light blue. They had patches of hair sticking out of their bald heads and the empty spots were covered with blisters and rot.

Their eyes...Their eyes were the same as the gargoyles, many had pitch black while few had white.

"These are dead gargoyles from the past." Aamon's soft spoken voice had changed and so did his eyes, they were now black with fiery red irises.

His skin had the same blue tint as his legion of monsters and as everyone watched, his skin sunk all the way into his skull until there was none left. Only his sunken eyes and bloody muscle where his cheeks should have been. His long silver hair became ragged and from his head sprouted curved horns. He looked like the grim reaper.

This was Aamon's true from.

The leader of the army of undead gargoyles.

They watched the undead as they waited for them to attack, there had to be a hundred of them in the square but around the city were hundreds more. The creatures didn't move, they stood with their eyes on them, soft groans leaving their mouths.

"Every gargoyle I've ever killed since Lucifers fall." They turned back to Aamon as his voice boomed, his lipless mouth opening and the words falling out. "When I kill a gargoyle, their soul becomes mine. It took a lot to listen to their screams… but after awhile, it became like a lullaby to me."

Maya met the eyes of the dead gargoyle in front of her, something was telling her that she had known this creature but all she could make out was that it was a male. The features that remained from when he was alive weren't enough for her to remember.

She moved her attention back to Lucifer who she found was watching her, his smile engraved on his face. She swallowed, their past relationship was still so cloudy but they had been together.

Together.

The thought made her sick.

The three demons that stood around him smiled down at their enemies desperate but determined faces. Abraxas met Arthur's eyes first then moved to Reggie's and with a click of his teeth, the shadow holding them in the square disappeared and his shadow creatures emerged instead. Their glowing red eyes shining against their pitch black forms.

They were at their strongest at sunset after all and there were no gaps in their forms as they joined Aamon's undead army.

Aamon turned to Lucifer and his master nodded, giving him permission to give his army the go but before he could, The Venandi started slashing through them like butter but as another flash of red light filled their eyes, the creatures began to attack along with Abraxas' shadow creatures.

Screams and gunshots filled the air as they began their fight, the gargoyles eyes changing to their respective colors and their nails growing into points as they cut into the creatures. But like the demons, the undead gargoyles wouldn't die unless the heart was destroyed.

Maya kept her eyes on the others as she cut through her fair share of creatures while trying not to use too much of her power in case she needed it for later. They seemed to have the same idea as they stayed close and fought the creatures around her.

Even Kellan had jumped in to help her and he stood front and center as he forced his claws into the creatures chests and destroyed their hearts. He seemed to relish in the act but as he cut one down, another would appear and before long they were overwhelmed.

That was until Arely pushed through the crowd of monsters along with the other Venandi that had been arrested. Their swords piecing the creatures hearts and red blood poured on the ground as they fell.

"Brother!" Alvertos called to him with blood covering his face and Arely cut his way through to his brother.

Maya looked around, Arely's arrival could only mean one thing: *The humans were there.*

The danger the gargoyles were in had escalated, not only would the humans be able to kill the undead ones, but the living as well. They were unbiased as to who they were going to kill.

On cue more gunshots filled the air and not only were there American officers coming from the stairs with their bullets piercing the creatures, but Israeli officers as well. Amongst them were people dressed in army type outfits, they had brought who they could but it didn't even out their numbers as there were still hundreds more undead gargoyles.

Their bullets passed through the shadow creatures and the shadows would kill the officers as they materialized again. The undead gargoyles on the other hand would fall only to get back up as their hearts remained intact and they sunk their teeth into their victims. Screams filled the air as their flesh ripped from their bones.

Lucifer's laughter filled the air and Maya's body unconsciously moved to him but as she met his eyes, she froze.

To her left was an Israeli officer pointing his gun at her, there was no way he could've gotten through the creatures but she didn't have time to think about it as the bullet came for her. The sound of the gun had mixed with the other gunshots and as she tried to step out of the way, one of the creatures pushed her back into it's path.

Until Cale pushed her out of the way and took the bullet for her.

Right through his head.

Gunshots filled the air as men in blue old style army uniforms ran to the men dressed in gray.

Men fell by the dozens as bullets pierced them, neither side had an advantage and the living were surrounded by death.

A familiar laughter filled her ears and she turned to see Lucifer dressed in the same blue uniform as the union soldiers. He was sitting at the tree line watching the carnage unfold with a terrifying smile. His bottomless eyes filled with glee and blood splatter covered his face.

The American civil war.

His laughter in reality coaxed her awake as she collapsed to her knees beside Cale who had fallen harshly to the ground. Her tears fell onto his blood soaked face as she leaned into him, his eyes were closed and his lips shook.

"Cale!" She shrieked and Emily came crashing down beside her while the others protected them from the creatures as they leaned over his body.

Maya placed her hands on either side of his face, looking at the hole the bullet had made in the side of his head. It seemed to have passed through but it wouldn't stop the hydrochloric acid from eating him alive.

"Cale!" Their sobs mixed with the sounds of the battle as they waited for the acid to eat his skin but it didn't. Instead they noticed the skin around the wound trying to heal.

Could he even heal from this? His healing was better than the other gargoyles but getting shot in the head had to be different.

The undead gargoyles and the shadow creatures began to close in on them and Maya shot up, leaving Cale to Emily, and with tears in her eyes she roared at the beings.

The pressure in her eyes heightened as creature after creature fell due to the ferocity she used to take them down. The fear of using her power had gone down the drain and as she pulled out the heart of the gargoyle she had recognized, her heart thumped. Blood splatter covered her face as she squeezed his heart and it exploded.

Arthur stepped in front of her with his own share of blood covering him. "I got this, go to Cale." He demanded softly and she met his eyes. The battle had just begun and they were already falling apart. She turned and as she did so, she noticed that Lucifer's face wore a proud expression from her display of violence.

She waited for the lethargic feeling from using her power to hit but it never came as she knelt in front of Cale. Emily's tear stained eyes met hers as she looked down at the still closing wound.

"Cale..." her voice shook as her heart felt like it was going to explode with grief.

She couldn't lose him... she couldn't...

A sob escaped her lips as a groan came from his and the girls eyes widened as Cale's opened weakly and they met the two women hovering over him.

"Cale!" Emily exclaimed as a fresh round of tears fell from her dark eyes.

Cale shivered from the pain as his shaking hand reached for Maya and she gently twisted her fingers around it.

"Why?" She whimpered and he gave her a shaky smile.

"Because… you can't…heal…like I can…" His words were slurred but she could still understand what he was saying.

"It could have been an acid bullet… it could have killed you either way." She swallowed.

Cale Swallowed as she leaned down and pulled his hair out of his eyes.

"You can't live without me, right?" She asked softly, her voice shaking. "Well the same goes for me, I can't live without you either."

His eyes fell as she leaned further down and pressed her lips gently to his and as they kissed, he lost consciousness again.

Maya pulled her head up to see him breathing evenly, the skin around the hole the bullet had caused was still trying to heal. His blood had saved him, his birth father was protecting him even in death. But he wasn't out of the woods yet.

Maya looked over the creatures and their comrades to the buildings on the other side of the dome and she turned back to Emily. "Get him out of here."

Emily's eyes widened with panic and grief. "I can't…"

Maya understood where she was coming from, but this wasn't the time to have doubts.

She grabbed the sides of Emily's face and the blood of the undead gargoyles rubbed off her hands onto her cheeks. It was a good thing that the undead gargoyles blood was the same as the living gargoyles or Emily would have been in trouble.

"You can do this… you can save him." Maya turned to the first person that came to mind. "Trevor!" She called to him and he turned to face her as he killed one of the undead gargoyles.

He jumped down and met them as Arthur and Kellan got in the way to protect them from the creatures onslaught. Trevor's face paled as he took in Cale's unconscious form.

"Is he…?" His voice trailed off.

"He'll be ok if we get him out of here." Maya's tone was filled with anxiety. "I'm leaving it to you to help Emily get him out of here."

Trevor seemed apprehensive, he was shocked that out of all of the people that she could have called for, she had chosen him. His doubts quickly went away as he pulled Cale from the ground and Emily rushed to help him. Maya watched Cale's limp form fall onto their shoulders until she met Trevor's eyes.

"I'll make a path for you to get out." She stated as she allowed more of her power to flow through her while having no regrets of what it was going to do to her body.

She plowed through the creatures and with the help of Trevor who left carrying Cale to Emily, he made sure none of the creatures could get them from behind.

The power Maya used made her feel free, it was rightfully her's to use.

Finally she made it to the wall that closed them into the temples square and she punched a hole through it so they could escape into the city. She was glad to see that none of the creatures had made their way to this side of the city yet.

As Emily stepped over the wreckage of the broken wall, Trevor followed closely behind while Maya protected the opening. Her eyes moved to them and she thought of how badly she wanted them to find someplace no one would be able to find them.

She had to bring her attention back to the fight as Astaroth lunged at her and she blocked the demons attack. As she did so, she wrapped a hand around the demons neck who cackled at the feeling.

"Sam!" Emily called back to her but Maya didn't turn. "Live!" Her friends voice shook. "Make sure you come back to us!"

Maya's eyes narrowed as Astaroth grinned at Emily's words. She swallowed as pain and regret filled her again. "Just go, Emily."

She knew her words hurt Emily but she wasn't going to lie, this was war and there was no telling what was going to happen.

She listened to Emily's light steps and Trevor's uneven along with Cale's dragging feet as they walked away.

"Time to play." Astaroth's voice filled with glee.

With a light squeeze, Maya snapped Astaroth's neck and the demon fell to the ground, her red hair splaying across her face.

Maya turned her head back to the break in the wall and Emily, Cale, and Trevor were gone. With relief filling her, she ran to the group to help them, dodging bullets while killing shadow creatures and undead gargoyles along the way.

That was until Astaroth grabbed her by the back of her coat and threw her backwards.

She landed on her feet and with no hesitation, she ran to the female demon whose neck was still wobbling to the side. She looked like a puppet with no marionette as she came at Maya again who kneed her in the gut. While doing so, Maya brought her claws to her chest but it was to no avail as the demon disappeared.

"You're fighting a lot better now, is your power not killing you?" Astaroth appeared in front of her again as she brought her hands to her own neck and cracked it back into place.

Maya didn't know why, but she no longer felt the effects of using her power. She should have been filled with fatigue as her body rejected the power.

It was freeing to be able to use it but she wasn't going to use it fully until she truly needed it. Her eyes shot up from the demons smiling face as she noticed Abraxas going for Arthur while Reggie jumped in with his bullets barely grazing the shadow demon.

She began to run to them but Astaroth stood in her way, "I'm still playing with you."

"You're playing?" Maya mused as a growl escaped her lips. "I'm here to *kill*."

The demons eyes widened for the first time as Maya grabbed her head and smashed it into the concrete and with her free hand, she forced her way through the demons chest and grabbed her heart. The demons black blood poured onto her but she didn't feel the sting as she crushed her heart and the demon laid with her eyes facing the darkening sky.

She jumped over her body and ran to Arthur and Reggie, stopping Abraxas' shadow just before it got to the latter.

She was still off limits.

"You're always getting in my way." The demon bared his teeth and licked them. "You *did* give me a few good days to play with your brother though."

Venom flowed through her but before she could do anything, Arthur attacked the demon. Abraxas stumbled backwards as his tar like blood dribbled down his slit throat thanks to Arthur's nails.

"He's mine." Arthur growled, his face filled with rage. "I have to return the favor."

"You're going to have to share." Reggie cocked his gun as he narrowed his eyes. "I have my own reason to kill this motherfucker."

The shadow demon cackled, "Look at you! A gargoyle and a human fighting together!" He inhaled the warm air as his eyes twitched to where Lucifer stood.

"Although the idea of fighting you is enticing sweetheart," He brought his attention to Maya. "I think there's something else you should be worried about."

She moved her gaze from the demon and she almost collapsed from shock.

Still standing at the opening of the temple was Lucifer, his dark eyes on her as his claws rested at her best friends throat.

Mina.

Chapter 59

"Pick partners!" The teacher called to the class as she stepped to the blackboard.

They had to dissect owl pellets that day in class and they had to pair up to do so. Owls ate rodents but they couldn't digest the fur and bones so they would spit them up.

Samantha Knight was the ripe age of ten and she looked around as the other kids found their partners while she remained seated. She kept to herself and never bothered to branch out. Mina had just moved there and no one wanted to pair with the new girl so they ended up together.

Mina pulled herself up onto the lab chair and for a long moment, she stared at Sam as if she was something she had never seen before.

The little girl reached forward and Sam jumped as she grabbed something from her shoulder length hair. "I'm sorry..." Mina said in a squeaky voice. "You had a fuzzy in your hair."

"Thank you…" Sam furrowed her brows at the the blonde haired girl.

The teacher delivered their owl pellets along with their tools to dissect them and told them they could start. Mina looked on with apprehension while Sam gabbed ahold of the plastic tools and began to pull at the matted hair until she found a perfect rodent skull.

Mina shivered at the sight and Sam frowned, "You don't have to be afraid." She assured her. "It's just bone." She reached her hand out so Mina could touch the skull and after looking between Sam and the tiny skull, Mina finally reached and took it from her hand.

"Wow!" She exclaimed and Sam smiled.

"Neat, right?"

"I'm touching barf." Mina set the skull on the table with a mild look of disgust and Sam nodded. "Pretty much." She turned back to the pellet, "Do you want to dissect it?"

After a moment, Mina agreed and the girls joked and laughed while they set to work which was kind of morbid since they were picking at an owls spit up looking for bones.

Mina was the first person Sam had ever acted this way with, they were opposites but they got on well.

Both girls were naive to what was going to happen to them in the future but that's how life worked, you retained your innocence until you no longer could.

"Run!" Sam screamed as their attackers surrounded her, giving Mina the opportunity to get out of there. Mina ran with regret on her face as she left her best friend behind, the person the attackers didn't even want.

Sam would do anything for her best friend, she would gladly relive everything that had happened to her after she had been kidnapped if it meant that Mina would be safe.

But that's not how life worked.

Mina screamed as Maya ran to her and she pushed through enemy and ally alike until she stopped directly in front of the dome, knowing that if she got too close, Mina would be done for.

Lucifer's eyes filled with glee at the desperate look on Maya's face as she looked at her best friend with tears in her eyes.

No one bothered them, the undead gargoyles ignored her and the shadow creatures stayed away. Even the humans, what was left of them at least, left her alone.

Lucifer's influence had taken over them all.

"This is your friend?" Lucifer cocked his head as Maya shook, she had to stop herself from running to Mina, to get her out of his evil hands.

He turned his head to Mina and she squealed as tears poured down her cheeks.

"She's a good one, she came all the way from her home town to try convincing the humans that you were good." He pulled her head back by her long blonde hair so his nails had a better angle at her throat.

"Stop!" Maya yelled and as her eyes drifted, she noticed that Mina was wearing the same clothes that she had the day she had met her at the containment center.

The demons had picked her up there, it was Maya's fault that she was there.

She had wondered how Mina found out where she was but the answer was clear now: Lucifer had used his influence and told her where to go. He could have taken her before but he wanted Maya to see her one last time, he wanted it to sting. He wanted her to suffer.

"Please!" Maya begged. "She has nothing to do with this!"

Lucifer rose a brow, "But she does, for the simple reason that she is the only thing holding you to your life as Samantha Knight."

"No..." Maya stepped forward but Lucifer's nails dug into Mina's skin and a trail of blood ran down her front.

"I'm not holding onto to this life! Let her go!" There were so many emotions running through her: Fear, anger, pain, desperation.

Lucifer sighed as he moved his eyes to the ceiling above him as if he was thinking and Maya watched as an *aha* look appeared on his face.

"I have an idea." He grinned. "I'll let her go if you guess my name."

Everything froze: The sounds of the battle behind her, the screams. All of it was gone aside from her slow heart pounding in her ears.

His name?

"...Lucifer." She said as her jaw shook and he shook his head.

"Come on, you're smarter than that." He snickered and her desperation worsened as she listed off more names: *Satan, The devil, The serpent...* But none of them were the correct answer and with each incorrect name, Lucifer's patience grew more and more thin.

"I'm talking about the name I had when we first met." He hinted silkily and her teeth chattered.

How could she know his name from her time as Anna? She had no memory of that life nor did she know what kind of relationship she had with Lucifer other than that they…

"…I don't know." Her words were barely more than a whisper.

"What?" He cocked his ear closer to her but she knew he had heard her.

"I don't know!" Her knees buckled and she fell on her hands and knees as she kept her eyes on Lucifer and Mina who was shaking like a leaf as she watched with tear soaked eyes.

"*Please*!" Maya pleaded. "I DON'T REMEMBER!" She screamed as tears poured from her own eyes. "I *can't* remember…"

Lucifer was right, she was still holding onto her life as Sam. She chose to go by her past lives name, had accepted that she was Maya, had even taken more of her past lives traits after getting her memories back. But she was still undoubtedly Sam.

All of this had started because she saved Mina the night she was kidnapped. It was meant to be Mina but she stood in the way of that. Fate wanted it to be Maya, No, it wanted it to be Sam.

Her parents feared her after her transformation and she accepted that but she couldn't let Mina go. There was never a day that she didn't think about her best friend's smiling face.

Mina was the reason she was holding onto Sam.

"It doesn't matter." Lucifer clicked his tongue as his narrowed eyes rolled to Mina. "I was going to kill her anyway."

A loud crack filled the air as he snapped Mina's neck and as he let go of her body, she fell violently down the stairs leading to the dome.

Maya frantically crawled to her friend, sobs leaving her mouth as she did so.

She had to save her, she had time, she…

It was too late… she was gone…

Maya looked into Mina's blue eyes and along with her tears, blood began to trail from her nose and mouth.

Her best friend was dead.

Best friend was dead.

Friend was dead.

* * *

Was dead.

Dead.

And it was Maya's fault, she had dragged her into this due to her unknown relationship with Lucifer.

She rolled her eyes to her enemy and even though they were filled with tears, they held no grief. She couldn't allow herself to feel that emotion. Instead she was filled with rage and the proud look on Lucifer's face made it escalate.

"The *death* of Samantha Knight." He declared with a cackle.

"*Somethings coming*!" A familiar voice screamed and she turned to see Donato collapsed on the ground, his eyes looked like they were going to pop out of his head.

Arabella was protecting him from the monster's as he had his vision.

Maya could feel it too, something terrible was about to appear and as she turned back to Lucifer, something ran past her from inside the dome.

Her head unconsciously pulled to the creature but it was far too fast to see. Instead she saw Lucifer's grin widen in the corner of her eye and she turned in time to see ten of the Venandi's severed heads fall violently to the concrete.

Screams filled the air as the creature showed itself next to the bodies as they fell beside their severed heads. It had the head of a goat with horns as long as a humans's arm. It's torso was that of a man's but it's lower half was covered in hair all the way down to it's large hoofed feet.

The beast stood over eight feet tall as it towered over even the tallest of people. It's victims blood dripped from it's claws and the thick liquid fell to the ground next to it's hooves.

It's eyes glowed a fiery red as it cocked it's head towards Maya and it's master.

This was Lucifer's pet.

She felt a finger appear under her chin and it pulled her attention back to Lucifer where he now stood over her, his feet inches from Mina's body and his bottomless eyes filled silk. "Keep your eyes on me."

She swatted his hand away and he cackled as she jumped to her feet with venom in her eyes.

"Have you heard of Baphomet?" He questioned as gunshots filled the air but as the bullets hit the creature, they sucked into his skin and left no wounds.

She had heard of the creature, he was a deity that resembled both a man and a goat. A creature that many worshipped.

"You have." Lucifer knew the answer just by looking at her and his eyes moved from her as the beast picked up one of the Venandi and the man screamed as the monster smashed his head into the concrete. "I'll let my pet have his fun." He exclaimed with a hint of entertainment and Maya shook as he took a step back into the shadows and like a mist, his body disappeared from sight.

"I'll be waiting for you, my sweet Anna."

His voice echoed in her ears and a chill ran up her spine as she turned to help her comrades.

She passed Arthur and Reggie as they fought Abraxas, both were bloody but they continued their fight. Though it was clear they were in another battle to keep their eyes on the demon they were fighting instead of the beast behind them.

Kira and Ari were already fighting the beast but the creature didn't seem to feel any of their hits, as they slashed it's skin open, it sewed itself back up within seconds.

A growl escaped it's mouth as it cocked it's head to Kira and like a flame, it's eyes grew brighter.

"Arthur!" A voice called out her brothers name and as Maya almost got to the creature, Aamon appeared before her and the smell of rot filled her nose. Her eyes flipped between the skeletal demon and the group of people running to meet them at the entrance.

She understood right away who they were: The full blooded gargoyles.

There were four women and six men, all the same age as Arthur and Maya in looks but not in years.

A smile flashed on Arthur's lips as he dodged Abraxas' shadow. "You know what to do!"

They began attacking their enemies and Maya noticed how fluid they were in the way they moved. It had been a long time since she had seen a full blooded gargoyle fight aside from Arthur. Her senses made her want to fight with them, but she desperately wanted to help the Venandi, Ari, and Kira as they fought the goat man.

Her eyes flashed as the creature killed the Venandi and it's own comrades. The undead gargoyles limbs flew into the air as the beast slashed away and the shadow demons dematerialized only to come back seconds later after they were out of the goat mans path of destruction.

The beast held no qualms on who it was to kill.

As Maya continued to watch, it was easy to tell which human's were trained to fight the demons. More specifically to fight the gargoyles due to them thinking that the demons were gone. The few older men and women that remained from the days the humans and the gargoyles had worked together looked at Maya like she was a ghost.

They saw her mother in her.

"Your focus is on me." Aamon's voice boomed and her attention fell back to the demon as Alvertos and Arley joined in on the fight with the beast.

Suddenly there were more undead gargoyles around Maya and the demon and they circled around the two like a barrier. Mist filled the air as Aamon breathed through his lipless mouth and Abraxas' shadow creatures joined the fray to keep the others from getting in and Maya from getting out.

The sound of the battle was enough to drive anyone insane: The screams, the growls, and the gunfire. Maya thought of Mina's smiling face, the sound of her laughter helped her zone out the sounds. Aamon attacked and she barely managed to dodge his hit.

Kira and Ari were still fighting the goat man and the creature seemed to be fixated on Kira more than the others.

She couldn't lose them…

Ari always understood her, she never once questioned her actions nor did she leave when the going was tough. She would always be thankful for Ari.

Kira was the light of the group. Her wise yet funny remarks would always ease the situation and like Ari, she understood Maya. One could say that she stayed with them because she had no one else, but Maya knew it was because she cared about them.

Aamon's socket-less eyes swayed to Baphomet's giant form as the sound of Donato's screams filled the air as he remained in his vision.

The goat man roared as the sound irritated him and the creature went charging to Donato, knocking everyone out of the way as it did so. Arabella's eyes widened with fear as she protected him but she knew there was nothing she could do against the beast.

Ari and Kira ran after him along with Alvertos and Arley, Maya could see the fear in Alvertos' eyes as the creature drew closer to Donato, it's nail's longer than daggers as it pulled it's arm back to kill the seer.

Maya pushed past Aamon so she could help but the demon appeared from every angle that she turned.

"LET ME OUT!" She roared as she pulled her jacket off in one quick motion and her wings extended so she could take off from above.

Her attempt was futile as the demon grabbed her wings from behind and forced her to the ground.

"You can't fight him yet." Aamon's mouth opened and the words poured out as he looked down to her.

Lucifer had planned this, this is exactly what he wanted.

Arabella's blood curdling scream filled the air but Maya couldn't see what had happened, she could only hear the cries of the other Venandi and Arely as he called for his brother.

Maya knew what had happened before she could see it, and as she pulled away from the demon, her hunch was confirmed: Alvertos was in front of Donato's shaking form, his vision had ended but the fear remained in his eyes as blood splattered on his face.

The goat man's claws were going through Alvertos' chest and his blood was dripping from the creatures nails as they peaked through his back. His blue eyes were wide with pain but he didn't allow himself to show the others.

"Father!" Donato's clear eyes filled with tears as he called to the man who had adopted him, who had saved him from his terrible life.

A bloody smile appeared on Alvertos' lips at the word, he was more of father to Donato than his own flesh and blood.

"I'm...sorry...Donat-" he couldn't finish as the goat man lifted it's claws and flung him into the air and he fell against one of the pillars on the dome.

His head rolled to the side and his blank eyes stared at his comrades as they looked on with shock at their leaders demise.

"BROTHER!" Arely shoved his sword through the creatures chest with pure rage filling his features but it didn't falter and it cocked it's head to the infuriated man.

It's hand closed around Arely's wrist as a growl escaped it's long mouth but before the creature could do anything, Kira wrapped herself around it's arm and clawed at it's skin.

Ari appeared behind the beast, her eyes narrowed as she struck the back of it's knees, hoping it would fall.

It didn't.

Maya grabbed Aamon's jaw, his bone was cold against her fingers but the muscle that remained was warm. She pulled until it broke from it's sockets and as she did so, she brought her mouth down to the arm that was holding her, her teeth sinking into the bone.

As she pulled, his arm broke off and she let it fall from her mouth as she slashed her way through the creatures blocking her from getting to her friends. But Aamon appeared before her again, his jaw and arm back in place but as her desperation rose, so did her power.

She weaved around him with the same speed he had used, and with her leg, she kicked his out from underneath him but the demon caught himself and wrapped his cold arms around her back. She couldn't move this time, his cool touch made her breath hitch and her bones felt frozen.

His cold breath hit her neck as he spoke, "Her suffering will be over soon."

Maya's hair stood on end as she struggled against him but her body wouldn't allow her to move. His power had sunk into her and what she wanted was far from what she could do.

Who was he talking about? Who was suffering?

Her eyes widened as a group of undead gargoyles closed in on Arely, Ari, and Kira who had moved from the beasts arm and she crawled to it's shoulders and with her black eyes narrowed, she twisted the beasts neck, snapping it.

She fell to the ground as Baphomet wobbled but he was far from done.

It finally let go of Arely but it grabbed Kira instead, it's neck snapping back into place as it's fingers closed around her throat.

"NO!" Maya screamed in unison with Ari and Aamon leaned closer to her ear.

"She has been starved of love…*Famished.*" His teeth rubbed against her ear lobe. "She will find love in the after life."

Ari ran to the creature but it swatted her down as if she was a fly, it's claws slashing at her front as she fell. Kira's eyes widened for a second as a small wimper escaped her trembling lips.

The beast barely squeezed, but her head fell to the side, landing on the creatures claws as her neck snapped. What could have healed was too far gone, all of the blood vessels in her neck were crushed. Blood poured from her mouth and nostrils, her black eyes had returned to their human color as they bulged out of her.

* * *

Famine means starvation but there are different kinds of starvation: Your stomach growls and you eat to make it stop. Some people can't do that, they starve.

Another type of starvation is one that someone wouldn't normally think of.

This was a hunger for love… for acceptance.

Though Kira had found both with her little group, she was still starved by her families lack thereof. Her father neither loved nor accepted her.

She was famished.

Her body fell to the ground as the beast loosened it's grip. Maya's eyes laid on her lifeless form and Ari as she shook against the ground. The sight sent rage through her, it warmed her frozen bones and her limbs shook.

Her friends, the people who had accepted her, who had cared for her. One was dead and the other was dying.

Arley looked on with furrowed brows as dread washed over him, he had lost his brother and he now watched as two girls were cut down trying to save him.

Maya's teeth extended into points and horns sprouted from her head. She pulled away from the demon but he grabbed her again.

He wanted Kira to die, he *needed* her to die and even with it done he still wouldn't let Maya go.

Her face curled into a snarl but as she forced her body to turn, a hand emerged from Aamon's chest and in it was the demon's heart covered in his tar like blood.

Maya looked past Aamon's eyes as the light in them began to fade and she was met with Kellan. She could only see his head as he stood behind the demon but she took in his bared teeth and his eyes that were filled with the same amount of rage as her's.

He tried to destroy the heart but the pain the blood caused made his fingers freeze. He groaned from the pain but no matter how hard he tried, his fingers wouldn't move.

A gun shot filled the air and a bullet went flying through the heart, barely missing Kellan's hand. The organ fell to the ground and Kellan pulled his arm out of the demons chest.

As the two gargoyles turned to see where the bullet had come from, they were met with Lucas, his blonde hair covered in his own blood and his eyes narrowed as his face twisted with anger. His gun was still pointed to where the demons heart had been.

He nodded to them as he lowered the gun and he turned to join Tori and the other remaining human's as they fought the undead gargoyles and shadow creatures.

"Fuck!" Kellan spat as the blood ate through his skin and the intense feeling of a bullet almost getting him.

The red in Aamon's eyes turned to gray as his bones began to splinter and break off one by one.

"You..." His voice echoed as his head fell to the heap of bones at Maya's feet. *"Are doomed."*

In the next second the bones turned to ash and not even his cloak remained.

With the death of their leader, the undead should have fallen, but they didn't. They continued to fight as if he was still there.

Maya met Kellan's eyes as he rushed to wipe the blood from his arm with his trenchcoat that he pulled off to do so. The blood had already taken his top layer of skin and it was working it's way further into his arm. Maya thought of the pain she had felt as Cain forced his blood down her throat, how it had almost killed her.

The blood that landed on her now didn't even sting, it only left small holes in her battle suit.

"Let's go kill that fucking thing." Kellan smirked though she could see the pain hidden underneath.

Even with her heavy heart and tears filling her eyes, she turned to the beast as it reached for Ari's shaking form. Arley was hacking at it's arm along with the other Venandi as they tried to get it to stop. Maya couldn't see Kira's body anymore, the undead gargoyles covered her as they rounded on the Venandi.

She had to fight the creature, she had to kill it or she would lose more of her friends.

She choked back the grief and allowed anger to flow through her instead. With a snarl she rounded on the goat man and Kellan followed close behind. Not in a million years did she ever think that they would work together like this but here they were.

As she pushed the creature backwards, almost getting cut by one of the Venandi's swords in the process, Kellan jumped with his wings extended and he landed on it's shoulders. He grabbed ahold of the beasts mouth and he gritted his teeth as he yanked but his strength did nothing.

Maya brought her arm back and with the help of Arely who

distracted the monster, she impaled him as if she was killing a demon: By aiming for it's heart.

But as she felt around it's insides, she found nothing.

Her eyes widened with shock as the beast grabbed her arm and her bones cracked from the force. Arley slashed at the creature as it brought it's other arm down to her, it was going to squish her like a bug. She pulled frantically but no matter how hard she tried, it's grip wouldn't loosen. It's other hand was about to close around her head, her life flashing before her eyes as she focused on it's palm but it stopped inches from her face.

She looked past it's giant hand and she noticed that the creature was looking down at her, it's eyes glowing and it's head cocked.

It's grip loosened and Kellan jumped down and cut it's wrist only for it stitch back up in seconds. The beast pushed Maya down as it clawed the front of Arely and he fell on top of Ari who laid in her own pool of blood, her once blue eyes staring blankly at the sky.

More and more of the Venandi fell along with two of the full blooded gargoyles that had come to help as the creature rampaged. The undead gargoyles turned to dust as they were clawed through their chests and the shadow creatures disappeared only to reappear where they once stood.

Baphomet had only been there for minutes but it had already sent them into devastation. The Venandi's numbers had gone down drastically and their leader was dead.

It had killed Maya's comrades, had killed it's own comrades.

It killed and killed and killed.

And the battle had only just begun.

The beast continued to rage until it's sight landed on Maya again as she shot to her feet, her eyes meeting the beasts glowing red.

A purr like sound came from it's mouth and as it stepped to her, she found herself frozen, not in fear but as if she was mesmerized by the creature.

It wrapped it's hand around her throat so fast that she didn't even have time to move and she gasped as it picked her up so her face was level with it's own.

It cocked it's head back and forth as if mesmerized by her as she had been with it and as Kellan jumped to help her, it proved to be futile.

The goat man grabbed him by the front of his shirt and he struggled against it's grip, growls ripping through his throat as frustration lit his face along with the lowering sun.

The creature turned as more Venandi came to their aid but it ignored their attacks as it looked off into the distance. The orange hue that the sun beamed on them made it impossible for Maya to see what it was looking at.

Her heart lurched as the beast lifted her higher along with Kellan who looked equally afraid. The beast recoiled back only to use all of it's strength to throw them into the air and there was no stopping even with their wings.

The strength the creature had used was too much for them.

The air rushed past them, making them deaf to the sound of their comrades yelling for them and their limbs swung in unnatural ways from the force.

Kellan struggled to reach for her, his face filled with both pain and determination and Maya just managed to grab his hand as they continued to violently rush through the air.

The Temple Dome growing further and further away.

Chapter 60

"Maya!" Arthur who was bruised and bloody called as he saw his sister and Kellan being thrown over the dome and the buildings surrounding it.

A gunshot filled the air as Reggie who had blood pouring down his own head shot at Abraxas as the demon went for Arthur.

"Pay attention!" The detective demanded through gritted teeth as smoke swirled around the gun and Arthur turned back to the human and the demon with apprehension on his face.

Abraxas cackled as the wound the bullet had caused on his shoulder began heal and he brought his hand to the black ooze coming from it and let it drip from his fingers. "Baphomet is having quite a lot of fun."

Arthur's jaw shook as Reggie reloaded his gun and they watched as the beast began to walk in the direction that it had thrown Maya and Kellan.

The two were no longer in the air and were nowhere to be seen although Arthur could hear the crash of their landing a distance away.

The beast was going for them, it had to be stopped.

"We're letting the beast go." Abraxas smirked as his shadow wrapped around the perimeter behind the beast as it walked heavily away, growls coming from it's goat-like mouth with every step. The Venandi and the full blooded gargoyles almost fell as they slid to a stop before they fell into the shadow. "You're sister will realize her destiny."

The demon twitched his fingers and more of his shadow creatures appeared beside him and in front of the other fighters, their glowing red eyes narrowed as they took in their prey.

"....You don't have much longer," Reggie breathed as he took in the carnage around him, gulping as he saw most of his comrades dead along with the humans who had came to help. Only Lucas, Tori, and a few others of the original group of detectives remained. His eyes returned to the demon in front of him. "The sun is going down."

"It is." Abraxas nodded, his pink eyes blending into the light. "And I could kill every being here before that happens but I choose not to."

Arthur who was watching Baphomet tread through the hole Maya had made so Emily, Trevor, and Cale could get out turned to glare at demon. "Then why don't you?"

"*Because-*" Abraxas' voice filled with silk as he placed his bloodied hand in his white hair and soaked the strands with black. "That would ruin the fun… plus I want to see your reaction when *he* gets here."

He?

"It's been a long time, demon." A man with blonde shoulder length hair approached Arthur and Reggie and behind him were five more people.

A woman with short brown hair, two men who looked to be twins with red hair and freckles. A man that towered over the rest, his brown hair falling into his brown eyes. Lastly a woman with long blonde hair in a braid over shoulder.

They were full blooded gargoyles.

"It has…" Abraxas' voice drifted as he cocked his head. "In fact it's been so long that I don't know who you are."

"I happened about you forty years ago in a bar." The blonde haired male gargoyle explained with narrowed eyes. "I knew from the start what you were and you almost killed me when you filled the bar with your shadow."

"Ah…" the demon closed his eyes at the memory. "You tried stopping me as I recall."

The full blooded gargoyle remained silent as the other five got into their stances to fight.

"This has gotten even more entertaining." Abraxas' cackle echoed through the square and the Venandi, Lucas, Tori, and the remaining humans looked on with fear.

Arabella and Donato who looked completely broken as they laid next their dead comrades gritted their teeth and their tears fell into their mouths.

Donato picked up the sword that laid at Alvertos' side and stroked the handle with his shaking fingers. "Arabella…" His thick accent was harder to understand through his pain but his ally understood him as clear as day. "Cover me."

Donato began to fight with the sword that belonged to the man who was like a father to him, and with Arabella's help, he slashed through the undead gargoyles.

Seeing him fight brought the remaining Venandi's morale up and they began to fight with the same ferocity. As Lucas cut down the last undead gargoyle that surrounded his group with a sword he had taken from the ground, they dodged past the shadow creatures around them. Killing some as they materialized until they joined Reggie and the rest as they stared Abraxas down.

Only Arthur looked away from the demon as his eyes twitched to where the goat man had gone but the beast was no where to be seen.

"Well then, *demon.*" Arthur's eyes fell on the bodies of Kira, Ari, and Arley as he turned to him.

A long drawn out growl rolled off his tongue and as rage flowed through him, his wings sprouted from his back and horns from his head, his skin turning light gray.

He curled his claws into the palm of his hand and his long pointed teeth grew sharper still. Black veins appeared under his white eyes while the other gargoyles eyes turned black as they transformed along with him.

Gray skin, horns, wings, pointed teeth and ears, monstrous eyes, and their faces twisted into an animalistic stare. They looked like their stone counter parts but they still held onto their human features. The Humans looked on with terror at their transformations, even the Venandi got distracted from their own fights to look on.

"Let's have our fun." Arthur sounded as monstrous as he looked as the words rumbled out of his mouth.

The sun was almost down as Trevor and Emily rounded a corner of a house, almost tripping over a flower pot as they did so.

Cale had woken up and although there was no sign of the wound left on his head, it was clear that whatever the bullet had injured in his brain was still trying to heal. His legs wobbled as he tried to walk so Trevor and Emily had to help him and his words were still slurred.

The city was hard to maneuver, there were so many turns and dead ends and a lot of the buildings looked the same.

They were lucky that none of the creatures followed them but that could change at any moment. The sounds of the battle behind them filled their ears and set them on edge, they wanted to go back to help their comrades but Cale was far too weak to do so.

He felt the worst out of the three, not because of his injury but due to it preventing him from being in the battle. He had saved Maya but the battle had just begun, he needed to be there.

He needed her to be safe.

An extremely loud noise from a distance made them stop in their tracks and over a hill they could see dust rising from whatever fell.

"*Where do you think you're going*?" A familiar girlish voice came from behind them and their hair stood as they turned to see the demon Maya thought to be dead: Astaroth.

There was a hole in her white blouse between her breasts, the skin underneath was healed but a long trail of dried black blood stained her front.

She noticed them looking and she smiled.

"*This*?" She placed a hand over the hole and her fiery red hair fell over her shoulders as she leaned forward. "Your girl stole my heart and left me for dead." Her bottomless eyes landed on Cale as she spoke.

They knew right away that she was talking about Maya.

"You should be dead if she took your heart." Emily shook as the fear she already felt escalated.

Cale was out of commission while she and Trevor weren't the best fighters, there was no way they were going to get out of this.

"You're right," The female demon shrugged. "If I was a *normal* demon I would have been dead." She kept her eyes on Cale the entire time she spoke and she licked her red lips. "There has been a change in you…I sensed it in the black and white eyed gargoyle too."

Cale tried to stand on his own and even though he achieved his goal, he still had no strength to fight. His motor skills were off as his brain healed, his speech was getting better as the minutes passed but walking was another thing.

Astaroth took a step toward him and Emily stepped in the way, an arm pushing him back. "You're not going to touch him." She didn't show fear anymore as she faced the demon, the girl that cowered in the face of a monster was no more.

With her dedication to save her friends, something had awoken inside of her. Something that even full blooded gargoyles had a hard time achieving.

She achieved her wings.

The new limbs tore through her trenchcoat and they stretched almost as long as she was tall. While Cale and Trevor looked on with shock and admiration at their friends achievement, Astaroth looked smug. There was no time to gawk at her wings, they would do nothing against the demon. Even with the power boost the wings gave her, Emily still wouldn't be enough to take on the demon and Astaroth's smugness confirmed it.

"No." Trevor's voice was strong as he stepped between the bloodied gargoyles and the demon.

Cale and Emily looked at the back of his head as he stood tall, their faces confused.

What happened to the scared man they had met almost five months ago?

"You guys go." He demanded. "I'll stay here and fight."

"You?" Astaroth snorted as she grabbed the stitch in her side. "That's hilarious!"

"Trevor..." Cale stumbled but Emily caught him, her wings folding into her back so she could get his arm over her shoulder.

"Go." The once fearful man demanded as he turned slightly towards them. "I'm going to have to break that promise that I made to you and Sam." His voice was defiant, strong.

The total opposite of how he used to talk when it was Maya's brother's who were after them.

He turned and met the demon's eyes, if he was afraid, he wasn't showing it.

"Sam changed her mind about me, she doesn't see me as that weak man who followed you from that cave." His voice grew stronger with each word. "She told me to help you because she trusted me so I'm *not* running away."

Cale gulped as Trevor brought up the promise he and Maya had made the others agree to over and over again. Maya had joked about it before they left the cabins and even though they had expected for the battle to be rough, leaving Trevor alone to fight a demon was impossible.

Maya trusted Trevor but Cale was sure that she didn't expect this to happen.

"Run if things get rough... save yourself."

Those were the words that neither Cale nor Maya lived by, it was time they stopped being hypocrites.

Cale inhaled sharply and with his jaw set with all of the regret that he felt at what they were going to do, he nodded to Emily.

Her eyes filled with both shock that he would agree to such a thing and worry for Trevor but she turned all the same. They began to walk away from their comrade, their friend. They could very well be leaving him for dead.

The two had remained silent until they turned to another alley.

"No more promises...this is a demand." Cale's voice called out and Trevor's ears twitched back as he kept his eyes on the smirking demon.

"Stay alive." Cale finished, his voice rough.

Trevor lowered his head as he listened to Emily's steps and the dragging of Cale's as they started down the alley.

"You're not going to chase them?" He asked with a tinge of surprise as he noticed that Astaroth hadn't moved an inch and only watched as Cale and Emily retreated.

"I don't think I will…*yet* at least." She brought her attention back to him. "Theres no sense in chasing them now if it's only going to take a minute for me to kill you."

Trevor lifted his chin as he took another step closer. "I bet I can last longer."

Astaroth bursted into laughter again and he waited for her to be done.

"Fine." She wiped a fake tear from her right eye as both of her irises turned blood red. "But since my *borrowed* heart was destroyed, I'll have to use my original power."

Trevor's expression changed.

Borrowed?

There was a reason why she had lived even after Maya had destroyed her heart.

The warm air blew against the opposing forces.

Weak versus strong.

Astaroth was stronger in both body and mind.

There was no way Trevor could win.

She cocked her head at his expression and gave a gentle smile. "You don't know much about demons, do you?" Her hand fell to her chest where Maya had wounded her. "Astaroth is the name of a male demon," She declared silkily "He was Lucifer's duke until he met his end." Her fingers curled into where the hole would have been but it looked like she was groping herself instead. "But like with all men, I took his heart."

She looked into the distance as if she imagining the event while Trevor listened on and contemplated if he should attack her but he knew a surprise attack wouldn't work.

"Just before he died, I took his heart and made it my own, we had a deal that if something happened to him that his soul would be mine… for over a hundred years he's lived in me until Lucifer's sweet Anna destroyed it." The female demon squeaked as she rolled her eyes back to him.

"What are you?" Trevor snarled but the air changed and a chill ran up his spine.

"Each demon is special." She declared as her red hair picked up in the breeze. "Azazel was good at possessions, Aamon stole the soul's of the beings made by God and made them fight for him." She closed her eyes as she smiled. "Abraxas is the master of shadows and Cain can control the body and make the creature look into itself and I-"

Trevor looked on as her skin changed to a light shade of red and it scaled like a reptile.

Long horns began to form from the top of her head and they curled to the sky as she brought a claw to her red lips and licked it with her too long tongue that ended in a point.

"I-" She repeated, her voice was seductive and drawn out. "Am the Succubus."

Wings the same color as her skin fell from her shoulder blades as she made her declaration and her glowing eyes filled with glee at the feeling of revealing her true form.

Air ran up Trevor's leg and he took a step back as he reached down to stop it just before the thing reached his groin.

The Succubus was well known, a lot of people even joked about the demon seductress but she was known nonetheless. The rumor was that she would prey upon sleeping men and seduce them, in doing so she took over their minds and even their health would deteriorate as she sucked out their soul and when she was done with her meal, the man would die.

"I took Astaroth's heart the same way I would take any other man's, it just worked out better for me since he was a demon." She licked her pointed teeth as she watched Trevor quiver, the sight giving her great pleasure. "The same as when I take in a human male's soul, as I eat their heart-" A soft moan crawled up her throat at the thought of her past meals. "I can eat the heart of another demon and make it my own, Astaroth's was nasty but it kept me alive and in turn I kept him alive inside me." She shrugged with a careless look. "He's dead for good now…Lucifer's sweet Anna killed him a second time."

She twisted her claws through her red hair and the red tint of her skin as it brushed against her hair made her look all the more monstrous with her gray horns and sharp teeth as she grinned. Trevor found himself wondering what made her so desirable to the men whose soul's she had sucked out.

Although there was another reason why she didn't interest him…

The trail of air began to crawl up both of his legs now until the limbs buckled and he fell to his knees. The trail curled around his knees up into his inner thighs and before it reached it's highest point, the Succubus who they once knew as Astaroth glided over to him and leaned her forehead on his and their eyes met.

"I would rather have played with that other man especially since he's with the black and white eyed gargoyle but you'll do for now." She mused and her hot breath blew into Trevor's face.

He shivered as she brought her index finger to the underside of his chin and trailed it along his skin. His eyes widened as he fought against her will and as he found strength in his legs, he got to his feet.

His heart pounded in his ears and the Succubus looked on with an intrigued expression. "You're the first man to ever back away from my advances…" She shrugged as the intrigue wore off. "You won't be able to for much longer though-" She stuck her tongue out and ran it over her sharp teeth. "They never can."

"You'd be surprised." Trevor breathed as he stood ready for the demon's attack.

The succubus smirked as she flapped her wings and she was in front of the half blooded gargoyle in a millisecond. She slashed at him again and again and he dodged all of them aside from one that he had managed to catch with his right arm instead of his gut where the demon had aimed. Blood poured from the three slash marks and the liquid splashed onto the demon as she continued to come at him. She could have killed him right then and there but she brought her fingers to his forehead instead and pushed.

As he fell, a daze washed over him: There was a buzz in his ears that ran all the way down his spine and his teeth chattered as his eyes glossed over. He tried to push himself from the ground but only made it to his hands and knees.

The demon appeared behind him and gently rested her arms over his shoulders and as she leaned over him, her breasts pushed into his back.

"Don't fight it." Her seductive voice filled his left ear. "I don't want to kill you… I just want you to be happy…be happy… with *me*."

Trevor inhaled sharply as she brought her hand to his chin again and turned his head so his brown eyes met her red. His jaw shook as he looked into her brilliant orbs, they were like an illusion and he wanted so badly to be lost in them, to be lost in her.

He needed to have her, he needed to make her his, he needed-

His breath caught and he stiffened.

* * *

He needed to protect Cale and Emily.

He began to rise and she clung to him like a child would a new toy.

"Still trying to fight it?" She purred. "It's no use."

Trevor swallowed as he turned and the demon pressed herself further into him, he could feel her every curve. He remembered how Cale had killed Azazel, a demon more monstrous than this wench. Maybe, just maybe, he could kill the succubus how Cale had killed Azazel.

He leaned into her front and he allowed a long exhale to leave his mouth, his jaw shaking with want. The succubus grinned as she leaned her lips closer to his, she had won and with a kiss his soul would be her's. She would enjoy this weak fools soul and would later feast on the man that the black and white eyed gargoyle loved.

Oh how it would hurt the gargoyle, she would try to kill the succubus in the most violent way. She would hold no qualms in killing this monster since she was a monster herself.

"Y-Your plan would have worked if it weren't for one thing..." Trevor moaned as he leaned into her.

The demon cocked her head, she had won no matter what this weak fool said, there was no man that could deny her.

"What's that?" She encouraged as her lips brushed his.

Trevor's shivering came to an end as his claws plunged into the demons chest, his fingers wrapping around her beating heart and her eyes widened as his narrowed.

"I'm *gay* bitch!" He snarled and with his declaration, he squeezed her heart and it popped in his hand. He ripped it from her chest for good measure and he watched as tiny gasps escaped the demons lips as her skin dulled along with her glowing eyes.

Blood leaked from her mouth as her jaw shook, her gasps turning into laughter until her mouth began to rot with the rest of her.

Her heart fell through Trevor's fingers as it turned to ash and his eyes fell to the pile now at his feet. He didn't have time to take in his victory as the demons blood began to eat his flesh and he quickly took off his coat and wiped it from his arm. It had already eaten the top layer of skin and left blisters. The pain was almost unbearable as some of them popped but he had other things to think about.

It was luck that had helped him kill the demon.

That and the demons stupidity that she could take any man and make him her own. She had fought the wrong one, she had fought a man who had no interest in a woman's sexual advances.

His eyes fell to the ash once again as he dropped his now blood drenched coat to the ground beside it. He wasn't going to waste time in taking solace in his victory, he couldn't believe it but he didn't think much of it.

He had to rejoin Emily and Cale.

As he ran in the direction the two had gone, he thought of Maya and how she had trusted him. She believed in him as he believed in her, she would save them all…he was sure of it.

He rounded a corner and whispered their names knowing they would hear and from a building ten feet away, a door opened and out came running was Emily, her arms wrapping around him and she shook as tears filled her eyes.

Her wings had dissolved back into her shoulder blades and she had ditched her coat.

"You…?" Her voice drifted as she pulled away and he replied with a jerky nod as another bout of pain hit him where the blood had eaten at his arm.

Emily's eyes fell to the hundreds of blisters that covered the limb and she met his eyes with a fresh round of tears in her own.

She pulled him inside the building she had came from and he was met with a small library. The little building was dim but even through the dusty haze Trevor could see the body of a woman that had been killed by Abraxas' shadow.

He thought of how she could have been sitting at the desk that was set in the front of the library just days before, how she went about her business until the shadow swallowed her whole.

In the present, Cale was in the chair, his eyes closed as he focused on healing.

"It's nice to know you listen." A smile appeared on his lips, he didn't even need to open his eyes to know who was there and Trevor was glad to hear that his voice was stronger as he talked about his demand for him to stay alive before he had left him with the demon.

Trevor smiled in reply but flinched at the pain in his arm.

They didn't bother to ask how and he didn't tell them the circumstances of his victory or what the demon really was.

Now wasn't the time and if they were lucky, they would live to see another day in a world of God's creation, not Lucifer's.

That's if they lived at all.

"As soon as I'm healed, I'm going back to the dome." Cale opened his eyes and Trevor noticed that not only did his voice get stronger, but the rest of his features did as well. He was beginning to look his old self. The wound that should have killed him was gone and his brain was almost healed. His healing proved to be a gift from God and the spirits of his ancestors.

"I have to help Sam and the others." He turned to Trevor who nodded, after killing the succubus a fire had lit inside of him.

He wanted more, he needed to kill more demons.

The gargoyles were made for this and even with most of them being half blooded and originally human, they still felt God's will running through them.

"We'll go together." Emily declared with an even expression as she looked out of the large window at the front of the Library but it quickly changed to fear as the earth shook.

Trevor held onto the desk as his feet threatened to fall from under him and Cale used it to keep his chair steady while Emily fell backwards into Trevor who caught her with one arm as the other still held on for dear life.

"What the hell was that!?" Trevor asked with panic in his tone as the shaking calmed and when he turned to the window, he almost fell again.

He stepped to the door with Cale and Emily in tow, their eyes as wide as his as they opened the door to see if it was the window causing what they saw but it wasn't.

The sky was red and the clouds had turned black, the air was dense and hot as if a fire had been lit close by. They shifted their eyes to the moon that was angled over them and their hearts lurched.

It was as red as fresh blood and it drowned the world in it's color.

It was a blood moon.

Suddenly the sound of what seemed like thousands of creatures roaring filled their ears and the beasts sounded like they were howling in victory.

It was as if they had been freed from a prison and they were filled with joy and bloodlust.

Dread filled the three gargoyles as they turned in the direction of the dome.

Where the noise came from.

* * *

A few minutes earlier

Abraxas was smiling ear to ear and while he was uninjured, the gargoyles were bloody and wounded and some even laid on the ground with their injuries too severe to continue the fight. Arthur panted along with his comrades as he took in the demons proud face.

Reggie, Lucas, and Tori had their guns pointed at the demons heart but their hands shook and made their aim off. More of the humans had been killed by Abraxas' shadow, it seemed that whoever didn't provide him a good amount of entertainment would be killed right away.

The gargoyles remained in their true forms as they and the demon sized each other up again, "I'm surprised you haven't ran yet." Abraxas smirked at the blonde haired gargoyle. "Like your kind always has."

"Silas." Arthur warned as the gargoyle stepped forward with a snarl on his face.

"We were here for days waiting for you after we got Arthur's call, we knew you'd know we were here if we replied to him." Silas' voice shook but it wasn't from fear. "We wanted to live peacefully but that's impossible with you heathens around and we-" His already black eyes seemed to darken. "Are done running from our fate and before long the rest of the gargoyles around the world will do the same."

"That's sweet." Abraxas mocked him with a soft chuckle. "And when it comes to the other gargoyles, they will never join you, they will continue to run even when this world ends."

Through their anger at the demons words, they were relieved to see that as the sun's orange hue turned gray, he seemed to weaken.

For the first time the shadow demon turned from his prey and looked instead to where Maya and Kellan had landed. He looked like he was waiting for something until his eyes flashed to the dome, his eyes crazed and his smile impossibility larger.

His shadow began to curl around his feet until it expanded further around him, his shadow creatures disappeared and many of the fighters found themselves swinging their swords and raising their guns at nothing.

The shadow demon's red eyes glowed against the gray mixed with orange. "She did it!" He sang. "Lucifer's sweet Anna did it!"

A loud explosion came from the dome and the building began to fall, gold mixed with light blue collapsing to the ground.

The gargoyles, humans, and the remaining Venandi watched as the gold top of the dome fell to the heap of stone from the rest of the dome and the undead gargoyles stopped to look.

"....It's happening." Donato's voice filled the square and the gargoyles could barely hear his racing heart over their own.

From where Maya and Kellan had landed, a flash of red light appeared until it expanded and the earth shook. They all fell as they lost their footing and landed amongst the dead and injured. As they looked up with wide eyes, they watched as the sky turned red and the clouds black.

What would have been a brillant light coming from the rising moon was replaced with blood red. They had heard of the phenomenon but had seen it as a myth, now they were forced to look truth in the eyes as they were engulfed in the light of a blood moon.

The end was here.

Abraxas' cackle echoed through the red and sent them all over the edge and as they stood, their knees buckled as they prepared themselves for an attack. But they were met with growls from where the opening of the dome had been instead.

"Hello, *old friend*." Abraxas called over to the being as it appeared in the rubble, its bare feet echoing through the square.

They all turned from the being before it formed completely and took in the new beasts that now surrounded them along with the undead gargoyles. Their gray skin was sunken in and rotted, their eyes red and long horns wrapped around their scalps like a goats. They looked like hairless mutated goats. Amongst them were human looking creatures but it was clear that they were demons in their fooling forms.

Alvertos had said that the end would bring more demons and Arthur's group was caught in the crossfire. The creatures filled the square completely, there had to be over a hundred of them and what was even more sickening was the fact that there was sure to be more demons arriving all over the world.

The creature that Abraxas had acknowledged materialized completely and like a force was pulling them to it, all of the fighters turned from the monsters that surrounded them to look at the being. They took in the demons fooling form that took the shape of a man, his skin was pale and his hair blonde, the wavy strands fell over his forehead into his bottomless eyes. He was wearing a monks robe, the black fabric made darker by the red hue of the blood moon.

The demon had a small grin on his face, he didn't look as excited and blood thirsty as the other demons but that was even more alarming.

This demon was different.

As he spoke their hearts lurched as their bodies froze with fear.

"Lucifer has succeeded." Many voices came from his mouth, the deep tones of men, the soft chimes of women, and even more terrifying, the innocent voices of children.

He ran a hand through his wavy hair. "I am finally free." His eyes met Donato's who looked on with fear even though the newcomer couldn't be seen with his eyes.

"I know who you are…I've seen you in my dreams." The seers voice shook as he trembled against Arabella who held onto him, her face twisted with terror

The new demon smiled at Donato's knowingness. "Say it *seer*," His voice was only one now, the low tone of a single man. "Say my name."

The blind man swallowed. "Legion… the man who was possessed by multiple demons."

"*Was*?" The demon known as Legion chuckled as he flattened his monks robe. "*I still am*."

He turned from Donato who had flinched and faced Abraxas instead, his head cocked. "It's been a long time, shadow demon." He acknowledged his comrade with a nod. "But I'm unsure of which demon that dwells inside of me missed you the most."

Abraxas gleamed at his old friend and as he did, his shadows that had darkened significantly due to the blood moon twisted but they didn't turn into the shadow creatures.

They turned into monsters.

The first one turned into a wolf that stood seven feet tall, its eyes red and it's teeth were solid even though they were made of shadow.

The second looked like a dragon, it's neck long and it's sharp teeth pressed into a snarl. It's claws planted into the stone underneath and it's shadowy wings flapped.

"You are one and we are all, my dear friend." Abraxas reached to Legion who smirked at the shadow demons display.

Some of the humans whimpered as the Venandi and the gargoyles tried to hide their terror. Legion turned to the whimpering creatures and all of his voices echoed again as he spoke:

"Don't worry, you won't die-" He inclined his head to the blood moon. "*Yet.*"

At Legion's words all of the creatures and demons howled in triumph. They were free from their prisons, even the angels who had waited for this moment to fall. Their sounds of victory echoed through the city, bringing dread to every creature that still lived.

Chapter 61

20 minutes earlier

"Wake up!" A voice called to her as the owner tapped her cheek. "Get up, damn it!"

Maya's eyes fluttered open and the first thing she saw was stars as her head pounded but as she settled and her eyes cleared, she found Kellan looking down at her, the side of his head covered with blood. He helped her up and she swayed as she took in where Baphomet had thrown them: They were surrounded by graves that were covered in leaves and in the distance there was a large fence.

She turned and through her dizzy spell, she noticed that there were countless graves behind them as well. Further back was a large brick structure hidden by trees and leaves and her eyes laid on it a second longer than she meant to. The trees that towered over the cemetery protected them from the sun's orange haze and they found themselves staring at the large gate that led into the cemetery.

"That big fucker is coming." Kellan gritted his teeth as his eyes narrowed at the gate. "He purposely threw us here."

Maya listened and she could hear the drag of Baphomet's hooves as it made it's way to them.

"We need to get back to the dome before-" She started but her voice drifted as Abraxas' shadow creatures surrounded the perimeter of the cemetery and blocked them in. Many began to step towards them, their eyes blending in with the sun's hue as their dark forms glided over the graves.

"Go find a way out and I'll catch up." Kellan directed as he flicked his fingers and his claws emerged out of them.

"I'm not leaving you here." She said as she looked down at his injured arm and how it shook as he tried to keep it up.

"I never thought I'd hear you say that to me." He chuckled although his eyes never left the goat man as the creature loomed in the distance.

"I guess I don't hate you as much as I used to." She smirked and he returned it.

"I guess I feel the same way."

After a minute and as the shadow creatures grew closer still, her feet still hadn't moved and it annoyed him. "Do you think I'm weak?!" He growled although she knew it was his way of trying to get her to leave him.

She took a step back.

He was right… she had to help the others.

"You better catch up to me." She demanded as she turned and began to run towards the brick structure to see if there was some kind of opening she could make it through.

Shadow creatures appeared around her but none of them attacked and she looked on with confusion as they stepped out of the way, making a path for her to run through.

She turned her head slightly to find Kellan ripping through the group of shadow creatures that surrounded him and the goat man as he walked through the front gate. She turned away so she wouldn't change her mind about leaving Kellan behind. He had to make it, he was strong and if they were lucky, the goat man would come for her instead.

She approached the brick building and the shadow creatures blocked her way from going further, the path they made would bring her into the structure.

It obviously wasn't a good idea to go in if they wanted her to do so but she found herself walking towards it, her eyes glazed over as she found a light inside.

Her legs shook as she tried ignoring the pull but as she stepped inside, both her daze and her need to break out of it disappeared as the light illuminated the sitting figure of Clarke.

A smile hidden under his gray mustache.

His long white coat covered his short stature but the fabric couldn't hide the blood stains on his hand. "Ah," He met her eyes as he looked up from where he sat on the tiny building's floor. "It's you."

"...What are you doing here?" She asked with a snarl.

He had tortured her and the half blooded gargoyles and she was sure he had done much more with the gargoyles in the past. This man was nothing but a mad scientist, he didn't need to be here.

"I came to Jerusalem with the other forces but I somehow ended up in here." He explained as he brought his gaze to the ceiling. "It seems the devil wanted us to meet here and now."

With his eyes off of her, Maya looked around: The shack was small and leaves were scattered on the ground. At the far side were steel bars between the bricks that the building was made of. It looked as if someone had placed mattresses between them like a bunk bed.

"It seems fate has brought us together." His voice echoed and as she brought her gaze back to him, she found him watching her as if she was the most interesting thing in the world.

"Why do you think fate has brought us together?" She asked roughly.

Of course Lucifer had brought them together but fate was another thing entirely.

He smirked, his yellowish teeth peaking out of his pale lips. "Because I'm the one who killed your parents."

She looked on with her teeth pressed tightly together, her mouth in a thin line while her eyes were as sharp as daggers. Clarke chuckled at her lack of reaction."You knew that already, didn't you?"

"...I had my hunch." Her voice shook with anger or sadness, she wasn't sure. "You killed them with those hydrochloric acid bullets, didn't you?"

"You're smart." The doctor closed his eyes and leaned into the bricks behind him. "Unlike your parents."

Her heart thumped at his crack at her parents. "What do you mean?" It was clear that her voice shook with anger now.

"Your parents knew my feelings towards them, I worked with them yes, but I never trusted them." He shrugged and his lab coat rubbed the dirty bricks behind him. "Who could ever trust a monster?"

"My parents weren't monsters," She snarled. "They fought with you against the demons and you betrayed them in return."

This man was testing her patience, she had to tell herself that she had changed. The words of her friend's echoed through her mind, that she was born new and she had left her murderous life behind.

She would have killed this man right now, would have ripped his throat out and would have stood back and watched as the light left his eyes as he gasped his final breath.

The feeling of satisfaction at watching her parents killer being sent to oblivion would be the greatest feeling to the old Maya.

She had changed.

"It's true." He opened his eyes and met hers. "If one didn't know they were gargoyles, they would never know. Your parents were as human as any of us but I saw their power, especially your mothers." He was looking at her but she knew he wasn't really seeing her, he saw her mother instead. "She was the only white eyed gargoyle and she had no control over her power, she was a loose cannon until she met your father."

He looked into her eyes and when he found that they didn't match her mother's, he looked away. "He got himself kidnapped by one of the demon's and she was beside herself with grief until we found where they were keeping him." He smiled as he remembered Layla's need to find the man she loved. "She honed her powers that day, she killed all of the demons in that place and she brought your father home." He blinked as he came back to reality. "You look just like her… you even act like her, you inherited nothing from your father." He took a breath that sounded like a laugh. "Though I'm not sure where those gray eyes came from."

"You killed them because of their power?" Maya asked simply.

She had changed.

"Of course I did, even though I have to admit that it hurt since I was taken with your mother." He stared blankly ahead. "I had feelings for her but it never left my mind that she was a monster. With the demons gone, your parents could have turned on us. We knew they had children, there was no doubt that they had that kind of relationship but they spoke nothing of you and your brothers when the new director sent out his call for help."

"But you didn't need help…" her voice drifted. "You wanted to kill them and you waited until you perfected your bullets before doing so."

"You really are smart." He smiled as his eyes grew wide with insanity, his face glowing from the light he had placed beside himself as the sun went down outside. "You killed innocent people for revenge and I'm the reason why." His grin widened. "You died right?" He asked with a chuckle. "Why did you die?"

She swallowed down her hatred, this man was the reason why she had killed people. It was her choice, it was her hand that killed them but his actions drove her to it. He was the reason why she had lost it all: Her family, her innocence, and her mind.

He had turned her into a monster.

She had changed.

"My brothers tried using a bomb to blow a city off the map." She announced casually as if it wasn't a big deal although the thought used to send her into a panic attack. "I sacrificed myself to save it."

"So you wanted to change your ways? Did you feel guilty for what you did? Were you tired of being a monster?" With each of Clarke's questions, her rage shined brighter on her face.

"…What are you going to do now?" His voice evened as she turned away from him, her eyes on the shadow creatures guarding the door. "You won't kill me, will you?" She could hear the smile on his face. "You don't want to be a monster anymore."

She ignored him.

"Your brothers," He continued after being met with silence. "What happened to them?"

She had changed.

"I killed two of them after I got my memories back and another was killed by a demon."

"Hm." She could hear Clarke shuffle behind her and she began to wonder why he hadn't gotten up during their conversation. He was met with a blood thirsty gargoyle but he had yet to move, to distance himself from her.

"That's a shame." He actually sounded disappointed. "But you have another brother and he didn't kill like you and the others." His voice was cold. "But he was the one who changed all of those poor humans into gargoyles."

Her eyes blurred as venom filled her, he was the reason why her family had fallen apart. Her older brothers were blood thirsty fools but Arthur wasn't. She was the reason why her brother had gone down this path but so was Clarke.

The people who had died so far during this battle suddenly flashed in her mind: Ari, Kira, Alvertos, Arely, countless humans, and *Mina.*

She had changed.

But she wanted so badly to see this monster rot.

She had changed.

But the image of his lifeless eyes was so enticing.

Her breaths came out heavy as she thought of the smiling faces of her comrades until they switched to her parents. Her mother who she looked exactly like and her father with his gentle blue eyes and blonde hair, their smiles wide as they watched their children.

They didn't know their family would turn into this.

She gritted her teeth and with each breath, her chest rose in an uneasy way as her slow heart tried to quicken. She knew Clarke had been placed here by Lucifer, like how he had showed Mina the way to the research center.

But the thought escaped her mind as she turned back to the man.

She had changed.

"I *am* a monster." She snarled as her eyes turned black and white. "I'll always be a monster and so will you." She took a step closer as he looked up at her with wide eyes. "I'm not the monster I used to be but I'm a monster all the same."

Her claws popped out of her fingers and Clarke tried getting up as fear filled his eyes but his body wouldn't move. Maya's chest swelled with pride at the terrified look on his face and wondered if her parents had the same look when he had killed them.

With no hesitation, her nails swiped across his neck and hit his jugular, his blood spurting out of the wound, some of it hitting the front of her shirt and the warm liquid ran down her front.

She watched his body fall to the ground as he convulsed, his shaking hand going to his neck as if it could stop the bleeding. She could have stood there and watched as he bled out but she had to help the others and the shadow creatures weren't going to be able to stop her.

The memory that Cain had showed her flashed into her mind, the pride of her kill had shown on her face at that time but this time her expression remained even.

She had changed but she also hadn't.

She turned to the door again but the creatures were gone, what stood there instead was the goat man, it's glowing red eyes on her as it ducked to enter the building. The beast filled the room from it's height and it had to duck to accommodate.

Maya stood ready for it's attack but to her surprise, it walked past her to Clarke and fell to it's knees as it examined the dying man. Baphomet watched until the doctor took his final breath, his body shuddering before it fell limp. A small growl escaped the beast's mouth as it sat up and with one hand, it touched the puddle of blood around Clarke's head and brought the other to it's own chest.

Deja vu filled Maya as she watched the beast use its claws to rip it's own skin apart, black blood pouring out as it reached into it's ribcage until it found it's own heart. She could see why she couldn't reach the organ before, it was much too small compared to the body it dwelled in and the ribcage was much too large.

She watched with wide eyes as the beast curled it's fingers around the organ and as it beat against it's palm, it squished it, the organ exploding in it's hand and it squirted black blood around the building. Some of it landed on Clarke and it began to eat away at his corpse while Maya had covered her body with her arms but once again, the blood didn't burn her and only left marks on her long sleeves.

She lowered her arms as the goat man fell and upon impact, the earth shook. She steadied herself against the doorway as shock filled her and when the shaking stopped, her eyes rolled outside as she noticed a red hue shining in the building: The sky had turned red and the clouds were black.

Her breath caught on the hot air as she stepped outside and her knees wobbled as she turned the corner that led from the building.

Laying amongst a pile of the shadow demon's ashes was Kellan, his gasps and grunts of pain filling the air. Maya ran to him, almost falling in the process, and she let herself do so as she came upon him. Her knees hit the hard ground as she scooped him into her arms.

There was blood pouring from his stomach and it blended in with the moon that rose above them. There was even more pouring from his mouth and it covered his teeth as he spoke.

"That…fucker…got… me." His dimming eyes wandered as he took in the red moon and as they widened, more fear washed through her. "What… did… you… do?" More blood poured from his mouth and his voice became weaker.

"I killed the man who killed my parents." Her voice shook as she looked down at his dying form. Not only did she know that it was her fault that this was happening, but so did he.

He chuckled softly as a smile appeared on his bloody lips. "Good for you."

"It's my fault." She swallowed, "I know this is because of what I did." She closed her eyes tightly as if it would make it all go away.

She was a fool, a stupid fucking fool.

Lucifer had pulled the strings and like a puppet she had moved to his will.

She knew it, she knew he had placed Clarke there so she could kill him and like the monster that she was, the temptation was too great. The end of the world was here and it was her fault. She could imagine the look on Lucifer's face as he found out that she had done exactly as he wanted and she couldn't breath as she thought of his smile and his bottomless eyes filled with glee.

This was his world now, this was his hell.

She closed her eyes tighter as she tried to stop the tears from falling but they flew open as Kellan pushed himself up and kissed her.

She could taste iron as his blood drenched her lips and her eyes softened as they met his. He fell again and she caught him in her arms, his eyelids shaking as he clung to life a bit longer.

"Haha!" More blood poured from his mouth as he laughed and the air caught in his throat. "I wanted to do that at least once before I kicked the bucket!"

She brought her hand to his cheek as her lips quivered, the taste of his blood still on her tongue. His eyes began to close as his strength left him but he had enough to leave her with a final message: *"Give em hell…Sam…an…tha… Knight."*

His head fell limp against her arm as his eyes closed, his mouth hanging slack.

Maya's jaw tightened as she laid him gently on the ground and got to her feet. She had already given them hell but Kellan didn't mean it that way and she knew what she had to do next. She had brought hell to the world but she had a different kind of hell to give her enemies.

The sound of victorious roars filled the air and she knew it was coming from the dome.

From where her comrades were.

She had unleashed more demons onto the world, this was their dwelling now.

"The hand of God will bring about the end of the world but will also save it."

She didn't know what the prophecy meant but she was the one who had caused the end of the world. She inclined her head and her eyes found the blood moon, her mouth going dry as she took in the result of her stupidity. She had no time to think about what she had done, Lucifer was waiting for her and she was going to meet him. Fate had brought them together in the past and had reunited them in the present.

A life for a life.

Old and new.

Lucifer was her fate and she was his.

Chapter 62

Welcome to the end

She didn't know where she was going but her leg's continued to move down the long road that led away from the cemetery. She had left it with two more bodies, she didn't count the shadow creatures or Baphomet.

The rocks crunched under her boots and she found solace in watching the blood moon as she walked, her eyes had quickly adjusted to the red but her mind hadn't.

She had to fix what she had done, she had to face Lucifer.

She could sense him like she had after their first meeting in this life but the pull was much stronger than before. Her mind didn't know where he was but her body seemed to, it was as if she was programed to find him and the end of the world had strengthened it.

Before long she found herself in front of The Temple Mount and as she looked up at the rubble that used to be the dome, she knew right away that it was Abraxas' handy work.

She heard no sign of the battle that had been going on there and with worry for her comrades, she went against what her body wanted and stepped inside the square.

Arthur and her comrades weren't there, only ash from the shadow creatures and Aamon along with the bodies of the undead gargoyles and the bodies of those who fought against them.

She couldn't see Mina's body anymore, it had been covered by the wreckage of the Temple Dome.

With grief threatening to spill over, she took in the carnage around her, her eyes landing on each of the bodies, hoping that it wasn't someone who she had left alive before she had been thrown off by Baphomet. She didn't recognize most of them but she grieved their deaths all the same. It had been a long time since she had seen death like this.

It reminded her of her time spent with her older brothers.

She continued to look and a small whimper escaped her throat as she took in the people she had cared for: Ari, who had been killed by Baphomet. Kira, who had met the same fate moments prior. Alvertos, who had protected Donato from Baphomet. Arley, who had fought on just because he had too. The bodies of the humans Reggie had brought with him.

She inhaled sharply as she turned from them, she remembered their faces from when they were alive and she wanted to keep it that way.

She almost recoiled back as she was met with a man in a black trenchcoat and as she took him in, she realized that it was one made by Ari.

His bare feet echoed through the square as he took another step towards her. His wavy blonde hair blowing in the warm breeze as he stopped just a few feet away and as her eyes met his, she realized they were as bottomless as the other demons eyes.

"Hello!" He called to her in a deep voice and she noticed that he had a bit of an accent.

She ignored him but it didn't seem to bother him as he grinned, his pearly whites were red against the blood moon. "I know who you are…" He cocked his head as his eyes lit up. "You're God's warrior."

The title sent a rush of anger through her, "I fight for no one other than the people I care for." She narrowed her eyes. "Especially not God."

The demon chuckled softly, "So I'm guessing the group that was here were your friends?"

Her eyes widened in fear, she wondered where they had gone and now that she was met with this demon she expected the worst.

"What did you do to them?" Her voice shook and unlike the other demons, he didn't seem to relish in her fear.

"Don't worry," He smiled gently and it caused her more alarm than a mischievous one would. "I didn't kill them but I did scare them enough to make them retreat… I made the other demons leave and spare their lives… their lives are my offering to you."

He bowed his head as if she was royalty but she didn't feel relieved by the demons words, in her time fighting these creatures, she had learned to never trust one.

"Your offering to me?" She rose a brow. "Why would you do something like that?"

"Because you freed me!" He sounded like she should have known the reason and of course she did, but it still didn't explain why he would allow her friends to live.

"Thousands of other demons and myself that have been either exorcized or banished by God, Jesus, or any of their fighters." He inclined his head to the moon hovering over them, it was set at it's highest point now.

"I am many demons possessing one body and I caused Jesus quite the amount of trouble to exorcize me...Well," He snorted. "*Us.*" He brought his gaze back to her. "It killed the body we were possessing and his body remained ours even after we were banished to limbo, where all banished demons go. We were lucky enough not to be killed but were unlucky to be cast into an eternal prison. Demons don't go to heaven when they die, they go to nothing." He sighed. "Demons should be killed as soon as they turn from God but he's weak when it comes to his people, he thinks we can change so he banishes us instead with exorcisms...though I do suppose that I must thank him," His bottomless eyes flashed. "During my time in limbo, all of the demons that dwelled inside this body became one and I became Legion."

Maya looked on as she took in the demons words, her too slow heart beating a tad bit faster.

"*Legion* is my name because that's what I am."

She didn't care about his name nor did she have the time to listen to him anymore. She stood tall as she readied herself for a fight but the demon didn't seem to notice as he still looked at her like she was the most glorious thing he had ever seen.

That seemed to be happening a lot lately.

"No need to tell me your name," He began again. "Lucifer's power has reached us all and we know everything he wants us to know." He acted like an awkward teenager as he rubbed the back of his head but his demeanor quickly changed and she watched as his expression went serious and his black eyes narrowed, *"I want so badly to fight you."*

She felt the air change and she couldn't breath as she prepared herself for the fight that was sure to come but as fast as his demeanor had changed, it went back to friendly.

"But you are lucifer's." He smiled as he closed his eyes. "He'd kill me if I touched you."

She could try killing him since his eyes were closed but she knew it wouldn't be that easy, this demon had an air about him, one that the other demons could never hope to achieve.

"It was so nice to meet you and I do hope that we meet again, but you must go to Lucifer." He opened his eyes and he retained his smile. "He's waiting for you."

She had to go, there was no more halting and she somehow knew that the demon would let her go. She turned but kept an eye on him in case he tried to attack her from behind but sure enough his feet remained planted and his smile had turned into a grin.

"Goodbye, Anna."

She stopped as his voice changed and her hair stood up on the back of her neck as a chill ran down her spine, her skin filled with goosebumps. She knew she wasn't mistaken when she had heard the number of voices that came from his mouth.

The voices of Men, women, and children all mashed into one.

"Goodbye, Legion." She began to walk again and she could feel his eyes leave her as he disappeared.

They'll meet again.

Crows flew overhead as she stepped through the streets leading to Lucifer, her legs knew the way while her mind focused on it's destination. She watched as the crows flying overhead did a nose dive as the hot air became too much for them and they fell on top of a nearby building. She didn't know if they died or they were simply too weak to move in this climate and she wondered if the other creatures around the world were feeling the same effects.

A buzz filled her ears as she grew closer to her destination until she stepped next to a large opening and turned to find a square that led to a brick building with intricate markings. There were different levels to the building and the highest peak looked like a top of a castle. The windows had bars in them and the lights that were attached underneath did nothing to break through the red hue coming from the blood moon.

Nonetheless, Maya could see Lucifer's illuminated form standing on the other side of the square in front of the most intricate of the building. The blocks looked like a large archway over the hole that led into the building behind him. His black hair and dark clothing blended in with the red and it looked like he was covered in blood.

Perhaps he was.

She could barely see the darks of his eyes but she knew they were on her as she stepped down a ramp into the square until they were twenty feet apart and Lucifer smiled.

"I knew you'd come, Anna." He gleamed as he spread his arms in a welcoming way. "As I knew you'd do *this* for me." He gazed at the moon with a gleeful expression.

This as in the end of the world.

"You had this planned." Her words came out as a statement, not a question. Of course he had this planned.

He reached his right arm towards her as if she was close enough to touch. "Of course I did sweet Anna, I knew you'd do this for me."

He saw the questioning look on her face and his smiled broadened. "Are you familiar with *The four horsemen of the apocalypse*?"

Maya could feel the lump in her throat form as the words came from his mouth, she was very familiar with the horsemen. They weren't literal horsemen but each of the four brought something different to the world and together they would bring the end.

But how did they play in with her causing the end of the world?

"First *death*," Lucifer started and her eyes widened. "Your dear friend who you sacrificed everything for, with her death you could no longer hold onto your life as Samantha knight. You're innocent life is gone and the girl that made you hold onto it is gone as well. "

She felt like she was going to be sick, it truly was her fault that Mina had been killed.

"Second is *Famine*," He brought two fingers to the air to signal the number. "The girl that you met in the cave who decided to stay with you because she had nothing. Her father didn't love her nor did anyone else in her life, they wouldn't accept her for who she was so she ran away. Kira was starved of love, she was *famished*."

Maya had always felt bad for Kira about her family, she had joked about it but Maya had always known that it caused her great pain. She was starved of love as Lucifer said.

"Third is *conquest*," A third finger appeared amongst the other two. "The doctor who killed your parents, he wanted knowledge about your kind and it was his quest to gain it. He killed your parents not because they were a threat, but for the simple reason that he wanted to know if he could kill them or not." Lucifer shrugged as he met her blank expression. "You didn't have to be the one to kill him but for theatrics sake, it was necessary." He chuckled until his voice went even again. "Fourth is *war*, Baphomet was the perfect symbol of the fourth horsemen. When one thinks of war they think of death, power, and fear and Baphomet was the representation of them all."

He pulled his dark hair out of his equally dark eyes as he used the arm he was reaching for her with to point at her. "Their relation to you and your relation to God is what made them all perfect candidates." He took a step closer to her but she held her ground. "You are still clueless to how much of a player you truly are in God's game."

"As I have been in yours?" She tested and the square filled with Lucifer's laughter, the sound carrying like the cries of a dying animal until he wiped the imaginary tears from his dark eyes and turned his head to the building behind him.

"This is The Church of the Holy Sepulchre," He declared. "It hold's a lot of power due to Jesuses influence and the fact that he had been buried and resurrected here. I chose not to destroy it since I thought it would be a good setting for our coming together. It didn't need to go anyway, the damage was already done by using you."

She took in the building again and remembered how Alvertos had told her and the rest that this place would be where Lucifer would be called to the most.

What a perfect setting.

As if the ground had been an illusion before, when she looked down she realized that there were bodies scattered around her, their hearts ripped from their chests.

Lucifer noticed her looking and cocked his head with intrigue. "No one has ever satisfied me the way you have." His voice was filled with more silk than usual. "They all begged."

She swallowed as she looked up, "I don't know what my relationship with you was-" she began with a hitch in her tone but Lucifer interrupted her.

"We were *allies*, *friends*, *lovers*, and *enemies*."

"I'm not your sweet Anna." Her voice shook as she furrowed her brows at how he described their relationship in the past.

"You are Anna as you are Maya and Samantha, although you have nothing to hold you to this life anymore." He lifted a hand to his dark hair again and tugged at the wavy strands, the red light fell into his eyes with his hair out of the way and it looked like they were glowing. "Names don't matter, you are a warrior made by God, fighting for him is your one and only purpose."

"I have plenty to hold me to this life…the others have to be alive."

Her brother, Cale, Emily, and Trevor had to be out there somewhere and Reggie and the rest had to be ok as well. She didn't trust Legion but perhaps he had told her the truth, she hoped so at least.

Lucifer closed his eyes and as he lifted his head to the moon, he opened them.

"I know you met with Legion and he assured you that he didn't kill them but the other demons won't care about thanking you for freeing them. Now that Legion isn't here to watch them, they will hold no qualms in killing your precious brother, your lover, and your friends.

The only reason why you got here with no problem is because they know better than to touch you…Even with his strength, Legion would be dust if he laid a hand on you." As he looked back down and met her eyes, his expression changed. "You are *mine*."

"I belong to no one, especially you nor God." Her voice was rough and filled with annoyance.

Lucifer stepped towards her and the hand that was still reaching for her almost touched her face. "But you play into our games so perfectly, do you honestly think all of your actions are your own?"

She swallowed as his finger tips brushed her left cheek and she wondered if it was true that God controlled everything.

Her knees buckled as an intense weight fell on her and she fell to the ground next to Lucifer's heartless victims, his dark eyes rolling down to her struggling form.

He was using his gravity power on her and like last time, she pulled herself to her knees but went even further, she managed to set one of her feet on the ground.

The force that was pushing on her made it feel like all of her bones were going to break and as she looked up at Lucifer with her eyes narrowed and her teeth bared, he licked his lips.

As fast as his power had pressed onto her, it let go and she fell from the pain in her joints.

"You certainly have gotten stronger." He closed his eyes as a chill from his excitement went down his spine while Maya panted at his feet. "Is this the power you used to kill Cain?"

"I didn't kill your demon." She breathed as she got to her feet and the two met face to face. Her gray eyes met his black and for the first time she noticed they were the same height.

"You know what's funny to me?" He cocked his head as their breaths hit each others faces. "I can see what all of my demons are doing…I can tell how they died but I can't see how Cain met his end." He leaned his head forward and his forehead practically touched hers. "I saw how that man of yours forced his arm down Azazel's throat and pulled his heart out from his mouth. I saw how that other man tore through the back of Aamon and a human finished him off. Of how that man you trusted to protect your injured lover and your friend killed Astaroth due to the fact that he couldn't be fazed by a succubus." His sharp canines popped out of his mouth. "And yet I can't see Cain's death."

Confusion filled her by what he had said about Astaroth, she thought she had killed the female demon but it seemed she had played her and went after her friends instead.

What confused her more was that Lucifer had called her a succubus, it didn't weigh on her mind much though as she thought of how Lucifer had said that Trevor had killed her.

In the midst of her thoughts, he began talking again and she listened on.

"You can't use your full power because your genetic code as a human can't take it so there's no way you could have bested him." He smiled against her face and his eyes didn't leave hers. "But I know better when it comes to you… It seems you haven't felt the effects of using your power during this battle but I've also noticed that you haven't used your true abilities…you must be scared to use them."

She knew what he was going to say before it left his mouth, not only because she could read him, but because she thought the same. "But in not doing so you have allowed your friends to die."

She could feel the pain in her heart and although she tried her best to not show Lucifer her weakness, her face betrayed her.

She should have bit the bullet and used her full power, she should have made the sacrifice and perhaps with her death, the world wouldn't have ended. She imagined what the freed demons were doing to the humans and the lump in her throat grew.

"I won't use my power against you…*yet*." Lucifer declared as he backed away. "Let's see how much you've improved since your first life."

They took each other in: Their expressions, how fast their hearts were beating, the twitch of a finger. It continued until Lucifer appeared before her and although she didn't notice that he had moved, she quickly dodged his attack.

He didn't lie when he said that he was going to hold back.

His fist met her elbow as she protected her middle and although her bone didn't break, she could feel the shock run through her nerves. This was the first time they had fought in this life and with having no recollection of how he had fought in her first life, there was a great disadvantage.

And this was only a taste of his power.

The two continued their humanlike fight all the while keeping their eyes locked on the other. They fought like it was the most important thing in the world. Lucifer had waited for this day since the death of Anna, no one was like his sweet Anna, no one could ever compare.

"This feels nostalgic." He gleamed as his nails slashed at her throat and she narrowly dodged what would have been a fatal wound although she was sure he wouldn't have killed her yet.

A thin line of blood dribbled down her throat from where his nails had grazed her.

He continued speaking as he attacked and Maya's breath hitched as she tried her best to dodge, the warm air burning her throat.

"Do you remember when we used to spar like this?" He questioned.

Although it was cloudy, she did start to remember.

In her minds eye she saw flashes of Lucifer in black slacks and a white buttoned up long sleeved shirt along with black suspenders that looped around his shoulders as he fought her with a playful smile. It was simular to how he looked now only he was much more modern.

Maya found herself remembering a less than playful battle that the two had: Lucifer's red eyes glowing against the normal moonlight like a flame against the snow, the bright moon illuminating his form as he towered over her as she crawled backwards to get away from him.

She woke from the memory as he wrapped his hands around her throat in the present and she brought hers to his. She stumbled from the force and fell backwards, the ground scraping her back as Lucifer fell on top of her.

Their fingers clenched tightly around each others necks and their palms pressed down as they squeezed tighter but Maya was the only one who seemed to be fazed by her air being cut off.

Lucifer leaned down so his face was only inches from hers, his legs pinning her down so she couldn't move. A grin on his face while Maya snarled.

Her hands were beginning to shake and she could feel the cartilage in her neck beginning to collapse from his strength. She was all too familiar with the feeling since Oberon had almost killed her the same way.

She started to gasp and her hands slackened on his neck until they fell to her sides and Lucifer removed his own but remained on top of her as she gasped for breath.

"It would be a waste to kill you now." He declared as he kept his eyes on her watering ones, he looked insane with the blood moon shining above him. "You have yet to show me what you can do." He reached down again and trailed his finger along the marks he had left on her neck.

As a shiver burst through her, Maya twisted her body and Lucifer fell sideways, giving her enough time to free one of her legs to kick him away.

She rushed to her feet as she felt the cartilage in her neck extend back into place and her eyes remained narrowed as she took in Lucifer's gritty laughter.

"You used to love when I touched you." He teased with a cackle.

"Shut the fuck up." She snarled.

"You used to be so quiet," he exclaimed after hearing her colorful word. "You didn't know as many words as I did so most of your thoughts remained unknown but now you can speak them freely." His expression softened as if his intentions weren't less than friendly.

"I wonder what goes through your mind." He let out a long exhale. "You die and you reincarnate into someone else, unaware that you had a past life. You die again and this time the memories of your second life haunt you until you're forced to get them back and now you learn there's another." He shook his head. "It must take quite the toll on you."

Her jaw shook as she held her tongue, she couldn't give him the satisfaction that his words had hit her. He didn't need to see a reaction though, their connection was far too strong for her to hide anything from him.

Without another word, he continued their fight and Maya prepared herself for him. He came at her with more strength now as his excitement for their fight grew to a new length and Maya found herself having a hard time keeping up with him.

Having the air choked out of her had dulled her vision and he pushed her into a corner so she had no where to go.

She didn't have time to think about it anymore, she had to risk using her power.

The pressure in her eyes built as she allowed the power to flow through her and she caught Lucifer's hand in hers before he could claw through her shoulder. His nails protruded out of the back of her hand but it felt less intense as her power dulled the feeling.

She met his dark eyes with her black and white and he grinned.

"Oh?" He exclaimed with a light igniting in his eyes. "We're using our powers now?" He cocked his head as he focused on her mismatched eyes. "The power you could have used to save your friends?"

Maya growled as rage flowed through her and Lucifer continued his mental assault. "I never took you as someone who was afraid to die and would allow others to die for you."

She lost it finally and slashed at him, his nails leaving her palm as he narrowly dodged with a gleeful noise coming from his mouth and as he stopped a few feet away, his smile was as wide as ever.

For the first time since her second life, Maya didn't care what the power would do to her, she was willing to die if it meant shutting Lucifer's mouth permanently.

As fast as he had dodged, she went at him again and as she did, the pressure in her eyes deepened. Her teeth extended into points along with her ears. Gray horns extended from her temples and stopped as sharp points. Wings of the same color emerged from above her shoulder blades as her pale skin turned to match her new limbs.

Her heart raced as she attacked him but it had nothing to do with the strain the power had on her body, it had everything to do with the adrenaline from allowing herself to let go.

She hadn't even used this much power to fight her brothers after her reawakening.

Lucifer dodged all of her attacks with ease but the more she let go, the harder it got for him to get away without using some of his power. As he would jump away, she would appear in front of him again but she was always met with a smile and it infuriated her to no end.

A loud growl escaped her mouth as she brought her right hand forward as she distracted him with her left and for the first time, she landed a hit on him.

Lucifer recoiled just a bit as her fist collided with his cheek and his smile turned into a grimace. Maya wasted no time in enjoying the fact that she had wiped the smile from his face and instead she continued her attack, but as she brought her dagger like nails to his heart, he caught her and her nails pierced into his hand instead.

The two now had matching wounds on their palms.

He gripped her hand and their fingers intertwined as black blood dripped from the punctures and like with the other demons blood, it no longer stung her.

Her hand shook as she tried to pull away but her fingers wouldn't budge from his no matter how hard she pulled.

"You are everything I wanted and more but you're still no match… So tell me-" He looked up and through his black bangs, she could see that his eyes had turned into flames. "How does it feel to be God's failure?"

Maya swallowed and her heart leapt as Lucifer tightened his grip and leaned in closer, an intense heat rolling off his skin and it burned her face.

His other hand drifted to the base of her neck and his fingers wrapped around it, his nails digging into her skin. "Out of all the warriors he's sent to end me, you've been the most entertaining by far." His lips were only an inch from hers and she could feel the vibration on her own as he spoke. "But you were also promised to be my undoing but you've been a failure." Suddenly he disappeared from sight.

She could still feel where his warm skin had touched hers and the vibration of his lips.

She turned on her heel to see where he had gone but all she could see was the heartless bodies at her feet. She blinked as fear filled her and a panicked voice made her jump.

"Help…me…!"

Amongst the other bodies laid Arthur, his arms weakly holding himself up and his eyes filled with tears. He lacked all of his teeth and blood poured from his mouth. Maya's eyes wandered to his hands and there were puddles of blood around them and a whimper rolled out of her throat as she noticed that he was missing his fingers.

She ran to him with tears in her eyes while thinking of Abraxas' torture and how she had left him with the shadow demon again

"Arthur!" She called as she reached out to him but stopped dead in her tracks as she met his eyes. She knew something wasn't right, the air around him was too dense, an air she only felt when she was with Lucifer.

"Ma..ya…" His voice whined again as he begged for his sister and although it stung, she ignored his cry.

"I know it's you." She kept her voice even although the lump in her throat threatened to ruin her fake composure and sure enough, a toothless smile appeared on the fake Arthur's mouth.

"You certainly *are* better than you used to be." Lucifer's voice left his mouth and as she watched, her brother disappeared. The skin bubbled at first then he turned into a black mist as it materialized into something else.

"You killed my parents…" Her heart thumped as Cale's voice filled the square and he materialized where the mist had been, his dark eyes filled with hatred.*"You're the reason I don't have a family…you're a*

monster…a worthless monster."

Although it was all a ploy to break her, he still told the truth.

She was a monster.

But she had also changed, the real Cale had taught her that.

She would always be a monster but she wasn't the kind of monster that she used to be.

His expression changed as he took in her reaction, the smile that had given her so much solace appearing on his lips. The way he looked after he had taken a bullet in the head for her filled her mind. He wouldn't be able to protect himself while he healed, the others had to protect him while they protected themselves.

They had to be safe, they had to run, they had to hide.

As she was about to take a step back, she stopped and looked the fake Cale in the eyes.

This wasn't going to work.

"You don't think you're a monster anymore?" The mist materialized again and changed to Clarke, his bushy mustache hiding his smile as it always had. *"You're just a different kind of monster now…you said it yourself…it's in your blood to be monstrous."*

He reached for her as blood poured from his torn jugular, the wound she had caused. *"You killed me, you haven't changed…if you truly changed, the end of the world wouldn't have happened…you should have walked away."*

Maya's eyes widened as the bodies that surrounded her stood, the mist covering their faces until it disappeared and she was met with her dead comrades.

"You could have saved me…I was alone and you left me to die…" Kira's rotted form swayed in front of her, her crushed neck rolled to the side and her bulged eyes practically fell from their sockets.

Maya gripped her stomach as she backed away, tears filling her now gray eyes.

"You weren't there to help me save her…I was always there for you…" Ari's voice filled her ears as she backed into the corpse Ari was controlling. *"You should have made the sacrifice to save us."*

Maya turned to find her blue eyes glowing against the blood moon, the only bright color that shined through the dim light.

An intense pressure built in Maya's heart and she couldn't breath, her mind was beginning to cloud and the rest of her body changed back to human like her eyes had.

"I'm sorry…" Her voice broke as she backed away but they

followed. "I'm *sorry…*"

"How sorry can you be?" Mina's voice filled her ears and Maya jumped as her dead friend walked between the other two. *"You left me to be kidnapped by the demons…you didn't care enough about me to bring me with you…you didn't want me around…"* She motioned to Ari and Kira's zombified forms. *"I was replaced."*

"No…" Maya stepped to her, her eyes wide with desperation to make her friend realize what she had done for her. "I did it all for you!"

"You did nothing for me!" Mina roared and Maya recoiled back, she had never heard her friend yell like that. *"You've been played by fate!"*

"We've all been played by her fate." Alvertos, Arely, and the rest of the Venandi that had been killed appeared next to the girls. *"She sacrificed us all."*

"No…" Maya's voice drifted as tears fell from her eyes. "I didn't-"

"It's ok, sweetheart." A voice that she hadn't heard in over a lifetime came from behind her and she almost snapped her own neck as she turned to the source.

Her father stood in front of her like he had never died, his blonde hair clean and his skin fresh unlike the other mirages. Beside him stood her mother and it was like looking into a mirror, they really did look the same with their viking hair and their pale features.

The only difference was that her mothers braids were neat while Maya's were loose from the battle and long strands fell from the twists. While her mothers skin was clean, Maya's was dirty and her clothes were torn with two types of blood splattered on her front.

Her mothers lips curled into a dainty smile and her eyes looked crazed.

"Everyone has their day to die, some just die earlier than others."

"As you have died twice already." Lucifer's chilling voice filled the square as the mirages fell and the black mist lingered around the bodies that had never moved.

A shiver ran up Maya's spine as she turned to him and when she realized that he was only inches away, it was too late and he hit her so hard that she fell to the ground and the concrete broke underneath her.

"This world is mine and you have delivered it to me." He declared as he stepped to her and the red light illumined his venomous expression. "I found you in your first life and I had my fun with you." He didn't move his head to look at her but his bottomless eyes fell to her and it made him look all the more terrifying. "In your second life I looked on and enjoyed the show, I can change my form to anything I want so I would watch you as you killed all of those innocent people."

She began to crawl away from him, her limbs shaking as they threatened to collapse.

"I am darkness, pain, truth, and death and of all the forms I choose to use, this one will always be my favorite, do you know why?"

He leaned down and grabbed the front of her shirt and lifted her halfway so her face was inches from his. His dark eyes were psychotic but they also looked entertained while Maya looked on with dread.

"It is the form I wore when I met you, no one has ever been deceived by me as much as you have." His voice was filled with an unnatural amount of silk as he pulled her to her feet only to knock her harshly to the ground again. "It's so entertaining to see that *God's warrior* has turned out to be just like *me*."

He grabbed her throat with one hand and twisted his fingers in her hair with the other as he pulled her up to make her meet his bottomless eyes.

"I was deceived by God, I was his equal but he wanted the power all to himself so he banished me. When he found out what I was planning, he sent his *angels* down to stop me but I tore them apart with ease." He licked his pointed teeth as he carried her by her neck to the side of the church and smashed her into it. She screamed as her spine broke and her legs went temporally numb.

"When I heard the whispers that he had sent down a stronger being to stop me… I had to find you, but you were oblivious to it all… you knew nothing of your power and you were weak until you finally woke up." His lips shook with excitement as his eyes drifted to her chest then back to her eyes.

Instead of begging for her life or screaming for help, Maya's eyes narrowed and her jaw set tight and instead of it angering Lucifer, the look seemed to excite him more.

"I killed you in a certain way in your first life and since then, it's all I've done when I've killed my prey."

Her eyes flashed to the bodies on the ground and she knew right away how he had killed her. The pain she got in her chest as she thought of her impending death made sense now.

"But no one is as good as you." Lucifer's voice brought her attention back to him and through the red hue, she saw her own death.

As the feeling in her legs began to return, she kicked against the ground but he lifted her higher and she kicked the building and his legs instead but there was no moving him.

Her hand wrapped around the wrist that held her neck and she looked at him with all of the ferocity that he had been lacking in his kills for over a hundred years.

He inhaled sharply as his signature smile returned, "I wish you hadn't died in an explosion in your second life… I would have loved to have seen this expression three times."

He brought his free hand forward and wiggled his fingers in anticipation, "But I suppose two times will do."

She only had time to widen her eyes as an excruciating pain filled her and blood poured from her mouth onto lucifer's gleaming face. He had forced his hand through her skin into her ribcage where he tore through muscle and bone.

He pulled his hand out as quickly as he had gone in, the muscle and cartilage that he had pushed though tore further and small whimpers escaped her throat but they came out as gurgles instead as she choked on her own blood.

Lucifer lifted his bloody hand to his exhilarated face, his teeth stained with her blood as he grinned at her still beating heart that rested in his palm.

Chapter 63

Anna

There was nothing like the sweet embrace of death, the very second you knew your life was over. The chill, the shock, and everything you wished you had done differently in your life. For Maya there was so much to regret. So much that even though her heart had been ripped from her chest, it still hurt with it all.

"That's the face!" Lucifer cackled as he watched her face turn to shock. "That's the same face you had when I killed you the first time!"

She should have been able to feel the pain in her chest but shock dulled the feeling. She should have been dead already but her body was trying to heal and it made her hold on just a bit longer. But without her heart, she had no chance, it would all be for naught.

More blood poured from her mouth as tiny gasps escaped her lips and she looked on as Lucifer examined her paling face.

"You haven't disappointed me!" He gleamed as a huge smile spread across his face, his bloody teeth threatening to cut his own lips. "I've waited so long to see that face again!"

Even as she died, Maya couldn't help but think of how poetic it was that she was meeting her end the same way she had killed someone for the first time in this life.

Her heart had been ripped out of her chest like how she had pulled Camilla's from her's.

Her body had given up on trying to heal and it began to shut down. The last time she died it had been quick, She wasn't able to appreciate death to it's fullest extent.

She could now.

Her eyes remained on Lucifer as he looked between her organ that laid in his blood drenched hand and her face. He looked like a butcher with her blood splattered over his face and his fiery eyes filled with glee.

Her vision began to dull as she watched the organ beat one more time, the final bit of blood that it pumped trailed down Lucifer's arm.

Her fingers fell from Lucifer's wrist and he placed a hand on her cheek to keep her head up as he leaned his forehead against her's, "Goodbye, *my sweet Anna*."

She couldn't see nor could she hear him but she felt his lips press to her's, the taste of her blood filling both of their mouths and as he pulled away, it trailed between them.

He had ended his sick game with a kiss.

He licked her blood from his lips as he enjoyed the last seconds of her life, the light leaving her eyes and her head falling forward as he removed his hand.

She was engulfed in darkness again and with her death, she knew this place wasn't simply a part of her mind, it was her personal limbo. She collapsed to her knees and gripped at the hole in her chest. This was just like the time she had gotten her memories back. She had promised that she wouldn't fail but she had died again.

"I will not fail…." Her voice trembled along with her bottom lip.

"I know." The voice that she had heard for months echoed through her ear drums but it only agitated her.

The feeling didn't last long though as she was too filled with regret from her own failure.

She had always wondered who the voice had belonged to but it didn't matter anymore, they were both wrong. If Lucifer's words were true, she was sent by God to fight him but she had turned out to be nothing but the devil's play thing.

She swallowed the lump in her throat as she thought of Arthur and the pain he was going to feel when he found out that she had left him again.

Of Cale who she had fallen in love with, her arms shook as she could still feel his wrapped around her.

Emily who had became her best friend, practically like a sister. Trevor who had looked up to her even with her being a monster. Reggie who had joined her even though she could have betrayed him.

They would be joining her soon and it was her fault, she brought about the end of the world and with it a legion of demons. She had fallen for Lucifer's tricks and became his greatest player.

She thought of Ari, Kira, Kellan, Alvertos, Arely, and the other fighters that had died. She thought of the people who had died before this battle: Carma, Daniel, Jeannie, Cam, and Dylan.

She thought of Mina….. of her second lives parents.

* * *

She had failed them all.

"...I failed." Her voice drifted as tears stung her eyes.

Would she be stuck here forever?

No matter, it's what she deserved.

But as her voice echoed through the darkness, it changed.

As if it was dissolving, the dark began to fall through the floor and before long, it was replaced with gold. The change in light made Maya squint and her tears glimmered on her cheeks. The same voice that had answered her all those years ago replaced her own and it bounced around her.

"You haven't."

Suddenly her mind went blank and she was neither met with darkness nor gold but with the sight of livestock in a snowy field, a makeshift fence holding them in.

As she stood and watched the reddish colored cows munch on their hay, memories of Anna's life before this point filled her mind until they stopped where she currently stood.

She watched the vapor leave her mouth as her warm breath hit the cold air and with her black slacks wet from the knee high snow and her black coat that had more holes than fabric, she decided it was time to go inside.

"Anna!" Her father called to her from the small wooden hut behind her, a thin line of smoke coming from the chimney.

"Comin'!" She called as she turned just in time to see him pull his head back into the hut's back door.

The year was 1860 and they were in the middle of a harsh winter in the north. Anna had grown up in a poor family that had consisted of her father, mother, and herself.

She had known for a long time that she had been adopted, the only blood child that her parents had was her older brother who had died from influenza a year prior to her birth. She was seventeen now and instead of going to school or spending time with friends, she spent her time working with her father on their farm.

While at home she would dress as a male, she didn't like dresses much and the only thing that gave away that she was female was her long wavy hair and the obvious.

As she opened the back door to the hut it creaked and she gritted her teeth at the noise. She could hear things better than other people but she chose to keep it to herself, it had to be nothing.

She stepped inside and was met with her mother and father who were sitting at a small table that was placed in the middle of the tiny building. There were plates of vegetables in front of them that they had saved from their garden before the snow had fallen. The little shack was a mess although it wasn't dirty, their clothes and other items were scattered amongst the beds and shelves but it was otherwise clean of dust and grime. Their dwelling was made of wood so their walls were brown and tiny drafts of wind came through the cracks.

Even with all of it's imperfections, it was still home.

Her father was in his forties, his brown hair graying and his skin dulling. He wore black slacks that had an equal amount of holes as Anna's coat and his white long sleeved shirt was stained with dirt from their summers work.

Her mother who was the same age as her father had an equally stained white frilly shirt and dress combo, her blonde hair twisted into a bun.

Anna removed her coat, exposing the same kind of shirt that her father was wearing, and hung the ripped thing on their makeshift coat hanger beside the fire so it could dry.

Even though the hut was small, all three of them slept, ate, and lived comfortably. Anna's bed was at the far side of the hut while her parents was at the other, the musty smell didn't bother them as they had grown used to it a long time ago.

Anna sat across from her father and took one of the green beans from her plate that her mother had warmed over the fire and began chewing. The sweet but salty taste filled her mouth and she closed her eyes as the heat from the fire warmed her cold limbs.

"Slow down, Anna." Her mother's blonde brows lifted over her blue eyes as her daughter reached for more beans. "You won' feel well later."

"Let er eat." Her father picked up a hand full of beans and shoved them in his mouth. "It's a small meal."

Anna smiled as her father winked at her and she remembered the day they had picked them together.

It felt like a lifetime since she had been in the garden, this winter had been the longest she had witnessed in years. Winter was a bad season for her, summer chores would keep her distracted from her lack of education and friends. Her parents couldn't afford school but she didn't resent them for it although she would have loved to learn how to read and write, to even speak better.

"I don' know 'ow much longer we can salvage though." Her father met his wives eyes with his hazel. "Another few months and winter should be gone."

"But even longer before the ground thaws an dries." Anna swallowed her share and pushed her plate away. "There's no way to plant tha crops with the ground ta wet."

Her father smiled at her words, "Ya know ow to live like a farmer, I just wish ya could have a chance to live like a lady."

A lot of girls her age were going places in their frilly dresses and flirting with the towns men but she lived a life of farming and she wouldn't complain.

She had never met her birth parents, she could have died where they had dumped her next to a river but she was found by her adoptive parents on one of their evening strolls. She was a baby girl who had been left to take on the world all on her own and with their son's death, her parents thought that finding her seemed to be a sign of God's good faith.

As they sat and talked about their plans for summer, the sun had gone down and before long, it was time to hit the hay. Her parents laid in their bed with their blankets wrapped tightly around them, they made a point to lay close together to obtain each others body heat.

Anna laid in her own bed with a book that her father had given her to practice with but with no one to teach her, she couldn't understand a thing.

Soon the room filled with her fathers snores and she sighed as she closed the book with a thump and her head ached as she looked into the fire. Her hazel eyes were transfixed on it as if it was the most intriguing thing she had ever seen. A chill ran through her as a dark figure formed in the middle and it began to move with the flames. It began to rise until it was in the shape of a tall man but it was void of any color other than complete darkness. It stepped towards her, the indents that were his eyes finding her wide ones.

Before she knew it, she was was reaching for the creature and he for her.

"Anna?"

Her mothers voice made her blink and as she did, the creature disappeared from sight.

Her mother didn't see it?

"What ar ya doin'?" The blankets rustled as her mother rolled to face her.

Anna swallowed as she continued to blink in case her eyes were playing tricks on her. "...Warming ma hands."

Her mother didn't look convinced but she didn't ask anymore of it, "Go ta sleep, ya have lots ta do morrow."

Anna leaned her head into her pillow which was way too thin to be comfortable and kept her eyes on the fire. Her brows furrowed as she wondered what the creature was and why only she could see it.

Was she going insane? Her jaw clenched, she knew what happened to people who were marked insane and she didn't want to go down that road.

As she fell asleep, her mind filled with a man made of light and the shadow man that she had seen in the fire. They stood in a multicolored realm and it looked as if they were floating in space, the stars glimmering as the outlines of other forms watched amongst the small glimmers of light.

The shadow rounded on the glowing man, its flame like eyes narrowed as anger surged through him but the figure made of light remained unfazed. In the next instant the shadow creature was falling from the sky and as it fell it's voice boomed. "I'll get you for this brother! You'll never stop me!"

"Anna!" Her fathers voice filled her ears. "Anna!"

Her eyes flew open, her face twisted in a silent scream but she quickly settled as she met her parents confused faces.

"What ya dreamin' about?" Her father asked in an exasperated tone, his hazel eyes blinking.

"Nothin'." She lied as she shot up.

"You said you'd get your brother." Her mother accused with a sad look. "You seen him?"

"No." She got up from the bed, pushed past her parents, and pulled on her coat and boots. Before she could step out of the front door, her eyes rolled to the fire that had burned to cinders, the figure was still gone. "I'm gonna check on tha cows."

She left her parents inside to wonder if their daughter had gone insane.

After a long morning of haying and milking the cows, Anna found refuge in the hay loft.

She sat on the softest bale of hay that she could find and ran her fingers though her knotted hair, tears forming in her eyes as she yanked the knots out and her scalp ached.

The barn was bigger than their house, but it was more important, it was their lively hood.

She sighed as she finished, she was now able to run her fingers through her long wavy hair with no restrictions. She dropped her aching hands to her knees and through the the dark loft window, she could see their neighbors house. Her eyes drifted to the smoke coming from the chimney and the creature that had formed in the fire came to mind again, of how he had gone after the other that was made of light.

"I'll get you for this brother!" His infuriated voice filled her ears again.

"You'll never stop me!" His tone was deep but there was a small amount of silk that laid within his anger.

A chill ran up her spine that had nothing to do with the cold and her fingers began to shake. As her eyes rolled to the darkest corner of the loft, she saw something stirring and when it stepped from the shadows, she realized it was the shadow creature from the night before.

In a daze, she reached for the creature again and it did the same.

It felt so right… they needed to touch… this was their fate.

When their fingers were inches from touching, a burst of cold air hit her and her eyes rolled into the back of her head.

She found herself standing in a garden, the air was warm and the gentle breeze blew through the holes in her coat. In the middle of the garden was a large tree filled with apples, the sounds of birds chirping filled her ears and she closed her eyes as she enjoyed the heat on her cold face.

"Eat it." Her eyes flung open as she heard the voice that she recognized as the shadow creatures. Standing next to the tree was a woman with long blonde hair that fell over her bare breasts, the rest of her exposed to the world.

"Why should you not?" The voice echoed again and Anna watched as the woman's eyes lowered to the ground and she saw a large snake at her feet, it's scales a mixture of green and gold and as Anna watched, the thing coiled up the woman's leg and stopped around her chest.

"He doesn't want to share his power…He's selfish."

"I shouldn't" The women said nervously as her body began too shake. "I mustn't."

"You should." The serpent coaxed.

The woman's hand shook as she reached for the nearest apple, her eyes never leaving the creature that coiled around her. As Anna watched the woman pull the fruit from the tree, she knew right away that something horrible was going to happen.

She stepped towards them, she had to stop her… she couldn't let her do this.

But as she took another step, the woman brought the apple to her mouth and the snake was replaced with the shadow creature, a smile carved into it's colorless face as it stood in front of the woman.

As soon as she took a bite, everything around Anna fell and she was flung into complete darkness, a blood curdling scream pouring from her mouth as she fell.

She woke with her fathers hand on her cheek, his face twisted with concern. "What are ya doin'!?"

She had no strength to answer him, all she could feel was the fall. She had fallen backwards off the bale of hay and she laid flat on her back.

"Jesus Anna wha in thu world is happening ta ya?" He got out of the way as she shakily pulled herself up, the hay rustling underneath her. "I could hear ya screaming from the house, the neighbors will think there's a murder goin' on!"

As he saw the terror on his daughters face, his gentled. "What are ya dreamin' about Anna?"

She met her father's eyes and her lips curled as she realized what she had had just seen, she wasn't educated but she knew the story of Adam and Eve.

"I-I think I saw tha..." here voice drifted as she began to think that it'd better that she didn't tell her father what she'd been seeing.

Her poor parents, one child had died from influenza and now the other was going insane. But she wasn't insane, what she saw was real and they had to understand, the gentle look on her fathers face assured her.

"I think I saw tha devil."

The loft was filled with silence aside from the creaks of the barn as the breeze hit it from outside and as her father registered what she had just said, his eyes widened. "The devil...?"

"I'm not mad!" She shot in nervously.

"No...Yer not mad." Her fathers voice drifted and she knew he was lying.

"It was only a dream." She assured him quickly and he nodded although his eyes were still filled with disbelief.

"Only a dream." He repeated.

At that moment, she didn't realize how much trouble her honesty would get her into.

It had been days since she had talked to her father about her dreams and although her parents tried to act normal around her, her dreams continued to worry them. It didn't worry them quite as much as it worried Anna though. She forced herself to stay awake to prevent the dreams from coming and she kept her gaze away from the fire but neither worked and the shadowy figure of Lucifer would still work his way into her mind.

Her chores had suffered from her lack of sleep and paranoia but she continued to retain some kind of normalcy.

She was on her way to the house after carrying water to the chickens which she had managed to spill on herself and her clothes were already frozen from the frigid cold. She wanted nothing more than to sit next to the fire and thaw herself out but as she turned the corner of the barn, she noticed a horse drawn carriage at the front of the house.

Her eyes landed on a man in a black suit as he held onto the two bay horses that were attached to the carriage. The bucket she was holding fell from her hand into a heap of snow as fear filled her. She swallowed as the worst came to mind but she couldn't bring herself to think that her parents thought she was insane. Maybe it was someone looking into getting milk, or perhaps the visitors were looking into using their service on their own farm.

She began to tread through the snow while ignoring the man at the carriage and she placed her hand on the front door but didn't push it open, instead she stood and listened to what was going on inside:

"She'll be fine, I assure you sir." A voice she didn't recognize appeared and she felt a pressure behind her ear's as she heard her father and mother shuffle.

"She'll be treated right?" Her heart thumped at her mothers question.

Treated right? What was that supposed to mean?

She was about to make a break for it when she heard the snow behind her crunch and she turned on her heel as the carriage man appeared behind her, another had stepped out of the carriage to hold the horses.

"Hello, miss." He drawled in a deep voice. "May we step inside?"

She gave him an untrusting look but she was far too obedient not to do what he had asked. She turned to the door again and she pushed it open, her hands shaking as she did.

Her parents and three other men in the same suits as the carriage man turned to her and their associate as they stepped inside, her parents eyes were wide with fear while the mens expression's remained even.

"Hello, Anna." The man nearest to her smiled gently, his frosty hair shining against the fire behind him. "How are you dear?"

"I'm na sure yet sir…" her voice drifted.

The man's smile widened, "Your father has told me you've been having a little problem and he would like us to help you."

She met her father's eyes as she began to feel sick, but he quickly looked away from her as if he was ashamed that he had ratted her out. She turned back to the men as the carriage man stepped closer behind her.

"I don' have a problem."

"You don't think it's a problem miss," He picked up a top hat that she hadn't noticed he had in his hand and he placed it on his head. "But we think it is."

Suddenly the carriage man had his arms around her middle and she fought against him. "I'm not mad!" She screamed. "I don' need to go! Arseholes!"

"She'll be fine sir." The man in the top hat assured her father over the sound of Anna's struggles to get free.

"Mother! Father!" She begged with tears in her hazel eyes but her parents

turned away, unable to look at her. "Don' do this!" Her struggling and begging didn't amount to much as the man who had a hold on her was twice her size and was much stronger than her. He turned as another opened the door for him and he carried Anna's thrashing body outside as the others followed.

That was the last time she saw her parents.

Anna's slacks and buttoned shirt had been replaced with a white dress, the sleeves ended in cuffs around her wrists and the fabric was stained from the patient who had worn it before her.

The asylum was dull, it's walls white and the floors the same color. The point of being inside this time of year was to escape from the snow and the frigid temperatures but it was practically the same with the color of the walls and the lack of warmth.

Worst of all, it smelt like shit, vomit, and piss. There wasn't a better way to describe it.

The other patients screams had filled Anna's ears since she had arrived there two weeks ago. The doctors attempted to bring her visions to light but she always insisted that she was sane. Though if she wasn't insane now, she would be by the time she got out of there.

If she ever got out of there.

She had kept to herself since her arrival and watched the neglect that the other patients went through with anger flowing through her veins. These people came here for treatment but instead they were treated like they were monsters, many of the caretakers thought the best treatment was a good beating.

She was currently sitting in the lunch room where they would supply the patients with three meals a day, although the food was far from nourishing.

A man's pained yells filled her ears and she turned to find a nurse force feeding him porridge that was clearly too hot to eat. He attempted to pull away but he was confined to a wheel chair and the disorder he had prevented him from using his hands.

Insane asylums in this age didn't help their patients, they kept them away from the sane.

The nurses and the doctors spent their time treating their patients like scum but the scum helped them earn their money so they tried not to be too rough with them. Although from what Anna had seen, being rough was nothing to the physicians, they just tried their best not to kill their patients.

"No!" A blonde haired girl whined as a man who Anna recognized to be a caretaker who relished in abusing his patients grabbed ahold of her wrist as his

face twisted with anger.

"I told you to sit!" He chastised her as she tried to pull away but he smacked her across the face so hard that she yelped, the sound of skin hitting skin echoing through the lunch room.

"You crazy-" His eyes drifted to Anna who had shot to her feet as the echo of the slap made the patients and the other nurses go silent.

"You gotta problem girl?" He narrowed his eyes and Anna's jaw locked to prevent herself from saying anything. "Cause it looks like you do."

He let go of the girls wrist and he strutted to Anna who nervously stood her ground. With each step, the man's shoes echoed through the now silent room, and Anna had to stop herself from flinching at the noise, her hearing had gotten abnormally better in the past few days.

A few of the more mentally unstable patients began to wimper and jeer as Anna looked into the man's intense eyes, his brown hair falling over his brows as he leaned to meet her eyes.

"I ain't gotta a problem sir." She answered steadily, "It's just I'm wonderin' how slappin' 'er is gonna fix anything?"

The man looked insulted by her words even though it was a valid question.

Without warning, he slapped her harder than he had the other girl and she fell roughly to the ground only for him to pick her up by her long brown hair.

"I heard about you girl, how you been seein' the devil." His hot breath hit the side of her face where his hand print was already starting to show and the pain seared. "You insane bitch."

Anger flared through her and maybe she truly had gone insane as she spit in the mans face, her saliva splattering on his pale skin.

The room was silent again, even the worst cases seemed to be surprised by her stupid courage.

The man didn't look angry at first, he seemed to be as surprised as the others were but as realization hit him, he picked her further up by her hair and slammed her head into the hard floor.

"You crazy whore!" He growled as she whimpered from the pain. "I'll beat the crazy outta you!"

"Joseph, I think she's had enough..." One of the quieter nurses approached but backed quickly away when she saw the look on his face.

He turned back to Anna as he tightened his grip on her hair, "You've got pretty hair girl, I heard before you came here that you used to dress like a man..." He pulled her up so she would meet his saliva covered face as it filled with rage. "Let's make you look like one again."

Anna faced the window as she sat in the mess hall and she watched as the snow fell gently outside.

In her reflection she could see the bruises that were already healing from Joseph's assault and her now bald head. She didn't care much about her hair being gone, what really bothered her was the looks she got as the nurses realized that she was the girl who had stood up to the abusive man. Every chance he got, Joesph would harass her, everything she did was wrong to him and he made sure she knew it.

"Excuse me?" A small girlish voice appeared beside her and she turned her head to find the blonde haired girl smiling awkwardly at her. "...Thank you for the other day."

"It's nothin'" Anna assured her as she moved her eyes back to the window but she could still feel the girls blue eyes on her bald head.

"What's your name?"

Anna turned back to her as she picked up on how well the girl spoke, she must have grown up in a wealthy family before she ended up in there.

"...Anna." She answered softly. "You?"

"Mary." The girl smiled gently as she pulled out the empty chair that Anna sat across from and planted her butt. "You seem like you don't belong here." She said quickly as if it was wrong to say and Anna met her eyes, "Neither do you."

Mary looked around nervously, her blonde hair swaying against her fair skin until she turned back to Anna and leaned forward. "I heard you saw the devil."

"I had a dream and that's it." Anna wasn't lying but she wasn't telling the truth either. "I'm not mad." She added quickly.

"I don't think you are." Mary assured her and she leaned back in her chair as the sound of one of the other patients screams covered their conversation. "I landed myself here because I panic at small things...I don't think it has anything to do with me being mad."

"...No." Anna dropped her gaze and ran a hand over her prickly scalp, her hair was already growing back.

"I'm sorry." Mary apologized and caught her off guard.

"Why?" Anna rose a brow even though the reason was obvious.

"You got hurt because you protected me."

Anna gave Mary a confused look, "What's protected?" She asked with an air of embarrassment for not not having a proper education but Mary smiled.

"To look after someone." She explained it easy enough for Anna to understand.

"Like I do with the cows?" Anna pressed on and Mary nodded with a soft

chuckle.

"A former farm girl and a former rich girl, maybe with each others help we'll make it in here." Mary's smile widened but Anna could see the pain hidden underneath.

She returned the smile and her's was real, she never had a girl friend before but it wasn't long before she and Mary became good friends.

Almost inseparable.

Four months had gone by and Anna's hair had grown to her ears and like she always had, she pushed most of it to the left to get it out of her eyes. Her right eye was currently black and blue from a hit she had received from Joseph just days before because she had defended Mary again.

She had taken her beatings for the past four months but with every bruise or welt, she healed faster than before and before long, she was known as the witch of the asylum.

Her lungs were currently screaming from having her head held under water. It had happened hours ago but she could still feel as Joseph grabbed the back of her scalp and plunged her head into the bath. Her lungs had felt like they were going to burst while her legs trembled and her eyes burned. Gasps and coughs had erupted from her throat as he pulled her up so she could get a quick breath before he pushed her back down. He tortured her because he wanted to, he said the beatings would heal her but it was bullshit.

Even with the pain in her lungs, Anna appreciated todays session of torture, it had given her an idea.

When he had pushed her back down into the water, her hands had unconsciously gone back and she had grabbed at his keys that laid in his left pocket.

She played with her cold soup as Mary sat across from her after maneuvering around a woman who thought her doll was a living baby.

"He's looking over here again." She informed Anna as she settled in her chair and Anna knew right away who her friend was talking about.

"He's goin' to say I'm eating my food wrong and smash my face into it." She joked and although what she said was funny, what made it messed up was the fact that Joseph would really do something like that. Anna was his favorite toy and he would find any opportunity to torture her.

Her eyes wandered to Mary's soup then back to her own bowl, "I wanna get-"

"Want to get." Mary corrected her and Anna fixed her words, "I want to get out of here."

Mary had been teaching Anna the proper way to speak and although Anna desperately wanted to learn how to read, they were supplied with no books to learn with.

"Don't let anyone catch you saying that." Mary's eyes wandered to see if anyone had heard. "But it would be nice to get out, huh?"

Anna's eyes wandered to the window and she looked down onto the courtyard where lush green grass laid instead of the snow that had melted a few months ago.

"I'm gonna...I'm going to get out of here." She turned away from the window and glanced at Joseph who was swinging his keys around as he stood at the doorway of the lunch room as if he was begging for someone to take them. There were four keys but Anna was sure that at least one of them was to the door at the front entrance.

"You can't be thinking what I think you are?" Mary leaned above her soup, pretending that she was blowing on it instead of whispering to her friend.

It wasn't a good cover up though, the soup was always cold so it didn't need to cool down.

"I alway's think." Anna said as she chewed on a piece of chicken and spit out a tiny bone that had been left inside, her eyes falling to it as it landed on the table between her and Mary.

Someone could have choked on it, someone who was actually insane.

"I've dealt with his beatings for a reason... to get close." Her hazel eyes narrowed and as Mary looked into them, she noticed a gray ring around the outside of her irises.

For the first time since she had been thrown into her first lives memories, Maya realized that she was simply reliving them, that she wasn't Anna anymore.

When she had regained her memories from her second life, she had seen some of them as if she was a different person until she regained them from her own point of view. She knew now that she had seen them the way the being who had created her wanted her to see them.

God.

Her eyes opened to the dark limbo again and she shook as she remembered all of the beatings and the fear that she had felt from the dreams of Lucifer. They had continued during her stay at the asylum, eating away at her, making her question the reason why she had them.

She never told Mary that the dreams had continued even though she had trusted her whole heartedly.

She would never get the chance to tell her.

Maya knew what was going to happen next, she had seen it already and she knew it was her fault.

Mary was the first of many to die due to her weakness.

Anna's ear's rang from the force that Jospeh had used to smash her head into a wall.

She had purposely crossed him, she didn't have to do much though, all she had to do was walk in his direction. As she fell to her knees in front of him, the pain etched on her face, she grabbed ahold of his pants, reaching her fingers inside his pocket and grabbing his keys.

She wrapped her fingers around them and closed her fist as fast as she could to stop the jingle and in the next second, he punched her and she fell to the ground.

"You fuckin' bitch." He growled as he pulled her up by her hair and she had to stop herself from spitting at him again. "You really are crazy to keep testing me."

He dropped her as he walked away, the sounds of the patients who had watched around the lunch room filled the air and Anna turned to watch Joseph leave as the sounds filled her ears, the cool keys chilling her hot skin.

"I got em." Anna had snuck into Mary's room and the girl shot up from her bed that matched the white walls around her.

"No way." Her eyes widened in disbelief.

"I 'ave ta hurry before he finds out…are you coming?" Anna sounded hopeful that she wasn't in this alone but she wouldn't be disappointed if Mary had changed her mind, what she was about to do was far too dangerous.

Mary's eyes fell to the keys between Anna's index finger and thumb, "I-I don't know-"

"It's fine if you don't wanna go, It's safer if you don't but I promise I'll find a way to get you outta 'ere." With Anna's words, Mary got up from her cot and wrapped her arms around the taller girl.

"I hope you get out." Anna could hear the pain in her friends voice, the only friend she ever had.

"If I don't, we'll see each other soon…or Joseph will kill me." Anna pulled away from her friend and took one last look at her. "I love you Mary."

Mary smiled at her words. "I love you Anna."

With one uneasy step, Anna stepped back then turned to go, her feet guiding her to the front entrance.

She didn't want to leave Mary behind but she had to go, she had to find the reason why she had her visions and she wouldn't find it here.

She had to plan this out carefully, she couldn't run into any guards on her way to the entrance and that's why she made sure to stir up the other patients on her way there.

She screamed in the faces of the one's the nurses had left in the halls and they screamed back, setting off a chain reaction. It was strange how they had never bothered her, some would lunge at the nurses and at each other but it was as if they didn't dare to with her. They looked at her with fear, they even cowered as she walked by.

Mary sat back down on her bed with tears in her blue eyes, Anna was the only friend she had in the cold asylum and now she was trying to leave.

She didn't hate her for leaving, she wanted to go too but she was too weak and she wasn't as brave as Anna. They were two girls committed to the asylum by chance and became friends.

She smiled gently as she heard the screams of the other patients echoing through the halls and she knew it was Anna's doing. Her heart thumped as she heard Jospeh's furious tone over the screams.

"I'll get that fuckin' bitch!" He roared as he walked by Mary's room and she feared that this was the final straw and he would actually kill Anna.

She shot up and watched as he turned the corner into another hall, pushing someone in a wheel chair out out of the way as he did so. She had to help Anna, her desire to help her friend made her forget her fear and she followed Joesph, his blood lust chilling her bones.

Anna's nerves were starting to get the best of her but she kept going, it was far too late to stop now.

She could have ditched the keys and acted like Joesph had simply dropped them but she knew she was going to be beaten either way. She had decided to go up the stairs instead of down so she could take the long way incase they saw her coming. She had scoped the place out, had made her plan well but her doubts were still there. She was two floors away from the entrance now and the sounds of the Asylum filled her ears, the noise was so loud that she didn't notice Jospeh coming from behind her.

He grabbed her by the back of her neck and slammed her head into the side of a wall, her head leaving an indent as he yanked her away. Blood poured from the cuts on her head as he slammed her down again, the pain splitting her head open.

"You damned whore!" He roared as he slammed her into the wall over and over again. "You mad bitch!"

Anna's head fell limp as he pulled her up again and flipped her around so she was facing him, his hands wrapping around her neck. Her lungs screamed as her air was cut off and she thrashed against him until a pressure started to build in her eyes.

Suddenly his hands were away from her and she gasped for breath, her vision going blank.

When she came to, she found Mary, her neck snapped as she laid on the ground and her blue eyes were staring at the ceiling. She had been killed by Joesph, he had snapped her neck and it was because she had tried saving Anna.

Anna's vision cleared as the pain in her head diminished and rage filled her eyes.

The pressure reached it's peak and as Jospeh brought his already shocked expression from the girl he had just to killed to Anna, his eyes filled with fear.

"W-What are you?" He stammered backwards as he tried getting away from Mary's corpse and the monster growling in front of him.

Anna unconsciously got up and before Joseph could run, she was on him, her hands wrapped around his neck. "Please!" He begged as he thrashed to get her off but there was no moving her. "I didn't mean it! I don't want to die!"

Anna didn't care.

There was a beautiful satisfaction that came with killing the person who had tormented you, had brought you close to death so many times. Had killed the person dearest to you.

She snapped his neck as his eyes watered over and she threw his body like a rag doll against the radiator. His body falling with a clunk.

When she woke from her intense bout of rage, she found herself on the floor, confusion filling her but most of all fear as she found Jospeh against the radiator. Grief filled her as she found Mary's orb like eyes on her, her head had fallen to the side, her neck no longer having the strength to hold it in place.

The sound of footsteps coming up the stairs filled her ears and her heart leapt, she had to get out of there or Mary's sacrifice would be in vain.

Her feet moved on their own as she ran down the hall, she wasn't sure how she had killed Joseph, she wasn't even sure where the pressure in her eyes had come from but whatever strength she had, she had to use it to get out of there.

She made it to the front door but the guards were already there waiting for her. A tall burly man took a step towards her and as her hand shook around the keys, she felt the pressure build in her eyes again.

The man didn't notice them change as he lunged foreward to subdue her but she punched him square in the face with one of the keys sticking out of her clenched fist. The metal went through his cheek and he yelped with pain as his blood spurted on Anna.

"You-" Another came from behind the now thrashing guard as he attempted to pull the key from his cheek. She narrowly dodged the wounded man but found herself in the other guards arms.

"Got you." He said in a gritty voice but his eyes widened as he met hers. "What in the world-"

A growl escaped Anna's lips as she stomped on his foot and he jumped as the the pain hit.

What would have been a simple stomp turned into the man's toes being broken, Anna's strength was more than human. His shock had given her the upper hand and with his toes broken, she had time to get to the front door.

She took a deep breath as her mind gave her the image of the door being broken down.

Could she do it?

She had no time to play with the keys which had fallen to the floor as the guard pulled them from his cheek, she had to use the power she had used to kill Joseph.

Like her body knew what to do, she curled her hand into a fist, dodging one of the guards as she did so and punched the door so hard that it broke apart, the wood falling on the blacktop outside with a crash.

It even slid several feet and Anna's eyes widened at her own strength but she had no time to gawk. She had to get out of there. Her ears stung from the noise but she ignored the pain and ran, the warm air hitting her face as she stepped outside for the first time in months and she took in the fresh smell.

She didn't have time to appreciate it though as more guards rounded on her and with tears in her eyes she continued to run to the iron gates that were blocking her from freedom.

She grabbed ahold of the bars and even though they bent a few inches, she couldn't pull them apart enough so she could step through. She had no control over this strange power of her's but it had gotten her this far.

She turned on her heel to find ten guards coming at her and in desperation, she screamed.

Only it wasn't a scream.

It was a roar.

* * *

As she stopped, she had the same confused look on her face as the guards and they stopped dead in their tracks before they got too close.

"....The devil." Whispers began to spread amongst the guards as they looked on with fear and Anna almost fell as dread overcame her.

She wouldn't even be allowed to move if they caught her, she'd be treated worse than the most insane person in the asylum. She would be treated as if she was a monster.

Which she clearly was.

She closed her eyes as they began to approach her again and her ears pressed to the back of her head as she sensed something coming from behind her.

As her eyes flew open, she noticed that the guards had stopped dead in their tracks and their eyes were focused on whatever she had sensed.

Before she could turn to see for herself what had appeared behind her, more than a dozen people landed in front of her, their backs to her as they faced the guards.

Directly in front of her stood a man in dark slacks, his torso covered in a white buttoned up shirt and black suspenders that matched his wavy hair. The man beside him who had short brown hair and peachy skin turned to Anna and she jumped as she took in his ink colored eyes.

He had a gentle smile on his face as he spoke to her. "We heard your call for help, fellow gargoyle."

Chapter 64

Samuel

They ran into the woods that surrounded the asylum but Anna found it hard to move after what she had just seen. The people who had showed up to save her had eyes that were pitch black, nails that curved into points, and teeth like daggers.

The man who had spoken to her before they attacked the guards had called her a 'fellow gargoyle' but she didn't know what that meant. With her lack of education, she didn't have an idea what he was talking about nor what she supposedly was. They ran and ran and Anna followed them like a lost puppy, there was no way the guards were going to follow them, the gargoyles had left them injured but killed none.

As they made it to the outer edge of the woods, more gargoyles stood waiting for them and they came to a stop in front of them, panting from their fights with the guards and their run through the woods.

The gargoyles who had waited brought their eyes to her and with her lack of education she couldn't tell that there were more than twenty of them including the ones who had saved her. She swallowed as they took her in, the mental patient.

"So this is the gargoyle who called for help?" A girl with curly red hair, green eyes, and freckles drawled with a southern accent.

"It is." The brown haired man stepped beside Anna and she jumped even though the fact that his eyes had turned to a normal shade of brown calmed her. "They had her in the asylum over there."

"So ya picked up a crazy woman?" A tall man with a bald head furrowed his brows. "Gargoyle or not, it's risky."

"I'm not mad." Anna assured them as her voice shook, she didn't know who or what these people were but they had saved her. "I was put in there by mistake."

"Doesn't seem mad to me." The brown haired man placed his hand over his heart. "The names Leroy, it's nice to meet yet another gargoyle."

Anna's eyes wandered over the people around her, some of them gave their names while the others remained silent. Her eyes landed on the black haired man that had landed in front of her back at the asylum. He was staring at her with an even expression and she found that his normal eyes weren't too far off from his gargoyle color.

His irises were as dark as his pupils.

"...I'm Anna." She said as she turned away from him. "I'm sorry but..." it was going to be a stupid question and she felt embarrassed that she didn't know what she supposedly was. "What are gargoyles?"

She was met with strange looks but none of them seemed judgmental, they were just confused that she didn't know about her own kind.

They had left the town that the asylum was in and found refuge in the town over. They had broken someone out of an asylum and people would be looking for them. It was dark now and they were sitting around a fire in the woods.

Well, fifteen of them were while the rest sat against the trees around them.

"I guess now's a good time." Leroy said as he watched the chicken they had stolen from a farm on the way there cook over the fire.

They had yet to explain to Anna what they were or what she was.

"Gargoyles are known as the creatures that sit on top of buildings... churches for example, and they protect the building from evil spirits." He explained over the crackle of the fire and he kept his eyes on Anna's illuminated face as the others listened."There is some truth to how the humans made the creatures on the buildings but there's more to it. We were made by God to protect the world from the devil and his demons. Gargoyles have been around for a very long time and some of us-" He looked around at the gargoyles around him. "Are over a hundred years old."

Anna blinked as she looked around at them all as Leroy had, none of them looked over the age of twenty.

There was no way that she was one of these creatures, she had lived as a human her entire life and only seemed to get her 'power' after her visions of the devil began...

Her eyes widened as they landed on Leroy again.

Gargoyles protected the world from the devil and his demons...Her visions were coming full circle.

"We stop aging young so we can remain in the world and defend it until the end of time, but even though we're immortal, it doesn't mean we can't be killed." Leroy pointed at the black haired man who was sitting next to Anna. "Samuel's parents were killed by demons four years ago and he was alone

until we found him."

Anna turned to Samuel and noticed that his expression was stone cold as if he was reliving the memory. She turned back to Leroy as Samuel turned his head slightly towards her, she felt strange looking at him.

"You said you heard my call for help…what was that?" She asked so the hard subject could be changed.

"You roared and we happened to be in the woods traveling to our next location." The red haired girl answered and her tone was softer this time, her southern drawl was intriguing to Anna.

"Not all of us have dead parents by the way, we've disbanded from them to make our own group…" her eyes fell to the fire and it made it look like her hair was on fire. "The demons have been restless lately and we've even had to join the Venandi on occasion." She looked up again and found the questioning look on Anna's face from the strange name. "The Venandi are humans that know of our kind and we work together to fight the demons." She looked into the dancing fire again. "They are our allies sent by God."

Anna thought of her visions of the devil and as she looked back on how she felt when they first began, she would have never thought it was due to her being a creature that was made to fight his demons.

Were her dreams a warning? Did God show them to her?

There was no way any of this was real.

Her heart fell as she thought of the possibility of both God and Satan being real, that she wasn't human but a creature that could change to look like a monster.

She held her breath as she thought of her linage, where did she come from? Were her real parents gargoyles? No, that didn't feel right.

"What is it?" Leroy rose a worried brow and as she brought her attention back to the fire, she found that they were all leaning towards her.

"…I was adopted." The words poured from her mouth, "I was raised by humans and I had no idea about my power until today… I could hear and smell better for the past few months-" She thought of the smells in the asylum that had been heightened due to her sense of smell and it made her sick. "But I thought it was normal until…" her eyes fell to the top of the dancing flames as she realized that she had actually killed someone.

Should she tell them? Should she tell them about her dreams? Did they have something similar?

"I-I killed one of the workers in the asylum… he killed my friend… he abused me." She felt odd making excuses for herself, she wasn't even sure if she felt bad for what she did.

The gargoyles eyes landed on the bruises on her face from Joseph's attack from earlier, they were yellow already as they were on their final stages of healing.

"You blacked out?" The bald headed man pressed and she nodded, "I don't remember doing it."

"We've all blacked out at least once, it's nothing to hate yourself for." His voice softened. "It just means you have to learn how to use your power, living with humans might have halted it until you needed it to help you."

She nodded again as her jaw relaxed, "You'll teach me how to use it so I won't black out again?"

"We will." Leroy gave a gentle smile.

It was still hard to believe that all of this was true, that there were beings who fought demons, that there were humans that fought with them against their common enemy.

That Anna was one of those beings even though she had lived as a human her entire life.

"How did you end up in the asylum anyway?" The red haired girl asked.

Anna swallowed, she knew this would come. "I-I had visions of the..." She didn't know why, but she felt if she told them that she had seen Lucifer, it would cause problems so she settled for his followers instead. "Demons." Her voice shook at the word. "My parents caught on and got worried."

They didn't look at her like she was crazy, her visions didn't seem like a big deal to them... although she had left a lot out.

"We're built to fight demons, it's only right that you would dream of them." The red haired girl smiled gently. "And when it comes to learning how to control your power...You'll learn a lot from us." She motioned to everyone until her eyes landed on Leroy. "But I don't know about Leroy." She gave him a devious grin.

"I'm Ida by the way." She turned back to Anna and Anna noticed that she had calmed after hearing her story, she seemed to trust her words.

"You're all evil." Leroy blushed as he laughed and for the first time other than when she was with Mary, Anna smiled.

She was leaning against a tree, her head resting against the bark and she watched as the girls sat and chatted in their casual dresses with the men in their slacks. She was filled with envy at the sight of the men in their attire since she was still clad in her white asylum dress.

They all munched on their pieces of chicken and as she watched she found herself wanting to go back home but she knew she could never go back.

She would never see her parents nor the farm ever again.

"Are you hungry?" A voice came from beside her and she found Samuel standing over her, a piece of chicken in each hand.

She found herself looking into his dark eyes before answering.

"I-I'm ok." She assured him but her stomach betrayed her and a growl filled his ears and he smiled at how red her face got.

"We have good hearing so it's easy to tell that you are." He sat beside her and handed her a piece of chicken as he did so. "It's not much but we have to take what we can."

"It's better than cold chicken soup." She sighed as she brought the piece of chicken to her mouth and it watered with excitement before she took a bite.

It was true that it wasn't much, but Anna relished in the taste of something warm and fresh.

"Thank you." She smiled softly after she swallowed.

He returned her smile then brought his attention to the fire. "I suppose I should properly introduce myself," he said as he watched the fire dance and Anna found herself mesmerized at how well he spoke. "I'm Samuel." He turned to her again and she nodded as if she was greeting him. "Anna."

"It's nice to meet you, Anna." He reached a hand towards her and she nervously took it. "…You as well."

"I'm sorry about what happened to you." He said softly as they let go of each others hands and Anna shook her head as she thought of what had happened to her in the months that she had been locked in the asylum. The abuse, the torture, the harsh conditions. She thought of what happened earlier…what happened to Mary.

Her fault.

In an effort to change the subject, she met Samuel's eyes. "I'm sorry about your parents."

"It happened years ago," He shrugged. "I still feel the pain but it somewhat dulled over the years."

"That sounds good." She compared his pain to her's and hoped that her's would dull as well, but as she thought of what she had just said, of how she sounded, her eyes widened. "I didn't-"

"I know what you meant." He assured with a smile.

"You…talk so nice." She complimented and she wondered if it was normal to compliment someone for such a thing. Mary had taught her how to speak better but Samuel was on another level. "You must have gone to a nice school."

"I did." His shoulder brushed hers as he leaned further into the tree."Even with my parents being gargoyles, they still posed as humans." His eyes found the fire again and Anna could see the flames dancing in his dark orbs. "My

father was a lawyer so naturally he made enough money to send me to a good school." He smiled as if he was remembering his old man, "He wanted a somewhat normal life for me, he didn't want me to fight demons."

"I learned how to speak better from a friend in the asylum..." Anna swallowed the lump in her throat. She felt like she could talk to Samuel and perhaps if she did talk about what had happened, she would feel better. "She died today."

"I'm sorry." He said gently and as Anna lifted her eyes, she found that his were on her again. "No one should have to go through what you have."

She closed her eyes, "It doesn't seem real...especially that I'm a creature made to fight demons..." She chuckled at how stupid it sounded. "I was only a farmer four months ago."

"It's real sadly," Samuel said with a hitch in his tone. "I know personally since my parents were killed by one and I've been fighting them with my fellow gargoyles ever since." He looked around at his comrades as they chatted and ate during their moment of peace.

"What are they like?" Anna asked softly, she had never felt this kind of fear before, the fear of the unknown.

Samuel met her eyes and for the first time, they weren't gentle, they were strong.

"They're terrifying." He said simply and when he realized that he was scaring her, he continued with a softer look. "But that's the reason why we're here, to stop them."

Anna narrowed her eyes as she thought of the creatures, maybe this was her calling. Everything that had happened to her in the past four months had led her to this point and although it still felt so unreal, she would accept her fate and would fight with the other gargoyles.

Running away wasn't an option, it was in her genetic code to fight the demons.

Fate brought the gargoyles and the demons together, they were two sides of a coin.

Different but the same.

In the month that she had been with the gargoyles, Anna had learned how to fight as one but hadn't gone out on any of the fights that the other gargoyles had with the demons.

Some would return bloody while others didn't return at all.

Leroy came back from this run with blisters trailing up his arm and since he had explained to Anna awhile ago of what would happen if she was touched by demon blood, she knew exactly what had happened.

The stuff was toxic, it would dissolve a human's skin like an acid and while it had the same effect on the gargoyles, it wasn't as fatal. That's if they washed it off quick enough.

Samuel's clothes were torn and underneath the rip in his white shirt was a claw mark that had already began to heal. Anna ran to him and met his eyes, they were the same height so it was easy to do.

"What happened?" She asked shakily as she pressed her hand to his injured chest.

The two got on well and while Anna would worry about the others, she would think constantly of Samuel's gentle eyes and that he was out there fighting his parents killers.

"It was Astaroth's demons." Leroy answered and both she and Samuel turned to him as Ida helped him stay upright as he winced from the pain in his arm. "He's proving himself to be quite the problem so we'll need all the help we can get to stop him."

"Do you know what that means?" Ida nodded to Anna and Anna's face lit up.

She would finally be able to test her abilities.

"Are you ok?" Anna asked for what felt like the hundredth time as she handed Samuel a fresh shirt.

He was sitting against a tree with his eyes closed and at the sound of her voice, his eyes opened.

"I'm fine, sweet Anna." He assured her but she could hear the strain in his voice. "You're just worried that I'll rip all of my clothes and you won't have anything to wear."

She had been wearing his clothes ever since he had heard about her dismay at wearing dresses. His clothes fit her well due to them being the same height but they were rather loose due to the fact that they were made for a male while she was indeed not.

"You know that's not it." She shook her head but smiled as he grinned.

"I guess It'll be my turn to worry soon." He dropped his gaze to Leroy as Ida tended to the wounds on his arm. "Maybe I'll finally get to see what color eyes you have."

Anna's eye color had yet to show itself even during her training, the odd pressure that she had felt in them hadn't returned since she had escaped from the asylum.

The other gargoyles had taught her how there were two eye colors that a gargoyle could get: Black or white. They told her how black was the average color while white was harder to come by, both colors were powerful but having white eyes made the gargoyle more of a loose canon and they weren't sure why.

None of the fifteen that remained since Anna's arrival in the group had white eyes nor did the one's that had died.

"I'm sure they'll be the same as yours." She said matter of factly, there was no way she was going to have a color that was so rare.

"We'll see, won't we?" Samuel smiled as he pulled off his ripped shirt and replaced it with the new one. Luckily his wound had healed and it didn't leave any blood on his fresh shirt.

Anna acted like she was ready but she could feel her nerves tingle at the prospect of fighting the demons. She had trained with the other gargoyles everyday since she had joined them, she had learned how to use her powers to an extent, but was she ready to fight a demon? Was she strong enough?

Samuel watched her nervous expression with an even one, his dark eyes filled with both curiosity and wonder.

A few days had passed since the others came back wounded and they had remained in the woods that they had settled in since their last bout with the demons.

Anna was plucking the feathers off a chicken for their meal that night, it's reddish brown feathers falling to her feet. Samuel was off gathering twigs for the fire and when he returned, he dropped them in front of her, the clatter making her look up with a brow in the air. "What is it?"

"They're coming back." His head turned to the woods to Anna's right, his dark eyes narrowed.

She listened in and she could hear the snaps of breaking twigs and the rustle of leaves as the others made their way back. They had left Anna, Samuel, and a few others behind as they went to town to gather more information on the demon named Astaroth.

"He's here." Leroy said as they entered the clearing ten minutes later with Ida and the others behind him. "He's smells different from the other demons… he's gotta be a top ranked one."

"Where is he?" Samuel stood straight as Anna settled beside him.

The look on Leroys face confused them, he looked like he was too nervous to answer. "He owns a saloon in town… we tracked his scent to the place and sure enough he was sitting in the corner dealing cards for poker." He spoke as if he was having a hard time believing it even though he had seen it with his own eyes. "He's been doing all kinds of illegal stuff in there: Booze, gambling, and whores."

Anna wondered what a demon would get out of such things but even more, she wondered what the demon looked like. The others had told her that the demons had 'fooling forms' so they could play with the humans but she still wondered what that entailed.

It looked like she would find out soon.

She wondered if she'd be able to pick up on the smell of the demon like the others could, wondered if she could be of any help.

"He had one of his patrons handing these out for an event tonight." Leroy handed Samuel a small piece of paper with fancy hand writing.

Anna looked at the fancy swirls as Samuel read the invitation and the others came up behind them to get a look as well. Samuel handed it to Anna and she awkwardly took it, she couldn't bring herself to say that she didn't know how to read. Her eyes followed the loops and swirls in the writing but she couldn't understand a word.

"Were you noticed?" A man named Henry asked directly behind her and the group in front of them shook their heads.

"He was too focused on his work." The bald headed man whose name was Arry replied. "And we made sure to disguise ourselves with clothes the humans wore."

Anna took in their outfits that they hadn't left in. "Stole em off a clothes line?"

"Yep." Leroy flashed her a grin and a wink.

"And we got more." Ida who they wondered why had a heap of clothes in her hands, threw the pile in front of them and Samuel handed them to the others until he got to a frilly dress and handed it to Anna.

The fabric was silk and the color was dark blue with floral designs.

She slid the smooth seam over her fingers and she met Ida's eyes who gave her a determined look.

"It's your time to shine."

Anna sat with her frilly dress on her lap and the invitation between her fingers, she pressed her head against the tree she was sitting against as she tried to sound out the words but failed.

Her head began to ache so she gave up and as she lifted her head, she found Samuel making his way to her. He was already dressed in a fresh pair of black slacks, suspenders, and a white long sleeved buttoned up shirt.

He kneeled in front of her and took the paper from her hand, "This thing sure has you intrigued." He chuckled. "You've been looking at it for hours."

She gulped and his face fell. "What is it?"

"I-" her heart raced and she hoped that he couldn't hear it but that was wishful thinking.

You couldn't hide anything when you were in the company of gargoyles.

"I…don't know…" She exhaled sharply as her face turned red with embarrassment. "I… don't know how to read."

She flinched like she was about to be hit but instead, she was met with a gentle look, his dark eyes softer than usual.

"A lot of people don't know how to read." He assured her with a smile that matched his eyes. "It's not something to be shy over."

She gave an awkward smile as relief filled her.

"You know what?" He sat down beside her and she watched as he did. "I can teach you."

Anna couldn't hide the delight on her face as she nodded enthusiastically.

She could finally learn, she could pick up a book and read and what's more, she could understand a simple invitation.

And so they spent the rest of their time until their departure for the town going through the words on the letter and before long, Anna had managed to read the first sentence.

She found that learning and being by Samuel's side had calmed her nerves of the impending fight but alas, the time came and she found herself dressed in her frilly dress.

The other gargoyles looked her up and down as if she was an intruder.

"I don't think this is going to work." She exclaimed as she pulled the bottom of the fabric up, she had left her slacks on but they were well hidden by the dress. "I don't look like a woman aside from the dress."

Ida and a few of the other girls looked offended since they had helped her clean up to look the role.

"You do look a woman." Samuel who had pulled on a black jacket moved a strand of her now shoulder length hair out of her eyes."You're actually too good for the roll."

She fought to hide her blush but it didn't take much as she found herself distracted by her nerves.

She looked down to the leaves at her feet and thought of the plan they had put together: Anna and the other girls were going to be the 'damsels' while the men would keep watch incase Astaroth tried anything. When the time was right, they would try to take the demon down.

She wouldn't allow herself to show fear, Samuel had told her that the demons thrived off the emotion.

Her visions of the devil had diminished since she found the reason for her existence, her purpose was set and she was ready.

Don't fear, keep moving forward.

The men remained back but kept their eyes on the girls as they took in the saloon named 'The Hierarchy'. Anna couldn't understand or much less read the word hours before until Samuel had explained it to her: The name was used to describe a system that showed power amongst levels. Anna wondered why the demon would name his saloon such a thing.

She inhaled sharply as she prepared to meet her very first demon.

The girls stepped inside and were met with music played by an older man in the corner, his banjo resting against his legs and his long calloused fingers pulling at the strings.

A chill went up Anna's spine and as she turned from the man, a strange smell filled her nose.

"It's him." Ida whispered and Anna found a short man sitting at the end of the bar with cards in his hands and a woman on his lap. Anna blinked through the hazy light as she took in his graying hair and his wrinkled skin and she found herself wondering if he was truly a demon but her mind screamed that he was.

The demon lifted his dull eyes and Anna quickly looked away and in doing so, she missed the light in his eyes as he saw her.

"Hey fella." Ida swept her red hair behind her shoulders as she leaned on the bar, the top of her breasts on show to distract the bartender.

The young man who had a huge selection of brew as his background grinned as his eyes wandered to where Ida wanted them to be. "Hi pretty lady."

The girls had agreed to stay together but Anna found herself drifting to the middle of the dance floor, leaving her allies to their flirting as more men joined in who obviously thought the girls were here for their 'shifts'.

The old building was made completely of wood and smelled of both cigarettes and booze, the only thing that distracted her from the smell's was the demon standing at the other end of the floor, his dark eyes on her as she took in the air around him.

"Hello, sweet." He drawled as he glided over to her and Anna could see the woman he had left behind looking infuriated.

She found it laughable that he would even think that posing as an older man would give him the chance with a younger girl. Nonetheless, she put a fake smile on and for good measure, she curtsied.

"Hello." She replied in a sweet voice.

Acting wasn't her forte. It was obvious that he knew what she was and that she was aware of what he wasn't. The two looked into each others eyes and Anna didn't feel any fear, she felt like she was right where she belonged.

"You're new around here, aren't you?" He asked softly and she nodded with a grin. "Sure am."

His eyes narrowed, "You and your people don't know what your messing with girl."

For the first time, Anna's eyes left the demon and they met the people inside.

There wasn't enough people in the saloon for this to be a real party, especially this time of night when the party should have been at it's rowdiest.

She inhaled sharply and the smell of the demon filled her entire being, it was sweet smelling but had a tinge of rot. It was all a ploy to get the gargoyles there, there was no party nor were there any humans in the old building, only the opposing creatures.

The demons had the same idea as the gargoyles: To hide their scents with human clothing and for good measure, they masked in the sweet scent of the booze and cigarettes. Anna could smell them now, the humans scents were long gone and not even the booze could hide the demons distinct scent.

The music came to a sudden end.

"It's a trap!" Anna screamed but Astaroth wrapped his arms around her and she struggled against his short stature.

The girls turned to her but the bartender who was really a demon grabbed ahold of Ida by her long hair and yanked her behind the bar.

"Move and I'll kill her." His eyes were on the entryway and Anna moved her own to find Samuel and the rest at the wide doorway with nervous looks on their faces. Samuel stood front and center, his eyes on Anna.

Astaroth's foul breath was hitting the back of Anna's neck and she wanted so badly to swat him away.

Did she even have the strength to do so?

"We're looking for someone who may be amongst you," The demon began with a smile. "You may not know yourselves who this person is but we'll surely find out tonight."

"What are you talking about?" Leroy's voice shook as he kept his pitch black eyes on Ida.

"Show me your eyes." The demon demanded but the gargoyles looked on with confusion instead of doing what they were told.

"Don't test me-" The demon sharpened his nails and brought them to

Anna's throat as the demon who held onto Ida did the same. "Both of these girls will die."

Ida flinched while Anna narrowed her eyes as Astaroth's nails threatened to cut her jugular.

The gargoyles did what they were told and the demons were met with pitch black eyes.

"You too, girls." Astaroth demanded of Ida and Anna after he took in the other gargoyles eyes.

Ida changed hers and the demon looked almost let down to see the normal color until he leaned forward to see Anna's still hazel eyes with the gray ring. "What did I say?" He growled but she shook her head as a cold chill went up her spine. "I can't…" Her voice drifted. "I-I don't know how…"

She rolled her eyes to Samuel who looked like he was about to attack the demon, his teeth pressed tightly together and his dark eyes narrowed.

"You don't?" The demon asked softly as he leaned his face into her neck and took in her scent."What kind of gargoyle doesn't know how to change their eyes? Maybe you need something to rouse them on."

He brought his dark eyes to the demon that was holding Ida and he nodded.

On cue the demon smashed Ida's head on the bar, her red hair flying around her along with drops of blood. As she tried fighting back, the demon grabbed her neck and pulled back to smash her head again, the bar breaking under her skull and blood poured from her mouth as the demon pulled her up.

The demon's dark hair and pale skin had her blood splattered over them and he peaked his tongue out and licked it.

"NO!" Leroy began to run to her but the demon who had been playing the banjo appeared in front of him.

Anna fought to break free but Astaroth was too strong for her so she was forced to watch as the banjo demon flung Leroy back and Samuel caught him before he was thrown into the rest of the gargoyles.

"Eyes now or the girl dies." Astaroth whispered in Anna's ear and she whimpered. "I can't!"

"That's too bad…" The demons voice drifted. "I guess I'll have to kill them all."

His arms disappeared from around her and he was in front of Samuel who swung at the demon with his claws out but the demon was quicker and grabbed ahold of his throat. He threw him to the ground while the banjo demon kept the other gargoyles at bay.

The other demons that had posed as bar goers simply watched the show with grins on their pale faces.

"No!" Anna screamed as her eyes flew between Ida who had been knocked out, her body laying against the now broken bar then to Samuel as he struggled against Astaroth on the ground.

"No..." Her voice drifted as her mind went to Mary, how she had saved her from Joseph, had sacrificed herself for her.

The pressure built in her eyes again and she held onto her sanity this time and allowed the power to course through her. The other gargoyles found her eyes and they almost fell back with shock as they took in not only an ink filled eye but another that was as white as snow.

"Demon." She said in a voice that sounded nothing of her own, it was strong.

Astaroth stopped his assault on Samuel to look at her, his eyes wide as he met hers.

The power told her what to do, told her go for the demon, it begged her to do so.

She complied.

She was in front of him now, her hand in his gray hair and his demons came to help him but without even breaking a sweat, she reached for their chests as she let go of Astaroth's hair and pulled their hearts out.

The other gargoyles had told her the only way a demon could truly be killed was by destroying their heart's. If the heart remained whole, the demon could come back even stronger than before.

But Anna didn't think of the others directions now, she was relying completely on instinct.

She crushed their hearts and their tar-like blood poured from her hands, the sting was excruciating and she quickly wiped it on the hem of her dress before it could do any real damage. The blood had already started to eat at the top layer of her skin.

As she lifted her eyes from the demons who were now ash at her feet, she looked into Astaroth's eyes.

"You're the one..." He managed to say before she reached into his chest like she had with the others and destroyed his heart.

Only she didn't do it right, we know that. His heart was already taken by the succubus, he had sacrificed his soul to the Astaroth we know and she took his heart before Anna could take it for herself.

A destroyed heart meant nothing in this case, the power of the succubus had already taken it's toll.

As the demon began to turn to ash, his eyes flashed over Anna's shoulder to Samuel but he quickly brought them back to her and smiled.

His body fell to her feet but unlike the other demons who had turned to ash and remained that way, he disappeared completely as wherever the succubus was now, she took him completely in and she became the fiery female demon that we knew as Astaroth.

Behind Anna stood the rest of the gargoyles, their eyes wide as they tried to come to terms with what had just happened. Leroy had already grabbed Ida who was beginning to wake up, her tired eyes finding Anna's strong form.

Samuel who stood only inches from Anna grinned as a light gleamed in his dark eyes.

Chapter 65

Anna and Lucifer

Things had changed since what happened at Astaroth's saloon. The gargoyles had been in shock about what had happened especially with Anna who not only had black or white eyes but both. They didn't question her on how it was possible, she was as clueless as they were. She wondered why she had mismatched eyes while the others had two of the same color. It didn't matter after a few days anyway, they were all alive and they had healed from the demons attacks.

She thought of the instincts that ran through her as she fought the demons, how it came to her like she had done it a hundred times before.

It was like she was an animal with the need to feed, drink, and kill.

It all came naturally.

Her friends acted different in her company now but not in a bad way, they didn't look down on her, they looked at her as if she was a God. She led them on their fights against the demons now, they won more often than not since she had discovered her power.

She hated that they saw her as this all powerful being, she was still the same old Anna.

Samuel was the only one who didn't treat her differently and she had solace in that.

They sat away from the others as they winded down for the night and they could hear the snores of their comrades. Anna had her head resting on Samuel's shoulder and she focused on the feeling of it moving up and down as he breathed. He had continued to teach her how to read in the days since the saloon and she had managed to learn how to read a little of the newspaper they had taken from the town they had moved to.

She read what she could but Samuel had to read the rest of it out loud to her. It was written that Abraham Lincoln, a man that had been a lawyer was in the running to win the presidential election against three other contenders. His election would spark change since he wanted to abolish slavery and the southerners feared the end of their way of life.

Anna wanted the end of such an evil thing and welcomed Abraham's election.

"There's going to be a war." Samuel had said after reading it to her and she couldn't tell what his even expression meant.

Now she thought of the prospect of the war that would surely come. It wouldn't just be the humans, the gargoyles and the demons would surely fight amongst the strife and chaos that war casted upon them.

Humans were monsters, demons were monsters, and gargoyles were too.

Was Anna a monster? She had killed Joseph and more demons than she could count. All of them were monsters in their own way but she had killed them all the same.

"What are you thinking about?" Samuel asked softly and brought her back to reality.

"Everything." She answered with a hoarse voice.

He leaned his head against the tree they were sitting against as he looked up to the moon whose light was shining though the leaves. The leaves were already beginning to fall again and orange, red, and brown would soon cover the ground and not too long after winter would be upon them.

"Me too." His voice drifted.

"...Do you ever think you're a monster?" She asked suddenly and he turned to her with confused eyes.

"Anyone can be a monster but we're a different kind of monster, we can grow claws, horns, fangs, and our eyes change color." She lowered her gaze. "I blacked out and killed someone without a second thought and I haven't felt bad for doing it."

Samuel dropped his eyes to her twisted fingers, "Sometimes I think of how things could have been for me if I was more of a monster..." She could hear the sadness in his voice and her frown deepened. "If I was stronger, my parents would still be alive...If I had been a monster."

"I was a monster but my friend still died." Anna's voice shook as Samuel's eyes met hers and she found that they were darker than usual while her's had turned completely gray.

It was random but the change had happened after their fight at the saloon and none of the others knew what it meant.

Their eyes remained locked for a moment and they sat in silence.

Anna would have been lying to herself if she said that they didn't have a connection, it was the first time she had ever felt this way towards a man.

"I guess we're all monsters…" He whispered as he leaned closer to her and his warm breath hit her face. "No matter what form we take: human, gargoyle, or demon."

"And monsters we'll always be." Anna leaned her forehead against his and took in his scent that smelled of the woods surrounding them.

Their eyes closed as their lips touched, Samuel's hands going to her hair as he pulled her closer while her own twisted in his shirt.

Anna pulled herself up and straddled his waist as his hands wandered first to her breasts then to the buttons between them, his shaking fingers pulling them away from the fabric until her shirt fell from her shoulders.

Anna quickly unbuttoned his shirt as he worked his fingers over the goosebumps on her chest. She pulled his shirt from his shoulders and her hands fell to his neck then down his toned chest. He pulled her closer to deepen their kiss and their hands wandered to their slacks.

Samuel wrapped his arms around her back, his lips finding her neck as he laid her down on the leaves.

He groaned along with her until he pulled his slacks the rest of the way down. Anna didn't bother to look, she kept her eyes on his dark ones as he kept his on her gray. She wiggled her legs so her slacks fell from her ankles and Samuel lowered himself down, their lips connecting again.

Allies.

friends.

Lovers.

And enemies.

Something was wrong, the town they had moved to next turned to disarray as soon as they got there. Leroy expected the cause to be the demons that they were looking for since they could influence the humans feelings.

In the days since their coming together, Anna and Samuel had spent more time as just the two of them, going to town alone and wandering off into the woods as the others slept.

The two walked through the busy streets of the town, watching the bar goers and shoppers as they laughed and drank. Anna felt relieved that the humans were starting to act normal again, she had seen so many fights and crime in the past few days that it made her long to go home to her parents where things were a little more sane. She wondered if they would approve of Samuel, she was sure they would since he was kind and proper.

But that would never happen.

She stopped as she realized that he wasn't beside her anymore and she turned to find his dark eyes staring off in the distance, his lips twitching.

"Samuel?" She walked back to him and placed her hand in his. "What is it?"

"Hurry! We're gonna miss it!" A woman yelled and the two quickly turned to a crowd blocking the horse drawn carriages as they ran in the middle of the road.

Anna and Samuel met each others eyes as they were pushed through the crowd and they found themselves going to the place the others were headed to.

Anna's heart thumped as she came upon what all the commotion was about: There were gallows set up in the middle of the towns square, in them were five men, begging and pleading for their lives.

"I didn't do it!" A pale faced man cried, his blue eyes bloodshot. "Please!"

Anna felt Samuel stop behind her but she only had eyes for the men with the ropes fastened around their necks.

A woman's too loud whispers filled her ears from beside her. "They murdered that family that lived in that small hut down the way." She told her friend as they looked anxiously up at the men and her friend scoffed. "Serves them right then."

Anna's eyes widened as a man dressed in a black suit walked to the gallows and stopped where a long rope that held the panels in place under the mens feet was tied. One pull and the floor that kept them from having their air cut off would be gone.

Death waited for his offerings, the men's souls were so close to being his.

Anna's ears filled with the begging of the men along with the whispers and jeers of the crowd and she couldn't breath as she saw the glee in the executioners eyes.

It was too late by the time she noticed the demons influence over the man and without even giving the men their final word's, he pulled the rope and the panels fell from under their feet.

Their ropes tightened around their necks, suffocating them while one died right away as his neck snapped from the force of the fall. Anna could see the lights leave their eyes as they struggled for breath until their bodies fell limp.

She could feel the energy flowing through the crowd but the biggest chill came from directly behind her. She turned her head to find Samuel, his black wavy hair had fallen into his dark eyes and on his lips was a malicious grin.

"S-Samuel?" She stammered and as soon as he heard her voice, his smile was gone and his eyes were on her.

"We need to tell the others." He turned without another look back as he pushed through the crowd and Anna followed close behind with fear in her heart.

After finding out what had happened from Samuel and Anna, Leroy and the rest of the gargoyles knew they had to get to the bottom of the towns demon problem.

There didn't need to be anymore deaths due to the demons influence and although they knew it wouldn't be easy to stop them, they figured since they had Anna by their side they would be able to handle it.

She didn't like the fact that her mismatched eyes had spread amongst the gargoyles, before long the news would spread to the Venandi if it hadn't already. She wondered why Astaroth had wanted to see their eyes and she remembered his shock as he saw her's and that he had said that it was 'her'.

What she wanted to know the most was why Samuel found the death of innocent men so entertaining.

She looked at him now, her eyes rolled to the corner as she kept her head forward and she watched him walk beside her. His expression was even but something was off.

The town was empty due to the fact that everyone had gone to sleep but the shadows moved in way's she had never seen before. They swirled and swam where the light touched.

They made it to the square where the executions took place and with Leroy and Ida in the lead, they looked upon the now empty gallows. Anna placed her hand on the wood and she found drops of blood that had slipped from the men's nostrils and mouths.

"They're here." Leroy said with a rough tone and Anna looked up to find them looking around at the empty spaces around them. Samuel had his eyes on his feet, his hair covering them while his mouth was set in a thin line.

Anna rolled her eyes to the sky as a deep voice filled the air, "Only I am here."

She dropped her gaze in time to see an older looking man in a monks robe approaching them, his hair silver and his beard the same color, they both reached his waist.

His eyes glowed an intense red against the darkness, "I expected there to be more souls to take." His voice boomed as he stepped closer.

"Who are you?" Leroy stepped in front of the rest of the gargoyles as if guarding them.

"Aamon, the killer of God's warriors."

The demon stopped a few feet away from them and his eyes flashed to Samuel who had yet to look up from his feet. Anna watched with confusion and with her brows furrowed, she took a step closer to the demon and his eyes found her's.

"Weak." He said simply as he brought his attention back the others. "I've fought many gargoyles in my existence and I can tell I will be disappointed with you."

The gargoyles began their attack but Aamon was far too powerful for them, this demon was different than the rest. He swatted the gargoyles away like flies while zombified creatures manifested around him, their eyes the same color as the gargoyles.

"This-" The demon rolled his tongue. "Is your fate."

The undead gargoyles started towards them, their sharp teeth bared and their nails ready to slash.

Anna's eyes twitched as Aamon made his way to Samuel who with everything going on around him, still hadn't moved an inch.

"Samuel!" She screamed to wake him up but he remained still until the demon was in front of him and his claws pierced his chest.

"No!" Anna's scream was blood curdling as tears filled her changing eyes.

"There she is." Aamon cocked his head as he took her in, his hand wrapping around Leroy's neck as the gargoyle went for him with rage filling his face. Leroy's strong expression was replaced with shock for only a second before the demon snapped his neck and he fell to the ground with a thud.

Ida's screams filled the air as she saw him fall and with being distracted by her lovers death, one of the undead gargoyles shoved it's claws through her back and blood poured from her mouth.

Through the shock of seeing her friends and lover being killed along with some of the gargoyles running away from the fight. Anna gritted her teeth as her power surged through her again and with her eyes switching between Ida, Leroy, and Samuel, she stepped through the fighting gargoyles to the demon who looked at her with an uninterested expression.

"This fight won't end the same way it did with Astaroth girl." He warned her. "He was weak."

A growl crawled up her throat and the demon smiled as he moved so fast that she had no time to dodge the attack to her leg and it broke. Her scarred hand from the last time she had touched demon blood swung at him with her claws out but she only made it inches from slashing open his chest.

"You don't know how to use your power." He exclaimed as he grabbed her wrist and broke it. "Instinct alone cannot save you nor your friends."

She fell to the ground beside Samuel and she reached for him with her uninjured hand and it shook as her fingers found his black hair.

She had lost someone she loved yet again and it had started with Mary.

Tears streamed from her mismatched eyes and as her bones popped back into place, she got to her feet again and faced the demon.

His red eyes laid on her and they filled with intrigue, "You and I are more connected than you know, we are both at the mercy of one being."

She didn't let the confusion at his words take over as she swung at the demon again and this time, as he attacked her, she dodged and it seemed she had the upper hand until she found herself distracted by an intense energy behind her.

The demons eyes looked past her and the living gargoyles looked on with shock filling their eyes. The undead gargoyles went back to nothing as the demon coaxed them away.

Anna turned and her heart practically stopped as Samuel stood where he had fallen, his wound healed and the same smile that she had seen earlier on his face. He licked his sharp teeth as his eyes lit up at the look on Anna's face.

"Aren't you happy I'm alive?" He chuckled. "My sweet Anna."

Her comrades fell to the ground while she and Aamon remained standing. They struggled to get up but the more they tried, the harder it became for them to breath. Within seconds, gravity crushed them and they fell limp, their blank eyes resting on Anna as she looked on with shock and grief.

"Leave us." Samuel demanded and without a word, Aamon bowed his head as he turned to walk away.

Anna watched the demon as he stepped away but she quickly turned to Samuel who was watching her with his smile still etched on his face.

"...You're not Samuel." Her voice shook along with the rest of her and his smile widened at her fear. "I don't think you ever were...it was all fake... wasn't it?"

She had been comrades and friends with Samuel for months, had fallen for him and now his entire demeanor had changed.

"My sweet Anna, I'm sure you know already." Even his voice had changed. "I'm the reason you're here, I'm the reason why you've lived your worthless life." His sharp teeth hung over his lips as his smile extended into his cheeks. "I'm the devil, although I do prefer being called Lucifer."

Anna looked on at the being that she had dreams of, the warnings were there all along.

Why did he single her out? How was any of this possible?

An intense feeling washed over her and she knew he was telling the truth. Lucifer had hidden who he truly was for years as he worked with the gargoyles but now realization hit Anna full force.

Her legs buckled but not from the shock but from the same power Lucifer had used on the others. She laid completely on the ground as she fought against his gravity, the heat making it hard to breath.

"I fooled you." He said in a silky voice as he stepped towards her. "That was the plan from the start but I didn't know how far it'd go…" He snickered as Anna's face twisted in disgust.

"You bastard…" She managed to choke out and Lucifer cocked his head. "What's the matter? You clearly enjoyed it."

Tears filled her eyes, "Why?"

"Why?" He mocked her as he kneeled in front of her and lifted her chin with his index finger. "Do you know how many holy beings God has sent down to stop me?" He sniggered. "None of them could stop me… no one aside from God himself could ever wish to but he was weak and showed me mercy instead of ending me." His eyes narrowed as they met Anna's. "He sent me here to live out eternity for my greed but didn't expect me to use it to my advantage."

He leaned closer until their faces were only inches apart. "I heard rumors that God sent down a warrior strong enough to beat me and since I knew the gargoyles were already his warriors, I knew the being would be amongst them." He leaned into her ear and whispered. "I hung around the gargoyles for years until you came along, I had my suspicions but many gargoyles had joined and I learned to keep my expectations low…that was until I met you and I finally saw your eye color." He pulled away and made sure their eyes met. "You are God's promised warrior."

Gravity eased as he got up and Anna gasped at the release and watched as he stepped backwards over Leroy's body. "But I thought you would be so much more, you have been the most entertaining but I'm still a little disappointed."

Anna shakily got to her feet as she watched him place his boot on Leroy's head. "You could have saved them.. perhaps you didn't want to."

"It's not over yet…" She couldn't hide the fear in her voice.

"No…" He smirked. "It's not."

He was behind her in a flash and he grabbed her shoulder length hair as he leaned into her neck.

"But it is for you."

As he pushed her forward, he kicked in her knee and she screeched from the pain. She fell roughly to the ground, gasps of pain pouring from her mouth. This break was far worse than Aamon's, it completely shattered her knee.

She twisted herself around and she froze as she took in Lucifer's eyes: They were red like the other demons but a flame danced in the middle.

"You failed." He said roughly as she began to crawl away until her back met with the gallows.

She had nowhere left to go.

She narrowed her tear filled eyes and her teeth locked against each other as his words cut her like a knife.

Lucifer stopped in front of her, his body still disguised as the man she loved. He took in her Valiant expression and it seemed to heighten his glee.

"Until next time, My sweet Anna." He reached forward so fast that she didn't have time to stop him, his hand reaching into her chest and her eyes widened with both pain and shock.

Blood poured from her mouth as her vision blurred and she could see the outline of Lucifer as he smiled down at her with her heart in his hand.

His cackle filled her ears as her body shut down, she couldn't feel the pain anymore but she could still feel the regret from her failure. As she died, her body began to rot away until she was dust at Lucifer's feet.

"See you in the next life." He jeered as he licked her heart before the organ turned to dust as well.

Maya stood in her void with tears streaming down her pale cheeks, her first lives memories leaving her more empty than before.

She fell to her knees as a sob escaped her throat, why would she get her memories back now? She had failed again… She had failed three times…She was made to fail.

She was deceived and played as if she was nothing more than a toy.

"I failed!" She screamed into the void again and this time, she reached for the voice.

"You haven't." It repeated and where her hand rested a ball of light appeared in her palm.

She watched as it extended around her and she took in her new limbo: There were hints of blue and purple as if she was kneeling in a brightened galaxy. There was no darkness here, only brilliant light.

In front of her stood a man made of pure light, he was even brighter than the space around him.

With her memories back from her past life and her prophetic dreams still fresh in her mind, she knew who this being was without explanation:

God.

Chapter 66

God

His shining form stood over her and although her eyes shouldn't have been able to take the glare, she looked on with ease. He was in the shape of a man but his body was made of pure light and on his face she could make out the indent of his eyes, nose, and mouth.

Her eyes drifted down his front as she noticed there was a blur where his right hand should have been while his left was still intact. She got to her feet, his light pulling her to meet him, and she looked into his brilliant face.

"Hello, Anna." His voice was smooth unlike Lucifer's silky tone and it echoed through the light.

It was his voice that she had heard, the one that had said that she wouldn't fail.

At the mention of her first lives name, she looked down to find herself dressed in her old clothes, the one's Samuel had loaned to her. Her white shirt was covered in dirt and her black slacks in dust, her hair falling to her shoulders. She furrowed her brows as she met the indents that were God's eyes.

"I would say this isn't real but I know better." She chuckled softly to herself, not because anything about the situation was funny, but because of the irony of it all.

With all of her failures, it was only right that her maker would come to take her soul for good.

She didn't need to see his eyes to know that he was looking at her, at the creature he had made to defeat Lucifer but had failed not once but three times.

"You have a lot to learn." He said suddenly and she chewed her lip.

"What could I learn that could possibly change everything I've done?"

"You could learn the reason behind your existence." He pointed to her chest and she looked down to find a hole in her shirt and a gaping hole where her heart should've been.

"To defeat Lucifer?" She asked shakily as she looked away from her fatal wound.

God shook his head, "There is so much more to it than that." He dropped his hand and a chill ran down her spine although his presence had filled her with so much warmth. "But to explain what your destiny truly is, I must start with the story of two brothers, of Lucifer and I."

She inclined her head and looked into the never ending ceiling, the blueish swirls had grown brighter as the purple danced along with them. As She brought her gaze back to God, she nodded for him to start.

"I am light while Lucifer is darkness, we have no physical forms… only what we choose to manifest."

Maya watched as his mouth opened and the words poured out as he spoke. She thought of the images people would use to show what God looked like: A pale skinned man with a beard and shoulder length hair.

What a lie.

"But light doesn't always mean good while darkness doesn't always mean evil," His sweet voice filled her ears and she only had eyes for him. "Lucifer and I were comrades, brothers, and friends, but we were two halves of a stone… we both wanted power and we both got it. My brother began to be seduced by his strength… and so was I." His gentle voice echoed through the light as Maya watched him speak. "But what we choose to do with that strength is what truly defines us."

"Then I'm a monster through and through." Maya swallowed as her nonexistent heart thumped. "I chose violence, death, and misery."

"You are a monster." He agreed. "But you've accepted that, haven't you?"

"I have." her voice drifted. "But I'm not the monster I used to be." Her gray eyes met his clear, "And you're a monster in your own right for making

such a failure."

"I suppose so." He leaned his head further down to meet her eyes since he stood a head taller than her and he continued with his story. "Lucifer used his power to be a tyrant, he wanted more strength."

His change in subject threw her off but she listened all the same.

"He wanted my position, he wanted to be the leader of all the angels and to bring his power to the world to make it's creatures his play things." She could hear the edge in his voice as he paused. "Instead of killing him, I sent him to earth to live with the first humans so he could understand his misdoings. I thought he could come to accept them, to even cherish them, but it didn't work. He used my pity to his advantage and caused the fall of mankind when he tempted Eve."

The light around them turned to the Garden of Eden and Maya watched for the second time as Eve bit into the apple and everything shattered around her.

"And so Lucifer's plan for hell on earth was set in motion."

As the light returned, Maya brought her gaze back to God, ready for him to continue. She had seen the fall of mankind before, she wanted to know how she came to be.

"I sent many of my warriors to earth to stop him but they were no match, even the greatest of them failed. They were powerful but Lucifer was stronger and most of all, they were pure while he was not."

"Why didn't you stop him yourself?" Maya challenged but he didn't seem to be fazed by her tone.

"I can't leave this realm or heaven will fall, I hold the universe together and my absence would cause the true end of the world. What the earth is going through now is only a taste of what could happen." Their eyes met. "But that's why I made you."

Maya shuffled and her eyes fell.

"It began with the birth of Lucifer's demons," he continued. "Demons are angels that have changed by their own negative wills and with the help of Lucifer, their forms changed completely and their powers became dark much like Lucifer's true form. The demons weakened themselves by sacrificing their spiritual forms, they could no longer evade a physical attack completely and their hearts were made their weaknesses. If the organ is destroyed, there's no going back for them." He picked his head up an inch. "And so I created the gargoyles to fight the demons even though they're not strong enough to stop Lucifer himself." He looked into the void. "I created gargoyles with both light and darkness in mind. For example, when a gargoyle has black eyes, it is their blood reacting to their power but it also has to do with the darkness itself. Gargoyles have a human base but what they transform into is what their form

truly is."

Maya looked on with her face filled with confusion but she allowed him to continue in the hope that she would get her answers without asking.

And she did.

"It doesn't mean the gargoyle is evil or their power is dark, it's the opposite. Their eyes change to black due to the fact that they have accepted the darkness that dwells inside them and they didn't allow it to consume them. White eyed gargoyles on the other hand are filled with light and their darkness has yet to come to the surface. Even when it does, the gargoyle can't accept it's darkness and they become uncontrollable. That is why white eyed gargoyles are stronger, not due to their strength, but due to their darkness burning brighter, it causes a reaction in their power."

He dropped his gaze from the void and it landed on Maya again. "You'd be amazed at how easy it is to accept who you truly are, that's why the black eyed gargoyles are more common. Gargoyles cannot age so they can protect the world for eternity but they can be killed and for my gratitude for their hard work, I bring them back as humans so they can get the chance to live peacefully. Even with their power and immortality, the demons still proved to be too strong for the gargoyles and Lucifer's power was beginning to rise, and before long, his plan to make earth his kingdom would come to effect. His influence caused wars, famine, and death and I knew I had to make someone who could rival him..." He narrowed his eyeless sockets. "But it came with it's sacrifices. You were made with the eyes of a black eyed gargoyle and a white eyed gargoyle. The perfect balance of light and dark. You are the most conflicted of all the white eyed gargoyles and the most pure of all the black eyed gargoyles."

Maya gritted her teeth and she found it hard to talk, her mouth felt so dry. "And so Anna was made."

"Yes," He nodded. "You were brought to earth by my own will... you were not born from anyone, I simply made you and I wanted your adoptive parents to find you... I wanted you to live a life of hardship, to suffer, to fight. I orchestrated the dreams you received, they were your warning for what was to come and what you were made for. The asylum was another part of my plan and I knew you would escape and lose your dear friend....I knew Lucifer was looking for you and that he would deceive you in ways he never had with anyone before you."

His face met hers and he saw the pain in her expression, her recently regained memories were still fresh in her mind.

"...I knew you'd be killed by his hand and that too was a part of my plan." He reached for her face with his non existent hand but without it he wasn't

able to touch her. "I kept your soul in limbo for many years and in your next life I decided to have you be born into the world with a family of the same blood."

Her body changed and she adorned her viking hair style, she was also clad in her mothers trenchcoat.

The hole in her chest still remained.

"And so you became Maya," he exclaimed. "I wanted you to love, lose, and hurt and in doing so, you would go down a path that Lucifer would have gone on himself."

Maya thought of all the death she had caused, the fear in her victims eyes. She had enjoyed it, Cain showed her that, but now it took on a whole new meaning.

"I've always wondered why you didn't strike me down for what I've done… and now it makes sense…" her voice drifted as she met his eyes as rage filled hers. "You wanted me to kill those people….innocent people."

"That was my will."

"Your will was for innocent people to die?" She tested with a strangled smile. "I never believed in you, when something bad happened people would say it's your will but how could someone as holy as you allow people to die in war, from sickness, and by the hands of their own kind? I thought either you were a fake or you were just as bad as they made Lucifer out to be."

He watched as she fumed, the tears in her eyes threatening to fall but she didn't allow them to.

"I didn't pull the strings completely, I simply set in motion what you would do." He cocked his illuminated head. "I wanted you to do what Lucifer would have done and sadly there had to be sacrifices."

"Why did you want me to be like Lucifer?!" She challenged but he ignored her as he dropped his nonexistent hand back to his side and continued with his story.

"I wanted you to regret what you did and like I knew you would, you did." His eyes fell to the glowing floor under Maya's knee high boots. "But I needed to plant the final seed to make you change, so I showed you the sight that would shape you in your third life: The little girl crying over her mother."

Maya's anger diminished as she thought of the little girl, her cries for her mother to get up, it was the sight that reminded her so much of the love she had for her own mother.

It reminded her of how much of a monster she really was.

"I knew your three brothers would be the cause of your death, they were filled with jealousy for your power. Unlike you, they never once thought what they were doing was wrong. I didn't need to influence you to sacrifice yourself

to save that city, you would have done it anyway." He lifted his eyes, "You've alway's wondered why you had the power to take energy, I gave it to you for that moment, I wanted you to die in the way you did."

Maya looked on with wide eyes and her teeth chattered, wherever her heart was now, it was racing with every emotion possible.

"I wanted you to be snuffed out completely. Lucifer wouldn't kill you in your second life, it wasn't time for him to use you. Your sin's were erased in that explosion and like what the humans call the Big Bang, you were born anew as a whole new being: A human."

Her own voice echoed in her head. "I will not fail!"

As God watched her skin grow paler still, he said the words he had spoken to her all those years ago.

"I know."

Her body changed again and now she stood in blue jeans and a black band t-shirt, her long wavy hair falling to the middle of her back. Her eyes had gone back to hazel and she looked much younger due to her lack of memories from her past lives.

"I wanted you to be reborn as a human, I didn't want you to get the memories of your time as Anna in your second life. But in this life, I wanted you to get the memories of your second." He began to explain again. "Your memories leaked through the seams but I made sure you wouldn't get them until you were ready. So I influenced your brother to create his army to protect you and in the meantime, look for you."

"Y-you influenced him?" She stammered with widened eyes.

"I suppose influence is the wrong word, I apologize." He bowed his head but lifted it again in the next second. "He was going to do it anyway, he loved you…his sweet little sister, he loved you through all of your sins, you were the only one aside from your parents who loved him in return. He worked with the man known as Archie and together, they found a way to turn humans into gargoyles. Since gargoyles are made with a human base, the two bloods can be combined. They are essentially the same but gargoyle blood is much stronger due to gargoyles being made by me to fight the demons. Humans can only take so much of the blood and Arthur figured that out. He only gave you and the others half the dose of blood and so everything went as it was supposed to: You were turned into a gargoyle once again but you were far weaker in comparison to your past lives. You received white eyes due to your denial of your memories and the wrongs committed in your past life. You rejected your brother and your past although you knew all of it was true."

Maya thought of Carma and how she was the only one aside from herself that had received white eyes out of all the humans that had been kidnapped by

Arthur.

After God's explanation, she understood why Carma had gotten them: With her identity disorder, she didn't have a hold of her own darkness and that's why the power seduced her.

Kellan had gotten the color due to his pride and Camilla got it due to her savagery and her illusion that her wrong doings were merely fun and games.

"With your rejection of your past life, you ran off and you were met with your most savage brother: Oberon. After his attack you were left close to death and with the full dosage of Arthur's blood and your acceptance of him, your power crept upon you once again." He continued. "When your brothers attacked you, you saw your friends in the same way you saw the little girl crying over her mother. In desperation, your memories came back to you and you were able to defeat your brothers."

The indents that were his eyes remained even as he spoke and Maya continued to listen.

"You are designed to want to fight Lucifer, you kept your oldest brother alive to tempt him to come to you although you didn't know who your enemy truly was. But similar to how you're drawn to Lucifer, he is drawn to you, ever since he took your heart in your first life. He came to you after biding his time and preparing his plan. He needed you because of your connection to me, he says that you're merely entertainment but he needed you. Due to your connection with me, the sacrifices close to you worked: Your best friend was the death of your innocence. Your new found friend who was starved of love. The man who killed your parents, Baphomet made sure you would make it to the doctor so you could deal the final blow. Finally, Baphomet himself as he is the image of war. Your power is my power and what happened to you weakened me. That is what caused the end of the world along with the rest of the terrible things that Lucifer has done."

Everything replayed in Maya's head as he spoke and she knew what he was going to say next so she said it for him."You wanted me to cause the end of the world."

"I did," he nodded. "I knew it would bring the demons that were exorcised out of their limbos... I knew of the repercussions, especially the revival of Legion who Jesus, the being I made to spread my will, exorcised himself. Even with knowing the consequences, that was the only way for me to get both you and Lucifer where I wanted you."

Maya's body shook, the nerves under her skin were shot and her throat felt like it was closing in on itself.

"Everything has gone to your will..." Her voice cracked. "Lucifer was right, I'm as much a player in your game as I am in his..." She furrowed her

brows as she fought to hide her emotions. "I was beaten, defiled, betrayed, and killed." She swallowed the lump in her throat but it wouldn't go down. "In my second life my hands were covered with blood and I was killed again…In this life I was beaten, played, and killed again…I chose to do all of these things but it wasn't really my will…" An emptiness filled her chest that didn't have anything to do with her missing heart.

"You're wrong," Gods voice filled her ears and she looked into his face with her cloudy eyes."You chose to love your brother after everything he's done, you found friends and comrades along the way, and you even fell in love on your own… those and many more have been your own will."

Her jaw shook and like before, she tried to talk through the lump in her throat. "You gave me life and took it away only to give it to me again for it to be taken." She did an exaggerated movement with her head. "So here I stand, my third life was killed as well… the cycle continues."

"No," God shook his head. "This is it."

This was it? Perhaps he finally had enough of her failures.

What was the point of this? What was the point in her existence?

Her mouth hung open, her mind going to her friends in her first life: Mary who saved her, Leroy who met his death too early by the hands of Aamon, of Ida who met the same fate and so many more. She now realized that Leroy was the undead gargoyle that she had recognized in Aamon's undead army.

She closed her eyes as she thought of Mina's smiling face, her blonde hair bobbing up and down as she got excited over something…Maya would never see that smile again.

She thought of her parents from her second life, how they had fought with the humans against the demons, how they loved and cared for their children until the very end.

Her mind drifted to her current parents who didn't accept her for who she was but she cared for them anyway along with her current lives brother.

She thought of Carma, Daniel, Jeannie, Cam, and Dylan.

Ari and Kira's laughter filled her ears and as she imagined them, Trevor was standing in the background smiling at how goofy the girls were. He was weak and scared but became strong because he had no other choice.

She remembered Deluca's sacrifice…it was in vain now and she had let Reggie down.

It felt like her nonexistent heart was going to explode as Arthur's laughter replaced the girl's and his bright smile filled her mind. He loved her, she was his only sister and she had hurt him because of her sacrifice. The years he had spent alone still haunted her and would forevermore.

The sad truth chilled her: She had left him alone again.

She thought of Emily who after their bout of uncertainty at the beginning of their relationship had became like a sister to Maya. She had only known that kind of love two other times: With Mary and Mina.

Cale filled her mind now, his gentle smile, his warm touch on her skin. The laughter they had shared as they looked into each others gargoyle eyes after they had realized their feelings for one another.

He couldn't live without her.

She finally allowed the tears to fall from her eyes and they came down like a stream.

"I don't want to die anymore!" She sobbed as her knees buckled and she fell to God's glowing feet. He watched as her shoulders shook while she whimpered, her lips quivering as the emotions she had been hiding for so long finally poured out.

"I'm sorry, but you already have." He said with a hint of pity. "But you will be reborn right where you need to be… and it's all thanks to Cain."

Her body changed to her current state in reality and she was bruised, wounded, and covered in two types of blood. She looked up with tear stained eyes to meet God's face as more blood poured from the wound in her chest.

"Everything Cain told you was true aside from his alliance with Lucifer," God declared as he looked down at her, his glowing form illuminating her face." He was born from Adam and Eve and in a jealous rage, he killed his own brother due to the fact that I accepted his brothers offering over his. I punished him by forcing his home to collapse on him while he was in exile. He felt remorse for what he did for many years and my final punishment was his breaking point."

Maya's tear stained eyes widened as he explained Cain's story and like before, a part of her knew what he was going to say next.

"He begged for my forgiveness, he wanted repentance for his sins, but what could make up for killing your own blood over such a trivial thing?" He cocked his head slightly and Maya thought of how strange he looked with his lack of facial expression. "I knew exactly what he could do to make up for his sins, and that was to join Lucifer as my double agent. A demon is born from their own desire to branch from me and that's precisely what Cain did."

His voice grew stronger with each word, it was the type of tone someone would use when everything was falling into place.

"After I told him my plan, he branched out to be with Lucifer, he became a demon from his own will and the power that I had chosen for him became a plaything for Lucifer. He became my brothers favorite demon and he never once suspected that he was really working for me. Lucifer thought Cain had joined him due to his anger towards me for choosing his brothers offering and

the punishment that I had casted upon him. Cain played his role well while he waited for a sign from me and he finally got one when I sent you to earth. But he knew you were not yet ready for your task so he stood back while Lucifer played with you. In your second life, I knew Lucifer wouldn't bother with you, so in the meantime, I prepared you further for your destiny. In your third, I knew destiny would arrive for both you and the rest of the players in my game and Cain finally had his chance for repentance."

God took a step back as Maya inclined her head further to get a better look at him. Things were starting to come together and somehow her body understood before her mind did.

"I gave Cain his ability to test you, to see if you were ready for your task and on that day, he knew you were."

He lowered his head and took in her dumbfounded expression, she had known something was up with Cain's death but she didn't expect this.

"He sacrificed himself to give you his blood, I told him to do so if he believed you were ready and I trusted his judgement. With your power killing your body, you would need a way to use it, and so Cain took the risk of you being killed by his blood so you could use your power once more. His blood should have killed you but your relation to me saved you. I wanted your original power to cause your body harm so this could happen, you needed his blood."

He lifted his gaze from her and looked into the glimmering light ahead of him while Maya only had eyes for him.

"Even with your full power as the black and white eyed gargoyle, it still wouldn't be enough to defeat Lucifer and I knew he would take your heart again."

Maya could see it, ever so slightly she could see a smile appear on his glowing face as he spoke of his plan and it's success.

"But with demon blood running through your veins along with your gargoyle blood, you're healing is that of both creatures. Your power cannot hurt you with the healing of a demon, there is nothing left of you that is human anymore and you cannot truly die unless your heart is destroyed."

Maya inhaled sharply as he turned to her again, his glow spreading even more warmth through her.

"But even with the power of the strongest gargoyle and the abilities of a demon, Lucifer remains far too strong for you." He announced after he had acted like he had Lucifer backed into a corner. "There is no way to kill him."

"Then why!?" She blinked as anger filled her and fresh tears fell from her gray eyes as God met them.

"Your eyes changed from hazel to gray in all three of your lives due to your

acceptance of your power," he told. "But also for a reason far more important than that: Your body has been preparing itself for three lifetimes for what it was made for, it was your mind that needed the work."

From nothing, a golden chest appeared in the space between them and Maya's eyes widened as she recognized it: It was the same golden treasure chest she had seen in her visions.

The light reflected off the gold and she thought of the bolt of lightning that had struck it and killed the men who were carrying it through the dessert.

"You've seen this before, haven't you?" God's voice wrapped around her as if it was a physical being and with a cold chill running through her body, she lifted her head from the treasure chest and nodded.

"This is The Ark of the Covenant." He declared and Maya dropped her gaze back to the chest that she now knew the name of. It was quite large, half as long as she was tall and the handles made it longer. On top were angels bent in prayer, their wings touching as they curved.

The Arks gold finish glowed against the light of the limbo and it shined on Maya's face as she continued to examine it as God started to speak.

"I encouraged the construction of the Ark many years ago, before you were even thought of."

Maya's heart thumped as she tried to stop her hand from touching the Ark, it was like it was calling to her. In her daze, she still listened to God's explanation, her face illuminated in gold.

"It holds tablets of my secrets and commandments, but it is much stronger and can hold items of much more power. As time went on, the Ark became stronger and it would have to remain covered from the sun since it's rays would add fuel to the Ark's power and before long, no one could touch it. It suddenly disappeared without a trace after many of years of opposing sides fighting for it's power. Many believed it was hidden and they thought going back to the Ark's roots would help them find it, but it was to no avail." He reached for the Ark with his handless arm. "They will never find it since I have brought it into my own hands."

Realization filled Maya as her eyes finally left the Ark and they rose to God again. "Theres no beating Lucifer so you're going to seal him?"

"No," he replied simply. "You are."

Silence, complete and utter silence at his words as she took them in, and when she finally spoke, she didn't bother to hide the disbelief in her tone.

"...How can I seal him? How could I if he's too strong for me?"

A hint of his smile returned and it only fueled Maya's confusion.

"Only I can touch the Ark of the Covenant in it's current state, no mortal could ever hope to touch it due to it's power but there is one exception as to

who can-" He moved his handless arm from the Ark and brought it to Maya instead. "The being made from my hand."

"The being made from your hand...?" She asked breathlessly as a chill went up her spine.

"You were made from my right hand, my blood and power flows through your veins so you can touch the Ark." He dropped his arm as he explained but Maya's gaze remained on where his right hand should have been. "The Ark alone will not be enough to hold Lucifer, you must take it within yourself and become one with it. You are compatible with the Ark due to you and it being made from my will, both you and the Ark were made for this. Even before I decided to make you, the Ark's fate has always been set."

He caught the disbelief on her face and his smiled widened. "You are the hand of God."

"T-The prophecy..." her voice broke as she thought of Donato's prophecy and how it was unraveling right before her eyes. "The hand of God will bring about the end of the world but will also save it..." her hands shook as she pushed herself up from the shining floor. "That was me...?"

He nodded, "You caused the end of the world by killing the man who killed your parents, you played right into Lucifer's hands and allowed the world to end."

Donato's prophecy made perfect sense: Maya, who was sculpted by the hand of God, ended the world by playing into Lucifer's game. She fulfilled the first half of the prophecy, all that was left was the second half.

"I didn't believe you were real until now, if Lucifer was real then you surely were but I couldn't bring myself to believe." She stammered. "I never understood how anyone could ever believe in you."

"Mankind is given their choice to believe or not, it does not matter either way." God admitted with an even tone. "But if there are souls and spirts, how could anyone not believe?"

"That's your reason? How could anyone believe that there is a being that makes everything all right?" She mocked. "All creatures suffer and when they ask for your help, they still suffer. You choose to punish humanity for Eve's stupidity."

"I don't make anything right, mankind follows their own path and I simply watch."

Maya swallowed and furrowed her brows, "You gave Donato the prophecy?"

"I did."

"You're not making sense." She swung her arm back in frustration. "If mankind follows their own path, how did you have all of this planned out?

Why did you make Donato a seer? How did he know where to find me? How did he know where the demons would attack? Why did you give him the prophecy about me?"

"Why did I make anyone a seer?" He blinked his nonexistent eyes. "Seer's don't see everything, they see hints of what is to come but nothing is ever set in stone. Seer's tell curious souls what their future will be and no matter how pleasant or cruel it may be, the actions of the receiver is what makes the future told to them come true. I have the future planned but it is the being that makes their future unfold."

He cocked his head. "When it comes to the prophecy about you," he raised the index finger on his good hand and pointed at the hole in her chest. "I whispered in Donato's ear what Lucifer would do, I pulled the strings to get you here. You're not an average being sent to earth to simply live your days until death, you have a purpose. Nothing would have gone the way it had if the prophecy had been told to Donato completely." He stepped closer to the Ark. "You would have tried avoiding it, that would have changed everything, and as I've explained, I needed the end of the world just as much as Lucifer to get you where you are now."

"...In others words," Maya looked God straight in the eyes as if she could see them as plain as day. "The second half of the prophecy is up to me."

"Yes." He replied simply.

"You can't control if I win or lose?"

"It's up to you."

She felt like she was going to be sick, how could she be strong enough to do such a thing? If she didn't have the power to fight Lucifer, how could she ever contain him?

"I can't do it..." her voice broke. "How could someone as monstrous as me do such a thing? I'm a killer and a failure... I'm weak and broken, I'm just as bad as Lucifer."

"No." God's gentle tone had been replaced with a stern one. "The fact that you and Lucifer are alike is precisely why you can contain him. You've done monstrous things, you know how it feels to waver from the light, but most of all, you changed your ways and have become something so much more. You have shown regret for what you have done, you willingly sacrificed yourself to make up for it and would do it again." He bowed his head slightly. "But it's as Cain said: You need to lose the notion that you need to die for what you've done...You've realized that, haven't you? That you have found a reason to live."

She thought of the people she cared for, of the people she loves. She wanted to stay with them, to love, to smile...to live.

She said so herself: She didn't want to die anymore.

But with her fate, they were no longer going to be the only reason why she had to go on. If God was saying that fate was what you made it, then she freely chose to do this. She was going to fight, she was going to take everything Lucifer had to offer if it meant the world would be safe. All of this could be passed off as her mind telling her to do what she was made to do, but she knew better than that. Having three lives made her certain of one thing: That she would always fight.

It was who she was.

"Rise, my hand." God directed as his voice changed from it's stern tone to determined.

Maya stood straighter, her shoulders broad and her head held high. Her eyes remained on the indents on God's glowing face as he took her in.

"Can you do it?" He asked.

"Yes," Her expression changed and it matched God's new tone. "I will not fail."

There was no more room for doubts, either she would do it or she wouldn't. There would be no lack of trying.

She caught a hint of a smile appear on his face again.

"I know." He placed his handless arm to the Ark and it looked like he was actually touching it. "It will be a heavy weight to hold."

"I know," her determination didn't waver. "But this is what I'm choosing to do…I choose my own fate."

He nodded with a smile, "You have a gargoyle base but I sacrificed my hand to make you." His expression went even as he explained. "My spirit and power flows through you, you will know what to do."

Three lives, driven by fate.

Anna, the girl who was deceived.

Maya, the girl who had lost her way.

Sam, the life that would end it all.

She brought her right hand forward and placed it where God's should have been and she felt a warmth as if it was still there. It was there, she was his hand, and she was where she needed to be.

The ark tingled under her palm and it felt as if electricity was flowing into her.

Her eyes moved to the light above them and she could see the outline of angels watching them amongst the colors like they had watched the fight between God and Lucifer. She recognized Cain's form amongst them, his face filled with ease.

"Goodbye, Anna."

As God's voice rang in her ears, she brought her attention back to him and her body changed.

To Anna, to Maya, and then finally to the body of her final life: Samantha Knight.

The Ark of the Covenant glowed until it turned into golden dust between her and God. It's particles started to flow into the hole in her chest until there was nothing left of it and her wound was healed.

Inside her chest was a brand new heart, a heart that pumped blood like others but had the power to hold the foulest creature to have ever existed.

She met God's eyes one last time as her body, starting at her feet, began to turn gold like a statue. It crept up her body until it covered her completely and she stood still, her blank expression on God until starting at her head, her body began to dissolve.

God and his angels watched as her form turned to gold dust until she was completely gone.

She will not fail.

Chapter 67

The hand of God

The red hue of the blood moon filled her half lidded eyes as she came to and the second thing she saw was Lucifer.

He was looking at her heart that still rested in his palm like it was a prize he had just won. Even through the blood moon's haze, she could see how dark her blood was. It was the color of mud and she knew it was due to her red blood being mixed with Cain's black.

She watched as the blood seeped through Lucifer's fingers as did her heart as it turned to ash.

It gave her great pride that his expression changed to shock as it fell to a small pile at his feet. He turned to her, his eyes landing first on her chest which had healed then to her face, a face filled with the ferocity of a beast. Her mismatched eyes shined against the red as she brought her claws forward and slashed at his throat.

Lucifer dodged her attack but it didn't matter to her, she didn't want to injure him, she only wanted him to let her go.

Her feet laid flat on the concrete as she fell from the side of the church and she watched Lucifer take her in with a confused expression. She was healed, the only proof that he had taken her heart was the hole in her shirt and the small pile of ash at her feet.

His eyes bored into the woman who had been his plaything for three lives. The moment he had waited over a century for had fallen apart and she stood in front of him with an even expression, her eyes set on his bottomless ones.

"Hello, *Samuel*." Her voice filled with silk and Lucifer's eyes widened a fraction at her knowledge of the name he had used to fool her. "What's the matter?" She cocked her head. "It's your *sweet Anna*."

His eyes narrowed and he regained his monstrous look as the blood moon shined directly on him as his back faced the opening of the square in front of the church.

"You shouldn't be alive."

"You can thank your favorite demon for the fact that I breath." She took a step closer as his eyes grew narrower still.

"My favorite demon?" He questioned with a hint of annoyance.

"I'm not the only one who was played." She declared as she settled over the body of a girl the same age as she was when she had died as Anna. "Cain was never your demon, he was God's double agent. He wanted repentance for what he did to his brother and God made a plan that would give him the forgivness that he needed."

She lifted her head to the moon as it made the setting all the more sinister. "The plan was to help me against you, he forced me to swallow his blood and although it nearly killed me, it had the effect he had hoped for: I have the healing of a demon and you were too prideful to destroy my heart."

"He couldn't have betrayed me," Lucifer growled as his dark eyes filled with rage. "He was loyal, he did as I said, He-"

"You already said so yourself," Maya retained her even expression. "You couldn't see him the day he died due to the fact that his loyalty wasn't with you."

"It doesn't matter." Lucifer smiled with his teeth bared like an animal, his clawed fingers digging into his palms and black blood dripped from the wounds. "You can't beat me!"

"No, but I can contain you." She declared as she stepped over the body of the girl and now she and Lucifer stood only a foot apart.

"Contain me?" His insane smile widened and a cackle escaped his mouth. "Someone as weak as you could never keep me at bay."

"You misunderstood me." She narrowed her eyes. "I'm going to *seal* you."

Lucifer's expression changed as he looked on with confusion and Maya explained, "You have a point that I'm weak, but I have the means to seal you: The Ark of the Covenant." She cocked her head. "Have you heard of it?"

His eyes continued to examine her healed body until they landed on the hole in her shirt over her chest, her pale skin had covered her new heart.

The look on his face confirmed that he knew of the golden chest that now dwelled inside of her. "That thing?" His eyes narrowed. "I fail to see how that can seal me, it's only a treasure chest and it hasn't been seen in centuries."

"Always so cocky." She said simply. "I *can* seal you but the only obstacle in the way is that only God's touch can make it work." Her focused eyes met his. "But I am *the hand of God* so I can in his place." She declared with an air of confidence. "God made me, his strongest warrior, from his own hand. He made me go through all these trials, made me kill and be killed, made me suffer… all to be able to keep you in the Ark."

Lucifer chuckled, her declaration meant nothing to him. "Where is the Ark of the Covenant anyway?" He looked around with a smug look as if it was going to appear.

"*I'm* the Ark." Maya proclaimed and Lucifer's eyes fell on her again.

"*You*?" He took one long step and his face was against her's, his fingers twitching as his hand drifted to her chest again. "*You're* the Ark? *You're* going to contain me?" His breath hit her face as he laughed. "I knew we were fated to be together but not like this…was your time with me in your first life not enough for you? My *sweet Anna*?"

"Thats your mistake, *Samuel*." She leaned into his face, their lips only an inch from touching. "Thinking I'm sweet." Her tongue crept out of her mouth as she licked her lips along with her pointed canines. "How could I, someone who has killed so many, be sweet? I'm a venomous bitch, my existence is built on violence and I crave to see that smile ripped from your face." Her mismatched eyes narrowed with bloodlust, "You wanted hell? *I am your hell*."

Lucifer attempted to close the gap between them, her words exciting him more.

Maya grabbed ahold of his wrist as he went for her heart again. As she did so, she acted as if she was going to kick him and he dodged but she instead jumped up and wrapped her legs around his waist, pulling him to the ground with her.

Lucifer looked up as she straddled him, his grin had gone nowhere.

"Brings back memories, doesn't it?" His question drifted into the air as he met her eyes and his widened with shock.

While her eyes were still black and white, they were different: Where her irises should have been missing, they were filled with crimson orbs.

She not only had the healing of a demon, she also had the power.

She opened her mouth and exposed teeth that were as sharp as Lucifer's and he looked on as she brought herself onto him, her teeth brushing his neck.

Before she could do any damage however, he kicked her off with more strength than he needed and she slid into the rubble and the bodies, knocking them away until she came to a stop and knelt amongst them.

"*Hand of God*!?" He roared as his eyes turned to flames. "*Ark of the Covenant*?!"

Maya stood as she took in his rage, she had to hurry or it would be too late. With God's power flowing through her, she knew exactly what she needed to do.

But she knew it would take a fight to get there.

She watched as Lucifer's skin pealed back and his true form shined through, he was the densest shadow she had ever seen and his flame-like eyes narrowed as he took in her unfazed expression. She had seen this form in her dreams when she was Anna, in every fire she had laid her eyes on.

She was pushed violently to her knees as Lucifer's gravity fell on her, her teeth grinding ever so slightly as she fought against his pull.

"I'll just have to take your heart again." Lucifer declared as he stepped towards her, his voice echoing through the square. "It'll give me great pleasure to do so."

Maya's eyes rolled up as he stepped closer and with a thump of her new heart, she pulled herself up until she stood halfway.

Lucifer stopped and curiously watched as she pulled herself completely up, his gravity no longer had an effect on her. It was like the time with Cain's power, he had said that she was the only one who had broken out of it.

It didn't seem to impress Lucifer though and out of his mouth made of shadow came a cackle. As it carried through the square, flames began to form around him and they illuminated his dark form. Flashes of memory filled Maya's mind, what a familiar sight this was.

The pressure pushing down on her stopped as the flames around Lucifer began to extend and they now ran the length of the square. The flames flared and along with his laughter, Maya could hear the crackle of the flame as it rushed towards her like a bullet and it expanded so she couldn't step out of it's path.

She wasn't going to run though, she was going to take the flame.

Lucifer watched as the flame engulfed her and the fire began to disperse as he willed it to do so and slowly, the flames dulled and it showed the charred bodies of the already dead.

In the middle of it all was Maya as she kneeled.

Her arms were in front of her and her hands laid flat on the ground, tiny flames dancing between her fingers.

Peaking though her brown hair were two curved horns as black as midnight. Her mismatched eyes mixed with crimson shined against the flames along with her fiery expression.

Her form continued to change: Her wings now connected with her arms as her skin turned a light shade of gray as the new and old limbs became one. Her sleeves ripped along with the sides of her shirt, the only thing keeping the shirt on her now was the vine-like fabric around her neck. Her claws turned into talons as her ears grew into longer points. Her horns widened and curved further, the two points almost touching as the horns shaped her head like a headdress. Along the horns were gold scales, they twisted up the bone and shined against the blood moon.

Lucifer's power had given her strength, a charge you could call it. She had only just combined with the Ark and although it was only an object to be used, it felt alive inside of her. It thrived off of Lucifer's power and it made her do the same.

The Ark knew it's purpose and now so did she.

She was monstrous but beautiful.

She was a gargoyle sculpted by God's right hand and the blood of a demon flowed through her veins. The Ark of the Covenant was her heart made over. Her current form was the result.

"Look at you," Lucifer's voice danced off the flames and ricocheted around her. "Still playing God's game."

Maya stood as her eyes fell to the ash around her along with the broken pieces of the church and the glimmer of glass against the blood moon.

"I play my own game." Her voice was smooth. "I make my own choices and I chose to stop you when I could've walked away."

"That's God's influence, my sweet Anna." She could hear the smile on his face although she couldn't see it, the indents on his face weren't as easy to make out as they were on God's.

"No," She flicked her sharpened nails as she laid her glowing eyes on Lucifer. "I just wanna watch you burn."

"You're a hypocrite! You're a killer just like me and if I burn, you burn with me!" The silk in his voice returned.

She stepped closer and as her right foot touched the ground, light filled the square and snuffed out the flames. Lucifer watched as God's power flowed around him until his head snapped back to Maya who took in his shock with an even expression.

"How?" Disbelief filled his tone for a second and Maya's mouth curled into an icy smile.

"I am the hand of God, therefore I hold some of his power." She cocked her head and the weight of her horns felt strange. "I was made to fight you, I was forged by my own mistakes to be your undoing and I plan to be just that."

"I'd like to see you try." His silky voice came out as both a laugh and a growl as his shadowy form began to wander closer.

The square filled with the sound of footsteps as they began to circle each other. They moved as if they were new lovers, feeling each other out as their eyes met, waiting for the other to make the first move.

But this wasn't the first time they fought, nor were they playing at being lovers anymore. There was nothing new about this and there needn't be any hesitation.

Maya's ears pressed to the back of her head as he disappeared and even though she couldn't see him, she could sense him. She stood still until he appeared behind her and as he swung, she turned and swung back, their arms meeting and with the clash came a splash of shadow and light as their powers combined.

With each new hit, the world was filled with the opposing forces: Dark and light.

The square filled with the ricochet of power as the two beast's fought with the valor of vikings. This battle was always meant to be since the day Anna had seen Samuel's back when he had saved her from the asylum. This was no longer a game, games were meant to be played and neither of them were playing anymore.

Fuck the strings of fate, Maya had enough of being a puppet.

She was free.

She held her ground but as God had said and as she had known, her strength wasn't enough to take on Lucifer. He may have been the weaker of the two but he still had some of the power that God held and Maya only had a fraction.

He grabbed her new horns and broke the top of one off, his fingers curling around the bone as he plunged the sharp point to her heart. She brought her arm up and the horn stabbed through it instead, the pain searing as it tore though skin and muscle but it was nothing she hadn't felt before.

The horn remained in her arm as she kicked at Lucifer but like the shadow demons, he dissolved and appeared again when he wanted to attack. When he reappeared for the last time, he was back in the form he had called Samuel, a soft smile on his lips.

Maya flapped her new wings and she glided to him with her talons outstretched. She barely scraped the front of his neck as he jumped back and his smile widened.

"Do you think I'd hold any qualms in slashing the throat of the motherfucker who deceived and killed me?" She snarled as she took him in.

Now that he had gone back to his human form, she could see his cocky expression. She watched his dark eyes turn back to flame and her loved ones appeared around her again, their voices calling to her.

"Why didn't you save me?" Ari's voice came out clear as her zombified form stepped towards her.

"I'm so alone." Kira cried.

"You left me…" Mina whimpered.

"You will fail." Alvertos and Arely's voices echoed in unison.

They stepped closer to her until they turned to ash and they fell to the ground only to be replaced by her parents.

"Maya…" her mothers voice drifted as her father placed his cold hand on her shoulder.

Unlike last time, Maya was unfazed by Lucifer's ploy and her eyes flashed as he stepped through her parents forms and they fell to the ground along with the rest of the ash.

A wide grin filled Lucifer's face as he positioned his claws at her chest and she grabbed his wrist to stop him. His other hand came down on her right shoulder to keep her in place.

He was inches away from her heart and their arms shook as they fought against each other, a demented smile on Lucifer's face while Maya's wore a snarl.

Even with a flap of her wings, there was no getting out of his grip and the Ark fluttered against her ribs. He was too strong and she wouldn't be able to hold on, he would take her heart again and that would be the end, she would fail.

"I'll destroy your heart and you'll finally be able to join your precious dead friends and family." Lucifer teased through his laughter. "It'll be so much easier for you, you won't have to regret what you've done anymore."

The thought would have been enticing not too long ago but she was driven by something else now: The world as it should be, the skies clear and the oceans blue. The safety of the people she cared for.

She swallowed her anxiety as her eyes started to close from the weakness she started to feel in her arms. She had to use all of her strength to stop him from taking her heart while he only used one arm.

In her mind, she reassured herself.

"If I close my eyes, I'm dead…I'll fail."

She growled as a fire as bright at Lucifer's flames burned inside her.

"I will not fail!"

His dagger like nails reached the hole in her now loose hanging shirt and as Maya's eyes fell to his tilted neck, she saw an opening.

She let go of his wrist but before he could pierce her chest, she twisted and his fingers clawed through the middle of her ribcage instead and pierced one of her lungs.

Through the sharp pain and the rush of air that left her lung, she leaned forward with her teeth bared and sunk them into Lucifer's neck.

Since he had gone back to his physical form, it had given her the means to get what she wanted. The thick black liquid filled her mouth along with something that felt like air. She swallowed the tar tasting blood and the charcoal air and she could feel the warmth of both crawling down her throat into her chest.

She was pushed back in the next second and Lucifer's claws left her lung.

The two looked at each other, Lucifer with a gash in the side of his neck and Maya's mud colored blood dripping from his fingers, a monstrous look on his face.

Maya's mouth was covered in black blood and as she opened her mouth, a trail of steam the same color as the blood came from her mouth.

"You think this can beat me?" He let out an insane cackle as he pressed a hand to the wound on his neck. "You weak-"

He began but stopped abruptly as starting at his feet, he began to turn into the same steam that had left Maya's mouth.

This is what God's will had told her to do, she had given the Ark a taste of what it was going to seal and now it wanted more.

By taking some of Lucifer in, the seal was set.

Lucifer was her's.

"Checkmate, Lucifer." Maya repeated the words he had spoken to her after he and his demons had destroyed the monuments in Washington.

His eyes filled with confusion as he watched the steam that was once his feet and ankles flow into her chest.

"All I needed was a part of your spirit." Maya explained as she allowed the steam to flow into her heart through the hole in her shirt.

Lucifer didn't wear the look of a man defeated, instead he began to laugh. "Don't think you've won!" He cackled. "I'll always be with you, haunting your thoughts!"

Of course he would find this funny, he would never give her the satisfaction.

She nodded, "You were right, we *are* fated to be together."

Shock registered on Lucifer's face for a millisecond, if one wasn't paying attention, they would have missed it and in the next second he continued with his laughter.

As his uncontrollable laughter filled the square, his body began to dissolve further and as it entered Maya, she felt the weight of Lucifer's immeasurable power.

"Yes! I'll always be with you until I rip out your guts and escape that worthless body of yours! I'll look into your weak eyes as I kill you again! You are mine! Your life is mine!" He cackled with a hint of venom in his voice.

"Ok." Maya agreed and once again, Lucifer's face filled with shock until his laughter returned. Even as his body fully dissolved, it's particles running into her chest, Maya could still hear his laughter.

She closed her eyes and although she had never uttered the words before, she spoke them perfectly: *"In nomine Patris et Filii et Spiritus Sancti…Amen."*

Her body began to glow with a light similar to God's and as she opened her eyes, they too began to glow a deep shade of gold.

Her hair picked up as if a strong breeze had blown past her, the now gold strands flowing around her shoulders like a shawl.

Like in the light filled limbo with God, she turned into a gold statue only this time it didn't take her with it as it dissolved. It broke away until she stood in her human form, her wounds healed and her ears clear of lucifer's laughter now that the seal was complete.

Lucifer now dwelled inside the Ark of the Covenant, inside her heart.

She groaned as her chest felt like it was going to explode and her knees buckled.

She fell to her hands and knees as she felt the weight of being the Ark and the power it was fighting so hard to keep at bay.

She had sacrificed her normal heart in exchange for the Ark of the Covenant so the chest now served as both her new heart and the Ark at the same time. The organ ached and Maya heaved as she felt Lucifer trying to break free. She struggled to take a good breath and she felt like she was going to suffocate.

But slowly the pain in her heart eased and as the dark blotches that had formed in her vision dulled, she was startled to see that the red hue was gone and she was instead covered with the moons bright light.

She lifted her head and she found that night had fallen on her, the night that should have been. Lucifer was the key that had held onto the end of the world and with his sealing, the world had gone back to it's normal state.

She leaned on the back of her legs and stared at the moon, the light coaxing the pain to stop. Her illuminated face carried an expression filled with wonder.

Although it was true that she would keep the world safe, she hadn't won. She would always have Lucifer to deal with.

She didn't do it for God, she did it for the people who made her worthless life worth living.

She needed to find them, she needed to see their faces… to see if they were ok.

She forced herself to stand and after a few wobbles, she managed to walk. As her feet carried her, she realized her heartbeat was still intensely slow, it's beats coming at an even lower rate than before. God had said that she had died but would be reborn where she needed to be, maybe she was a dead person walking.

Like before she had met with Lucifer, she didn't know where her feet were taking her until she was half way though the square and she turned to get a final look at the Church of the Holy Sepulchre. The place where everything had changed.

Most of the side had been burned away but it's foundation held true. How fitting that she would be reborn there, at the church of the resurrection.

Her eyes fell to the ash at her feet and she knew where she wanted to go. She turned around and made her way to the place she had last seen everyone, the place she had been before she and Lucifer had their final battle. She couldn't help but think of how naive she was even though it was less than an hour ago. She would have never expected that Lucifer would be a part of her, that she would be his vessel.

She walked down the streets that were lined with the bodies of the undead gargoyles and ash from the shadow demons. She hoped she wouldn't see a face that she would recognize but she pushed forward, her friends had to be alive, what was left of them.

If the others were dead, there was no way she could hold Lucifer, she was prepared for this role but without the others she would never make it.

She knew even though she had stopped the end of the world, there would still be repercussions. She could sense them, the demons that had been freed from their limbos. She knew they were still there, their master may have been sealed but they still walked freely.

They would pose a problem, especially Legion.

God's voice rang in her ears as if he stood behind her, *"Be weary of Legion."*

She would be weary of him of course but she also knew that neither he nor the other demons would strike now, they would embrace their freedom until it was time to play.

Everything was a game to the demons and Maya was their greatest contender, they would surely show themselves.

She and Legion will meet again.

The hand of God will bring about the end of the world but will also save it.

She was the reason the world had met it's end but she had saved it and she will continue to protect it.

She stepped to where the Temple Dome used to be and although she could have ignored the bodies since she had seen them before, she owed it to herself to look.

This was the reason why she couldn't be weak, *this* was the reason why she would hold onto the burden she was destined with. She had said so herself that her existence had been built on violence and perhaps this was her punishment for all her wrong doings.

She skimmed over the bodies of the officers from both here in Israel and her homeland and mixed amongst them were the white coats of the Venandi and the black coats of her fellow gargoyles.

Ari and Kira laid close to each other and Maya's jaw tightened as she noticed that it looked like they were reaching for each other.

Alvertos' body laid amongst the rubble of the temple while Arely's laid along with Ari and Kira's. He had bled out from his wounds caused by Baphomet.

Maya's eyes moved away from them as the sight became too much to bare.

It was enough, the message was clear and she would never let their sacrifices be in vain.

Her heart fluttered as she looked to where Lucifer had met them at what used to be the entrance of the Temple Dome. Her eyes fell again but widened as she found a clump of black fabric on the ground and she found herself jogging to it.

At the foot of the wreckage was her mother's trenchcoat, *her* trenchcoat. It was tattered and torn but the silver gargoyle clasps held true. With her backless battle suit ripped at the sides due to her wings, her front was a gentle breeze away from being exposed so she pulled on the coat and clasped one of the buttons.

She walked from the Temple, her feet sliding down the broken stairs, and after turning to the path that led away from the dome, she noticed there were people standing there.

She looked on as they did the same until the one leading them ran to her and she stood still.

As the others that were with him followed, the moon shined on them and revealed that it was Arthur and the others.

Arthur being the one running to her wrapped his arms around her and relief filled her bones.

"Maya!" His breath hit her ear as he held on tight and she wrapped her shaky arms around him.

"My brother." Her voice cracked as she laid her forehead against his shoulder. He was wounded and bloody but he was alive.

"...You did it." He placed a hand on her cheek as he pulled away, his hazel eyes filled with tears.

What had happened between her and Lucifer would come later, she only cared about seeing the people she loved alive and well.

Emily came from behind Arthur along with Trevor, their expressions sad but they still smiled as they looked at her. Their arms wrapped around her as Arthur stepped out of the way and Maya placed her hands on their backs, their heart's beating against her palms.

A sob escaped Emily's lips and Maya leaned her head against her shoulder, her eyes closed as she thought of what Trevor had done.

"I'm glad you didn't run." She turned to him. "I knew you'd turn out strong."

His smile had widened as the three pulled away from each other, "It wasn't just physical strength…" His voice drifted as he gave a nervous chuckle.

A footstep echoed through the path and Maya's smile fell as Emily and Trevor moved to join Arthur to the side of her.

Her slow heart thumped as she saw him standing only a few feet away from her, his head completely healed and a relieved smile on his face.

Cale.

She didn't see the twenty Venandi or Reggie and the remaining humans, all she could see was Cale. Her jaw shook as she met his dark eyes, her legs wobbling as emotion overcame her.

They ran to each other, Maya throwing herself into his arms and as he caught her, their lips connected. The taste of salt filled their mouths as Maya's tears spilled over and fell on their lips. They slowly broke apart and looked into each others eyes, Maya's silent tears still streaming down her cheeks. He pulled her closer as she wrapped her arms around his back and she buried her face in his chest, his comforting smell filling her nose and a sob finally escaped her lips.

Chapter 68

Eternal

She stepped through the tunnel leading to God knows where, her slow heart pumping against her ribcage. The cave was desolate and cold, drops of water fell around her as her feet echoed along with the noise.

She could barely see what was in front of her or why she was even there but she continued on.

She came to a stop as a flicker of light went off at the end of the cave and she rose a curious brow. Her boots scrapped the ground as she began to walk to the light, the shine mesmerizing her.

She reached her hand out as she drew nearer and the flame danced in her palm.

Light and flame.

Life and death.

That's what God and Lucifer were and she was both.

She wondered where the flame was coming from as there was no candle or any other source, but the light went out. She unconsciously reached out again, her eyes turning gold as the Ark reacted to the power coming from the space in front of her until a growl filled the cave and her glowing eyes widened.

The air was excruciatingly hot as the light flipped on again and on the other side of it stood a beast, it's face glowing in the flame. It's curved horns hugged the sides of it's head and it's bloody teeth bared as another growl rolled off it's tongue.

Maya simply stood and watched as the beast eyed her with it's black eyes, the smell of rot coming from it's breath as it opened it's snout and a gust of wind blew its brown fur.

The sound of men, women, and children screaming for their lives filled her ears and what sounded like water splattered the walls. She imagined the beast dragging it's large animalistic feet through puddles of blood and Lucifer's laughter echoed through the cave.

"Sam!" A warm hand cupped her cheek and eased her out of her dream. Her eyes opened to find Cale leaning over her, his worried eyes on her pale face.

She pulled herself up, Cale's hand sliding from her face as he moved out of the way and leaned against the headboard of their bed. She inhaled sharply and his fingers found her's as she leaned her head back and met his eyes.

"Lucifer again?"

"...It wasn't as bad the others." She assured him with a smile and caressed the top of his hand with her thumb. "Waking up makes it worth it." She turned, leaned into his face, and kissed him.

As they broke apart, he seemed assured that she was alright. His dark eyes met her gray and she knew he was looking at the thin gold ring that circled around the outside of her irises.

It was one of the side effects of becoming the Ark of the Covenant but it was small compared to the others.

Especially the dreams.

This is why God prepared her the way he had, only she could take Lucifer's will, she knew his game and she knew how to play it herself.

Her heart slowed back to it's too slow pace after the dream had caused it to rush and she grinned as she looked at the time on the digital clock sitting on the dresser.

"We still have some time before we have to meet the Venandi-" Cale smiled before she got the rest of the words out. "Do you wanna spar?"

The two shot up from the bed and they got dressed in something quick. Maya pulled on a pair of sweats and left Cale's shirt on that she had worn to bed while he dressed in a fresh one and his own pair of sweats.

After they were done, they ran through the cottage to the sliding doors leading to the backyard. The morning sun shined on them and burned their eyes until they adjusted to the light.

Six months had passed since the events in Jerusalem, they were back in the states and had moved location and although Maya found herself missing the old cabins, they had upgraded. They had electricity, television, and warm water along with being close to civilization.

They were no longer on the run, the director in charge of the force that had green-lighted the experiment's on the gargoyles had been killed by Clarke before he had gone to Jerusalem.

The new one was a younger man who had worked under the ex director for years and he took his place. He wanted to work with the gargoyles the same way his predecessors had but now the Venandi were in the mix. It was hard to believe the new director's deal, especially for Maya and Arthur after what had happened to their parents.

But there was no need to fight each other anymore, they had a common enemy: The demons.

It was true that even though the end of the world had been halted, the demons that had been brought back still remained. Not only that, but new demons were created from angels who sympathized with Lucifer, they had waited for the end to change their allegiance.

Even though there was still some lack of trust, the three allies remained close in location and met often as the demons became more and more rowdy.

The creatures never strayed too far from where Maya was, even though she was his vessel and the seal had worked to seal Lucifer's power, it could still be felt and the demons thrived off it. Although they were much weaker in comparison to when Lucifer was moving on his own.

Maya had explained everything that had happened after she was thrown off with Kellan by Baphomet. They knew she had killed Clarke, they knew he and Baphomet were the final straws in causing the end of the world. By killing one of Lucifer's horsemen, she was the cause of the end of the world along with the sacrifices being related to her.

They knew about her fight with Lucifer, how he had killed her by taking her heart and she regained her memories from her first life. She explained how she talked to God and that he told her the reason behind the gargoyles creation and the reason their eyes were the way they were.

She told them that she was sculpted from his hand and there was no other way to defeat Lucifer other than to seal him with the ark that she now possessed.

She also told them that all she went through in her past lives and the current were to ready her for what she was made to do.

"So," she smiled at Cale as she pulled her hair into a pony tail, it had grown past the middle of her back but unlike before, she enjoyed the length. "I think we should play a game."

He rose a brow as he stretched and Maya hopped over to him, "The winner gets to-" she whispered to him as she leaned into his ear and when she stepped back, she was met with a look that only meant that he was in.

The winner would be a lucky person.

"You're on." He agreed.

Maya backed away with a devious smile until they were a good length apart and without warning, the two went at each other.

They dodged punches and kicks alike, even landing a few on occasion. Neither fought seriously but sparring seemed to be an enjoyable past time for the two. They had done it from the very beginning of their relationship and it stuck with them.

Maya recoiled back as she went in for another attack and Cale brought his arm in front of him to block the hit. They grinned at each other, their heavy breaths hitting each others faces as Maya leaned closer, her eyes on his dark ones.

She lifted her left leg and kicked his out from under him and he fell to the ground then for good measure, she pinned him down as he smiled up at her.

"I won." She purred.

"I lost." He placed his hands behind her knees and she rose a brow. "You meant to lose, didn't you?"

"Maybe." He chuckled and she snorted as she leaned further down, her lips brushing his and their expressions changed.

She hovered over his face as if teasing him until her lips crashed into his. He hungrily kissed her back, his hands trailing up her thighs to her bottom then to her back where he twisted his finger's into her long hair.

Maya moved her hands up his abdomen, feeling every muscle through the fabric of his shirt and at his chest she could feel his heart pounding against her palms.

Their ears perked as they heard someone at the front of the cottage and they reluctantly pulled away from each other. There were two people and by the way the first person stepped, they could tell it was Emily. The Second walked heavier and they knew right away that it was Trevor.

Maya quickly rolled off Cale as she heard them talking about how they were probably out back. She glanced at Cale as he sat up and their eyes met long enough for them both to understand that they intended to finish what they had started later.

"There you are." Emily rounded the corner of the cabin, her dark hair had gotten longer and she wore it in a loose braid that fell over her right shoulder.

Trevor who had gained a good amount of muscle in the past six months wore his light brown hair in a shorter style.

They were both dressed in their backless battle shirts, though only the top parts of their backs were cut out unlike Maya's.

"You two are freaking animals." Trevor reached his arms out to help them up and they both grabbed his wrists.

As they stood and dusted themselves off, Emily approached Maya.

"I'll help you braid your hair." She told her as she pulled a leaf out of her brown locks for her.

Maya had taught her how to do the viking style braids and Emily liked to practice when she could since she had trouble doing it with her own hair.

She agreed and Emily pulled her inside and the boys followed but stayed in the living room where they sat and flipped on the tv.

The world was somewhat normal after what had happened but people always talked about the events that had transpired in Washington D.C and Jerusalem and were always on guard.

Before they left Jerusalem, they had set the square in front of the Temple dome on fire, burning the bodies of both their enemies and comrades. They couldn't leave behind proof of what had happened there, even with the sorrow it caused them.

Arthur and the rest of the full blooded gargoyles had gone to the cemetery to retrieve the bodies of Kellan, Clarke, and Baphomet but they had returned with only Clarke.

Kellan's body along with the beasts were gone.

Emily closed the door to the bedroom and she turned first to the white sheets on the bed that were in disarray then to her friends clothes from the day before on the floor.

"Trevor's right, you guys really are animal's." She snorted.

"Em!" Maya squeaked and the girl's could hear Trevor's laughter and Cale's embarrassed groan from the living room.

* * *

Maya sat on the end of the bed while Emily set to work on her side braids and she directed her what to do when she got stuck.

After what had happened in Jerusalem Maya would have never thought that the humans would want to work with the gargoyles especially after everything they had done. Maya and her brothers weren't forgiven for what they did, but it was a lifetime ago and the demons needed to be dealt with. The demons that were freed from their limbos joined with the freshly made ones and attacked places they thought would bring them entertainment.

The thought never left her mind that she was the reason the world had ended in the first place. She had freed the demons that had been exorcized and had encouraged more to join. She played right into Lucifer's game and although she tried to convince herself that it was a fate that she had chosen for herself, she knew God had planned this.

He wanted her to end the world as much as Lucifer did.

The end not only gave Lucifer and his demons strength, but it also gave God the means to talk to her. He needed her heart destroyed so it could be replaced with one combined with the Ark of the Covenant. He needed her to go through what she did so she would be prepared for the weight that she would hold.

She understood Lucifer's desires and what drove him, a pure being would never stop him and she was far from pure. She and Lucifer were one in the same only she didn't act on her darkness the way he had.

"We're gonna run out of time if we don't hurry." Maya joked as Emily got to the final twists of her braids and she heard her swallow nervously as she twisted the last hair tie.

As she finished, she took in her handy work and let out a sigh of relief.

Maya smiled at her as she placed a gentle hand on the braids. "Perfect." She complimented. "Now you just need to learn how to do it on yourself."

She got up after she thanked Emily for her help and opened the wooden closet door.

She and Cale shared both the dresser and the closet though her clothing took up more space on the hangers. On the far left, the last two hangers held her new battle suit and her old trenchcoat.

She hadn't worn her mother's coat since Jerusalem.

"Why won't you wear it?" Emily asked from the bed as her eyes fell to the gargoyle clasps that Ari had picked out and sewed on.

"The coat represents my past," Maya didn't want to sound deep but there was no beating around the bush. "It was my mothers and it was mine, it's seen so much battle and death along with every wrong thing I've done." She turned her head and met Emily's brown eyes. "I want to leave it all behind me."

Emily smiled, Maya's reason was good enough to settle any kind of worry that she had until her eyes moved past her into the closet. "Ari would be glad that you wear the battle suit she left you."

Maya turned back to the closet and her eyes found the last creation Ari had made on the other side of her coat: It was a type of corset, of course the back was missing all the way down to the waist like her previous battle suit, but this one was far more eye catching.

Along the middle going up the belly to the chest was a black floral design. Running along the sides was white and at the bottom was a black belt. At the neck was a belt style cuff attached to the sleeves and it was adorned with bronze buckles that were carefully placed in the floral black running up the front.

"She out did herself with this one..." Maya's voice drifted as she thought of when they made it back to the cabins after the battle.

When she went to her cabin, she found the top on her bed and a note placed carefully on top. She swallowed the lump in her throat as she recalled what it had said: *"Embrace what you are."*

Maya remembered the tears that had streamed down her cheeks as she read the letter.

She began to wonder if half blooded gargoyles reincarnated like full blooded gargoyles but she could only hope. Ari had made the top to match her eyes, the colors of both light and darkness, the acceptance of darkness and the lack thereof.

She was the perfect mix of both.

She wore the top with pride when she fought the demons with her black skinny jeans and knee high boots. She would embrace all that she was, Ari had told her to do so and she was going to honor her wish.

She took off Cale's shirt and replaced it with the corset then pulled on her skinny jeans to finish the look.

Emily grinned as Maya faced her, the outfit was like a warning to the demons, when they saw the flash of black and white, they knew they were done for.

Maya returned her smile and her ears perked as she heard a knock on the front door and as she listened to Cale answer the door, she heard Arthur's voice asking if they were ready.

She opened the door and their faces fell on her and Emily as they stepped out.

Arthur was dressed in a black coat and Cale had pulled on a fresh pair of jeans he had grabbed from the washer.

Behind Arthur stepped Archie in a t-shirt and jeans, he chose to be the doctor for the fighters and left his coat at their base.

"Let's see if there's any demons to kill." Maya's gray eyes narrowed while the gold rings in them glimmered.

Their base of operations was in the least obvious place there could be. Although the public knew of the gargoyles existence and the end of the world was witnessed by all, they still kept what they were doing a secret.

How could the public accept the fact that the government was working with the creatures that attacked and killed them? Perhaps one day the gargoyles could fight with the humans out in the open but for now, keeping it hush was for the best.

They pulled into the parking lot of an old town building with the vehicle that had been provided for them. They wore jackets over their battle suits to not bring attention to themselves but with it being the middle of april, jackets were a bit of an overkill to some.

Perhaps they didn't need to wear their backless suits but it was much more useful to wear something that didn't get holes in it every time they had to use their wings. They seldom had to use them against the demons that they fought but there were some that required more attention. The Venandi could deal with many of the demons themselves but sometimes the gargoyles had to step in.

Maya wanted to fight every demon she could, she had brought them into this world and she wanted to be the one to take them out.

They walked up the stairs of the old building, it had a musty smell that was almost unbearable to the gargoyles but they controlled their heightened senses and continued on.

At the top of the four floor building was a door with no window and it could only be opened from the inside unless one had a special key.

Arthur was about to knock when it opened and on the other side stood Arabella, a smile on her face as she saw Arthur.

"About time you got here." She teased and Arthur shook his head with a grin. "Some of us have lives to live."

She stepped out of the way to let them in and as they entered, they realized right away how Arabella had known that they were there: In the far corner of the large room where there were chairs set around a large round table sat the full blooded gargoyles. They had heard the other gargoyles approaching and had given Arabella the hint that they were on their way.

There were only three of them now as the others were out scouting with the other Venandi but the long haired gargoyle named Silas who posed as the leader was present.

Filling the rest of the chairs was Reggie, Lucas, and Tori who had joined the Venandi instead of rejoining the humans. Donato sat with them, he and Arabella were the only two who remained from the original group of Venandi and Arabella was made the leader of the sector.

"I hate to disappoint you guys but I haven't heard anything from our scouts about the demons." She made her way to the table and looked down at the map that was placed there. As said, the other Venandi were out scouting with the full blooded gargoyles and the map was marked where the demons had struck before. A different color marked where they thought they would attack next, that's where the scouts were now. None of the locations were too far away that Maya and the rest couldn't get there in time.

"Let's hope there's no demons that require your attention." Lucas placed his hand on the map as Maya and the others removed their jackets. "Though I can tell you're all rearing to fight." He said at the sight of their battle suits while he and the other Venandi along with the other gargoyles wore their street clothes.

"Landen left these for us and wanted me to give one to each of you." Arabella moved to a cabinet on the other side of the table and opened it with a creak.

Landen was the new director of the human and gargoyle alliance, he was usually there for their meetings but there were times when he got caught up in his work at other places. He was a blonde haired man with striking blue eyes, he always wore a black suit and tie combo.

Arabella pulled out guns for each of them and handed them out, the cool steel touching their warm skin.

They could feel the acid resting in the bullets inside and they felt uncomfortable. The director had suggested that the gargoyles learn how to shoot guns for long range fights and since they had supernatural eye sight, they would have better aim.

Trevor and Emily sat down on the black couch that was placed in the middle of the otherwise all white room aside from a few wooden tables and chairs. Archie who had already sat down watched as they set their guns down on the wooden coffee table in front of them with an uneasy look on their faces. One of these bullets had killed Dylan, there was no way they could use this weapon with ease.

Maya set her's down on the table, its hilt covering the bottom of the map. "As the director knows," She tried to sound as polite as she could though her voice shook. "I'd rather not use the weapon that killed my parents and my friend."

Arthur stepped beside her and placed his gun beside her's. "With all do respect, I feel the same."

Cale sat down on the arm of the couch as he placed his gun beside Trevor and Emily's. "I'd much rather use one of *your* weapons."

Arabella's eyes wandered to the cabinet that not only held the guns, but their swords, daggers, bows, and sage.

"It's takes some getting used to." Reggie met Maya's eyes. "But it's nice to use something other than a gun."

She gave Reggie a grin, "You've taken to it well…All three of you have."

They had killed a good amount of demons since joining the Venandi.

Her eyes fell to the gold watch on Reggie's wrist, it was his father's and he wore it whenever he went out. "Your father would be proud."

His eyes fell as everyone else's landed on him and when he looked up again, he met Maya's eyes. "He would be proud of you too."

She inhaled sharply and her eyes fell from his soft smile.

"We need to talk about the problem at hand." Donato's thick accent echoed through the room and they brought their attention to him. "I can't see the way you can but I know these weak demon's are leading to something greater." His clear eyes fell on Maya. "The real problem is what Legion and Abraxas are planning."

Legion had told Maya the truth when he had told her that he had let her comrades go in return for her setting him free.

As she looked around at her comrades aside from Cale, Emily, and Trevor who weren't there when Legion arrived, they all looked like they had seen a ghost.

They had filled her in on what Legion did, how everything had gone pitch black and they saw visions of their own death's by his hands.

Each of them had different versions of him killing them.

Arthur's eyes fell on her as she thought of what he had seen: Legion had projected himself as her and made it look like she was the one killing Arthur. The others didn't like to talk about what they had seen but it weighed on them like a boulder.

They had also told her how the demon could control Aamon's army of gargoyles and the other demons cowered in his presence, even Abraxas did as he was told.

He only showed off his power for a moment until he and Abraxas disappeared in the latters shadow. The two of them were the biggest threats of all the demons and Legion's true power had yet to be seen. He was biding his time, waiting for the right opportunity to strike and Maya knew they would meet again.

"How is the seal?" Donato's voice woke her from her thoughts as she met his eyes and she was turned into the center of attention.

"It's good," She assured. "It only weakens when I'm asleep but not enough to cause any alarm."

"How often does he try to weaken you?"Arabella asked and Maya answered as if the answer was obvious. "Every night."

Cale's eyes remained on her while the others looked awkwardly away, he was with her when she had the dreams and saw first hand Lucifer's attempts to break her.

He knew she could handle it, she was chosen for this, but it was rough seeing her wake in a cold sweat every morning.

"I don't dwell on dreams anyway, I've dealt with them in my first life and the entirety of my current." She placed her hands on the table, her eyes landing on her right hand as she thought of God's missing one. "God planned on this and prepared me for it." She looked out the large window into the parking lot below. "He and Cain had everything right where it needed to be."

She had told them where Cain's loyalty really lied, how he had forced his blood down her throat to give her the means to survive against Lucifer. Her body had taken it in and absorbed it's power, she was just as much a demon as she was a gargoyle now.

She would use this power to fight the demons and she would take what Legion and Abraxas had to give her. The gargoyles were made for this, half blooded or not, they would continue to fight until all of the demons were wiped from the world.

The male gargoyle she had saved from the experimental center was out patrolling with the other gargoyles and Maya held onto hope that the others she had saved that day would come to fight as well someday.

"I always knew I'd be fighting something," Cale declared and they turned to him as he stood, a smile appearing on Maya's lips as she met his eyes. "The fact that It's demons doesn't bother me."

"It's all I've ever known." Arabella sighed with a chuckle. "I never thought I'd end up being the leader but I know Alvertos and Arely are looking down on us and are proud of what we're doing."

Donato's eyes fell. "All of our fallen comrades would be proud."

Silas got to his feet, his long hair falling to his shoulders and his eyes shining. "All of our comrades throughout the ages would be proud and I'm hoping someday the other living gargoyle's will join us."

"It's a heavy weight we hold." Donato shook his head with a sad smile. "Especially you." He pointed to where Maya stood. "You're the most dangerous woman in the world, not only due to your power, but due to who you have trapped in your body." His milky eyes met her gray with the gold rings. "One slip and he'll be back and this world will be his."

"And you know what that means," She looked at the people around the table, they were the only ones she could trust to do this if the time came. "If it ever seems like I'm going to let him take over, you know what to do."

The room was silent as her words set in and she could feel their nerves. "Don't worry," She assured them. "I'll never let that happen."

After a few hours of simple sparring, the gargoyles made their leave and Reggie, Lucas, Tori, and Arabella walked them out.

Arthur and Arabella walked side by side and she gleamed at him as they joked and Maya had to turn to hide her laughter from the dorky smile on her brothers face.

"I guess we're getting a taste of our own medicine." Cale lifted her as he whispered in her ear and she squeaked.

"Do we look that bad?" She asked with a chuckle as he set her back down.

"Yes." Trevor and Emily said in unison.

Arthur looked up as he heard the other's laughter along with his sister's embarrassment and he smiled as Arabella watched along with him.

His sister, the only person remaining from what felt like a different life. He hadn't reincarnated like she had but he had certainly changed.

He could see that she was happy but in her eyes, he could still see the weight of her sins.

She had changed but it would never take away what she had done.

What assured him was that she was no longer the girl who allowed her faults to bring her down a path of death and despair.

She had something to live for.

Maya and Cale laid in the darkness of their room, her head resting on his bare chest. She wore the shirt he had for the day and it hung loose. She was quiet as her mind filled with their conversation with the Venandi from earlier.

"What's wrong?" Cale pushed himself up and Maya lifted her head to look at him, even through the dark she could still see his worry.

How could he not worry about her when she had to fight every hour, minute, and second to keep Lucifer contained.

"It's nothing." She smiled gently to reassure him. "I'm just wondering what Legion and Abraxas are planning." His eyes fell to her's as she leaned her chin on his chest, "I don't feel this kind of unease with anyone aside from Lucifer… Legion makes my skin crawl."

"He can't be too much for you to handle." His eyes deceived him and Maya could tell that he would rather her not fight him at all.

She sighed as she sat up, "You didn't meet him so you wouldn't know," she twisted her fingers in the sheets. "The other's fear is justified, even when I met him for a few minutes, I could feel the power in him. He earned his name due to many demons possessing one body."

Being in limbo made Legion all the more stronger, as it did for the other demons.

"We will meet again." Her face was covered in the moonlight shining through the window as she said the words and Cale watched as the gold ring shimmered around her gray orbs.

"We'll face him together." His voice was strong and his face matched his tone. "We'll *all* face him together."

"…Thank you," Her voice broke. "For everything…even after everything I've done."

He chuckled softly and it caught her off guard. "You'll never change." He leaned up on his elbows. "You are Anna, Maya, and Sam...The black and white eyed gargoyle, The hand of God, The Ark of the Covenant, and the woman I love."

He placed his hand on her's and squeezed. "In your times of doubt I will always remind you of what you truly are." He smiled at the tearful look on her face. "There's not a person in this world that's not a monster."

His words were true, when she doubted herself he would always remind her of why she was here and why she was doing it. She had changed and she wouldn't allow the cycle to consume her any longer.

She surprised him when she positioned herself on top of him, her lips crashing into his and his surprise didn't last long as he returned her kiss.

He lowered himself back down as she traced her fingers along his stomach and chest until she placed her hands on his cheeks.

She rocked her hips and rough groans escaped his lips, the vibration hitting Maya's as she pulled away. Their lust filled eyes met as she straightened and pulled his shirt over her shoulders, goosebumps covering her breasts as the cool air touched them.

She leaned down again and their faces met, "Let's start where we left off this morning." She whispered with a grin before their lips connected again.

After a moment, Cale held her tight and pushed his heel into the bed as he flipped their positions.

They chuckled at the squeak that came from Maya's mouth, "I thought I get to top tonight?" She questioned slyly. "Isn't that the reason why you let me win?"

Cale snorted as he placed his forehead on hers, "It was the plan originally but I prefer it this way." he gave her a quick peck and she caressed the back of his neck. "It's easier to look in your eyes."

Their hands wandered over each others bodies as they kissed until they had enough of exploring and went straight to the destination.

Maya's face twisted in a silent scream against his neck as she wrapped her limbs around him and pulled him impossibly closer. Cale's fingers twisted in the sheets as he came undone, his teeth pressed tightly together against her pulse.

They laid with their bodies covered in sweat as they tried to catch their breaths until Cale pulled himself up, kissed her brow, then leaned down and pressed his lips gently to hers.

They embraced the after glow as if it was the best thing to ever exist, the feeling of the other as their damp skin pressed together. The smell of their mixed scents filling their noses and the emotion that overcame them as they deepened their kiss.

The sun shined on her, the gentle breeze brushing her face. She knew where she was, she had seen it before in another dream.

The garden of Eden.

"Tempting, isn't it?" Lucifer's voice came from behind her as she looked up at the forbidden tree and she turned to find him in the form he had named Samuel, his dark eyes on the tree. "It was easy to fool that weak minded woman." His gaze moved to her as she looked on with an even expression.

"This is quite the change from the other dreams." She narrowed her eyes. "What brings us to this warm atmosphere?"

"I wanted to talk to you." He gleamed, she was like an old friend to him after all.

His sweet Anna.

"Talk then get the hell out of my mind." She growled. "You can try as hard as you want but you won't get out of the Ark."

"Out of you." He corrected her. "You are the Ark, therefore I am inside of you." His smiled changed into a grin, "Look at you living your happy life." He snorted as he stepped closer. "You don't feel guilty that many of your comrades are dead while you still breath?"

She only looked at him, her nostrils flaring and her eyes narrowed. She knew his game and that was precisely why she wouldn't allow herself to be fooled by him. He always tried to hit her where it hurt the most.

Her lack of emotion didn't seem to bother him, he knew it was eating her up inside.

"You're a savage bitch, aren't you?" He tried a different approach. "You killed your own brother's without batting an eye and you watched Azazel kill Eli without flinching." He shrugged. "No wonder why God chose you for this, you're a beast."

He stepped the rest of the way to her but she didn't move, she looked into his dark eyes and allowed him to play his game."Before long his plan will backfire on him," He licked his sharp teeth. "I will crawl my way out of you and I'll watch the light leave your eyes again, nothing has ever given me greater pleasure."

He was gone suddenly and there was no trace of him.

That was until she felt something crawling up her leg.

She looked down to find Lucifer in his serpent form and he was coiling up her leg, his scales shining and scrapping her skin as he slithered to her neck and wrapped around it.

She closed her eyes as she tried to remind herself that it was only a dream but that failed as he tightened around her throat. It felt so real, the feeling of her airway being blocked, her lungs screaming for release.

She grabbed at him, her shaking hands desperately trying to get him off as her wide eyes filled with tears and she gasped for air.

She woke with a scream, her body flying from the bed as she sat up. She gasped for air as she tried to calm herself, her lungs filling with air and her heart slowing. In an attempt to ease herself from Lucifer's dream, she didn't realize that Cale didn't get up to help her as he usually did.

With a cold feeling in her chest, she turned her head slowly to the right where he laid, her fingers shaking against the sheets.

"...Cale?" Her voice shook as she looked at the mound under the blankets, unease filling her. "Ca-" She began again but the blankets fell flat as whoever had been laying there disappeared.

She leaned forward to examine the spot, tears filling her eyes as her lips quivered but as she did so, she was met with the shock of her life: In front of her appeared a refection of herself, it matched her in every way aside from the insane grin on her lips and the black bottomless eyes that matched lucifer's.

"What's the matter?" The reflection asked with excitement and she almost screamed from it's voice: It was a mixture of Lucifer's and her own.

It reached inside her chest and blood poured from her mouth and it splattered on the creatures face. It wasn't a creature though, it was Lucifer wearing her face, he was trying his hand at torturing her further.

Their mixed voices filled the room as he cackled with her lips, their bottomless eyes filling with glee.

She jumped awake but made no noise, she only wiped the tears from her eyes and sat up like she had in the dream. She turned to Cale who slept peacefully beside her, his body facing her and his right hand laying where her head had been. The room was dark still but as she looked out the window, she could see the light haze of the rising sun.

She inhaled through her nose and exhaled out of her mouth as she turned her gaze back to Cale. His breaths calming her and his sleeping expression brought a smile to her face.

It was alright, it was just a dream.

She got up and pulled on a pair of jeans and a t-shirt and before she even knew where she was going, she had left the cottage. Her feet leading her to the damp morning outside.

She found herself sitting on the beach that was only a mile down the road. She listened as the waves crashed as she sat in the sand, her knees to her chest and her arms wrapped around them.

She could see the top of the sun causing the dark sky to turn orange in the horizon.

Her heart had finally slowed down to it's too slow pace. It only ever fastened after one of her Lucifer induced dreams and although the dreams caused her emotional stress, she knew it had to do with his power putting strain on the Ark.

She remembered what it had taken for her to become The Ark of the Covenant: She had to do evil things, she had to suffer, she had to die.

What a feeling it was to die three times.

She wasn't a hero for what she had done, she was a monster and she always had been one. The world had needed a monster to contain an even bigger monster.

She could still hear the sound of Leroy's, Ida's, and the rest of the gargoyles voices as they sat around the campfire and Mary's laughter mixed with them.

She imagined Eli, Peyton, and Oberon who had replaced the people from her first life around the campfire, their voices filled with excitement as they talked about their fun for the day.

She could also picture Arthur sitting quietly as he tried to ignore their conversation.

She thought of Ari, Kira, Jeannie, Daniel, Cam, and Dylan.

Of Carma.

And of Mina.

She blinked away the tears as she thought of the day she had met Mina along with the day she had lost her.

Her ears perked as someone appeared behind her and even though the sand muffled his steps, she knew it was Arthur.

"I thought you'd still be asleep after talking to Arabella all night." She joked without turning to him.

"I thought you'd be as well after doing whatever you do with Cale." He shot back and even though he sounded disgusted, she could still hear the playfulness in his tone. She normally would have felt embarrassed but she smiled instead.

Arthur stepped to her right and settled beside her, his face turning to her.

"I had another dream." She admitted.

"What was this one about?" He asked softly, the worry clear in his voice.

"He'll try anything to weaken me." She twisted her fingers. "He's been trying harder as of late." She turned to him with a gentle smile. "But I won't fail, that's why everything happened the way it did…so I could do this."

Arthur dropped his gaze then turned to the rising sun, it's rays expanding further into the horizon. "It's hard to believe it's almost been a year since I found you again."

Maya thought of when she was merely Sam, she was so ignorant to what was to come.

She remembered the fearful determination she had felt as she fought off Kellan so Mina could escape. She remembered her desperation to escape the cave and the despair she had felt as she found out that she would be changed into a gargoyle.

She thought of the way Arthur had treated her before she knew who she truly was. The emotions that had filled her after he had told her that he was her past lives brother.

So much had changed since then.

"We've come a long way, Artie." She snickered and he playfully scowled until he smiled.

"We have." He agreed. "Mom and dad always said there was a reason for our existence." His voice cracked as his hazel eyes met the one's that had matched his own until their change to gray. "I like to think that they'd be proud."

Maya dropped her gaze. "I'm sure they would be."

They sat in silence for a moment as they watched the sun continue it's journey to take over the sky.

"I'm happy…" Maya's voice drifted and Arthur turned his head slightly as she continued. "Should I be happy? Especially after everything I've done?"

Arthur inhaled as his eyes fell on the ocean, the scent of it filling his nose. "I feel guilty everyday for what I've done…I brought most of these people into this fight and to their deaths because of my selfishness."

His selfishness was what gave him his white eyes. The need to have a family no matter the cost made him unable to contain the light inside of him.

But he would never truly admit to his true darkness.

He looked at her with sad eyes. "You're not the only one who feels guilty for the things you've done."

She swallowed as she looked into his eyes, his words hitting her. "And when it comes to you being happy," He continued. "I'm sure *they* would want you to be."

"As happy as I could be with the devil in my head right?" She tried her hand at a joke although it was a morbid one.

It didn't mean anything to her: She had fought Lucifer in her first life, had unknowingly prepared for him in her second, and it came full circle in her third.

Her battle with Lucifer would never be over, they would fight forevermore.

"But we continue on." Arthur started and she watched as he turned to her again, his eyes filled with something she hadn't seen in a long time. "We fight for what is right but we also live."

She smiled as she turned to the horizon one last time, they would have to go back soon before the others woke up and wondered where they were.

"I've died three times now," She looked at the orange hue the sun was casting across the sky, the darkness being swallowed by it's light.

The large star reminded her of her own being, of how her lives ended and started new the same way the sun drifted away, plunging the world into darkness only to rise again with a brand new light.

She leaned her head back and watched as the stars were swallowed by the light.

"This is my last life," The sun shined on her face. "My eternal life."

It was frigid, the landscape dark and the tree's leafless. There was no life nor hope, only solitude. The breeze that whispered through the dark echoed with the sound of tortured souls. It was like a melody to the cloaked being as he sat on a rotted log.

He lifted his bony fingers, his breath bringing vapor to the air.

In his eyeless sockets, he saw the hand of God.

Cover art by Sydney Height.

CPSIA information can be obtained
at www.ICGtesting.com
Printed in the USA
LVHW031554130320
649996LV00001B/2